The Amarnan Kin
Scarab - Smenkhkare

By Max Overton

Writers Exchange E-Publishing
http://www.writers-exchange.com/

The Amarnan Kings, Book 2: Scarab - Smenkhkare
Copyright 2011, 2015 Max Overton
Writers Exchange E-Publishing
PO Box 372
ATHERTON QLD 4883

Cover Art By: Julie Napier

Published by Writers Exchange E-Publishing
http://www.writers-exchange.com

ISBN **ebook**: 978-1-921636-50-9
Print: 978-1-925574-03-6 (WEE Assigned)

Dedicated to Julie Napier,
my beloved wife and devoted reader.

Who's Who and What's What in Scarab - Smenkhkare

In any novel about ancient cultures and races, some of the hardest things to get used to are the names of people and places. Often these names are unfamiliar in spelling and pronunciation. It does not help that for reasons dealt with below, the spelling, and hence the pronunciation is sometimes arbitrary. To help readers keep track of the characters in this book I have included some notes on names in the ancient Egyptian language. I hope they will be useful.

In Ancient Egypt a person's name was much more than just an identifying label. A name meant something, it was descriptive, and a part of a person's being. For instance, Amenhotep means 'Amen is at peace', and Nefertiti means 'the beautiful one has come'. Knowledge of the true name of something gave one power over it, and in primitive societies a person's real name is not revealed to any save the chief or immediate family. A myth tells of the creator god Atum speaking the name of a thing and it would spring fully formed into existence. Another myth says the god Re had a secret name and went to extraordinary lengths to keep it secret.

The Egyptian language, like written Arabic and Hebrew, was without vowels. This produces some confusion when ancient Egyptian words are transliterated. The god of Thebes in Egyptian reads *mn*, but in English this can be represented as Amen, Amon, Ammon or Amun. The form one chooses for proper names is largely arbitrary, but I have tried to keep to accepted forms where possible. King Akhenaten's birth

1

name was Amenhotep, though this name can have various spellings depending on the author's choice. It is also sometimes seen as Amenhotpe, Amenophis, Amunhotep and Amonhotep. I have used the first of these spellings (Amenhotep) in the *Scarab* books, and every name that includes that of the same god is spelled Amen- or -amen. The god himself I have chosen to call Amun, largely because the word Amen can have an alternate meaning in Western religious thought. The god of the sun's disc I have called Aten, though Aton is an alternative spelling. The City of Aten I have called Akhet-Aten (the Horizon of the Aten), rather than Akhetaten as it is normally written, to distinguish it easily for readers from the similar name of its king, Akhenaten.

The names of the kings themselves have been simplified. Egyptian pharaohs had five names, known as the Heru name, the Nebti name, the Golden Falcon name, the Prenomen and the Nomen. Only the Nomen was given at birth, the other names being coronation names. The Heru name dates from pre-dynastic times and was given to a king upon his coronation. All kings had a Heru name, but by the eighteenth dynasty it was seldom used. The Nebti name dates from the time of the unification of Egypt and shows the special relationship the king had to the vulture-goddess Nekhbet of Upper Egypt and the cobra-goddess Wadjet of Lower Egypt. The Golden Falcon name conveys the idea of eternity, as gold neither rusts nor tarnishes, and dates from the Old Kingdom. It perhaps symbolizes the reconciliation of Heru and Seth, rather than the victory of Heru over Seth as the titles are usually non-aggressive in nature.

By the time of the eighteenth dynasty, the prenomen had become the most important coronation name, replacing the Heru name in many inscriptions. Since the eleventh dynasty, the prenomen has always contained the name of Re.

The nomen was the birth name, and this is the name by which the kings in this book are commonly known. The birth names most common in the eighteenth dynasty were Tuthmosis and Amenhotep. Successive kings with the same birth name did not use the method we use to distinguish between them--namely numbers (Amenhotep III and Amenhotep IV). In fact, the birth name ceased to be used once they became king except by family members, and the coronation prenomen distinguished them. Amenhotep (III) became Nebmaetre, and Amenhotep (IV) became Waenre.

Another simplification has occurred with place names and titles. In the fourteenth century B.C., Egypt as a name for the country did not exist. The land around the Nile Valley and Delta was called Kemet or The Black Land by its inhabitants. Much later, Greeks called it Aigyptos from which we get Egypt. Other common terms for the country were The Two Lands (Upper and Lower Kemet), and the Land of Nine Bows (the nine traditional enemies).

Similarly, the king of Egypt or Kemet was later known as pharaoh, but this term derives from the phrase Per-Aa which originally meant the Great House or royal palace. Over the years the meaning changed to encompass the idea of the central government, and later the person of the king himself. The Greeks changed Per-Aa to Pharaoh.

During the eighteenth dynasty, the kings ruled from a city known variously as Apet, No-Amun or Waset in the Fourth province or sepat of Upper Kemet, which itself was also called Waset. This capital city the Greeks called Thebes. The worship of Amun was centered here and the city was sometimes referred to as the City of Amun. I have retained the ancient name of Waset.

The gods of Kemet are largely known to modern readers by their Greek names; for instance, Osiris, Thoth and Horus. I have decided to keep the names as they were originally known to the inhabitants of Kemet--Asar, Djehuti and Heru. The Greek names for some unfamiliar gods can be found in the section *Gods of the Scarab books*.

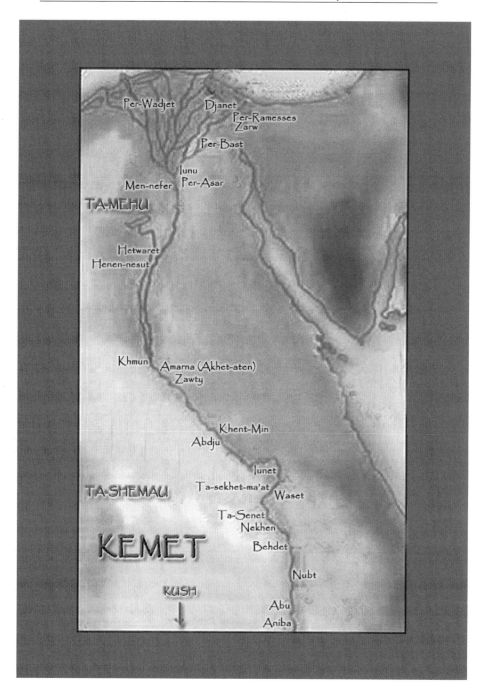

$\mathcal{P}rologue$
Syria 1960

D
r Dani Hanser climbed down from the truck and stood on the dusty road looking up at the cave. The sides of the stream valley rose in a gentle but steepening curve from the trickle of water gurgling over the rocks in the stream bed up to a narrow ledge in front of the cave entrance. A narrow path zigzagged its uneven way toward the cave and Dani's heart sank when she saw the flicker of movement in the shadows beneath the rocky overhang.

"They've let goats into the cave, Marc," she complained. "The owners of the land assured me they wouldn't."

A tall, young man with a full beard of chestnut hair jumped down from the bed of the truck. "So what are a few goats? We'll clear them out before the others get here." He stretched and yawned, looking around.

The truck was parked at the end of the dirt road that led back to the Hims-Tudmur highway. Several tents of varying sizes had been set up over the past few days by the Syrian crew of the British archaeological expedition. Small two-person tents would house the members of the expedition and larger ones would contain stores, a kitchen cum dining room and the equipment necessary to run the archaeological dig over the next four months. The tents of the Syrian crew occupied a level area fifty metres upstream. Despite the reasonably cordial relations that existed between the Syrian government and the Midlands University running the dig, the predominantly Moslem crew was under orders not to fraternize with the foreigners. They worked around Dani and Marc, nodding politely if they caught a glance but otherwise ignoring them.

"At least we have better weather this season," Marc commented. "That bloody rain we got last year drove me bonkers."

Dani smiled. "It will be pleasant without the mud," she agreed. She gestured toward the cave. "Coming up to have a look at the dig site?"

"Sure, though I think I have a wee bit more interest in our chamber." Marc glanced around to make sure they were not overheard. "Any news on that, by the way? I'm guessing not as we've been allowed back."

Dani led the way up the rough track to the cave. "Well," she said over her shoulder. "The minister was a bit curious as to why we would be interested in continuing a dig that yielded so few results last season, but I spun him a yarn about how a negative result would be just as important scientifically as a definite presence. I said that if we found nothing at such a good site, it was a reasonable conclusion that the Neanderthal migration did not follow the Orontes Valley."

"And he bought it?"

"Yes, though I had more trouble from the university authorities back home, especially as I couldn't tell them exactly why I wanted to return. However, in the end they trusted my judgment and funded us for another year."

"Excellent."

Dani grunted. "Except that the minister here will be ordering more random inspections, spot checks really, at intervals. I think he's suspicious about something."

Marc muttered an imprecation under his breath. "That's going to make it harder to work on the chamber."

"I've had a few thoughts about that. Let's see what the inside of the cave is like first."

A goat ran past them when they walked under the overhang, bleating as it bolted out into the bright sunlight. The interior of the cave was dry, with a thick layer of earth and dried mud extending over the entire floor. The earth was patterned with hoof prints and small mounds of dry dung. Apart from a slight farmyard smell, the goats appeared not to have done any damage. A hard-packed track disappeared into the gloomy recesses where last year's dig had taken place.

"Damn, I forgot to bring a torch."

Marc shrugged. "Never mind, we only really came up here to check on the chamber." He walked along the track for about twenty paces before turning and facing a sheer wall of rock. He grunted, but nodded with satisfaction. "Doesn't seem to have been disturbed."

Dani came and stood beside him, staring at the rock face. "Only because nobody who saw it had any curiosity. That mortar we used really stands out."

"What do you expect? Modern cement over ancient brickwork. We were lucky."

Dani's hand went to the pocket of her jeans and she drew out a heavy object that glinted despite the dim light. "Lucky?" she whispered. "I don't think so."

Marc glanced at her and saw the gold in her hand. "Jeez, Dani. You brought it back? I would have thought it would be in a museum back home. Can I have a look?"

Dani hesitated then passed the object across.

Marc examined the object in his hand. It was a large gold scarab beetle, its legs and head tucked under a carapace which was carved and lined in a way as to make the artifact extremely lifelike. He turned it over to reveal a symbol carved into the belly of the beetle, nestled between its legs. The symbol looked like a circle with lines extending from it, each one ending in a tiny hand. Marc recognized the symbol as that of the ancient Egyptian god Aten, which for some reason had been carved into the belly of the sacred scarab beetle, symbol of the god Khepri. The carving was fine and delicate, the whole a work of art.

"This belongs in a museum, Dani. It's an incredible piece of work."

Dani took back the scarab, clutching it tightly in her hand. "It's not going to a museum. It...it has always been in my family, Marc. Don't ask me to explain. Not yet."

"How can it have been in your family? We only found it here last year. In fact it was in the mud beside where we found the chamber." Marc turned and looked at Dani, his forehead furrowed in puzzlement. After a moment he nodded. "All right. You tell me when you're ready."

Dani slipped the scarab back into her pocket and pointed at the wall. "As soon as anybody with a bit of technical know-how sees that they will know that's artificial. My idea was to put up one of the larger tents in here, ostensibly so we don't have to cart everything down to the camp. We can have trestle tables in it and set out a few artifacts so anyone popping in--the minister, for example--will only see what we want him to see."

Marc grinned, his teeth white in his gleaming chestnut beard. "Not bad. We can rig the back flap of the tent so we can draw it up to allow us access to the chamber."

The other members of the expedition arrived the next morning. Another truck with the logo of the National History Ministry pulled up and four men and two women clambered down from the back. While the support staff emptied the truck and took the baggage and personal belongings to the tents, Dani led them all to one of the larger tents that would serve as a conference room. She sat them down on the camp chairs and officially greeted them, after which she smiled warmly, hugging the women and shaking hands with the men.

"Welcome to all of you," she said softly. "I'm hoping you had successful university years and you're all raring to go on the dig this summer."

A small, dapper man with a shock of wavy black hair leaned back on his chair and put his feet up on another. He started rolling himself a cigarette. "Thank you for that delightful welcome, Dr Hanser," he said in a lilting Welsh voice. "But I think I speak for everyone here in saying we'd like to know what's happening about that other matter."

"I'm sure you would, Daffyd," Dani said. "I'm sure you all would." She looked around the tent then went to the entrance and looked out at the camp before returning to her chair. "We are all going to have to be very careful what we say, especially around camp." She told them about the proposed visits by the minister and the idea she had about erecting a tent within the cave, backing on to the chamber wall.

"We're all really excited about this," smiled a tall blond girl. She looked like she would be more at home on a catwalk than grubbing in the dirt after stone and bone. "We talked it over in the truck on the way up and Doris and I," she put her hand on the shoulder of a smaller, less overtly demonstrative woman with short mousey-brown hair. "Well, Doris and I just want to assure you of our support, no matter what."

"Come off it, Angela," drawled one of the men. "We all agreed on that last season. Majority rules and we all voted on it."

"Al's right," added one of the other men. "We're in this together."

8

"Hey, guys," Marc interrupted. "It's okay. We all made our promises and I'm sure we've all kept them. Not a word to anyone until we know what we've found. That's right, isn't it?" He looked around the little group. "Daffyd, Angela, Doris? Al, Will, Bob?"

The others nodded or murmured agreements. "Er, well, not quite," Bob muttered.

Dani stared at the man. "What do you mean?" she asked quietly.

"I...I told my brother. I'm sorry guys." Bob looked around the group apologetically. "I just had to tell somebody, but he didn't believe me, so it's okay."

"No, it's bloody well not," Will said, "If we find anything and decide to go public, he could put two and two together and everyone will know we sat on this for a year."

"I agree," Marc added. "It puts us in an untenable position."

Daffyd shrugged. "I agree it's not the best news I've heard, boyo, but there's not much we can do about it, now is there? Let us just hope your brother can keep quiet, Bob."

"Perhaps Bob should return and make sure his brother keeps quiet."

Dani shook her head. "No. Bob's part of this expedition, Will, just like the rest of us. We're going to find that second chamber and we'll all be there to see what it contains."

They erected the tent in the cave the next day, and while Al and Will set about the demolition of the filled-in wall hiding the first chamber, Dani led the others deeper into the cave to the site of the Neanderthal excavations of the previous season. Though the site was deep within the cave system a shaft of sunlight from a section of collapsed ceiling lit the dirt floor.

"We have to have this site active and being worked on in case of any surprise inspections. How would it look if the minister found nobody doing any work on the dig that is our sole reason for being here?"

Dani supervised the setting up of the pegs and guidelines for future excavations, then helped clear the rubbish and debris from the trenches. When all was clean and professional looking again, she nodded in satisfaction.

"I'm going to roster people for days on the dig, then on the chamber." Dani held a hand up as a chorus of protests rose. "We have to show progress on this site and for all we know, there may not be another chamber." Her hand crept to her jeans pocket and her fingers touched the gold scarab. "Nobody will miss out on a thing. If we find another chamber, everyone will get a chance to see it. Now, Daffyd, you're in charge here. I'd like you to organize Doris, Angela and Bob on preliminary work on the north trench."

Daffyd nodded. "And you, Dr Hanser?" He took out his tin of tobacco and papers and started to construct another cigarette.

"I'm going to take Marc and see how the others are doing. I'll check back here in a couple of hours." Dani turned and walked back through the cave with Marc.

"You could have problems with your authority this season," Marc said quietly once they were out of site of the excavations. "Everyone wants to work on the chambers. It wouldn't be so bad if we were actually getting something from the dig, but that seems to be a wash out. You'll have people grumbling because they're rostered on a useless dig instead of working on the exciting Kemetu tomb."

"I know, but we have to show progress on the dig site. Hopefully we'll find the next chamber soon so everyone can share in what we find."

When they arrived back at the tent they found that Al and Will had not wasted any time. The back of the tent was rolled up out of the way and a hole had been punched through the mortar and mud brick wall behind. The blocks were stacked neatly to one side of the gaping hole and light glimmered from the interior of the chamber. Al poked his head through as they entered the tent.

"Oh, hello Dani. We're all set to turn the lights on. We just need to start up the generator, if you'd be so kind, Marc." He pointed to a small generator in one corner of the tent, the exhaust outlet pushed under the tent side.

Marc primed the generator and wound the cord. He pulled it sharply and the engine spluttered into life, coughing and kicking for a few moments before settling down into a throaty purr. Lights flickered on in the chamber, brightening and shining out to illuminate the tent.

"I think we're going to need some sort of solid screen over the hole," Dani said. "If we get any surprise visitors, they're going to wonder why there's a bright light coming out of the cliff face." She ducked and stepped through the hole into the dazzlingly bright chamber, Marc following close behind. Dani pivoted slowly on her heel, taking in the view. It was exactly as she remembered it from the previous year.

Three of the four walls of the large chamber were covered in tiny hieroglyphs, the picture writing minute and cramped, sandwiched between paintings of Egyptian scenes, the figures of men and animals lovingly depicted, realistic rather than stylized. One of the scenes showed a young woman, not much more than a girl, still with the side hair lock of youth, looking at a large scarab beetle as it rolled a ball of dung across the sand. The face of the girl showed a marked resemblance to that of Dani. The back wall was a gigantic mural depicting a semi-circle of gods facing a young woman on her knees before them, back turned to the chamber. The ceiling of the chamber depicted a huge golden Aten sun disc, gleaming richly in the bright lights. Rays from the disc extended down the walls, all around the chamber, each ray ending in a small hand clutching the ankh, the symbol of life. One of these hands touched the head of the kneeling woman in the mural in an act of blessing and protection.

"Bloody hell," Marc muttered. "I'd forgotten how beautiful it was."

"Please, Marc," Dani whispered. "Have some reverence for the place."

Al grinned as he looked around the covered walls. "So where's the next chamber, do you think?"

"I don't know, but I'll bet there is one."

Marc looked at Dani curiously. "Are you going to do your finding trick again?"

Will frowned and looked at Marc, then at Dani. "What trick?"

"Remember last year when we first found the scarab? Dani led us right to the entrance to this chamber." Marc smiled apologetically, realizing he had put Dani on the spot. "I reckon she's psychic or something."

Al laughed. "Maybe it's because Dani looks like this Beketaten lassie in the paintings. Maybe the gods of Egypt are leading her."

"The goddess Nut ruled the heavens and was the deity of direction," Dani said. "If you want to find something, ask Nut."

"Or ask a nut, anyway," Al chortled. "Well, we found the first doorway by looking for straight line irregularities in the plaster, so I suppose we can do the same here." He turned down the rheostat, dimming the lights in the chamber. As the shadows swept in he flicked on a flashlight and, holding it close to the wall, squinted along it, looking for the tiny straight ridge that might imply the presence of a door.

Marc and Will followed suit, taking a wall each, moving slowly along, then back at a different level. Dani stood in the middle of the chamber with the golden scarab in her hand. She bowed her head and muttered beneath her breath. She waited, the only sound in the chamber being the intermittent scrape and whisper of clothing as the men moved, and the muted hum of the generator from the cave.

"It's behind there," Dani said at last. She pointed at the mural on the back wall. "The woman is on the panel and the sides are delineated by those two sun rays that extend to the floor."

Al stared at her quizzically for a minute before crossing to the mural and shining his torch parallel to the wall, squinting along the beam. "Shit. She's done it again. Just what are you Dani? Some kind of miracle worker?"

Marc stared at the mural and shook his head, a horrified expression on his face. "Please be wrong. Not behind the mural. We can't destroy that, not for anything."

Al fetched the rest of the team from the dig and they stood or sat in the once more brightly lit chamber and stared at the mural.

"We can't destroy that picture," Angela said. "It's a work of art. It would be like...like vandalizing the Mona Lisa."

"I agree with you," Doris said firmly.

Daffyd puffed on his cigarette. "Time to call in the big boys I think. We turn this over to the experts. They'll figure out a way to get past it."

"Shit." Al slammed his hand against the plaster wall. "I was all for doing that last year, but now...well, I've got to know what's behind there."

"What's that painting on?" Marc asked. "I mean, I know it's on plaster, but is it plaster over brick or over solid stone? And what's likely to be on the other side? Empty space or a passage filled with rubble? Dani? What would an Egyptian tomb be like?"

Dani thought. "Rubble-filled passageways are more likely at a tomb entrance. At a guess I'd say the wall is dressed stone..."

"Why not mud brick?" Al interrupted.

"A professional tomb builder would use stone. Remember the lower courses of the wall we came through are stone, the later ones being brick. They'd use stone deeper in the tomb...always providing this is a tomb."

"So you think it is empty space on the other side of dressed stone blocks?"

"I think so, yes. Why?"

"Let me bounce an idea off you all, then." Marc approached the wall and felt the faint irregularities with his fingertips. "Let's say we cut a narrow groove vertically down both sides of the doorway, keeping damage to a minimum. Once we know where the levels of each course of stone are, we cut horizontally along the mortar. Couldn't we lift out each block without destroying the artwork?"

"Hey, that might work."

"I think it might depend on how fine a cut you could make, the strength of the plaster and probably half a dozen other factors," Daffyd commented. "More likely it would shatter as you lifted it out."

"What about if we just lifted the bottom two feet out? We could wriggle through the gap."

"Without causing much damage," Angela added.

"Of course, two feet might not be enough for you, Angela." Al grinned and winked, laughing as the buxom girl flushed.

"Okay, keep it seemly," Dani said. "That might be the best we can hope for." She made a rough measurement on the wall with her hands. "Two feet comes to about here. We'd only be taking off a small part of her feet and most of the rock slab she's kneeling on."

"So we'll try that?" Marc asked. He looked around at the group, smiling as he received nods and grunts of affirmation. "I'll get the cutter and an extension cord to run it off the generator."

"There is one other vitally important thing to do before we start destroying art," Daffyd commented, pulling out his tobacco to roll another cigarette. "It's something we should have done last year and I kicked myself for not doing it." He looked round at the blank expressions. "Take some holiday snaps. We need a complete photographic record of this whole chamber. If you remember, we took photos of the outside of the chamber before we broke down the wall, but the excitement of the inscription rather drove everything else from our minds."

While Marc found the stone cutter and extension cords, Dani went back down to the camp to find her camera and a box of flash bulbs.

She then spent the next hour and several rolls of film carefully photographing the whole chamber, paying special attention to the mural on the back wall. At last she nodded and stepped back, tossing the last spent bulb back into the empty box.

"Your turn, Marc."

The stone cutter ripped through the soft sandstone easily. Marc worked his way down each side of the hidden doorway from waist height to the floor, then awkwardly held the cutter parallel to the floor and cut through the base. Several flakes of painted plaster fell away and he slowed his cutting rate. He switched off the electric saw and it cycled down rapidly, the scream of metal on rock only slowly fading in their battered ears.

Al picked at the cut edges of the rock and found the position of the tiers of dressed stone blocks. He indicated a position nearly three feet up the wall.

"The blocks look to be nearly thirty centimeters high--that's twelve inches for you non-scientific chappies." He smiled. "We'd find it a tight squeeze getting under just one or two tiers--he winked at Angela who grinned back--so I suggest we cut through the mortar here, allowing ourselves nearly three feet."

Marc went to work again, slowly cutting through the mortar between the tiers of stone in a more or less straight line across the doorway. He switched off again.

"That should do it. I'm definitely into open space behind the blocks. I can tell by the feel of the saw blade."

Al picked up a hand drill with a masonry bit and laboriously scraped out two deep holes about a foot from the floor and a foot in from the sides. He screwed in two eye-hooks and attached ropes to each one.

"Time to show us what you're made of, guys. Let's pull this sucker out of here."

Grabbing the ropes, they braced themselves and heaved backward. The slab of stone scraped forward a fraction then stopped. They tried again with a similar result.

"We need a lubricant," Bob panted. "Squirt some oil under the stone or something."

Al shook his head. "We don't need oil, just an even pull." He pointed at the slab of painted stone. "See how it has pulled out about a centimeter on this side but less than half that on the other? The block is moving at an angle and is catching on the sides. Sorry girls, but you need to be in different teams. We need equal muscle on both ropes."

Under Al's direction, he and Will pushed the slab straight again before reorganizing the teams on the ropes. This time the stone, after an initial reluctance, slid free of the wall with a grinding noise. They altered the angle of the pull and coaxed the block to one side, revealing a dark cavern beyond the painted wall. Stale air oozed out into the lighted chamber, mingling with the sharp smells of burnt rock and excitement.

"Over to you, Dr Hanser," Daffyd murmured. "I believe the honour is yours."

Dani nodded and flicked on a flashlight, playing the beam into what looked like a passageway. She ducked down and, bending double, edged under the hanging wall. The beam from the flashlight surged ahead of her, lighting floor and bare walls of a short passageway cut through the sandstone and into a second chamber.

"What can you see?" Doris called.

"There's another chamber," Dani's voice echoed back. "It's much larger than the first, but it's covered in writing again. Come through, and bring lights."

The others entered, tentatively, waving flashlights ahead of them as they crowded through. Daffyd plugged in another long extension cord and brought an electric light in with him. The harsh light threw the shadows back, revealing a long chamber that on first sight looked a lot less interesting than the first one. The whitewashed plaster walls were again covered with minute hieroglyphs but there seemed to be very few paintings. There was no gleaming Aten disc on the rough rock ceiling and their overall impression of the chamber was that it was utilitarian rather than artistic--until they saw the back wall.

"My word," Daffyd said, holding the light high.

"Damn."

"It's glorious," Angela breathed. "Who are they?"

Two men faced each other on the wall. Both were young, one no more than a youth and they both wore the blue war-crown of Kemet. Wearing nothing more than the crowns and short military kilts, the artist had captured the young kings--for that was what they must be--in the act of battle. The older man strode forward as if eager to get to grips with his enemy, a set expression on his face, curved bronze sword held aloft. His opponent, though in a similar pose, one leg extended toward battle, looked more hesitant. He clutched a spear in both hands, the point held at stomach level. Behind the fighting kings stood other figures, smaller to denote lesser importance in the traditional artistic mode. A woman stood behind the older king, reddish glints in her hair and sword held ready. The younger king was supported by an old man, dressed in the long white robe and leopard skin cloak of a priest of Amun, the crook and flail of kingly authority in his hands. Cartouches above the heads of the figures held hieroglyph symbols which Dani translated.

"The woman is our old friend Beketaten again, and the old man is Ay, her uncle." She whistled as she turned her attention to the kings. "The older one is Smenkhkare and the younger Tutankhamen."

"That can't be right," Angela protested. "I did some reading on the eighteenth dynasty and Smenkhkare died almost immediately after Akhenaten. Tutankhamen succeeded him but he was only a boy of about nine. They couldn't possibly have fought."

"It's a bit of a conundrum, isn't it?" Daffyd agreed with a smile.

"Perhaps it's only supposed to be representational," Marc said. "I mean, Tut took the worship of Kemet back to Amun from the worship of Aten under old Smenk, so maybe that is what this means. The two are battling for their respective gods."

"That would work," Bob agreed. "After all, that scene in the first chamber must be representational." He grinned. "Unless you think our little Scarab really did meet the gods of Kemet?"

The others laughed, except Dani. "Legends say she did," she said.

"What legends would they be?" Daffyd asked.

"I told you my mother was Kemetu? Well, her grandmother used to tell me stories about a great hero called Scarab, her ancestor, a woman who lived thousands of years ago. One of the legends says she met the gods." Dani laughed into the silence that greeted her words. "Well, we didn't read anything about that in the hieroglyphs, did we? So perhaps the pictures really are just allegorical."

"And what about this lot?" Doris gestured around the chamber. "Are you going to read it to us? Tell us what happened?"

"Pictures first," Daffyd interrupted. "Take pictures of everything here before we start."

16

"I don't think I have enough film. Does anyone have 35 mm film? And flash bulbs?"

Doris shook her head. "I've only got a box brownie."

"I do," Al said. "I've got half a dozen rolls. I think I have some bulbs too. Hang on a sec and I'll get them." He ducked out of the chamber, to return some ten minutes later, breathing hard. Handing over the rolls of film and flash bulbs to Dani he went and sat with the others as she proceeded to litter the floor with spent bulbs.

"Okay, that should do it," she said after about half an hour. "I'll send these off for developing as quickly as possible, so I'll know whether I need to take any more."

"Are you going to start translating now?" Doris asked, the tremor in her voice betraying her excitement.

"Yeah," Al added, "Time to find out what happens to Scarab, Dani."

"All of this?" Dani asked, waving her arms to encompass the packed hieroglyphs on the walls. "You know it's going to take weeks."

"Better get started then," Marc grinned.

"Well, okay, but I'm not going to try reading it all at once. We'll do some tonight, some more tomorrow, and so on."

"Just like chapters in a book," Doris said happily. "I love a good book."

"I've got to find out where all this starts, first," Dani said with a smile.

"Already done, Dr Hanser." Daffyd pointed to the wall just to the right of the entrance way. "While you were taking photos I was looking for the beginning."

"Well then, I suppose I'd better start." Dani stretched and looked around at the eager faces of her graduate students. She giggled. "You all look like a bunch of kindergarten kids at story time." Crossing to the wall she examined the script, running her fingers down the columns of hieroglyphs before scanning portions on either side of the door and at a couple of other places on the wall. "Yes, you're right, Daffyd. I'd say this is where it starts." Turning back to the group, she smiled. "Are you all sitting comfortably? Then I'll begin." Dani examined the wall again and took a deep breath.

"I am glad to be back in Waset," she read. "It is a city that is full of history and of the gods of our ancient land. The city of Akhet-Aten is new and clean but it is empty, being dedicated to a god that speaks only to the king and offers little to anyone else. Here in Waset, the disc of the sun seems less remote and people can worship it through the old familiar forms of Re and Khepri.

The three years that elapsed between the accession of my brother Smenkhkare and the end of Akhenaten's reign were probably the most peaceful years for Kemet since the death of my father Nebmaetre and for twenty years to come. The people loved Smenkhkare and he achieved a good working relationship with the priests of Amun at Waset, despite the worship of all gods other than the Aten still being proscribed. Akhenaten stayed in his capital city and left the running of the country to Smenkhkare and Ay, the co-regent and the Tjaty. This arrangement was not always amicable as the two men of Waset were strong-willed..."

Chapter 1

The young man brushed past the guards and walked into the upstairs antechamber of the king's apartments, tossing the double crown representing the two kingdoms that made up the land of Kemet, onto a great gilded ebony chair. He stretched and yawned, pushing his shoulders back with a grimace before pouring a cup of wine from the chilled pitcher on an inlaid ebony table and carrying it over to the great window overlooking the royal gardens. Clad in a fine white linen kilt and sandals, he leaned casually on the marble-lined balustrade, only the muscles in his broad back betraying his tension.

An older man followed him into the room, moving quietly. The man, likewise clad in white kilt and sandals, also displayed several items of jewelry and badges of office. A broad heavy gold chain hung about his neck and armbands of gold revealed his power and wealth. Short and stocky, the older man's skin was creased and displayed the signs of incipient old age, hanging in wrinkles as his body lost its muscle tone. A shock of white hair topped his head, and his hands which hung by his sides, trembled slightly, matching an intermittent tremor below his left eye.

"The temple of the Aten in Hazor has been burned to the ground and the priests slaughtered."

"Why am I just hearing this now, Ay?" The young man did not look round but sipped at his wine, looking out at the heat-rippled air above the city. The heavy odors of dust and the effluvia of crowded humanity wafted up from streets and alleys.

"I only received the news yesterday."

"Then why did you not raise this issue at the morning audience?"

The young man, King Ankhkheperure Djeserkheperu Smenkhkare, co-regent and Lord of the Two Lands excepting only the City of Aten turned from the window of his apartments in the old Waset Palace to stare at his Tjaty and great-uncle, Ay. Although only of middling height, perhaps three cubits and two palms tall, the young king stamped his presence on any room. Still young, rising nineteen years, Smenkhkare had all but ruled Kemet these last three years after coming to the throne at the behest of his half-brother Akhenaten, called by many the Heretic King. Smenkhkare was unaware that Ay had engineered his co-regency, in the hopes of maintaining his failing grip on the power of the king.

Akhenaten had himself inherited the Two Kingdoms seventeen years before from his father Nebmaetre Amenhotep, when the old king fell victim to a stroke from the gods which rendered him a dribbling cripple, unable to walk or talk, incapable of ruling Kemet. His queen, Tiye, with advice from her brother Ay, had ruled for six months before giving in and enthroning her son Waenre Amenhotep as co-regent. The young king took over the reins of Kemet at the height of its power, with a full treasury and an experienced army. With resolute ministers and experienced generals even a young, untried king could do little damage to Kemet's strength and reputation; but the young Waenre Amenhotep was also a religious fanatic.

Raised in Zarw in the Delta region, Waenre Amenhotep's early life was spent among his mother's people, the Khabiru. His mother Tiye was the daughter of Yuya, a prophet of the Khabiru who had arrived in Kemet in the time of the old king's father Tuthmosis. Prophesying of famine and harvests, and interpreting dreams, Yuya became powerful in the king's court, eventually being appointed Tjaty. He had three children, Tiye, Ay and Aanen. The Khabiru, a tribe of wanderers from the north, worshipped a strange god, one who had no form, yet whose face shone with the brilliance of the sun. This god had no name but in the Khabiru tongue was addressed as 'El' which meant 'god' and as 'Adon' which meant 'Lord'. By a twist of fate the word 'Adon' is pronounced 'Aten' in Kemetu, and two generations of Kemetu kings had gradually raised the Kemetu god Aten, a minor aspect of the sun god Re, to the status of a major deity. The young Waenre Amenhotep went further. First he changed his name to Akhenaten or 'servant of the Aten' to honour his god, then he moved his capital city from Waset, the City of the god Amun, to a new city dedicated to the sun god, Akhet-Aten or 'the Horizon of the Aten'. Not content with raising his god to this level, Akhenaten decreed heresy. He ruled that all other gods were false and that their temples were to close, their worship to cease. Amun especially was singled out, his treasury confiscated, his lands sold and the very name of the god was chiseled off monuments and expunged from the records, even where it occurred in his dead father's name. For this sacrilege he earned the undying enmity of the priests of Amun, of which his own uncle Aanen was Second Prophet.

Wrapped up in his religious fervor, Akhenaten channeled gold from the temples and the state treasury into building rich new temples dedicated to Aten. Not understanding the delicate balance, or Ma'at, that governed Kemet, he pardoned all criminals, releasing hordes of murderers and thieves; and stripped the army of its strength, fostering rebellion and warfare amongst Kemet's vassal states and enemies.

Then plague struck the Two Lands. Three of Akhenaten's daughters by his beautiful young wife, Queen Nefertiti died, and the king was suddenly brought face to face with his own mortality and the extinction of his family line. He had no sons to become king after him, so in desperation he followed the example of his father.

Nebmaetre Amenhotep had married his own daughters Sitamen and Iset, fathering sons on them: Smenkhkare and Tutankhaten. Akhenaten decided to do the same in the hope of similarly fathering sons. First he married his eldest daughter Meryetaten. This act estranged Nefertiti, leading her into an act of rebellion which was quickly put down by Paatenemheb, General of all the Armies. Nefertiti was banished but the other rebel, Ay, Nefertiti's own father, managed to clear himself of the charges, and keep his position as Tjaty. Meryetaten became wife and queen but the hope of sons died quickly. She gave birth to a baby daughter and Akhenaten, husband and father, put her away and married his next oldest daughter Ankhesenpaaten. She too, produced a daughter and was eventually put aside.

The deposed daughter-queen Meryetaten proved an embarrassment at court, refusing to accept her new status and Akhenaten sent her up-river to Waset to marry his co-ruler Smenkhkare. Neither party desired this union but they accepted it for the sake of Kemet's peace. The marriage was never consummated and the king and queen maintained separate apartments within the palace.

Ay, though technically Tjaty to king Akhenaten, rapidly saw that the real power in Kemet was to be found in the court at Waset. He moved south using the pretext of guiding the new co-regent Smenkhkare, whereas his real reason was to rule Kemet through the young inexperienced man. Here, Ay made one of his rare errors of judgment. Smenkhkare may have been young and inexperienced but he was highly intelligent, possessed a will of hardened bronze and had firm views about how Kemet should be ruled. He allowed himself to be guided by his great-uncle Ay but always questioned his advice, never allowing him the freedom he desired. Increasingly, Ay became discontented with his situation and started to look for ways to work around the king.

Ay shrugged at his nephew's question, though he knew the easy familiarity encouraged by Akhenaten was frowned on by Smenkhkare. "I regarded the matter of little importance."

Smenkhkare stood silently, staring at his Tjaty, waiting. After a few moments, Ay reluctantly added the honorific, "Your majesty."

"Remember who is king here, Ay. I will not have my commands questioned or my wishes ignored by anyone. Even you."

Ay hid a scowl by bowing. "Of course, your majesty. Forgive me."

"So tell me about this act of violence in Hazor."

"There is not much to add, my lord. I received a letter from the governor of Hazor telling me that a mob torched the Aten temple and killed the priests. He acted immediately, of course, and hanged the ringleaders."

"A mob from within Hazor? Not a foreign army?"

"Apparently not. The ringleaders were put to the question but could reveal only that gold was paid, by persons unknown."

Smenkhkare raised the cup to his lips and sipped the strong wine, looking at the older man over the rim. He swallowed and lowered the cup. "And why did you think this news was not important, Ay?"

The Tjaty shrugged again, ignoring the muscles that clenched on the king's jaw in response to his renewed disrespect. "It was only a temple to the Aten. It is time that heresy was put to rest."

The king frowned. "You were an ardent supporter of the Aten not so long ago. A priest in fact. Have your beliefs undergone such a radical change? I would question your motivation."

"I was father to the queen and uncle to Waenre Akhenaten. I could not do otherwise." Ay pursed his lips before continuing. "When you have more experience of Kemet and its people you will realize the necessity of expedience."

"I will not lie--not about my beliefs, or about my actions."

"Then let me act, my lord, for I have your good at heart."

"Act how? By trampling on the beliefs of my subjects?"

Ay allowed himself a slight smile and bowed, thus missing the ripple of anger that played over the young king's features. "The worship of the Aten is heresy and those who still cling to that religion are heretics, misguided at best."

"The only heresy was worshipping the Aten to the exclusion of all the other gods. Aten is a Kemetu god and the destruction of his temple is an affront to the majesty of our Two Lands."

"Atenism is still the official religion and Akhenaten is still the king. Must his delusions continue to rip our country apart?"

"Waenre Akhenaten is king but so am I," Smenkhkare said softly, his dark eyes boring into Ay's. "I am working to soften the effect of more than a decade of monotheism, but I will not act precipitately."

"I would strongly advise you..."

"I do not want your advice, Ay."

Ay shrugged once more, making his king's jaw muscles jump again. "That is my function. I am Tjaty and King's Adviser. It is my duty to guide the king using my experience and wisdom."

"You are not my Tjaty, nor my Adviser, even though you are my uncle. I did not appoint you. If you desire that function, then return to Akhet-Aten so my brother Akhenaten may make use of you."

"Akhenaten rules only his City of the Sun. He has no use for a Tjaty, whereas you..."

"I have my own advisers, uncle. And ones I can trust."

Ay stared at his young king. His hands clenched into fists beside him and his breath came faster, his nostrils dilating. "You do not trust me?"

"I did not say that. I said only that I have advisers I can trust and that I do not need Akhenaten's Adviser to help me in my task."

"And what of my services these past three years?" Ay stepped forward, his eyes flashing. "Have I not guided you, supported you and advised you through a time that would surely have overwhelmed a boy unused to power and court intrigue?"

"I am no longer a boy."

Ay opened his mouth to further his attack, before catching sight of the young man's expression. He swallowed his words and kept a tight hold on his anger. "You are right, your majesty. You are no longer a boy but surely my experience and wisdom are still useful currency in guiding our country?"

"You want my thanks, uncle? You have it. You want honours? You already have them, all that a man could want. How can you rise higher in Kemet? You are but one step below the kings. You want rewards for your services to three kings? You shall have them in abundance. I am going to give you vast estates in the Delta, uncle. Rich farmlands with many servants and huge herds of cattle. Return to Zarw, to your people the Khabiru, to your ailing daughter Mutnodjme, and enjoy your well-earned retirement."

"You would not dare..." Ay bit his lip, stifling his anger. After a moment he resumed in a calmer voice. "You do not mean it, your majesty. You cannot. My function is to advise you..."

"I have other advisers."

"Who? Who could possibly advise you as well as me? Do you mean that pack of misfits you call a council?"

Smenkhkare's eyes narrowed for a moment before he relaxed. He turned and walked back to the window, perching himself on the sill and sipping his wine. "Go on, Ay. Tell me of my misfits."

Ay hesitated then tossed his head defiantly, his wavy white hair gleaming in the bright noon light that poured in from the wide windows. "Very well then, I will advise my king one more time." He crossed to the table and poured himself a cup of wine without bothering to ask the king's permission. He used the time and the simple actions to gather his thoughts.

"Your council--if it can be called that--consists of a physician, a priest, a scribe, a merchant, a couple of dirty commoners and a girl. There is only one legitimate member, Treasurer Sutau. Physician Nebhotep is competent enough in his field, I suppose, but hardly a man to decide the fate of Kemet. He is more at home among his pills and his knives."

"I thought you liked Nebhotep. Did he not save the royal household from the worst ravages of the plague?" A shadow crossed Smenkhkare's eyes as he remembered the death of his own grandmother Tiye from the plague.

The same shadow darkened the old man's face for a moment. He recalled his granddaughters lost to the disease that swept through Kemet, killing nearly one in ten. "What has liking a man got to do with it? I look for ability in the men I use, not their charm. He is a fine physician--as physicians go, but not a man to advise a king. As for the priest--well, he is my brother Aanen and I am quite fond of him for all he is a rabid follower of Amun."

"I seem to remember you were a priest of Amun before you turned to Aten," Smenkhkare murmured.

Ay flushed. "Yes, I was. But my outlook was never narrow; I was always open to alternative ideas."

"You bend with the wind, you mean." Smenkhkare flicked his hand nonchalantly. "My apologies, Ay, I have interrupted your diatribe against my council. Please continue."

Ay inclined his head toward his king, his expression tight-lipped. "The priest is only interested in one thing," he continued. "The return of his wealth and power."

"Not just that, but yes, he seeks the reinstatement of Amun as first god of Kemet. I see nothing wrong in that. Amun is the god of our royal house."

"Then there is the scribe Khensthoth. A pedantic old fool who is better employed as a teacher of foolish boys than as a statesman."

Smenkhkare smiled, though not at Ay's cynical remarks. "I was one of those foolish boys once. You should take the time to get to know the old man. He is a repository of wisdom."

Ay waved a hand dismissively. "At least those members of your council are educated men and can talk intelligently. What of your four commoners--the grain merchant, the toymaker, the farm boy and the pimp? What possessed you to give power to such as these?"

"They are good men. Well, Kenamun the toymaker is anyway. The merchant Meres seeks profits; he wants the economy running smoothly again. The farm lad Khu stuck by my sister in a time of great danger. I value loyalty. Mahuhy is a businessman and knows how the city works. I have seen them all as they went about their work and I can recognise their abilities."

"But they are common. Their families are nothing. How can you raise them so far above their station?"

"My family was common once," Smenkhkare said softly. "Before the god Amun raised them to become Per-Aa, the Great House, they were mere soldiers. And what of yourself, Ay? Your father was a common shepherd of the Khabiru before my grandfather raised him to the nobility. Do not be quick to judge others on the circumstances of their birth."

Ay bowed once more, hiding the fury in his eyes. "I stand corrected, your majesty," he murmured.

"And what of the last member of my Council?"

Ay turned away from his king and stared out through the wide window at the city. "Yes, your sister Beketaten." He remained silent for a long time, his fingers slowly twirling the wine cup by its long golden stem. "A beautiful child," he said at last. "But willful."

Smenkhkare held his voice carefully neutral. "Would you care to explain that?"

"Come, your majesty," Ay chided. "Everyone knows of Beketaten's part in my daughter Nefertiti's supposed rebellion. She overheard me talking to my daughter when she was angered and not thinking straight and the girl leapt to false conclusions. Instead of going to Akhenaten with her accusations she fled the city to protect what she thought was a danger to her own life. It was only when she was discovered that she concocted this fantastic tale of my own treason." Ay turned and looked hard at Smenkhkare. "Akhenaten himself heard my case and ruled me innocent."

"But not your daughter."

Ay shook his head and brushed the back of his hand theatrically against his dry eyes. "Alas, no. Still overcome with her anger, she admitted her guilt."

"Yet you did not plead for her?"

"Your majesty, I am a loyal servant of the king Akhenaten. I would not defend my daughter's admitted guilt. I do, of course, grieve my loss, but for the sake of Kemet, I would give up everything."

"You have given up much for Kemet, uncle, and served the Two Lands faithfully for a lifetime already longer than most men's. I think it is time you enjoyed what time you have left in the peace of your own household, with the reward of your king to sustain you."

Ay stared at Smenkhkare, his mind seeking a way out of this disaster. "I do not wish to retire. I can still be of service to Kemet."

"But I wish you to retire, Tjaty Ay, and I am king. Would you disobey me?" Smenkhkare held up a hand as his uncle opened his mouth. "Think before you speak again. I am not a king like my brother Akhenaten that you may bend to your own will. I am my own man and know my own mind. Take this retirement with the blessing of your king or go serve my brother in Akhet-Aten. You have until the end of the month to get your affairs in order."

Chapter 2

Waset, the city of Amun, sat sweltering in the summer heat, the burning disc of the sun blazing down from a cloudless sky the colour of lapis lazuli. The dust of the land rose up to meet the sun in the rippling atmosphere, tainting the air with an acrid smell, a mixture of ground rock, sweat, incense and ordure. Men worked in the heat, having no choice. If they did not work to support their families, no-one else would put bread on their tables for them. It was a feast day of the goddess Tefnut, yet the business of the city went on. Every day was the feast day of one or more of the gods, but who had the leisure to observe them all? The priests chanted their rituals, made the offerings, and perhaps carried a statue of the god through the crowded streets, but the average citizen paused only to salute the passing deity before hurrying off about his business.

In the wake of a small gaggle of white-robed priests bearing a gilded statue of Tefnut, two people, a young man and a younger woman, walked slowly down the Street of Potters. To an observer, it might have seemed that the young couple was part of the procession, but when the priests turned into the Street of Weavers, the man and woman kept straight on without a glance, their heads bent in conversation.

"They are daily growing bolder, my lady," the young man murmured. "They forget the old religion is still prohibited."

"Enough of the 'my lady', Khu. It is time you grew bolder and called me Scarab. You did once before, in the desert."

The young man sketched a brief bow and grinned. "As my lady wishes. Seriously though...Scarab, the old gods are still banned, yet everywhere you look you see gods and their priests."

"That is because my brother Smenkhkare is bringing back the old ways, as well you know. The people have lived without the solace of the gods for too long. Only the prohibition of Akhenaten prevents the temples being opened and freedom of worship flourishing once more in the Two Lands." The young woman shook her head, making the carefully braided wig on her head swing. She smiled at Khu, revealing strong white teeth in a coppery complexion. Dark eyes twinkled beneath full lashes and her breasts quivered beneath the fine linen of her garments. "It is too lovely a day to be serious Khu. Let us enjoy our beautiful city and the new peace and prosperity my brother brings to Kemet."

For a space they walked in silence, taking in the familiar, yet ever-new sights, sounds and smells of the city. Crowds of men and women thronged the streets, dressed for the most part in plain linen kilts or shifts, the poorer men often naked, contrasting with the occasional flash of colour and gold as a rich man passed, a slave holding a wide sun-shade above his shaved head; or a lady, her maids dancing attendance around her as her jewels flashed in the sunlight. Children swarmed, running and darting between the legs of the adults, their shrill cries piercing the deeper muted roar of a thousand voices in conversation. Dogs snapped and snarled in the alleys, fighting over scraps of food, disturbing the clouds of flies that dipped and hovered over food and waste alike. From the edges of the street came the cries of the shop-keepers, of merchants and of whores, each extolling the virtue of their particular commodity. Soldiers, gripping tall spears and with curved bronze swords hanging from leather belts, patrolled the streets in small groups, their eyes roving. Medjay too, the local police, stood at the street corners, their short cudgels in hand, looking for any disturbance, ready to crack a few skulls to restore order. They looked faintly resentful that the citizens were careful not to give any cause for their interference.

Although not much past mid-morning, the heat of the sun beat back from the packed and hardened clay of the streets, reflected off the mud brick and stone walls of the buildings, and rippled the dusty air. The odor of a thousand years of life, baked into the brick and earth, rose as a familiar miasma, noticed only by strangers to the city. Women had been thronging the streets since early morning, seeking out the daily necessities for their households, bargaining and arguing with shopkeepers and merchants, beating down the price of bread, onions, beer, or a handful of dates. Now they took their leave of the merchants, hurrying home to escape the midday heat and prepare the noon meal for their families. The men remained, backs bent and heads bowed, carrying produce or waste, bearing loads or repairing walls, carving wood or fashioning metal, carrying out the myriad tasks that brought in the pittance they needed to keep their families fed.

Yet people smiled, or at least went about their business with an air of contentment. Their muscles might ache and their skin burn under the fierce heat of the sun, the sweat drying to leave a dust of salt on their tanned skin, but they were doing what their fathers had done before them, and their fathers, back through the generations. They helped maintain Ma'at, the crucial balance of god and man, everyone in his place and doing what he was born to do. From the exalted gods, through their representative-on-earth, the king; the nobles, priests and scribes down to the poorest peasant who worked the land or emptied the latrines, all worked to keep Kemet stable and prosperous.

The heretic king had changed everything, overthrowing the gods and setting up his own god Aten in their place, creating a new capital city and disturbing the balance of the world. The gods had struck back, bringing plague and famine, war and poverty, until the land of Kemet tottered on the brink of anarchy and chaos. Then Smenkhkare became king over Waset, and the land staggered away from the precipice. Despite the continued presence of the heretic in his city, the new king had fought to bring prosperity to his people and the gods back to their worshippers.

Scarab and Khu paused where the Street of Potters debouched into the great Avenue of Rams, the broad thoroughfare that led to the huge expanse of the temple of Amun. Although not yet open to the people, Smenkhkare had been working with the priests to refurbish the temple and make it a fit place for the god once more. The ceremonial lake of purification had been dredged and refilled, the walls white-washed and the temple itself, open only to the elements and the wild creatures, thoroughly cleansed as it became once more the abode of ever-living Amun.

30

"I know Amun must be returned to his pre-eminence," Scarab murmured. "But it worries me that Kemet will return so completely to the old days."

Khu frowned, his young face beneath its unruly thatch of black hair, screwing up in concern. "What do you mean? I thought you wanted a return to the old ways?"

"I do, but think, Khu. We have had but one god these last six or seven years and where has it got us? Kemet has been brought to the edge of disaster. Now we return to the old ways but we have that." Scarab gestured toward the great white-washed walls of the Amun temple, reflecting back the glare of the sun in coruscations of blinding light. "We put ourselves under the dominance of one god again."

"But the other gods are allowed, at least unofficially. We just saw Tefnut in the streets."

"I know, but why can we not get back to where all our gods are important in our lives? Why does one god have to be dominant?"

"He is the god of your family," Khu reproved gently. "Your ancestors made him great, and he in turn brought greatness to them. Look at your father, the great Nebmaetre. Was he not one of the greatest kings who ever lived?"

Scarab smiled. "True. And my brother Smenkhkare will surpass him." She shrugged and set out across the wide Avenue, heading for the Street of Glass. "If I had my way though, I would make all gods of equal importance, give them all a proper respect."

"Perhaps that is just a problem of the cities, my la...Scarab." Khu hurried to keep up. "Back on the farm we had an awareness of every god. My father Pa-it greets the sun every day, not just as the Aten, but also as Khepri, Re, Heru and Atum. A farmer is always in debt to Geb of the growing things, Su of the wholesome air, Tefnut of the night dew that freshens the crops, Hapi who brings us the blessed inundation every year..."

"I understand, Khu," Scarab interrupted. She placed a slim hand on the young man's bronzed arm. "I understand. You are closer to the land, to the very essence of Kemet, to our Two Lands. You can see the importance of the gods. That is why we must make everyone aware of the great debt we owe to all our gods, not just one or two or fifty."

"So we need to get back to our old worship and remove the taint of Atenism."

"Aten is a god too, an aspect of the greatest of them." Scarab gestured up at the sun, now close to the zenith. "We must find a way to let all gods be a part of our lives." She looked around at the street they now found themselves in. "Enough of this talk for now, dear Khu; we must remember what we came here for. There is Ahhotep's workshop."

They stood on the Street of Glass, outside a great walled enclosure, peering in through a wide opening. Two heavy wooden doors lay flat back against the crumbling mud brick walls, as if holding them up. Within the courtyard a large tamarind tree shed dappled shade over the bare, dusty earth of the interior. Leading the way into the courtyard, Scarab made her way toward the figure of an old man seated on a wooden stool and leaning up against the gnarled bark of the tree. As she entered the shade, she felt the temperature drop and she smelled the sharp acid-sweet tang of fallen tamarind pods. Her mind leapt back years to almost-forgotten memories of the palace gardens and her naming-day.

She studied the old man on the stool for a few moments. Head bent forward on his bare chest that was pocked and scarred with innumerable small blemishes, the man snored softly, one hand on his lap, the other hanging beside him, close to an overturned pot of beer.

Clapping her hands together softly, she called out. "Ahhotep!" After a moment she repeated her call, a trifle louder. The old man's soft snores broke off abruptly and his head half-lifted, his eyes blinking and squinting.

"What? What is it? Nakht, is there a problem?" He came fully awake and looked up without recognition at the young woman standing in front of him, backlit by the glare of the noonday sun. Then he rubbed his eyes and leaned forward peering at her. "My lady Beketaten, is that you?" He fumbled for the stick that lay propped against the trunk of the tree, forcing himself upright on shaky legs.

Scarab moved forward quickly and put a hand on Ahhotep's shoulder, gently pushing him back down. "Sit, Ahhotep. We will not stand on ceremony today."

Ahhotep struggled for a moment before giving up. "It is not right, my lady, that I should sit while you stand." He coughed, his breath hard and rasping within his chest and he hawked to spit before thinking better of it and swallowing convulsively. "Let...let me call for a chair for you."

"Khu will get one; you sit quietly and catch your breath." Waiting until her young man trotted off toward the buildings, Scarab knelt in the dust and picked up the fallen pot, smelling sour barley beer. Fluid slopped within the earthenware container and she handed it to the old man. "Here, you look as if you need it."

Ahhotep took the pot with a trembling hand and drank, beer dribbling over his chin and onto his chest. "Thank you, my lady," he whispered, stifling a belch. "The days are long for an old man with little left to do."

"Not so old, Ahhotep." Scarab looked searchingly at his lined face and white hair. She hesitated and subtracted ten years from her guess. "Why, you can be no more than fifty. A fine age but by no means decrepit."

"Sixty-five, my lady, and not much longer for this world." Ahhotep sighed and ran a hand through his long hair, sweeping it back from his face. "I am ready. My wife died three years back and I have a fine tomb waiting for me in the hills. If it were not that Nakht needs me still I would go now."

As if called, Khu trotted back across the courtyard with a stool, a short but robust young man in a leather apron hard on his heels. Setting the stool in the shade by the old man, Khu withdrew a few paces but remained attentive.

Ahhotep gestured toward the young man. "You remember Nakht? Boy, pay attention. This is the lady Beketaten, sister to both kings. You pay her proper respect now."

Nakht smiled and bobbed his head. "I remember, father." Turning to Scarab, he bowed his head. "Greetings, most beautiful lady. You are indeed welcome in my father's humble workshop."

"I thank you for your kind words of welcome, Nakht, son of Ahhotep." Scarab inclined her head slightly, a gentle smile on her face.

"May I offer you water?" Nakht drew a small pitcher from behind his back, the earthenware sides beaded with condensation. He carefully extracted a delicate blue cup from a small leather bag at his side and poured a cool stream of clear water into it, then held it out. The dappled sunlight glinted on the cup, throwing out gleams of deep blue like the early evening sky.

Scarab took the cup delicately and gave a small cry of delight. "Glass? But it is so blue, so delicate. How did you make it?"

33

Nakht blushed and looked away. "It...er, my father..."

"Nonsense, boy. Take credit for it." Ahhotep smiled indulgently and leaned closer to Scarab, dropping his voice as if vouchsafing a secret despite being heard by everyone. "He made it himself, but how I don't know. He won't even tell me...me who taught him everything he knows."

"Then I will not ask him for the secret," Scarab said. "It is truly beautiful, Nakht." She sipped and smiled again. "It even makes the water taste better."

"Thank you, my lady." Nakht bowed again before turning and hurrying away across the courtyard.

Ahhotep watched him go, a tear glistening in one eye. "I have never regretted the day I adopted him," he murmured. "Never, for one instant." He shook his head and brushed at his eyes with the back of a gnarled hand. "To business, I think. You are too busy to waste your time on the maundering of an old man."

"I'll always have time for you, Ahhotep. You were good to me when I was a little girl."

The old man turned to where Khu stood by the trunk of the tamarind tree. "You see what she is like? Royalty, sister to the king, no less...two kings, yet she still has time for a commoner."

"What did you want to see us about?" Khu asked. "It was rather surprising you asked us to come out here, rather than presenting a petition with everyone else at the Hall of Justice."

"Yes. Yes, I am sorry for that, but I had my reasons. I did not truly think you would come yourself, my lady. I thought perhaps you might send a trusted servant." Ahhotep's eyes twinkled. "Someone like this young man here."

"I am on the King's Council, old man. I am not a servant."

Ahhotep stared up at Khu blandly. "Are you not the king's servant, lad? And this lady's too? I seem to remember it was not so long ago you were a gawking farm lad."

Khu flushed. "That was in the past. I am a trusted member of the council now and..."

"Enough, Khu," Scarab broke in gently. "Nobody here thinks less of you for your origins. You are what you are, my friend if nothing else." She turned back to the old man. "What were your reasons for not wanting to come to the Hall of Justice?"

34

Ahhotep sat in silence for a moment then spoke in a low voice, as if afraid of being overheard. "You know how I make glass, my lady? Not the details, you understand, just that I need various salts, minerals, even metals to mix in when the glass is molten. Well, these things I have to bring in, often from far away. I get alum from the Dekla oasis, certain ores I get from Nubia and Mitanni, and others can be mined here in the Two Lands."

"Yes, I know these things."

"Recently, I have been buying minerals from a certain merchant called Ptahwery, a man who owns a caravan that plies a route south to the second cataract. Down near the old king's gold mines. There is a rock there that yields an additive that gives the glass a unique yellow-green tinge, so bright it almost seems to glow." Ahhotep shrugged. "It is not a popular colour, but that is beside the point."

"I was wondering when you might get to the point," Khu growled.

Scarab raised a hand in warning. "Go on, Ahhotep."

"Robbers are a problem sometimes. The caravans are safe enough close to the mines where the presence of soldiers is enough to protect them, but further away, closer to Waset, it is another story."

Scarab frowned. "Robbers I can understand. Since my brother Akhenaten emptied the prisons there has been lawlessness in the land..."

"As well we know," Khu grunted.

"...but this is a matter for the authorities. Why does your friend Ptahwery not just bring this to the attention of the Medjay or the local garrison commander? Even bringing a petition at the morning audience would probably yield results."

"Because of who leads the robbers, my lady."

Scarab regarded the old man in silence for long seconds. "Who?" she asked softly.

"Mentopher, steward of Tjaty Ay."

"Your friend must be mistaken," Khu laughed. "Can you imagine a man with that sort of position and wealth stooping to rob a few camels in the desert?"

"Do you know the man?" Ahhotep asked.

"No, but the idea is preposterous. A man that well-known would have been recognized long since."

"Exactly what I said to Ptahwery."

35

"But there is more, isn't there, Ahhotep?"

"Yes, my lady. Other merchants have reported the same thing. The robber leader is always cloaked, even if it is very hot, and he wears a veil across his face."

"Oh, well in that case Mentopher is obviously guilty. Hand him over to the Medjay and be done with it." Khu turned to Scarab. "We have surely heard enough of this rumor and innuendo."

"Shh, Khu. Go on."

"A month ago, Ptahwery's caravan was robbed again, by the same band. The leader was cloaked as usual but this time the neckband slipped and Ptahwery caught a glimpse of a scar on the man's chest, just below his left armpit." Ahhotep demonstrated the position.

"Lots of men have scars," Scarab said gently. "Even you, old man."

"True, but few have the sign of Heru branded on their side." Ahhotep glanced up at Khu. "You know that Tjaty Ay availed himself of many of the released criminals when Waenre Akhenaten emptied the prisons? He branded his slaves with the sign of Heru. Well, Mentopher has risen in his master's service but he still retains the Heru brand. It is interesting that this robber also bears it."

Khu frowned. "Ay has many slaves. No doubt some have escaped."

"Surely that is more likely, Ahhotep? It is a great leap from seeing some brigand with a Heru brand to accusing the steward of Tjaty Ay."

Ahhotep snorted. "Do you think I would trouble you if that was all?" he sighed and leaned back against the trunk of the tamarind. "Forgive me, my lady, but of course that would not be enough. Last week I was at Ay's estates across the river. He has a glass foundry there and Ikhnapu, the manager, is an old friend of mine. Over a pot of beer he told of this beautiful glowing yellow glass vessel the steward had brought back from Nubia on his recent trip there. He went and got it, to show me that it really existed."

Scarab waited as Ahhotep closed his eyes, his head against the rough bark of the tree. "And? Did it exist?"

"Oh, yes. I knew even before he brought it out to me. It was mine. I made it myself, here in my own foundry."

"You are sure?" Khu broke in. "I know you turn out good pieces, but could not someone else have made it?"

"It had my mark on it. I put five small lines overlain to form a star on the bottom of my best pieces. It is so others can tell who made it. I made two of these vessels and sent one as a gift to the governor of Qerert, from whose territories the colouring ore came. Ptahwery carried it for me, until he was robbed by the man with the Heru scar."

"And he brought it back to the house of his master." Khu nodded grimly. "How do we handle this, Scarab? Confront Ay or just go to the Medjay with it?"

Scarab shook her head. "Neither. We do not know how high the rot has spread. If it is just Mentopher seeking to augment his wealth, then if we report it, Ay will cast his steward loose to face justice. If Ay himself is involved, then we must carefully consider our actions. One cannot impugn the highest in the land without strong evidence of complicity."

"So what do we do?"

"I will take it to my brother Smenkhkare." Scarab turned back to Ahhotep, who was watching her with interest. "Who else knows of this?"

"Only Ptahwery. He came to me as a friend and I have told only you."

"Not even Nakht?"

"Especially not Nakht. He is young and his craft is starting to bring him to the notice of the rich and powerful. If he suspected Ay of wrongdoing, his face would shout it out though his tongue was silent."

Scarab nodded. "Good. Keep it so. I will talk to my brother and he will decide where we go from here." She rose to her feet and smoothed down her linen dress. "We will take our leave of you, dear Ahhotep. Come up to the palace soon. I would like to commission a glass goblet from you as a gift, and we will need to discuss it."

Ahhotep forced himself up onto tottery legs. "I would be honoured, my lady." He bowed, then stooped to pick up the blue glass cup with a little bit of water still pooled in the bottom. He tipped it out onto the dry ground and handed it to Scarab.

"Please accept this small gift from the workshop of Ahhotep and Son."

Scarab smiled and lovingly cradled the glass in her hands, holding it in a sun-dapple so shards of blue light flashed and spun. "It is beautiful, Ahhotep, but I cannot accept it. It was made by Nakht, by a process that he holds dear. I could not take it."

"It belongs in a king's palace. It would please me...and Nakht, if you would house it in a fitting place."

"Very well. I shall send it to Akhet-Aten, to the young prince Tutankhaten. He will be nine shortly and already he appreciates beautiful things. It will do them good to see that the best things still come from Waset."

Ahhotep beamed, his broad grin of pleasure showing up many gaps in his discoloured teeth. He handed Khu a piece of cloth and the young man carefully wrapped the cup. They bade the old glass-maker farewell and left him underneath the tamarind tree.

"Where to now, Scarab? Back to the palace? We need to get this somewhere safe." Khu hefted the cloth-covered glass.

"Soon. I want to talk to Shenfer, the wine merchant, first. I hear he has a new vintage and I am eager to try it."

"The quickest way would be through the docks if you don't mind a few smells."

"When have I ever minded a few smells, Khu?" Scarab grinned. "Come on, we can cut through here." She led the way down an alley that snaked out of the main business area into the seamier side of the city.

The alley broadened out into a street as it wound its way west toward the river. The streets in this area were potholed and dirty, littered with the refuse of a crowded populace. The people were still plentiful, buying and selling, arguing and conversing, but there was an edge to their voices, their faces harder and eyes more watchful. Children swarmed as they did everywhere but many appeared undernourished and covered in sores. Dogs still fought for scraps but as they neared the river, rats joined them in their search for food and over everything was the roar of flies, darkening the air and adding to the growing stench.

"I'm not sure we should have come this way, Khu. The stink is greater than I thought. Why don't people clean these streets?" Scarab brushed at the flies buzzing around her.

Khu shrugged, kicking at a stray dog that wandered too close. "Where are they going to dump the refuse? At least in the richer areas the merchants hire men to cart it away. Here nobody has the wealth to waste on good works."

"The city fathers should pay...look, Khu." Scarab pointed. "A rat just bit that child." A minor commotion erupted on the far side of the street as the screaming child was snatched up by its mother, the older children stamping and hitting at the rats with yells of laughter. Scarab hurried on, dragging Khu with her.

"Up here." Khu directed them out of the narrow street into one that if not much wider, was at least a little cleaner. Fewer people walked the street and these mostly men. Scarab's clean white linen dress and finely coiffed wig attracted a few looks, as did Khu's brightly coloured kilt, leather sandals and armbands, very evidently of gold.

Scarab looked around her at the buildings, noting the lack of shops and the wide, low windows with women sitting within them. "I know where we are. These houses are brothels and this is the Street of Whores."

Khu looked at her with an expression of curiosity mingled with wariness. "Do you know what a whore is, my lady?"

"Don't start with the 'my lady' again, Khu. Yes, I know what a whore is and I've been here before." Scarab laughed. "If you could see yourself, Khu. I came here when I was a child. Smenkhkare brought me into the city on one of his expeditions and we got lost."

A woman had been staring at the young man and woman talking on the street and as Scarab laughed, she pushed away from the darkened entrance to one of the brothels and stood in front of them, holding the folds of her dirty diaphanous gown closed.

"You is the young lady from the palace, isn't you? They says you listens to common folk."

Khu, after a moment's hesitation, stepped forward and shouldered the woman aside. "Out of here, woman. We have no time for you."

The woman ducked under the man's arm and confronted Scarab again. "Wills you listens to me, then?"

Khu grabbed the woman's shoulder, his face reddening with rage. "I told you to..."

The woman turned on him, cutting his outburst off. "Be quiet boy. I don't know whats you is doing in this street, but I doubts you know what to do with it except pee." She swung back to Scarab who was gaping at Khu's discomfiture. "Please, miss. You is me only hope."

Scarab held out a hand to restrain Khu, and nodded at the woman. "All right, I'll listen. What did you want to say?" Looking at the woman intently, Scarab saw that she was not the young woman she first thought. Heavy makeup, rouged cheeked, stained lips and eyes sticky with kohl imperfectly masked the wrinkles and lines in her face. The hand stretched out imploringly was cracked and worn, trembling slightly, and beneath the dirty and faded gown her body sagged, revealing the ravages of time and ill-use. "What is your name?"

"Tio, miss. I was once a maid to...to Lady Sebtitis, but I fells on hard times."

"You want alms, Tio? I have nothing with me, but if you go to the temple of Amun at sunrise or sunset they will feed you."

"I has been there, miss, and priests or no, theys wants something in return for the god's bounty. No, I don't wants alms, miss, I wants to stop whats I doing."

"So stop," Khu growled. "Seems simple to me, woman. If you don't like whoring, then stop and find yourself honest work." He flushed and bobbed his head apologetically. "Sorry Scarab, I got carried away there, but really, her fate is in her own hands."

"What woulds you fornicating well know about it, boy?" The woman burst into tears and pushed roughly at the young man. "Yous men are all the same. You use us 'til we's worn out thens you casts us aside."

"So what do you want, Tio?" Scarab asked gently. "You want to stop your...your line of work?"

Tio spat at Khu and turned back to face Scarab, the kohl around her eyes streaking her face so that it looked like some harsh caricature of an old woman. She blew her nose with the fingers of one hand and wiped them on her dress. "Yes. Yes, miss, I do. Will you helps me?"

Scarab pursed her lips, a tiny frown creasing her forehead. "What would you have me do?"

"I needs a job, miss. I is willing to do anything." Her face brightened into a gap-toothed smile. "I used to be a lady's maid, p'raps I coulds be one again?"

One side of Scarab's mouth twitched. "I think we won't reach quite so high to start with, Tio. Would you be willing to work in a kitchen?"

"Yes, miss, anywheres. You finds me a job, I works real hard."

"Come up to the palace...you know where the palace is, don't you? Then come to the rear entrance, by the shrine of Nut by the servant's quarters. Ask for the overseer of the kitchens, Horshir." Scarab looked carefully at Tio's face. "Can you remember that? Rear entrance by the servant's quarters, overseer Horshir."

Tio nodded, hope brightening her eyes. "I'll go there right now, miss."

"Not now, Tio. Tomorrow. I must speak to Horshir first, so he knows you are coming. Go at noon tomorrow and do not wear makeup. Wear your cleanest dress."

"Thanks you, miss." Tio sketched a crude curtsey, grinning broadly. She turned to go before stopping and looking back over her shoulder. "Does...does this job pay much, miss?"

"No, Tio. You will get food and a place to sleep. Maybe a little copper if you work hard and do everything Horshir tells you, but it is a start. At least you will not be living here." Scarab waved her hand vaguely at the buildings.

Tio's face fell and tears started trickling down her cheeks again. "I needs to earn gold, miss."

Khu, who had been pacing the street, glaring at anyone who looked in their direction, whipped round and gave a harsh laugh. "Gods, you overprice yourself, woman. You'd be lucky to earn two copper pieces spreading your legs. And you want gold for washing pots and pans?"

Tio spat at him again before dropping her voice so only Scarab could hear. "I owes my...my pimp, miss. I owes him a deben of gold at least. He won't let me go unlesses I pays him."

"How did you come to owe so much, Tio?"

The woman shook her head. "I don't know. He makes me buy me dresses and pots of makeup out of me earnings." She sobbed again. "No matter how hards I works, I always owes him more."

Scarab put a hand on Tio's arm. "Maybe he'll let you pay him off slowly."

"No, miss. He'd kills me first." Tio stared up at Scarab. "Maybes you could talks to him, miss? Make him leaves me alone?"

Khu snorted loudly. "I can see it now, my lady. A princess, sister of the king talking to a common pimp. Why not just pay the man yourself and be done with it?" He strode forward and interposed himself between the two women. "You've talked long enough to this...this person." He rounded on Tio, pushing her back. "What makes you think you can talk to a high-born lady like that? She is sister to the king and

41

a member of his Council. I am a Councilor too, for that matter. And you dare to ask us to talk to your sniveling pimp?"

"He be a Councilor too," Tio yelled.

"What?" Scarab restrained Khu with one hand. "What did you say? Who is your pimp?"

"Mahuhy."

"Councilor Mahuhy?" Khu goggled, his mouth dropping open.

Scarab's mouth curled in distaste. "I knew Mahuhy had unsavory dealings, right from when I first met him, but I did not think he was still a brothel keeper."

"Not just brothels, miss." Tio glanced around at several passers-by who were looking curiously at them, attracted by the raised voices. She lowered her voice. "He has at least three brothels with over twenty girls and...and many other things. He..." Tio shook her head and fell silent.

Scarab regarded her for several minutes before nodding decisively. "I will talk to him, Tio. Come up to the palace tomorrow as we agreed. We will find you a job and work something out with Mahuhy."

"Bless you, miss," Tio murmured and walked slowly back to the brothel as Scarab and Khu walked off down the street. She did not see the two young men leaning against a wall, who immediately started after them.

Khu and Scarab walked in silence, each keeping their own counsel, along several streets, working their way down through the city toward the docks. The air grew moist, a rank stink of mud and effluent and the mingled scents of fish and spices drifted from the wharves, overlain by the sharper smell of pitch. The population changed around them by degrees, fewer women and children venturing onto the streets, their places taken by almost-naked laborers and sailors. Their palace garb drew more looks and Khu started to look around with a touch of unease.

"I don't think we should have come this way," he muttered.

"Nobody should be enslaved like that woman," Scarab replied, ignoring his remark. "It angers me that in a land that is free and just like our Kemet, a woman can be so used by immoral men."

"Eh? Oh, the whore. Well, she chose her life in the first place, Scarab. Women do it all the time."

"If it was solely a matter of her choice, Khu, I would not mind so much," Scarab snapped, a touch of asperity in her voice. "But how much choice does she have? You heard she is in debt. A deben of gold is an enormous sum to a woman who earns no more than a few copper pieces in a day."

"She was born to it. You should not worry about injustice so much, the gods know if a wrong is being done."

Scarab stopped dead in the street and glared at Khu. "You are saying a woman cannot be in charge of her own life, cannot better herself?"

Khu frowned. "We all have a position in life that comes from the gods. It is given to us to change a little, but what would happen if everyone decided to become what they are not? A laborer becoming a noble, a soldier becoming a scribe, or..." he laughed. "Even a fisherman becoming king."

"Or a farm boy becoming a King's Councilor?" Scarab asked quietly. "Do not forget that even Per-Aa, the Great House, my own family, were mere soldiers once. A person is not what they are, Khu, but what they can make of themselves."

"I suppose you are right, my lady." Khu grunted and looked away. "I still think it is dangerous to seek to change too much."

"How much is too much? Is it too much to change a whore into a kitchen servant? She was once a lady's maid."

"So she claims." Khu raised a hand defensively. "All right, I will allow that some people can change...or be changed, but there are limits. Where would our dear land be if those in power changed?" He grinned suddenly. "Are you thinking of changing, Scarab? Do you have a sudden desire to be a soldier? Or a scribe?"

"Could I not be? At least I have the position and influence to change my station in life if I chose."

Khu snorted. "You could not. You would not be allowed to. You will marry your brother and raise sons to rule Kemet. That is your lot in life."

"If I choose it to be. My brother Smenkhkare will not hold me against my will. I may yet decide to...to, I don't know, marry a soldier or a farmer."

Khu stared at her solemnly. "If you marry your Paramessu, I will dance at your wedding, Scarab, but you know it will never happen.

Your brother loves you but you are too important to Kemet. Any man who marries you will have a claim on the throne." He shook his head. "You will marry a king, almost certainly your brother Smenkhkare."

Scarab opened her mouth to defend her soldier love Paramessu, feeling a hot flush of embarrassment stain her cheeks. A man brushed against Khu and he stumbled forward, almost knocking Scarab over. "Careful, Khu," she cried. "What's the matter?"

Khu half-supported himself on Scarab's arm, staring in disbelief at a smear of blood on one hand. "I...I've been cut." He stared at the back of the retreating man, then back at Scarab as another man moved swiftly forward, a dull gleam of copper in his hand. Launching himself forward in a leap that stumbled and faltered, he screamed out a warning, dropping the cloth-covered glass as he did so.

Scarab turned as the man stabbed, the blade ripping through her linen dress. She hit out at the man ineffectually and danced back against the wall of the building on the edge of the street. "Help," she cried out to passers-by. "Help us, good people." With hardly more than a glance in their direction, the street emptied, leaving Khu and Scarab backed up against a wall and three armed men facing them.

"What do you want?" Khu gasped, holding his side where bright blood trickled slowly through his fingers, staining his kilt. "All we have are these armbands. You are welcome to them."

One of the men grinned, revealing yellowed and rotting teeth. "Toss them over here then and be quick about it."

"Enough," growled one of his companions, a tall, thickset man in a voluminous cloak. "We are not here for the gold." He glanced up and down the almost-deserted street. "Finish them before someone alerts the medjay."

Rotten Teeth and the other man moved forward, copper knives held at the ready, their faces relaxed, expecting a swift killing of an unarmed man and a girl.

Khu did not wait, throwing himself forward to grapple with Rotten Teeth, one hand gripping the man's wrist, the other seeking for a grip. They swayed in the street, the blood pouring out of Khu's side and spattering the ground.

Scarab moved away, her eyes watching the other man's, her sandaled feet stepping back carefully. "Who are you?" she asked.

"Why do you do this?" The man came on in silence. "Do you know who I am? I can reward you if you turn and leave."

The man grinned. "I know, but I have gold enough, lady." His knife arm thrust forward, the blow low and straight. Scarab gasped and swayed to one side, the blade cutting into linen again. Her dress fell open, revealing her sole item of underclothing, a short kilt. "Pretty young thing, aren't you?" the man said calmly, as if discussing the weather. "Too bad I have to kill you."

"Finish it," the thickset man yelled. "I can hear the Medjay coming."

The man in front of Scarab nodded and stabbed, grabbing at her at the same time. She eluded the blade but his grasping hand grabbed her ripped dress and hauled her close as his other hand drew back the knife again.

Scarab gave a cry and wriggled free of her dress, feeling the fabric rip. She glanced quickly over to where Khu lay on the ground, still fighting with the other man, then back to her own opponent. As the man grinned at her nakedness she stepped forward and planted her sandaled foot squarely in the man's testicles. He fell forward with a strangled cry of pain, dropping the knife and clutching his groin. Another pace forward and Scarab's knee rose with a satisfying crack under the man's jaw. The man's head snapped back and he dropped and lay still. Scarab scooped the knife up from the ground and, sparing a glance for the suddenly indecisive leader, dropped on her knees beside Rotten Teeth as he pried Khu's grip from his knife-holding hand.

"I think not." Scarab slipped the copper knife between Rotten Teeth's ribs and the man juddered, his surprised eyes opening wide. His own knife fell, narrowly missing a blood-covered Khu, before he collapsed sideways to the dusty street.

The thickset man stepped forward, drawing a short sword from beneath his cloak, and then looked round toward the sound of shouting and drumming feet. He hesitated a moment before taking to his heels as a troop of Medjay, short kilts flying, raced down the street toward them. The men ran past, shouting to the thickset man to stop but he disappeared around the corner and out of sight.

The Medjay officer stopped, his eyes widening at the sight of a disheveled young woman, her bare breasts heaving from her exertions, standing beside two still forms and a young blood-covered man.

Scarab smiled and nodded toward Khu. "Send for a physician at once, officer. And take that man..." she pointed at her opponent. "... into custody. The other one is dead." Reaching up, she adjusted the wig on her head as it threatened to slip off.

The Medjay officer gaped then snapped off a series of orders to his men. One ran off at high speed while others set about staunching Khu's wound and examining the other men.

"I want that man questioned, officer. They meant to kill us and knew who we were."

"And who are you?"

"Princess Beketaten, officer, and that man your men are roughly attending to is Councilor Khu. If he dies because of his treatment, you will follow him over the river."

The man flushed and bowed. "My pardon, lady, I did not recognise you...ah, dressed as you are." He turned and yelled at his men and their ministrations at once became gentler. Picking up her shredded linen dress he offered it to Scarab who held it to her, quickly seeing it was pointless trying to cover herself with it. She threw it to one side. One of the Medjay troopers slipped his kilt off and, standing unselfconsciously naked, draped it around her shoulders.

The physician arrived, together with a litter and quickly had Khu transferred to it and hurried off to the palace. Scarab indicated the fallen assassins. "What about them? I want to know who planned this."

"Thems both dead, miss," commented the naked trooper. "Thisun with a knife in his heart, thatun with a broken neck."

"Have their bodies brought up to the palace," Scarab told the officer. "And the one who ran off if your men catch him. I mean to get to the bottom of this." She looked around at the gathering crowd before picking up the fallen glass, finding it still intact. Turning, she mustered as much dignity as she could and walked after the physician and his patient. The officer, after a few moments hesitation, sent a squad of his men after her, detailing others to clear the bodies from the street.

Chapter 3

❚❚ I send you and two others to take out a raw youth and a girl and you cannot even manage that. Can you think of any good reason why I should not have you thrown to the crocodiles?"

The thickset man, now without his cloak, dropped to his knees on the marble floor of the great chamber and held out his arms imploringly, revealing a whitened brand in the form of a hawk on the side of his chest. "Master, the Medjay arrived before we could do anything."

"But not before the girl killed your two men. How is that possible?"

"It happened so fast, master. Mende took on the youth and almost had him, but Nupher toyed with the girl. I was as surprised as he when she kicked him. It was a lucky kick." The man hesitated, his eyes flicking to the two guards standing by the walls of the chamber, then back to the old man standing in front of him. "Then she killed Mende with Nupher's dagger."

"And what were you doing while all this happened?

The man licked his lips before answering. "I...I was keeping watch."

"Really? Watching for whom? The Medjay did not arrive for several minutes and the streets were deserted."

"I was sure they could handle them," the man whined.

"Mentopher, you have failed me. You know the penalty for failure." The old man noted the guards tensing with anticipation, and concealed a smile.

"Please, master, I beg you, have mercy."

The old man turned and walked over to a balcony that overlooked a small garden. He looked out at the flowering shrubs and ornamental pond and at the gardeners hard at work raking leaves, on hands and knees trimming the grass, and weeding the beds of flowers. Stretching, he raised his arms above his head and relaxed, feeling the serenity of the garden flow over him.

"Mentopher, report to the drill sergeant. You are to have twenty lashes for your failure. Tell him blood is to flow."

"Y...yes, master." A pause... "Thank you for your mercy, master." Mentopher arose and stumbled from the chamber, closing the door behind him.

The old man closed his eyes and breathed deeply, the warm scented air from the gardens filling his lungs. Without turning he snapped out orders to his guards. "Bring wine, and send for my guests." He breathed deep again and leaned on the balustrade, watching the gardeners. A smile played across his lips as he noticed their sudden fear and redoubled efforts.

Wine arrived with a muffled knock on the cedar wood doors of the chamber and a muttered apology from a servant as a pitcher of river-cooled wine, another of river water and a tray of faience goblets were set on the wide ebony table inlaid with gold and ivory. The old man did not turn from the window, ignoring the servants and their mission until he was sure they had left. Then he turned and walked over to the table. He picked up one of the cups and examined it, turning it to follow the pattern. His finger picked at a tiny flaw in the rim and he put it back on the tray, frowning. Selecting another cup he repeated the performance and, satisfied with the beauty and perfection of this one, filled it with dark, sweet wine from the pitcher. He raised it to his nose and inhaled the strong aroma, a mixture of scents--fruit, ripe and succulent; the good, rich earth of his vineyards far to the north in the delta lands near Zarw; the sharp tang of the oaken wine-press and even a trace of the mellow wax that sealed the wine-jars. He sipped, and closed his eyes, savoring the taste, remembering days long past when he was more concerned with the management of his estates than the running of a kingdom.

The cedar doors creaked and the old man's eyes snapped open as he swiveled to face the men who trooped into the room. Dismissing the guards, he ushered his guests toward the table and the wine, then toward several couches and chairs at one end of the balcony.

"Be seated, gentlemen. I believe you all know each other, though this may well be the first time you have gathered together." The old man put his wine cup down on the balustrade and turned to face the five men seated facing him. "Bear with me a few moments while I enumerate your strengths and attributes so you may each take comfort from the very special skills and abilities each of you brings to the task in hand.

"Bakt, third prophet of Amun, whose strong hand guides the priests of Amun and whose wisdom is god-given. Save for the present Hemnetjer and my brother, the most powerful man in the realm of the divine.

"Kheper, Overseer of the guild of Corn Factors, leading businessman of Waset and a man whose counsel is listened to in every city of our Two Lands. A man whose trade empire extends into every land that borders on Kemet and into many that do not.

"Usermontju, Chief of the Medjay of Waset. A man whose civil power and authority, while not officially recognized by the mayor, is absolute within the city boundaries.

"Psenamy, General of the Army and ex-commander of the Amun legion here in Waset, until his untimely and unjust dismissal by Paatenemheb. Although no longer in command of an army, he commands the loyalty of many individual men and has, with the aid of much gold, raised and trained a small army of his own.

"And lastly, Maya, treasury scribe, without whose creative manipulation of the treasury records, none of this would have been possible."

Maya stirred in his seat. "Thank you, Ay. Let us not forget that you, Tjaty and most powerful man in Kemet, after the kings, are the one that recruited us all to your cause--now our cause. You have made promises to us all, effectively bought us. Have you now reached a time when these promises can be fulfilled?"

A ripple of interest washed over the other men. Psenamy stopped with his cup of water halfway to his lips. "This is true? The time has come?"

Ay nodded. "In a word, yes."

"Can you elaborate on that?" Usermontju put his wine down and leaned forward, a hunger growing in his eyes. "Are we talking about resistance or...or rebellion?"

"Hush," Kheper whispered. "Let there be no overt talk of that." He glanced toward the open balcony. "Who knows who could be listening?"

"None listen," Ay said flatly. "My security in this palace is absolute."

"Very well. I accept your assurances," Psenamy answered. "The time has come for action, but what action are you talking about?"

Ay slowly walked over to the other men and stood with his legs braced and fists planted firmly on his hips. His posture lent him an impression of youth and strength, a look belied by his wrinkled skin, a growing paunch and dark veins scarring his bronzed legs. "Too long has Kemet suffered beneath the yoke of the heretic," he said softly. "Too long have our people done without their gods. We must strike a blow, a righteous blow, for the freedom to worship as we will and to restore the honour of Kemet in the eyes of the nations. Akhenaten must fall."

"And be replaced by whom?" Bakt asked. "Smenkhkare will not sit idly by and watch us remove his brother. Or will he? Can you control Smenkhkare?"

Ay shook his head, his white hair flying. "No, the king no longer takes my advice, preferring that of a gaggle of commoners and incompetents. He must be removed also."

"So who is to reign as king, Ay? You?"

"I have no desire to be king. I am a faithful servant of Kemet."

"You would let anarchy rule?" Psenamy scoffed. "Come, you and I both have had command of men. We know there must always be a leader, a ruler. Who is it to be if not Smenkhkare or you?"

"Tutankhaten."

Kheper laughed. "But he is a boy, not yet nine summers. How can he reign?"

"He is of that cursed blood too, bearing that cursed name," Bakt added. "At least our present ruler in Waset puts his faith in Re."

"Names can be changed, Bakt. Have you forgotten how the heretic was once named Amenhotep? We can crown him without the 'aten' and put 'amen' back in his name."

The priest nodded. "That would be pleasing to Amun."

"But his age," Kheper repeated. "He is too young to reign alone. If he was co-regent at least he would have proper guidance."

"He will have proper guidance."

"Eh? Who from? You, Ay?"

"Can you think of anyone better?"

"So you will not sit on the throne of Kemet," put in Maya. "But you will control the king anyway."

"Is there anyone better suited? I have been adviser and confidant to three kings, why not another? And this at a time when Kemet surely needs my talents."

"Very well," Maya agreed. "Let us say you can control the boy. How will you topple the kings? I seem to remember you had some difficulty toppling one king three years ago."

Ay stared unblinking at the treasury scribe, reminding himself how useful the man was to his enterprise. The man met his gaze for several seconds then looked away. Ay suppressed a smile. "I went into that on the behest of my daughter Nefertiti, before I was ready, and even then I nearly succeeded."

"Paatenemheb." Psenamy spoke one word which hung in the air between them.

Bakt nodded. "Yes, our illustrious General of the Armies. No enterprise will succeed without that man's support. Do you have him on our side?"

"Yes," Usermontju agreed. "The man is a fanatical supporter of Akhenaten and he has the army behind him. I want no part of this if he is against us. I have no desire to end up staked out in the desert."

Ay frowned. "No, he is not on our side." He held up a hand to stem the shudder of unease in his listeners. "But we do not need him. Listen and I will tell you why. First, he is not the fanatic you think. He has no real love for Akhenaten, only for Kemet..."

"He changed his name to encompass the false god," Bakt commented.

"And has since changed it back to Horemheb. He did that in the first place because he sought gold to pay his armies. I was there when he did so and I talked to him. I know the real reason. His love is for Kemet and he will do anything to strengthen our Two Lands. If we topple the heretic and present him with a stable replacement, he will not move against us."

"And if he does?"

"He will not. Besides, he is on our Eastern borders. By the time he hears of our coup it will be too late for him to do anything. We shall send him a gift of gold, many deben of gold."

"You'd try to buy him?"

"No. The man cares nothing for personal wealth. He will use it to equip his army and he will remember where the gold came from when he needs more."

"I do not trust him," Psenamy muttered.

"I am not surprised. He dismissed you from your command. But you need not trust him; trust me when I say that he will not move against the only surviving member of the royal house, Tutankhaten."

"The only surviving male member."

"We have no desire to return to the days of a female monarch. The women will serve to cement legitimate claims to the throne. I have in mind to marry Ankhesenpaaten to Tutankhaten. Nobody could dispute his claim to the throne then."

"What of Meryetaten?"

"The widow of both Akhenaten and Smenkhkare," Ay sneered. "Well, if her sister does not produce an heir, we can always marry her to a third king."

"And Beketaten?"

"She dies."

"Why does she need to die?" Kheper asked. "She is beautiful, unmarried and a princess; one of Nebmaetre's daughters. I would have thought her a prime candidate for your plans."

"I have my reasons." Ay hesitated before continuing in a flat voice. "She is too close to her brother Smenkhkare and she has connections to Paramessu, Horemheb's adjutant. No." He shook his head. "She is too dangerous to live."

The other men digested this information in silence, drinking from their wine cups. From outside the room came the murmur of gardeners' voices and more muted, like waves on a distant shore, the ebb and flow of city life.

"Then how are we to proceed?" Kheper asked at last. "This is something that must be planned to the last detail."

"Indeed?" Ay commented dryly. "Then it is well you have me leading you. You will all have your parts to play, but you take your cues from me. I want no initiatives, you understand?" He waited for agreement from each man, pointedly staring at them until they nodded or grunted their assent.

"Very well, then. It must be soon. Smenkhkare has forced me to retire, effective at the end of the month, a mere twenty days away. Once I am officially retired, any power I have is severely restricted. So, our blow falls on the eighteenth day."

"Why then?" Maya asked.

"Because in three days time Smenkhkare leaves the city and plans to return around the end of the month, I suspect to be sure I retire."

"I have not heard of plans for any such trip," Maya commented, his forehead creasing. "I am sure I would if it were so."

"That is because it is not a formal occasion, warranting a withdrawal from the treasury. The king has heard of a lion near Djeba that is terrorizing a village, killing the cattle. He plans to hunt it down. He means to take a dozen men and enjoy a quick and pleasant hunting trip." Ay smiled and walked back over to the balustrade, leaning against it and picking up his wine cup.

"That was a fortunate turn of events."

"Fortune had nothing to do with it. My men brought him the report."

Usermontju snorted. "Then there is no lion?"

"There is a lion, though maybe not a cattle killer. It will take him a week to get to Djeba, but when he does, he will find more than a lion awaits him. I have a company of picked men who will kill him. Another week to get the news back to Waset and in the chaos, we strike."

"You mean for my troops to take the city?" Psenamy asked.

"No, Usermontju's Medjay will be enough for that. You will be busy elsewhere."

"Oh, doing what?"

"In a moment. Now, news of the death of Smenkhkare arrives in the city. Immediately, for their own protection of course, the Council is placed in custody by the Medjay. Bakt announces the temples closed in mourning, including the temple granaries; and Kheper, as head of the

Guild of Corn Factors, closes the markets, effectively shutting off food from the city."

"What of Amenemhet and Aanen, first and second prophets?" Bakt said worriedly. "If they countermand my orders there is nothing I can do."

"Amenemhet will be in Ineb Hedj and Aanen in Iunu by then. I have asked them to check on the return of the worship of Amun in those cities."

"And what of me?" asked Kheper. "You are casting me in a less than favourable role, cutting off food supplies. There will be rioting when food runs short and they will blame me."

"There is enough food in the city for two days before the granaries need be breached. Usermontju's Medjay will keep the councilors locked up and keep order in the city. If any complain, they will explain that the food has been cut off on the orders of the King's Council."

"And after two days...?"

"News will reach the city that Akhenaten has gone mad and abdicated in favour of his brother Tutankhaten. The boy's first act as *de facto* king will be to open the granaries. The citizens will be feeling the first bite of hunger by then and will praise his magnanimity. Then he will formally renounce the Aten heresy and restore freedom of worship. The people will love him."

"And I?" Psenamy asked. "What will I be doing while Waset falls?"

"You will leave Waset with your legion on the day after Smenkhkare sails south and will be in Akhet-Aten, taking the heretic into custody. The timing is not too important here as a messenger will arrive from the capital with the news of the king's abdication on the right day, even if it has not happened yet."

"But I am to only capture him rather than killing him?"

"Gods, yes. He is heretic but he is also an anointed and consecrated king of Kemet. Such an action would be god-cursed. It would shake the foundations of our society, destroy Ma'at, if he were assassinated, so he will not be killed, just locked up for his own good." Ay smiled broadly. "The news of his brother's death will no doubt completely unhinge his mind, making it necessary for the only other male relative to step in."

Psenamy frowned. "But you would kill Smenkhkare? He too is a consecrated king."

"True, but he will die as the result of a hunting accident. Also, he is only co-regent, the lesser king. Do not worry about that aspect, Psenamy...or any of you. I have thought it through most carefully. We will arrange to get Tutankhaten down to Waset within the month and I will have things prepared for his coronation."

"So soon?" Bakt looked faintly shocked. "It is usual for the heir to bury his predecessor and that cannot happen for the seventy days of the Preparation."

"There will be a burial. The Seventy Days of Preparation will take place, the king, what is left of him, or his effigy will be buried, and the new king crowned. Akhenaten will be alive but in custody and Smenkhkare will, for all people know, be in the belly of a lion."

"So we have Smenkhkare dead, the Council in custody, Akhenaten locked up and Tutankhaten crowned as king," Maya said. "What then? What is my role in this?"

"Treasurer Sutau is a councilor and regrettably will have succumbed to anxiety." Ay shrugged. "He is an old man, after all. That is where you come in, Maya. I will appoint you Treasurer, an interim position of course, until the king can confirm your appointment. You will, as Treasurer, provide us with the funds necessary to complete our task."

"I don't like the idea of just locking the heretic up," Bakt said. "He could be a focus for disaffection. The Aten still has supporters. What if he escapes?"

"Psenamy will make sure he does not. It will only be for a while, just long enough for people to forget him, and then he can quietly die of snakebite or some disease or other. Something from the gods."

"Where will he keep him?"

"The North Palace for a start. Make sure he is comfortable but do not allow him access to anyone important."

"But that can only be a temporary measure," Bakt grumbled. "Too many people will know he is there."

"Nonsense. People will be glad to be rid of him and he will be powerless. After a month or two, Psenamy can return to Waset leaving a competent officer in charge until such time as the former king meets with an accident."

Bakt scowled. "It seems to me that everyone here has a task that can easily be explained away as working to save Kemet from anarchy, but I am doing nothing except closing the temples. What do I get out of all this?"

"Why, the satisfaction of knowing you had returned Amun to his full power, glory and wealth." Ay smiled, watching Bakt's eyes carefully. "Of course," he added softly, "I planned on making you First Prophet of Amun and Hem-netjer. Would you be willing to take on this extra burden?"

Greed glowed in Bakt's eyes. "First? What of Amenemhet? And your brother Aanen for that matter?"

"Let me worry about that. In a month's time, Amun will have a new Hem-netjer." He looked around at the five men preparing to take over a kingdom. "I will visit each of you in the next few days and go over in detail the part you will play in our venture, but for now I bid you farewell." Ay raised his wine cup with a smile. "Gentlemen, let us drink to a new Kemet and the health of our young king Tutankhaten."

Chapter 4

Ankhkheperure Djeserkheperure Smenkhkare, co-regent, King of the Two Lands, Lord of the Land of the Nine Bows and highest in the land save for his weak brother Akhenaten in his far off city of the Sun; paced the floor of the upstairs reception chamber in the old palace at Waset. Although rich beyond the imagination of most men, having the treasury of Kemet at his disposal, he dressed simply in a fine white linen kilt and ordinary leather sandals. His sole ornamentation was a plain gold band around his upper left arm and a large emerald ring on the middle finger of his left hand. The fact that the ring alone would have kept a small town supplied with food for a year did not register on his mind. In his own eyes the ring was just one he liked.

"It is intolerable that my sister should be attacked on the streets of Waset, in broad daylight." Smenkhkare stopped and glared at Scarab. "What were you doing down near the docks anyway?"

Scarab raised an eyebrow but otherwise kept her face expressionless. "You sound as though you hold me responsible for my own attack." She smoothed her own thin linen gown and played absently with a large blue and red scarab brooch on her left shoulder. "As for being near the docks..." She shrugged. "Have you not taken me there yourself?"

Smenkhkare ignored the question and started pacing once more. "Would you recognise the man if you saw him again?"

"I've already told you, brother. It was Mentopher."

"Ay's steward, yes I know."

"But you don't believe me. Why not?"

"When you first told me I sent Usermontju, the chief of the Medjay to Ay's palace with a squad of men to arrest this Mentopher. Do you know what he found?"

"That he had fled, of course. I did not think he would meekly wait to be caught."

"No sister, he had not fled. He was there but he could not have done it. At the time you say he was leading an attack on you and Khu, he was lying in agony on his sleeping mat. It seems he broke one of Ay's favourite cups and was beaten for his clumsiness."

Scarab's calmness cracked and she frowned. "You took Ay's word?"

"Not just Ay. Usermontju saw him and examined the wounds. He could not have moved off his pallet yesterday."

Scarab turned away and moved to the balcony overlooking the river and the far bank with its great mortuary temples. She gripped the ledge hard, her knuckles whitening. "And what of the report from Ptahwery and Ahhotep?"

"Usermontju investigated that too. Ay released his records and revealed seventy slaves branded with the Heru emblem. Of those seventy, thirty-four have died, thirteen escaped, five were sold on and eighteen remain in Ay's employ."

"One of whom is Mentopher."

"Five witnesses swear he has not stirred outside the palace or its grounds this past month."

Scarab turned to face her brother across the room. "All Ay's men of course?"

"Of course, but in the eyes of the law they are still witnesses and even two are enough to exonerate a person."

"You know as well as I that Ay and Mentopher are guilty. Could you not have them..." Scarab's voice trailed off and she looked down at the floor.

"Have them put to the question? Is that what you were about to say?"

Scarab shook her head but would not meet her brother's eyes. "No. I didn't..." With an effort she looked up at Smenkhkare's expressionless face, searching it for her brother rather than the king. "Yes, that is what I meant, but I withdraw my words unspoken."

"Good." Smenkhkare looked away, scanning the room and its rich furnishings as if they could inspire his thoughts. "I could do it, sister. I could use my power as king and have Ay and Mentopher executed and few would mourn them. Fewer still would blame me and none to my face, but I cannot, will not, be that type of king. I will rule my people, all my people, with fairness and justice."

Scarab sighed and turned to look out of the window once more. "So he escapes again."

"Mentopher? You know of another occasion?"

"I meant Ay."

Smenkhkare crossed the room and stood close to his sister. "We shall soon be rid of Ay. I have retired him to his estates in Zarw. He leaves office at the end of the month. He is an old man and will soon be harmless."

"I'd like to believe that."

"Believe it. After this month you will probably never see Ay again. Now forget him." Smenkhkare turned his sister to face the open balcony and pointed. "There, what do you see?"

In the distance, where the great plateau of the western desert crumbled and broke into great dry valleys that opened out onto rich farmland surrounding the mortuary temples, a thick black shroud folded over the land, blurring the junction of land and sky. As they watched, thin jagged pieces of light as bright as the sun lit up the valleys momentarily. A fresh cool wind, heavy with moisture, blew toward them, invigorating the air and ruffling the dust laden palm fronds. The gaily coloured flags hung from the temple walls snapped and fluttered, their hues muted as the bank of cloud moved over the sun. The doves and pigeons that roosted amongst the palace roofs fell silent, edging together and looking at the sky askance.

"Set's breath," Smenkhkare murmured.

"Rain! Is it going to rain again? You remember last time, down by the river?"

"I remember, little sister, but this will be far more. See those...those gray veils that connect the cloud to the land? That is rain, heavy rain."

"But it will not hurt us will it? Even heavy rain can only be a bit of water falling from the sky."

"It will not hurt us, but it can do damage. There was a storm there last night and now another one. Already the tombs of the kings in the Great Place are flooding."

"But it is so dry there. Surely the water will just soak into the soil?"

"Not if the rain is heavy enough. Dry stream beds become raging torrents within minutes, sweeping away rock and dirt and anything that gets in its way. Remember that, sister. If you ever should find yourself in a dry valley and it starts raining, get out. Get to high ground." He squeezed Scarab's shoulder hard, making her wince. Abruptly, he dropped his hand and turned back toward the room. "I am going over to the Great Place today to inspect the damage. Do you want to come?"

Scarab nodded. "What can you do if it is flooded?"

Smenkhkare smiled. "You've never seen the workmen's village over there have you? The place where the craftsmen live, on the threshold of the valley of the dead kings? You'll see; there is a lot I can do."

Smenkhkare and Scarab boarded the royal barge not long after the noon meal, being joined by the Royal Scribe Ahmose, whose duties included the administration and oversight of the Great Place, and one of his assistants, a young scribe named Paser.

The barge-master ordered the lines cast off and the vessel moved ponderously out into the current, the oarsmen straining to overcome the movement of the oily waters. The storm clouds had vanished and the sun shone forth brilliantly once more, but the wind had died with the rain and the only disturbance on the face of the river was a low cresting wave from the prow of the boat, the chunking of oars dipped in unison. Crabbing sideways across the flow, the barge pulled into the dock on the western bank.

Priests of the mortuary temples met the royal party, the king's chariot standing ready, along with several other less richly ornamented ones. Smenkhkare helped his sister up and then climbed aboard, shaking the reins and setting the pair of white horses off at a trot through the rich farmlands. Quickly, the priests and scribes followed suit until a long pall of dust hung over the road that arrowed toward the fractured cliffs. Peasants worked in the fields, backs bent and heads down, scarcely looking up as the god on earth drove by.

"I don't see any sign of the rain," Scarab said. "I expected the ground to be wet." She flapped a hand ineffectually at the billowing dust.

The cliffs parted as they rode closer, widening and stretching back, deep into the desert. Immediately ahead, Scarab could see, through groves of palm and acacia, tamarind and willow, the brick walls of the new palace, long abandoned and the massive stone constructions of the mortuary temples. Their own father's, Nebmaetre Amenhotep, dwarfed the others, its gaily-painted walls and limply-hanging flags and banners silent testimony to one of the greatest kings Kemet had seen. They passed the long walls of their father's temple on one side, and the small one dedicated to that other Amenhotep, the son of Hapu, on the other.

Twisting around, Scarab saw the following chariot, bearing the Royal Scribe, slow and the men inside salute the small temple. She peered around her brother to stare to the north first, then the south, but all she could see was the rich farmland merging into a hazy green stain, glints and flashes of light reflecting off innumerable canals and channels that fed water from the river to the fields. She knew that somewhere to the south lay the great palace of her father Amenhotep and the great lake that he had carved out of the farmlands to please her mother Tiye. It had been many years since she had seen it and she felt a touch of wistfulness, wishing she could see it again. She looked ahead once more and saw that they were about to leave a land brimming with life for a dry and dusty land. The sun shone suddenly hotter and she felt the life and moisture sucked right out of her.

The road turned left, then right into one of the smaller valleys, the crumbling rock, limestone and shale, mounting up on either side. The roar and grind of the chariot wheels, the pounding drive of horses' hooves beat back at them from the walls of the valley and the dust, no longer borne away by the faintest of breezes in the open country, enveloped them in an acrid cloud. The road passed a village, walled and crowded, and started climbing up toward what Scarab could now see was a ridge sweeping from south to north across the real entrance to the valley.

Smenkhkare leaned closer to Scarab and spoke loudly, pitching his voice over the clatter and roar. "The tombmakers' village. This is where all the men who work on the tombs, masons, sculptors, artists, live. Their wives and families too."

"It looks dreadful. So dry and...and there are no plants, no living things."

Smenkhkare grinned, the dust lying ashen on his coppery skin, his teeth white through the dirt. "There are plenty of living things here, sister. Scorpions, snakes and sometimes other things. You'll probably see hawks and if we are here when night falls you'll see bats and hear crickets singing. The Great Place is a place of both life and death." He pointed into the hills and cliffs on their right. "You know what's up there? The tombs of the nobles. They seek to be close to their king in death as in life."

Scarab peered up through the dust clouds. "I don't see anything."

"Nor should you. The entrances to the tombs must remain hidden else thieves would rob the tombs of their gold, consigning the nobles who lie within to an afterlife of poverty."

Scarab sneezed from the dust and rubbed the tip of her nose with the back of her hand. "Why is it so dusty if it has just rained?"

"The land is dry and soaks up the water. Only if the rain is heavy enough will it flood for an hour or two before the ground and the sun soak it up."

The road veered east of north but still climbed up a gentle incline. Ahead lay a camp, an arrangement of brown linen and hide tents and lean-tos, interspersed with crumbling mud brick walls. A few men stood around, but when they saw the royal party, dropped to their knees, bending forward until their heads were in the dust. The small procession thundered past, up the road which led them along a flat ridge for a while before descending in a steep curve to join another road from the north. The horses' hooves slipped in the loose stones and Smenkhkare kept his charges under firm control as they made their descent. Scarab clung to the railing at the front of the chariot, bracing herself against the side.

"Normally we would come up the main road there." Smenkhkare pointed to the north. "But this way is faster and more exciting."

Scarab looked up at her brother through the enveloping dust. "What is wrong? It is not like you to be so...so...not like a king."

A grimace quirked the corner of Smenkhkare's mouth. "You remember when we used to sneak out and wander around Waset without a care in the world?" He stared straight ahead and did not see his sister's smile and quick nod. "I miss those times and sometimes wish I had not become king."

"You are a good king, brother. Compassionate but just. Would you leave our people in the hands of people like Ay?"

"No. A king stands before the gods on behalf of the people. I feel called to do that. It is just that sometimes...sometimes I want to do something daring and dangerous." He shook his head, and then suddenly swore at the horses, pulling them up hard in a shower of stones as the chariot slid sideways in front of the gate that guarded the entrance to the Great Place. The horses stamped and blew, shaking the dust from their manes. Smenkhkare stared straight ahead at the opening gates and the hurrying guards. "I must learn to control my desire for action, little sister, else I shall precipitate my people into a war of conquest and glory."

"You will not go to war, surely? There is no reason."

"No, none." Smenkhkare took his linen headpiece off and shook the dust out of it before slipping it back on. "I will go hunting instead. A lion is terrorizing the villages near Djeba. I leave tomorrow but I mean to be back by the end of the month."

The other chariots with the scribes and priests pulled up behind them and Ahmose, as senior official, dared to call out to the king. "My lord, do we drive on?"

"Feel like a walk, sister? I think these temple priests and scribes could do with some exercise." Smenkhkare leapt down from the chariot, helping Scarab down. "I think we will walk from here," he called back.

Without waiting for the others to dismount, the king set off at a rapid walk past the guards and into the burial valley. Scarab hitched up her long dress and hurried after him, grinning at the startled looks on the faces of the soldiers.

"I meant to ask you. How is it that you beat off those men yesterday? I am told Khu was injured early on, yet two men died."

"The gods smiled on me."

Smenkhkare stuck his tongue out and blew. "That for your luck. Tell me, Scarab. Where did you learn to fight?" He pointed toward a broad track that led off toward the right hand side of the valley. "Up there, I think."

"What are we looking for?"

"We are not looking for anything; I know what is up here. Who taught you to fight?"

"Slow down, brother. What is up here?" Scarab glanced sideways at the lithe young man striding beside her. "Paramessu taught me."

"Paramessu? But he is up north and you have not seen him these last three years...or have you?"

Scarab shook her head. "He left me his Leader of Fifty, Meny, with strict instructions to look after me. The man interpreted that rather liberally and taught me to fight."

Smenkhkare stopped and stared at his sister. "You fight with men?"

"Who else is there to practice fighting with?" Scarab grinned. "I cannot see the palace women doing anything more than pulling hair and scratching."

The king snorted and started forward again. "That is true; still, I do not think it is seemly for a woman to fight with men."

"It kept me alive yesterday, and Khu."

Smenkhkare strode ahead in silence. They crested a small rise and started down a smaller trail that led toward a great slope of loose rubble where several men stood around talking or shifting rocks.

"How is he? Khu."

"He will live, the wound was not deep. It will be some time before he fully recovers, but he will be up and about in ten days or so."

"You like him, don't you?"

"Khu?" Scarab's eyes opened wide. "Of course, he is a friend."

"Not Khu." Smenkhkare's voice betrayed a tinge of impatience. "Paramessu."

"I scarcely know him," Scarab said carefully. "I last saw him three years ago, as you said. I am grateful to him for giving me Meny but..."

"Do not harbor affection for him, Scarab. He is a soldier and beneath you."

"I did not think to hear you talk of stations in life, brother. Did not you always teach me to look at the inner person, not what he is on the outside?"

"That is not what I mean." Smenkhkare stopped again and waved back the following priests out of earshot. "I have no doubt he is a good man and an able soldier, but he is just that whereas you are a royal princess, destined to raise royal sons to rule Kemet."

Scarab stared back at her brother. "You mean to marry me off? To whom?"

"When I return from Djeba, and when Ay is safely in retirement, I will marry you myself and make you my queen. You shall bear my sons and rule Kemet with me." Smenkhkare cocked his head to one side. "This does not please you, Scarab? I told you when we were children that I would marry you."

Scarab looked down at the rocky ground at her feet, feeling her heart pounding and the blood rushing through her temples. "As...as my lord commands," she whispered.

"I do not command you, sister." Smenkhkare stepped forward and lifted Scarab's chin with one hand. "Do you love some man? Do you want his arms around you instead?" His eyes narrowed. "Or is it lust? Have you been indiscreet?"

Scarab blushed and jerked her head away. "I have not forgotten who I am, brother. Have you?"

The king's eyes flashed and his lips tightened. "I am the king." His shoulders slumped and he uttered a deep sigh. "But I am also your brother, and come next month, your husband also. I care for you, little Scarab, and will not see you throw your destiny away." He turned and signaling the priests, started toward the men on the rubble slope, who knelt with heads bowed low as their king approached.

Scarab stared after him, her mind in turmoil. Ahmose and Paser nodded to her, their eyes curious as they passed. The priests looked away, but hurried on after the scribes and their king. Scarab dropped the folds of her bunched up dress and she smoothed it, dusting it down. She patted her wig, liberating more dust, then adjusted it and walked slowly up to the group of men. The rocks here showed signs of the recent rain though already the fierce sun baked the ground dry again. In the hollows between the boulders, the dust had turned to mud, now rapidly drying.

A plain-kilted man stood talking to Smenkhkare, his paunch and plump limbs revealing an occupation that did not involve manipulating rocks or any form of manual labor. Scarab edged closer to listen.

"...I have teams of men on that already, majesty. As I said, we only had a small cliff face collapse and the excavations of the buried tomb entrance are almost complete."

Smenkhkare nodded, his face serious. "And water damage? There was a large storm last night, I hear."

"Only minor flooding, majesty. We were lucky. If the dry valleys on the other side of the Great Place had flooded..." The fat man swung round and pointed a pudgy finger across the barren floor of the burial valley. "Several tombs would have been damaged."

"But none were?" Smenkhkare persisted.

"No, majesty." The man hesitated and licked his lips, his eyes flickering across the men behind his king. They lingered on the figure of the beautiful young girl for a moment, before moving on. "There...there is something else."

"I was wondering when you were going to get to that, Kenhirkhoshef."

The fat man's eyes widened. "You knew of it, majesty?"

"Knowledge comes to me from many sources. You must not imagine that the overseer of the Great Place is the only eye of the king."

Kenhirkhoshef bowed. "Then you also know whose tomb, majesty."

"No, that was not revealed to me." Smenkhkare stared at the man, seeing a mix of emotions in his face, but fear starting to get the upper hand. He did not enjoy lying to the man but needed to see if guilt lay in his face. Abruptly he turned to the captain of the valley guard who was dressed like the other soldiers but wearing a headdress with the blue stripe of office. "Hori, you have seen it?"

The captain saluted. "Yes, majesty, I have seen it."

"Very well then." Smenkhkare turned back to Kenhirkhoshef, noticing the sweat breaking out on the man's face despite the shade over this part of the valley. "Whose tomb is it?"

Kenhirkhoshef cleared his throat and swallowed. "Your grandfather and grandmother's, majesty."

"King Tuthmosis?" Smenkhkare feigned shock and anger, though he felt the real emotions grow inside him.

"No, majesty, the parents of...of your father's er, queen...er, your majesty's moth...grandmother..." His voice trailed off. Kenhirkhoshef took a deep breath and stared at a point above his king's head. "Lord Yuya and Lady Thuya, majesty."

Scarab saw her brother's shoulders tremble slightly and stepped up beside him, placing a hand lightly on his arm. "What is it, brother? What has happened?"

"The tomb of our mother's parents has been broken into," Smenkhkare replied quietly, a faint tremor slurring his words slightly.

Scarab's hand convulsed, gripping the king's arm tightly. Ahmose and Kenhirkhoshef looked shocked but refrained from speaking. "Who did this?" she asked. "Who committed such a sacrilege? Or rather, how did this happen?" Scarab rounded on the captain of the guard. "Where were your men while my grandparents' tomb was being plundered?"

The captain glanced at the king, hesitating.

"Answer her, Hori," Smenkhkare said quietly, his voice controlled again. "This is my sister Beketaten."

Hori saluted again. "Yes majesties." He wheeled and stabbed a finger at spots on the valley rim, high above them. "I have guard posts there, there and there. They are manned at all times with watchmen who keep guard of the main trails leading down into the valley from the desert plateau. I have a post at the valley gates also." Turning back to face the king again, he went on. "I have fifty men, sir. Divided into two watches, I have ten men at each of the watch stations and twenty at the gate. If they see any unauthorized activity in the valley, they send a runner to the main gate and I investigate."

"So how is it that my grandparents' tomb was violated? Were your men asleep?"

"No, majesty. The valley is large and it is very dark at night. I believe some men took advantage of the storm last night to descend along one of the lesser trails and break into the tomb. I do not have enough men to guard every trail or goat track."

Smenkhkare turned to Ahmose the chief scribe. "Why is it that there are only fifty men guarding the royal tombs?"

Ahmose sketched a quick bow. "Your royal brother cut back the numbers some years back. He felt that the fact the tombs were buried in loose rock was a greater protection than more soldiers." The scribe ventured a small smile. "There are no records kept of the site of each tomb."

"Evidently not protection enough." Smenkhkare faced Hori again. "He has a point, captain. How can robbers find the tombs among all these piles of rubble, particularly if even the officials do not know the position of the tombs?"

"Perhaps one or more of your men is less than honest, captain." Scarab stared at the impassive face of the guard. "A word passed to a thief..."

"Begging your pardon, lady, but there is no need for that. Any burial that occurs within the Great Place is observed by many eyes. The valley rim is impossible to guard properly and all someone has to do is note landmarks and they can find the place later, even at night. I keep watch with my men after each burial, camping near the site for forty days, but after that I must attend to my other duties. Sometimes the location of a tomb is passed down from father to son until years later it is broken into."

Smenkhkare looked at Hori's rugged but open face for several minutes. Abruptly he nodded and addressed Ahmose. "See to it that the guard here is doubled immediately. The captain cannot be expected to carry out his duties with so few men. Kenhirkhoshef. Lead me to the tomb. I will see this desecration for myself."

The Overseer of the Great Place led the way as best he could, heaving his bulk over the loose rubble, scrambling down to the floor of the valley. He puffed and panted, sweat running down his body, carving runnels in the ubiquitous dust. Smenkhkare strode beside him, forcing the pace, refusing to let Kenhirkhoshef slow and catch his breath.

"You are too fat," Smenkhkare growled. "Evidently I shall have to cut your rations and have you train with the guards."

"With...with respect, majesty." Kenhirkhoshef gasped. "My f...fat has nothing to do with what I eat...my parents were both fat. I have to...to eat to sustain my body."

"Where is this tomb?" The king scanned the walls of the valley, the scree slopes and jumbled dusty piles of rubble.

"Up there, majesty." Kenhirkhoshef pointed up a side valley, his trembling arm wavering as he drew in great lungfuls of air.

Smenkhkare stopped and looked at the Overseer's flushed face and sweat-soaked body. He beckoned to Hori, the guard captain. "You know where the tomb is? Then take me there. Kenhirkhoshef, stay here until you are ready, and then follow." He turned away and trotted after the guard captain.

Scarab followed at a slower pace, feeling the heat of the sun beating back from the valley sides, the light blinding on the pale rock. She squinted and held a hand up to shade her eyes. Sweat trickled down her back and between her breasts, mingling with the dust to stain her dress. Used to a dry heat, Scarab found the increased humidity in the air made the afternoon sun harder to bear. Ahmose and Paser slowed their pace as well, as did the priests of the mortuary temples. They made a show of keeping her company, being part of her official entourage, obsequiously asking after her well-being, loudly wishing they could shield her from the sun. Scarab suspected they were hanging back just to avoid undue exertion.

They caught up with the Overseer as he turned to leave the track along the valley floor, preparatory to scrambling up the twenty or thirty paces of rock debris to where a carved lintel beam and door pillars could be seen, half buried in the rubble. Smenkhkare and Hori were nowhere to be seen.

"They have entered the tomb," Kenhirkhoshef explained.

Scarab leaned down and peered into the space cleared by the robbers. A short flight of stairs, still choked with debris, descended to a bricked up wall, the seals of the mortuary priests still visible, pressed into the clay before it dried nearly forty years before. A ragged hole in the brick wall gaped, the blackness within seeming to throw an inky shadow out into the sunlit world above.

"How can they see in there?" Scarab muttered.

As if in answer a faint light flickered in the blackness, growing stronger, until her brother pushed his head and shoulders through the gap, scrambling out and dusting himself off. Hori followed, grasping a lit torch.

The king called the mortuary priests over. "The tomb has been breached, though the burial chamber seems intact. Send someone back to the temples for seals and to the village. We will need bricklayers and plasterers. Ahmose, please make a quick inventory of the tomb goods, have anything damaged removed and organize replacements." He looked around at the assembled men, his expression somber. "There is no worse crime than desecrating the place of the dead. An attack on the living can be defended but the dead ones rely on us to ensure their happiness in the afterlife. I ask you all to work now to right this dreadful wrong."

The priests bowed and hurried off on their errands. Paser took out writing materials from the pouch at his waist and followed Ahmose into the tomb, taking with them another torch from the bundle of them at the tomb mouth.

Smenkhkare watched until everyone was out of sight except for Hori and Scarab. "Come, sister," he said. "Let us pay our respects to our grandparents." He picked up another torch and lit it from the one burning outside the entrance, then held it high for his sister to climb into the grave.

Scarab felt a tiny prickle of unease at the back of her neck as she hitched up her dress and descended the steep steps cut into the stone. She stood looking at the yawning black hole until her brother touched her on the shoulder.

"Do not be afraid," he said softly. "They are your grandparents and love you."

Scarab climbed over the lip of the wall, ducking under the rough overhang. She waited uncomfortably in the dark, feeling the eternal night of the tomb press in upon her, until Smenkhkare passed the torch to her. The air was still and the flame burned low and constant, the shadows trembling only as her hand shook. Dimly seen within the small circle of light, wall paintings told a story in pictures of the fate awaiting the dead when they came face to face with Asar. A musty smell pervaded the steeply-descending corridor. At the far end came a glimmer of orange light and a murmur disturbed the air, beating up the long dark corridor from the tomb below. Scarab felt the hairs on her arms rise until she realized the voices were those of Ahmose and Paser. She fought down an urge to giggle and looked at her brother in the dim light.

"Come," he said and took the torch from her, leading the way downward through the pieces of wall rubble.

The corridor, though seeming to stretch into darkness was short, a mere ten paces. Despite the flickering red light of the torch, they shuffled along, afraid of tripping over something they could not see, their fingertips brushing the walls. A second doorway, open this time, framed another steeply-descending flight of stairs. Scarab counted out five steps before the corridor opened out, though the stairs, hewn out of the rock, continued in the central part. At the bottom of the stairwell lay another walled-up entrance, with a rough breach hacked in the lower left corner. Bending down, Scarab could see the glow of a torch and hear the voices of the scribes as a low murmur. She scrambled through, followed a few moments later by her brother. The scene that greeted her was a devastation of broken and ruined furniture, broken pots and here and there a glint of gold or semi-precious stones.

"The thieves got through to here, but thank the gods, no further," Smenkhkare said grimly. "The Medjay will make inquiries, of course, but the chances of finding who did this are not great."

"What would happen to them if they were caught?"

"They would be tried, either in a local court, or perhaps before the mayor of Waset. If the evidence was good, like recovered grave goods, a confession would be extracted and sentence passed. Probably just a simple execution." Smenkhkare scowled as he looked around the ruins of his grandparents' tomb. "If it was up to me, death would be a while coming and they would pray for it."

Scarab shivered at this talk of death in the darkness. She moved closer to where Ahmose and Paser were making notes of the contents of the room.

"... linen clothing," Ahmose was saying, as Paser made notes on a scrap of papyrus with a charcoal stick. The chief scribe unfolded the cloth and examined it. "A dress, fine linen, for formal wear." He picked up another garment and unfolded it. "A dress, plain, with a large tear. And here is a wooden box with cosmetics, still intact, a jar of unguent, sealed and a small image of Re."

The two men ignored Scarab and she moved over to the edge of the light, picking her way through a jumble of furniture and equipment, everything that a married couple would need for eternity. She recognized chairs and a bed with a carved hippopotamus headrest, a hunting bow, a spear and shield and a scatter of papyrus scrolls and pens. Coming to the wall of the chamber, she ran her fingers along the rough stone surface, her forehead wrinkling as she tried to work out what was wrong.

"Where are the paintings? And why is the wall rough and unplastered?"

"I do not know," Smenkhkare replied. "It may be that the tomb was finished in a hurry. There were a few paintings near the entrance. Or it may be that our grandfather Yuya did not want foreign gods in his tomb."

"What do you mean by foreign?"

"Lord Yuya was Khabiru, remember? He came to Kemet as a youth and an interpreter of dreams, and grandfather Tuthmosis made him Tjaty. He must have kept his Khabiru god."

"The Aten? Like brother Akhenaten?"

"No, not Aten, I mean the nameless Khabiru god that Akhenaten identified with the sun disc. Anyway, we shall probably never know the reason. All we can do is tidy the place up, replace what is left and make a fresh offering of food and drink for their outraged spirits."

"Wh...where are the bodies?"

Smenkhkare stepped over the debris until he reached the back wall. Holding the torch aloft, he pointed at the seals and the inscriptions carved in the plaster wall. "Here it is plastered and behind this wall lie the undisturbed bodies of our grandparents. See, the seals of the mortuary officials are intact. Whatever the thieves plundered, they did not reach the gold that lies here."

Scarab stood and stared at the blank wall for a long time, the light from the torches steady though reddened in the still, musty air of the burial chamber. The only sound was an intermittent murmur from the scribes, a rustle of cloth or a soft clatter as they moved or put down an item, and the faint crackle and spit of the burning brands. Her mind seemed detached from her body and she wondered what it would be like to lie still in the blackness of her grave, her body packed with resins and spices, wrapped in tight linen, dreaming the years away. Or would she be with the gods? Would she wander star-lit fields or sunny meadows with Re or Nut, Het-Her or Djehuti, or any of the myriad gods she knew existed? Would they remember her as she had remembered them? Remembered them and striven alongside her brother to bring their worship back to the people of Kemet. A sound intruded and her mind swept back into her body and she looked round.

"Come sister," her brother said, his hand on her arm. "Let us leave these men to their work. When I return from my hunt at Djeba, we shall offer new grave goods and seal the tomb again. In the meantime, the mortuary priests will replace anything that is missing." He turned and led the way out of the burial chamber, up the steep flights of stairs and into the dazzling warmth of the Great Place.

Although it seemed like they had only been underground for minutes, Scarab could see that Heru, the Ascended Light was dropping toward the western cliffs of the valley. Already the edge of shadow that marked the valley rim was sweeping inexorably over the rubble of white rock. Far down the valley, she saw a line of men heading up toward them, priests and soldiers and many laborers carrying bundles. She pointed.

Smenkhkare nodded in satisfaction. "Good. They will repair the tomb and guard it until I can return." He turned to Overseer Kenhirkhoshef. "I will leave you in command of this valley for a little longer. Make sure that you look after the tombs here as if they were those of your parents." He left the overseer bowing obsequiously and set off down the valley toward the gates, Scarab following more slowly. Halfway down, the shadows claimed them and a little later, as Smenkhkare drove the royal chariot down the road toward the cluster of mortuary temples and the river, the great sweep of shade cast by the setting sun stretched out and over the water, leaving only the high walls and columns touched by the golden light of the god.

Smenkhkare drove in silence, his face set and immobile, seemingly lost in thought. Scarab respected his mood and looked out at the farmlands and the peasants trudging home after a long day in the fields.

They reached the waterfront and the king dismounted, holding a hand out to help Scarab down from the chariot, turning the horses over to a stable hand. He waved away the officials who came toward him and, holding his sister's hand, walked past the docks and mudbrick buildings onto a grassy ridge that lay parallel to the river. After a hundred paces he stopped and sat down, tugging Scarab down beside him. Pulling his knees up under his chin, he wrapped his arms about his legs and rested his chin on his knees, staring out over the darkening water.

Scarab sat quietly beside her brother, legs tucked underneath her. She looked at his profile in the fading light and frowned at his serious look. "What is it, brother?"

For a few moments longer he sat in silence. "What is it all for? Why are we here?"

Scarab thought for a moment. "Why are we here on the riverbank, or why are we alive?"

Smenkhkare gave her a swift look before staring out into the dusk again. "Alive of course. Why am I king and...and those men we passed just now are mere peasants."

Scarab shrugged. "Because the gods knew your Ka before it was united with your Khat, your physical body. They saw your nobility of spirit, knew you were kingly, whereas the peasants...well, no doubt they have other talents that suit them for their lives."

"You say I am kingly. What is a king?"

"One who rules."

Smenkhkare shook his head. "That is not enough, sister. What else is a king?"

Scarab thought about her answer, not quite sure what her brother meant. "A king is one chosen by the gods to lead his people."

"You know that is wrong. I am king because my brother is king; my father was king and his father before him. How is there any choosing in this?"

"The gods chose our ancestor Ahmose to be king though. Our family has been strong and has governed our Two Lands well. Do you not think they would choose another man, another family to become Per-Aa, the Great House, if you displeased them?"

"What of my brother Akhenaten? He abolished the gods. Why have they not rid the country of him?"

Scarab smiled gently and put her arm about her brother's shoulders. "Perhaps they have. Akhenaten is now king over a single city whereas you are king of the rest of Kemet. They know you will bring back true worship and have confirmed you in your kingship."

Smenkhkare nodded grudgingly. "Perhaps you are right, little sister. I had not thought of that."

The sun finally dipped below the desert cliffs and the glowing dusk faded into night. A cool breeze ruffled the unseen water and rattled the palm fronds above them. Scents of flowers from the fields, of lotus from the irrigation canals, tickled their senses and a low susurration of sound carried over the wide river from a city settling down into night.

Scarab caught faint movements in the dusk along the ridge and she turned her head but the motions ceased when she looked, only to resume elsewhere. "They are here," she whispered. "The dead have arisen from their tombs and stand beside us, looking back to their old city where once they lived."

A cry came, faint but distinct, carried on some vagary of the evening wind. Smenkhkare smiled. "The dead around us and an infant cries in Waset. New life to replace the old." The aromas of countless evening meals drifted over the water, frying fish, new-baked bread and even the sharp tang of sour beer. The king stirred and looked at his sister. "I am hungry."

"Eat and drink and be happy while you live, dear brother. Who knows what the gods will send our way?"

"Oh, I know, little Scarab. They have spoken to me."

"Really? What did they say?"

"That I am king for a great purpose. I will restore true worship in all of Kemet. I will be a great and powerful king, making Kemet's name resound among the lands around us. Our enemies shall fall at my feet but I shall be merciful. I shall be a father to my people, leading them to happiness and prosperity." Smenkhkare sprang to his feet with a whoop of joy, dragging Scarab up beside him. "I will marry the most beautiful princess Beketaten, make her my queen and father a thousand sons on her. We shall reign together for a hundred years before descending into the richest and most awe-inspiring tomb, there to enjoy the company of the gods for a million more years."

Scarab frowned. "Do not tempt the gods, Smenkhkare. You wish for too much."

"It is no mere wish, little Scarab. You shall see. I feel invigorated and I can accomplish anything." He took her by the hand and they ran back along the riverbank to the torches of the waiting officials.

Behind them, on the dark deserted riverbank, the breeze swirled and whispered in the palm fronds, as if generations of ancient ghosts, scores of the forgotten dead, remembered their own youth, their own overweening desires, and laughed at the folly of kings.

Chapter 5

T he hymn to the Living Aten rose clear and strong from the Great
Temple in the centre of Akhet-Aten, City of the Sun. Alone at
the altar as the first rays of the rising god caught the great beaten
gold representation of the disc of the sun, King Neferneferure
Waenre Akhenaten, 'He who is useful to the Aten', lifted up his worn
and troubled face to the warmth, praying that this day he would once
more gaze upon the face of his god. He ended the hymn in a single
high note and the choir of lesser priests broke into the free-form
response, their voices less pure but still enthusiastic. The king strained
to see, his other senses fading and he found his thoughts wandering.

Flashes of light, formless and multi-coloured, broke the darkness
that so often enveloped him these days. Surrounded by the beauty of
his own temple to Aten, he was unable to see it. Four years ago, a
lifetime, in those calmer days when Nefertiti was queen beside him, he
had sought communion with his god, staring into the face of the sun
until he fell blinded and insensible on the desert sand. Only the
ministrations of the court physician Nebhotep had saved his sight. Yet
from that day the darkness had gained a hold on the king, first on his
vision, then on his heart and his happiness.

Queen Nefertiti, hurt and angered by the king's decision to take his
own daughter as wife, had rebelled and attempted to take over the
throne of Kemet. The attempt failed, despite the connivance of her
father, Tjaty Ay. Kemet's greatest general, Paatenemheb had put down
the rebellion almost before it started. Now the queen, *my beautiful
queen*, was in exile. Akhenaten was not even sure where, only that

Paatenemheb had taken her from the Great Hall of Justice and marched into the desert with her. She might even be dead. *No.* Akhenaten shook his head. He would feel it in his soul if she died.

The response faded away and Akhenaten, without conscious thought, took over the chant, the sounds of sistrum and lute accompanying him. He poured his heart into the culminating praise song, pleading silently that he might be given one more day, one hour even, of clear sight. The notes of the song died away and the unseen audience sighed and moved away, leaving the hunch-shouldered king in silence and darkness. A hand touched his bare arm.

"Father, it is time to go." The speaker, a young girl of some twelve or thirteen floods, looked scarcely old enough to have lost the side lock of youth, but was arrayed in a beautiful white linen gown, her small rouged breasts just visible beneath the sheer fabric. A gold necklace broke the gauzy white sweep of her garment and complemented the gold *nefer* beads that adorned her short, curly black wig. Elsewhere in Kemet it might be the fashion to wear long wigs that fell in straight tresses below the shoulders, but here in the capital, the Nubian style reigned supreme.

"Ankhesenpaaten." The king smiled and put out a hand to feel for his daughter. She stood still and let the wandering hand stray to her breast but before it could slip down her body she deftly moved aside, taking her father's arm gently and started forward, leading him out of the temple. Ankhesenpaaten, third daughter of Akhenaten and Nefertiti, was also queen, wife of her own father.

Four years ago, in a desperate attempt to have the son he so badly wanted, he had taken an example from his own father and married his eldest daughter Meryetaten. This betrayal of their private marriage vows had finally turned Nefertiti against him and into rebellion. The rebellion and the marriage to Meryetaten had failed. The mother went into exile and the daughter gave birth to a girl and Akhenaten put his new queen away, sending her to Waset to marry his brother and new co-regent Smenkhkare. That marriage too had failed, though as far as he knew it was because the co-regent never consummated the marriage, having accepted her in his palace for form's sake.

The previous year Akhenaten had tried once more for a son, marrying his other daughter Ankhesenpaaten. The birth of another girl brought Akhenaten's dreams of dynasty to an end. Seldom now could he arouse himself to any semblance of interest in women, and that suited his daughter-wife. She had her eyes on another man--well, a boy really--the king's youngest brother Tutankhaten. Son of Nebmaetre Amenhotep and his daughter Iset, the nine year old boy was being raised as a prince and subconsciously at least, for the idea was never voiced, as Akhenaten's son.

Ankhesenpaaten led her father out of the temple and, with a handful of waiting courtiers, walked slowly back to the palace. She would have rather taken a sedan chair for the short journey but the king still wanted to be seen by his people and insisted on walking. *It is just as well he is blind*, she thought. *He cannot see that his people have lost interest in him and his god.*

Back in the palace, she made sure that the king was placed in charge of servants she knew would look after him, bathing him and dressing him again, before she crossed the great covered bridge with its Window of Appearance to the women's quarters in the palace of the queen. Other women resided here as well. A king was not judged as potent and kingly without a stable of wives, even though Akhenaten had agreed to have no other bed-mate besides Nefertiti. Since the fall and exile of the former queen, Ankhesenpaaten's mother, the king had forsaken his promise and slept with his other wives, notably the Lady Kiya, a Mitannian princess whose beauty rivaled that of the younger Nefertiti. Children had resulted from his union with the lesser wives, all girls though, leading to Ankhesenpaaten's instalment as queen and wife in a renewed attempt to engender a son and heir.

Although she was still technically queen, she thought of herself as a princess, a daughter. Her face clouded momentarily as she remembered her own daughter by her father. Already the little face, almost always crying, had slipped into obscurity. The disease that carried her off in the first months of her life had been a recurrence of the plague that killed three of her sisters and her grandmother Tiye. This latest outbreak, though mild by comparison, had claimed the life not only of her little daughter, but also of her sole remaining sister in Akhet-Aten, Neferneferoure. Of all her sisters, only the eldest, Meryetaten, survived, and she was in Waset.

Ankhesenpaaten walked to her rooms where her many maidservants stripped her naked, putting her jewelry away in the great chest and her golden-beaded wig on one of the wig stands. She went into the tiled bath chamber and despite it being not long after dawn, bathed again quickly. Other servants sluiced her down with tepid water, then with cold and patted her dry with soft wool cloths, under the watchful eye of the Supervisor of the Bath. Dressing again in a plain dress, she spent a long time pawing through her jewelry with the Guardian of the Jewel Boxes before selecting a plain gold bracelet and a gold brooch with carnelian and lapis in the representation of the all-seeing eye. Her Keeper of the Cosmetics signaled and trays of ointments and unguents, powders and brushes were brought forth and a small army of women applied themselves to perfecting the already beautiful. A while later, after the princess-queen had examined herself in a polished silver mirror; she dismissed the servants with a wave of her hand and set out for the courtyard of the main palace.

At the far end of the long open space, lined with statues of the king carved in the new fashion, accentuating length of limb and face and increasing the girth of belly and lips, sat the old scribe Keneben. So old and frail that he looked like a body the embalmers in the House of Death had misplaced, he was nevertheless imbued with a vitality that put many younger men to shame. He sat on a magnificent carved chair, as befitted his rank and importance, his long robe arranged in neat folds about him. Arrayed before him on the grass, sat three boys, upright and attentive, and hanging on to every word of the old scribe.

Ankhesenpaaten approached quietly and sat down on a bench nearby, under the shade of a small flowering tree. The red blossoms gave off a faint perfume that competed unsuccessfully with her own perfumes. Keneben acknowledged her presence with a tiny nod, not interrupting his lessons. She nodded back, slow and regal, content to sit back and listen to the old man expound to the boys. One of them, the smallest, caught the old man's nod and turned to look, grinning delightedly as he saw Ankhesenpaaten.

"Pay attention, Prince Tutankhaten," Keneben snapped, before resuming his dissertation. The small boy started guiltily and looked back, one of the other boys, a tall Nubian boy, smiling at his discomfiture.

"It is in my mind to talk of mathematics today, children," Keneben said. "Mathematics, or the language of numbers, comes from the gods and governs every aspect of our Kemet, our lives and our deaths." One of the boys groaned and Keneben stopped talking, fixing the culprit with a steely eye. "You do not approve, master Hiknefer?"

The tall Nubian, who had smiled a little earlier, looked embarrassed at first, before putting on a show of bravado. "I can see that it might be useful to count one's herds, or..." he sniggered. "Or one's wives, but why should a king need to do more? He will have scribes around him for that."

Keneben nodded amiably. "You are sure you will be a king, Prince Hiknefer? Miam, where your father governs as a vassal of Kemet, will need a strong ruler, one who can discern the truth for himself rather than just take the word of his servants." He turned to the other Nubian boy, on the other side of Tutankhaten. "And what of you, Khai of Kush? Do you see any other uses for mathematics?"

Khai squirmed under his tutor's gaze. "Yes master," he whispered. "Tall and mighty trees of ebony and mahogany come from the land of Kush. If I, as governor of Kush, am to meet the quota set by the king, I must be able to calculate the volume of each tree, work out how many men I will need, how much bread and beer to give them."

"Well done, Khai." Keneben smiled broadly. "Learn from your friend, Hiknefer. Now, young Tutankhaten, have you anything to add to this discussion? How would you use mathematics in the service of your king?"

"I...I would build temples to glorify the gods," the young prince said slowly. "For this I would need to know how much land to clear and level." His high-pitched voice quickened as he warmed to the subject. "The quarrymen would need to know how many blocks of stone to cut and what size. How many men would be needed if twenty men are needed for each block and there are fifty thousand blocks in the great temple of Amun? I would have to calculate..."

"How many men would you need?" Kenemen interrupted.

Tutankhaten screwed up his face, his eyes raised to the clear blue skies above, his lips moving silently. "A...a million," he concluded doubtfully.

"There are not that many men in all Kemet, boy."

Hiknefer laughed. "You won't get to build your temple to Amun then."

"There is a way," Kenemen said. "Think."

"Bring men in from other lands?" Khai's face brightened. "We shall declare a great war and conquer the Hittites, the Mitanni and the Babylonians, taking a million captives. They will build the temple."

Tutankhaten shook his head, smiling. "We do not need a million men. If each gang of twenty men moved a hundred blocks, we would only need ten thousand men. We could find that many in Kemet."

Keneben clapped his hands with delight. "Excellent, prince Tutankhaten. Your example of the temple was a masterly one, for in the temple we see a microcosm of Kemet and of the world."

"Which temple, master?" Hiknefer leaned closer, as if he dared not speak louder. "Is it the temple of Aten here in the City of the Sun, or..." He licked his lips and flicked a nervous glance toward the young girl on the stone bench beneath the blossoming tree. "Or is it the temple of Amun?"

"A good question, Hiknefer." Keneben leaned forward in his turn, beckoning the boys closer. "I will tell you a secret, a sacred secret, one known to scribes and priests but few others. All temples are the same."

Khai gasped. "The gods are the same?"

"Did I say that? I said the temples are the same, not the gods, you foolish boy. No, each god is different and you will find different things in each temple, but the plan of them, the mathematics, is the same. The temple can be called the Divine House, the Per Neter, in which the divine principle, the god or Neter, resides while on earth. It is the halfway point between the heavens, the abode of the Neteru, and the earth, the abode of man, and as such reflects both." Keneben settled back on his chair and the boys recognized the signs of one of his lectures, reclining on the grass in front of him.

"You are already aware of how everything in life is paired? We have had lessons on the innate bifurcation of all things. Look around you and you can see this--the living and the non-living; the living further divided into plant and animal; animals into human and non-human; humans into man and woman. It goes further. Our Kemet is made up of two kingdoms, Upper Kemet and Lower Kemet. The River divides both upper and lower into East, the realm of Life and Light; and the West, the realm of Death and Darkness. So too, there are the gods and men. The temple is the sacred space where they meet and it is no accident of design. When the gods first created man, they set out ways for him to worship the gods. The place they chose was the temple. The gods set out the temple in such a way that it reflected their divine laws."

Ankhesenpaaten paid scant attention to Keneben's lecture. Some she already knew, for even princesses have their tutors, other bits she did not know, and did not care. Her attention was on the young boys lounging on the short-cropped grass of the courtyard. She amused herself by reminding herself of what she knew of them.

Hiknefer was the eldest, about the same age as she, a prince of Miam from the province of Wawat or Lower Nubia. The hot land to the south went through cycles in which it was conquered by Kemet, then shook off its tyranny before falling once more. Many soldiers in the Kemetu army came from Nubia, being tall and strong, though undisciplined unless they were ruled with firmness. Ankhesenpaaten smiled to herself, examining the strong straight limbs of the youth, the dark skin almost black with a sheen of blue like a ripe grape. She knew he was tall, having stood next to him many times. She was no stripling herself, yet if he held out an arm parallel to the ground, she could have walked under it without touching. The boy's nose was straight, his teeth gleaming and his gaze, which drifted in her direction from time to time, were warm and inviting. She considered his unspoken invitation for several delicious seconds before putting the thought away. She was after a bigger prize.

"There are four parts to sacred mathematics," Keneben was saying. Ankhesenpaaten felt a flush in her young body and dragged her attention away from Hiknefer and back to the old scribe. "Four dimensions." He lifted a hand and marked them with his fingers as he talked. "First, the dimension of number. We can define a temple by its size, the area it occupies, its boundaries. Number provides the plan of a temple. Second, there is the dimension of Time. We can orient the temple in relation to the Nile, central to our physical world, and the celestial world above us. Time defines the purpose of a temple."

Purpose, Ankhesenpaaten thought. *I know what purpose Hiknefer would have. Very different from the other one.* Khai, from the land of Kush or Upper Nubia was as different from Hiknefer as two Nubians could be. Only a year younger than the tall youth, Khai was short, shorter than herself, but broad and muscular. She had seen this type of body before and knew that when he was an old man, as old as...well, in his twenties or thirties, he would be fat. Already, dimples of fat could be seen beneath the earth colour of his skin.

Ankhesenpaaten did not enjoy Khai's gaze. He seldom looked at her, but when he did, she felt as if she were being examined by a crocodile, a hungry one. The looks he gave her were calculating, comparing their stations in life and how they might be turned to his advantage.

With a shiver she turned to an examination of the young prince Tutankhaten. Four years her junior he was actually her uncle, being the youngest brother of her own father Akhenaten. You could tell he was the king's brother, being slim, but without the strength of Hiknefer. A sickly child, still wearing the side lock of youth, he had, until recently, spent more time inside the palace than outside it. Where other boys ran and played and fought, he spent his days in the cool shade being looked after by nurses and tutors, or playing games of dice or senet.

Only last year, when the political situation in Nubia abruptly changed, necessitating the taking of hostages, did Tutankhaten's life also change. Into his life came the two boys Khai and Hiknefer, hostages to their fathers' good behavior. Despite the very different backgrounds, and ages, which often meant more to youngsters, the three boys became firm friends and were now seldom seen apart.

It was at this time that Ankhesenpaaten really became aware of the young prince for the first time. She knew he existed, of course, but she had never had reason to talk to him. She was a woman and a queen, also a mother at twelve years and was not interested in a boy still with his side lock of hair. Then things fell apart. Her baby daughter, darling little Ankhesenpaaten-ta-sherit, died and her father-husband put her away, though he still tried a half-hearted grope or fumble when the heat rose in him. Worse was the fact that with her estrangement came a distancing from the affairs of state. True, the court at Akhet-Aten was limited; the governing of the country being under the aegis of Smenkhkare and Ay at Waset, but it was a start. Then just as she acquired the taste for power it was snatched from her. Rather than complain or become bitter, she sat down and thought it through, made her plans. She jumped as Keneben's words echoed her thoughts.

"...a plan. Geometry is the growth plan of a temple. Lastly, there is Volume for the choice of building materials evokes associations with the divine forces. Volume provides the goal of a temple."

What is my goal? Ankhesenpaaten asked herself. She found herself looking at Tutankhaten again, considering his place in her plans. Akhenaten was senior king in name only. His sway held only as far as the city limits. Smenkhkare was the real force in the Two Lands--and Ay the Tjaty, her grandfather. She put no faith in her family relationship with Ay. Had he not consigned his own daughter, her mother Nefertiti, to exile and possible death? The royal family of Kemet was sparse now, the dynastic hopes rested on very few individuals. The old king Amenhotep had been virile, fathering a profusion of sons and daughters on lesser wives--they did not count-- yet only two sons by his queen Tiye. The first, Tuthmosis, had died before ever gaining the throne, her father Akhenaten benefiting from his death. Then Amenhotep fathered the princes Smenkhkare and Tutankhaten, and Akhenaten fathered six daughters. Yet who was left to carry the hopes of the family into the next generation? Two kings and a prince, two queens and a princess.

Keneben's lecture wandered on, leaving behind the mathematical aspects of temples and entering the realm of colour. "Blue is the colour of the sky, and hence of the cosmic divinities, while green is a colour of growing things and is associated with Hapi and Asar. Black is the land itself, a colour of death and putrefaction, yet out of it springs white, the colour of life, and red signifies animation and the completion of the cycles of life."

Full circle. Young and old. Akhenaten is past it, she thought dispassionately. He represents the old. Smenkhkare will be king for a time, but my sister Meryetaten will not be his queen. Her life is past. Besides, rumor has it that his sister Beketaten will soon take her place in Smenkhkare's bed and beside him on the throne. Who does that leave? Tutankhaten and myself.

"The gods themselves are associated with colours. Blue and black are the colours of Amun, red and black with Set. Auset is blue and green, Asar black and green, Djehuti, blue and yellow."

"What of the Aten?" Hiknefer asked.

"Aten is the disc of the sun. All the solar gods are associated with yellow and white, save Heru, the Ascended Light, who as he sinks toward the western horizon is coloured red and yellow."

Smenkhkare will soon be senior king. Ankhesenpaaten nodded to herself and unseen by her, Keneben preened, thinking she praised his erudition. That leaves Tutankhaten as junior king here in Akhet-Aten. Beketaten will be queen in Waset, but I could be queen here. And why stay here? Two kings and Two Lands. Smenkhkare could rule Upper Kemet while Tutankhaten and I could rule Lower Kemet from the old residence at Ineb Hedj.

Ankhesenpaaten felt a rising surge of excitement. Here was her purpose, and all it took was marriage to this little boy lolling on the grass in front of her. *But how to make him king?* She pondered the question. There was only one man in the whole of Kemet strong enough to make a king, grandfather Ay. She must write to him immediately and suggest it.

Keneben cleared his throat, breaking into the young girl's thoughts. "Well boys, you have been a most attentive audience. Tomorrow we shall investigate some of the intricacies of measurement, area and volume. All these things will be of immense use to you in the service of your king. But for now, the morning is well advanced and I feel the need of a little...er, refreshment." The old scribe rose to his feet, wincing as his joints protested his actions. The princes scrambled to their feet also and sketched enthusiastic if somewhat clumsy bows of respect for their departing tutor.

"What shall we do now?" Khai asked. He stared at the young girl sitting on the wooden bench nearby and a slow smile upturned his lips.

Hiknefer glanced at the position of the sun. "It is nearly time for archery practice. We should get something to eat and drink beforehand."

Ankhesenpaaten ignored the two Nubian boys and concentrated her attention on her young uncle. "Tutankhaten, come here please." She smiled as he immediately obeyed. As the other two princes followed their friend however, her smile slipped and she lifted her head up, staring at a spot above Khai's head but of necessity, to one side of Hiknefer's. "I will speak with the prince alone. You other boys have my leave to go."

A few moments of hesitation and first Hiknefer, then Khai, nodded at Tutankhaten and left. After a few backward looks they broke into a run and soon disappeared among the tall colonnades of the surrounding palace halls.

"Come and sit beside me." Ankhesenpaaten patted the bench and smiled encouragingly.

Tutankhaten sat down, staring sideways at the beautiful young girl, but said nothing.

"I was listening to Keneben and I heard what you said about wanting to build temples. Only kings build temples."

The boy sat with his bony shoulders slumped and his narrow chest caved inward, staring at his hands which rested on his thin legs. He swung his legs back and forth slowly. "I know," he whispered.

"So what makes you dream of doing so?"

A shrug. "The king has no sons. Maybe he will make me his heir."

"Is that what you want?"

He looked up and met her eyes. "Yes," he said simply.

Ankhesenpaaten met his gaze and held it, looking into the depths of his deep brown eyes. "Why do you want to be king?"

Tutankhaten looked away again, reaching down with one bare foot to trace in the sandy path. "The gods need me."

"Are you sure you have that the right way round?"

"Yes, the gods need me. They want me to build them temples and bring their worship back to the people."

"I thought Smenkhkare was doing this already."

The boy shook his head, the single lock of hair swinging. "He brings back Amun and Amun will be a tyrant like Aten. The people need all the gods. Besides, he is...is oppre...oppress...taxing the people too much, and he is spending all the taxes on jewelry when women and children are hungry."

"How do you know these things, Tutankhaten? I have access to the couriers from Waset and I have never heard he was anything but upright."

"Kadore tells me. He brings me letters from uncle Ay."

Ankhesenpaaten sat and thought about this for a few minutes. The sun rose above the surrounding palace roofs and the shadowed light fled before the burning rays. The strum of insects in the shrubbery faltered. A breath of hot wind stirred the blossoms and a single red petal fell, slipping through the thickening air to land on the gauzy white of her dress. The scarlet petal looked like a splash of blood.

"What does Ay say?" she asked at last.

"Many things. He tells me how the rest of Kemet is troubled and looking for a strong leader. He says my brother Smenkhkare is failing to unite the people."

"Does he indeed? And does he tell you what the remedy is?"

Tutankhaten nodded. "He says that when Akhenaten failed, the gods sent a king to replace him in the person of Smenkhkare. Now that he has failed the gods will provide another king, a stronger one."

"Does Ay say who this king will be?" Ankhesenpaaten's voice trembled.

"No."

"A king must be of the family of Amenhotep. There are only three living males in this family--Akhenaten, Smenkhkare and you." She looked sideways at the little boy fidgeting on the bench beside her. "Who do you think he means?"

"Me. I will be the next king."

Ankhesenpaaten took a deep breath and exhaled slowly, composing herself. "I can help you become king."

"How?"

"A king needs a strong queen beside him, someone who can help him bear the burdens of ruling a great nation, someone who can bear him many fine sons and daughters. You cannot marry just anybody, Tutankhaten, you must marry within the family. Later you can do as you please but your first wife, your queen, must be a family member." Ankhesenpaaten paused, listening to her hammering heart. "Only by marrying a family member can the king and queen present a strong and united house, one that the people will have faith in." She reached out and took his hand in hers, turning it over and tracing the lines in the palm with one finger. "Meryetaten and Beketaten are too old for you and are tainted by Smenkhkare's failings. I am the only other princess. You must marry me."

Tutankhaten's eyes grew large. "Me? Marry you?"

"Yes. Don't you want to?" Ankhesenpaaten drew back slightly, dropping her head modestly. "Don't you find me beautiful?"

"Oh, y...yes. Of...of c...course I do," he stammered. He blushed, his bronzed skin turning a shade darker. "I mean, you want to? But I'm only nine."

"You are older than your years, everyone says so. Besides, we don't have to share a bed yet." Ankhesenpaaten smiled demurely and glanced at the little boy. "We can get betrothed and when you become king, I will marry you and become your queen on the same day."

"I don't know that I can be betrothed. I'm only a boy."

"Then it is high time you lost this." She reached out and flicked his side lock of hair. "I shall write to Ay immediately. Kadore can take the letter back to Waset when he goes."

Ankhesenpaaten stood and pulled Tutankhaten onto his feet also. He only came to her breasts so she bent down and kissed his cheek. "Now kiss me, husband-to-be, then go and play. I have many things to do."

The prince reached up and put a clumsy kiss on his niece's lips, before turning and scampering away over the grass.

Ankhesenpaaten watched him absently, her mind already elsewhere, turning over phrases for her letter to grandfather Ay. She could not entrust this to a palace scribe, she would have to write it herself.

Chapter 6

Jebu the Amorite sat in the feasting hall of his lord and master Aziru, king of Amurru, in the city of Taanach and lifted his cup of wine in salute, politely drumming on the table with his other hand. He wiped the wine that spilled into his beard with the back of one hand and set the ornate silver cup back on the table with a thump, whereupon it was at once refilled by an attentive servant. Resting one arm on the side of his great carved chair he settled back to listen to the rest of the speeches, idly picking at the remnants of the feast that covered the tables and a good part of the floor of the hall.

The Babylonian ambassador was on his feet now, resplendent in his long woolen robes and tall, braided hat that, together with the matted, greasy hair and plaited beard, sent cascades of sweat pouring off the man's face. The ambassador paused in his speech and pulled a linen cloth from beneath his robes, wiping his face. King Aziru made a comment that was lost in the general noise of the hundred men in the hall, but was evidently heard, though not appreciated, by the ambassador. He glowered, but was careful not to direct his outrage at the king. Putting away the cloth, he resumed his speech.

Jebu listened attentively, dismissing the platitudes, the praise phrases and the empty promises he had heard before, centering his attention on the nub of the speech. He found himself scowling and hurriedly calmed his features, putting up a hand to his mouth in pretence of finding a distasteful morsel of food. Casually he leaned over to the younger man seated on his right.

"As I predicted, Ephras. The Babylonian king will not support us."

The younger man glanced hurriedly to see whether they were overheard. "He did not say that, General."

"Listen to what he does not say." He waved a hand dismissively and sat up straight again.

The speech came to an end and the over-heated ambassador bowed, taking his seat again. King Aziru thanked the mighty kingdom of Babylon for their gifts--he gestured to a small open chest in front of the raised throne--and for their considered reply to his inquiries. Aziru leaned close to his chamberlain who stood attentively beside the throne and muttered a few words. The chamberlain stepped forward, angling his stance so as not to present his back to the king, and addressed the feasters.

"King Aziru calls on Satturata, the ambassador from the illustrious kingdom of Mitanni to answer the king's question." The chamberlain stepped back as a short man arose from one of the seats and strode forward, bowing to the throne.

"My lord Aziru, high sovereign of Amurru, suzerain of the disputed lands of Sinai, my lord and master Mattivaza sends his greetings and presents a gift of a twenty fine fleeces of wool." He gestured and a string of slaves ran into the hall, each bearing washed wool fleeces in their arms. Satturata waited until the slaves had withdrawn, leaving a gleaming white pile of fleeces in front of the throne, before resuming. "Further, he gives to lord Aziru, twenty fine horses and twenty bulls from his own herds." Satturata smiled and bowed again. "In deference to the customs of Amurru, I have left the livestock outside."

"Good of him," Jebu growled. "You notice the son of a...you notice he brings nothing that will aid the war."

Ephras leaned across, an expression of concern wrinkling his weathered face. "General, have a care," he muttered. "The horses will be welcome, surely?"

"Spavined nags the lot of them, I expect." Jebu said loudly, smiling at the men around him. He lifted his wine cup toward the ambassadors before sipping from it.

The Mitannian ambassador ignored the interruption and continued his speech, taking many minutes to say very little, before sitting down again. The Assyrian ambassador, Arik-Den-Enlil, followed, with much the same performance. Several copper ornaments and a few antique weapons joined the small pile of gift offerings in front of the Amurru king.

Jebu drained his cup once more and gestured to the attendant to bring more. He belched, and remarked loudly to the other men at his table, "It appears we have no real friends." Heads turned, including that of Aziru. The king looked at his general from under hooded eyes for a long time while the room hushed, waiting for his reaction. Aziru turned to his chamberlain again and the Hittite ambassador was introduced.

Mutaril got to his feet and bowed deeply before Aziru, then turned toward the hall and sketched a bow toward the Amorite general. "Mighty king Aziru, lords and ambassadors, and esteemed General Jebu, I too bring the greetings of my monarch, Shubbiluliuma and an answer to King Aziru's question." Mutaril paused and advanced further into the open space in front of the throne. He walked slowly over to the gift offerings of the other ambassadors and stirred the trinkets and fleeces with one foot. "I share General Jebu's disdain for this refuse. If these ambassadors from Babylon, Mitanni and Assyria had insulted my king with such offerings, they would have left their heads with them."

The hall erupted into a roar of anger and applause, the ambassadors rising to their feet in a rage. The Mitannian strode out into the middle, red in the face and demanded of Aziru an apology for such behavior.

The king raised a hand and waited for the hall to quiet. As the sound died away he spoke in a soft voice, encouraging everyone to strain to hear him.

"You ask an apology of me, Satturata? Have you not been listening? It is Mutaril the Hittite who draws attention to your insult, not I."

The Mitannian stuttered and paled as he realized the path that unconsidered anger had set him on. He bowed and gestured toward Mutaril. "My apologies, King Aziru, if I seemed to imply you were at fault. I merely sought to have this man's tongue curbed. He insults both my master and you when he claims you are held in low esteem by Mitanni." An angry agreement came from the Babylonian and Assyrian ambassadors.

"I will decide when and if I have been insulted. Now be seated, Satturata, I would hear the words of my brother Shubbiluliuma." The ambassador bowed again and resumed his seat, casting angry glances at the assembled listeners. When all was quiet again, Aziru inclined his head toward Mutaril. "Please continue, ambassador."

Mutaril smiled and bowed again. "Shubbiluliuma, king of the Hittites and overlord of the Hittite Confederacy sends his greetings to his brother Aziru, son of Abdiashirta of the Amorites. He reminds my lord Aziru that the land of Hatti has been a loyal ally of Amurru these last ten years and more. Hatti has supplied gold and corn and meat that Aziru might pursue his just and honourable claim of lordship over southern Syria and Sinai, long held by the usurping kings of Kemet. All that Hatti has asked in return is the loyal friendship of Amurru. Is this not so, your majesty?"

Aziru's chamberlain leaned over and spoke a few words in the king's ear, listening to the reply, before he spoke to the hall. "Aziru, king of the Amorites, recognizes the debt of friendship he owes to his brother Shubbiluliuma."

Mutaril ignored the outraged whisperings from the ambassador's table behind him and bowed once more. "Lord Aziru, my king answers your question thus--I remember my friends in time of plenty and of want. Ask, and you shall receive it." The ambassador turned and clapped his hands. Through the main doors of the hall trotted a stream of slaves, each laboring under a burden he held in both arms. "As a token of my king's respect and affection for his brother Aziru, king Shubbiluliuma sends a gift worthy of a king."

A buzz of voices broke out as the slaves passed the first tables and the gathering caught sight of their burdens. The voices rose to a roar as the first of them placed his burden on the steps of the throne dais, hurrying back and out of the way. Others followed, as the hall erupted in shouts of wonder and applause. Even Aziru got slowly to his feet, staring at the golden bricks piled in front of him.

"Gold," Mutaril called out clearly above the noise. "Gold worth a thousand times the gifts from lesser kings, Aziru."

The chamberlain picked up one of the bricks and brought it to Aziru. The king held it, stroking it with a gleam of greed in his eye. "Thank you, Mutaril...I send my thanks to my brother Shubbiluliuma, and assure him that the friendship gift he bestows on me will be repaid a hundred-fold."

The feast broke up into a milling mass of nobles, senior officers and courtiers, all wanting to see the fortune in gold close up, avarice and lust showing in almost every face. The ambassadors left quickly, shamed before the gathering and urgently wanting to send news of this extraordinary gift to their masters. In this they were unlucky, as the chamberlain ordered the gates of the city locked, denying exit to any until the wishes of the king became known.

Jebu, with Ephras keeping close company, moved out into the hall as servants cleared the remnants of the feast and pulled the tables back to the edges of the room. Other servants strewed clean, scented sand on the floors, where hounds fought and snarled over scraps. Few men met Jebu's eyes, turning aside or suddenly becoming engrossed in a conversation as he neared.

"That was not wise, General," Ephras murmured. "You will not get another appointment by being rude to the king or his guests."

"He is not angry with me, Ephras. You saw the way the ambassadors acted. I was merely saying what he already thought."

Mutaril approached through the throng, people bowing respectfully and moving out of his path. The Hittite ambassador nodded and smiled. "Well met, General. I enjoyed your comments tonight."

Jebu jerked his head toward the dais and the ring of guards surrounding the gold. "You surprised me there, your Excellency."

"Oh? How so? Hatti has always been a friend of Amurru."

"A friend, yes, but one notably slow in giving gold."

Mutaril sighed. "Your words pain me, General. My king has always tried to provide your king with the means to resist Kemet."

"Enough to resist, but never enough that we might accomplish our aims."

The ambassador looked at Jebu carefully, lowering his voice so that they could not be overheard. "You are an intelligent man--and an able soldier. Why don't you tell me why that might be?"

Jebu paused, considering for several moments before uttering a bark of amusement. "Shubbiluliuma guards his borders by using Amorite troops. He weakens the enemy by fostering Aziru's claims over southern Syria, yet he can still pretend to be a loyal ally of Kemet and accept gifts of gold from their king."

Mutaril smiled. "General, you are wasted in the army. With your insights you should be a diplomat."

"Is that where the gold came from? Kemet?"

"A delicious irony, is it not? Their king Akhenaten bleeds his army dry to provide the gold he gifts to his loyal allies."

"I hear the situation is changing in the south though. This new king of theirs, the king of Upper Kemet...I forget his name..."

"Djeserkheperu."

"Yes, that is it. I hear he is striving to return Kemet to the old ways. He is strengthening the army and I would wager the gifts of gold will cease."

"Too little, too late, General. With this gold, Aziru will be able to sweep all before him."

Jebu stroked his beard thoughtfully. "What of their General Paatenemheb? Gold will not sweep him away."

Mutaril smiled again and inclined his head. "That will be your problem. I bid you goodnight, General...Lieutenant." The Hittite ambassador swept past, toward the throne and Aziru. Jebu watched him go, a small smile on his lips.

"He is right, Ephras. With gold, much can be accomplished."

"But he is wrong about it being your problem, General. Surely he knows you were...well, relieved of your command?"

"I would imagine a man like him would be well-informed." Jebu shrugged. "Never mind, we will find out soon enough. Let us find some more wine. This talking is thirsty work." He led the way over to the slaves by the stacked amphorae and took two filled cups, passing one to his lieutenant. "Drink, Ephras, either to drown our grief or celebrate our good fortune. Either way, we can get drunk." Draining his cup he refilled it and moved toward the sound of music and merriment.

In the open area of the great hall furthest from the throne dais, musicians had set up camp and were sending out a rhythmic pulse that caught at the senses. Drums beat and sistra rattled, overlain by the wild scaling of a flute. A score of slave girls dressed in little to nothing, swung and gyrated in the open space, a few of them tumbling and leaping. The surrounding men, for the only women that attended formal feasts were entertainers, hooted and yelled, faces flushed with drink and lust. One of the tumblers miscalculated and landed close to the circle of onlookers. A man reached out and grabbed her, hauling her close and nuzzling her naked breasts with his greasy bearded face. The girl screamed with laughter and dragged the man to one side, through the crowd to a side door. Others followed and as the girls paired off, fresh dancers emerged to keep up the entertainment.

"Not to your liking, Jebu?"

Jebu swung round and cocked his head at the short-bearded man of middling height in front of him. "I know the voice, but I do not recognise you."

A gap-toothed smile broke through the hair. "Nor should you. It has been a while, Jebu. The Gezer road. A caravan with gold under the copper in panniers."

"Ashraz?" Jebu's eyes opened wider. "It has been a while." His eyes flicked to the plain black robes and unornamented hands, the lack of distinguishing features. "The last time I saw you, you were a spy. Are you still?"

"I would not be a very good one if I admitted it to everyone I met." Ashraz stepped back as a drunken man lurched by, the naked girl on his arm bumping into him. Ashraz delivered a sound slap to a naked buttock and turned away grinning. "Let's just say I keep my eyes and ears open."

"Fair enough. And what brings you here today? Or shouldn't I ask?"

Ashraz eyed Ephras coolly. "Who's this? He looks familiar but I can't place him."

"Ephras. He is my lieutenant. You actually met him on the Gezer road, though he was only a pup at the time."

"You trust him?" Jebu nodded. "Good enough for me." Ashraz took Jebu by the arm and steered him out of the way of the revelers. Ephras followed a few paces behind. When they reached the wall, the spy turned his back to it and surveyed the room for a few minutes. "I like walls," he said matter-of-factly. "Good safe things to have behind one. And yes, you can ask."

Jebu took a moment to understand what the spy was talking about. Then he nodded. "What are you doing here today, Ashraz?"

"Guarding the gold."

"You knew about it? Before Mutaril brought it in?"

"Of course. I suggested it to Shubbiluliuma in the first place. Of course, he won't remember me. He'll think it was his own idea, but something had to be done and I judged the time was right."

"Right for what?" Ephras asked.

"War."

Ephras looked at Ashraz, then at Jebu. "What war?"

"There is always war," said Jebu softly. "But I have it in mind you mean something special."

Ashraz looked over to where the girls were still tumbling and dancing. "A fine crop of slaves," he commented judiciously. "I fancy some of them are Kemetu too. Have you ever had a Kemetu woman, Jebu?"

"Can't say that I have. What did you mean about war?"

"You should try one." Ashraz smiled and picked his teeth with a long, blackened fingernail. "Not as inventive as a Babylonian, nor as abandoned as the sluts of Byblos, but they have something else." He faced toward the girls but he was watching Jebu.

"What?" Ephras' voice was rough with sudden emotion. "What do they have?"

Ashraz laughed. "I'm glad someone here thinks about the normal pleasures of life. You are too wrapped up in your army, Jebu. Ah..." He snapped his fingers. "I was forgetting, you do not have an army." Grabbing Ephras by the arm, he turned him toward the tumbling girls and pointed. "See the one on the left, yes, that one, the one who has just completed the somersault...she is Kemetu. Tell me how I know."

"She has coppery skin."

"Pah, so do other girls. Watch her boy, think about it." Ashraz turned back to where Jebu was leaning against the wall, playing with the tassels in his belt. "Why is it you do not have a command, O General of Aziru's army?"

"I feel sure you are about to tell me."

Ashraz sighed and stretched, grimacing as he grabbed at his side. "I'm not as young as I once was, Jebu."

"Age comes to us all, Ashraz." A smile quirked Jebu's lips. "Not always wisdom though."

"What did you think would happen to you after losing your army to Paatenemheb? Did you honestly think Aziru would just turn round and offer you another one?"

Jebu's jaw muscles clenched and he looked away. "My army was raw and untrained. They fled before the hounds only to fall to the huntsmen's spears."

"A bad commander blames his men," Ashraz murmured. "Is that not how the proverb runs?"

Jebu's hands curled into tight fists and his nostrils flared. "I am not blaming my men," he grated. "I state a fact. I was given that army only a week before and asked to perform miracles. If I had had time to train them..."

"What a pity you do not have men now, Jebu. You surely have had time to train any army." The smile on Ashraz's face was crueler, his voice edged with scorn.

"Three years, Ashraz," Jebu said softly. "I have spent three years wasting my time recruiting farm lads and townsmen who would neither know their members from a spear, nor which one to stick in a woman, or which in an enemy. Then I did not even have the satisfaction of whipping them into shape. I had to turn them over to others."

"Yet you stay? Have you not thought about hiring yourself out? There are many kings who would pay good gold to secure the services of a seasoned warrior. You might not be a general but you would have a command again."

Jebu shook his head. "I serve my king."

Ashraz clapped his hands together slowly, several people looking around before turning back to the entertainment. "Good Jebu. Poor but loyal."

"You mock me, Ashraz. Why? Or are you for sale to the highest bidder?"

"No, but I choose carefully those whom I serve." The spy pursed his lips and edged closer to the general. "I do have an offer for you though, one that I think you should consider."

"I have it!" Ephras called. "Look, Ashraz." The young man grabbed Ashraz and pointed to where the tumbling slave girls were walking on their hands and feet, bodies bent backward in a bow. All displayed a rough triangle of dark hair between their thighs, all except one, and she also had coppery skin. "Kemetu women are hairless."

"Not naturally, boy. They shave." Ashraz looked back at Jebu's impassive face. "I need to talk to the general in private. Why don't you go and sample the Kemetu girl? I guarantee you an unforgettable experience."

Ephras looked round, pleasure and anticipation on his face. "That'd be all right, General?"

Jebu nodded. "Go and have fun." He watched as Ephras stumbled over to the Kemetu girl and they ran from the hall together. "What offer?"

"I find that in my line of business I visit many places, talk to many people. Kings even. Why, just last month I was talking to Shubbiluliuma, the Hittite."

"So you said before. Get on with it."

"Patience, Jebu. I'm coming to it." Ashraz glanced around again, waiting a few moments for a servant to pass. "The Assyrians seek an experienced officer to lead an attack against certain hill tribes on the border of Assyria and Amurru."

"Surely they have experienced officers of their own?"

"One would think so," Ashraz agreed. "However, your name was mentioned in the same breath as rather an intriguing amount of gold." He watched Jebu carefully and, after a few minutes when he got no reply, frowned. "You do not want to know how much gold?"

"And for this gold I must leave Amurru and fight for the king of Assyria against hill tribes who may well be allied to Aziru?"

"Well, perhaps. But at least you would be exercising your talents for soldiering."

"If I agree, you will carry word back to Assyria, where no doubt you will be paid."

"Of course. It is only reasonable that I get a fee for all my hard work. So, you agree?"

Jebu whirled and caught Ashraz, pinioning one arm and slamming the smaller man against the stone wall. He slipped his eating dagger from his belt and held it to the spy's throat. "Guards!" he yelled. "Guards, treason!"

The hubbub in the hall vanished as if hewn by an axe. Heads swung round and the soldiers around the king started across the hall at a run. The chamberlain followed more slowly, his face thoughtful.

Jebu released Ashraz as the soldiers surrounded them, the press of the crowd jostling the guards. He grabbed a sword from a guard and held it to the spy's chest. Ashraz said nothing, just massaged his arm and smiled.

"What is the meaning of this, General?" the chamberlain asked. "Have you had too much to drink that you must assault the guests?"

"This man offered me gold to fight for my king's enemies. He is a traitor."

The chamberlain looked at the slight figure standing with his back to the wall, the point of a bronze sword pricking his robes. "This man?" He glanced at Ashraz's clothing and looked in vain for jewelry. "He does not look rich enough to offer anyone gold."

"Not his own gold, you fool. Assyrian gold."

The chamberlain bristled. "Remember yourself, General. You have seen this gold?"

"No, I..."

"What is happening here?" King Aziru walked up behind Jebu, the soldiers parting to let him through.

"Your majesty." Jebu bowed awkwardly, trying not to take his eyes off Ashraz, nor let the sword point waver. "This man is a traitor. He offered me Assyrian gold to war against your allies."

"Indeed? Then you have done well to apprehend him...what is your name?"

"Jebu. I was once a general in your army."

"Ah. I remember a Jebu, but that Jebu would have killed a traitor, not captured him."

"You wish me to kill him, your majesty?" the point of the sword rose slightly to prick the base of Ashraz's neck.

Aziru stood in silence for several minutes, drawing the tension out. "No, ex-general Jebu. Bring him to the chamberlain's room, I will have him questioned." The king turned and walked away, the crowd parting in silence before him.

Jebu jerked his head and stood aside, pushing the spy after the king, the squad of soldiers falling in around them. "For the sake of an old friendship, Ashraz," he murmured. "Admit your guilt at once and I will petition the king to grant you a swift death."

"Yours would be the hand with the sword, old friend?" Ashraz smiled and sauntered on, displaying no signs of fear.

The chamberlain's rooms off the great hall were small and cramped; being dominated by a large table covered in papyrus and clay tablets. The king pulled out a sturdy chair from behind the desk and after inspecting the seat, sat down.

"Dismiss the guards, Jebu. I will talk with you and this man alone."

"Your majesty, that would not be wise...this man is a traitor and dangerous."

"Can you not protect me?"

"Yes," Jebu agreed grimly. He moved slightly, positioning himself between Aziru and the spy.

"Good." Aziru stared at the small man and nodded. "Why did you talk to ex-General Jebu, Ashraz?"

Jebu's head swung round, though the sword did not waver. "You know this man?"

"Do not interrupt me again. Go on, Ashraz."

"Yes, your majesty. I talked with General Jebu to determine whether I could buy his services for the Assyrian king. I offered him a large but indeterminate amount of gold. He refused, drawing a knife on me."

"I told you he would."

Ashraz opened his mouth to protest then wisely kept quiet. Instead he bowed. "Indeed you did majesty."

"Now tell him why you did it. You can put that sword away, Jebu," Aziru added.

Jebu lowered the sword a fraction, his eyes narrowing thoughtfully. "You meant to test me? Test my loyalty?"

Ashraz grinned. "No hard feelings Jebu? We had to be sure."

"We?"

"General Jebu," Aziru gestured at Ashraz, smiling gently. "Meet my spy-master. I have need of you, Jebu. I have need of an experienced general."

"You had one three years ago, Aziru, yet you dismissed me."

Aziru's smile slipped. "It is not wise to remind kings of their...well, shall we say...not fully thought out actions." The king sat in silence for a few minutes. "War is coming, Jebu, real war with Kemet. Now that we have sufficient gold I mean to raise a proper army, a professional one. I cannot think of anyone I would rather have lead it. Will you accept?"

Jebu nodded, his mind suddenly racing. "Yes, my lord, I will."

Chapter 7

T he king's barge pulled out of the current, heeling over slightly as the river tugged at it, and into the lee of the great wharf that ran out from the harbor at Djeba. The master rapped out a command and the rowers shipped their great red-tipped oars, water streaming off in rivers of crimson-gold in the early morning sunlight. The slightest of impacts and naked men leapt aboard from the wharf, hauling heavy ropes with them, rapidly securing the barge in place.

Smenkhkare, resplendent in a pleated kilt of finest linen with a blue and gold cloth tied around the waist and hanging down in front, stepped from under the awning set up in the middle of the barge and looked up at the small city of Djeba on the west side of the river. Around his shoulders and covering his chest almost to his nipples was a heavy gold pectoral, inlaid with semi-precious stones--red, yellow, green--and blue glass paste. The centerpiece was a carved topaz scarab, wings outstretched as if folding the king in its protective embrace. The double crown of Kemet, surmounted by the royal uraeus, raised the king's stature from middling height to regal proportions. A heavy gold ring, carved with the cartouche of his royal names, glinted on his right hand as he strode to the gangplank, accompanied by several young courtiers from Waset.

On the wharf to greet his king, stood the mayor of the city, the chief of the Medjay and the senior priests of Heru, whose temple dominated the mud brick town. Behind them, crowding the riverbank and the closest streets of the city, stood throngs of people, chanting and waving, all overjoyed to be in the presence of their god-king.

Smenkhkare greeted the officials briefly before walking over to the closest citizens and greeting them warmly. Most stared open-mouthed at such an unprecedented move, but a few plucked up the courage to offer blessings or prayers for the king's health and long life. One young woman timidly reached out and touched Smenkhkare's arm. He turned to her and smiled, at which she covered her face with her headdress scarf, blushing furiously. After a few minutes, he returned to the priests and walked with them up the short incline of the lower city toward the small temple of Heru.

The temple was oriented East and West and as he entered through the narrow gate between the two entrance pylons, the morning sun threw his shadow ahead of him, as if he raced to meet the god in his sanctuary. A great black granite statue of Heru as a falcon, wearing the double crown of Kemet, stood in the great open-aired peristyle court, just at the entrance to the first hypostyle hall. Smenkhkare stopped and contemplated the god basking in the rays of the rising sun.

"Heru is the sun reborn to the dying sun of Asar," the high priest intoned. "It is fitting that he greets himself rising anew each day."

Smenkhkare nodded and passed through the first hypostyle hall with its lotus-topped columns bearing up the weight of the roof, then into the much smaller second hall before he reached the sanctuary of the god. Here, the light of the new day scarcely lit their way and bright torches smoked and guttered, shadows making the dim halls come alive. The priests reverently opened the great doors and revealed the god worked in gold, standing on the great bark of the sun as it sailed through the heavens. Bowing to both Heru and the god on earth, the priests withdrew, leaving the king alone.

Smenkhkare exited the temple before the sun reached midway to its zenith. Bidding farewell to the priests and promising to gift gold to them, the king gathered his friends and courtiers and headed for the mayor's residence. A great crowd of people accompanied them, a happy throng content to be in the presence of their monarch.

At the residence, Smenkhkare waited patiently while the mayor organized refreshments, though he refused to allow a feast to be prepared.

"When we return," the king said. "First we must do what we came here to do--kill the lion that has become a cattle killer."

"What, er...Oh, er, yes, your majesty," the mayor stuttered. "In that case I will, with your permission, withdraw and allow you to prepare." He bowed and hurried off, mopping his brow with a small cloth.

Smenkhkare picked up a small flask of beer as a dozen slaves brought food and drink. Turning to his friends, he raised his beer high. "May the gods grant a successful hunt."

A slim young man with a full head of his own black hair grinned and downed his beer in a single gulp, snatching up a bunch of plump red grapes. "What's the plan then, Djeser? When do we leave?"

One of the courtiers hissed with displeasure at hearing his king addressed in such a familiar fashion and with a contraction of his holy prenomen as well. Smenkhkare just frowned slightly but let the slip pass.

"As soon as the guides get here, Psamtek. I'm told the village in question is about two hours away, south and west on the borders of the great desert."

"How are we going to hunt it? On foot or by chariot?"

"That depends on the nature of the terrain. Really Siwadj, how can I tell when I've never seen the place? And before you ask, Merybast..." Smenkhkare forestalled a small sallow-complexioned youth. "Yes, we can hunt other things beside the lion. The lion is a necessity but if the hunting is good, we can stay a few days and try for some antelope and ibex. If not," he shrugged. "We can always return to the river and hunt wild fowl."

The guides arrived, a surly-looking man who claimed to have lived near the village in question all his life, and a taller quiet man who just bowed to the king and his nobles. The party set out, the king being accompanied by Menkure, Siwadj and Merybast, as well as Psamtek, son of the Keeper of the King's Furniture and Raia, son of the Controller of the King's Funeral artists. They had all, at one time or another, been students of Waset' foremost scribe, Kensthoth, now a King's Councillor. Several prominent men of Djeba had asked permission to hunt with their king and, with the guides and servants, nearly thirty men sped out of the city in a cloud of dust just after noon.

Smenkhkare led, driving the royal hunting chariot unloaded from the barge during the morning. With him rode Raia and Merybast, the rest of the party following by pairs in heavier ceremonial chariots. The baggage, of which there was a considerable amount, for one cannot expect a king to be without his comforts, trundled at the rear in a large wagon.

Two hours became four and the king fretted, forcing himself to travel at the pace of the slowest chariot. Already, the supply wagon lagged at least an hour behind. The rich farmland of the river plains dried out, a margin of trees giving way to sparse scrub and thorn thicket. Patches of sand showed through the vegetation, presaging the great desert to the west. Raia pointed out a pair of ostriches picking their way slowly through the scrub and Smenkhkare immediately turned off the track, urging his horses into a gallop as he raced over rough ground to cut them off from the open desert. The chariot bounced and slid, threatening to tip them off, but the horses, full of the joy of running after the enforced idleness of the boat voyage from Waset, gave their hearts to the chase. Another lurch over stones then they were into an open patch and closing with their prey. The great birds accelerated, stepping high, kicking up puffs of dust with each enormous stride. Passing the reins to Merybast, Smenkhkare braced himself against the swaying sides of the chariot and picked up his bow.

The first arrow winged its way toward the male bird just as the ostriches reached the open ground, the striding birds starting to pull away from their pursuers. The shaft entered the straining chest beneath the left wing and, between one stride and the next, the cock bird fell dead, tumbling and somersaulting in a spray of feathers and sand. The drab hen bird veered sharply and the second arrow missed, but as she turned back, the next struck her in the upper thigh. She slowed abruptly and fell, then struggled up again and limped slowly away, uttering cries of distress. The chariot came up alongside and Smenkhkare leapt to the ground, pulling out a short bronze dagger. Avoiding the half-hearted kicks of the wounded bird, he grabbed the long neck and slashed it nearly through, jumping back as the animal collapsed in a welter of blood. They left the corpses for the servants to collect and joined the others on the distant track, grinning and waving as the men cheered the king's hunting prowess.

The track to the village ran in a southerly direction for a while longer then curved round to the west, running parallel with a large dry sandy stream bed. Another hundred paces or so and one of the guides ran up alongside the royal chariot and shouted out, waving toward a stand of trees. Merybast, who was still managing the horses, pulled them to a halt.

"A good place ter camp, yer majesty," the guide explained. "There's shade an' a bit a water." He smiled ingratiatingly, exposing rotten teeth. "The lion's 'ereabahts too."

The site lay on the edge of the old stream, where water at some stage had undercut the bank, bringing an old acacia tree down and effectively blocking what had once been a rushing flow. The debris and rocks trapped by the fallen tree had accumulated on the upstream side and now, long after the rains had disappeared; a pool of water lay hard up against the steep bank, a scum of green slime around the edges.

Smenkhkare left the servants to await the wagon and set up camp, taking his friends and the guides apart to discuss the lay of the land and the plans for the next day.

"All right, relax and take your time," Smenkhkare said. "We will have no formality out here." He pointed at the guides. "What are your names?"

The two men looked at each other, and the taller one nudged his companion who said "Bey, sir." The man pointed at the taller man. "An' 'es Baki...sir."

"Very well, then Bey. Tell me about this lion."

Bey screwed up his face in puzzlement. "'Es a lion, sir. I means, what else could 'e be?"

"Sorry, sir," Baki broke in. "Bey is a little dim-witted at times. He means well though. The lion is a large one, with a black mane. He favours his left front paw on account of a wound."

Smenkhkare regarded Baki with interest. "You are not from around here, are you? There's a hint of city in your voice, and educated too."

"That's right, sir. I was a servant to a scribe in Djeba but I came back home when my mother died." Baki shaded his eyes from the setting sun and pointed almost due west. "The old river bed runs down there, maybe five thousand paces or so, and passes between two patches of dense scrub thicket."

"How big are these patches of thicket?"

"The one to the north is many thousands of paces long sir, running between here and the river. The smaller one to the south is shaped like...like a radish, maybe fifty paces across and a hundred or so in length. It is where the lion always lies up."

"Always?" Merybast asked, "You seem to know a lot about this lion."

Baki nodded. "That's true, sir. My village has lost eight cows and three bulls in the last two months. Last week, a nephew of mine, six years old, was mauled." Baki looked down at the ground and scuffed a bare foot in the sand. "He died. So yes, I know a lot about this lion. I've made it my business to."

Smenkhkare clapped Baki gently on one shoulder. "Do not be despondent, Baki. Tomorrow we shall kill the beast that robbed you of your nephew."

"So what's the plan?" Menkure asked.

Baki looked at his king. "If your majesty will permit me?" Smenkhkare nodded and the guide continued. "We tried to hunt the beast once before when he lay in his lair during the heat of the day. We beat drums and rattled sticks and shouted, hoping to drive him down to where three men with spears stood waiting." Baki shrugged. "He scattered them and escaped into the northern thickets. There we would not follow."

"Why not?" Raia asked.

"We are not huntsmen," Baki replied simply. "Whereas the lion hunts to live."

"So what are we going to do?" Menkure asked again. "Organize another drive?"

"I would recommend it, sirs. The thickets are too dense to resist the lion if it should attack, but brave and resolute men could take it as it crosses between the south and the north."

"That would be me," Menkure said modestly.

"And I," added Siwadj.

The others joined in, clamoring for the positions of honour.

"Enough," Smenkhkare interrupted with a laugh. "I shall take the honour. It is mine by right." He looked round at crestfallen faces. "However, I shall have two companions to share the danger. Menkure? Merybast? Will you protect my flanks?"

"Yes!" Menkure yelled, stabbing his fist at the sky.

"I would be honoured," Merybast replied calmly.

"Do not think the rest of you have escaped all danger," Smenkhkare went on. "This lion has been hunted before and this time he may decide to break through the men who disturb his rest, rather than flee before them. I would have you three with the men of the village, to strengthen and support them. Also to protect them if the lion breaks out."

"Willingly, Djeser," nodded Psamtek. He looked up at the sinking sun, then around at the dry landscape. "Baki? Any chance of some hunting? We could always do with some meat for tonight."

Baki shook his head. "The land is too dry for much game, which may be why the lion has come close to the villages. There may be a few antelope around, but I could not say where. There is little forage."

Raia frowned. "It is hard to believe there is nothing. What about you, Bey? Do you know of anything?"

"Me? No, sir, I don' know nothin'. I is just a farmer, sir. I knows nothin' 'bout 'untin'."

"Meat will not be a problem, sirs," Baki said. "I have arranged for several goats to be brought out from the village."

"Goat?" Psamtek mimicked being sick. "Well, I suppose if there's nothing else..."

"There are always the ostriches," Raia grinned. "They can be quite tasty."

"Try and think of something beyond your stomachs, gentlemen." Smenkhkare shook his head gently. "We are not at a palace banquet. There will be time for hunting game after we have disposed of the lion." He pointed toward the setting sun, now touching the horizon. "Let us give praise to Re and pray that he will look upon our hunt tomorrow with favour." The king raised his arms to the golden-red light and lifted his voice in song, the others joining in after a heartbeat.

"Praise be to Re," Smenkhkare sang. "Giver of light and banisher of the dark places. Praise be to Re, who makes all things grow. The plants praise him, lifting up their limbs toward the light. The good animals walk abroad in his light, partaking of his sustenance, while the wicked animal shuns the light of day, hunting by night. Yet even he must face the day, when the golden eye of Re seeks out his iniquities. Let Re look down on us tomorrow and guide our hands, giving us a resolute eye and filling our hearts with courage that we may slay the killer who hunts by night. Praise to you, O Re! Bless us, thy sons."

Smenkhkare went on for several minutes, chanting the words, some of them the old words of praise from the ancient songs of the priests, others newer, from the heart. His friends followed along, their repetition a syllable or two behind. The voices died away at last as the last edge of the sun disc dipped below the edge of the world, a brief flash of emerald green teasing the eyes, gone almost before it was seen.

The king turned to his friends and smiled. "Come, supper awaits us." He led the way through the twilight to the camp under the trees where a roaring fire, tents and the scent of roasting goat meat welcomed them.

Three tents comprised the camp--one for the king, a second for his five friends and the third for the dozen or so servants. The guides slept outside, huddled near a smaller fire for warmth and security against a possible man-killer that stalked the night. Smenkhkare sat up late, at least until the waxing moon rose, shedding a pearly light over the barren landscape. His friends sat with him, companionable yet quiet, respecting his mood. His edict, issued over dinner, restricted their drinking, so they sipped on wine rather than drinking great draughts, and told stories over the campfire.

"It is quiet," Smenkhkare remarked, sitting in his carved wooden chair and staring out over the dry stream bed to the plain beyond. Below him, from the pool's edge, came faint sounds as small nocturnal creatures braved the presence of men to slake their tiny thirsts. From further away, crickets and other insects kept up a constant muted chirring, underscoring the silence. Far out over the plains a night bird called, once, twice, high and piercing. The smell of wood smoke and charring meats lingered faintly in the still air.

"A lovely night, Djeser," Raia agreed. He, and the others, sat cross-legged or sprawled out on the sandy soil beside the king's informal throne. Menkure and Siwadj murmured together and Psamtek was drawing designs in the sand with a broken twig. Merybast had his head over the edge of the small drop to the pool below, straining his eyes into the night, in the hopes of seeing whichever animal was drinking. "So quiet and peaceful."

"Too quiet. There is a lion out there, hurt and hungry. Why is he not proclaiming his presence?"

"Perhaps he is not hungry," Psamtek said from the shadows. "Maybe he killed today and is lying up with his meat, content to survey his kingdom."

Merybast turned and looked back toward the others, grinning. "Rather like you, Djeser. You killed today and now you sit with a full belly, regarding your kingdom."

Smenkhkare laughed. "Two kings cannot share a kingdom. Tomorrow, one of us must die."

"Hsst! Do not speak words of ill-omen, my lord." Psamtek threw down his stick. "Say a prayer to Heru, averter of evil."

"I saw my brother Heru in his house today. He will protect me."

"I pray so, Djeser," Raia said. "But my lord, you know that tomorrow is an unlucky day. Why do you not put off the hunt until the next lucky one?"

"And when is that, Raia?

"Three days hence, Djeser."

Menkure broke off his low conversation with Siwadj. "How is it you know which day is lucky and unlucky, Raia? I have to ask the priests when I want to know."

"My father is Controller of Funeral Artists. It is important that the sacred artwork is only carried out on lucky days."

"And how many lucky days are there in a month?"

"It varies. Between nine and thirteen."

Menkure laughed. "I must become a funeral artist. I can have most of the month off."

Raia shook his head disapprovingly. "They can work on unlucky days too. They just have to offer up a sacrifice through the priests to avert the evil."

"Ah. So if I really want a rewarding life I should become a priest and have all the artists bring me meat."

"Enough," Smenkhkare laughed. "But you see why I cannot wait for the next lucky day, Raia? There are too few of them and the villagers are relying on us to kill the lion. We will just have to make tomorrow a lucky day."

The next day's sun rose redly, casting a bloody look over a thin mist that swathed the landscape. Raia looked worried but said nothing, helping to prepare for the hunt. The sun mounted through the morning sky, yellowing to its usual blazing disc set in a lapis sky. The heat increased and the mist disappeared. As if they had been hidden by the mist, people appeared, men and women both, carrying an assortment of drums, horns and sticks. Baki and Bey set about organizing them into chattering groups, giving them their instructions and at last, led by the village elders, they trooped off into the plain. Raia, Psamtek and Siwadj went with them, armed with spears and bows.

Baki returned to the king and his other two friends. "If you would follow me, sirs." He bowed and led the way down into the dry stream bed, turning east and south toward the distant river. Smenkhkare carried a double-curved Nubian bow with a quiver of a dozen strong bronze-tipped arrows. Menkure had armed himself with a long leather sling and watched the ground as he walked, stooping to select rounded stones the size of pigeon's eggs.

"Are you any good with that?" Merybast asked. He thumped the shaft of his long spear into the sand close to Menkure's hand as he reached down for another stone. "Or am I going to have to guard you while you throw stones at rabbits?"

"Good enough," Menkure replied coolly. "I can hit a target at fifty paces four times out of five."

Merybast nodded grudgingly. "Better than me with my spear."

"Please sirs." Baki turned with an apologetic look, a finger placed on his lips. "We must be quiet now or the lion may hear us. If he hears sounds from here, he may escape in another direction."

They walked further along the stream bed, moving more cautiously as the vegetation grew thicker on both sides of the stream bed. At last Baki called a halt and pointed toward the northern side. "See, the track the lion takes."

Smenkhkare trotted over to where the path disappeared into the trees and started casting about in the loose sand.

"Sir, sir," Baki hissed. "With respect, the lion will appear from the other direction. From the southern thicket."

"He may appear from there Baki, but he does not leave by this path. There are no pug marks, no footprints, save those of ibex." He turned and stared at the guide quizzically. "Why not?"

Baki shrugged. "I know not, sir, but I have seen him myself walk across this stream bed and disappear into the trees just there."

"A lion leaves tracks, Baki, yet this one does not." Smenkhkare scrambled back down to the dry bed and confronted the guide. "I can think of two reasons why not, and I do not like either of them."

Menkure looked puzzled. "A lion without tracks? Are we talking about a ghost lion?" He glanced toward the trees uneasily.

"Three reasons, then, though I think yours very unlikely. No, either our guide has brought us to the wrong place or he has lied from the start."

"Lied how?" Merybast leaned on his spear and looked at the impassive guide with interest.

"Well, Baki? What is the answer?" Smenkhkare slipped an arrow out of the quiver and swiftly fitted it to his bow without taking his eyes off the man. "I think you had better start talking, Baki."

"Talking about what? What lie?" Merybast stared at his king, then at the guide. "What are they talking about, Menkure?"

"The man lied to us," Menkure growled. "There is no lion."

"No roaring during the night," Smenkhkare said softly. "And now no tracks to be seen." He glanced at his two companions. "Have either one of you seen any actual evidence that there is a lion here?"

"Sir, you are mistaken," Baki muttered. "I tell the truth. There is a lion here that kills our livestock."

"What I want to know is why I have been lied to." Smenkhkare brought his bow up slowly until the sharp arrow point covered the man's heart. "Speak, Baki. Why have I been brought here?"

Sweat broke out on the guide's face and he swallowed convulsively. "Have mercy, great king. I have not lied. There is a lion and in all probability he lies in yonder thicket awaiting the beaters to drive him out." As if waiting for his words a horn sounded in the distance and a great shout arose, drums beating and sticks rattling a cacophony.

Smenkhkare's eyes never left the guide's face. "Merybast," he said. "Run and tell them to stop. There is no need..."

The din faltered and an echoing roar of rage split the air. Merybast, in the act of turning to run up the slope, stopped dead, head turning back in consternation. Smenkhkare's stare wavered and he lowered the bow slightly, easing his aim from Baki's chest.

Baki licked his lips. "You hear, my lord?" he croaked. "The lion comes."

"I think he's right, Djeser," Menkure muttered. He shifted from foot to foot, drawing the sling cord through his fingers.

Smenkhkare nodded, reaching a decision. "Baki, stand back out of the way. Merybast, on my right, Menkure, guard my left." The king positioned himself a couple of paces in front of his companions, facing the dense southern thicket and the narrow game trail that debouched from it into the stream bed.

The noise of the drums and horns grew louder, and the tension grew. Merybast wiped first one hand, then the other, on his kilt, while Menkure swung the sling in his right hand, the left in the pouch at his waist, the clicking of river pebbles loud in the still air.

"Quiet, Menkure," Smenkhkare said coolly. He drew several arrows out of his quiver and stuck them into the sand in front of him, calmly selecting one and eyeing its true lines before fitting it to his bow.

"He comes," Merybast murmured.

A tawny shadow slipped through the undergrowth from right to left, heading for the opening that led over the lip of the stream bank. A large head, surrounded by a great dark mane, thrust itself over the edge, then, muscles rippling, the huge cat bounded down the slope toward them. Abruptly it paused, its legs digging into the sand as it caught sight of the three men in its path. It crouched and stared, its round yellow eyes boring into them, assessing the risk. The lion snarled, and then changed its tone to a guttural cough that grew into a shattering roar of anger and defiance, its hind legs gathering under it for the charge.

A bowstring thrummed and an arrow leapt at the moment the hind legs released their energy, launching the great cat forward. A rock slid under one paw and for an instant the lion stumbled, lurching downward, the sharp-tipped arrow piercing the lower jaw and glancing off the bone rather than burying itself in the feline chest. The deep roar climbed to a scream of rage and the lion threw itself forward again.

Smenkhkare snatched at the next arrow and knocked it sideways. He reached for the next and pulled it into his bow blindly, never taking his eyes off the rapidly closing beast. Something whistled past his ear and hit the lion a crack on its skull. The charge slowed a fraction and another stone hurtled in, cracking a cheek bone. The lion's head whipped to the side and upward as the pain made it flinch.

Smenkhkare's second arrow plunged deep into the base of the beast's neck. Still it came on, slower now, stumbling forward, death in its eyes and blood pouring from its mouth and nostrils, jaws agape and slavering. Another stone thudded into it, knocking it to the side. Merybast threw his spear, the point scoring a red line down the lion's flank.

Smenkhkare stood and watched the lion coming, a third arrow fitted and ready. Hot blood from its mouth sprayed his legs as it roared again in pain and frustration. It lurched and the king stepped swiftly to one side and loosed his last arrow into the side of the lion as it brushed by him. The shaft ripped through the golden hide at point-blank range, tearing through muscle and sinew, passing between the ribs and burying itself in the massive heart. With a sigh, the great beast toppled and fell forward, one paw reaching out with talons spread to claw at its tormentors even as life fled. Menkure staggered back, one hand clutched to his raked leg.

The three men stood in silence and looked down at the lion stretched out on the ground. Merybast walked past the lion on shaky legs to retrieve his spear, while Menkure sat down abruptly, looking in wonder at the claw marks on his leg.

"A noble sight indeed, Smenkhkare." A cool voice issued from the edge of the thicket behind them. "What a pity your bravery will never be known."

Smenkhkare turned. Baki jumped down from the stream bank, a dozen soldiers behind him. More appeared from the scrub, spears leveled at the king.

"What is the meaning of this, Baki? Who are these men?" The king looked past the guide to a soldier displaying an officer's armband. "What unit do you belong to? What are you doing here?"

"He will not answer you, Smenkhkare. He does not understand Kemetu, only Assyrian."

Smenkhkare's eyes narrowed but he said nothing. He glanced quickly down and spotted his quiver with at least six arrows lying a few paces away. "What is an Assyrian officer doing in the heart of Kemet?" He took a step sideways, casually, as if coming to Menkure's aid. Merybast moved forward, worry showing on his face, his spear clutched tightly in both hands.

The Assyrian officer snapped a command and the soldiers spread out in a semicircle, drawing their crescent swords.

"You dare to draw weapons in the presence of the king," Menkure hissed. Forgetting his wounded leg, he jumped up, moving in front of Smenkhkare. "Tell them to put up their swords." The king took another step closer to the quiver, stumbling a bit to make it look as if he was avoiding Menkure.

"I think not," Baki said smoothly. He added a few phrases in Assyrian and the officer nodded. "Please do not take this personally, Smenkhkare. You are a decent man and you treated me with respect, but I have my orders."

"Which are?"

"I regret to say that Kemet must have a new king, one who will lead us back to Amun. To accomplish this, I am afraid that..." Baki shrugged. "Well, you are a king and a god. You will be welcomed into the afterlife."

Smenkhkare staggered another pace to the side, lifting a hand to his forehead and bowed his head. "Who? Who has ordered this?" He stifled a sob.

Baki sneered. "I thought you were braver than this Smenkhkare."

"It was Ay?"

Baki nodded. "Enough of this." He snapped an order to the Assyrian officer.

Smenkhkare dived for the quiver, snatching it up as he rolled, one of the arrows slipping into place and being loosed as he came onto his back. It struck one of the soldiers in the thigh and he went down with a curse. The king continued his movement, rising to one knee. Another arrow--and another soldier fell. Now the sling whistled its arc and a man fell as if pole-axed. Another clutched his throat and fell choking. Baki screamed and urged the remaining soldiers in the thicket above, down into the stream bed.

The king and his companions fell back toward the path across the stream bed, past the dead lion. Smenkhkare's bow strummed again and Menkure's sling slashed the air again.

Merybast hung onto his spear, stabbing at any soldier who got too close. "We are winning," he panted. "They only have swords and they are six down, seven. Soon our friends will be here."

"I have two arrows left," Smenkhkare remarked calmly. "What of you, Menkure?"

"Down to my last stone." He glanced down at the sand as they backed away. "Nothing here either." Glancing at his king, he jerked his head toward the path leading north and east through the thicket. "Go, Djeser. Merybast and I will hold them as long as we can."

"Look!" Merybast screamed. "It is Siwadj...and Raia." He pointed up the stream bed to where two men had emerged from the edge of the southern scrub and were racing toward them. Behind them streamed more men, glints of metal on head and breast and hand showing their profession. Tiny darts rose and fell like gnats and their two friends died, sprawling loose-limbed in the sand. The men behind came on at a run.

"We are dead if we stay," Smenkhkare said. "Use your last stone, Menkure." He loosed an arrow, striking down the Assyrian officer. "Throw your spear, Merybast, then run. Maybe we can make it to the river." The last arrow found its mark and he cast away the bow, grabbing Menkure and pushing him toward the path. "Merybast, come!" Smenkhkare turned and raced after Menkure as the remaining soldiers surged forward. He glanced back as they reached the scrub and saw that Merybast had disobeyed his king for the first and last time.

The young man stood on the path below the bank. His spear transfixed one Assyrian and he grappled another with his bare hands. He died even as his king turned back to help him.

"It's too late, Djeser," Menkure yelled, dragging his king into the slight shelter of the scrub. "We must run if we are to live. Run, Djeser, run!" he screamed at Smenkhkare's hesitation.

"I will avenge him," the king muttered. "I will avenge them all."

Menkure slapped Smenkhkare across the face. "Forgive me, Djeser, but you will have to run now if you are to avenge them later." He turned and fled down the faint game trail. A moment later, Smenkhkare followed, only paces ahead of the pursuing soldiers.

Chapter 8

"You are sure he is dead?"

Baki hesitated for no more than a fraction of a second before nodding. "Yes, Tjaty. I am certain."

Ay sat back in his padded chair and looked at his servant with a sour expression. "Of what worth is your certainty? Very well, tell me again. Leave out nothing."

"They fled from the soldiers--Smenkhkare and Menkure. The others died. Our soldiers were hard on their heels when they entered the scrub but the fugitives were unencumbered and ran faster. Even so, when we emerged on the banks of the river over three hours later, we were no more than two or three hundred paces behind them. They ran south along the open ground until they reached a lagoon choked with weed and rushes."

"There were no people on the riverbank? No farmers? Nobody to see what happened?"

"None, Tjaty. The land is not farmed there. So, they look back and see us come out of the trees. Well, we are still inland of them so we angle across to cut them off."

"How could you cut them off? How could you intercept them at all if you were hundreds of paces behind?"

"The lagoon, sir. It meant they had to turn back inland to get around it. Well, they saw we would be very close by the time they got there, so they dived into the water to swim across. I cursed then, sir, as I knew the Assyrians would not swim after them. We ran to the shore and saw them nearly across when the water swirled behind them and one was pulled under. A moment later the other one disappeared too."

"You are certain it was a crocodile? They did not dive down out of sight?"

"We saw the tail, sir, and blood. I sent men around to the other side and they probed the rushes as best they could but they saw nothing. I saw nothing, sir, and I was watching the whole time. A crocodile took them and they are dead."

Ay nodded. "You have done well, Baki. Not perfectly, for then I would be gazing on the corpse of Smenkhkare, but well enough. Go and see my steward. He will see that you are suitably rewarded."

Baki bowed to Tjaty Ay, then quickly to the other man sitting half-seen in the shadowed corner, before turning and leaving the room.

"A man with dangerous knowledge, Ay," commented the man. "At least the Assyrian soldiers are incapable of being understood."

"All taken care of, Usermontju. My steward Mentopher has his orders." Ay smiled thinly. "And the Assyrian soldiers are even now on their way north under their original commanders, laden with gold. They will not be seen again, at least not in Kemet."

"A pity about the ring though."

"Yes," Ay agreed. "I needed the royal signet ring to help cement Tutankhaten in place as heir."

"There is no doubt there?" Usermontju asked. "The succession will be unbroken? It is very important for the Ma'at of Kemet."

"Psenamy will have secured the heretic by now and be bringing the boy back to Waset. Another week or two and we will have another king on the throne."

"What of the Councillors?"

"That is your next job. You have the resources to carry it out?"

The chief of the Medjay nodded. "I can detach a hundred men without compromising the security of the city." The big man grinned hugely, his full lips with sparkling white teeth splitting his bald melon-shaped head. "I have even arranged a meeting with the full Council for late this afternoon to discuss the king's triumphant return. By dusk they will all be in custody."

"For their own protection, of course. There is no telling what may happen now the king is dead. A crocodile took him in a tragic hunting accident, but who knows what unscrupulous people might take advantage of the turmoil." Ay regarded Usermontju calmly for several minutes before nodding suddenly and rising to his feet. "Go and carry out your instructions, Usermontju. I have other things that need to be set in motion. I shall announce the news at dusk."

The chief of the Medjay left Ay's palace and hurried through the city toward the king's palace, a troop of his men trotting behind. Citizens who saw them coming stepped aside hurriedly or suddenly decided they had business elsewhere. When the Medjay moved in force and with purpose, one did not want to find oneself in their way.

The palace guards saluted and let the force through, where they were joined by others previously stationed outside the council chamber.

Usermontju beckoned to his lieutenant. "They are in the chamber?"

"Six of them, sir. I couldn't find the others."

The chief swore. "Who is missing?"

"The lady Beketaten, Councilor Khu and Councilor Mahuhy."

"And Aanen, of course. He is in Iunu..."

"No, sir. He is here too."

Usermontju wiped his brow with a stained linen cloth, darting quick looks around him as he thought. "Well, no matter, we must do the best we can. The other councilors are probably just late. Wait out here and show them in when they arrive. The rest of you come with me." Usermontju threw open the great doors to the Council chamber and marched in at the head of twenty men.

The six Councilors present sat around a large table, talking quietly. Treasurer Sutau broke off his conversation as the doors crashed open and started to his feet, anger building in his face. "What is the meaning of this, Usermontju? How dare you bring armed men into the Council chamber, and so noisily too. Dismiss your men and explain yourself."

"Sit down, Treasurer. The rest of you also." Usermontju signaled to his men and they surrounded the table, weapons drawn. Kensthoth the scribe sat quietly but the others showed varying degrees of interest, concern or agitation at the events.

"I bring news of the utmost importance; and I would appreciate your co-operation. Smenkhkare is dead and there is a possibility of foul play. Until we know the circumstances surrounding the king's death, we must ensure the safety of the king's councilors. You will therefore be placed in protective custody. Please now accompany my men and..."

"On whose authority do you act, Usermontju? None of us gave the order."

"Physician Nebhotep." The chief of the Medjay bowed briefly. "Tjaty Ay gave the orders. In the absence of the king, his is the greatest authority."

"Actually, no." Aanen, a small man with more than a passing resemblance to his brother Ay, pushed himself to his feet, and stood clutching the table. "If my lord Smenkhkare is dead, then full authority reverts to our other king, Akhenaten."

"Would that were so, Aanen." Usermontju hesitated. "What are you doing here? You are supposed to be in Iunu finding out about the temple situation there."

"You seem remarkably well informed. Ah," Aanen snapped his fingers. "Of course, you are in my brother's confidence."

"I am privileged to be a servant of Lord Ay. But what are you doing here? Have you disobeyed the Tjaty?"

"Not at all. His request was that I ascertain the strength of the people's response to the return of the gods in the city of Iunu. I do not need to be there to do that. I have efficient priests to do my bidding. I judged it better to remain in Waset while the king was absent. It appears I was right. My brother seems to want more power than he should."

"With respect, Second Prophet Aanen, there are reports of fighting in Akhet-Aten, and no-one knows how serious the situation is. Until we hear the commands of the king, we must consider ourselves as the servants of the Divine Father, Tjaty Ay."

"There is a measure of truth in what he says," Kensthoth agreed calmly. "We must behave in a responsible manner. Do you not agree, Kenamun?" He turned toward the old man beside him, who nodded nervously, looking around at the others for reassurance.

"I think we are overlooking one serious aspect of this business," Nebhotep said. Usermontju flicked his eyes toward his men and they tensed, waiting for a signal to act. "The lady Beketaten is not only a Councilor, but also the king's sister. The news must be broken to her with tact and sensitivity."

"Where is lady Beketaten?" the chief asked. "And Mahuhy and the farm lad for that matter?"

"I do not know," Nebhotep said. "But I think it would be more important to secure her safety than the rest of us put together. If there is indeed a plot against the throne, then she is in real danger."

"Agreed." Usermontju nodded. "So if you gentlemen would accompany my troops without fuss, I will be free to take the rest of my men and search for the lady."

"I think I will accompany you, Usermontju. I have no desire to be locked up, even for my own safety, and I'd feel of more use searching for the lady."

"I too," added Sutau. "In a time of trouble and uncertainty I think it important that people see the King's Councilors still about their business as usual." He faced the others seated around the table. "Who else will be seen with Nebhotep and me?"

"I cannot stay here anyway." Aanen got to his feet, pushing back his chair. "As a priest of Amun I have a duty to be at the temple. People will need the comfort of the gods."

"That is already taken care of," Usermontju said, a note of agitation creeping into his voice. "Bakt is even now closing the temples and securing the granaries. There is really no need..."

"Bakt?" Aanen looked incredulous. "He does not have the authority. And besides that is the wrong thing to do. The temples must remain open." He pushed past the chief of the Medjay. "I am going to stop him."

"Arrest him," Usermontju snapped. "The others too." He smiled with satisfaction as the troops with him immediately restrained the six men. "I am truly sorry you will not do this willingly, but you are going to obey the orders of Tjaty Ay. He commands that you be taken into protective custody and that is what I will do. Now take them away." The chief watched them hustled from the chamber, and wiped more sweat from his face with his now damp cloth. *Now to find the others. Where in Re's holy name can they be?*

Scarab was in her suite of rooms putting the final touches to her makeup. Earlier in the afternoon she had bathed, before spending nearly an hour selecting jewelry and perfume, sandals and wig, with a bevy of ladies-in-waiting attempting to accentuate her beauty. She nodded at a servant who brought a highly polished silver plate and held it up. The reflection left a lot to be desired, but at least she could see enough to fit her earrings--long tear-shaped red glass beads wound around with gold wire. Nodding to the servant, she turned away, adjusting the shoulder wings of her long sheer dress. The linen sheath, elegantly pleated, fell in a cascade from just beneath her full breasts, which were themselves almost concealed by the wings. She smiled to herself, feeling a touch of guilt at having so many people at her beck and call, but also feeling pleasantly pampered. *Why not?* she thought. *I like to look beautiful sometimes.* She dismissed the servants and sat herself down by the balcony in her bed chamber, looking out over the palace gardens. The late afternoon sun mellowed the harsh angles of the buildings and the din of the city came muted to her ears.

A servant coughed discreetly from the doorway, then bare feet slapped gently across the tiled floor to her side. "Lady," whispered Tami, Keeper of the goose-down pillows. "There is a man here to see you. Shall I send him away?" The girl sounded vaguely shocked.

"Who is it?"

"Councilor Khu, my lady."

Scarab jumped to her feet in a most unladylike fashion. "And you kept him waiting? You bad girl." She grinned to take the sting out of her reprimand but then pinched her lightly on the arm. "Send him in." She smoothed down her dress as Tami hurried off.

"Khu! Welcome." Scarab smiled warmly as the tall lad walked painfully into the room, one hand pressed firmly against his side. The smile slipped, to be replaced by a tiny frown as she saw the shadow in his eyes. "Should you be up? You know the doctor said you should rest."

"Ah, lady, who can rest on a glorious day like today?" The young man glanced toward the balcony and frowned. "Strange. I thought the day most beautiful, but it becomes quite ordinary when compared to your presence."

"You are a liar and a blatant flatterer, Khu, and I shall send you back to your farm unless you start telling the truth." Scarab fought to

121

hide how pleased she felt. "But tell me honestly, Khu, why are you here? The meeting does not start for another hour."

"Honestly, Lady Scarab? I hoped to enjoy your company for a while. I thought perhaps we could walk in the gardens or sit by the fish pond."

"That would be nice. Before we have to attend another meeting and talk for hours about all manner of dull subjects." Scarab took Khu's arm and half supporting him, walked to the door of her chamber and into the hallway. They turned toward the colonnade that lined one side of the palace gardens.

Gardeners were hard at work in the flowerbeds and among the scented shrubs that crowded the edges nearest the palace. A heady scent of blossoms filled the air and the drone of insects coupled with the perfume, thickened the air.

"I used to play out here all the time when I was a child, Khu, but it has been over a year since I was here. I had a place under the great tamarind tree which was..." Scarab looked around the garden with a frown. "Where is it? It overhung a large, almost-wild pool with fish and frogs and dragonflies. I cannot see it." She marched up to one of the gardeners.

"Where are the tamarind tree and the pond?"

The gardener cowered on his knees. "Please, great lady, I don't know. I think there was one over there." He pointed a shaking finger toward the corner of the palace. "It...it died, lady, and they replaced it with another."

Scarab started to walk away before remembering herself. "Thank you," she said. She resumed her journey, Khu falling into step beside her. "I do hope he's wrong. That tree held memories."

They rounded the corner of the palace and Scarab saw the man had not been mistaken. The giant tree was gone but the pool remained, now only partly shadowed by a mere sapling. They walked closer and Scarab scuffed the toes of her sandals in the fine sand. A large circle of bare ground almost surrounded by close-cropped grass revealed the site of the old tree. The young one, still straight of limb, was crowned by bright new growth. Scarab looked up into it and grimaced. "It is not the same at all. There are no pods, no bird nests, only..." she touched the bark gently. "Only a few ants. And there are no scarab beetles either."

Khu grinned. "Must feel funny having an insect named after you."

"It was the other way round. I was named after the scarab because I always played with them."

"Your father named you for a beetle?"

"Not just a beetle, Khu. The sacred scarab beetle, Khepri. And it wasn't my father, I never knew him. It was my brother Akhenaten who gave me that name." Scarab wandered over to a stone bench that lay beside the now manicured pool with its lilies and schools of tiny silver fish. She sat and contemplated the dark water.

The young man came and sat beside her, respecting her silence for several minutes before saying quietly, "Your brother returns tomorrow."

Scarab nodded. "Or the next day. He said he'd be back by the end of the month."

Khu sat and fidgeted. "Do...do you love him?" he blurted out.

Scarab turned, her eyes widening in surprise. "Of course I do, Khu, he's my brother."

"Th...that's not what I m...meant." Face burning with embarrassment, he looked down, unable to meet Scarab's eyes. "When the king returns he means to marry you and make you his queen. I...I just wondered if you loved him...like that."

Scarab regarded the young man for several long minutes before turning back to her contemplation of the pool. "That is a very impertinent question, Khu," she said quietly. "You must learn to guard your tongue. But because it is you who has asked, I will not think ill of you." She bent and picked up a handful of fine gravel from the path, opening it out in the palm of her hand. Picking out small stones, she flicked them into the pond, the tiny silver fish darting from one small splash to the next in the hope of food.

"When I was a young girl, I could not imagine anything I wanted more than to marry Smenkhkare. He was so bold and daring, so strong yet gentle. He was going to be king and I was going to be his queen. Together we would rule Kemet with justice and compassion, bringing in another golden age." Scarab smiled. "Of course, we were only children, playing at being grown up." She threw the rest of the stones into the water and watched as they sank through the clear liquid, the fish scattering in panic. "Then we grew up. He stayed in Waset and I went to live with the king in Akhet-Aten. It did not matter for we were promised in our hearts and we knew we would one day be together. Then came Ay's attempted rebellion and...and somehow everything changed."

"Smenkhkare became king," Khu said softly.

"And later married Meryetaten. Yet that did not matter. He did not love her and never slept with her. She lives alone in her rooms at the palace with only her little daughter Meryetaten-ta-sherit for company." Scarab shook her head. "No, she did not change things for me." She dusted her hands off and held them out in front of her, palms up. "They say you can tell a person's life by the lines in their hands--what they will do, whether they will marry, to whom even. Do you think that is true, Khu?"

"Honestly? No. I think they are just creases in the skin. We all have them in more or less the same places."

"There was an old nursemaid up in Akhet-Aten who used to sing to the young princesses, a Hittite slave called Hati, Hatia...something like that. She told me this line gave me a long life." Scarab pointed at the crease encircling the flesh of her thumb. "And this one a death in a foreign land...and here that I would marry but not for love, and here I would love but my heart would break with it."

"Then that proves it is all nonsense." Khu forced a laugh. "You are a beautiful princess of Kemet. You will marry your brother whom you love and live a long and wonderful life as queen, having many children before finally dying and joining your husband in his royal tomb."

"I love my brother, but I do not love him as I would a husband, Khu. Oh, I will marry him if he asks it of me, but if I have a choice..." Scarab shook her head. "I love another."

Khu sat in silence for several minutes before clearing his throat and uttering a single word in a strained voice. "Who?"

"Paramessu," Scarab said, a tremor in her voice. "I know I shall almost certainly never see him again, and if I do, never be allowed to be alone with him, but I love him."

"But he is an old man..." Khu broke off, before picking his words with care. "My lady Scarab, Paramessu is a fine soldier..."

"More than a soldier, he is almost a general. He commands a whole legion."

"But he...he is what, fifteen years older than you and surely married."

"Closer to twenty and he was married but his wife died, together with his son, in the plague many years ago."

"He is a soldier, my lady, and you must marry a prince or a king."

"That is with the gods, Khu. All I know is what my heart tells me. I love him, though it can never be." She stared at the pond and missed the tears in Khu's eyes.

He brushed them away without fuss and essayed a tentative smile. "We should be getting to the meeting, Scarab. Judging by the sun it is almost time." Khu got to his feet and brushed his gown absently, looking toward the palace where a woman in the short kilt of a servant hurried toward them. "I think we have company."

Scarab looked round, then rose, shading her eyes with one hand. "It is Tio. What is she doing out in the living area of the palace? If the Overseer of Kitchens catches her she will get a beating."

Tio the scullery maid hurried across the lawns to Scarab and threw herself on her knees, her bare bosom heaving with the exertion. "My lady," she cried. "Oh, my lady, there is great danger. You must flee at once."

"What are you talking about, woman?" Khu exclaimed roughly. "And what are you doing out here? You know you are required to stay in the kitchen area."

"Enough, Khu. Get up, Tio, there is no need for this. Tell me what the matter is."

"Oh, my poor lady, such terrible news and such danger." Tio started weeping. "You must flee at once to safety."

"Oh, get up, Tio." Scarab bent down and hauled the older woman upright. "Now what is this all about? Dry your tears and start from the beginning."

"Scarab," Khu interrupted. "We are starting to attract a bit of attention from those guards over by the portico. I suggest we move somewhere more private."

Scarab nodded. "Over here." She led the way across the gardens, out of sight of the guards and the gardeners, and into the shadow of the house of old Her-uben, one-time Head Gardener, but now retired, though still allowed to live in his house in the palace orchards. "We will not be seen here. Now, Tio, start from the beginning and tell me your news."

The maid nodded and backhanded away her tears. "Yes, my lady. Well, I is working in the kitchens like I always do...only today I was tending the fires as the boy 'oo usually does it is sick. I think he got a flux by drinking bad water 'cos Wia says 'e was throwing up all..."

"Tio," Scarab cut in. "The news. What is it?"

"Yes, lady." Tio bobbed respectfully and took a deep breath, her lips moving as she positioned herself further along in her story. "Well, Roma--'e's the man what brings the onions, 'e 'ad just come from the Tjaty's palace and 'e say the place there is in an uproar. A man of the Tjaty's just got back from Djeba where the king was."

"Just a minute, Tio," Khu asked. "Roma told you this?"

"Nah, the like of 'e won't talk to likes of me. I was tending the fires an' I 'eard 'im talking to Hay, the Overseer. 'E said...well, I don't likes to repeat it..." Tio glanced around and lowered her voice to a whisper. "'E said the king was dead."

Scarab gasped and Khu broke in hurriedly. "That is just a nasty rumor, Tio, put about by gossips with nothing better to do, and you should not be repeating such things. Don't you know my lady here is the king's sister?"

"Yes, sirs, I knows an' I is not wanting to bring such news, my lady, oh no, but that weren't all I heard."

"What did you hear, Tio?" Scarab asked quietly.

"Come on, Scarab, you don't believe her, do you?" Khu remonstrated. "I mean, if anything like that had happened it would be public knowledge. It would be all over the city."

Tio shivered, despite the warmth of the late afternoon sun. "I don't knows about that, sirs, only whats I heard."

"And what did you hear, Tio?" Scarab asked again, putting a hand on the maid's arm.

"Roma says 'e spoke with the Tjaty's man what jus' come back from Djeba, an 'e said the king had been took by a crocodile and the rest of his frien's was dead too."

"That shows this is all a pack of lies," Khu said, relief showing in his voice. "The king was hunting a lion nowhere near the river. And to claim five of his friends died too." He shook his head and laughed. "This Roma should be reported to the Medjay...and that friend of his in Ay's palace for starting such a story."

126

"Well, you coulds have Roma arrested, but not the others one. 'E was killed by the Tjaty's so'jers right after 'e talk to Roma...'e saw it an' it scared 'im plenty."

Scarab's fingers dug into Tio's arm. "Ay's soldiers killed this man of Ay's who had just returned from Djeba with news of the king's death? Is that what you are saying?"

"This tale just keeps getting more far-fetched."

"No Khu." Scarab's voice trembled. "That part tells me my Smenkhkare is dead." A single tear marred the surface of her cheek. "Ay has had my brother killed and the man who did it has been silenced."

"Killing a king is god-cursed. Not even Ay would do that."

"Ay may reason he did not do it, he merely caused it to happen."

Khu frowned, not wanting to believe. "And...and the crocodile?"

"The crocodile is a fabrication. I have no doubt Ay will use the story so he does not have to produce the...the body." Scarab sobbed and her tears streaked the kohl around her eyes.

"Lady," Tio said. "You has got to 'ide. The so'jers will be lookin' for you. I saw lots of Medjay go to the Council rooms an' they was armed."

"The Council will have called them, Scarab. When news of this breaks there will be panic, so we'll need the Medjay to keep the peace." Khu looked toward the palace and took a few steps in that direction. "We should join them immediately, Scarab." He looked at her tear and kohl-streaked face with sudden realization and returned to her side, putting an arm around her. "I'm so sorry, Scarab. We should get you to your ladies first. We can get the Medjay to guard you if you like, then..."

"Shut up, Khu. I do not need my ladies and we do not need to be joining the other Councilors." She dabbed at her face with the wide shoulder wings of her dress, succeeding more in marking the dress than in cleaning her face. She raised a hand as Khu opened his mouth again and he remained silent, though fidgeting with a need for action. "Give me a moment, Khu. I must think."

"No, my lady. You mustn't stay 'ere. You got to 'ide before the so'jers or the Medjay find you an' cart you off to prison or worse."

"If Ay is behind this," Scarab said slowly, "Then he must have a plan to take power. A real one, not like the last time when his daughter

Nefertiti forced his hand. He could not hope to do it without the backing of the army, so we cannot trust the troops. Nor can we trust the Medjay. Usermontju is a friend of Ay. We cannot help the Council if we are in prison or dead, so we must remain free. But where to go?"

"We could go to my father's farm in Akhet-Re. Nobody would think to look for us there."

Scarab's lips twitched. "Not until they remembered Councilor Khu was once a farm lad from Akhet-Re. No, it will have to be somewhere safer than that."

Tio wrung her hands and looked around, casting scared glances toward the palace. "You must 'urry, my lady. You has got to get away."

"Akhet-Aten then?" Khu said. "Appeal to your other brother. When he hears that Ay has...has had his co-regent killed, he will act. He would have to."

Scarab nodded. "Perhaps. Either there or north to find Horemheb."

"Horemheb? Oh, you mean General Paatenemheb. I thought you said you could not trust the army?"

"He has changed his name back again, Khu. He only took the Aten name to get gold for his army. Now he has remembered his allegiance to Heru. I think he would help us. He has no great love for Ay."

"But the army?"

"Horemheb is loyal. That is one of his virtues. And he is not the army of Waset. I am sure Ay has subverted the local garrison."

"My lady, please." Tio started tugging on Scarab's arm, dragging her toward the palace.

"She is right, Scarab. We can talk about where we mean to go, but first we must get you to safety." Khu broke Tio's grip on the dress. "Safety does not lie in the palace though."

"Course not sirs, but we has to get through the palace to gets out. I thinks I can smuggle yous through the kitchens."

"No, there is another way." Scarab chewed her lip, remembering. "Smenkhkare used to take me out to the city when we were children. Behind Her-uben's house there is the garden wall. It used to be in ruins." She walked around the corner to the narrow aisle between the mud brick house and the tall stone wall of the palace gardens, now deep in evening shadow. "It's narrower than I remember, and more overgrown."

She eased herself between the walls, stepping over the tangle of weeds and loose stones, praying silently to Wadjet that there were no cobras hiding there. The air was still, cool and damp, and small things rustled and scurried in the undergrowth. A few paces and she came to tumbled stones and the gnarled roots of the old acacia tree. "It's still here," she called back. "We can climb the wall easily. Come on."

"No lady, I cannot," wept Tio. "I would 'old you back wheres a man and a woman can go unnoticed. I wills go back to the kitchens an' meets you later."

"Where, Tio?"

"The old place wheres I used to work. Mahuhy's brothel. 'E'll be on the run too." The older woman turned and ran back through the orchard.

Khu forced his way into the narrow gap and came up behind Scarab. He looked up at the ruined wall, measuring the handholds on the stones and tree. "What's on the other side?"

"The great temples of Amun. I think we can find refuge there, at least temporarily. I know...or knew one of the priests, a man called Pa-Siamen. Smenkhkare used to bring me here. He always said I was welcome."

"That was many years ago, Scarab. You are now the princess Beketaten, sister to the king who banned his god. Remember he is a priest of Amun."

Scarab shrugged and clambered up the tree and stones. She straddled the wall and looked down into the ill-kempt gardens surrounding the temple, then back at the carefully manicured orchards and gardens of the royal palace. "We must make the best of it, Khu," she said. "Can you think of a better place to go?"

Khu followed her up the tree and swung his leg over the wall, sitting beside her. "And here I was thinking I'd had all my adventures. Seems like I only have to stick close to you." He grinned and jumped forward, landing in the long grass and rolling over. Getting to his feet, he held out his arms to the princess on the wall. "Come on then, Scarab. I'll catch you."

Skirts flying, she jumped.

Chapter 9

General Psenamy arrived in Akhet-Aten by the desert road in the middle of the morning, after a forced march from Waset. He brought with him the Waset legion, fifteen hundred strong and ostensibly dedicated to Amun, though still circumspect about openly carrying the symbols of the god, particularly here in the stronghold of the Aten. Curious eyes watched the troops as they poured through the narrow gap in the southern valley, past the vast cattle pens and into the crescent-shaped plain that held the City of the Sun. The audience grew as the army approached, by degrees curious, then welcoming and at last alarmed as the size of the army became apparent. Citizens who had lined the streets at the southern end of the city fell silent and withdrew, watching from doorways and behind shuttered windows. At length the soldiers came to the grand Royal Road and the palace.

Psenamy halted the troops and rapped out a series of commands, spreading his men out to guard the exits from the palace. Five hundred were dispatched to the north of the city with orders to subdue the local garrison and take the North Palace, securing that end of the city. Another five hundred set out to quell any disturbance from the populace, though most citizens had already left the streets. The general led a hundred men inside the palace, brushing aside the guards at the main doorway.

"Kill any who resist," Psenamy snarled to his officers. "But the Heretic is not to be harmed."

A servant, in terror of his life, led them to the chamber of justice where the king sat, hearing petitions from his nobles. Throwing open the great double doors, Psenamy led his men into the chamber, interrupting the king as he sat dispensing justice to his subjects. His soldiers rapidly disarmed the surprised royal guards and herded the nobles to one end of the hall. He strode up the middle, his sandals slapping the bare tiled floor loudly in the sudden silence. Halting before the throne where Akhenaten sat in stony splendor, he saluted.

"Lord Waenre Akhenaten, I bring greetings from Tjaty Ay."

Akhenaten sat still, as unmoving as a statue, his heavily-made-up eyes betraying the only signs of life. He sat stiffly, his feet tucked neatly beneath the throne, his arms crossed over his bare chest with the crook and flail of office held firmly in hands that, by the whitening around the knuckles, displayed his tension. A shendyt kilt, dyed a rich red, with gold-threaded border, girded his loins. The double crown of Kemet soared above the king, red and white, and the curved and carved symbolic beard protruded from his chin, held by a thin strap.

"Akhenaten," Psenamy repeated. "I bring greetings from Tjaty Ay."

The king stirred and his eyes sought out the man standing before the throne. "Who are you and what are you doing here?" he said in the direction of the man's voice.

"I am General Psenamy of the Waset legion, and as I said, I bring greetings from Tjaty Ay."

"I did not command you here." Akhenaten's eyes drifted over the armed soldiers filling the room. He could not see them clearly but he remembered what the man had said. "Why is the Waset legion off-station? And why are they armed in my presence? Send them out at once."

Psenamy ignored the king's command. "I also bring news, Akhenaten," he said, a touch of arrogance creeping into his voice as he realized he controlled the situation utterly. "Your brother Djeserkheperu Smenkhkare is dead."

A sigh swept through the room and a few of the women cried out before being hushed. The king looked hard at the general for several minutes before asking, "How did he die?"

"A hunting trip. He was taken by a crocodile and dragged beneath the water."

"Why did his companions not save him?"

"Only one was nearby. He was killed too."

"Was his body recovered?"

Psenamy shook his head.

Another long pause ensued before the king sighed and shifted his position on the throne. "I will pray to my father the Aten that his spirit may enter the blessed fields despite his body not being buried." He looked away from Psenamy. "You have my leave to go. All of you; leave me."

"I cannot do that, Akhenaten." Psenamy signaled his men and they closed in around the throne.

Akhenaten frowned. "You disobey me? Have you taken leave of your senses?"

"I have come to my senses at last, as has Kemet herself. You have brought the Two Lands to the brink of ruin by your actions and your inactions. For the sake of all, you must be protected, even from yourself."

"You are mad." Akhenaten gestured with his flail. "Guards, remove this madman from my presence."

Psenamy smiled and stepped closed to the seated king. "Your word no longer commands obedience, Akhenaten," he said quietly, so only the king could hear. "You will be taken from here and another shall rule in your place."

Slowly, the king got to his feet and stood erect, back straight. He looked out over the head of Psenamy toward the gathered nobles. "So, it has come to this. You would kill your anointed king. Know that Aten sees all and will curse you and your men down the halls of eternity." He drew himself up and looked disdainfully at the general. "Strike then and be damned."

Psenamy laughed. "You are not going to die, Akhenaten, nothing so melodramatic. You will be incarcerated while we get Kemet strong again. Who knows? Maybe you will be allowed a wife and freedom to worship your god from your prison. Maybe if you cease your madness you will be allowed back."

Akhenaten's shoulders sagged and the crook and flail drooped to his sides. His already long face lengthened and the symbolic beard slipped, dropping around his neck. "You will allow me my beloved Ankhesenpaaten and the Aten?"

Psenamy reached up and removed the tall double crown from Akhenaten's head, placing it on the ground, before taking the crook and flail, symbols of royalty from his unresisting fingers. "Not Ankhesenpaaten, we have other plans for her. You may have your lady Kiya instead." The general signaled to his men and they surrounded the king. "Akhenaten, you will now accompany me to the North Palace where you will remain under guard." He regarded the immobile, crushed figure in front of him. "Must I order my men to use force, or will you come willingly?"

Akhenaten's eyes flashed briefly, dark behind the cloudiness of his failing eyesight. "I am still the king, anointed and chosen by the god. You may have me in your power but I am still your lord and master until you kill me." He smiled sourly. "And then I will be with the Aten and you will be nothing." The king pushed forward and Psenamy hurried to catch up with him, his troops walking fast, their spears held threateningly outward.

Servants and slaves crowded the palace halls and porticos, held in rapt fascination by the spectacle of the king in custody. They watched in silence save for a few muffled sobs and a collective sigh as the procession passed. Ankhesenpaaten watched too, from the entrance to the women's quarters, apprehension and excitement gripping her heart. A little further down the hall leading to the main palace gate, they passed prince Tutankhaten, standing with his two Nubian friends. Psenamy hesitated, as if to speak to the prince, but Akhenaten did not pause, walking swiftly toward the gate, so the general passed by the young prince with merely a nod.

As the king and his guard passed from the palace, the servants started to disperse, slowly finding their way back to their duties, though moving half-heartedly, as though unsure of themselves. Ankhesenpaaten left the women's quarters and headed for the palace gate, where Tutankhaten still stood, talking to his friends.

Hiknefer was the first to greet her, his voice warm and pleasant, the smile in his eyes matching the white sparkle of his teeth against his dark skin. "Welcome, princess Ankhesenpaaten. Perhaps you can tell us what is happening. We were playing outside when someone said the king was dead. Great is our relief to find that the rumor is unfounded."

Ankhesenpaaten smiled in return, then became serious. "The king is dead, but not my...my father Akhenaten. It is the co-regent in Waset who has died."

"Then what is happening to King Akhenaten?" Khai asked. "Where is he being taken? He did not look as if he went willingly, despite his hurrying step."

"I do not know. You have heard nothing?"

"If my brother Smenkhkare is dead, then I can be king," Tutankhaten said brightly. "Does this mean we will be going down to Waset? Are we going to marry, Khese?"

"Hush, you silly..." Ankhesenpaaten caught herself. "Be circumspect, Tuti," she said calmly. "Let us wait and see what other news there is first. We need to find out what is happening to my father."

"I thought he was your husband now," Khai said. "But then you Kemetu change family relationships so often it is hard to know. Tomorrow, he will no doubt be your aunt...ow!" Hiknefer's hand cuffed his wooly-haired head.

"Keep a civil tongue in your head, Khai," the tall Nubian admonished. "Your pardon, lady, but I agree, we need to know what is happening here in Akhet-Aten. There may not be much we can do, but we should know the situation."

"There may be more I can do," Ankhesenpaaten reminded them. "I am queen, after all, and that must still mean something." She caught sight of a nobleman coming out of the Chamber of Justice. "Wait here," she ordered, hurrying down the corridor. "Lord Mahmose, a moment if you please."

The nobleman was standing by the door of the chamber with a group of men and women. He looked bemused, unsure what to do, but on hearing his name called, a look of relief crossed his face. He was a man happiest when told what to do.

"Ah, my lady...I mean your majesty. How may I be of service?" He gave a deep bow, edging away from his companions.

"Lord Mahmose, you were in the Chamber with the king, were you not? What happened in there? Where is my...husband going?"

The man looked uncomfortable and he looked up at the painted ceiling as if for inspiration. "Ah, General Psenamy brought news of the death...of the most unfortunate death of the co-regent Smenkhkare. It appears that he..."

"That much I know. The how and why of it can wait. What else did the general say? About my husband the king?"

"Ah...er, your majesty...ah, he...he is deposed. Or so I understood," Mahmose rushed on. "I suppose I could be mistaken. I do not have any real understanding..."

"Stop it!" Ankhesenpaaten stamped her sandaled foot, cutting off the flow. Heads turned, curious, and she moved closer to the nobleman, lowering her voice. "Just tell me exactly what was said by the general."

Mahmose flushed and stammered, finally getting a measure of control before starting again. "General Psenamy reported that co-regent Smenkhkare died on a hunting expedition. When the king gave him leave to go, he refused, saying...saying his rule had come to an end and that he would be imprisoned in the North Palace. The general stripped his majesty of the crown, crook and flail and marched him out."

"Did the general say anything about...about me or prince Tutankhaten?"

"Not about the prince, your majesty. The king asked whether you would be allowed to join him in prison..." Ankhesenpaaten gasped, partly in shock, partly in outrage. "...and the general replied he had other plans for you."

"Did he say what they were? Or what he planned to do next?"

"No, your majesty, save that he was escorting the king to the North Palace." Mahmose hesitated and stuttered again as he raised a topic that was seemingly now in everyone's minds. "Er...what will happen now, your majesty? If...er, if both kings are...are gone, who will rule us? Are we to...to see a queen rule over the Two Lands as in the days of Ma'atkare Hatshepsut?"

"Would that be so bad, Mahmose?" Ankhesenpaaten smiled grimly. "However, you may rest easy. I have no desire to rule as king. Besides, my husband has a brother, the prince Tutankhaten. He surely has the greatest claim to the throne of Kemet. Remember, he is the son of the great Nebmaetre Amenhotep himself."

"Ah." Mahmose nodded sagely. "A wise choice indeed your majesty. May it come to be so."

"A king needs a queen though, Mahmose, a royal wife," Ankhesenpaaten said softly. "Who can you suggest as a suitable queen for King Tutankhaten?"

Mahmose raised his eyebrows. "I, your majesty? Well, let me think." He frowned, stroking his chin with one hand. "There are not many royal women, unless we count the daughters of lesser wives and concubines."

"Let us not consider them. He needs a truly royal wife, one of the line of Amenhotep."

"There is your elder sister Meryetaten."

"She is barren. After the birth of her daughter Tasherit, she has not had another child to Smenkhkare in three years. A queen must be fertile. Who else is there?"

"Er, Beketaten?"

"Too old and too independent. She was infatuated with Smenkhkare and I cannot see her being subservient to a young king. Who else?"

"There is no-one else, your majesty."

"What of myself?"

"B...but you are already queen and married to...to the king, your father."

"He is king no longer. You just told me. And if he is not king, I am not queen." Ankhesenpaaten preened, smoothing her fine linen gown with her hands, gazing into the nobleman's eyes. "I am royal by birth, of the ancient line of Amenhotep. I am fertile, having borne a daughter already, and I am close to the age of prince Tutankhaten. Do you not think I am the logical choice, Lord Mahmose?"

Mahmose, caught between truth and expediency, bowed deeply. "I am your servant, your majesty. Tell me what to do and I will do it."

"You are a rich man, Lord Mahmose, one of the richest in Akhet-Aten. You know every family of influence here in the City of the Sun. I ask you to remember your princess Ankhesenpaaten and your prince Tutankhaten. Talk to others, persuade them, converse with the general and use all your gold and influence. You will not find the next king and queen of Kemet ungrateful. Think how high the house of Mahmose could rise in the land."

Greed flared in Mahmose's eyes. "Indeed, your majesty. It will be my pleasure to champion your cause. Surely you and the prince are the only hope for our poor lands." He bowed again. "With your leave, majesty, I will set about my business at once." Mahmose hurried off toward a small group of nobles that were leaving the palace.

Ankhesenpaaten smiled and nodded before walking sedately back to where her uncle and his two friends waited, the Nubians patiently, the young prince fidgeting and chattering.

"What happened, Khese? What did you talk about? Can we go now? I want to go and watch the soldiers."

"Yes, Tuti, I think you should go and do something more interesting, but it might not be a good idea to be near the soldiers just now. Why don't you go and practice your archery?"

"I don't want to," the boy whined. "I want to see the soldiers."

Ankhesenpaaten dragged the prince to one side and, gripping his arm tightly, leaned close and whispered fiercely, "Do you want to become king? Then you will do as I say, right now." The boy's eyes widened in shock and she forced a smile. "I really do love you, Tuti, and want what is best for you. Right now you need to be away from the soldiers. Will you do that for me?"

Tutankhaten nodded, still frightened of the girl. "Yes, Khese," he whispered.

Ankhesenpaaten nodded and released the prince's arm, stroking his shaved head and the black lock of hair on it. "Hiknefer, will you and Khai take the prince to archery and see he remains dutifully at his lessons? I ask this favour as queen."

Hiknefer smiled broadly, his teeth sparklingly white against the blue-black sheen of his skin. "Yes, your majesty."

Ankhesenpaaten watched as the three ran off until they rounded a corner and disappeared. Noticing the Under-Chamberlain of the Bed Linen nearby, she called him over.

"Nebre, find General Psenamy and bring him to me."

The Under-Chamberlain gulped. "Your majesty," he said, wringing his hands together. "I am merely in charge of the linen. A great general is not going to listen to me."

"Then you must make him listen. Tell him Queen Ankhesenpaaten commands...no, make that requests, Nebre. Tell him I request an audience with him in..." she thought quickly, dismissing the throne room and the Hall of Justice. She did not want to appear as queen to this man, yet somewhere informal like the gardens would put her at a disadvantage, make her appear empty-headed. She needed to present herself as a woman. "...in my rooms."

Nebre's agitation turned to shock. "My lady, you cannot receive a man in your rooms. It is not seemly."

Ankhesenpaaten raised one eyebrow and drew her slim thirteen year old body erect. "You are telling me what is seemly?"

"N...no, my lady, of c...course not," Nebre stuttered. "I merely wished to...to point out that..." His voice trailed off and he hung his head miserably. "I will do as you command, your majesty."

"Then go and do so, Nebre. You will find General Psenamy in the North Palace, whence he was escorting the king." She clapped her hands sharply. "Go, hurry."

Ankhesenpaaten turned on her heel and stalked back to the women's quarters and her suite of rooms. She called her maids to her and ordered them to prepare a bath, stripping off her linen gown which already felt soiled and tossing her wig onto a chair. While the water and scented oils were prepared, she used the flushing toilet so loved by Akhenaten. She sat and thought on her coming ordeal, knowing she must somehow find the balance between woman and child, showing she was mature enough to be a queen, not just of Akhet-Aten but of Kemet, yet young enough to be a true wife of the young Tutankhaten. She was sure neither Psenamy nor her grandfather Ay welcomed the possibility of another Hatshepsut. That woman had so completely dominated the young Tuthmosis that Kemet had come to hate her.

She flushed the basin, releasing a stream of pure water down the channel, before walking in to the bath chamber where she dipped herself in the cool, scented water then allowed herself to be patted dry on wool towels. Another gown, scents and unguents, a mere hour spent touching up her makeup, a freshly combed wig and a careful selection of jewelry and she was ready to face the general. *If he comes*, she thought. *What if he does not?*

Ankhesenpaaten put that thought firmly from her mind and walked into the large room bordering on her bedroom. Ordering the servants, she arranged the furniture so that two padded couches were pulled close together near the balcony overlooking the Queen's Gardens and a small table, ebony inlaid with lapis and topaz, bore two of her favourite cups--blue faience with the handles being the winged goddess Auset. She smiled wryly as she remembered Akhenaten's anger when he first

138

saw them. They had remained hidden lest they be removed and smashed, but she brought them out now. Hopefully they would help impress the general that she believed in other gods beside the Aten.

She sat on one of the couches and dismissed her servants, instructing them to notify her the instant Psenamy entered the queen's palace. Ankhesenpaaten relaxed, breathing slowly and calming herself. The day was heating and the air still and humid, the scents from the flowering shrubs mingling with her perfumes. She closed her eyes--just to relax--and dozed.

Voices in the corridor outside her apartments woke her. The shortened shadows told her it was near noon as she came instantly awake, her heart speeding up as excitement gripped her. A maid knocked on the wooden doors before opening them and putting her head round the edge.

"My lady, General Psenamy is outside. He wishes..." The maid broke off with a squeak of alarm as the general pushed past her and into the room.

Psenamy glanced round the room, ending with the young woman on the padded bench by the balcony. He grunted and walked into the middle of the room. "What nonsense was that bed linen servant spouting? He commanded me into the presence of the queen. I take it he meant you?"

Ankhesenpaaten forced a smile. "Welcome, General Psenamy. I apologize for the behavior of my servant. I shall discipline him. Meanwhile, please join me in a cup of wine for I really do need your help and advice." She clapped her hands softly. "Hatia, bring wine for my guest."

Psenamy shook his head. "I do not drink wine before the evening. It befuddles the mind."

"Then cool water, General. It is hot outside and I can tell you have been busy. Hatia, quickly now."

Psenamy opened his mouth to refuse but instead nodded and walked over to the balcony where he leaned with his back to the balustrade and stood looking at the queen. "Why did you call me here? If you think to plead for your husband it will do no good."

"General, you have done me a service," Ankhesenpaaten laughed lightly. "For all that Akhenaten is my father, I prefer him in your care to myself in his."

"Then why?"

"My father was king of Kemet and he started a grand enterprise. At least in the beginning it was, the power of the priests of Amun was too great. Raising the Aten to supreme god undermined that power and in a fashion restored Ma'at to the Two Lands. After all, we are all the children of Re and the Aten is but an aspect of Re. But then advisers counseled him falsely and his wits left him. He made the Aten the only god and attempted to kill the other gods. That was his only real sin. The Aten is but one god of Kemet and all gods should be given their measure of worship."

"Commendable sentiments," Psenamy sneered. "But this story of false advisers is not the tale I heard."

"Then you heard wrong," Ankhesenpaaten said sharply.

"And you are wasting my time." Psenamy pushed himself upright. "I have my duties to perform."

Ankhesenpaaten got up quickly and crossed to the general. "Forgive me, Psenamy. I did not mean to offend you. I can only plead female emotion at suddenly finding myself demoted from queen to nothing."

Psenamy huffed and looked away. "Far from nothing, lady," he muttered.

"Please, General. Stay with me a short while and advise me. Look, here is my servant with water cool from the river. Will you not take a cup with me?" Ankhesenpaaten took the tray from Hatia and set it down on the table, busying herself pouring water into one cup and watered wine into the other. She handed Psenamy his cup with a smile. "Do you like the cup, General? My husband never liked them, so I had to keep them hidden."

Psenamy turned the blue faience in his hands, nodding at the fine craftsmanship of the winged goddess handles. He raised it to his lips and took a long swallow of the water. "You have good water here, my lady."

"It is river water drawn from above the city. I am told it makes a difference." She sipped her wine, gesturing to one of the couches. When the general sat, she took her place on the other one, demurely arranging the pleats of her gown.

"What advice do you seek of me, lady?"

140

"I am only a woman and understand little of the ways of rulership and governing, but I hoped you could explain a few things for me."

Psenamy nodded. "If I can."

Ankhesenpaaten furrowed her brow and bit her lip gently as if perplexed, but her eyes watched the general carefully through her long lashes. "If I understand correctly, Smenkhkare has been killed in a hunting accident and you have, for reasons that escape me...no, no, general, I'm sure they are good reasons...you have deposed my husband Akhenaten. Is...is that what has happened?"

"Indeed it has, my lady. You display a remarkable understanding for a woman."

Ankhesenpaaten made a show of being pleased. "Thank you, General. You do me much honour. But what will happen now? Kemet has lost both its kings. Who will ascend the throne?"

"There is only one living male member of Per-Aa. Tutankhaten must become king."

"Oh, but of course! Why did I not think of that?" Ankhesenpaaten laughed gaily, and then suddenly frowned. "But he is only a boy? Will that matter?"

"No, lady. There are experienced men who can support him until he comes of age."

"Ay, you mean?" Psenamy looked sharply at her and Ankhesenpaaten hurried on. "He would surely be the best choice. He has advised three kings already."

"Indeed. Who better?" Psenamy drained his cup and set it down on the tiled floor. "If that is all, my lady, I will be about my business."

"Please, Psenamy. One more question. One that concerns me much, I suppose because I think of womanly things." Ankhesenpaaten took a deep breath and looked the general straight in the eye. "So Tutankhaten will be crowned king but who will be his queen?"

"Eh? As you said, he is only a boy. Time enough to think of that later."

"Oh, I agree, Psenamy. There is plenty of time, but who will it be when the time comes? There are not many choices."

Psenamy looked at the young woman warily. "No? Then enlighten me. Who then, are the choices?"

"He must marry a royal princess of Kemet."

"Must? There is no great necessity, lady. Any young woman of good family will do. Look at the great Nebmaetre, marrying his Tiye, a commoner. And even the Heretic your father married Nefertiti, daughter of Ay." Psenamy smiled. "I'll warrant some nurse has fed you a tale of kingship being passed through the female line. It is not so, lady. A king will marry whom he chooses."

"I am glad of it, General. I believe in love, even for kings. But no," Ankhesenpaaten shook her head. "That was not what I meant. I have heard the tales but know it for the gossip of old women with too much time on their hands. But if you leave a princess unmarried she may become the object of other men's ambition. Surely it would be more...more economical to marry him to either Meryetaten, Smenkhkare's widow, or Beketaten, his sister."

"An interesting thought, lady, but your elder sister is tainted too strongly with Atenism. She has remained a devotee of the heresy, despite her husband's attempts to restore order. Why, she even talks of returning to Akhet-Aten to be with her father."

"And Beketaten?"

"She is dead, lady." Psenamy forestalled the young girl's question by raising a hand. "I do not know the whys or wherefores but a messenger brought the news to me as I arrived this morning."

Ankhesenpaaten sat silently, head bent, observing Psenamy surreptitiously, willing him to reach the right conclusion.

"There is one other possibility," the general remarked casually. "You, my lady."

Ankhesenpaaten fought down her triumphant expression and managed to look confused instead of incredulous as she had been trying for. "Me? But I am queen...no, no longer queen but still married to...to Akhenaten."

"A marriage can be dissolved, my lady. Easily. Think on it. You are the sole surviving untainted princess and Tutankhaten is the sole surviving prince. What could be better than the two of you marrying and producing heirs that will rule Kemet after you?"

"The idea has merit," Ankhesenpaaten said slowly. "But it should not be my choice, Psenamy, or yours, or even that of my grandfather Ay. A king should marry for love, or if not for love, at least by marrying the woman he chooses. Ask him, General Psenamy. Ask the king to be, prince Tutankhaten, who he will take to wife. If he chooses me I will do my duty to Kemet."

"Nobly said, my lady." Psenamy got to his feet. "My next duty was to apprise the prince of his future. I will now ask him to name his future wife as well." He bowed low, whirled on his heel and marched from the room.

Behind him, Ankhesenpaaten allowed herself a smirk of triumph.

Chapter 10

"**Y**ou cannot remain here, my lady. I regret it deeply for the sake of our past acquaintance and the, dare I say it, friendship I enjoyed with your illustrious brother, but it is too dangerous."

"Come on, Scarab. I told you this poxy priest was a waste of time," Khu snarled. "He is afraid and I would not want to stay around a fearful man. He is likely to betray you next."

Scarab looked from Khu to Pa-Siamen the priest and back again. The two men stood close together, the farm lad turned Councilor and now fugitive, tall and upright, his fists clenched by his sides, his eyes blazing with contempt and anger. The priest, by contrast, stood with downcast eyes, his body slumped and weary, not meeting the hostile gaze directed at him. The room too, reflected this dichotomy of spirit, a blazon of bright sunlight through a window aperture high on one wall, a deep gloom of tinted green where the light of morning filtered through shrubbery long untended outside a lower window.

The previous evening Scarab and Khu had come to Amun's temple, fugitives from an unseen menace and had been admitted by an old porter. Shown into a musty guest room and supplied with water and crusty bread, they passed the night in fitful sleep, afraid that at any moment, Ay's guards would come for them.

Pa-Siamen arrived with the first light of morning, in company with his immediate superior. Recognizing the woman whom he had last seen as a small girl tagging along with her brother, he kept silent as to her true identity, introducing her only as Scarab. The elder priest passed the care of the supplicants to Pa-Siamen and took his leave, instructing an acolyte to bring fresh bread, figs and water.

"You cannot remain here," the priest repeated.

"I would not put you in danger, Pa-Siamen," Scarab said gently. "We shall leave at once."

Pa-Siamen brought his head up sharply. "I am not the one in danger, Beketaten, sister of the Heretic. If anyone here guessed your identity, you might not live long enough to be taken by Ay's guards."

Khu gave Scarab a long meaningful stare, edging between the priest and the door, a gleam of bronze showing near his right hand.

"You are named the Handmaiden of Aten, lady," went on the priest. "Do you in fact still live up to that name?"

"You know I do not, Pa-Siamen. I was named Beketaten by my brother but the name I now go by is simply Scarab, the name by which you knew me when my other brother, Smenkhkare, brought me here. I believe all gods should be worshiped, not just one."

The priest scratched his beardless face. "Scarab, eh? Khepri, the sacred beetle--well, that is a good name--as is that of Smenkhkare. There is much sorrow in Waset today, much mourning that even Ay cannot suppress."

Scarab made a surreptitious sign to Khu who glowered but edged away from Pa-Siamen, the knife disappearing back into his robe. "What do the people believe?"

"They believe Smenkhkare is dead." Pa-Siamen shrugged. "Of course they will believe what Ay tells them, he is next to the king in power and authority. Besides, he produced evidence to back up his story."

"What evidence?" Khu growled. "I thought a crocodile took him."

"Has Ay produced my brother's body?"

"No, my lady. He produced a kilt, ripped and bloodied, of fine linen such as the king wore and stained by the river mud. Also the bodies of five of the young nobles who accompanied him. They died of wounds--spear, arrow, and sword--that Ay says were inflicted by bandits."

"Bandits? Why would they kill nobles instead of ransoming them?"

"I do not know, but Ay says the king and one other fled from the scene of the ambush and attempted to swim the river, only to be dragged down by crocodiles."

"And the servants that were with them?" Scarab's face took on a puzzled look.

"All dead, my lady."

"Then who was it that saw the ambush and the king and one other taken by crocodiles? Are we to believe the bandits obligingly reported the matter to Ay?"

"It makes you think, doesn't it?" Khu mused. "There was no love lost between your brother and Ay. Now your brother is dead and somehow Ay knows all the details."

Pa-Siamen looked shocked. "You are not thinking the lord Ay, or anyone for that matter, actually killed the king? Such an act is god-cursed and the wrath of Amun would be swiftly visited on such a miscreant."

Khu snorted derisively. "Even the Heretic, Akhenaten? If someone killed him, Amun would rejoice."

"No, Councilor Khu. Though Akhenaten cursed the gods and sought to obliterate Amun from the minds of men, he is still a consecrated and anointed king. Why, it was in this very temple that the Hem-netjer of Amun crowned him as king. The gods may exact vengeance on him after death, but no respecter of the gods will hasten his demise."

"All right," Khu grudgingly agreed. "So Ay did not have Smenkhkare killed, but how did he know if none witnessed it? It is suspicious."

Pa-Siamen shook his head. "You seek complexities where there are none. All in the royal party died, but men live by the river, hunting and farming. Ay says a hunter spied them from afar, too far away to come to their aid."

"Too far to help? Yet near enough to recognise the king?" Scarab made a sour expression. "You cannot convince me Ay did not have a hand in this. He stood to gain too much."

"More than likely, but what are you going to do about it?"

"I don't know, Khu. There is probably little I can do. If I could find Smenkhkare's body with stab wounds in it, I could perhaps rally the nobles against Ay, but he is certain to have the army behind him."

"That I wouldn't be too sure about. Horemheb is his own man and if nothing else he is loyal. I mean, look at his actions when Ay attempted that first rebellion. He tried hard to get Ay executed or exiled along with Nefertiti. Do you think he will support Ay if he really has had the king killed?"

Scarab nodded. "There is Akhenaten too. Pa-Siamen, I know what you think of him, but in your own words, he is the anointed king of Kemet still. If he speaks out against Ay, the people must surely rally to him."

"Perhaps," Pa-Siamen said. "What I do not understand is why the Tjaty would attempt this thing. From what I have heard, his daughter Nefertiti rebelled in the hope of overthrowing the Heretic--and now you say he was implicated in this. Why would he now remove the king he helped place in power, just to give sole authority back to the Heretic?"

"Because Smenkhkare was going to relieve Ay of his position of Tjaty at the end of the month. In two days time."

"Ah. And did Ay know of this?" Pa-Siamen asked. Scarab nodded. "Then that which was unclear, becomes clear."

"So to get back to my question, Scarab, what are we going to do?"

"Akhenaten first. We must take our suspicions to the king and hope that he will investigate them." Scarab picked up a ripe fig from the plate on the floor and dusted it off before biting into it. "We will stay here no longer than we must, Pa-Siamen. I would not expose you to any more danger."

The priests head came up sharply. "As I said before, you are the one in danger, my lady. For myself I care nothing if I may serve you, but you are in great danger if you stay here."

"Nobody knows we are here," Khu said. "Unless you have spread the word."

Pa-Siamen gave Khu a disgusted look. "Forgive me, Councilor, but at heart you really are just a farm lad. Nobody knows you are here? What of the porter last night, of the priest Amenhotep this morning, and the acolyte? Do you think they have kept silent or perhaps might have gossiped about a young man and a young woman seeking refuge in the temple?" He started pacing in agitation. "'Seeking refuge from what?' they will ask. Then will come news that the Tjaty is looking for two of the Councilors, by coincidence a young man and a young woman, and before we know it, Ay's soldiers arrive. They may already be on their way."

Khu looked at Scarab. "Then we had best get out of here. But where?"

Scarab considered a few moments. "Akhet-Aten," she said hesitantly. "The first step must be to see the king, see if he can rein Ay in." Turning to Pa-Siamen, she said, "Can you get us horses? And provisions? Speed is important."

Pa-Siamen laughed, cutting it off in a fit of coughing. "Amun may be rich, but I am not, my lady. If I tried to procure horses I would immediately attract attention."

"It will take too long to walk," Khu said. "If you remember, we tried that once before and look where it got us."

"There is another way," the priest said. "Though I hesitate to mention it, er, with you being a princess and the king's sister..."

"I am Scarab. Say what you need to."

"The First Prophet of Amun, Amenemhet, has journeyed to Ineb Hedj to oversee the dedication of the new temple...hmm; it has just occurred to me that he went at Ay's suggestion. I wonder if that means anything."

"The other way?" Khu prompted.

"Oh, yes, as I was saying, Amenemhet is in Ineb Hedj and Amenhotep who is second only to Bakt the Third Prophet..."

"Get on with it," Khu muttered softly.

"...is sending a boat down river in the morning to apprise the Prophet of recent events. Well, supplies are also being sent and some of the temple servants will be traveling too, to fetch and carry as needed. I, er, I thought perhaps you two could, er, become servants..." Pa-Siamen looked from one to the other uncertainly. "It is all I can think of," he added miserably.

Scarab thought it over for a few minutes. "What do you think, Khu?"

Khu grinned. "It beats walking or sitting on a horse."

"Wouldn't we be recognized?" Scarab asked.

Pa-Siamen smiled. "Do you know what your...let's say, Keeper of the Unguent Jars, looks like?"

"Wa'bet? Yes, she is young, barely fifteen summers and she has a cast in her left eye. Why?"

"All right, a bad example but let me say also, lady, that it is unusual for servants to be noticed. I have heard some say that servants all tend to look alike. If you do not attract attention to yourselves, I dare say you could walk aboard under Ay's nose and he would not see you."

Scarab fingered her fine linen gown. "I suppose I shall have to leave this behind?"

"Er, yes, lady." Pa-Siamen looked uncomfortable again. "The, er, temple servants are not like the palace servants. They are more, shall we say, menial and do not dress as well."

Scarab sighed. "I shall have to walk around naked, you mean?"

"Amun, no!" Pa-Siamen looked shocked. "Only slaves go naked. But you will only have a short kilt." He glanced at Khu. "At least you will look the part. That shock of hair you have is definitely servant class. A short kilt and you will pass for a servant anywhere. As for you my lady..."

"I have walked the streets wearing nothing but a servant's kilt before, Pa-Siamen." She smiled at the priests upraised eyebrows. "I am sure I can comport myself with proper humility again."

Pa-Siamen kept Scarab and Khu in his rooms that day while he found servant's clothing and some basic possessions for them. He also prowled the priests' quarters, listening to gossip, alert for the slightest hint of suspicion that the two fugitives had attracted attention. The main topic of conversation, however, was the death of Smenkhkare and whether or not the Heretic would replace him with another co-regent. The consensus seemed to be that the death of the king was, at least in some degree, a judgment by the gods. Most recognized that Smenkhkare had been a true believer, a good man and a good king, who had honestly striven to ameliorate his brother king's heresies. However, perhaps he really was tainted by Atenism which attracted the wrath of the gods. If that was true, then Kemet would not achieve true prosperity until the whole line of Akhenaten had disappeared.

As dusk approached, the priests congregated in the great temple of Amun once more for the end-of-day ceremonies, the god's evening meal and the sealing of the inner sanctuary. Pa-Siamen excused himself, pleading ill-health and hurried back to his room with a bundle of clothing and some food.

"Here," he said, handing over a pitcher of beer and a bag of fresh bread and fruit. "This is all I could sneak out of the kitchens without attracting attention. I've also got kilts and sandals, fairly roughly made, I'm afraid, but anything too well made will seem odd." Pa-Siamen lit a candle from a small fire-pot and its flickering glow cast swaying shadows around the bare room. "I...I also found you a decent wool cloak, my lady, so you can...er, can preserve your modesty."

Scarab smiled and fingered the weave of the coloured cloak. "It is a very nice cloak, Pa-Siamen, but it is not the sort of quality you'd expect a servant to be wearing." She shook her head. "I must refuse it. I cannot afford to attract any attention."

Pa-Siamen bit his lip but nodded. "It is probably a sensible decision, my lady. I will leave you for a few minutes so that you can change, then I must take you to the servants' quarters. It would look suspicious if servants came from here in the early morning."

"There is no need to leave, Pa-Siamen," Scarab said. "It will take me but a moment and I must get used to a lack of privacy." She unhooked the clasps of her gown and let it fall to the floor. Tossing her wig down beside it, she loosened the fine linen under kilt and added it to the pile. Completely naked, she crossed to the stool and took one of the coarse brown linen servant's kilts, fastening it about her waist. She looked up to see Khu studying the ceiling intently, and Pa-Siamen tracing patterns on the stone floor with the toe of one sandal. "You can look now," she grinned. "Though I don't know why you looked away. You can be sure nobody else will. Your turn now, Khu."

Khu disrobed and knotted the kilt around him. He blushed as he realized Scarab was watching him with a smile on her face. It was all he could do not to turn his back on her, knowing she would probably laugh if he did so.

"I'll wager you didn't know high-born ladies were so immodest, did you Pa-Siamen?" Khu growled. "Even the queen and princesses in Akhet-Aten used to walk around naked half the time."

"Immodest?" One of Scarab's eyebrows lifted. "Men and women work in the fields naked, sailors are naked and so are slaves. The gods gave them those bodies so why should they feel ashamed. Besides, it is much more comfortable wearing little or nothing." Abruptly she laughed. "Your faces. You should see your faces."

Pa-Siamen conducted Scarab and Khu to a small cottage in the servant's area as the temple grounds darkened. To any who observed, it would have appeared commonplace, a priest on an errand with two servants in train, carrying the priest's burdens and doing his bidding. He left them in the little one room cottage with an oil lamp and their bundle of provisions. In a corner lay two wrapped and bound bundles, about the length from a man's fingertip to his elbow along a side.

"At dawn, bring those bundles to the main gate. Try and act like servants, do not speak unless you are spoken to and then merely to give an answer. Do not volunteer for any task, try and stay out of the front rank and please, my lady, you especially, do not look anyone in the eye. There is no mistaking an expectation of obedience." Pa-Siamen started to close the door, then stopped and looked in on them. "May the gods of Kemet be with you both. I will pray for Amun's blessing tonight."

"Thank you Pa-Siamen," Scarab said. "Will we see you again?"

"No." The priest shook his head. "I will be on hand in the morning. If anything goes awry, maybe I can help, but do not look for me. I cannot acknowledge you." He closed the door, leaving them in the dim light of the guttering, smoky oil lamp.

Khu put down his small bundle of food and looked around at the bare room. "Makes me glad I'm not really a servant of Amun," he murmured.

"I've seen better," Scarab agreed. "However, we will endure what we must. We should get some sleep. Are there any bedrolls in here or do we have to sleep on the floor?"

"Gods, I hope so." Khu scuffed the dirt floor with one foot and listened to the rustlings in the palm frond thatching of the cottage. "We had a dirt floor at home in Akhet-Re, but it was never this filthy." He lifted the oil lamp and threw the shadows back a bit. "Here." Setting the lamp down, Khu pulled two stained mats from a corner and shook them out. Something small and black fell from one of them and fled chittering in outrage toward the shadows.

Scarab shrugged. "If a mouse is the worst of it, I shall sleep well tonight." She laid the two bedrolls out in the middle of the room and lay down on one of them. "Goodnight, Khu." She blew the lamp out.

Scarab woke in the pre-dawn chill, shivering. The door creaked loudly but she cracked it open, peering out into the first faint light of the new day, then drew it wider. She walked around the side of the hut and squatted, relieving herself. Rubbing her arms briskly, she turned back to where Khu sat on his mat, a dimly seen shadow in the hut's darkness, knuckling away the night's grime from his eyes.

He yawned hugely. "That was one of my worst night's sleeps," he complained. "I hardly slept for all the fleas and rodents."

Scarab laughed. "Really? So every time I woke up you were just pretending to snore?"

"Hmmph." Khu rolled over and up onto his feet. "Excuse me a minute." He ducked out into the darkness, returning a few minutes later to rummage in the bag of provisions. "Are you hungry?"

"Not really, but I suppose we should eat something. It's nearly dawn." She accepted a few dates and chewed quickly.

Khu pulled out the jug of thin beer and sniffed the opening. "The stopper fell out and I think it's flat, but it still smells good." He upended it and took a pull, suddenly turning his head and spitting out the contents in a spray of liquid. "Ugh, there was a cockroach or something in there." Putting his eye close to the opening, he peered into the container. "Can't see a thing. Oh well," he shrugged and took another drink.

"I think it's time to go." Scarab got to her feet and looked out into the gray light where people moved across the grass and along the sandy paths through the unkempt temple gardens toward the main gate, many of them carrying burdens. She turned toward the bound bundles and tugged experimentally on the ropes binding one of them. "They're heavy."

Khu bound up their small bundle of provisions and came across to heft the bundles by the door. "Not too bad. They are about the same, but I'll take our bundles as well."

"No you won't." Scarab grabbed the flat package of their old clothes and slipped it under one of the cords binding one of the bundles. Gripping the bundle firmly, she bent and hauled the bundle up, grunting with exertion as she wrestled it up onto one shoulder. "There, not so bad," she panted, moving to lean her burden against the wall of the hut.

Khu grinned and picked his up in a fluid motion, swinging it up onto his shoulder. Holding it in place he squatted to retrieve the provisions which he kept in his free hand. "Well, my lady, shall we go?" He gestured toward the doorway.

"Don't call me that, I'm just plain Scarab now." Pushing away from the wall, she walked slowly through the doorway, having to turn her shoulders slightly to negotiate the opening because of her large bundle. Khu followed and they walked slowly toward the main gate.

A small retinue of priests gathered in a group by the main gates which were still shut. Twenty or so servants stood off to one side, mostly men but a few women too, their bundles at their feet, awaiting the command to move. Scarab and Khu joined them, keeping their eyes averted from priests and servants alike. Dropping their bundles to the ground they sat on them, turning away and leaning together as if talking. Nobody took any notice of them.

A few minutes later a senior priest arrived from the temple and things started to happen. The gates swung open and the servants, with much groaning and grumbling, shouldered their burdens, forming up into a double line. Scarab and Khu jostled their way into line near the rear. The priests shouted out a command and the procession moved off. The broad avenue outside the temple gates was already thronged with people despite it being just after dawn. Normally the life of the city rose and fell with the sun and no matter how hard the work, the city hummed with a cheerful energy. Today though, the mood was somber and quiet, the faces of the people lined and anxious. Tradesmen and laborers both started early, though the womenfolk would not be on the streets until the sun rose higher. Their early duties were in the home, cleaning and preparing, planning and performing the myriad tasks that kept a home running smoothly. The crowds parted in front of the procession, flowing smoothly around the short line. Except for a few glances at the priests, the people ignored them and Scarab felt her tensed shoulders relax.

The priests led them down into the West quarter and along to the docks. The temple of Amun boasted its own docking facilities and several vessels. Tied up on the pier in front of them was one of the barges used to transport the god himself on the holy days. Small, but sleek, and gleaming with fresh paint and gilt, the barge and the rows of naked oarsmen that stood alertly on the gleaming deck, waited expectantly for the god or his representatives in the Two Lands. Between the procession and the barge stood a troop of soldiers.

An officer barred the way, his eyes flicking down the line. "What have we here then?" he asked.

The senior priest flushed and pushed up to the front of the line. "I am Ephenamen, priest of Amun. By what right do you stop us?"

The officer inclined his head respectfully. "I am under orders from Tjaty Ay who has taken charge of the city until a new king is crowned. I am looking for two people, a man and a woman."

"And why would you imagine I have them? Who are they, thieves?"

"Princess Beketaten and Councilor Khu."

Ephenamen roared with laughter, his fellow priests joining in, and it was the officer's turn to flush.

"My orders are that every person leaving the city is to be stopped and questioned. Do not hinder me in my work."

"Very well," replied Ephenamen with a sneer, "Examine my servants." He snapped out a command and the servants lowered their bundles to the ground. "You can see for yourself we have princesses, queens, lords and ladies among them."

The officer bowed stiffly and stalked down the line, his eyes flicking lightly over each face in turn. Ephenamen accompanied him.

"What does this Beketaten look like?" the priest asked.

"I do not know, only that she is the king's...the late king's sister."

Ephenamen was incredulous. "If you do not know what she looks like, how will you recognise her?"

"Breeding must show. A lady cannot hide her quality."

Ephenamen snorted. "I wish you well with your impossible task, soldier." He pointed down the short line of servants. "Do you see your lost princess?"

The officer's eyes passed quickly over the females in the line, stopping on Scarab's fine features. He moved closer and peered at her face, dropping his eyes smoothly over her breasts and legs. "Quite a beauty we have here. What is your name, girl?"

"Neferkhepre, sir," Scarab murmured, keeping her eyes lowered.

"Beautiful scarab, eh? Not a bad name. Where are you from, little scarab?"

"Waset, sir. My father is a baker."

"Why are you not working for him?"

"I seek to better myself, sir, working in the temple."

"You speak well for a servant."

"Thank you, sir." Scarab sketched a brief bow. "I have tried to imitate those around me."

"You do not miss grinding the flour and putting it in the ovens to bake?"

"It is easy to see you have never stepped into a baker's, sir. The flour must be worked into dough with water in which grape skins have been soaking; else you will not get it to rise."

The officer grunted. "You are wasted as a menial servant, beautiful one. Hard work will rob you of your beauty. Say the word and you can become my bed-mate, living a life of leisure and pleasure." He grinned and slipped his hand between Scarab's thighs, pushing up under her kilt.

Scarab kept a firm grip on herself but stepped back calmly with a smile. "What, officer? No gifts, no sweet words? I do not think much of your romantic technique. I like my men to be slow and sensual. Are you as hurried in bed?"

Beside her, Khu growled softly, his muscles flexing. The officer glanced at him, his eyes narrowing. "And what is it to you, fellow? Do you dare challenge me?"

Scarab laid a hand on Khu's arm. "This is my brother Mena, and he is a little slow-witted. He is protective of me. It is all right, Mena. The officer means no harm, do you sir?"

The officer snorted and turned away, casually examining the rest of the servants before coming back up the line. "All right," he said to Ephenamen. "You may pass."

The officer watched as the procession moved onto the dock and boarded the barge. One of the soldiers sidled up alongside him. "I saw yer talkin' ter the pretty one, sir. She be beautiful enough ter be the princess, I thinks."

"Don't think, Hem, it doesn't suit you. A real princess would have had my eyes out for slipping her one like that. She's good looking but she's common. She knows how to make bread, which is something no princess would know. Now fall in, soldier. We have other ships to check."

Chapter 11

messenger arrived from Waset three days after the fall of
Akhenaten. Written dispatches from the Tjaty were delivered to
General Psenamy in the North Palace. Psenamy took them
from the hand of the dirt-covered rider and verified the seals
were intact.

"You have a verbal message for me?"

"Yes, General. To be given after you read the scroll."

Psenamy nodded and waved the messenger away, retreating into
the next chamber to read and consider the information. He poured
himself a cup of earthen-cooled water and sat by the balcony,
examining the seal once more. It was definitely the Tjaty's private seal,
he decided. Cracking the wax with his thumbnail, he unrolled the scroll
and scanned the columns of writing.

"Greetings, General Psenamy," it read. "By now you will have
given the king the sad news of his brother's demise. I trust that you
have given the king every assistance and support in his time of grief."
Psenamy shifted in his seat, feeling a faint frisson of unease at the tone
of the letter. "Remember that in this troubled time, Kemet must be
assured of the safety of our beloved king, so stop at nothing to ensure
he is protected and guarded in a safe place. As a suggestion, I would
recommend the North Palace as it is a secure and comfortable
temporary accommodation until such time as the stability of the Two
Kingdoms returns." He nodded, comprehending Ay's purpose. In the

unlikely event the letter fell into the wrong hands, it contained only a loyal concern for Kemet and its king.

"I have need of you here in Waset. Leave as many men as are needed to guard the king, keeping his sacred person secure from any who might importune him and return to Waset as quickly as you can with the rest of your legion. Bring with you such personages as you deem useful in settling the peace of the Kingdoms, as we talked about before." It was signed "Ay, Tjaty of Upper and Lower Kemet, Divine Father, Fan Bearer on the King's Right Hand," followed by another sentence that Psenamy read twice, a frown wrinkling his forehead.

The General let the scroll roll up as he gave vent to a few fine curse words. *What has happened?* he thought. *Ay wants me down in Waset after just a few days. Has the city rebelled?* He drained his cup and marched out into the foyer. "Where is the messenger? Bring him at once."

The messenger arrived a few minutes later, still chewing and swallowing a hasty meal. His face was still caked with the dust of the road and he walked hesitantly, as if in pain. Coming to attention in front of the General, he saluted.

"Do you know the contents of this scroll?" Psenamy held up the message.

"No, sir. I was told to deliver it into your hand, wait until you had read it then give you my verbal message."

Psenamy dismissed the guard at the door, sending him outside the chamber. "Do you know why I am recalled to Waset?" he asked.

The man looked mystified, shaking his head. "No sir, only what I was told to tell you."

"Go on then."

"Yes sir. I am to say that the sister has escaped and that the Tjaty greatly desires the third daughter to visit him when the boy cousin does."

"That is all?"

The messenger nodded and Psenamy tapped the scroll in his palm as he looked at the weary man. "Do you understand any of that?" he asked. "It seems a bit vague to me."

The man hesitated then shrugged. "I think the third daughter might mean Ankhesenpaaten, sir, though she is more properly titled queen. That would make the boy cousin prince Tutankhaten."

"And the sister?"

"No idea, sir. Unless it means the sister of Ankhesenpaaten--you know, Meryetaten, the queen of the late king."

Psenamy nodded. "I don't have to tell you to keep silent about all this, do I? Though nothing has been said that is treasonous or even impolitic, in the wrong hands these words could be embarrassing."

"No sir, I know how to keep quiet."

"Good man. Well, I won't keep you. No doubt you have a meal and a bed waiting for you."

The man saluted again and turned toward the door. Before he had taken more than two steps, Psenamy dropped the scroll and whipped a dagger from his belt. Three strides and the General slammed the dagger home into the messenger's back, his free hand coming round to snatch the head back. Another plunge of the dagger and the surprised shout of pain faltered and died. Psenamy lowered the body to the blood-spattered tiles and thrust the knife once more, between the ribs. Standing up, the general ripped his tunic, and then lay down on the floor near the dead man, smearing himself with some of the blood. He took a deep breath.

"Help! Guards, to me, help!"

Moments passed before the door to the chamber burst open and three guardsmen poured through, swords at the ready. They stopped and stared at the sight of their general scrambling up all covered in blood.

"Well, don't just stand there, you fools. Help me up." As one man grabbed an arm and awkwardly hauled him up, Psenamy gestured toward the dead messenger. "The son of a whore tried to kill me. See to him, I want to put him to the question."

The other soldiers bent over the man, lifting limp eyelids before straightening with a grunt. "He's dead, sir. Won't get nuthin' outa him."

Psenamy huffed in exasperation, shaking off the hands of his helper. "Curse the man; I need to know who sent him."

"Perhaps this might tell you, sir." A guard stooped to pick up the papyrus scroll. He half-opened it and almost dropped it when Psenamy snatched at it.

"Leave me." He gestured at the dead man. "Take that offal out with you." He waited until the door closed behind them before unrolling the scroll once more. He re-read the last sentence, added as a postscript after Ay's signature.

"To be safe; kill the messenger."

Psenamy took the scroll over to a wall torch and held the message in the flames until it caught. He let it fall and watched until the papyrus turned black, the borders winking in tiny red crawling sparks, before grinding his sandaled heel into it. Leaving the mess on the floor, the General left the chamber and walked swiftly to his own where he stripped and sponged the blood off his body before donning a clean kilt. He chose his adornments with care, selecting a heavy gold and malachite pectoral and solid gold armbands that matched the rings on his fingers. Opening the door, he called a servant over to him, bidding him run to the Southern Palace and notify the Chamberlain that General Psenamy would be calling on Prince Tutankhaten and her majesty princess Ankhesenpaaten within the hour.

Satisfied, Psenamy turned toward the inner chambers of the North Palace where the Heretic, Akhenaten, held solitary court watched by the half dozen Nubian soldiers that stood guard over him. They had been picked for their strength and loyalty to Amun. Guards came to attention as the General strode deeper into the palace, spear hafts clunking dully against the tiled floor. The chambers that now held the king of Kemet had once been storerooms, shut away in the middle of the palace, far from the fresh air and blazing sun. In lieu of daylight, orange-yellow rush torches and oil lamps lit the bare rooms, cramped and poorly furnished, while dark and shifting shadows crouched in the corners, dragging down the spirits of the occupant.

Akhenaten was sitting on the small, low bed against the far wall staring fixedly at one of the tall Nubians guarding him. He looked up as the doors swung open to let Psenamy into the chamber. The king stared at the general blankly for a few moments before recognition crept into his face. "General Psenamy, why am I being confined to this room?"

"For your own safety."

"Your tone is insolent, General."

Psenamy smiled mockingly and made an exaggerated bow. "My apologies, your divine majesty. You are here for your own safety though."

Akhenaten got to his feet and though he had been stripped of all the royal regalia, he still managed to look like a king. "Safety? Where lies the danger, if not from you?"

"Your brother Smenkhkare is dead. I would not want to see harm come to you too."

"I thought you said my brother died by crocodile. Do you imagine I am in danger from them too?"

"From men who see in your brother's death a chance to rid the Kingdoms of heresy."

Akhenaten drew himself up, staring stonily down his long face at the General. "Have a care what you say. My word is Law and the truth of the Aten is self-evident to any whose hearts are pure."

Psenamy shrugged. "I did not come here for a philosophical debate, your majesty. I came to tell you that you will be staying here a while longer but that I must leave today for Waset."

The king flicked a hand nonchalantly. "It is of no importance to me where you go."

"Then I will bid you farewell, your majesty." The General bowed again and turned on his heel. Behind him he heard a ragged breath and looked back over his shoulder.

"Where is my dear wife, Ankhesenpaaten? I greatly desire to see her."

Psenamy turned back to face the slumped figure of the king. "I told you I would not allow her here. You have the Lady Kiya to console you."

"I don't want the Lady Kiya." Akhenaten stamped his foot petulantly. "I want my wife Ankhe. Bring her to me."

"No. Ankhesenpaaten is required in Waset, together with your young brother Tutankhaten."

The king stared at the General, then his full lips began to quiver. "Please, bring her to me--or let me see the sun and the sky. My father Aten lives in my heart but if I cannot see his glorious face I must be allowed to commune with my wife. My little Ankhe supports me."

Psenamy smiled, enjoying the king's discomfiture. "Yes, but princess Ankhesenpaaten does not wish to see you. She knows where her future lies and it is not beside a broken down heretic king." He turned toward the door once more, laughing. "Pray to your Aten, your majesty. Maybe he will come and save you." Psenamy locked the door

160

behind him and set off back through the corridors of the North Palace, still chuckling.

He found his second-in-command on duty at the main palace gate. Gesturing to the officer to join him, Psenamy set off in the dusty heat of the fore-noon toward the southern city and the main palace.

"Khaemnum, I am leaving you in command."

The officer looked surprised and pleased. "Where are you going, sir?"

"Waset. I have received orders to take Tutankhaten south to be crowned as co-regent."

The two men continued on down the great Royal Road in silence for several minutes. Normally bustling with activity, this backbone of the city lay stunned in the blazing sun. The people that moved on its wide thoroughfare did so as if preoccupied. Commerce had insufficient motive to move them, the shaking of the normal order of things having produced a lassitude and uneasiness about the future. Men watched the soldiers covertly, hoping to divine some purpose in their travel, some hint of what lay before the City of the Sun.

"Your most important duty will be toward the king. Do not be misled by his deposition, he is a devious man and will attempt to deceive you."

Khaemnum nodded. "Don't worry, sir, I'll keep him safely locked up."

"No, that is just what you must not do. Akhenaten is still king in Kemet, and will be as long as he has life in him. We must just make sure that saner minds have control of the reins of government. That is why Tutankhaten must be crowned as co-regent as soon as possible, so he can bring Kemet back to the old gods."

Khaemnum frowned. "So if he is still king and I am not to keep him locked up, just what am I to do, sir?"

"Watch him, limit his contact with others, and do not ever leave him alone." Psenamy stopped in the middle of the street, close to where the Great Temple of the Aten lay. He pointed at the enormous edifice. "That is what happened when Akhenaten was free to do as he pleased and it has brought nothing but misery to Kemet. Atenism is not yet dead, Khaemnum, it has merely become less obvious. If the gods are willing, in time it will disappear. But while Akhenaten lives, he could become a focus for pro-Atenist trouble makers."

"Then would he not be better dead, sir?" The officer looked troubled.

"Of course, but are you going to do it? Will you kill an anointed king? If you are willing to give up your eternal life and face the curse of all gods, then tell me. I am sure certain people would be most interested in the news." Psenamy watched the younger man's face for a moment before smiling wryly. "I thought not. That is why you must keep him alone and away from anyone who seeks to use him for their own purposes. Keep him in his chambers for a few days more, then you can let him out into the gardens, under guard of course. If he remains calm and pliable--use your own judgment--you could even let him serve in the courts again. Just monitor what is said and if he tries anything, lock him up again." The General resumed walking toward the palace gates.

Khaemnum nodded pensively. "I think I can do that sir. But how many men will you leave me?"

"More than enough. Ay needs the legion back in Waset but I intend leaving you two hundred men. Now, I must talk to the prince before we depart, so I want you to get your command set up. Pick your officers and get their men into position. Have the rest assemble by the docks." Psenamy clapped his second-in-command on the shoulder and entered the palace.

The chamberlain awaited him in the dim, cooler interior and after bowing, set off along the corridors toward the king's apartments. Servants stood around and watched the two men, rather than being about their duties. The whisperings and mutterings of conversation died away as Psenamy approached, picking up again after he passed. Guards, his own men, stood at the entrance to the king's suite and they saluted, the butts of their spear shafts thumping solidly into the tiled floor. The chamberlain opened the door for the General and gestured him to enter.

The large airy room that formed the antechamber looked as if the strong desert winds that carry the sandstorm had swept through. The few pieces of furniture had been pushed back out of the way and a litter of toys, wooden carvings and weapons littered the floor. In the centre of the room was an open space where two boys heaved and strained, their bodies locked in a wrestling grip, each trying to throw the other to the floor. Prince Tutankhaten, though slight of build, held his own against the larger frame of Hiknefer, sheer determination neutralizing strength, limbs the colour of beaten copper appearing pale against the rich blackness of the Nubian prince.

As Psenamy entered the room, Tutankhaten glanced toward the movement and his muscles relaxed for a moment. Hiknefer felt the tremor and needed no further encouragement. With a heave, he toppled the prince and threw him to the floor, dropping to his knees beside the young boy with a wide grin of mirth on his face.

"Two to one, Tuti," Hiknefer crowed. "You owe me the dagger with the carnelian inset."

Tutankhaten scrambled to his feet full of hurt indignation. "That wasn't fair Hiknefer; I had you until he came in." He pointed an accusing finger at Psenamy. "It doesn't count, does it Ankhe?"

The General glanced across the room to where Ankhesenpaaten sat on the bed with her legs curled up under her. The girl put down the polished silver mirror and looked up at the boys with a bored expression. "What doesn't count, Tuti? What are you talking about?" She straightened her legs out and stood up gracefully, smoothing the pleats of her transparent dress. "General." She inclined her head a fraction, acknowledging his presence. "To what do we owe this...this summons?"

Psenamy bowed deeply to the former queen and the future king. "My lord, my lady, I thank you for acceding to my request."

Tutankhaten ignored the adults and punched Hiknefer in the arm. The tall Nubian boy danced backward, his white teeth showing in an infectious grin.

"It's not fair," Tutankhaten repeated sulkily. "That bout doesn't count."

Psenamy coughed and said, "If I might make an observation, my lord."

Tutankhaten stopped in the act of throwing another punch. "What?"

"It seems to me, my lord, as if a valuable lesson might be learned here today. If this had been a real fight on the field of war and not just a play fight, then your moment's inattention might have brought you death. You must learn to control yourself, become single-minded in your every action, become kingly. Today, you need to accept your defeat gracefully, for the gods hate unseemly pride and complaints against what life throws at us. Be gracious and embrace your friend--and learn how to defeat him next time."

"You will too, Tuti," Hiknefer murmured.

Prince Tutankhaten looked from Psenamy to Hiknefer and then to Ankhesenpaaten, his brow furrowed in thought. He faced the General again and cocked his head on one side. "You said kingly--that I must learn to become kingly. Why?"

"I received a letter from Tjaty Ay today. He requests your presence in Waset." A small smile crept under calculating eyes. "There is a small matter of a vacant throne and a young prince ready to become king."

The prince's eyes grew large. "Me?" he squeaked. "You mean me?"

"But of course, my lord. Who else could be king except the sons of the great Nebmaetre Amenhotep? Your elder brother Akhenaten has asked to remain king here in Akhet-Aten so he may continue his worship of the Aten, but he has agreed with the Divine Father Ay that you should rule all Kemet, save this city, from Waset."

"Your majesty." Hiknefer dropped to his knees beside the small boy, only to find his head still topping the youngster's by two fingers. He quickly bent and touched his forehead to the tiled floor. "I offer my life and my loyalty to King Tutankhaten."

Ankhesenpaaten too dropped onto one knee. "My heart is yours, great king," she said softly.

Tutankhaten giggled and he raised one foot and wriggled his toes in Hiknefer's curly hair. Beside him, Psenamy coughed softly.

"Be gracious, my lord," he murmured. "Be kingly."

The future king gave his friend a gentle nudge with his foot. "Get up Hiknefer. Come on, you're still my friend." As his friend rose, Tutankhaten turned to Psenamy again. "What about Ankhe? I want her to come to Waset too."

"Of course, your majesty." The General bowed in the direction of the former queen. "Tjaty Ay specifically asked that she accompany you."

Ankhesenpaaten walked over to the prince and put her arm about the boy. She looked Psenamy directly in the eye and a fleeting flicker of guarded acknowledgement passed between them. "I will always be with you, Tuti," she said calmly. "I have given you my promise."

Tutankhaten hugged her. "Are you going to marry me, Ankhe?" He looked up at Psenamy. "Is she? Is that why she's coming to Waset?" His bottom lip trembled slightly. "You won't take her away from me?"

"Marriage?" mused Psenamy. "That is a very good idea, my lord. I wish I had thought of that. She is the last female of the royal line."

"So it is true, then?" Hiknefer looked from prince Tutankhaten to the young Ankhesenpaaten. "I have heard stories but was unsure of them. The right to be king resides in the females and a king must marry his sister or close relative to become king?"

Psenamy laughed; a barking explosion devoid of mirth. "You heard wrong, boy, though there is a kernel of truth in it. The right to be king belongs to the male heir but a king would be a fool to leave an unmarried female where any ambitious man could find her and marry her. He would not be king long. To be safe, he marries her himself so there can be no rivals for the throne. In-as-much as a female carries the bloodline of the king as well as a male; it makes sense for the new king to deny that bloodline to others by marrying his female relatives."

"I see." Hiknefer nodded. "But does not prince Tutankhaten have a closer female relative than queen Ankhesenpaaten--forgive me mistress," he bowed to the lady. "Is not princess Beketaten a sister of...of the new king? Should he not be marrying her to keep the bloodline safe?"

"The bitch is dead," Ankhesenpaaten snarled.

"That is true, General?" Tutankhaten asked. "Why was I not told?"

"The news came yesterday, my lord. I conveyed the message to the queen, but we decided you had enough to concern you without adding to your worries. If I have done wrong, I beg my lord's forgiveness."

"You are forgiven," Tutankhaten said with a grin. "I did not really know her. Besides, it's Ankhe I want to marry. We'll have such fun, Ankhe. We can all play together and...and go on river voyages and hunt lions..."

"And govern the Two Kingdoms properly, Tuti." Ankhesenpaaten pursed her lips. "You will have to lean on me for a while. I will help you be a king."

"When do we leave for Waset? Can I take all my toys?" The young prince's grin slipped. "Is Hiknefer coming? And Khai too? I don't want to leave them behind; I want to make Hiknefer my Tjaty."

"You will be king, my lord; your wishes will command us all." Psenamy bowed low before the little boy again. "We leave for Waset this afternoon, and the princes of Nubia will be accompanying us. As for being Tjaty, well, my lord, the Divine Father Ay is Tjaty and prince Hiknefer will soon be going back to his people to govern Lower Nubia for you."

The prince nodded. "We'll find something else for you then, Hiknefer. Come on, let's go and pack our toys and pick out which dogs we are taking." He grabbed the tall Nubian youth by the hand and scampered to the door.

Psenamy watched them out of sight before turning to Ankhesenpaaten. "You'll be able to keep him in hand?"

The girl nodded. "Leave him to me. He will be king, but I will rule Kemet with the help of my grandfather Ay."

Chapter 12

The two barges passed each other less than half a day south of Akhet-Aten, the great breadth of the river between them. The land on either side of the river at that point lay green and lush, reeds and papyrus stretching back to fields of long grass before the desert. The hand of man lay light on the riverbanks and flocks of ibis and egret wandering the muddy shallows, taking flight in a storm of white wings at the approach of the barges. Water swirled and rippled as crocodiles, tips of snouts and armored eyes barely breaking the surface; sank beneath the flow.

The priests of Amun, shading their eyes against the dancing glare of the low evening sun, recognized the other barge as it forged slowly upriver, its red-tipped oars chunking into the water, pulling slowly backward and lifting again, golden drops spattering back into the oily calm of the current. The royal blazon flew in the prow--the gold flag with the red and white double crown of Kemet.

Ephenamen ground his teeth at the sight. "The Heretic," he snarled. He found himself in a quandary, not wanting to make obeisance to the champion of the Aten but knowing if he did not, their lives could be forfeit. He growled, and as the royal barge approached, dropped to his knees, staring down at the water so as not to look at his hated king. The other priests followed suit as did almost everyone else on board.

Scarab stood near the railing, looking curiously at the approaching barge, until Khu pulled her down.

"You're supposed to be a servant," he muttered in her ear. "Servants don't look at kings."

Scarab shook his hand off and crouched by the low railing, staring across the water. Around her, the other servants and sailors lay flat on the deck, waiting for the god to pass. As the barges drew closer, the figures beneath the huge linen awning amidships became clearer.

"That's not Akhenaten," she said softly. "It's only a boy, actually boys." Scarab shaded her eyes. "Tutankhaten. Why is he going to Waset?"

Khu tried to quieten her, putting a finger to his lips. "Shh. Remember who you are supposed to be."

The barges sped past one another, few eyes on the royal barge bothering with the other one heading downriver with the current. They passed and rapidly receded from one another. Ephenamen the priest rose to his feet with a venomous look at the back of his enemy. He spat into the river, the gobbet drifting alongside until it dissolved.

"Why does the Heretic leave Akhet-Aten?" he asked of his fellow priests. "What mischief does he seek to cause in Amun's City?"

The others offered opinion based on ignorance, being all they had to offer and Ephenamen cut through the babble, chopping down with one hand.

"Enough. We will break our journey and put in at Akhet-Aten. The First Prophet will want to know why the Heretic leaves his lair."

The chief priest retired to the small awning on the deck and the servants went back to their positions, busying themselves with the countless small tasks of a personal nature that they only had time for when not called upon to serve their masters. Scarab and Khu sat a little apart from the other servants and leaned toward each other, talking. A few curious eyes watched them and two of the younger women stared hungrily at Khu.

The young man was personable enough to attract the attention of young women, who had made their moves on him the first night out from Waset. Amused and a little pleased by the attention, Khu had responded positively until Scarab had left his side with a muttered remark about the minds of men. Khu followed, and when the women continued their advances, turned on them and sent them packing amidst screeched abuse. Rumor had quickly spread that the two new servants were not in fact brother and sister, but were lovers, possibly running from a cruel master.

Khu turned his back on the watching women and sat cross-legged in front of Scarab, pulling the front of his kilt down between his thighs for decency. "Does it matter?" he asked casually. "What importance is the boy? Another week could get us to Ineb Hedj and with luck we can find passage to Zarw."

"I hate not knowing." Scarab worked with a borrowed needle and a length of linen thread, repairing the torn edges of her gown with clumsy stitches. It was still grimed and stained but she could not bring it out in the open to wash it without inviting awkward questions. She drew her breath in sharply and popped a finger into her mouth. "How do they not bleed over the clothes? I'll never look down on seamstresses again. Besides, Khu, it is fairly obvious that Tutankhaten is being brought to Waset at Ay's instigation to be made king."

"Then what is the problem? We just sail by to Ineb Hedj and on. We find Horemheb and enlist his aid against Ay."

"What of Akhenaten?"

Khu shrugged. "What of him? He rules his City of the Sun while the rest of Kemet gets on with its own business."

"I hate to say this, knowing the damage he has caused to Kemet, but I think Akhenaten is preferable to Ay. With Akhenaten, at least the rule of law stood firm, but with Ay we might as well have a brigand chief ruling us."

Khu eyed Scarab warily. "So what do you want to do?"

"See Akhenaten. Tell him what's going on. See if we can persuade him to help."

"And how do we do that? Firstly, we cannot just walk up to a priest and say 'Thank you for the ride, please let us off at Akhet-Aten', and secondly, if by some miracle we did get off, how are two servants going to get in to see the king?"

"I don't know...yes I do. It will be dark by the time we get there. We can slip over the side and swim to shore."

Khu snorted. "I don't suppose you've noticed there are crocodiles in the river. I would have thought with a brother lost to them already, you'd be a..." He broke off as he realized what he was saying. "Scarab, I'm sorry, really I am. I just...I just forgot and...please forgive me."

Scarab's eyes filled and she brushed away tears angrily. "That's all right Khu, really it is. I just haven't had a proper time to mourn for Smenkhkare. But I will, soon."

Khu sat silent for a time, letting Scarab gather her thoughts and emotions. The sun sank below the distant cliff tops on the western shore, dark shadows racing out over the water. The air cooled, a welcome respite from the day, and servants hurried to light the cooking fires. Large slabs of rock were set up on the deck and small fires kindled, the cooking pots filled and soon the welcome scents of food filled the evening air.

When the priests had eaten their fill, the sailors were served, and then the servants had their turn at the bread and vegetable stew, fried fish fresh from the river and thin, sour beer. Khu took two servings back to Scarab by the eastern railing and squatted beside her. Wordlessly, he held out the bowl of food and a mug of beer.

Scarab took the food with a smile and ate hungrily. When they had finished she motioned Khu to stay and picked up the bowls and mugs, taking them back to the cooking fires and the buckets of water, to wash them out. She kept her ears tuned to the snippets of conversation around her, and when she returned to Khu in the starlit darkness of the night, she was grinning.

"We are stopping at Akhet-Aten. The priests think Akhenaten was on that barge we passed and they want to know why he travels to Waset."

The moon rose, casting a weak silvery path over the rippling water just before they saw the lights of the city. Mooring at a vacant dock was a tricky business in the darkness, but the sailors were experienced and the task was accomplished with no more than a single jarring shock and two oar blades snapping. Ephenamen organized the priests and as soon as the gangplank was down, marched them off into the city. Because of the lateness of the hour, few people were near the docks and the sight of priests of Amun in the city of Aten did not excite as much interest as might be expected.

Scarab and Khu sauntered over to the gangplank but were turned away by a guard. "Nobody goes ashore," he said in a bored voice. "The priests will be back soon and we leave then."

They wandered back to their position by the railing and leaned close to each other, Scarab whispering, "We'll have to go over the rail, and soon. It won't take those priests long to find out Akhenaten has not left the city."

Khu stared down at the dark lapping water with distaste. "If we have to," he grumbled. He scanned the barge, noting the huddled mass of servants preparing for sleep, the sailors sitting around waiting for the return of the priests, and the guards. Looking toward the stern, he saw the only relatively deserted part of the boat. "We'll have to leave through the latrines."

Picking up their small bundle of clothing, he walked casually to the stern, followed a few moments later by Scarab. The latrines were used by both sexes as Kemetu were used to the naked human body and bodily functions were regarded as quite normal. Two sailors were present when they walked behind the low screens that divided the latrines from the rest of the boat. The screens served the purpose of deflecting any smells that might waft from the area, rather than protecting the privacy of the occupants. A framework of timber hung out over the side, with a chair suspended over the water. A hole cut in the seat allowed for the elimination of waste in such a way as to not soil the sides of the barge.

The sailors talked as they urinated, two curved streams splashing into the water below. They did not even look up as Scarab and Khu entered, merely shaking their members dry and leaving.

"We've got to go silently," Khu said. "Lower yourself into the water rather than jumping in."

Scarab nodded and slipped her kilt off, standing naked in the darkness.

"What are you doing?"

"I want my kilt to remain as dry as I can and unsoiled by anything we may touch as we leave," Scarab murmured. "I can swim holding my kilt out of the water."

"Good thinking," Khu agreed, taking off his own kilt and adding it to his bundle. He pointed to a mooring rope coiled by the screens. "I'll lower you first." Fastening one end to the railing, he lowered the other end into the water. Scarab climbed over the rail and gripped the rope, going down hand over hand before slipping into the cold water. She floated, holding her kilt out of the water, and looked up at the dark shadow that was Khu, framed against the starlit heavenly body of the goddess Nut.

The rope shook, then began to rise as it was pulled upward. "What are you doing?" she hissed. Khu did not reply but continued pulling until the rope disappeared entirely. Moments later, two ropes snaked down to the water and soon afterward, she saw Khu's naked body just above her. He slipped into the water and grinned.

"What were you doing with the ropes?" Scarab asked, kicking gently with her legs as the gentle current tugged her away from the shore.

"I realized if we left the rope tied to the railing, someone might notice we had left." He tugged sharply on one of the ropes and the other flicked up. "So I looped it instead of tying it." The rope flew free and splashed into the water beside them, sinking rapidly out of sight.

Holding his own bundle out of the water as best he could, Khu worked his way along the barge. Scarab followed, stifling a cry as something live brushed her leg. *Not a crocodile*, she realized with a gust of relief. *Probably just a fish or an eel.* The water shallowed rapidly and they stood in the mud with the water still up to their waists, contemplating the open area they would have to cross to reach the relative safety of the shadowed streets. To make matters worse, the few lights at the head of the dock lit the area and anyone watching from the dock or the barge would be sure to see them.

"If you can't hide, be obvious," Scarab murmured. She took Khu's hand and waded out of the river onto the bank, clambering onto the open area sloping up to the darkened streets. As Khu joined her, she put her arm about his wet, naked body and walked slowly into the light, keeping her back turned toward dock and barge. She moved slowly, as if she had not a care in the world, exaggerating the movement of her hips. Glancing toward Khu, she saw him struggling to keep calm, his body betraying the turmoil in his mind. "Just pretend we are lovers, out for a stroll on the river bank," she whispered.

The challenge came, a loud shout followed by a chorus of ribald remarks from the sailors.

"Ignore them," Scarab said calmly. "Walk slowly," she hissed as Khu started to move faster. She pulled him to a halt then threw her arms around his neck, pulling his head down and kissing him. The catcalls and whistles of appreciation grew louder. Without looking toward the barge, Scarab gave them a rude gesture and resumed her slow gyrating walk toward the shadows, laughter following them as they disappeared into the darkness of the street.

"Oh gods," Khu muttered. He leaned against a mud brick wall, breathing hard. Refusing to face Scarab, he struggled to wrap his kilt about him, taking rather longer at it than normal. He jumped when Scarab lightly touched his arm.

"I'm sorry if I embarrassed you, Khu, but it was necessary. You mean a lot to me and I would not hurt you for the riches of Kemet but the best way to hide is to be out in plain view. Those men did not see anything suspicious, just two young lovers."

"So...so what's next," Khu asked, his voice unsteady.

"The palace. We have to try and find Akhenaten."

"I don't imagine we are going to get in to see him dressed like this." Khu fingered his rough weave kilt and glanced at Scarab, hurriedly looking away again as he realized she was still naked.

Scarab smiled, a touch sadly, at his reaction. "You've seen me naked before, Khu, and I've seen you naked. Why does it embarrass you now?"

The young man hung his head and looked down the street, away from the naked girl beside him. "Seeing is one thing," he muttered. "But you held me close and kissed me as a lover. You are a princess, my lady, and I am just the son of a dirt farmer. It is not right and...and I don't know what..." He broke off and took several deep breaths. "Forgive me, lady, I am thinking thoughts that are not proper."

Scarab shook her head gently before slipping her kilt around her waist. "Khu, you are a dear friend but you are also a handsome young man. Can I be blamed for taking a kiss, even if it was necessary to elude our enemies? Please do not think less of me for it."

"Less?" Khu whirled and confronted her. "I think less of myself for lacking control. I would do anything for you, my lady, even die for you."

"Let us hope it won't come to that. Now, I think we had better get to the palace. We can probably slip in as servants and when we find the king, we can change into our gowns."

Entering the king's palace in Akhet-Aten was less difficult than they imagined. The palace was in an uproar with all authority gone, the chamberlain and nobles striving to maintain order, but the servants giving only cursory obedience before hurrying off on errands of their own. Scarab and Khu came in through the kitchens, carrying empty baskets found outside. Putting them down, they tried to look busy, moving things or dusting objects with a cloth whenever anyone came close. They strained their ears to hear what people were saying.

"Tutankhaten's not here," Khu said, after two nobles had walked past them, arguing loudly. "He's gone down to Waset to be crowned co-regent."

"We suspected that, but where is Akhenaten? I cannot believe the palace would be so chaotic if he was here."

"Do you think we can make it to the king's apartments--wherever they are?" Khu looked up and down the corridors. "At this time of night, he'd be there if anywhere."

Scarab led the way, wending a path through the maze of rooms and corridors, into the great palace. Before long they stood outside the king's apartments, standing alone outside the doors. There was no sound, and no guards outside. A single torch burned in a wall sconce a few paces down the corridor.

"He's not here." Scarab pushed open the door of the suite to reveal chambers clothed in darkness. "Where can he be?"

"We'll have to ask somebody and hope they don't recognise you."

They walked quickly back into the main halls and headed for the servants' areas, avoiding any nobles or officials they saw. Nearing the kitchens again, they came across a young girl carrying a load of old bed linen.

"'Oo are you?" she asked. "I 'aven't seen you before."

"We're new," Scarab replied. "We are supposed to be serving the king but we don't know where he is. Can you tell us?"

"Ee, listen to 'er stuck up voice. Where you from then, ter talk like that?"

"Waset. We were servants in a temple there and the priests sent us up as a gift for the king. You must know of the barge that arrived tonight."

"Nah, they don't tell me." The girl shrugged, her bare breasts rising and falling in a way that mesmerized Khu. "You look pretty ratty though. Are them your best kilts? The king won't like you being dirty."

Scarab nudged Khu hard in the ribs. "Keep your mind focused," she muttered. "We'll clean up before we see him, but where is he?"

"North Palace, don't ya know nuthin'? 'E's under guard by troops from Waset." The girl regarded Khu with a sparkle in her eye. "Come an' find me after. I be Wai an' I works in the washroom." She turned and hurried off.

"Nice girl," Khu commented, watching her walk.

Scarab rolled her eyes. "The North Palace it is then."

"What about these troops guarding him? They must be Ay's men."

Scarab led the way out of the palace and into the Great Royal Road that ran the length of Akhet-Aten. The city lay dark and silent under the moon that glowed like polished electrum in the clear night sky. They started north, past the huge open portico of the temple of Aten. Looking in, they saw a huge open area silvered by the moonlight, the many carvings of Akhenaten that lined the walls standing like alien watchmen, hooded eyes dark over carved inscrutably smiling lips.

"It's more open and honest than the dark temple of Amun," Khu muttered. "But the god is distant and unconcerned with men. At least Amun speaks to men."

"The Aten only ever spoke to one man, my brother Akhenaten." Scarab turned away from the temple and started toward the North Palace once more. The streets were almost deserted, save for a drunk staggering out from a side street, looking blearily around him and moving back into the darkness. A dog ceased its scratching to follow the young man and woman, its tail signaling hope that slowly died as the streets passed and no food was forthcoming. At length it sat on its haunches and barked once as if in reprimand, before resuming its teeth-baring hunt for vermin.

The palace loomed out of the night at last, the guards at the main gates shadows backlit by the fire burning in the guardroom. The walls of the palace compound stretched into the darkness on both sides, too high to scale and offering no place of entry.

"We're not going to get past them," Khu said gloomily.

"There's another way. Remember I left this palace at night when I discovered Ay's plot--his first plot." Scarab led the way along the shadowed street that skirted the wall, heading further north. She pointed at another opening in the wall, guarded by a single figure lounging against the wall, apparently picking his nose. "The servant's entrance. We should be able to get in there."

"He'll just let us in?" Khu's voice resonated with doubt.

"Well, we are servants." Scarab thought for a moment then held out her hand. "Give me the bundle of clothes." She unwrapped the

175

garments still damp from the river and shook out her gown and Khu's ceremonial robe. "It'll have to do. Follow me."

The guard looked up from his studied contemplation of a dried piece of mucus to see a young man and woman walking slowly toward him, talking in low voices. He flicked his hard-won trophy away and pushed himself away from the wall, blocking their way.

"'Oo are you, then? What are you doing out so late?"

Scarab broke off her supposed conversation and turned toward the guard. "You don't remember me from earlier this evening?" She sniffed loudly. "I am insulted."

The guard grinned. "I only came on an 'our ago. That must 'ave been Menes you saw. I wouldn't forget a beautiful girl like you." He leered, running his gaze over Scarab's body.

Scarab preened, thrusting out her breasts and dipping her head in what she hoped was a gesture of coyness. "Mm, I can see now I was mistaken. You are much manlier than the other one. What's your name?"

"User-Re. And yours?" The guard ran his hand over Scarab's arm, the back of his fingers brushing her breast. Khu growled softly and moved closer. User-Re's eyes narrowed and his hand moved toward the sword in his belt. "And 'oo might you be?"

"He's my brother. Don't mind him, he's a bit simple in the head but he means no harm." Scarab thrust the damp clothes into Khu's arms and pushed him toward the gate. "Take these in and let me talk to this nice man. I'll be along in a few minutes." Khu stumbled off, risking a look back as he went through the gate and turned the corner. He saw Scarab standing close to the guard.

"What's yer name?" User-Re asked, his voice rough and his eyes gleaming.

"Nefer."

"Beautiful, eh? Well named." He moved closer and stroked Scarab's arm again. "'Ow about it? We could 'ave a quick one up against the wall 'ere in the shadows." His hand dropped and he flipped his kilt aside, exposing himself. "All ready for you, eh?"

Scarab laughed. "Later, User-Re. My mistress will skin me if I'm late back with her gown."

"Yer brother's got it," User-Re said sulkily. "'E'll take it to yer mistress. I could still give yer a quick one."

"I told you my brother's simple. He'll stand in the hall all night waiting for me and my mistress will be screaming the walls down." Scarab smiled and walked her fingers up User-Re's arm. "Besides, why should I have a quick one when I can have you all night? What time do you get off duty?"

User-Re swallowed noisily and adjusted his kilt. "Midnight."

"Then wait for me, my big man." Scarab turned and ran lightly in through the gate and almost knocked Khu over in the darkness.

"Simple am I?" Khu growled. "You couldn't think of a better story?"

"It worked, didn't it?" She shuddered and glanced back toward the gate. "I need a bath. I can still feel that man's hands on me."

"I thought I was going to have to kill him. I wanted to."

Scarab flashed a quick grin. "I'm just glad men think the way they do. It makes them easy to manage." She put a hand on her friend's arm. "Not you, Khu. You're different."

Khu allowed himself to be persuaded. He shook out the clothing he had crammed under one arm and handed one to Scarab. "Time for these?" he asked.

Scarab held up her gown and examined it critically in the light from the open doorway to the servant's wing of the palace. "I had intended to wear these to gain access to Akhenaten, but I don't think they will do." She flicked at a large smudge of dirt on one shoulder and grimaced at a tear in the front.

"And who might you be?" A high-pitched voice had them jerking round toward the doorway. A large, fat man stood blocking the entrance. Clothed in a gown that stretched from his waist almost to the floor, the folds of his stomach and breasts, together with rolls on his cheeks and neck, gave him the appearance of a gluttonous child, despite a few wisps of gray hair above his ears. His voice further confused the picture, being that of a young adolescent in tone and timber, but of an adult in content. A petulant expression crossed his face, decided it liked the neighborhood and settled in for the evening.

"The Aten knows I have enough to do around here without two grubby urchins wasting my time. Who are you and what are you doing here? Smartly now, before I call the guard."

"Sethos, overseer of the kitchens, a eunuch," Scarab murmured out of the corner of her mouth before bowing toward the fat man. "Lord

Sethos," she continued out loud, "My brother Khu and myself...my name is Nefer...were sent from the main palace to help attend on the king. At your direction of course," she added hurriedly.

Sethos beckoned them into the light and looked them over slowly, waddling around them, a sneer on his face. "And who sent you?"

Scarab racked her brains, covering her lack of knowledge of the current members of the court with another bow. "The chamberlain, Lord Sethos. I cannot remember his name as we are just arrived from Waset, but he picked us out to come and give you our service."

"Wenner." Sethos looked as if he had a mouthful of vinegar. "That misbegotten son of a...never mind." He smiled craftily. "I shall see to it that the king hears of his generosity." Shaking his head, Sethos ordered Scarab and Khu to follow him and led them into the bowels of the kitchen, wheezing and sweating. "Put your rags over there." He pointed to a pile of sweepings and refuse, waiting until they had tossed their gowns aside.

"Nefer, you will take that tray there. Khu, the pitcher and a cup. No, it doesn't matter which one, do you think the king can afford to be choosy?" Sethos waited until the two young people were burdened down. "You are going to take the king his supper. He likes everything to be perfect--good food, wine and cups, beautiful servants with clean bodies and neat clothing. What a pity he will have you to serve him tonight."

The Overseer of the Kitchens waddled off, the other servants fleeing before him like a school of little fish scattering before the lumbering progress of the *Pehe-mau*. He led Scarab and Khu slowly through the palace, not to the royal suite, but to the inner storerooms.

"Where is he taking us?" Scarab whispered. "The royal chambers are over there." She jerked her head to the right.

"Quiet," Sethos snapped in his childlike voice. "The king has been moved. For his safety, is the story we are told. They must think we are fools. Anyone can see the king is a prisoner."

They arrived at the inner rooms where a guard ran his eyes over Sethos with distaste, Khu with disinterest and Scarab with enthusiasm. Dragging his eyes away, he unbolted the door and opened it wide.

Sethos pushed through into the room that blazed with the light of several torches. Akhenaten stood at the head of the bed, his head downcast, a wooden carving in his long-fingered hands. He never stirred as the door opened. Two tall Nubians stood in the far corners of the chamber, appraising the newcomers, flickers of light glinting off their bronze spear points. "Your majesty," Sethos said, his head bobbing in the sketchiest of bows. "Your supper is here, brought by courtesy of Wenner, your Chamberlain, who supplied these two servants." Masking a sneer of contempt, he backed through the door and closed it, leaving Scarab and Khu standing with the food and drink.

"Put the food on the table," Akhenaten said, his voice tired and despondent. Scarab and Khu moved to obey. Scarab poured a cup of wine from the pitcher and carried it over to the king, boldly meeting his eye as he raised his head. His forehead wrinkled into a frown. "You look familiar, though your manner is insolent. Were you one of my servants in the other palace?"

"No, Akhenaten," she murmured. Scarab flicked her eyes toward the Nubian guards. "Can they understand us?"

Akhenaten nodded slowly, his eyes fixed on Scarab's.

She dredged her memory for lessons learned from Ay when he had been her tutor, seemingly a lifetime ago. Ay was half-Khabiru, as was her own mother, Tiye. Akhenaten had passed his early years in Zarw, city of the Khabiru. She forced her tongue haltingly into the half-forgotten language.

"Akhenaten, I am your sister Beketaten whom you named Scarab long ago," she said in execrable Khabiru.

Akhenaten's mouth twitched in amusement as he too fell into the Khabiru rhythms. "Indeed? I thought her dead." The king sighed. "Perhaps she is and you are just a joke played on a helpless victim." His eyes narrowed. "If you really are my sister, why and when did I name you Scarab?"

"When I was four, you came to the garden with your queen, the beautiful Nefertiti..." A shadow darkened the king's eyes. "...and found me watching Khepri, the sacred scarab beetle. As I was then no-name, you named me for the beetle I studied."

Akhenaten nodded. "So I did. Well, Beketaten..." He ran his eyes over her. "You appear to have fallen from favour, like me."

"I prefer the name Scarab now."

"You have forsaken the Aten too?" he asked sadly. Looking at Khu, he went on, "And who is this? A lord's son, no doubt? Still loyal to his king? Who are you, lad?" he added in Kemetu.

"I am Khu, son of Pa-it, of Akhet-Re, your majesty." Khu sank to his knees, his head bowed.

"Akhet-Re? The little mud village across the river? There is no lord there."

"His father is a farmer, brother. Yet Khu has risen to become a Councilor of...of... he is a loyal friend," Scarab finished.

Akhenaten nodded, dismissing the young man from his thoughts. "Why have you come to see me?"

"Your brother Smenkhkare, whom you raised to be king beside you, is dead."

"You do not tell me anything I do not know." Akhenaten stared at the little carved figurine in his hand then abruptly tossed it onto the bed. "How did he die?"

"They say he was taken by a crocodile, but I do not believe it. I think our uncle Ay had him killed." Scarab proffered the cup of wine again, glancing at the baffled look on the faces of the guards. "Take it, brother. They are starting to wonder what we talk about."

Akhenaten took the cup and sipped. "What do you plan to do?"

"I? I thought to ask you for help."

The king smiled sadly again. "As you can see, I am not in a position to help myself, let alone others."

Scarab turned away, the palm of her right hand slapping her thigh. She frowned, thinking hard, oblivious to the looks of outrage on the faces of the guards as she stood with her back to the king.

Khu moved forward and offered the tray of food to the king. As he passed close to Scarab he nudged her. "Turn around," he hissed softly. "You have your back to the king."

Scarab stood for a moment trying to decipher the significance of Khu's statement, then a glance at her stained and tattered kilt reminded her of the part she played. She whirled, and dropped into a deep bow, her head almost touching the floor. "Your pardon, great one," she said loudly in Kemetu. "Your words contain such wisdom I forgot myself as I contemplated their meaning."

"You are forgiven, child," Akhenaten said in a regal voice. He switched back to Khabiru. "Having found your king to be ineffectual, what will you do?"

"There are those still loyal to you." Scarab rose from her obeisance though she still kept her demeanor downcast. "I will find Horemheb. He has no great love of Ay."

Akhenaten nodded. "I should have listened to his counsel once before. But will you throw the Two Lands into civil war?"

"If I must, but you will see, Akhenaten. The people will not accept Ay."

"But they will accept Tutankhaten, with my Ankhesenpaaten as his queen." Akhenaten said softly, his eyes searching Scarab's face. "And Ay will rule through my young brother, as he did through Smenkhkare."

"Ay did not rule Smenkhkare," Scarab flared, before hurriedly moderating her tone. "That is why he killed him, before my brother could dismiss him from office."

"Ah, I wondered at the cause." Akhenaten took a fig from the tray Khu held and chewed noisily. "Well, if you can interest Horemheb, maybe we shall yet succeed. There is still a little time. Ay will not have me killed until his own hold over Tutankhaten is complete. You will have to travel into Kenaan to find the general though. He has left Zarw to counter the Amorite threat. I heard this just before...just before."

Scarab's shoulders slumped. "Kenaan? How can we travel there? I have never left Kemet."

Akhenaten looked at his sister dispassionately, his expression calm. "The Aten will guide you, child," he said, reverting to the Kemetu tongue.

Chapter 13

"Has he taken leave of his senses?" General Horemheb exploded up out of his seat, overturning the table in front of him and scattering papers and his wine cup. The heavy linked gold of his chain of office flashed and glinted as his broad chest heaved with anger. The courier backed away, his eyes wide, remembering the sayings of the barrack room as soldiers talked about their officers over a pitcher or three of strong beer. 'The last thing many an enemy of Kemet has seen has been Horemheb angry,' was a common saying. 'Flight may win you no gold but you may live longer,' was another. The man started to consider the wisdom of this one.

"What has he done that is so wrong?" Paramessu asked, bending and setting the table on its legs again. He started to pick up the fluttering papers. "Ay has acted as Tjaty on the unexpected death of the younger king and..."

"Leave those things alone," Horemheb snapped. "Use your head, Paramessu. This has the stink of Ay all over it. Do you not remember what nearly happened four years ago?"

Paramessu turned to the trembling courier and dismissed him, pressing a copper clasp into his hand. "Go and have a drink, soldier." His grip tightened on the man's hand. "But have a care what you say."

The courier nodded; his trembling increasing as he looked into the dark eyes before him. "Never a word, sir," he croaked. "On my life."

Paramessu smiled with his lips. "Just so," he agreed softly, releasing the man's hand. He followed him to the flap of the tent and called the captain of the guard over. "A perimeter of men fifty paces away. Allow no-one closer." After watching for a few moments to see the captain hurrying off, bellowing commands, Paramessu turned back inside the large tent and walked over to his General. "I have a feeling we are about to talk treason."

Horemheb snorted. "When has the good of Kemet become treason?"

"Ay is Tjaty of Upper and Lower Kemet, appointed by Akhenaten, our anointed king," Paramessu said softly. "Speak against him without good cause and you speak against the king. That is treason."

"Was it treason four years ago when Ay and his bitch-daughter Nefertiti tried to overthrow Akhenaten?"

"You know it was not."

Slightly mollified, Horemheb grunted and picked up his wine cup, brushing the sand out of the damp interior. He looked around for the wine pitcher and refilled the cup with the watered wine mixture, draining a cup in three long swallows. Belching mightily, he refilled the cup and handed it to the younger man. "On the face of it, Ay acts correctly. Smenkhkare dies under somewhat suspicious circumstances..." He waved a hand as Paramessu opened his mouth. "...maybe, maybe not, I won't argue the toss now...so he brings the young boy down from Akhet-Aten and means to crown him king in Waset in thirty days time." He shrugged. "Yet it does not feel right."

"A popular independent king dies and a young untested boy succeeds him? I know what you mean. Ay could see his control of Smenkhkare vanishing and replaced him with someone he can twist round his finger."

"Now who is talking treason?" Horemheb smiled wryly. "Are you going to drink that wine or just play with it?"

Paramessu looked down at the forgotten cup before raising it to his lips, drinking. He passed it back to the General who finished it and poured another.

Looking quizzically at his aide, Horemheb asked, "How do you know Smenkhkare was asserting himself?"

Paramessu looked down at the ground and coughed self-consciously. "I had letters from...from princess Beketaten, sir. She described the situation at court most fully."

"So you have yourself a spy in the king's household, eh? Or is it more than that? I seem to remember you thirsted after those rosy-tipped breasts once."

"Sir!" Paramessu strove for shocked but merely sounded embarrassed. "She is a princess."

"It wouldn't be the first time a lady of breeding has gone for a bit of 'rough', lad. If the opportunity arises, go for it, I say."

"That is not how it is, sir. I respect her."

Horemheb grinned. "Then remember she is sister to kings. Woo and marry her and you could find yourself with a strong claim to the throne of the Two Kingdoms. Ahmose, the first of her dynasty was a common soldier." He raised the wine cup in a mock salute and sketched a bow to his friend. "Health and long life, King Paramessu."

"Do not joke about it," Paramessu said in a tight voice. "I have the greatest regard for princess Beketaten and I will not have anyone hold her in low regard. Anyone." He fixed his General with a hard stare.

Horemheb nodded. "Point taken, young Paramessu, I meant no offense."

The tent lapsed into silence as the two army men sought for ways to heal this slight rift in their relationship. Paramessu tidied the mess of papers on the ground while his General watched him morosely, sipping the wine in his cup. After a few minutes, Horemheb sighed and punched the younger man on a shoulder, a sympathetic look on his face.

"I am sorry, Paramessu, but there is one other thing you need to consider."

Paramessu raised an eyebrow. "What?" he asked cautiously.

"If Ay has had Smenkhkare killed, what has he done with Beketaten?"

The young officer paled visibly. "He would not, surely? What reason would he have?"

"After what we have just discussed? Consider the princess Beketaten, Paramessu. With your mind if you can, rather than your balls. Smenkhkare dies; there are two males left, Akhenaten the Heretic who can be disregarded, and a malleable youngster. There are also three females; Meryetaten who by all accounts is drifting back to Atenism, Ankhesenpaaten the young queen of the Heretic, and Beketaten. All are royal; all would make good dynastic marriages."

Horemheb started pacing, falling into a lecturing mood as he so often did before a battle. He began ticking points off on his fingers. "Meryetaten can be ignored. She is so steeped in the heresy; no follower of Amun would accept her. Her sister Ankhesenpaaten is young, not much older than Tutankhaten, and her beliefs are not yet as strong. She could be accepted as queen." He stopped and stared at Paramessu. "Then there is Beketaten; sister to present king, past king and future king. Too old for Tutankhaten, in fact too headstrong and independent for any young man."

Paramessu frowned. "Then if she is not to be married to Tutankhaten, where is the danger?"

"I said she was more than a match for any young man, not any man."

"Ay?" Paramessu snarled. "He aims too high."

"You think so? Ay was Tjaty to Akhenaten, ruling Kemet in all but name. Then came Smenkhkare who limited his power, and died for it. Now comes a young boy whom Ay can manipulate as he will. He is all but king again."

The General drained his cup and busied himself refilling it. He held it out to Paramessu again but the young man shook his head.

"What happens when the boy becomes a man and asserts his manhood?" Horemheb asked softly. "Will he die too? He is the last of Nebmaetre's male heirs. Who do you think will claim the throne and whichever female relative is still alive?"

Paramessu picked up the chair from the corner whence it had tumbled and set it upright. He lowered himself into it with a groan, forgetting that he sat unbidden in the presence of his superior. Anyone less than Horemheb would have flogged him for the disrespect, but the General just smiled faintly as he watched his young protégé wrestle with the problem of Ay.

"What will you do, sir?" Paramessu asked after a long time. "You have no love for the Tjaty. I cannot see you standing by and doing nothing."

Horemheb grunted. "What is it you think I can do?"

"March the army down to Waset. Arrest Ay and set Tutankhaten up as undisputed king."

"To be guided by whom? He is underage."

"Yourself."

"You'd replace a tyranny of Ay with a tyranny of the army?"

"You are not a tyrant."

Horemheb grinned. "Ask the men out there and see what they tell you. But no, I am not a tyrant yet I could become one if I ruled Kemet, even on behalf of the king."

"Then a Council, like the one Smenkhkare had?"

"Possibly."

"It is the only course of action. Go to Waset, General. Take your army and confront Ay. Find out the situation and if you judge it in Kemet's interests, remove him and see the new king enthroned either with yourself as his strength, or with a Council to advise him."

Horemheb regarded the young man seated before him, who leaned forward in his eagerness, whose voice lifted stridently with excitement. He noted the tones of command in his powerful voice. "I hear and obey, O General of All Kemet's Armies," he said, his voice dripping with sarcasm.

Paramessu frowned, looking up at his superior. "But you are General..." The realization of where he sat and the things he'd said crashed in upon him and he leapt to his feet, his face ashen. "General, forgive me." He fell to his knees on the hard-packed earth and prostrated himself, dropping his forehead into the dirt. "Forgive me, sir. I meant no insult."

Horemheb walked around the prostrate figure of his legion commander and sat down on the chair. He regarded the prone form thoughtfully for several minutes before telling him to rise. Paramessu got to his feet and stood in front of the General, stiffly erect, arms by his side and eyes unfocused, lined on a point straight ahead of him.

"What are your wishes, sir?"

"Wipe that smudge of dirt off your forehead."

Paramessu hesitated as if trying to make sense of the command, then rubbed at his forehead with one hand. He looked down at his hand to check the results before resuming his rigid stance.

"I value your thoughts, Paramessu," Horemheb said softly. "You have a good heart and a good head on those broad shoulders of yours. You just need to remember to think a bit more often. Now let's have no more of this prostration nonsense. I am not a king to demand such subjection; I am just your commander. I know you acted without thought, not out of pride or malice." He smiled and extended his hand. "Will you accept me as your General *and* friend?"

Paramessu blushed, then grinned, at first uncertainly, then in growing strength. "Willingly, sir." He gripped his general's hand firmly, feeling the strength in the fingers of the old man seated in front of him.

Horemheb allowed Paramessu to pour him another wine, while the old general watched. He accepted the cup with a nod of thanks. "You are partly right, I will go to Waset."

The younger man opened his mouth to speak but shut it again, question unspoken. He stood silently, waiting for his general to continue.

"Good man," murmured Horemheb. "I will go to Waset, but not at the head of an army. I have no desire to rule, just to ensure Kemet is ruled well. If I went in strength, Ay's hand would be forced and we do not need a civil war."

"Then what will you do, sir?"

"I will talk to him."

"Talk? To Ay? What can..." Paramessu cut himself off with an effort. "Sorry, sir."

Horemheb nodded. "I will talk to Ay and find out his intentions. I will talk to Tutankhaten and Akhenaten, and I will watch and wait. I will not fight fellow Kemetu unless I am forced to it."

"When will you leave?"

"Immediately. It is imperative I get to Waset before the coronation in thirty days time."

Paramessu frowned. "Sir," he said hesitantly. "What of the Amorites? Our last reports had them marching south toward us. Surely...er, is this a good time to leave?"

"I feel confident their General Jebu will hang back as usual. No doubt he will harass the local villages, enjoy a spot of pillage. If you keep the units in close contact, he will fall back. With luck, I'll be back in two months and we can plan a major offensive that will end the Amorite menace."

"You are leaving me in charge, sir?"

"Can you think of anyone better?"

Paramessu considered the question carefully. It was a great honour to be picked to head the Northern Army against the enemy, but with the honour went responsibility. If he made a mistake and this led to a major defeat, his head would not stay on his shoulders long. He wanted the position, but he felt the weight of the command already. "No, sir, I cannot think of anyone better," he said at last.

Horemheb leapt to his feet. "Then let's get your appointment announced and I can leave." Striding to the tent flap he pushed it to one side and emerged under the hammer blows of the sun. "Captain," he yelled, as the perimeter of guards snapped to attention. "Assemble the legion commanders and officers down to Hundred level by the temple. At the double, man. Do you think I pay you good gold to sit on your fat ass all day?"

The captain, trim and fit, snapped off a salute and took to his heels. He grumbled to himself as he ran. "Good gold? When was the last time I got to see gold? Dust and flies and the flux more like." However, he grinned as he spoke, feeling the honour of being picked by General Horemheb for this task, however menial.

By the time Horemheb and Paramessu got to the makeshift army temple--panels of wood and cloth surrounding an altar and cedarwood chests containing the images of the gods--most of the officers were in place, the last of them running in from the sprawling camp. The General waited until the last of them arrived before speaking.

"Men of the Northern Army, I have no doubt that by now rumors of events back in our beloved homeland are running through the camp like fleas on an Amorite king." He paused for the ripple of laughter and appreciation that always followed his first words. "I will confirm those rumors for you. Our king Ankhkheperure Djeserkheperu Smenkhkare has been called to the gods and his young brother Tutankhaten is to be enthroned in Waset in thirty days time." The noise from the assembled officers changed to one of anguish, cries and groans ringing out at the news that the god-on-earth had passed away.

"I must be in Waset for the coronation. It is imperative that the army is represented at the inauguration of this new era in our history. Accordingly, I will leave for Waset today, accompanied by an honour guard. While I am gone, Legion Commander Paramessu will command the Northern Army. I raise him to the rank of General Commander and as a sign of my favour and authority..." The General's fingers went to the heavy gold around his neck. "...I bestow upon him my Gold of Office." Horemheb raised the links over his head, advanced two paces and slipped the mass of gold around the younger man's neck. He embraced Paramessu, and kissed him on both cheeks. "Make such appointments as are necessary," he murmured. "But only on merit." Drawing back, the General resumed his bold stance before his officers.

"Some of you are worried about the Amorites. Some have already voiced their concerns to me about their approach. Well, let me reassure you on that score. General Jebu, the Amorite leader, is nothing but a bandit chief who operates best when leading armed men against defenseless villagers and peasants. He will be very cautious about facing the armed legions of Kemet." Horemheb looked fondly over the officers of his legions arrayed in front of him, dark eyes staring back from determined, chiseled faces.

"I see before me the cream of Kemet's forces, the legions of Re, Heru, Set and Ptah, and I feel peace in my heart. I know that I can leave you for a time, returning to you in two months, secure in the knowledge that the northern borders are secure. With such men standing between the Two Kingdoms and the enemy, the people of Kemet can rest easy in their beds. I salute you, men of Kemet's Northern Army."

The men broke into cheers, fists stabbing upward as the officers voiced their enthusiasm for the task ahead. Horemheb let them cheer, walking among them, embracing some, clapping others on the shoulder, exchanging a few words with most. True to his nature, he did not neglect the lower ranks; letting the Leaders of Hundred see he valued them as much as the legion commanders. At last the cheering faded and Horemheb dismissed them. He walked back to his tent with Paramessu.

"I'll take a Fifty with me as honour guard. Who would you suggest?"

Paramessu considered a moment. "Kaha. He's young but he's keen and learns fast. I had him in mind for promotion but he could do with some experience outside of straight army affairs...and I know you'll work him ragged."

Horemheb nodded. "Who will you raise to Commander of Re Legion?"

"Hednakht."

"Really?" Horemheb's eyebrows lifted a fraction. "I thought you would go with one of the officers in your own Re legion."

"Only on merit, I believe you said, sir."

"So I did. Well, it's nothing to do with me. You are in command for two months. Just don't lose me my army."

"I won't sir," Paramessu said with a grin. He saluted his commander and hurried off, eager to issue his first orders as General, though in fact there was little that needed doing in Horemheb's Northern Army.

Horemheb watched him go, his face expressionless, before ducking inside the tent to pack his few belongings for the trek south.

Chapter 14

G eneral Jebu cracked his whip above the rumps of his horses, setting his heavy war chariot flying along the road through the Amorite camp. Soldiers and the inevitable camp followers jumped aside in haste as he passed, though none dared show open displeasure. Men stared after him, thinking thoughts of violence and women muttered imprecations as the chariot disappeared into its cloud of dust. Jebu stared fixedly ahead, ignoring the armed might that lay all around him, goading his horses to ever greater speed. His companion and lieutenant, Ephras, clung to the railing of the jouncing chariot with white knuckled intensity, thankful at least that the stiff breeze off the mountains kept the dust away from them. Instead it trailed west in a dense plume, covering the tents of the encamped army with a thin white pall.

The road branched, one curving eastward toward the distant coast, the other continuing north toward the camp of the Hittite mercenaries. Jebu reined the horses in and let them catch their gusting breaths, flanks zebra-striped with sweat, foam-flecked nostrils gaping wide. He stared to the north at the mercenary camp, ignoring the sentries fingering their small recurved bows as they looked at this intruder with suspicion.

"Martu give me strength," Jebu muttered. "Raman, Thunderer, deliver me from my enemies...and my so-called allies." He jerked his head toward the Hittite camp. "A pox on both Shubbiluliuma and Aziru. They give me gold to raise an army and buy mercenaries, and then hamstring me with such as these."

"The Hittite mercenaries, you mean?" Ephras' voice came hesitantly. One did not draw undue attention to oneself when the General was angered.

"Of course the fornicating Hittites," Jebu snarled. "Who did you think I meant?" Ephras kept prudently silent. "You were there with me in Taanach when they gave me gold..." Jebu caught sight of Ephras' mystified expression. "No, that's right, you weren't. Thank you for correcting me."

Ephras tried to think of a way to decline the dubious honour of correcting his General but could not think of a way that would not get him whipped. He stayed silent, trying to look calm and at ease, however much of a lie that was.

"Aziru gave me gold, much gold, which he said was a gift from that poxed Shubbiluliuma. Gold to buy arms, gold to hire mercenaries, gold to train an army good enough to defeat Kemet. All well and good, Ephras, but what does he do then? I'll tell you," he went on, overriding his lieutenant's silence. "I can buy arms from Hittite merchants only, who sell me bronze, not superior iron. I can hire mercenaries, as long as they are Hittites and I can train my army as long as it never gets good enough to defeat Shubbiluliuma's army. And that is a long way off being good enough to take Horemheb. The gold was a gift but it returns to its giver so fast it has not time to do any good."

Jebu stood motionless in the carriage of the chariot, his hands controlling the horses, his eyes roving over the Hittite sentries. "Look at them, Ephras. I am their Commander, yet they would cut me down without compunction. How does Aziru expect me to weld them into a decent fighting unit?"

"Per...perhaps y...you are not...not meant to, sir," Ephras stuttered.

"Eh?" Jebu dragged his eyes from a glowering contemplation of his supposed allies, and focused them on his shaking lieutenant. "What do you mean? Explain yourself."

Ephras took a deep breath and gripped the rail of the chariot tightly to stop his tremors. He stared ahead at the horses' backs and fought to find the right words. "The Hittites give gold to Aziru so Aziru may wage war on the Kemetu. But then they weaken the effect so Aziru cannot defeat the Kemetu. Who benefits from this situation?"

Jebu frowned. "Go on," he said quietly.

"Yes sir. Well, the Kemetu are weakened by a protracted war. It takes a lot of gold to keep a large army in readiness, even for a war that may not come. We Amorites do not achieve our aim of conquering Kemet and must continually fight our enemies on all sides. We cannot be a threat to any other kingdom."

"But Shubbiluliuma, the puppet master, benefits all round. By all the gods, it is so obvious." Jebu smacked his forehead with the palm of one hand. "The Hittites gain a weakened Kemet and an ineffectual ally in Aziru who will never be a threat but instead will be grateful for their supposed help." Jebu raised an eyebrow inquiringly at the young man. "You thought of this all by yourself?"

"Er, yes sir."

"Very good, Ephras." Jebu stroked his beard thoughtfully. "And have you also thought of a solution to my problem?"

Ephras shook his head. "No sir."

"Then it is as well that I have."

"You have, sir? May...may I ask..."

"Let me think on it, Ephras." Jebu turned the chariot in a wide circle, leaving the rutted road and bouncing over the uneven surface of the plain until they rejoined the road, heading back the way they had come. He kept the horses reined in, denying them their heads, as he concentrated on the problem in hand. The outlying tents of the Amorite encampment reappeared, set among the scrub of the foothill plains. Soldiers were seen in increasing numbers, doing all the things that soldiers do in the eons of boredom between the instants of death and terror. Weapons were sharpened, equipment repaired, fires tended and food prepared, clothes were washed and darned. Those with wives, or with a woman, whether of their own or shared, spent time in drinking and carousing, in making love or picking fights. Most ignored their commander in his war chariot but a few watched him drive by, wondering what his quiet mood presaged.

As they neared the centre of the camp and the large commander's tent, Jebu shook himself, turning his attention outward once more. He nodded, reaching a decision and swung down from the chariot, throwing the reins to a young groom. Ephras followed. The man led the horses off to be groomed and fed while Jebu snapped out a series of command to Ephras and the other men hanging around the entrance to his tent.

"Bring wine, Hittite wine. Find the senior officers, colonels and upward. Have the quartermasters ready to strike camp, but make sure the men have eaten first."

Ephras hurried off to issue further orders that would facilitate his General's commands. He was back at Jebu's tent before the last of the colonels arrived.

Jebu looked round the small circle of senior officers. Most had been with him or in similar armed units for several years, though the men they commanded might be young and ill-disciplined. He nodded to the servants to serve drinks to the officers and accepted a gold cup of fine Hittite wine. Raising his cup, Jebu waited until the murmuring died down, and proposed a toast.

"To victory over Kemet."

The officers dutifully drank--What fool would turn down dark, sweet Hittite wine?--But disbelief showed in their faces.

One of them, a heavily bearded, swarthy-skinned man with a sty in his left eye, lowered his wine cup and belched. "An admirable sentiment, Jebu, but did you bring us here just to voice platitudes?"

"Indeed, no, Simas," Jebu replied. "You, and everyone else here, will soon have the opportunity to strike a physical blow against the might of Kemet, instead of just mumbling into your wine."

The officers muttered among themselves but looked away, not wanting to meet General Jebu's eyes. At length, Simas spoke what was on everyone's mind. "We have heard a lot of talk, General. Even from Aziru when he was here last month, but we all know it'll take more than brave words and gold to defeat Kemet." He looked round at the other officers, hoping for support, but as none came, continued on alone. "Don't get me wrong, I, and most of us are here for the plunder and good Hittite gold is worth fighting for, but really, General, what chance do we have against Horemheb?"

Jebu smiled, twirling his wine cup. "We outnumber him."

Simas nodded. "True, but not by much. Perhaps fifteen thousand to twelve. And his troops are seasoned warriors whereas most of ours are raw mercenaries and half-trained recruits. Barely a third of ours know how to fight properly--or want to."

"Even a farm lad can kill a soldier with a stone or a spear."

"You are dreaming Jebu," Simas sneered. "Before the Kemetu soldiers got within spear range, these farmers would have wet

194

themselves and be half way back to their villages, crying for their mothers."

"Then we must find a way to get our lads behind the Kemetu."

"It will do no good," another officer broke in. "Horemheb is no fool."

"Defeated before you even start, Merru?" Jebu shook his head sadly. "So you will not fight Horemheb?"

"It's not a matter of will not, Jebu," Simas said. "It is just plain folly."

"What if I told you Horemheb is no longer with his army?"

"What?"

"Where is he?"

"How do you know?" A chorus of voices broke out, clamoring for news.

Jebu held his arms out, waving the noise down. "The news arrived last night. One of the Kemetu kings has died and another is to be crowned in Waset. Horemheb has left his army in the field to attend the coronation."

"Gods," Simas expostulated. "His king will have his head for that."

"If you left your men, or I did, no doubt Aziru would have ours." Jebu shook his head. "That won't be Horemheb's fate."

"Then of what significance is the news?" Merru asked.

"He has placed the command in the hands of an untried general, one Paramessu. I say it is time we showed this new general what it is to face an Amorite army."

"And Horemheb is definitely gone?" Simas asked. "How do you know?"

"I have a spy in the Kemetu camp. Gold buys more than soldiers. And yes, Simas--all of you--Horemheb is not with his army and we have the greatest opportunity handed to us. We are going to take the battle to Kemet."

"How, for Martu's sake? We are still out-classed."

Jebu grinned, picking up a long stick and moving to a patch of bare earth. "Gather round. I'll show you."

It takes a long time to uproot an army and goad it into moving, so it was noon the next day before Jebu's army started its slow trek southward. Ahead of them, maybe forty miles away, lay the army of the Kemetu. The Amorites could not hope to surprise the enemy-- moving fifteen thousand men plus their baggage tends to get noticed-- so Jebu sent a picked force of nearly a thousand men on almost all the horses ahead of the column. Their instructions were detailed and explicit and more than a little mysterious as the riders carried few arms; pack horses carrying instead a strange assortment of tools and equipment. They disappeared to the south, the pall of dust raised by their hooves blanketing the trudging men as they set out in slow pursuit.

The land through which they moved was green after the summer rains but already drying. The grass and the unkempt fields of barley were just starting to show the faintest autumn hues, jewels of red poppy and blue cornflower winking among the stems. The farmers had fled the land but the earth still moved in its cycles, the plants and animals largely ignoring the passage of humans. The broad front of the moving army filled the road and burst out on either side, trampling the nascent harvest beyond hope of recovery.

They camped that night by a small stream barely five miles onward, chopping down groves of willow and aspen to fuel the campfires. The next morning, Jebu's army moved on, leaving a great stain on the land where it had rested. Three days more and Jebu, ahead of his strung out army, halted his war chariot on a small spur of the chain of hills that broke the coastal plains north of the Kemetu border. Ahead of them stretched a flat plain, bounded on either side by fields of boulders. Even as Jebu and Ephras watched, trails of men burdened by rocks and boulders trudged from the valley floor to the sides, depositing their loads before retuning for more. Behind the ant-like strings of men lay an area of disturbed earth, strung across the base of the valley as if forming a backdrop to the open stage of the bare and level valley floor.

"Is that wise, General?" Ephras asked. "Clearing the valley of rocks will certainly make it easy for our chariots, but the Kemetu have many more."

"Yes, I suppose they do, but you were there, Ephras. Did you not hear my plan?"

"I heard it, but I did not understand it. How do lines on the ground translate into armies of men?" The young man shrugged. "I doubt others understood it better than I."

"Well, we shall see." Jebu shook the reins and guided his chariot down into the valley, skirting the area of disturbed soil. He gestured to an officer as he came close, gesticulating back at the ground. "Put some guards up there. The army is coming and we don't want accidents."

The man saluted and ran off, calling to his men. Jebu drove the chariot down into the centre of the valley and stopped again, carefully examining the view in all directions. He nodded. "It will do."

A horse and rider came over a ridge far to their left, down the great valley, and spurred toward the lone chariot. As the rider drew closer, they could see it was one of the many spies sent out days beforehand, scouring the ground ahead of the army for news of the enemy. The man reined in his horse hard, sending it down on its withers, dust and gravel showering out. Leaping off the trembling beast, the rider threw himself down on one knee before his general

"Kemetu, my lord," he gasped. "Not five miles from here."

"Are they approaching?"

"No, my lord, but neither have they camped."

Jebu looked up and scanned the skyline anxiously, but all he could see were his own troops still laboring at their tasks and the first of the army vanguard. Turning back to the spy he gestured him to his feet and tossed him a flask of watered wine. The man drank thirstily before belching loudly and wiping his lips and beard with one hand. "My thanks, lord. I needed that."

"Do the Kemetu know we are here?"

"Possibly, my lord, but I think they do not know exactly, just that we are close." The man grinned. "We found a few scouts but none of them made it home. That will tell them we are close, but not where."

"Good man." Jebu reached down and took the flask back. "Rejoin your men, you have done well." He handed the flask to Ephras as the man galloped off, back down the valley to find his unit. "Things are coming together." Urging the horses into motion once more, Jebu wheeled the chariot and walked it back toward the disturbed earth at the head of the valley.

"Ephras, if you had a choice of the time of day to meet the Kemetu on this field, when would you choose?"

The young man looked around, then back at his general, frowning. "I suppose when my men were rested and the Kemetu worn out from marching. If our army gets here soon, they will be tired, so we must camp until morning."

Jebu nodded. "A reasonable answer, but there is a better one. Where is the sun?"

"Down the valley."

"And how long to sunset?"

"Three hours maybe."

"So if we meet the Kemetu in the late afternoon, we will have the sun in our eyes; whereas if we meet them in the early morning, it will shine in theirs."

Ephras looked doubtful. "How will you make the Kemetu attack you when you choose?"

"Wait and see."

The first units of the Amorite army arrived in the valley just over an hour later and Jebu directed their officers as to the disposition of the troops. More arrived, strung out over several miles, and were patiently positioned. When most of his army was present, Jebu looked up at the sinking sun, its deep yellow rays turning the bare grass of the valley plain a gleaming gold. He called Simas to him.

"Simas, I need a cool head this evening. The Kemetu army is down there." He pointed into the lowering sun. "I want you to take your corps, a thousand men, and move down to meet them."

"The plan you made appears clearer to me now I see the field of battle, Jebu, but I do not see how attacking the enemy with so few men gives us victory. Did not your plan call for a battle here?"

"I do not want you to attack, Simas. Walk your men slowly, as if tired after a day's march and do not appear to notice the Kemetu until you are sure they have seen you. Then pull back but stay in sight and crowd together as if you expect an attack."

"What if they do attack? I cannot fight ten times my number on my own."

"They will not. It will be almost dark when you get there and Kemetu do not like to fight at night. Take wood with you and make campfires, let them know you are there. Then wait until the dark before the dawn before coming away in silence. The Kemetu must not know you have gone until first light."

Simas saluted and marched his men away. Jebu dismissed them from his mind and set about having his men fed. He would not allow a proper camp to be made, but allowed each troop and unit to make its own small fire and cook a meal. Bedrolls were laid out around the fires and under the watchful eyes of sentries, the men tried to sleep, putting the anxiety of the coming battle out of their minds as best they could.

Jebu drove his chariot out into the great valley plain until he was alone in the darkness. He looked back towards his army, seeing a constellation of tiny flickering stars littering the indistinct horizon--the fires that shielded them from the outer darkness. In the other direction, down the valley, lay only blackness and silence. Dropping the reins of the horses over their heads, he let them graze while he sat in the short grass and listened to the almost complete silence, broken only by the sighing of a soft breeze through the grass and the rhythmic rip of grass torn out by sharp teeth. A soft thumping noise from near the chariot brought, a few moments later, the sharp ammoniacal smell of fresh dung.

The stars slowly crawled across the sky, moonless until near dawn. Somewhere down the valley a jackal called, long and lonely, echoed by another. Jebu shivered, remembering the Kemetu had a jackal god. He did not doubt that tomorrow night the god, and his creatures, would be feasting on the dead. With a measure of luck, and the will of the gods, good Amorite gods, the dead would mostly be Kemetu.

The moon rose, its pale waning light doing little to dispel the shadows of night. Behind it, low in the east over the back of his waiting army, the sky faded toward gray. With the gray light came the sound of footfall on the grass, many and moving quickly. The horses, standing lock-legged in the chariot traces with heads down, dozing, lifted them and stared, ears pricked forward. Jebu rose to his feet, joints stiff, his tunic and trousers damp with dew. He yawned and faced into the still dark west, whence came the rhythmic sound of men on the move.

Out of the shadows came a figure, half running with sword drawn. The figure started on catching sight of the chariot and the figure by it, half-raising the weapon before recognition swept over him. With a sheepish nod, the man moved on, followed by another, then three, more, until the plain around him seemed alive with pale forms as if ghosts rose from the dark earth beneath.

"General."

Jebu half turned as Simas approached from his left. "What news?" he asked softly.

"They will come," Simas said somberly. "And more than we thought. I hope you are ready for them, General."

"What happened?" Jebu glanced at the soldiers streaming back past him in the growing light before turning his attention back to his officer.

"We found a regiment getting ready to pitch camp. We pulled back, making a show of it and they followed slowly, not really trying to close with us but keeping us in sight as the light faded. Just before dark we saw others come up behind them. We lit fires and posted sentries, making a lot of noise for a while then quieting down. At moonrise we slipped off, silently, leaving our fires smoldering."

Jebu nodded. "You did well, Simas. Now let us hope they take the bait."

Simas grinned. "Oh, they will. Just before nightfall we loosed a volley and killed a few. I think they'll want to avenge their comrades."

Jebu took Simas up into the chariot and coaxed the horses into first a stiff walk then as their muscles loosened, into a trot toward his encamped army. The sky ahead of them paled first then reddened as the sun neared the horizon. Strung across the valley, the vast body of men awoke and greeted the new day with a growing chorus of sounds. Metal clashed and leather creaked. The snorting of horses grew louder as they stamped and blew, shaking the night chill out of their limbs. Plumes of vapor arose, from breath and from urine. Standing to under arms meant no facilities so men and horses obeyed the calls of nature where they stood. Vapor joined the mists that gathered in the lower part of the valley, white and still as if a lake had formed there.

The lone chariot raced now toward the side of the valley and the slight rise on the northern edge where Jebu had made his command post.

Simas' eyes narrowed. "You do not lead the charge, General?"

"No. I will be where I can see what is happening. Look to your own unit, Simas and follow my signal." He slowed the chariot and Simas jumped off, hurrying across to where his men were forming up after their run up the valley. Jebu continued on to the rise and halted, jumping down and handing the reins to a charioteer who stood waiting. He called Ephras to his side. "Is everything arranged?"

Ephras stifled a yawn and nodded; his eyes red and bleary. "Yes, General." He pointed at a group of men standing nearby with tall poles lying in the grass with different coloured banners lying rumpled beside them.

"The men know what to do?"

"They have followed your instructions exactly, sir. Nothing can go wrong."

"Anything can go wrong, Ephras. Learn that if you learn nothing else. This is Horemheb's army we face, even if the son of a whore is not leading them." Jebu shook his head and smiled wryly. "However, my plan is a good one and if the gods smile on us, we will have us a mountain of heads today."

"They come, sir," quavered one of the junior officers. "The Kemetu."

"Be easy, Martas," Jebu growled. "You'll have your opportunity soon."

The lake of mist swirled and flowed, and heads appeared, bobbing slightly as they came. Minutes later the bodies appeared under them, the morning sun glinting off the bronze of the spear tips and swords, the gold of the officers. The tramp of marching feet grew audible to those who waited and a light breeze blew from the lower reaches of the valley, dispelling the mist and bringing with it the wail and bellow of the war trumpets. Jebu shivered at their call but was careful to keep his face impassive. He felt the eyes of his officers upon him.

The Kemetu army poured up the valley in a broad river of men before suddenly halting with a dull thump of hundreds of bare feet stamping into the soil. The units behind continued, veering to left and right before likewise halting. Behind all three, the last of the legions spread out in a thin line, not more than six or seven men deep, across the breadth of the valley. Behind the men could be seen a mass of horses and chariots. The army halted and the martial music died away into a breathless anticipation.

"Does anyone recognise the banners?" Jebu asked.

Ephras pointed. "That's Ptah in the centre, Heru on their left wing, but I cannot recognise the far one."

"Re is on the right," Martas added. "And Set in the rear."

"Horemheb's dog Paramessu is commander of the Re legion," Ephras mused. "Will he lead them today, or stay back to control the whole battle?"

"So we come to it, gentlemen," Jebu said briskly. "Does everyone understand what is to happen?" He scanned the officers around him, nodding grimly at the determined looks. "Good, then let us begin."

Martas signaled to the young men with their banners and as the first full rays of the morning sun burst over the hill behind them, striking low into the eyes of the Kemetu, a yellow banner flew high above the Amorite command post.

The centre of the Amorite army opened and fifty war chariots thundered out, picking up speed as they careened down the gentle slope of the valley toward the enemy.

Chapter 15

Scarab and Khu left the North Palace by the main gate, avoiding the attentions of User-Re, the guard. The king still claimed he commanded loyalty within the town and gave them a ring as a token of his authority. It seemed to work, as it brought help from one of the palace horse grooms who pointed them toward one of the principal artists of the city. The sculptor Neb, the groom said, always worked late in his workshop in one of the streets behind the main palace, torches blazing in a large room filled with slabs and blocks of stone--sandstone, alabaster, granite and marble. The steady hammer and chip of metal on stone could be heard a street away and drowned out the sound of their first tentative knocks. Waiting for a pause in the fusillade of blows, Khu hammered again on the wooden workshop door. The hammering started again then faltered. Faint footsteps approached from the inside, and the latch on the door lifted, a pale face peering out through the crack.

"Who is it? I haven't got time to waste."

Scarab held up the king's ring. "Do you recognise this?"

The man reached out a hand and grabbed it from Scarab, ducking back inside and slamming the door closed. A minute passed, then another, and Khu looked at Scarab with a scowl. He lifted his fist to beat on the door again.

"All right, all right," the man grumbled from inside the workshop, unlatching the door and standing aside to let the young man and woman in. "The ring is genuine, so I will give you help if I can." He eyed the two of them in their stained and worn kilts, the side of his mouth lifting in disdain. "Slaves? Or maybe common servants?" His eyes opened wide suddenly. "Did you steal this?" he said, opening his hand to reveal the ring.

Scarab shook her head and reaching out, took back the ring, slipping it onto the second finger of her right hand.

"How dare you?" the man snapped. "That is Akhenaten's ring and none save the king can wear it."

"He will not mind. I am the king's sister."

The man frowned and stared, first at Scarab, then at Khu. "And I suppose he is the prince Tutankhaten?"

"Do not be ridiculous. This ring is enough token for you to help us, or should I tell the king that Neb the sculptor refused to aid his sister?"

Neb cocked his head to one side and peered at Scarab. "Curious," he murmured. "There is the look of the old king Nebmaetre about you, and if that..." The sculptor broke off and grabbed the young woman's hand, dragging her over to a block of sandstone. Khu hurried after, his hand on the hilt of his small knife, secreted in the belt roll of his kilt.

Neb's eyes flicked over the carving in the sandstone block, then back to Scarab's face. "You do not have the long face or the protruding skull, but the shape of the eyes, the lips, the nose...you are kin to the king." The sculptor's hand traced the relief portrait of Akhenaten, his queen and daughters in the act of giving homage to the living Aten. "You are not the queen, nor one of the daughters..."

"I told you, Neb. I am Akhenaten's sister..."

"Princess Beketaten." Neb dropped to his knees in the powdery dust of the workshop floor. "Forgive my impertinence, great lady. I did not look to see you in the City of the Sun. I thought you in Waset."

"I came to see the king." Scarab motioned to Neb to rise. "But now I see it was a wasted trip."

Neb dusted the rock flour off his body, raising clouds of the fine debris. "You are talking about the imprisonment of the king."

"You know of this?"

"Everyone knows, my lady."

"And yet you do nothing?" Khu interrupted. "He is guarded by what? Fifty soldiers--a hundred? Why do the townspeople not rise up and free him?"

"Two hundred," Neb said quietly. "Of the Amun legion. They have no love of the Aten, or of his people. We cannot congregate in numbers greater than ten, save to praise Amun in his new temple. We cannot see the king. We cannot worship as we used to." The little sculptor shrugged and ran his fingers through his dust laden hair, releasing another billowing cloud. Coughing and sneezing, he led Scarab and Khu across the room to some makeshift furniture in one corner.

Neb dusted off a chair for Scarab and indicated another for Khu. "The king is father to the people, lady. How can we turn everything on its head by rescuing the king? Even if we had the means to do it?"

Scarab nodded. "I understand. I think in all Kemet there is only one man who can overturn this injustice. My friend and I will seek out General Horemheb in the north. He has the army behind him and will not leave the king in captivity."

"How will you find him, my lady?"

"He will be in Zarw, the garrison city, or east of there on the borders with Syria and Sinai, maybe even in Kenaan. People up there will know, but first we have to get there. Will you help us Neb?"

"I, lady?" Neb's jaw dropped. "How can I help?"

"The king said you would give us assistance. That you were loyal."

"To death, my lady, but how can I help? I have neither the skills to fight, nor the influence to sway others."

"Clothes," Khu rasped. "Do you have clothes we can wear? And gold? We can find a boat north to Ineb Hedj if we can pay our fare and if we look the part."

"Clothes I have, but..." Neb looked at Khu's tall figure. "...whether they will fit you is another matter. For you, my lady, I believe I can do a little better. My sister sometimes lives here when she fights with her husband." Neb grinned. "Wedded bliss she does not possess, for all her airs and graces...what I mean, my lady, is that she has left two gowns here. Not what you would be used to in the palace, but in good repair and respectable."

"Thank you, Neb. I shall remember your kindness to the king. He will reward you many-fold in happier times."

"And gold?" Khu reminded the little sculptor. "We must have our passage to Ineb Hedj."

Neb nodded and walked over to the corner of the room, opening a small battered wooden box. He removed some rags and scraps of papyrus before unrolling a cloth bundle secreted in the bottom of the box. Gold gleamed in the folds of the cloth.

"The king himself gave me this over four years ago," Neb said softly. "A chain of honour of twenty deben of fine gold, for a sculpture I made of the queen Nefertiti before her disappearance. I have lived on it for those last four years and now there are but two links left." He held them up in his hands, gazing at them fondly for several minutes before turning and handing them both to Khu. "Take them. They came from the king, it is only right they serve him now."

"We cannot take the last of your gold, Neb," Scarab said.

"We need it," Khu muttered, clenching his fists around the two links.

"Please, my lady. There is little enough I can do. Let me at least set you on the path to finding justice for the king."

In the pre-dawn darkness, Scarab and Khu found themselves down by the docks once more, this time clothed decently, if not in fine raiment, and with considerable wealth in a purse slung around Khu's waist. They kept a wary eye out for thieves but it seemed that even the lawless had decided sleep was to be preferred to wandering the empty streets. Khu found a spot out of the chill breeze off the river, in the lea of a building, and they settled down to wait the hours until dawn.

"We should have waited in the sculptor's workshop," Khu grumbled. "At least there we would be warm."

"I did not like to impose on him further. We already have his clothes and his gold."

A wash of gray light gradually revealed the river and a strangely lessened foreshore. The water lapped fitfully almost up to the base of the docks, green and cold in the wan light of the early dawn. City sounds intruded as the people woke to a new day of work. Softly at first, the murmur of voices and the muted clatter of wood on stone, the clinking of cooking pots on hearth stones, gradually grew in strength and frequency. Smoke tickled the nostrils and the aromas of bread, fresh from the ovens, mingled interestingly with less wholesome smells as each family emptied out the night soil into the drains that led to the river. An old man moved near the docks, busying himself with a long rope, easing the kinks out of it and coiling it. From time to time he looked down at the water near his feet, moving a small stone upward at intervals.

Khu watched with curiosity before suddenly nodding. "The river is rising," he exclaimed. "The floods are upon us. I had forgotten it was time."

"They are early," Scarab replied. "In Waset, the flood was not expected for another half month. How is that going to affect our journey to Ineb Hedj?"

"We have the means to hire a boat and buy food too, but I'm not sure it would be a good idea to be conspicuous here in Akhet-Aten. There are troops of Amun, and hence of Ay, present. We do not want to attract attention."

"We have to have a boat, Khu. We will have to risk it."

"There is another way. If we get someone like that old man to ferry us across the river before the docks get busy, we can get to Akhet-Re without undue notice."

Scarab pondered Khu's suggestion. "I can understand you want to see your family again, but how does that really help us? The villagers are farmers, not sailors."

Khu grinned. "So I have found an aspect of the common life you have not yet learned, noble lady? The harvest is in and the village will be selling a lot of their produce to the cities. Here in Akhet-Aten of course, but also downriver. We can ride with a load of cucumbers and melons to Ineb Hedj."

The old man did not own a boat, but his nephew did, and before the docks became really busy, Scarab and Khu found themselves rocking in a small boat as the nephew sculled away from the eastern bank and into the broad flow of the river. It was swifter than they remembered from the day before, and the middle was discoloured, muddy and swirling as the runoff from the distant source waters swelled the Life of Kemet. The rower cursed, battling futilely against the current, his efforts slopping muddy water over the edges of the boat.

"You will not get paid if you tip us in," Khu said sharply.

The man cursed again but gave up his uneven struggle against the fast-flowing water, angling instead across the current, allowing the boat to be swept downriver, its shadow on the water stretched out before them in the early morning sunlight. They landed at last on a muddy bank almost out of sight of the city. The man helped Scarab out of the boat and stood waiting expectantly. Khu fumbled in his waist purse and took out one of the gold links. The man's eyes widened momentarily, but his face fell as Khu scraped off a shaving of the soft metal with his sharp knife.

"My fee is more than that," the man said sullenly, taking the sliver of gold. "I risked my life out there and I have a long and dangerous row back."

"You already have more than your boat is worth," Khu said in a flat voice. The knife he had started to return to the purse remained in his hand and he shifted his grip on it.

The man's eyes followed the movement and he shrugged; turning and pushing the tiny boat out into the relatively calm water just offshore. Safely away from Khu's knife he turned and abused the pair of them, raining down curses on their heads. He ended with a threat to tell the soldiers before bending his back to the oar and sending the little boat out into the current.

"Set take the man," Khu spat. "I should have killed him. Now he will set the soldiers on our trail."

"How?" Scarab smiled and squeezed Khu's arm. "We have done nothing suspicious and they have enough to do in the city without following up every tale of travelers with gold."

Khu nodded reluctantly and started up the bank. At the top, he scanned the surrounding countryside to get his bearings before heading off at an angle to the riverbank. After a few minutes of scrambling through long grass and *Acacia* scrub, they stumbled upon a narrow dirt road. Scarab looked around and smiled.

"I could be mistaken, but I think I came this way the first time I crossed the river four years ago. It was dark then but this looks vaguely familiar."

"You did," Khu confirmed. "When Min put your bloodied cloak in the river to throw off the search, he found your boat a little further downstream. He told me that night when he returned from doing it."

The fields on either side of the narrow road lay deserted, devoid of crops and workers both, dry and parched in the summer sun. Turning off the road they walked along the edge of the shallow canal that ran inland from the river. In stark contrast to the fields, the irrigation ditch lay wet and glistening, with pools of water harboring swarms of insects and tadpoles. Every few moments a tiny surge would ripple up from the direction of the river, slowly connecting the ponds into a ribbon of water. The level in the ditch slowly rose up the steep banks as they

208

continued. The sun was halfway to the zenith before they reached the village. Dogs barked and children ran screaming from the two strangers as they walked into the space between the huts.

Faces appeared at the doors and a very old man sitting on an old tree stump in the middle of the village, looked up. He had a twisted arm and pock-marked face, his body above the brief linen flap hiding his genitals lined and wrinkled. His eyelids lifted in surprise and his toothless mouth creased into a smile. "Khu? Is that you? Khu, son of Pa-it and Asenath?"

Khu grinned and ran over to the old man, falling to his knees in front of him. "Ankhu, sir, it gladdens my heart to see you in health." He turned and beckoned Scarab. "You may remember each other. Scarab, this is Ankhu, one of the elders of my village. Ankhu, this is..."

"I remember," the old man snapped, his yellowed and rheumy eyes staring up at the young woman. "The last time she was here, the soldiers came and interrogated us. Is she bringing them again?"

"No, sir. Not this time. Nobody knows we are here. We have come to see my family."

"Then it is well you have come, young Khu, for your father Pa-it is unwell."

"Not so unwell I cannot greet my second son," rumbled a voice behind Khu. He turned with a cry of joy to find his father standing behind him, a young boy steadying the old man his father had become.

"Father!" Khu ran to him and fell on his knees, kissing his father's feet.

"Rise, my son." Pa-it's wrinkled hand ruffled Khu's long black hair. "Do you have no word of greeting for your brother?"

"Pa-it-pasherit? Little Pa-it? You have grown." Khu rose to his feet and looked down gravely at his younger brother. "I see a fine young man who is becoming the strong right arm of his father."

"Hello, Khu," little Pa-it said shyly. "I would like to come to Waset to see the King's Councilor from Akhet-Re advising the king. It must be so exciting. Nothing ever happens round here."

"He lies," Ankhu laughed. "Why just last month a dog died."

Khu joined in the laughter. "Believe me, Pa-it-pash, a quiet life in a village is better than an exciting one on the run."

"You are a fugitive?" Pa-it the elder asked. "From whom? How did this arise? I thought you were a respected Councilor."

"King Smenkhkare is dead." Khu went on to describe the events of the past few weeks, finishing with their flight from Waset and the meeting with Akhenaten. "So we must find General Horemheb. He is the only one who can stop Ay."

Pa-it looked past his son to where Scarab stood watching. Behind her, several villagers had come out to listen, standing silently as they heard about events from the wider world. "My lady Beketaten," Pa-it said quietly. "You have our sympathy for the loss of your brother. He was a fine king by all accounts. We will aid you in whatever way we can."

"Is that wise?" Ankhu asked. "Remember the trouble we had last time this girl was here?"

"I am not going to turn my son away." Pa-it's voice was edged with anger. "Nor will I refuse to help the sister of the king. Her enemies are my enemies." He looked around at the villagers. "You elected me head elder. Do you accept my judgment?" Noting the nods and murmurs of agreement, Pa-it turned back toward his hut, his hand on his youngest son's shoulder. "Please come inside, my lady, Khu. I cannot offer you more than bread, water and fruit, but that we have in abundance."

Scarab entered the small hut she had last seen four years previously, looking around as she did so. "Asenath?" she asked, tentatively.

"My wife is visiting our daughter Enehy and assisting her in the birth of our third grandchild."

"Three children! But mother is well? And Imiu and Min?" Khu sat down on a wooden bench by the table, a concerned look on his face.

"Well enough. Your mother is gray-headed and no longer young, but she can at least walk unaided, whereas I must use a staff or a strong young man." Pa-it gazed fondly at his young namesake. "As for Imiu, she still works as a maid in the city and hopes to marry soon--a young scribe with prospects. Min is in Ineb Hedj. He took a boatload of our harvest down there for the better prices."

Khu struck the table with one hand and swore softly. "We have missed it then? I had hoped we could travel to Ineb Hedj on the harvest boat."

"Why do you want to go to Ineb Hedj? You just got here."

"We must find General Horemheb," Scarab explained. "He is the only man who can stop Ay and restore peace to the Kingdoms. He is somewhere on the northern or north-eastern borders. I hope to hear news of his whereabouts when we get to the northern capital."

"You have a long journey ahead of you, and no certain destination. Do you have the funds to support you?" Pa-it frowned and looked at his elder son, then back to Scarab. "The village is poor but we can probably scrape up some barley you can trade." A wry smile flitted across his lined features. "You can take as many melons as you want, but they are difficult to transport in any worthwhile number."

Scarab smiled in return. "Thank you, Pa-it. You have already given me a son who is a strong and loyal friend. I could not have survived without your friendship and help. We have a small amount of gold, sufficient to get us to Zarw at least. We just have to get there."

"The boat has gone, Scarab." Khu grumbled. "Did you not hear my father? We have missed it."

"You missed the boat with the grain and vegetables. We are sending another one tomorrow with melons and cucumbers. You are welcome to travel on that one if the master of it agrees."

"Another boat? You never send two."

"Normally, no," Pa-it said. "But for a time people have been leaving Akhet-Aten and we sell less produce there. We have a surplus and we can get higher prices downriver. We have to act fast though, as the river is rising early this year."

"Yes, we saw the level rising as we came across."

Pa-it nodded. "Tomorrow we move inland to the flood village in the foothills, but first we send the boat north. Rest here and eat something. I will send one of the young men to buy passage for you both."

"We can pay." Scarab motioned to Khu and he took out one of the links of gold. Pa-it's eyes widened as his son cut off a broad sliver of the soft metal with his bronze knife.

"That is too much."

"Then bargain with it, father. Keep the rest for the village. It has been deprived of my labor these past four years."

Pa-it nodded and picked up the sliver of gold. Taking a staff from the corner by the door, he instructed little Pa-it to tend to his brother and the princess' needs, then left. The boy rummaged through the cooking pots and chests and served up a simple but tasty meal of bread, cucumbers and radishes, with draughts of cool clear water to wash it down. As Scarab and Khu ate, he peppered them with questions about Waset and the court, wanting stories of the doings of all the great and not-so-great. In the end, Khu had to order him to be silent, just so they could finish their meal.

Clearing away the dishes, Pa-it started the questions again and Khu, who now just wanted to rest, growled at him. Scarab took the young boy off to a corner of the hut, leaving Khu to sleep, and told him stories of her childhood and the adventures she had with her brother Smenkhkare in Waset. She removed her sandals and together they relaxed on one of the straw-filled pallet beds.

Young Pa-it looked from Scarab to the softly snoring form of his brother. "Are you going to marry Khu?" he asked quietly. "I'd like you as my sister."

"I'd like you as my brother too, but it is not that simple."

"Why not? Khu likes you, I can tell."

"And I like him, Pa-it, but...well, I am sort of promised to another man."

"Oh." Pa-it sat silently for a while. "Do you love this other man?"

Scarab nodded. "Yes."

"Oh." After another long pause, Pa-it looked into Scarab's eyes. "Why are you crying?"

Scarab burst into tears, clutching the boy to her and sobbing for several minutes before she got control of herself. She felt the boy trembling in her arms. "I'm sorry, Pa-it, I didn't mean to scare you. I just miss him so much." She took a scrap of linen from a shelf and looked enquiringly at the boy before wiping her eyes and nose.

"You didn't scare me. I miss mother sometimes when she's away visiting Enehy and I feel sad--but I never cry. It must be because you are a girl."

Scarab smiled. "Yes, that must be it."

The elder Pa-it returned in the late afternoon, a serious look on his face. He woke his son Khu and sent little Pa-it off on an errand. "There are soldiers looking for you. The boat master, Kheper-Atum, says that Akhet-Aten is abuzz with rumor about a young lord and lady that fled from Waset, having stolen the Tjaty's property. They will come here eventually."

"Then we must leave." Scarab shot to her feet and looked around for her sandals.

212

"Sit down, my lady," Pa-it said. "You need the boat and I have persuaded the master to leave at nightfall rather than tomorrow morning. The village has been busy loading the boat all afternoon. Truth be told, I think the master is anxious to leave anyway. The river has risen nearly half a cubit."

As the sun dipped below the western cliffs, sending long shadows drifting toward the river, Scarab and Khu, accompanied by Pa-it and little Pa-it with a burning rush torch, set out for the tiny boat dock that serviced the village. They had eaten again and took with them a rush basket of bread and cooked vegetables for the journey downriver. Unseen by Khu or his family, Scarab had removed the remains of the cut gold link and hidden it in a pot in the kitchen where it would be found after they had left. Her debt to this family was considerable, and Scarab wanted to repay them in some small measure. The remaining link would be enough to get them to Zarw, after which Horemheb would provide.

The dock was in darkness, a single rush torch burning at the back of the boat and an oil lamp flickering inside a small lantern of oiled paper at the prow. The master of the boat, a small wiry man with a shock of white hair, stood by the steering oar, his fingers drumming impatiently on the stock. A young boy sat on the dock, his fingers fiddling with the coarse hemp rope that secured the boat to the shore. The current tugged at the vessel, pulling it away from the dock until the rope stretched and tightened, then slowly drifted in again. The land around the base of the dock was already under perhaps two fingers of water and Scarab and Khu splashed through the rising river to the boat.

"About bloody time," the man in the boat grumbled. "If we wait any longer the current will be too strong."

"Patience, Amentep, it is only just nightfall." He and Khu helped Scarab aboard, then the old man embraced his son and kissed him. "Look after her, Khu. She is your sacred charge."

Khu nodded. "Remember me to mother. Tell her I think of her daily." He tousled the head of his younger brother and clambered aboard.

Little Pa-it handed him the basket of food. "May the gods be with you," he squeaked, emotion threatening to unman him. He knuckled tears away and waved as the boat boy untied the rope and leapt into the stern as the current, so long deprived of its prey, swung the heavily

213

laden boat out into the river. Within minutes all that could be seen was the dim flare of the rush torch moving swiftly downriver. Pait took his youngest son's hand and they started back to the village across the slowly flooding fields.

Chapter 16

General Psenamy arrived in Waset a scant three days before the formal burial ceremony of Smenkhkare. The royal barge from Akhet-Aten found itself forcing its way upriver against a stronger current as the floodwaters of the annual inundation raised the level and increased the flow of water. Instead of the expected fifteen days, the journey took nearly twice as long. Several times, Psenamy considered putting in to the eastern shore and continuing the journey overland. It was only the lack of horses and a chariot for the young royal couple to travel in that dissuaded him.

The barge finally put into Waset with an exhausted crew, the oarsmen straining one final time to bring the craft creeping into the raised flood docks hard up against the city walls. The land rose more steeply on this, the eastern side and the floodwaters seldom found their way into the city past the first few streets. The mud brick buildings tended to collapse when that happened but that concerned no-one important as the dock area was one of the poorest parts of the city. The waters stretched westward like a sea, the already wide river become a vast moving lake as the low-lying flood plain to the west became inundated. The waters washed right up to and into the funerary temples and almost to the new palace of Nebmaetre. Little used since the death of the great king, Ay had prepared the rooms and halls for the arrival of the new king Tutankhaten.

For the time being, however, the prince and princess stayed in the old palace, in rooms considerably less spacious and well-appointed than the palace of Nebmaetre, but having one superlative advantage--

they lay within the suite of rooms that Ay called his own. The prince would not be able to stir without the Tjaty's knowledge and no-one would have access to the prince without his permission.

After a day of settling in to their new rooms, Tutankhaten and Ankhesenpaaten were whisked off to a series of small ceremonies in the hastily refurbished temples of various gods, culminating in the great temple of Amun, where, with a notable lack of ostentation, the young prince and princess were formally married. The coronation would follow in about a week's time, when both young royals would be confirmed as King and Queen of the Two Kingdoms. All reference to Akhenaten would be removed from the ceremony, with people's minds fixed on the bright new future. In the meantime though, came the sad duty of the previous king's burial.

By custom, the heir to the throne led the procession through the city, led the prayers for the dead king's safe passage through the underworld, and was responsible for the ritual 'opening of the mouth' whereby the Ka of the king could once again enjoy the offerings left behind by the mourners. The problem was, Smenkhkare had no body to be buried and far from being in any danger passing through the underworld, had by now passed through the gut of the crocodile and was in no fit state to enjoy anything. It was necessary for the ritual to be carried out, however, if only to show Tutankhaten as the rightful heir to the throne of Kemet.

So it was that on the third day after arriving in Waset, Prince Tutankhaten and his wife Ankhesenpaaten walked through the streets of Waset in an abbreviated procession from the palace to the great palace of Amun. Behind them walked Tjaty Ay and Meryetaten, the ostensible widow of the late king, bereaved but not grieving. The King's Councilors were there too, though not all of them, and they walked hedged close about by guards. Priests met the young heir at the temple gates and he was guided into the inner sanctum where, under the watchful eye of the Tjaty and the new First Prophet Bakt, he stumbled his way through the prayers and offerings.

Devotions over, the young Prince and Princess moved toward the royal docks with the priests and high officials following. They crowded aboard the funeral barge, Tutankhaten and Ankhesenpaaten sitting in state beneath the central awning. The barge moved slowly out into the broad river, the oarsmen digging in their oars and straining as the strong current heeled the barge over. Spray flew, soaking the garments of the mourners and the call of the master rose urgently into the summer evening as he exhorted his men to greater efforts. The barge crabbed sideways across the river and drifted over the flooded fields on the western side. They made good progress now, the deep-digging oars stirring up great swirls of mud in the shallow water, the scarlet tips of the oar blades more often covered in the silty deposition of the flood as they raised aloft in the dying rays of the sun.

The barge ran aground just short of the great funeral temple of Nebmaetre Amenhotep, the funerary priests waiting by a gangplank of boards constructed to carry the mourners dry-shod from barge to land. Stalwart slaves lifted the young royals, the Tjaty, officials and priests from the deck and sloshed through the shallow water, depositing their burdens on the dry boards. The soldiers and their prisoners, the King's Councilors, had to walk unaided. One of them, Physician Nebhotep, lagged behind, making a great show of limping. The Captain of the Guard, anxious to perform his duties impeccably in the presence of Ay, snapped angrily at the physician before ordering another prisoner, Aanen, recently the second prophet of Amun and brother to the Tjaty, to help him.

Aanen waded back to the limping doctor and put his arm around his waist. "Are you hurt, Nebhotep?" he asked solicitously.

"Not at all," Nebhotep murmured. "I have seldom been in better health."

Aanen's arm slipped as the priest stopped suddenly. "Then why..."

"Keep walking, Aanen. You are supposed to be helping me." Nebhotep waited until they were both moving forward again. "I intend to escape."

Aanen said nothing but his expression expressed his doubt.

"It is my only chance. Once we return to the palace we will never leave it alive. We have only been kept alive to be seen with Ay and Tutankhaten. Once we have given our unspoken blessing on the succession, we shall be removed."

"I cannot believe that." Aanen shook his head. "Ay will not just have us killed. It is preposterous."

"No more so than killing the king. Do you doubt he did that?"

Aanen shook his head again. "How will you escape?" he whispered.

"I don't know yet. If all else fails I shall jump overboard on the return journey."

"You would drown in the flood."

"Better death at the hands of the gods than at the hands of Ay."

Once the prisoners had made it to the boards, the procession formed up again, and this time led by the priests of the funerary temple, made their way to dry land. Within a dozen paces they passed from waterlogged soil to bone dry dust, proof if any were needed that the flooding came from the river, not the skies. The doors of the funerary temple were wide open, a blaze of torches banishing the encroaching darkness. Smenkhkare, as son of Nebmaetre Amenhotep, was granted the right to lie in honour in his father's temple, attended by the priests dedicated to his rites.

"How is that possible?" Councilor Meres muttered, shifting his great bulk uneasily as the procession made its way into the inner precinct of the temple. "Smenkhkare's body was not recovered. How can he be here?"

"It is not his body, you fool," hissed Scribe Kensthoth. "No more than it will be his body that the prince applies the Pesheskef, the Seb Ur and the Ur Hekau to. They have an effigy of the king. That is all."

"Quiet!" the Captain of the Guard snapped. "Remember where you are."

The funerary priests lifted the ornately carved and painted wooden casket, so large it was almost the size of the great stone sarcophagus, carrying it reverently as if it truly contained the body of the king and carried it outside the temple to the waiting ox-cart. Wheel-less, the massive wooden sled surged and hesitated as the beasts strained and heaved, pulling it over the pot-holed surface of the road toward the Great Place, the Valley of the Burial of Kings.

Full night was on the funeral procession by the time it passed through the gates of the Great Place and into the Ka-haunted valley. Despite the crowd of burning torches and oil lamps, the blackness seemed impenetrable beyond the firelight. The prince looked warily into the darkness, his hand clutching that of his new wife. After several turns and an hour of heaving the great wooden sarcophagus over the rubble of the valley, the ox-sled ground to a halt near an unprepossessing mound of rocks and sandstone chips. The dark grave mouth yawned in front of them, waiting to be fed with the fruits of death.

The sarcophagus was unloaded by the funerary priests with much grunting and straining, the soldiers finally having to lend a hand to wrestle the casket upright in front of the tomb steps. The painted golden face of a stylized king stared out at them from the casket lid. Painted hands, crossed over painted breast, grasped the crook and flail of kingly authority, the cobra and vulture of the Two Kingdoms adorning the wooden brow. Other priests brought food and drink, bread, meat and wine, and laid it on the ground near the casket before stepping back.

Bakt advanced and started into the recital of the prayers for the dead king. His voice droned on and the watchers and listeners shifted uncomfortably on the stony ground, shivering in the chill wind that blew off the desert and shook the torch flames. The prayers finished abruptly and the Hem-netjer of Amun handed Prince Tutankhaten the Pesheskef, bidding him touch the lips of the image with the tip. The boy nodded and advanced on the upright casket, the adze-like tool raised.

"I open the mouth of my lord Djeserkheperu," Tutankhaten said in a loud but shrill voice, He strained upward with the Pesheskef but fell short of the painted lips. He tried again, giving a little hop, but was again unsuccessful.

"Let me help you, my lord." Ay moved forward and, old man though he was, grasped the young boy firmly and hoisted him up into the crook of one arm. "Open the king's mouth."

Tutankhaten dutifully touched the adze to the casket then handed it down to Bakt, who handed him the next implement, the Seb Ur. The Ur Hekau followed and Ay nodded gravely, lowering the prince to the ground.

"I am confused." Kensthoth's clear voice filled the circle of light. "Has the heir opened the mouth of our beloved Djeserkheperu or has Ay caused it to be done? Who is our next king?"

Ay whirled, his eyes and lips compressed, his fists opening and closing by his sides. "I am a loyal servant of the king," he hissed. "And that is more than can be said of you, scribe." He signaled to the Captain of the Guard. "Silence that man and keep him quiet. He disturbs the peace of this sacred occasion." The Captain nodded and a soldier cracked the old scribe over the head with the butt end of his spear. Kensthoth crumpled, a gash on his head leaking bloodily into the dry dust.

Ay nodded in satisfaction and turned back to the tomb. "Continue."

The funerary priests heaved at the heavy casket and slowly tipped it and lowered it into the tomb entrance. It teetered on the edge of the steep stone steps cut into the rock and finally, restrained by ropes and sweating men, descended into the depths of the chill earth. Lit torches descended with it as the priests wrestled the sarcophagus into a small chamber at the end of a short stone corridor. The priests returned to the surface and brought down the baskets of food and jars of wine, arranging them close to the casket. Others carried down grave goods, though the quality was not high and in many cases the finer articles were mere models of the right things. The burial itself was quickly finished. Three workmen, who had appeared tardily from the village outside the gates of the valley, filled in the stone wall at the bottom of the steps before applying a coat of plaster. One of the funerary priests pressed the official seal into the wet plaster and Bakt, as Hem-netjer of Amun, added his mark.

"That's it?" Aanen muttered. "A king of Kemet is buried with such a miserly display? They tempt the gods."

Leaving some of the guards behind to watch as the workmen filled in the stairwell with rubble, the funeral party started back down the valley, Councilors Kenamun and Meres supporting a dazed and groggy Kensthoth.

"We have a chance," Nebhotep murmured as he stumbled down the trail beside Aanen. "There are fewer guards now."

"Where will you do it?"

"Are you not coming with me, Aanen?"

The priest shrugged, falling silent as the Captain of the Guard walked back down the file. They passed out of the gates and down the road toward the funerary temple complex and the waiting barge. As they neared the temples, the oxen and sled was led off to one side and most of the priests departed also, bowing low to Ay and the Prince and Princess. The head priests continued down past the temples toward the vast sheet of water that spread out before them, the distant lights of the eastern city casting arrow-thin streaks of gold and copper on the glassy surface.

Tutankhaten, who had been very quiet since leaving the burial valley, walking arm in arm with his older wife, stopped suddenly. "I want to visit my father Nebmaetre in his temple," he announced, an obstinate look on his face.

Ay's face reflected surprise and annoyance. "This is not a good time. You can come back tomorrow."

"I don't want to come back tomorrow. I want to see him now." The boy screwed up his face and stamped his foot.

Ankhesenpaaten smiled at Ay. "Is my lord Tutankhaten not within his rights, my lord Ay? I understood that as heir, his word was law."

"Oh, very well." Ay looked edgily at the prince as he started back toward the temple gates, the priests fawning about him, then at the captive Councilors standing with the guards. He hesitated. "Captain, get the...the prisoners on board. I shall be with the Prince."

"Lord Ay," the princess called. "You are required to attend upon the heir, together with an honour guard."

Ay swore, signaling to the Captain and three soldiers to follow him. "Get them aboard," he hissed at the remaining three soldiers. They saluted and started herding the Councilors onto the boards that led over the flooded fields to the royal barge.

Aanen moved closer to Meres and Kensthoth. "We are going to escape," he whispered. "There will not be a better opportunity."

Meres looked fearfully at the remaining guards carrying burning brands and spears, then at the surrounding water. "Escape where? And why? We are well treated."

"Speak for yourself," Kensthoth grumbled. "But you are right, friend Aanen. You should try to escape. Find the princess Beketaten."

"You do not believe she is dead?" Aanen nodded. "Perhaps you are right." The priest glanced around, noting their positions near the end of the boards and the inky bulk of the barge lying in the darkness some twenty paces away. "The guards will have to put down either torches or spears to help us on board. There are only three of them. Either way, we scatter. They cannot catch us all."

Kensthoth shook his head. "I am injured and friend Meres here is too fat. Make good your escape, Aanen. I will distract them." The old scribe lumbered into the water and splashed knee-deep toward the barge. "Help me up, guards, I feel dizzy and my head hurts..." He fell forward, grabbing at one of the guards, pulling him down into the water.

The guard yelled and dropped both torch and spear as he tried to save himself. He rose spluttering, casting about in the muddy swirls for his spear. One of the others ran forward, hesitated, then stuck his spear point down in the mud, holding the torch aloft as he grabbed for his companion.

Meres splashed forward too, yelling that Kensthoth was drowning, and to help the man. Sailors looked down from the deck of the barge and laughed. Two started to climb over the sides to help the soldiers but the barge master waved them back. Aanen, Nebhotep and Kenamun edged backward on the boards, the guard beside them staring at the watery melee, laughing. A nod and Nebhotep grabbed for the burning brand, wresting it out of the guard's hand and whirling it away across the water. At the same instant, Aanen pulled at the spear but the soldier held tight, his laughter turning into a roar of rage. Kenamun hit at him with a fist and the guard fell backward off the boards into the water.

"Run!" Nebhotep yelled. He ran back along the boards but saw lights bobbing on the road that led to the temple and surmised the altercation had been heard. He jumped off into ankle-deep water and splashed off into the darkness.

"Over there!" a sailor yelled, pointing, but nobody took any notice, too caught up in what was happening closer at hand.

Aanen took to the water immediately, lifting his feet high as he attempted to leap free of the clinging water with each stride. Kenamun went with him, his feet slipping on the muddy bottom as he waded through the knee-deep water. He fell behind, his bulk slowing him.

Behind them both, the fallen guard got to his feet and shouted after them, hearing the loud splashes and seeing the white foam as they churned the surface. He raised his spear and cast, the wet shaft whipping thin scatters of droplets as it flew. The point entered Kenamun's thigh, just below the left buttock, and he fell with an agonized scream, cut off as his head plunged beneath the surface.

Aanen stopped dead and turned, looking back at the stricken toymaker-Councilor, then at the guard forging through the water, his sword drawn. With a muttered prayer to his god Amun, he resumed his floundering run, rapidly passing into the darkness of the flooded night.

From the shelter of a clump of flooded palms only a hundred or so paces away, Nebhotep watched the drama unfold. He saw the priest floundering in the ever-deepening water as he waded further from the barge and called out to him, softly at first, then louder and more urgently. He heard and turned, eventually coming to the meager shelter of the palms.

"Nebhotep, thank the gods. Did you see what happened to Kenamun?"

The physician nodded. "He is not dead. I saw the soldier help him up and half carry him back to the boards."

Aanen turned and watched the men milling about near the royal barge. He could easily make out the figure of his older brother Ay. "I don't see the prince."

"Ay turned him back," Nebhotep said. "When he saw the disturbance he gave the royals into the care of the priests and brought the other guards back at a run."

"What will he do?"

"Ay? You know him better than I," Nebhotep replied. "You tell me."

Aanen considered. "He will make the best of it. After all, what harm can we do him? Had we remained Councilors, perhaps we could have argued against his policies. We effectively resigned when we ran."

"Do you think he will pursue us?"

"Not personally, but I think the guards will have a good motivation to hunt us down. Look." Aanen pointed to where Ay confronted the guards and remaining ex-Councilors on the boarded path. Despite the loss of several torches, enough light was still shed by the remainder to reveal the anger of Ay.

"Fools! Imbeciles! I leave three trained soldiers to guard old men and fat slugs and you cannot even do that." Ay shook his fist under the noses of one of the soldiers, who quaked visibly. "How did it happen? You. You're the one who dropped his spear like some half-witted peasant. Answer me!"

The soldier stammered, wanting to edge away from the Tjaty's anger but not daring to, afraid of angering him more. "He...he was h...hurt, sir. I w...went to h...help him and...and he pulled me down. I...I couldn't..."

Ay backhanded him across the face, hard, sending the man reeling back a few paces. "Menre," he snapped. As the Captain of the Guard stepped up, Ay pointed at the man on the ground. "I want that man flogged. A hundred lashes."

Menre bowed but hesitated. "A hundred lashes will kill the man, sir," he murmured.

"Why should I care?" Ay turned away, his anger making his body shake. "A hundred lashes I said and if he survives he is to be dismissed. I will not have incompetents in my guard."

The condemned man moaned and rolled his eyes but said nothing.

"Yes, sir," Menre said reluctantly. "As soon as we return to the city." The Captain turned to his men. "Get these men aboard the barge."

"No." Ay snapped. "Captain, you will kill these men right here and now."

"Sir?"

"You heard me. Kill them."

Kensthoth shook off the arm of one of the guards. "What are you talking about, Ay? We have committed no crime. We are King's Councilors." Meres and Kenamun, the latter clutching his bloodied thigh, added their voices to the protest.

Ay swiveled his head and stared at the portly scribe. "You are no longer Councilors, your king is dead. As for a crime, you attacked one of my soldiers and fostered rebellion among the others so they fled from my appointed authority."

"That is not a capital offence, Ay. I know what I'm talking about."

Ay swung round on the Captain. "I gave you an order, Menre. Must I draw my sword and do your duty for you?"

Menre saluted. "Men, hold the prisoners." At once the soldiers leapt forward and grabbed each man by the arms, forcing them to their knees on the boards. Menre drew his sword.

"You cannot do this Ay," Kensthoth rumbled. "You exceed your authority. Only the king or the duly appointed courts can take lives."

"Fool, I have all the authority I need. Until we have a king, I act for him." Ay nodded to the Captain. "Do it."

Menre plunged his short sword into the scribe's neck, the sharp blade ripping through cartilage and arteries, sending a bright scarlet jet of blood fountaining across Meres next to him, bloody froth staining his lips. The merchant screamed, his cries cut short as the blood-spattered bronze sliced across his throat in a fresh welter of crimson. The two slaughtered men collapsed as the soldiers released them. Kenamun the toymaker struggled to his feet and stared at the Captain as he stepped in front of him.

"The gods will judge you Captain...and you Ay." He gasped and shuddered as the sword plunged into his belly. He sank back down to his knees with a deep groan of pain. The soldiers released him and he toppled face down into the water.

"Clear this mess away," Ay snarled. "And quickly. The prince will be returning to the city."

The guards hastened to drag the bodies back toward the dark shadows behind the funerary temples, while others sluiced water over the boards, sponging them down with the toymaker's own robes. The condemned soldier helped, adding his tears of terror to the wet boards.

The funerary priests appeared once more, escorting the prince and princess from the temple, leading them down to the water's edge. Ay bowed as the young royals approached.

"We should be getting back, my lord. Tomorrow will be a long day."

Tutankhaten yawned loudly, covering his mouth with one hand. "Where are the others, uncle?" He looked around. "I want to ask the scribe a question."

"He is staying here, my lord. He has already gone. Now if you will accompany me?" Ay gestured and the priests picked up Tutankhaten and Ankhesenpaaten, and carried them out to the drifting barge. The barge master released his sailors, who helped the young children on board. Ay was the last on board. He turned and stared back into the darkness stretching away on either side from the little island of light around the boards, the funerary priests and the guards.

"Find them, Menre. Find them and kill them. They cannot have gone far."

"Kill who, uncle?" Tutankhaten tugged at the Tjaty's arm. "Who are the soldiers going to kill?"

Ay forced a smile onto his face as he turned to face the young boy. "Nothing to cause you concern, my lord. Just some enemies of Kemet. I will always be here to protect you."

Chapter 17

"**M**y lord General? Do we advance?"

Paramessu ignored the question and scanned the battle lines drawn up across the valley. The early morning sun dazzled him and he squinted, one hand to his brow. The wooden platform he stood on moved slightly and his muscles tensed. His breakfast of beer, bread and stale meat bolted quickly at dawn sat like lead in his guts, the fear he dared not let his men see gripping his belly like talons. He belched and acid flooded the back of his throat, making him swallow hard. His stomach felt knotted and tight and had been getting worse in the days since he took over command of the combined legions of the Northern Army. Balancing on a hastily erected dais did not help, but at least it enabled him to see over the heads of the fighting men to gain some semblance of an overview. Fighting down a feeling of nausea he turned to look down on his legion commanders, a forced smile on his face.

"Well, gentlemen, are your legions ready? We have the Amorite army at bay and I intend to crush them."

His commanders looked from one to the other, then, almost to a man, nodded or gave audible signs of confirmation. Only one, a tall, thin, hawk-nosed man, by coincidence commander of the Heru legion, its hawk emblem not unlike its commander's profile, nodded reluctantly. "Permission to speak, General?"

"Of course Djedhor, but make it quick." Paramessu laughed. "We have Amorites to kill."

"I am suspicious. We clearly outnumber them yet they did not vanish in the night like they have before. And this morning we find them waiting for us."

"They probably did not know we were so many," observed a grizzled older man with a white scar down the left side of his body. "My Ptah legion met the vanguard of their army last night. They withdrew and no doubt reported a single legion." He spat to one side. "Five of my men died by their arrows. I have sworn to revenge myself a hundred-fold."

"Good, Amentep, well said." Paramessu nodded. "Hednakht, is Re ready for battle?"

Young commander Hednakht bowed; aware he owed his promotion to his new general. "We are, sir," he said crisply.

"And Khui? Is Set prepared?"

"Indeed we are. Just look around you." Khui waved his hands expansively at the legion that surrounded the dais. "We are just awaiting your orders, general."

"Then, gentlemen, I think we will begin."

"Just like that." Djedhor looked as if he had drunk sour wine, his face set in a disapproving grimace. "Do we not have a battle plan? Horemheb would..."

"...Would beat the excrement out of these dogs," Hednakt broke in. "Not only do we outnumber them, but a Kemetu soldier is worth three Amorites. We'll slaughter them."

Paramessu frowned. "Yes, we have a plan, Djedhor--a simple one. We will advance in battle formation until we are in arrow-shot of their front ranks. We loose a volley and send in the heavy chariots. We have nearly two hundred and they will smash their line, scattering it like geese before the fox. Then we mop up the remnants."

Djedhor grimaced. "It could work, General," he admitted. Suddenly he shrugged and smiled. "The Heru legion will be there when you need us, sir."

The General nodded. "I know you will all do your duty for Kemet. Now, back to your legions and wait for my command." He beckoned the small group of trumpeters over to him. They came at a run, clutching their instruments, and joined the group of runners just behind the General's dais.

Paramessu looked over his army carefully, waiting until all commanders were in position and the men ready. Somewhere ahead, behind the dazzle of the sun, stood the enemies of Kemet, the clean, stone-free lines of the valley rising up in a gentle swell. He muttered a quick prayer to the several gods and chopped down with his right hand. "Signal the advance," he said firmly.

The brassy wails rang out in the cool morning air and with a heavy sigh, all the legions except Set lurched forward, the ground trembling beneath the sandaled feet of twelve thousand men. The ragged lines swiftly settled into a march as they moved up the valley. Paramessu clambered down and instructed the soldiers to carry his observation platform forward.

"Nearly there," Paramessu muttered to himself. He counted out the paces and at fifty, called out to the signalers. "Sound the halt." A sharp, strident note suddenly cut off and a heartbeat later the feet crashed into silence. "Archers at the ready." A rapid series of notes. "Chariots prepared." A skirl dying in a flutter.

Paramessu climbed back up onto the platform and scanned the battle lines once more. The sun had risen slightly and while still full in his eyes, at least enabled him to make out the enemy lines, though in no detail. He lifted his arm to send the volley of arrows on its way and halted, arm upraised, head cocked to one side, listening. A low rumble grew in intensity, along with the cries of men and horses. "Chariots, by the gods." He swung round to the trumpeters and screamed, "Loose the arrows."

A thousand bows bent and a thousand shafts flew high, silhouetted against the blue of the morning sky for an instant before plunging into the dazzle that was the Amorite army--but over the heads of the light war chariots that thundered down the valley. Paramessu froze, his mind whirling. "Release our chariots," he screamed. The blare of the trumpet was drowned as the heavy war chariots of the Kemetu army rolled left and right around the central Ptah and Set legions, picking up speed as they trundled into the narrow lanes flanked by Heru and Re. Men from these legions, acting under orders from their commanders, Djedhor and Hednakht, as they reacted in a time-honoured way to the threat of chariots, spilled out into the narrow aisles. The men, armed with long spears, knelt, their weapons leveled and pointing in bristling hedges at the oncoming Amorite chariots. Kemetu chariots, unable to stop in time, unable to swerve because of the press of their fellows around them, overran their own troops, killing and maiming, before bouncing and bucking over the screaming obstruction into the level plain beyond the army.

The Amorite chariots, few in number and far more maneuverable, turned aside from their charge at the last minute, sweeping along the front of the Kemetu, releasing arrows in a stinging cloud that, while it did little damage, plunged the front lines into confusion. The chariots then turned and fled back to the safety of their own lines, leaving only Kemetu dead on the valley floor.

Paramessu groaned, his hands covering his face as he wept for his men. Lifting a tear-streaked face he called for the 'Stand to', waiting in an agony for the troops of the three front line legions to form up into ranks again. The chariots milled around in the front of the army, as their commander, Khaenmaat, tried to decide what to do. The dead and wounded were carried back behind the army where a small cadre of physicians got to work on the survivors.

"Runner, get to Khaenmaat, Commander of Chariotry. Tell him to proceed up the valley at speed and smash their front line. When he bursts through he is to turn and hit them again from the rear. The legions will support him." Paramessu called three other runners closer. "To the legion commanders, advance rapidly behind the chariots and engage the broken elements of the Amorite army before they can reorganize."

The runners raced off and after a few minutes resolution returned as the chariots formed up in a loose squadron, the legions muttering and heaving with the excitement of imminent conflict. An order rang out and the chariots leapt forward, Khaenmaat in the lead, his gold chain of office bouncing and gleaming as he turned to wave his men forward.

The valley sloped upward gently, enough to counter the vigor of the horse teams pulling the heavy chariots, though because the valley floor was for some reason devoid of rocks, smooth and level, the armed might of Kemet moved at a full gallop by the time they reached the Amorites.

The legions of Heru, Ptah and Re ran forward in the wake of the chariots, uttering a roar of defiance at the enemy. As they ran, they started bunching together. At first, the commanders yelled at their men to maintain their ranks, to keep formation, but as the advance disrupted, they saw that the valley sides were to blame. The low rocky edges of the valley moved inexorably inward as the army moved higher. The legions to left and right, Heru and Re edged sideways as they ran, avoiding the rocky ground but pushing inward, obstructing their fellow soldiers. The advancing army became a disorganized mob of armed soldiers.

Paramessu, still atop his shaky platform in the Set legion, saw the developing chaos and swore violently. Lifting his eyes above the mob he saw his chariots impacting the Amorite line and crashing through it. "Yes!" he screamed. "We have them, men. We have broken through." The men of the Set legion raised a cheer, shaking their spears in the air. Paramessu jumped down and pushed his way to the front of the line where Khui stood impatiently.

"Well, General? What are our orders? My men deserve to share in the victory."

"And they shall. Advance Khui, advance and conquer." Paramessu ran out in front of the troops and exhorted them to follow, turning and starting up the valley toward the sounds of fighting. With a great cry of joy, Khui and the Set legion followed. Unseen by the Kemetu, a red banner rose and fluttered above a slight rise on the right flank of the enemy.

At the head of the valley, Khaenmaat roared with triumph as his heavy war chariot tore into the enemy line ahead of his squadron. His triumph turned to surprise then rage as the Amorites melted away from the thundering chariots, drawing together into thin islands of men with open channels between them. The horses swerved slightly toward these openings, pulling against the reins of the charioteers, and ran down the aisles. The Kemetu chariots streamed through the Amorite army, doing little real damage, though many had succumbed to the trampling hooves and crushing wheels.

Khaenmaat saw open ground in front of him, a bare earth expanse and grinned. "Turn," he howled above the drumming hooves and metallic din of the battle. "Turn and hit the dogs from the rear." His chariot sped out onto the bare earth, his squadron behind him. The charioteers slowed their racing horses and started them into the turns, practiced so often before. Khaenmaat had turned his head to look back at the following squadron and suddenly saw one just disappear in front of his eyes. The clouding dust rose in billows but the chariot had vanished as if it never existed, not become enveloped in dust. Another...and another...his world lurched, and Khaenmaat flew over the chariot railing as the vehicle dropped away beneath him. Horses screamed in terror and men cried out. He tumbled, catching glimpses of a sky so blue it hurt, of rich brown earth and for an instant he remembered the golden and green river valley of his birth. He landed hard, the breath knocked out of him and he lay there trying to collect his wits. A deep silence descended over the earth.

What happened? Did I hit a rock? He struggled to rise but found himself unable to move. Looking down, Khaenmaat found himself staring at a bloody stake apparently rising out of his belly, the skin torn and ragged around the point where it erupted from him, his body and the surrounding earth soaked in blood. He stared uncomprehendingly, feeling no pain, hearing nothing. *I cannot be seeing that*, he thought. *I feel nothing. Am I dead?* Turning his head he saw the lip of the pit and the tangle of his chariot and the team of horses. The charioteer lay still, his head at an odd angle, but the horses lay thrashing, mouths open and bloodied yet strangely silent.

Comprehension dawned. "Oh, gods," he muttered. "A pitfall. I am dead--we all are." With his words, sound returned, at first as if muffled through layers of cloth but presently in full strength. He struggled to sit up again and pain swept over him, setting his body ablaze with ice and fire. Khaenmaat screamed, his voice rising in a wail of horror and agony from one of the pits that sprinkled the bare earth at the head of the little valley. Behind the shattered remnants of Kemet's chariot squadron rose the sounds of battle.

The rabble that was once the pride of Kemet's legions crashed into the firm ranks of Amorite soldiers that formed up as soon as the chariots had passed. The line was thin, but armed with long spears and the Kemetu had been expecting chaos following on the heels of the chariot squadron. The line held and pushed forward, the long spears stabbing. Kemetu found themselves hemmed in by their fellows, without the room to swing curved copper swords or wield the heavy stone maces. The noise of battle grew louder as the toll mounted, injured men falling to the ground clutching bloody wounds or crushed limbs, others pushing forward and trampling friend and foe alike.

231

Thought fled, mind and body working in the familiar drill routines as the Kemetu were slowly pushed back.

A tremor ran through the mass of struggling men and cries of "Set! Set!" echoed from the rear. The pressure built once more as the last of Paramessu's legions joined the battle. The balance of the swaying armies changed and abruptly the Amorite line gave way, so suddenly was the pressure released that the front ranks of the Heru and Re legions fell forward, weapons flying. If the Amorites had turned and attacked then great would have been the slaughter. But they did not, choosing instead to fall back. Picking themselves up, the stumbled Heru and Re soldiers joined their fellows running forward, cries of triumph and anger building their courage.

Djedhor laid about him with his whip of office, screaming at his men to listen, to form into units. "Stop, you fools. The battle is not yet won. Form into ranks." The men rushed by him, ignoring his threats and pleas as the Amorite troops jogged back up the valley, drawing the disorganized legions behind them.

The Heru commander saw Paramessu among the Set legion and fought his way across the flow of troops to his side. The General grinned fiercely, his unused sword in his hand as he pointed it up the valley. "We have them on the run, Djedhor."

Djedhor grabbed at Paramessu and swung him round. "They are not running. They are falling back in good order. It is a trap."

"Nonsense. Their spirit is broken. Khaenmaat's chariots broke their back and now we will mop up the remnants."

"Then where are the chariots now? If they succeeded they should be attacking from the rear."

A flicker of movement from the valley side caught Paramessu's eye as he opened his mouth to reply. A blue banner arose among the rocks and boulders and waved above the churning dust that filled the battlefield. "What in the name of Re is that?"

Djedhor looked then swore violently. "It is a trap. I don't know what it means but the Amorite general is still in control of his men, which is more than can be said of you...sir."

At the head of the valley, just short of the torn up earth where the pride of Khaenmaat's chariot squadron lay dead or dying, the Amorite troops, as abruptly as if they heard a command above the din of the pursuing soldiers, stopped and turned once more, shield fitting into shield, spears leveled. The intermingled legions burst on the shield wall and faltered.

Above the pall of dust a green banner rose. From the rocks and boulders that littered the sides of the valley, a mass of men emerged, armed with bows, and great quivers of arrows slung about their hips. The green banner dipped and a black cloud rose from each side, arcing high into the heavens to descend in a lethal downpouring from the cloudless sky.

Men died. Many more fell wounded and screaming as the massed Amorite archers rained down a deadly hail of arrows on the Kemetu horde. Within minutes of the first volley, the numerical advantage of Paramessu's army had disappeared. Paramessu saw the slaughter from the rear, where he stood aghast. Djedhor acted. He dived into the melee of men and pulled out a signals trumpeter.

"Sound the retreat," he screamed.

The signaler looked from the legion commander to his General, hesitating. Paramessu nodded and the trumpeter raised his copper instrument and blew the quavering notes of a 'general retreat'--seldom heard by a Kemetu army.

"Again."

The metallic notes sounded again, louder and clearer. Heads turned, questioning, then all through the milling mass of soldiers, men suddenly reached a decision, turning and fleeing down the valley. Many of them dropped their weapons in their haste to escape.

Paramessu shook his head, trying futilely to restrain the men as they streamed past him, determined to put as much distance behind them and death as they could. "It is too much," he yelled. "It is becoming a rout. If we don't stop them they won't stop running until they reach Kemet." He shook the trumpeter who was still sounding the retreat over and over. "Stand to," he urged. "Sound the 'stand to'...then the 'form ranks'...quickly, man, before we lose them."

The new calls resounded, alternating, over and over. For a long while there was little effect, the thousands streamed back down the valley, pursued by ragged volleys of arrows as the discipline of the Amorite archers became diluted by excitement. Paramessu and Djedhor, dragging the trumpeter with them, moved down the valley with the mob of men, out of range of the archers.

"We have a respite," Djedhor observed. "But the enemy will be down on us very soon and there will be no stopping them unless we can form up into some semblance of order."

"Not even that if they send their chariots again." Defeat sounded in Paramessu's voice.

"They cannot. Our dead litter the field too much to allow passage." Djedhor stared at his general then reached out and slapped him hard, snapping Paramessu's head to one side. First shock, then anger flared in the man's eyes and Djedhor nodded in satisfaction. "The first independent command is the hardest. So you have lost a battle. Don't lose an army."

Paramessu nodded, the anger leaking from his expression to be replaced by determination. "Take the left flank, Djedhor. Rally the men." He wheeled and strode off through the men who still ran and scrambled back down the valley. Their pace had slowed now that death no longer rained down on them and their limbs mindlessly heeded the trumpet calls. "Hold, men," Paramessu bellowed. "Heru, Ptah, Set, remember who you are. Re, my beloved legion, will you desert me now? Hold, take heart, and look to your fellow soldiers. Remember we fight for our beloved Kemet, our honour. Form your ranks and together we will come out of this with glory."

The downward motion ceased and soldiers stared about them, unable to meet the eyes of the men next to them. Eyes downcast, they sought out the legion colours and started to form rough lines, facing back up the valley. Officers, from legion commanders to Leaders of Fifty raced up and down the lines, pushing and bullying the men in their commands. Not all the soldiers were armed, having dropped their weapons in their haste. Now those who still had spear and curved sword, shared them. Others, without the means to defend or attack, stood behind the front ranks; stood ready to step forward when a man fell, ready to pick up his weapon and fight.

Long before they were ready, a gentle wind from the northeast carried the dust cloud over the rim of the valley and revealed the Amorite army on the move. They filed down from the rocky heights of the valley sides and picked their way through the dead and wounded, blades rising and falling, slowly quieting the screams and moans of fallen Kemetu. Paramessu's army muttered angrily at the sight, the outrage growing to a roar of disapproval and anger. Individuals ran out from the rough-formed lines, waving weapons and shouting threats, only to be herded back by whip-wielding junior officers. The commanders took advantage of the men's mood, goading them to anger and a desire for revenge while still urging discipline.

The Amorite regiments moved down past the bulk of the fallen and stood in ranks, facing the Kemetu legions. A lone chariot raced out from one flank and sped across the face of the army. A man stood in the chariot alongside the driver, shouting and waving his fist at the troops. A wave of enthusiasm and cheering erupted from the ranks as the chariot passed.

"The Amorite general," Djedhor observed. "He has a decent victory to hand his men and he's using it to whip up their fervor."

"He can rant all he likes," Paramessu growled. "He'll not get another victory over me."

"May the gods of Kemet grant us that, but do not get over-confident. We still have a tough fight ahead of us."

Paramessu looked at the old hawk-faced warrior covertly. "I think Horemheb made a mistake," he admitted. "You should be Commander-General, not I."

"Very true. I am senior officer and I've had vastly more experience than you, Paramessu," Djedhor said quietly. "I was expecting Horemheb to give me command." He glanced around to make sure they were not overheard. "I got where I am through merit alone, not by socializing with the General." The Heru commander shrugged. "You are a good officer, Paramessu, and in time you will make a great general--if you live to learn your lessons." Turning to face his superior, he dropped his voice further so even Paramessu had to strain to hear. "The first of those lessons is never--I repeat, never--admitting to your legion commanders that you do not have full confidence in your own abilities and judgment. Such knowledge can shatter morale."

Paramessu flushed and nodded tersely.

"Remember too, that the men appreciate a commander who leads from the front, rather than hanging back making observations from the rear." Abruptly, Djedhor smiled, his great hawk nose making his smile look hungry. "The enemy is coming. I suggest you get out there and show your men how it is done."

Paramessu swung round to face the front and saw, in truth, that the whole Amorite army was on the move, marching ponderously down the valley. "Yes, Djedhor, you are right." He stepped away then paused, a mischievous grin on his face. "Won't you join me? I'm sure the men of Heru would appreciate seeing their own commander up at the front."

"Very good, Paramessu." Humor flickered across Djedhor's eyes as he accompanied his general out beyond the lines into the space between the two armies.

"I will not waste time on empty words." Paramessu strode along the front ranks, his eyes flicking across the faces of the men. "I could prattle on about honour and the good name of your legion, but the truth is, men of Kemet, that unless we give a good account of ourselves here today, we will not live to see the sun go down tonight." He paused, and stood hands on hips as he waited for his words to be repeated down the ranks. "Worse than that, unless we stop these Amorite dogs right here in this little valley, they will sweep down into Kemet, our homeland, looting and pillaging as they go. Do you want to explain to your wife why she was killed? To your daughters why they were raped, to your sons why you failed to defend them? To your parents and grand-parents why their tombs were robbed and desecrated?"

A roar of anger greeted his words, swords drummed on leather shields, spears cracked together as they shook above their heads. Those who had no weapons slapped their hands on their leather armor or stamped their feet. "Follow me, lads," Paramessu cried. "Follow me to victory." He turned to face the steadily advancing Amorite army and drew his curved bronze sword, cutting through the air above his head in great sweeping slashes. The morning sun shone on the blade and Paramessu felt a great cry of exultation building in him. He suddenly shouted out a prayer to the gods of his four legions.

"O, Re, look down upon your sons this day and light our way to a victory over the enemies of Kemet. Heru, falcon god, lend us your fierceness and speed that we may drop like the thunderbolt on the Amorites. Ptah, god of craftsmen, help us to carve our names in glory today so that men for generations to come will remember us. Set..." he hesitated, wondering how to invoke this god. "...Lord of chaos; help us throw our enemies into disarray. Let them feel your dread hand upon them this day."

Leaping into the air, Paramessu let out a cleansing shout of pure joy, feeling his worries and fears slide off him. He pointed his sword toward the enemy and set off at a run. A heartbeat later, the legions erupted with a roar of triumph and charged after their General, rapidly overtaking him and enfolding him in the front wall of warriors.

The enemy line neared and the blur of armor, beards and weapons resolved into living men, intent on killing. Emotions reflected from the faces in front of Paramessu, from resignation and fear to determination and anger, and to the fierce joy that overcomes a soldier when the waiting is over and the killing begins. The two lines came together like the sound of an avalanche of rock and the screaming started again. Paramessu's eyes locked with an older man, his black beard streaked with gray. The man's spear dropped, swinging toward Paramessu's chest. He stepped aside casually, moving as if the enemy was a parade-ground training dummy and thrust with his sword, finding the thin gap between plates of leather armor. The body convulsed, almost tearing the sword from his grasp. Blood-stained teeth showed in a mouth suddenly gaping and the man slid down beneath the trampling feet to be replaced by a youth, terror and desperation in his wide eyes. Bronze blades met, clashing. The youth stabbed wildly and would have succeeded but for his fellow soldiers who pressed against him in their struggles, carrying him away. Another man came at him, sword in hand, hacking and slashing. Paramessu felt a blow on his thigh but felt no pain. He stabbed forward and the man screamed, reeling back, pushing into the crowd and disappearing.

The two armies were evenly matched numerically but the Amorites had expected an easy victory, harrying a retreating foe. Instead they found an army intent on recovering its honour, pressing forward with vigour. The time was past for tactics and trickery, strength of arms would now be the determining factor. The sun reached its zenith and began the downward slide to evening, and still the battle continued. After the initial fury of the Kemetu attack the Amorites, slightly better equipped and with the help of the gently inclining valley floor, pushed their foes back, step by weary step. Hacking and stabbing, the battle line crawled back down into the flatter plain at the base of the hills. In the late afternoon, the sun came to the aid of the Kemetu, shining full in the Amorite's eyes. The slow retreat halted and now the Amorites drew back but the legions did not follow.

The armies stood only fifty paces apart, the space between littered with bodies, and stared at each other. Men fought for breath, forcing back the pain of wounds and an overwhelming thirst that left their tongues like wooden blocks in the gritty cavity of their mouths. Sweat drenched loincloths and armor, fine crystals of salt dusting the skin. Neither side felt confident in carrying on the fight, nor could find the strength to do so, yet neither would yield the ground to the other. The balance was maintained.

And then the gods of Kemet stepped in. The sun was lowering when the light faded as a bank of clouds built up, driven by a west wind off the Great Sea. The temperature dropped, providing some respite from the heat of the battle but both sides desperately needed water. Streams ran off the hills nearby but neither army felt it could leave to look for water without ceding the battlefield and the advantage to the other. So they stood and faced each other, willing the others to leave, praying to their respective gods.

The clouds built into great storm clouds and rolled inland, flashes of lightning becoming more apparent as the light faded. Far to the west, rain fell, misty gray swathes connecting cloud and land, fluttering curtains that promised life. The rain grew closer, coming up behind the Kemetu army, but patchy now, the rain showers starting and ending abruptly. The wind changed, bearing the rain to the north but one eddy, a vagary of the storm, dumped a heavy shower on the rear of the Kemetu army. Cries of delight arose as the water fell, easing parched mouths and cooling and washing the blood and dirt from exhausted bodies. The shower advanced over the front ranks and into the space between the armies. The Amorites lifted up their arms and the throats as the first damp gusts of air blew over them.

And then, between one pace and the next, the rain ceased, the clouds sweeping up over the Amorites, giving nothing more. A groan of disappointment and religious fear swelled, and the Amorites drew back, the body of the army trembling as if with a fever. A banner rose, black and red, from the heights on the right flank and the weary men turned, moving back up the valley, leaving the Kemetu in possession of the battlefield.

Paramessu let his sword fall slowly, hardly daring to believe the battle was truly over. Deep within the ranks of exhausted soldiers, the young commander of the Re legion, Hednakht, let out a whoop of exhilaration.

"It's over boys," he yelled. "We've won." He saw his General and pushed through men who were too tired and in pain to celebrate the costly victory, to his commander's side. "We won, by the gods." He spotted Djedhor and Amentep nearby. "Did you see how my legion fought, Djedhor? And you, Amentep, I think my men outshone yours today."

"Yes, Hednakht, I'm sure you were the best soldier on the field," Djedhor said sourly. "I know for a fact my men just stood around all day." He dismissed the young man to his bragging and limped across to Paramessu.

Paramessu frowned and gestured. "You are hurt, Djedhor? You are limping."

"It is nothing, sir. A glancing blow from a mace has bruised my hip." His eyes narrowed. "What of yourself sir? I trust that is not your own blood."

"What? Oh, er, yes. Some of it anyway. I seem to remember a blade scratched me at some point." Paramessu brushed at his left thigh with one hand which came away smeared with blood.

"You'd better let me look at that."

"Later. Hednakht, stop boasting how you singlehandedly won the battle and start organizing the camp. We should march back down to the first decent stream. These men need rest, food and the attention of the physicians. Come on, get things happening."

"Sir!" Hednakht saluted and hurried off, shouting to the Leaders of Fifty and of a Hundred. Soon the army started moving away from the battlefield, most unaided, though many bore wounds, some only with the help of their more able comrades.

When the movement was well under way, Paramessu joined them, moving stiffly and almost falling as his weight fell on his left leg. He brushed away Djedhor's help and limped off.

Djedhor found Khui nursing a broken arm and assisted him down to the camp as an overcast dusk enveloped them. "A sorry day's work," he muttered.

"You think so? We won didn't we?"

"If you can call it that. Our entire chariot squadron lost, and over two thousand dead by my reckoning and more to come after the physicians have their way."

Khui looked worried. "A broken arm is nothing to worry about is it?" He winced and drew in a gasping breath as he turned and brushed his arm against the other commander.

"You'll live," Djedhor grunted. "It's always the ugly ones who survive."

Khui laughed then almost cried again as the broken ends of the bones ground together. Djedhor found a physician and left Khui to his tender mercies, setting off to check up on his own Heru legion.

Chapter 18

For young Prince Tutankhaten, his coronation day started just after dawn when he was awakened by the bevy of nobles that would accompany him through the ceremonies and travails of the day. With this dawn start, the boy was many hours behind the majority of his future subjects. Trumpets blared at midnight from the temple of Re as the aspects of the god changed--sombre Atum of the unified light became benign Khepri of the dawn light. The trumpets were a signal for rejoicing. This was to be the day when all of Kemet, the Two Lands of Kemet from the Great Sea to the cataracts of Nubia, could forget the sorrows of their dead king Smenkhkare and look forward to the bountiful blessings of their new king Tutankhaten.

The treasury and the temple granaries had poured forth largesse of barley for weeks before, bakers all through the city of Waset had prepared great golden loaves of crusted bread, much of which was soaked and fermented to produce huge vats of the thin, sour beer the people loved. Produce poured in from the countryside, fish from the flooded river, wild fowl by the boatload from the reed marshes downriver, and lowing herds of cattle. Huge fires burned through the night as a feast was prepared for everyone in the capital city.

Ay let it be known that the young prince had ordered this feast out of love for his people, but in reality, the boy understood little of what was happening, and nothing of the lot of the common people. He remained cocooned in a world of Ay's making but his own choosing, seldom leaving the confines of the eastern palace except to make offerings at the main temples, always under the watchful eye of the Tjaty.

Ay smiled a lot in the days leading up to the coronation. The young prince was proving nicely malleable and readily gave in to the Tjaty's suggestions. Ay looked forward to many years of power at the right hand of god-on-earth. Then in the evening of the day preceding the coronation, he received a nasty shock and for a while his whole world trembled. Horemheb arrived in Waset, at the head of a small cadre of professional soldiers.

Given scant warning, and hardly believing it, Ay hurried to the main entrance hall of the palace to meet the great general. A multitude of smoking torches lit the tall pillars of sandstone, painted in bright colours and symbolizing the papyrus and lotus of the Great River, that dwarfed the men as they stood in the Great Hall in tense confrontation.

Ay sketched a brief bow, his hooded eyes never leaving Horemheb's. "My lord Horemheb, I scarcely believed my ears when your arrival was reported. I was unaware you had been summoned."

"I was not summoned. I came of my own accord." Horemheb's eyes flicked over the men standing a few paces back from the old Tjaty, dismissing them.

Ay frowned. "You left your station on the northern border without permission? Was that wise, lord general? Was it...dare I say it, the action of a loyal subject of the king?"

"You are not a fool," Horemheb growled. "Do not take me for one."

Ay regarded the man who had almost caused his dismissal and execution for treason four years before. He had dreamed of the day when he would have Horemheb in his power and the time seemed opportune. He had deserted his station on the border, an offence that could have him hanging from the walls of the city by his feet, the vultures tearing at his privates. The man had arrived in Waset so precipitately that few in the city or palace knew of his presence, and only accompanied by a mere fifty men. Ay's hand twitched as he almost signaled to Mentopher in the shadows. One small gesture and the local palace guards would fall on the General and capture or kill him. The guards were loyal to Ay personally, not to Horemheb as General of all the Armies of Kemet.

His hand twitched again and he heard Mentopher move, shifting his weight, anticipating the killing. Surely Horemheb could not be so trusting, so stupid as to walk virtually unarmed into the lion's lair? He must have some hidden resource, an unseen advantage.

"Perhaps we should discuss the situation in private?" Ay said smoothly. "You must be tired after your long journey. A cup of fine dark wine, perhaps, before you pay your respects to Prince Tutankhaten?"

"Yes, there are things that must be said, questions that must be answered." He gestured with his right hand, his eyes never leaving the once-powerful but now wizened body of the Tjaty. "Kaha, you will accompany me with three men. The rest will stay here." Horemheb's eyes flicked quickly over the men standing behind Ay. "Chamberlain, you will have beer and meat brought for my men."

"At once, Lord General," the Chamberlain said, bowing low. He hurried off on his mission.

"I think it would be better if we talked alone," Ay said, looking askance at the young Leader of Fifty behind Horemheb. "You would trust your man?"

"With my life, but he will not be present. I value him too much."

Ay raised an eyebrow questioningly.

"People who know too much have a habit of dying."

The Tjaty smiled sardonically and bowed his head briefly. "Then let us talk together, General Horemheb." Ay led the way to a small sparsely furnished room off the main audience chamber. He took a burning torch from a wall sconce in the corridor outside and lit several of the torches inside the room, releasing a warm flickering light into the chamber.

Horemheb set Kaha and his men on guard outside the door, together with Mentopher and two of his cronies. Shutting the door behind him, the General stood and looked at Ay as he picked out a comfortable padded chair and sat down. "I know you are plotting something again, Ay. By rights I should have you arrested and brought before the king."

"Perhaps." Ay nodded thoughtfully. "Perhaps you could, perhaps not." He sat and watched Horemheb by the door, a small smile creasing his lined face. After a few minutes he said softly, "Shall I tell you why you won't arrest me?"

Horemheb grunted and walked across to another chair a few paces distant from Ay. "So tell me."

"Because you are an honourable man. You could have had me executed four years ago when my daughter and I rebelled against the Heretic. You knew I was guilty but you stayed your hand. Why?" Ay waited a few moments but Horemheb said nothing, just sat down and looked at the Tjaty from under hooded lids. "I'll tell you--because you obey the rule of law, whether it is right or wrong. The Heretic told you to spare me, so you did. You are an honourable man."

"Yet despite Akhenaten sparing your life and restoring you to your position once more, you turn on him at the first opportunity."

Ay laughed. "I never said I was an honourable man."

Horemheb frowned. "Do you not fear the gods?"

"Which ones? We Kemetu have enough of them. You'd think some of them would be genuine."

There came a soft rapping at the door. Horemheb rose quietly and walking across, opened it to reveal Kaha. The young Leader of Fifty held out a small jug of beer and two earthenware mugs. "We have bread and meat too, sir."

Horemheb nodded and took one of the loaves under his arm, grabbed a small chunk of roasted beef with one hand and the jug and mugs in the other, leaving Kaha to close the door for him. He carried the food and drink over to a low table and set them down. Pouring the beer, he broke off a chunk of bread and ripped a sliver of meat from the bone, carrying his meal back over to his chair.

Ay got up and poured himself a small drink, grimacing at the sharp yeasty smell and the thin sour taste. "The drink of the common people," he muttered. "And out of clay mugs too."

"You are of common stock, Ay, for all you are titled 'Divine Father'." Horemheb chewed noisily and swallowed his bread and meat before draining his mug of beer with relish. "I am common, too, but I am not ashamed of it." He belched loudly.

"Why did you come here?" Ay snapped the question out, staring at Horemheb with glittering eyes.

The general lowered his mug to the tiled floor and stretched out his legs, only his shoulders betraying the tension that suddenly came upon him. "Kemet's General of Armies belongs with his king on his coronation day."

244

"And leave your station unbidden? You do not believe that any more than I do. Why did you come?"

Horemheb hesitated. "To take the measure of the young boy who is to be king."

"He is only a boy. There is nothing to measure. Why did you come?"

"To talk to you, Ay," Horemheb snapped. "To find out your intentions and if necessary, oppose you."

"With fifty men?" Ay sneered. "Now if you had brought your army..."

"I do not need an army, any more than I needed one four years ago."

Ay stared, his eyes glittering with hatred. "You tricked me then. You will not do it again." He walked over to his chair and sat down, placing his mug on the floor at his feet.

Horemheb conceded the point with a polite inclination of his head.

"You will not trick me again," Ay reiterated. "And you do not have the strength to match me."

"You think not?"

"You have a mere fifty men, I have the city legion--the legion of Amun, loyal to me personally."

"Really?" Horemheb smiled and looked around the room. "I do not see them."

Ay frowned. "You are not a fool, Horemheb. Why do you talk like one?"

"I do not need an army, Ay. We are alone in this room and your precious Amun legion could not lift a finger to help if I decided to kill you. You are an old man, become soft with city living." Horemheb contemplated the Tjaty for a few moments, flexing the fingers on both hands. "I could snap your neck before you could even cry out. And my men outside that door are more than a match for yours."

Ay licked his lips but otherwise did not move. "That would not be wise."

"Then convince me that I should let you live."

"How? How can I convince you?"

"Try something different, Ay. Try being honest." Horemheb paused then lashed out with his question. "How did Smenkhkare die?"

Ay sat silently, his eyes hooded and face expressionless. "I am told he was taken by a crocodile."

Horemheb made an impatient gesture with one hand. "Did you have him killed?"

"Am I Sobek that I can command crocodiles?"

"Do not evade the question, Ay. Did you have a hand in his death?"

"Yes."

"You do not fear the judgment of the gods?"

"Which gods? They have had ample time to judge me, yet here I am. That is a stupid question."

"Then let me ask another. Why?"

"Because he got in my way." Ay sighed and got up, moving slowly over to the table with the clay mug. He poured himself another beer before turning to face the army general again. "You have never been a courtier, Horemheb. For you life is easy. You command and men obey."

"They do the same for you. You are Tjaty, second only to the king."

Ay nodded. "Yes, second. So what must I do when the king cannot see what must be done, or when shown what must be done, will not do it? Believe it or not, Horemheb, I have the good of our Kemet at heart. I saw Smenkhkare start to pull our Lands back down the path his brother so recently took us."

Horemheb looked up sharply. "I cannot believe he meant to take us back to the Aten. Not after what he started."

"Then why did he take on the name of my fallen daughter? He started to style himself Neferneferuaten, as if he was the consort of the Heretic. He even took to wearing women's gowns in private."

"Smenkhkare?" Horemheb frowned and shook his head. "I find this hard to believe."

Ay shrugged. "Not many knew of it and I made efforts to hide his worse excesses. Then he started talking about destroying the temples again, starting with the great temple of Amun. What was I to do, Horemheb? Allow Kemet to be plunged into heresy and chaos again?"

"No. No, that would be the worst thing that could happen."

"I acted for the sake of Kemet, Horemheb. I took the responsibility on my own shoulders and rooted out the last of the Heretic's taint. Now the young boy will be king and rule in wisdom and in fear of the gods."

"You are not worried that he too is tainted by Atenism? He carries an Aten name."

"Names can be changed, his cursed brother did it. Even you did it. He is young enough to be malleable. I can curb any tendency to bring back the heresy."

Horemheb nodded grimly. "And there we come to it, Ay. You could not control Smenkhkare but you can control Tutankhaten. Why did you not just eliminate the boy and make yourself king?"

Ay shrugged, spreading his arms wide. "I am an old man, Horemheb. I asked Smenkhkare many times to let me retire to my farms near Zarw and live out my old age in comfort. He always refused." Ay stood and after hesitating a moment, walked over to the seated general. "I do not want to be king, but if I can serve our beloved Two Lands, I will stay on and guide the young man until he can manage alone.

"You had Smenkhkare's Councilors killed."

"No, never. I put them under guard, certainly, but that was for their own protection. Despite my efforts, rumors of the king's Atenism had leaked, and I feared for their safety. Some of my guards thought they were prisoners and when they left, thought they were escaping. In an excess of zeal they killed them."

"I will want to speak to the guards."

"I had them executed." Ay pulled a chair close to Horemheb's and sat down. He leaned forward, peering into the suspicion that clouded the General's eyes. "I realize now that was a mistake, but I was incensed at their stupidity."

"So they are all dead?"

Ay hesitated. "No, not all," he said slowly. "Beketaten and Councilor Khu--and the pimp--could not be found and were never in protective custody. I have no idea where they are."

"I pray that they are safe--and you had better find a god to believe in so you can pray too." Horemheb leaned closer to the old man. "Let me be quite clear on this, Ay," he said softly. "I would take it as a personal affront if Beketaten were to die."

"Why?" Ay's brow wrinkled. "What possible reason could you have to be so interested in her?"

"The blood of Nebmaetre Amenhotep runs thin these days. I would not see an unwed daughter of his wasted."

247

Ay sat back with a leer. "You fancy her, Horemheb. You would make a bid for the kingship yourself."

"The boy is only nine and a lot of things can happen before he becomes a king in reality. We may need to find a young noble to become king after him. That would be so much easier if we could marry him to royal blood."

"There are always my two grand-daughters."

"They are tainted." Horemheb shook his head. "No, Beketaten is very important to any future king. Do yourself a favour, Ay. Find Beketaten and keep her alive."

Ay smiled. "So I am to live, after all?"

"A soldier would be a fool to throw away his bronze sword before a battle just because he cut himself on it. Hard times are coming for Kemet and her young king. I can think of no-one more experienced and able to guide him through these times than you."

Ay's smile broadened and he inclined his head graciously. "Thank you, Horemheb. It is good to know you trust me once more."

"Trust has nothing to do with it. I think you are hungry for power and for riches, but if my feeding that hunger will keep Kemet safe and stable, I am willing to do it."

Thus, six hours later, when the young prince Tutankhaten stood at the gates of the Great Temple of Amun, the two most powerful men in the kingdom stood behind him, Ay, Divine Father, Lieutenant General of Chariots, Grand Tjaty of the Two Lands; and Horemheb, General of all the Armies of Kemet.

Bareheaded, and naked save for a simple pleated loincloth, the future king stood in the dust outside the first pylon of the Amun temple, the one built by his father Nebmaetre, and shivered despite the hot sun. Hours of fasting and concentrating on the complex preliminary rituals had left the boy reeling with exhaustion and weak from hunger. Rituals taken in stride by men coming to the throne in the prime of life proved taxing on a boy just turned nine years and frail at the best of times. He lifted a hand to his face and fought back tears, fighting for the strength not to shame himself. Somewhere, he knew, his young wife Ankhesenpaaten was about to undergo similar rituals as she was anointed Queen and Great Wife in preparation of her life task beside him on the throne of Kemet.

Horns sounded deep within the temple complex and Tutankhaten started forward, his bare feet kicking up small puffs of dust as he passed into the brief but cool shade of the gateway before entering the wide expanse of the courtyard with its Lake of Cleansing. Priests thronged the open space, drawn up in two masses to either side of a broad path that led from the first to the second pylon. Up this thoroughfare the boy walked, a small and lonely figure. Twenty paces behind him followed Ay and Horemheb, then every noble, high official and person of any importance who could make it to Waset for the coronation.

Tutankhaten approached the second pylon and stopped suddenly, his heart hammering, as creatures emerged from the shadows in the gateway. A moment later he slumped in relief as he realized they were just men. These were the priests of every god in the city, masked and garbed in representation of their god--falcon-headed Heru, ram-headed Amun, Ibis-headed Djehuti. Others came too, human-faced but decked in rich robes and elaborate headdress. Asar, skin painted green with powdered malachite wearing the conical crown of Lower Kemet framed by tall feathered plumes, Geb, clothed in vegetation with a large golden goose sitting on his head, and Ptah, in closefitting garments and skullcap, bearing a staff surmounted by a great golden ankh.

The god-priests surrounded the small boy, towering above him and cutting him off from the nobility behind him. Heru of the Horizon held out a hand, the glittering garnets of his eyes staring down. Tutankhaten took the hand and allowed himself to be guided to a screen in front of the second pylon.

"This screen was erected by your ancestor Tuthmes, may he live forever," intoned Heru of the Horizon. "Contemplate the works that a king may do to honour the gods." The god-priest pointed to the white limestone lintel, twenty cubits high, carved with an inscription honouring Tuthmes, which framed the gate of the pylon. "That too, is his work."

"When I am king, I will surpass these things," boasted the young boy.

The god-priest Atum joined them in front of the screen and took Tutankhaten's other hand. The trio moved around the screen and through the gateway into the precincts of the temple known as Ipetesut. Entering the hall of the temple, the two guides left the boy in the charge of the other priests who stripped him of his loincloth and led him naked to a shallow, low-rimmed pool. Tutankhaten walked into the middle of it, looking scared and vulnerable in the knee-deep water. The priests withdrew, chanting in low tones the first hymn of enthronement as four god-priests drew closer--Djehuti with the ibis-beak, Set with his strange curved muzzle and erect ears, falcon-beaked Heru of Behdet, and Dunawy, also falcon-beaked. They walked to the four cardinal points of the compass and stepped up on the low rim of the pool. Each carried a tall golden ewer and they bent in unison, dipping the vessels below the surface of the sacred pool, then straightening, stepped down into the water and approached the young prince.

"The water of divine life transforms man to god," Djehuti said, the words muffled slightly by the beaked face. He lifted the golden ewer and poured a stream of water over Tutankhaten's head. "Enter into the presence of the gods and be welcome." One by one, the other gods poured their water and repeated the words.

The priests approached once more and led the boy out of the sacred waters and garbed him in fresh, clean linen, never worn. His guides, Atum and Heru of the Horizon again took him by the hands escorted him to the Hall of Jubilation. The light of innumerable burning torches reflected off the dazzling surface of two electrum-plated obelisks erected by his ancestress Hatshepsut. The many-columned hall marched into shadows, two rows of papyrus-shaped columns rising to a high ceiling and colossal statues. Two great pavilions in stone faced each other across the hall, carved in the archaic fashion of past ages.

Tutankhaten, released by Djehuti and Heru of the Horizon, walked alone into the House of the Flame, *Per-neser*, the Northern pavilion. The gods Nekhabet, Bout, Neith, Auset, Nebt-Het, Heru and Set greeted him, their voices raised in joyful hymns as the young king was greeted into the company of the gods. One by one the gods of the Psedjet bowed before the boy and spoke the ritual words of acceptance.

Passing from the Northern pavilion, Tutankhaten entered the Southern Great House, *Per-wer*, alone. The inside of the primitive temple was dark, lit by a single torch, and in the shadows at the rear, the young boy could dimly see the figure of the ram-headed god Amun. The silence was broken by a loud hissing and the sibilant scrape of scales over the tiled floor. From the shadows emerged Wadjet, Great-in-Magic, the cobra protectress of the kings. The giant snake slithered forward, scales slipping over the smooth tiles, its tongue flickering. When it reached the boy it stopped, investigating the bare feet for several long moments, tasting the fear that flowed from the boy, detecting the trembling of his limbs. With a hiss the cobra reared up, its eyed hood expanding behind its tiny head and it stared into the boy's eyes, mouth agape.

Tutankhaten stood frozen, wanting to run but unable to move his legs. The great column of the snake's body rose up in front of him and the breath caught in his lungs. The small glittering black eyes of the cobra mesmerized him and his attention focused on the reptilian head. Mouth open, the cobra's fangs stood out whitely, a drop of venom at the tips. The torchlight caught the drops, turning them into drops of liquid fire. They sparkled and drew the boy closer and in a rush, understanding flooded over the prince. This was Wadjet, sacred cobra of the kings of Kemet, a friend to be welcomed, not an enemy to be feared. Tutankhaten relaxed and smiled.

The cobra sank back down to the floor and moved closer, winding about the boy's legs, traveling upward in coils about his waist and chest. The young king staggered as the weight of the snake lifted from the floor. The cobra hissed again, angrily, and Tutankhaten braced himself, standing still once more. Torchlight threw a shadow on the wall of a two-headed beast, human and writhing serpent, then the snake lifted itself and spread its hood once more, a living uraeus above the king's brow.

The figure in the shadows stirred. "Amun accepts you as the heir of Kemet. Wadjet, daughter of Amun recognizes your royalty." The Amun-priest walked forward and lifted the cobra from the young king's head and shoulders, lowering it to the floor. It slithered off into the shadows.

Tutankhaten left the pavilion whereupon the priest styled Iunmutef, or Pillar of the Mother, approached. He represented the god Heru, welcoming his father Asar back from the dead. The prince had died to his former life in the ceremony with Wadjet, and been reborn as god-on-earth. Wearing a leopard skin and a great wig of plaited hair drawn to one side, the priest took the great white conical Hedjet crown of Upper Kemet and placed it on the king's head. The assembled priests cried out in exultation, praising the boy as king of Upper Kemet. Iunmutef removed the white crown and replaced it with the red Deshret crown of Lower Kemet. Again the priests shouted out and Iunmutef handed it back to an assistant. Next came the double crown, red and white, the Pasekhemty or Two Powerful Ones, followed by the Atef crown of Re, the Seshed headband for informal occasions, the Ibes crown and a whole series of ornate and simple headdresses that represented the monarch's power for any conceivable circumstance. The final crown to be lowered onto the young king's head was the blue war bonnet or Khepresh. This one, Iunmutef left in place and fastened a giraffe's tail, ancient symbol of the clan chieftain, to Tutankhaten's belt. Attendants approached with a pair of sandals and Iunmutef held them up so the king could see the figures of the nine subject peoples engraved in the soles. The king would leave the temple already treading down the traditional enemies of Kemet.

Atum and Heru of the Horizon fell into place on either side of him and guided the king deeper into the temple, passing through the third pylon. Within this deep recess he turned to the right and entered the shrine of Amun. Carved from a single block of rose granite, the walls had been ground thin enough to be translucent, the torchlight penetrating as a dim red glow. In this gloomy space, Amun, ram-headed, bearing the solar disc upon his head, waited for Tutankhaten. The young king knelt at the god's feet, his head bowed. Amun reached down and lifted the Khepresh from his head.

"Accept this crown from your father Amun," echoed a deep voice and Tutankhaten felt the Khepresh crown replaced gently. The god's hand touched the nape of his neck in a silent benediction.

Tutankhaten backed out of the rosy glow of the god's presence, his head still lowered, and found the priests waiting en masse. His guides, now divested of their god-heads, led the young king, still shivering from the touch of Amun to a low throne. Seated upon it he looked at a sea of upturned faces. Five priests moved to the front and in turn, addressed the young king.

"Let the aspect of Heru empower you," intoned the first priest. "Your name shall be Heru: Kanakht tut-mesut--Strong bull, of perfect birth."

"Nekhabet and Wadjet name you also," the second priest said. "Your name is Nebty: Neferhepu segeretawy--He of the good laws, who pacifies the Two Lands."

"The gods recognise you as their son on earth," said the third. "Heru Nebu: Wetjes khau sehotep neteru--He who wears the crown and satisfies the gods."

"Nesut-byt--King of the South and of the North," cried the fourth priest. Nebkheperure--Lord of the manifestations of Re."

"Sa-Re--Son of Re." The fifth priest paused for a heartbeat, a slight smile on his lips before completing the king's birth name-- "Tutankhamen, Living image of Amun."

Despite the solemnity of the occasion, the priests muttered and whispered. Tutankhaten, surely? Had the fifth priest made a mistake? The young king's forehead furrowed and he stared at the priest, wondering the same thing. He saw the knowing smile and knew it was no mistake. Amun had claimed the king for his own.

The priests led King Nebkheperure Tutankhamen out into the forecourt of the temple, now packed with people. Wearing only his plain white kilt and the blue Khepresh crown of blue leather, his whole being radiated a new-found confidence and sense of his own position, god-on-earth, nine year old Father of his people. They led him to a raised throne and presented him to the people, who cheered so loudly the pigeons roosting in the rooftops of the temples during the heat of the day took off in a startled clattering of wings. The priests performed the coronation ceremonies once more, to the acclaim of the assembled crowds, replacing the blue crown with the double crown *Pasekhemty*. They twined lily and papyrus around a pillar in the ceremony of *Sma-Tawy*, a symbolic uniting of the Two Lands, and the boy-king, donning the lightweight blue crown once more, raced around the walls of the sanctuary in symbolic representation of his fitness to rule.

Tutankhamen held in his hands the two traditional scepters for the first time, the crook or *heka* of Southern royalty and the flail or *nekhekh* of the Northern Kingdom. Invested with his full powers, the king of the South and the North left the temple through the great pylon of his earthly father Nebmaetre and rode through the streets of the city in an electrum-plated chariot driven by the most senior of the royal charioteers. Multitudes lined the streets, waving and cheering, happy that the times of trouble were at an end at last and even want and hunger were past now that the young king was there to lead them.

Hours later, as dusk fell, the chariot stopped at last at the eastern palace where a very tired boy, his head barely supporting the blue leather crown, was helped from the chariot and into the palace where he was reunited with Ankhesenpaaten, now officially Queen of the Two Lands. Sobbing with exhaustion, the king was led off to his bed where he fell asleep within minutes, his thumb securely in his mouth.

Chapter 19

Horemheb was in Waset. Somehow, in their passage down the flooded river, Scarab and Khu had passed him by; whether at night when the boat, wallowing heavily in the water under the weight of melons and cucumbers, tied up to the trunk of a tree; or just passed unseen during the day, the boats separated by the wide expanse of water. Certainly there had been many boats and any one of them could have held the General. On the other hand, maybe he had brought his army with him and traveled by the land route, bypassing the flooded valley. All Scarab could find for certain was that Horemheb had been in Ineb Hedj on his way south but left long before she had arrived.

"So what do we do?" Khu asked simply. "Turn around and go back to Waset?"

"I'm tempted," Scarab replied. "Even if only because I must see Horemheb. It's too dangerous though. If Ay caught even a hint we were near..."

"So what then?"

"We carry on up to Zarw. That is Horemheb's military base, he will be returning there."

Just north of the city of Ineb Hedj, the great river divided into several great channels and the number of smaller waterways and lagoons of the Delta of Lower Kemet. The annual flood turned the discrete channels into a broad sheet of water dotted here and there with clumps of trees, beds of papyrus sedge, the tops of their leafy stalks riffling the surface of the water, and low hillocks crowded with mournful herds of cattle. It was easy to get passage on a boat out of Ineb Hedj, especially heading north into the flooded lands. Farmers and herdsmen, out of work until the waters subsided, readily took on other work and there was fierce competition for the tiny shaving of gold on offer. In the end, Scarab settled on a boat owned by a young lad from a village that now lay under water. His name was Amenhotep, the same as her father, yet a more dissimilar person could not be imagined. Where Amenhotep the king was--or had been--tall and handsome, strong as a bull and beautiful to look at, the young lad Amenhotep was short and scrawny, with a squint that made his face a perpetual scowl. He had a sunny disposition though and he managed the boat with a consummate skill, as if born to the water trade.

The flooded river broadened as it reached the flat lands of the Delta, spreading out over the land almost as far as the eye could see. Only the pyramids, those mountains of stone so old not even the priests could truly say who had built them, men or gods, towered above the river valley on their own western plateau. The current carried them past and into Lower Kemet.

Khu looked over to where Amenhotep stood in the stern, lazily sweeping the rear oar as he kept the small boat stable, pointed down river. "Do you know where we are going?" he asked. "I don't see how you can navigate without landmarks."

The lad shrugged and swept a hand vaguely toward the sky. "The sun tells me." He went back to his sleepy contemplation of the sluggish waters.

"What does he mean, the sun tells him?" Khu complained to Scarab, who sat in the prow trailing her fingers in the water. "And I'd be careful of crocodiles too," he added.

Scarab lifted her hand sharply from the muddy green water. "I think he means just that the sun tells him east and west."

"So how can he tell north and south?"

Scarab lifted an eyebrow mockingly. "And this from a farm boy? The river flows from south to north."

Khu stuck out his tongue, then grinned. "How can he tell how far we have traveled? As far as I know, Zarw is on the eastern border somewhere. That means at some point we are going to have to leave the river and strike overland. How will he know when we have reached that point?"

"I don't know, Khu. I've never been this far down-river. Why don't you ask him?"

"He doesn't talk to me. You ask him." Khu leaned back against the side of the boat and closed his eyes.

Scarab sighed and got to her feet, dusting down her gown. She adjusted the shoulders, making sure her breasts were adequately covered before moving down the small boat to talk to Amenhotep. No seventeen year old in Kemet was ignorant of sex, but Scarab had found, before their travels north, that she had been somewhat protected as a princess. Here on the river, where as far as anyone was concerned she was only a lowly maid-servant or some such, she attracted a lot of attention from men, by no means all of it welcome. However, as with the guard in Akhet-Aten, she was learning to turn men's lusts to her advantage.

Amenhotep turned to face Scarab as she approached; his face lighting up as if the sun shone behind his squinting eyes. His perpetual scowl turned into a grimace that in the two days since they had engaged his services, Scarab had come to recognise as a smile.

Scarab sat down on the broad rim of the boat and, shading her eyes with one hand, looked out over the waters. A gentle breeze from the north ruffled the surface of the river and set the short reddish brown locks of hair on her head, waving. She had shaved her head for so many years she had almost forgotten she did not have the straight black hair of most of the population. Her mother Tiye had had hair like hers, probably as a result of her Khabiru roots. *At least when we get to Zarw, I won't look out of place,* she thought. *There are lots of Khabiru there.*

"Amenhotep?" Scarab asked quietly. "How is it you know exactly where we are? One stretch of river looks much the same as another."

The lad shook his head and pointed. "This is just a river with too much water in it at the moment. The land is still down there, but covered by water. See that slight ruffling of the surface? It means there are reed beds below. And over there, where the river runs smoothly, like oil? That is flat rock."

Scarab looked dubiously at the river, trying to distinguish between oily water and ordinary water, between calm and ruffled. Another patch of faintly rippled water came up and she hung head first over the edge, peering into the muddy water. A swirl of clearer water revealed a glimpse of vegetation, gone almost before she could register it. "Reeds?" she asked.

Amenhotep smiled and nodded. "You are learning. After a while you recognise the features of the river and surrounding land as if there was no water."

"So you'll know when we reach the place where we must go overland to Zarw?"

"About five days. We are only just passing the channel that leads to Iunu."

"Iunu? The place of pillars?" Scarab felt the hair on her head prickle. "I have heard of it but never been there. Where is it, Amenhotep?"

The young lad looked around, considering. "There." He pointed northeast. "If we sailed up that channel," he said, pointing at the open water to the right of the little boat, "We'd get there in about a day. You'd still have to walk though. Even with the flood, Iunu is not on the river."

"Take us there, Amenhotep."

Amenhotep frowned. "I thought you wanted to go to Zarw. If we go to Iunu, we'd have to come right back here before going north again. You'd lose two days--a day there and one back."

"I...I know, but I feel we must go. Take us there, Amenhotep. We'll pay you extra."

Amenhotep snorted. "I do not need more gold. It is my pleasure." He slipped a loop of rope around the steering oar, holding it in place, before scrambling over the deck to the small mast. Hauling on ropes, he raised a tiny triangular sail which billowed and luffed in the slight headwind, heeling the boat over and slowing its progress.

Khu's eyes snapped open as a splash of cold water wakened him. "What in Set's name is happening?" He looked around wildly, clinging to the side of the boat. "Why are we turning?" Scrambling to his feet he set off, awkwardly, for the rear of the boat, ducking under the sail. "What are you doing, Amenhotep?"

"Ask your mistress." Amenhotep jerked a thumb as he busied himself tying ropes.

Khu picked his way carefully over the covered bundles of the cargo toward the steering oar where Scarab stood staring out over the water. "What's happening? Why are we turning?"

"Iunu," Scarab murmured, without turning.

"So? What's Iunu and why should we want to go there?" Scarab did not answer so he lightly touched her bare arm and asked again.

She turned slowly, as if reluctant to lose sight of something. "You have never heard of Iunu, the place of pillars?"

Khu shrugged. "I am only a farm lad, Scarab. I've never been down farther than Ineb Hedj. What is this place of pillars? A temple or something?"

"Yes, a temple to Atum."

"Aten? Why do we want to go to a temple of the Aten?"

"Atum." Scarab smiled faintly and sat down near the steering oar, motioning to Khu to sit beside her. Amenhotep finished tying off the ropes and took his place by the oar once more, staring ahead at the new course of the boat, but sneaking glances at the young girl.

"Atum," Scarab repeated. "The creator god from whom all other gods came. The priests say he sat all alone on the Ben-Ben mound until he created the earth and everything in it. They say the city of Iunu grew up around him."

Khu nodded. "I remember the name now. My father used to pray to the sun god in his various forms. Khepri was his favourite..."

"Mine too."

"...but the evening sun was addressed as Atum. So this Atum is really just an aspect of Re?"

"The other way round I think. Atum came first, but the city is also known as the City of the Sun."

"So why are we going there?"

Scarab shook her head, the reddish highlights in her short hair catching the sun. "I don't know. I didn't mean to but when Amenhotep mentioned Iunu, I knew I had to go there."

Khu looked up at the young man standing at the steering oar. "I hope you like an adventure," he said, a trace of sarcasm tingeing his voice. "You'll find lots of exciting things happening around Scarab here."

Amenhotep squinted at Khu, then looked dreamily at Scarab. "If her name really is Scarab then I think she should go to the City of the Sun. It seems right."

"Thank you, Amenhotep. And that is exactly where we are going." Scarab got up and walked carefully up to the angled prow of the boat where she seated herself looking out over the water as the little vessel carved its path eastward toward the distant shore.

The voyage to Iunu took the rest of that day, despite Amenhotep praising the speed of his little craft. When they reached the eastern shore, he turned the boat north again, hauling in the sail and letting the current carry them onward. The sun was sinking low in the west when he turned the boat toward land again. Khu looked back at the setting sun. "I've never seen it plunge into water before," he said with a worried expression. "What if it goes out and there is no light tomorrow?"

Amenhotep pulled the little boat into the shallows near a clump of date palms and secured it to a fallen log. They set up camp in the shelter of the rustling palms and cooked a meal of fresh-caught fried fish that they ate with some stale bread and water straight from the river that was mildly gritty on the teeth but tasted pure. The sun set in the river waters, apparently without harm as there was no sound of hissing, as when a bronze blade fresh from the armorer is plunged into water. Khu listened for it but grudgingly admitted night fell without the sound of the sun's death.

The feeling of relief was obvious in his face the next morning when the first rays struck the ground, evaporating the light dew. He knelt, facing east, and bowed his head. "Now I know why the Aten is worshiped."

Amenhotep cleared away the pots and tidied the small fire. He pointed to the east. "Iunu lies over there, about half a day's walk. You will find a road before long if you continue toward the sun. It is the main Ineb Hedj to Iunu road. There should be lots of people."

"Thank you," Scarab said. "Will you be all right here? Do you want to come with us?"

Amenhotep shook his head. "I have to stay with my boat. How long will you be?"

Scarab shrugged. "A day or two. I don't know. I don't even know why we are going."

"I'll wait for three days then. If you are not back by then, I'll assume you are staying in Iunu or moving on overland."

The land in Lower Kemet was not at all like the red lands of the upper river valley. Scarab had thought the lush grass around the campsite owed its existence to the proximity of the floodwaters, but she quickly saw she was wrong. They moved inland, eastward, and soon left the river behind. The grass continued however, if anything becoming lusher, dotted with clumps of papyrus reed and stands of trees. Herds of cattle appeared, each tended by small naked boys armed with sticks. The boys paid no attention to Scarab and Khu, plodding along behind their charges, a swift crack of their staves across a loitering cow's rump the only sound. The cattle showed more interest, standing staring at these new humans with their large liquid eyes, their heavy dewlaps swinging. They stood their ground for as long as they could before snorting suddenly with alarm and plunging off, the naked boys running after them. Thick clouds of flies followed the herds, feasting on the fresh dung. Beetles were there too, sacred scarabs, fashioning miniature sun balls and trundling them across the sandy soil between the swards of cropped grass.

Scarab squatted and watched them for a few minutes, pointing out the iridescent colours of their grooved and ridged carapaces to Khu.

"I don't see how anyone in their right mind could think you looked like a beetle," Khu grinned. "You are not nearly as colourful."

They found the road just before noon, a hard-packed ribbon of rock and earth tamped smooth by countless feet. It ran northeast-southwest, connecting the great city of Ineb Hedj with Iunu and beyond. Traffic was light on the great road, a scattering of men and women on foot and a few ox-carts laden with produce, moving toward Iunu. They joined the other travelers who cast a curious eye on the young man and woman, but said nothing, turning back to their silent contemplation of the baked road ahead.

Scarab had been expecting another great city like Waset or Ineb Hedj, even something smaller, like Akhet-Aten, so she felt let-down when Iunu appeared suddenly over a small rise. A cluster of mud brick houses constituted the main town, surrounding an open space in which stalls and benches, laden with produce, attracted the travelers as they arrived.

"Where are the pillars?" Khu complained. "I thought you said this was the place of pillars."

"I did," Scarab said. "And the temples--where are they?"

One of the travelers stopped, letting his eyes travel appreciatively over the young girl. "This is the newer part of the city. The temples are further on. Just follow the road."

They stopped briefly in the market place, finding some new-baked bread and thin beer at one of the taverns lining the open place. Khu haggled for a minute, reluctantly parting with a scrap of copper. Shaking his head, he carried the loaf and mugs of beer to a rough wooden bench where they sat in the shade, eating and watching the people of Iunu.

"What do you hope to find here?" Khu asked around a mouthful of gritty crust. "You are normally so...so single-minded. It's not like you to wander away from your path."

"I don't know. It was like someone told me to come here."

Khu stopped eating and looked at Scarab, his mouth falling open. "You heard a voice? Of a god?"

"No." She looked sideways at her companion. "Close your mouth, Khu or you'll lose your meal." She shook her head slightly. "Like a voice but not a voice. I can't explain it. Perhaps more like suddenly remembering something I meant to do. Anyway, we are here now. Maybe we'll find out when we get to the temples."

The temples lay in a small depression half an hour's walk beyond the mud brick town. True to its name, pillars were the first thing seen, the tops rising above the gentle swell of the land. As they topped the rise, a forest of stone trees spread out before them, eight great stone temples arranged in a spiral dominated by a huge ninth one atop a gentle central pyramidal mound. After standing there a while, absorbing a sight that rivaled that of the great temple of Amun in Waset, Scarab and Khu started down toward the first of the temples. Priests came out to meet them, white-robed and shaven-headed, and guided them onto a road that circled inward toward the central mound, passing in front of every temple. Priests of the gods stood outside the temples, welcoming supplicants and those offering up a sacrifice for prayers to be said. Statues of the gods watched from raised plinths on the temple steps.

Scarab and Khu followed the direction of the priests, walking slowly along the supplicants' road from the left. A single priest walked with them, a few paces ahead. Other priests watched from the temple steps.

"Do you have the feeling we were expected?" Scarab murmured to herself. "But who knew we were here?"

"Why these gods?" Khu whispered. "I mean, I've heard of them, but except for perhaps Geb as god of the earth and growing things, I've never had occasion to worship any of them."

"Three is a holy number," Scarab replied in a quiet voice. "And three times three even more so. The nine gods and goddesses of Iunu are special. All the scribes and tutors said so, though they never explained to me why."

"Ah, there is a god I recognise." Khu walked on to the next temple and stood looking up at the statue of Asar, god of the underworld.

"And the next," Scarab observed. "Auset, his loyal consort and mother of Heru."

The priest ahead of them stopped and spoke. "Auset will bless you, young lady, but not yet."

Scarab frowned and walked up to the statue of Auset, a tall severe-looking woman with a tall crown in the form of a throne. "Mother goddess, queen of heaven. What do you want of me?"

"Not yet," murmured the priest. "She has nothing to say to you yet."

"Then...then why was I called here?"

"You have not yet completed your circle."

Scarab looked hard and long at the serene-faced priest before turning to face the road again. She passed the temple of Nebt-Het with an enquiring glance at the priest then strode on to the next.

"Oh, I hope not," Khu muttered as he saw the strange animal-headed figure of the statue in front of the eighth temple. Set the destroyer looked down from his plinth at the deserted steps and forecourt of his temple. "Why would anyone want to worship a god of chaos and destruction?"

"That is not his function here in Iunu," reproved the priest. "He represents the land of Lower Kemet, the god of the red desert, mighty warrior husband of Nebt-Het, the fertile lands of the Delta." A small smile crept over his face and humor glinted in his eyes. "In fact, young lady, he could be the one with the message for you. You have the red hair of people loved by him." The priest cocked his head on one side as if listening. "No, not yet. One day perhaps." They passed the temples of Shu and Tefnut, Geb and Nut. "Nothing here either," the priest said. "Today you are welcomed in the greatest temple." He pointed to where the road ascended the gentle pyramid to the forecourt of the temple of Atum.

"Me?" Anxiety and curiosity warred in Scarab's face. "The god asks for me?"

"Perhaps I have the wrong young lady," the priest said, a smile on his face. "The god said merely a woman with hair like the desert sands who was a daughter, sister and servant of the sun. 'Handmaiden of the sun' was how the god phrased it. Are you such a woman?"

"Handmaiden of Aten," Khu muttered, paling. "Beketaten."

Scarab licked her lips and nodded slowly. "I...I have been called that."

"Then come, the god waits." The priest set off up the gentle slope toward the temple of Atum, the creator god. After a few moments Scarab followed, with Khu trailing behind, fear on his face.

They passed through the entrance pylon and the open hypostyle. The forecourt of the temple was roofed, but still gave the impression of being open, the pillars marching in rows toward the shadowed depths of the building. A cool breeze blew through the columns despite the heat of the afternoon sun and the effect on Scarab and Khu was as refreshing as a dip in the river. A feeling of calm descended on them both despite their earlier feelings of anxiety.

They went deeper into the temple, the light fading to a gray gloom as they left the sunlight behind. The rooms and corridors were deserted, the only sound being the soft footfalls of the three of them. The priest led them into a darkened room and halted before a pyramid of granite that rose to perhaps twice man height, its featureless sloping sides hardly discernible, its summit clothed in darkness.

"Wait here." Without waiting for an answer, the priest bowed to the granite pyramid and left, disappearing before he had taken a dozen paces. The soft susurration of his gown and the gentle slap of his sandals stayed a while longer before leaving them in a deepening silence.

"Why are we here?" Khu said, dropping his voice to a whisper as his words echoed through the darkness, startlingly loud. "Why did he just leave us?"

"Wait," Scarab whispered. "The place is holy. Can't you feel it?"

The silence grew and with it a feeling of oppression, as if a great weight was settling on the temple roof, bowing the pillars outward like supple reeds. A glimmer of light appeared, so faint that Scarab rubbed her eyes to make certain it was still there. The glow strengthened and settled on the summit of the granite pyramid, growing until it enveloped the unseen tip. Within the glow the figure of a seated man slowly appeared, a king, crowned with *Pasekhemty,* the red and white crown of the Two Kingdoms. The formal beard jutted from the man's face and the sacred uraeus hissed and twined above his stern unblinking eyes. Crook and flail of kingly authority crossed on the man's bare chest, the flail quivering slightly. This slight movement of breathing was the only sign this was a living man, not a statue.

"What do you seek, child?" A voice, deep but hollow as if issuing from a tomb chamber rather than lungs and throat, echoed in the still air.

Scarab found her mouth dry and her limbs rigid as she fought down a fluttering panic growing in her breast. "I...I was b...brought here," she stuttered.

"Examine your heart. What is it you seek?"

Scarab forced a deep breath and stiffly rubbed her arms where the fine hairs stood erect. She recognized the aura of kingly authority that surrounded the figure on the granite pyramid. Whether this was actually the god Atum himself on the primordial Ben-Ben mound, of just his priest impersonating him, she could feel the power that washed over her. This was the king and she was a petitioner.

"Mighty king, live forever." She raised her arms and fell to her knees, craning her neck to look up at the enthroned figure. "My brother Djeserkheperure Smenkhkare, rightful and anointed king of our Two Lands has been murdered and his killer, my uncle, stands behind my other brother Tutankhaten, ruling through him though he is common-born. I ask justice, divine king."

The stern figure of the god-king looked down on the young girl on her knees. "How will you serve me, handmaiden of the sun?"

"Give me justice and I will do whatever you want, great king."

The figure shook its head, the gesture one of regal finality. "Give freely and without reserve, without seeking reward for your labors, and I may show mercy."

Scarab bit her lip, sure that this was the priest of Atum seeking some hold over a person he knew to be royal. She opened her mouth to refuse when she caught sight of Khu out of the corner of her eye. Her words died unspoken.

Khu yawned and stretched. "How long is that priest going to leave us alone?" he muttered. "He could at least have left us with a light."

Scarab glanced up at the seated king-figure, surrounded by a pearly glow, then back at Khu, his eyes wandering aimlessly over the pyramid. "You cannot see him? The priest?"

"Eh? Where?" Khu looked around in the shadowed chamber. "No, I do not see him."

Scarab looked back up at the seated man again, feeling tightness in her chest. "Forgive me, divine king," she whispered. "I am your servant. Command me."

"I am the creator of heaven and the earth. My children rule water, wind, fire and earth. My progeny rule life and death, order and chaos. Here in Iunu, the Nine govern Kemet and all nations. Yet lesser ones, mere aspects of the essential being, seek to rule men's minds, disturbing the natural balance, that which you call Ma'at." The voice fell silent, the last phrases rolling around the great darkened hall, fading into echoing whispers.

"What must I do, divine one?"

"Seek the balance, handmaiden of Atum. Bring others to knowledge of their creator, worship my children, and serve the Nine."

"I am only a woman, divine king. I have no power to make men listen."

"Live long, daughter, sister, wife and mother of kings. Nine you serve and nine shall rule while yet you live. Your brothers live and yet will die and your uncle will meet his judgment. Do not fear, for those who oppose you, oppose me." The glowing figure stood and lifted its right hand in a silent benediction. The glow flared brightly, shattering the gloom of the chamber in a soundless explosion, leaving Scarab blinking as violet afterimages danced and drifted.

"Scarab...Scarab...are you all right?" The drifting lights faded and she looked up into Khu's concerned face. "I just looked around and you were kneeling on the floor. Are you all right?"

She scrambled to her feet and clung to Khu's arm. "He spoke to me, Khu. He granted my wishes."

"What are you talking about? Who spoke to you? I didn't hear anyone."

Scarab looked at him strangely. "You saw no-one, and heard nothing?"

"No. The priest left us alone and hasn't come back. Why?"

"Never mind." Scarab pulled her friend away from the granite pyramid and started walking back through the temple columns toward the entrance and the light of a hot summer afternoon in the eighteenth, the fourth and the first years of the reigns of her three brothers. She blinked as they emerged into the bright light, feeling at peace for the first time since she had heard of Smenkhkare's death. *Could he truly be alive?* she thought. *If so, I will find him and marry him and bear him sons to rule after us. He said I would be wife and mother of kings. Or perhaps he did not mean...my thoughts are swimming. What did the god really say? Who else will father my sons if they are going to be kings?*

Chapter 20

Jebu sat alone on the hard stone bench outside the king's audience chamber. Since his arrival in Taanach three days previously, he had been treated like a leper, shunned by noble and soldier alike, relieved of his sword and ordered to await the king's pleasure. Now, as he sat in the courtyard of the palace, a thin cloak wrapped around his shoulders in a vain effort to ward off the biting wind from the mountains, he started to worry for the first time about his future. He had seen the king's anger fall on others before, from criminals who stole the king's wealth to soldiers accused of cowardice. Those unfortunates had begged for death for days before their mutilated bodies released their whimpering spirits. He had seen, too, the fall from grace of ministers and nobles. High station did not save one from death, but at least it granted one a swift release. The question was; in which category did Jebu's crime place him?

For crime it must be. Why else did he languish outside Aziru's chamber for three days, eating and drinking only what he could scrounge from the common soldiers' mess, using the open midden in front of all. Once he saw Ephras across the courtyard and saw him try to approach, only to be turned back by the guards. Professional palace guards these, as vicious as any soldier in his command, but without the discipline. They scratched and gossiped, laughing at Jebu's plight with many gestures that implied death in one form or another, but for all their seeming inattention, none were allowed close to him, nor was he allowed to leave. The only time they showed a semblance of training was when the captain of the palace guards made his rounds.

Toward evening of the third day, just as Jebu resigned himself to another hard, cold night on the ground, the captain made an unscheduled appearance. Marching up to the seated general, he dismissed his small cadre of guards, waiting until they were out of earshot.

"The king will see you tonight. You would be advised to wash before your audience. You stink." The captain curled his lip in disdain.

Jebu uncoiled and moved toward the captain in a fluid motion. He stood close, his face thrust forward. The captain overtopped Jebu by a hand, yet it was the captain who stepped back, his eyes widening.

"Until I am relieved of my command," Jebu growled. "I am still a general and you will address me with respect." He saw the flicker in the captain's eyes and his hand flashed to the officer's belt, drawing the dagger even as the man's hand fumbled for it. Thrusting the dagger upward until it just pierced the man's skin, he gripped the captain's greasy beard with his other hand, preventing him from pulling back. "Well, what do you say, captain?" He dug the tip of the dagger in deeper as the watching guards surged closer, weapons drawn. "Stay back," he warned.

Pain flared in the man's eyes, and fear. "G...general, sir," he stammered. "You misunderstand me. I meant no offence. I was merely suggesting you ready yourself before seeing the king."

Jebu smiled. "Perhaps I did misunderstand you, captain. What is your name?"

"Arnu, sir."

"Well, Arnu, I am going to release you in a moment. You will control your anger and dismiss your men. If the king truly wishes to see me, he will not take kindly to news of my death, will he?" Jebu let go of the captain's beard and stepped back, watching the man carefully.

Arnu flushed and adjusted his clothing, wincing as he moved. A small patch of blood showed on the man's tunic, low down on the left side, and Arnu's hand came away bloodied. He waved away the soldiers and they retreated, muttering imprecations as they put up their weapons.

"You had better show me where I can find water to wash with. And food, some decent food. I have had enough of the swill you feed the common men."

Arnu led the way across the courtyard and had a woman draw water from the well, splashing it into a tub. Jebu stripped to the waist and wet himself down, scrubbing at his matted chest hairs and soaking the long locks of his head and beard. Grabbing some folded bed linen he roughly dried himself before donning his clothing again. "Better," he muttered. "No chance of a clean tunic, I suppose?" He shrugged when Arnu said nothing and busied himself digging his fingers into his long hair, raking his ragged nails through it and combing it into a vague semblance of respectability.

Food came next, and the service was as cursory as the washing. Bread, some dried goat's meat with the fat on it congealed and faintly rancid, and copious amounts of water from the well. Jebu chewed and swallowed standing up, his back to the kitchen wall, his eyes roaming over the captain and his small group of men.

Evening fell, and the cooking fires cast a lurid glow over the waiting men, glinting redly from watchful eyes. Wiping his greasy hands on the damp linen, he drained his mug of water and nodded at Arnu.

"When does the king wish to see me?"

"At sunset." Arnu grinned and his men chuckled, fingering their weapons. "I'm afraid you have kept your king waiting and we all know Aziru does not like to be insulted like that. I would not give a dog's corpse for your chances now...General." He stood aside and waved Jebu toward the door and the courtyard beyond.

The guards at the doors of the king's chambers stood to one side, staring impassively at Jebu and his armed escort. Throwing the doors open, Arnu marched into the centre of the hall and saluted.

"Dread king, the traitor Jebu."

Aziru sat at a trestle table with two other men. Jebu recognized Mutaril, the Hittite ambassador from the court of their theoretical ally, Shubbiluliuma, and Ashraz, Aziru's spymaster. Aziru looked up as the squad of guards entered the hall, and watched stony-faced as his general was brought forward.

"Why is he late, captain?" Aziru asked softly. "I commanded him to be here at sunset."

"He insisted on washing and eating first, dread king. He would not be hurried."

Aziru turned a baleful eye on Jebu, noting the wet and straggly hair and beard, the grease stains on the man's tunic. "You put cleanliness and food before the wishes of your king?"

Jebu bowed low then straightened and smiled at Aziru. "Your majesty's presence satisfies my heart and my mind, yet I fear my body is weak and needs sustenance. I would be strong that I might serve your majesty well."

"He has the tongue of a courtier," Mutaril murmured.

"If I thought he had, I would rip it from him," Aziru growled. "I have need of a general, not another sycophant." He noticed Arnu and his guard avidly attentive and waved a hand dismissively. "Leave us, captain."

The king waited until the room had emptied of guards before addressing Jebu again. "What happened, Jebu? I expect my generals to win battles. If they do not, they should have the courtesy of dying with their troops."

"That is why you have a lot of inexperienced generals."

"Don't be clever, Jebu. Tell me why you lost the battle when you had all the advantages."

"I would dispute I lost the battle."

"You withdrew from the field."

"As did the enemy."

"My lord Aziru," Mutaril interposed smoothly. "Perhaps we could hear General Jebu's thoughts on the battle and our Kemetu foes."

Aziru grunted and sat back in his chair. "Go on then."

Jebu bowed again. "Horemheb is one of the reasons we are still sitting in Kenaan instead of living off the fat of the land in Lower Kemet. My spies told me he had left his army under the command of a junior officer. I thought it worth testing his ability."

"With what result, general?" Mutaril twirled his silver wine cup, staring into its ruby depths rather than looking at Jebu.

"I destroyed all his war chariots and killed nearly four thousand Kemetu."

"And your losses?"

"Less than a thousand."

Aziru leaned forward again. "Then how is it you left the enemy in possession of the field?"

"Horemheb was not present but his men were."

271

"Of course. What of it?"

"We thought Kemet weakened when their king denied gold to their armies. Thousands left and all that faced us were the ones who had little to lose. Those few became the core of Horemheb's army. They are well-trained, disciplined and fierce. They fight not for gold but for their country." Jebu started pacing, unaware of his growing unrest. "That is all that saved that raw commander from complete, ignominious defeat." He smacked a fist into his other hand. "They were in full retreat, almost a rout and he turned them. That bastard of a commander rallied them and they stood and faced my army again."

"His name is Paramessu," Ashraz commented. "Son of Seti, a former troop commander and judge of the garrison town of Zarw."

"Is that relevant?" Aziru asked.

"No information is irrelevant, your majesty. If we cannot see the relevance it is only because we...ah...cannot yet discern the pattern."

Aziru glowered. "If you were not so valuable to me, Ashraz...Go on, Jebu."

"The Kemetu fought us to a standstill. We were both in such straits that a camel straw could tip the balance. Then it rained--but on the Kemetu only. They were refreshed and we were not. Men started saying the gods favoured them, and I could hold them no longer. I moved my men back out of the valley of Bashra to the first watercourse I could find."

Aziru frowned, drumming his fingers on the oaken table top. "Did you offend Anu and Amurru in any way? Why would the rain and thunder gods favour our enemies?"

Jebu shrugged. "The priests offered the pre-battle sacrifices as usual. They even offered up some of the captured Kemetu after we withdrew, but it was too late then."

"You used signal flags in the battle, Jebu," Ashraz said. "Was it effective?" The spymaster caught another scowl from the king and shrugged apologetically. "It is all grain to my grindstone, your majesty. If I am to serve you I must have information."

"And how will signal flags...never mind, answer him."

"They served well enough. Certainly in the early part of the battle before the clouds of dust obscured them. I positioned my command post on a slight rise to increase my visibility."

"Better than sounding a horn, do you think?"

"Battles are noisy affairs, Ashraz. Too often the din of metal and cries of pain block the signals."

"Enough of this," Aziru growled. If you want to know more, ask him later." The king fixed Jebu with a stony glare. "If his head remains on his shoulders," he added. "My brother and ally Shubbiluliuma supplied you with five thousand troops to fight the enemy, yet you left them behind to attack the Kemetu. Naturally he takes this as an insult-- that we do not trust him. I have assured my Hittite brother that my feelings for him are unchanged and that the fault is yours alone. He asks for your head--or if I am inclined to be especially generous, the pleasure of separating your head from your body himself. Which is it to be?"

"I am your majesty's dog. My preferences are of no importance." Jebu bowed again. "I would ask that I may comment on this perceived insult, however." Aziru nodded and he continued. "The commander of the Hittite contingent, Mursilanda, has blocked me at every turn. He refuses to camp with my men, train with them or even discuss plans for the campaigns. He made it very plain that he represented the Hittite king alone and that the only time he would aid me is if his interests were threatened. When the opportunity arose to strike at the Kemetu, I took it, leaving Mursilanda behind to look after the interests of his Hittite master."

"Yet if you had taken them, the battle might very probably have been won," Mutaril said softly. "You would have had an overwhelming numerical advantage." The Hittite ambassador arose and smoothed his robes before coming around the table to stand close to Jebu.

"And if he had ignored my commands in the battle, I could have lost it. Then you would have no need to take my head, your majesty. The Kemetu would have taken it and be battering at your gates right now." Jebu fixed the ambassador with a sardonic gaze. "The Hittite king has given me one of the bright new steel blades, but then forbids me to draw it from its sheath in defense of my king."

Jebu swung round to face his king and took a step forward, flinging his arms wide. Ashraz tensed and half rose from his seat, his dagger glittering in his hand. Aziru waved him back down.

"King Aziru. My life is yours to command or take. I exist only to serve you. If you are determined on my death, then give me a blade and set me before the Kemetu army that I may take some of them with me into the afterworld."

Aziru pondered; his chin on his fist. His eyes flicked across to the Hittite ambassador and caught the faintest of nods. Ashraz the spymaster raised an eyebrow, slipping his dagger back in his belt.

"Agreed," Aziru said shortly. "When we find the Kemetu army you will meet them with a good blade in your hand." A faint smile creased his bearded face. "I would prefer it if you took the army with you and defeated my enemies, General Jebu, but I leave that to your judgment."

Jebu looked from king to spymaster to ambassador and back to Aziru. "I...you want me to take the army?"

"I believe that is the function of a general."

"Then I am still a general?"

"Yes."

Jebu's jaw tightened. "So what was the purpose of...of this playacting?"

Aziru waved a hand at Ashraz. "Tell him."

"Jebu, old friend, you must try and see this from a broader perspective. Our army engages the enemy having left what is arguably its most powerful unit behind. Then the battle is inconclusive and you withdraw from the field. Your loyalty was called into question and the king felt an investigation was called for."

"Mursilanda has been questioned and reluctantly admitted to an appalling misinterpretation of our king's instructions." Mutaril took a ring from his finger and held it out. "Take this, Jebu. It is the authority of Shubbiluliuma. Mursilanda will obey without question if you have this ring."

Jebu took the heavy silver ring molded in the form of a horned bull's head. He turned it over and over, then slowly slipped it onto the forefinger of his left hand. "I accept your words, ambassador, and those of my own king. I am, as ever, your loyal subject, but I would know one thing more. Who was it that called my loyalty into question?"

Aziru stirred, shifting uncomfortably in his chair. "My cousin, Lord Amalti. May I ask your intentions?"

Jebu's nostrils flared and his fists clenched by his sides. "He dishonours me. I will kill him."

"That is what I was afraid of. Did I not say that, Ashraz?"

"Indeed, your majesty."

"I cannot allow my only capable general to put himself in added danger by challenging a powerful lord."

"With respect, your majesty. I cannot be any sort of general until he is dead. My honour is more important than my life."

"Your words again, majesty," Ashraz murmured.

"You would never get near him, Jebu. My cousin Amalti lives in fear of assassination and has many guards. However, he also has many enemies, and it would not surprise me if one succeeded." Aziru smiled knowingly at his general. "I assume Amalti's death would wipe out the stain on your honour?"

Jebu pursed his lips and stroked his beard thoughtfully. "It would depend on whether the killer knew of my dishonour. If he did, then I could accept his death."

Ashraz laughed out loud. "Your majesty, you know your general so very well. It is exactly as you predicted. Shall I?" Aziru nodded and the spymaster pulled a leather bag from under the table, loosened the drawstrings and pulled out the bloodied head of the king's cousin, Lord Amalti. Gripping the head by its long, matted hair, he held it up for all to see. "He knew, Jebu. At the end he knew that retribution fell on him from Aziru and his General."

Jebu sighed deeply and ran his fingers through his still-damp hair. "Then I shall take my place at the head of your army again, majesty."

Aziru nodded. "I expect great things of you, Jebu. Train your army, and when you are ready, take bloody war to the Kemetu. With the help of the gods I will yet be king in Kemet."

Chapter 21

Four generations back, Zarw had been a small army garrison near the eastern borders of Kemet and near enough to the main trade route that led from the cities of the Great River north and east into Kenaan and the lands beyond, to be tactically important. When famine gripped the Fertile Crescent that encompassed the lands of Babylon, Mitanni, Hurri and Amori, people of those countries looked to Kemet. Rains might have failed, but the River always flooded, and grain was plentiful. Into the land of Kemet came a Khabiru seer, in the time of the great Nebmaetre Amenhotep's father, Tuthmosis. He settled initially in the rich Delta lands around Zarw, but his fame as a seer and a prophet brought his name to the attention of the king. Tuthmosis sent for Yuya, for such was his name, and tested him, pitting him against the prophets of his god Amun.

It is said that the god of Yuya triumphed, and that may well have been the case, for the priests of Amun declared undying hatred for the god of the Khabiru, the one with no name and no image. Yuya returned to Zarw and married, raising three children by his Kemetu-Nubian wife Tuya--Ay, Aanen and Tiye. The king's son, Amenhotep, came to Zarw fifteen years later and fell in love with Tiye, for great beauty was common in that family, and married her. It was almost unheard of for a prince to make a commoner his queen, but such was Tuthmosis' love for his son, that he raised Yuya to the position of Tjaty and caused to be built a great palace for his son and Tiye in Zarw, so she could be near her people, the Khabiru.

When Tuthmosis was called to the gods, Nebmaetre Amenhotep took his wife Tiye to Waset and ruled as king from the power base of his family. A city grew up around Tiye's palace in Zarw, and further out, in the rich fertile plains of the lower Delta, a community of Khabiru flourished and grew.

Scarab and Khu arrived in Zarw a month after leaving Iunu. They came overland with a small caravan of traders, paying their passage with another link of the gold chain. Scarab agonized over leaving the boat lad Amenhotep behind, but assuaged her guilt by arguing that they would be hard pressed to return before he left at the appointed time. Also, she felt a drive to be in Zarw. She had to reach Horemheb and though she knew the general had been in Waset, he surely would be returning to his army. Zarw was the one place she could be sure of crossing his path.

There is a small hill to the southwest of the city, no more than twenty or thirty cubits high, yet from the caravan route it hid the city completely. As the trail of mules, herds of goats and the few camels of their caravan started to round the hill, Scarab pulled Khu away from the line and hurried upward, over-riding his protests.

"I want to see the city before we arrive there and this hill is the best opportunity."

"We can see it quite well enough from down there," Khu grumbled. "I'm tired, and anyway, how do you know you can even see the city from up here? You've never been here before."

"Aram told me." Scarab saw the questioning look. "One of the Khabiru herdsmen. He comes from Zarw."

She mounted the top and looked across the green plain to the still-distant walled city of Zarw. The walls themselves surrounded the palace of Tiye and its gardens and temples, but the city itself lay outside, the tumbled and crowded mass of mud brick houses cowering under the walls like small children clinging to the skirts of their mother. The city of the Khabiru lay to the south and west of Zarw proper, a gaily coloured blazon of tents for the most part as befitted a traditionally nomadic people, but here and there were clusters of mud brick houses. To the north lay the army barracks behind its own set of walls. Between the two cities and the army lay a vast sea of cultivated land, a patchwork of crops and pasture tended by the Khabiru. Scarab pointed out the features she knew and guessed at others.

"That's the canal my father built for my mother." A broad channel of water arrowed out of the west from the distant river, the sunlight dazzling off its choppy surface. Small boats plied its surface, carrying people, animals and the wealth of the land. Surrounded by trees and reeds, the channel looked more like a river save for the abrupt way it ended close under the walls of the palace, cluttered by a mass of rickety wharves, refuse from the city bobbing in the water. "My mother used to tell me the channel was the most beautiful thing she'd seen," Scarab said sadly. "Look what they've done to it since she left." She wiped her eyes with the back of her hand and sniffed loudly.

"Never mind, it is not my concern now. That's where we have to go first," she said, pointing at the army barracks. "If Horemheb is not there, hopefully they will have word of him."

"What about the palace? It belonged to your mother."

"I cannot be known as a daughter of Nebmaetre. If word got back to Ay..."

"You don't think they'll recognise you anyway? You have a...a certain look about you. That hair for instance. Shouldn't you shave it off again?"

Scarab stroked her hair, knowing it was as short as a man's and made her stand out, but it was the colour of her mother's hair and she was not going to shave. "I'll pass myself off as a Khabiru woman. I look enough like one and I can speak the language after a fashion."

Khu nodded, knowing that once she got a thought in her head it was harder to shake out than a stick insect in a bush. "Hadn't we better be getting back? The caravan is past the hill already."

They ran down the hill and rejoined the tail end of the plodding caravan, walking easily along as the road skirted the outer edges of the Khabiru city before plunging through it to Zarw itself and one of the palace gates. The herds stopped in holding pens within the camp, but the mules, laden with trade goods continued on inward.

As they walked deeper into the Khabiru city, they found themselves immersed in a great sea of strangers, yet for Scarab, they were familiar strangers. She had known few Khabiru in her lifetime, her mother and two uncles, a scattering of servants within the palace, but these had dressed in the Kemetu way, speaking the language of the Two Lands. Here for the first time was literally hundreds of men, women and children who looked like her family and servants but, being dressed outlandishly, they struck her as strangely exotic.

Khu, together with the mule train drivers, looked Kemetu, but Scarab's features, and in particular her reddish hair, caught the attention of those they passed. Word spread faster than the pace of the mules and the crowds grew, looking and chattering in a language that the Kemetu could not understand. They kept a hand on their daggers and picked up the pace. Scarab on the other hand, could understand a lot of what was said and soon her face was nearly as red as her hair.

"Who is she?"

"Scandalous, has she no shame?"

"She is Kemetu, what do you expect?

"She is no Kemetu. Look at her hair."

"Khabiru?"

"Illegitimate, no doubt. Fathered by a wild youth on some river whore."

"Dressed like that too. See how she shamelessly exposes her breasts."

"A whore herself then."

Scarab's face coloured and she hurried on, clutching the thin linen of her gown about her shoulders. Always at ease with nudity, the pointed comments drew an unaccustomed flush of shame to her cheeks. She glanced at the women she passed, swathed in gaily coloured robes from head to foot, thin lips pursed in disapproving lines. Harried by cutting comments and hard looks, she found herself almost running by the time the mules entered the mud brick city beneath the palace walls.

"What's wrong?" Khu asked. "I couldn't understand what they were saying."

Scarab shook her head, thankful that in this street she once more blended into Kemetu society. She shivered and shook her gown out, folding her arms as she walked, suddenly self-conscious of her own breasts.

The military barracks proved to be little challenge to enter. The guards at the gate cast a bored look over the men and women that streamed in and out, laden with wares, carrying baskets of food or firewood, pitchers of water, wine and beer. Small herds of cattle and goats, rush cages full of squawking fowl and strings of fish, still glistening from the canal, all the bounty of land, water and air found its way into the domain of Kemet's protectors.

Scarab and Khu entered on the heels of a flock of goats and looked around in the spacious courtyard for the administrative building. Seeing several soldiers standing guard outside a closed door, Scarab pointed. "There. That'll be it, I'm sure."

It was the armory however, and the leader of the guard detail saw them off at spear point, soundly abusing them. As they moved away, however, he relented and shouted out to them, pointing at another building.

The door of the administration building stood open and inside the airy entrance hall sat a scribe busy tabulating a series of what looked like accounts. He looked up as they walked in.

"Yes? Can I help you?" His tone was mild though his expression conveyed an abstracted annoyance as if his mind was still in his figures.

"I'm...we are looking for General Horemheb," Scarab explained.

The scribe shook his head. "Nobody just sees the General. What is it about? Who are you?"

"I'm Bek...we are messengers from...from the Tjaty in Waset. We bear important messages for the General. Please tell us where we can find him."

The scribe looked them up and down slowly and sniffed loudly. "You are very young to be on government business and I have seen better dressed beggars."

Khu stepped forward and leaned toward the scribe, staring into his face. "I am Lord Mena of Akhet-Re and this is my sister Neferkhepre. We are not accustomed to being treated like this. You will direct us to General Horemheb immediately, and while we are with him you will find us fresh clothes and food. We were waylaid a day's journey south of here by bandits. That is something else we must report to the General."

The scribe lifted both eyebrows and reflexively leaned back out of Khu's reach and started to rise to his feet. "My apologies, Lord Mena, I shall..." He hesitated and he frowned. "How is it that you come from Waset to see the General? He is in Waset. How did you not know this?"

"He was there, we know," Scarab explained. "We came down from our estates at Akhet-Re for the young king's coronation. We saw Horemheb there. Later he left and the Tjaty asked us to go after him with a message..."

"Why you?" The scribe's voice hardened, suspicion blossoming again. "You I could believe were raised in a noble household, a ladies maid perhaps, but him?" He glanced at Khu. "He has a common voice. You cannot disguise it." The man got to his feet and walked to the door. He glanced out at the guards across the courtyard. "Why would the Tjaty send a message by the likes of you? Quickly, before I call the guards to arrest you."

Scarab smiled and looked down shyly before meeting the scribes stare again, flushing daintily under his scrutiny. "You are very perceptive, sir," she said softly. "I am indeed a daughter of a noble family--indeed my father was a son of the great Amenhotep himself, by a concubine of course. This young man..." She waved a hand vaguely at Khu. "He is one of my servants. I should have known we could not fool the General's scribe. However, some aspects of our story are true."

"Indeed?" The scribe's eyes moved appreciatively over the young girl's body, the interest showing in his voice. "What was true then?"

"We were robbed," Scarab said. She lifted her arms to display her ragged and stained gown, well aware of the effect the movement had on the man in front of her. "This is not the garb I am accustomed to. And we do have a message for Horemheb, though not from Tjaty Ay."

"The General is not here."

Khu groaned. "Gods. Then where is he?"

The scribe glanced at Khu, then back at the young girl and shrugged. "Still in Waset as far as any of us know. We expected him back a month past."

Scarab sighed, her shoulders slumping. "I...I had not thought past finding him, and now he is not here."

"You could talk to his lieutenant...no, for he is sick and may not recover. You could wait for the next legion commander back on leave. I believe Djedhor is due."

Scarab looked up at the scribe, her eyes widening. "Who is the lieutenant and why is he sick? Is...is it Paramessu?"

"You know him? Will he speak for you?"

"Yes. And yes." Scarab got up quickly. "Take us to him."

The scribe frowned. "He is with the physician. It is doubtful he will live."

"What has happened?" Scarab lunged at the scribe and gripped his biceps tightly. "What has happened to him? Tell me." She stared in his eyes, her own already moistening.

The scribe struggled to free himself and did so with difficulty, only to find himself penned in by Khu as he moved up beside Scarab. "It w...was a wound," he stammered. "In the big battle. He thought it nothing at first but it went bad and now his leg is as red and hot as the desert. The army doctors do not expect him to live."

"Nor would he if it were left to them," said a voice behind them. They turned quickly, Khu's jaw dropping, and Scarab's face breaking into a smile of joy.

"Nebhotep. What are you doing here? How? When?" Scarab laughed and ran to the physician, throwing her arms about him.

"A long story and one I am willing to tell you, my lady, but first I must wash and break my fast. Will you and Khu join me?"

"My lady? She really is a lady?" The scribe's face flushed with embarrassment.

"Oh, yes," Nebhotep said softly. "Very much a lady."

"Nebhotep," Scarab murmured. "Enough. The world does not need to know."

"What of the lad? He said his name was Mena, not Khu."

"Friend Hay," Nebhotep said, addressing the scribe. "Let it suffice that this is as great a lady as you should hope to meet, and this young lad here, while not of the nobility, has a trusted position in our government. He often uses the name Mena when traveling on business. Treat them with respect."

"Yes, honoured physician." Hay bent almost double as he bowed first to Nebhotep and then to Scarab, even sparing a bow of lesser proportion for Khu. "I shall, with your permission, fetch fresh clothes and food for your guests."

"Thank you Hay. We shall be in my rooms. Only disturb us when you have the clothing and food, or if the lieutenant's condition changes."

"Paramessu. Is he all right? What has happened? Can I see him?"

"Soon. Come with me now." Nebhotep turned and led the way deeper into the barracks' administration building. They walked down a long corridor before turning and entering a spacious room almost devoid of furniture. A cot bed lay along one mud wall and a table and three chairs occupied a position on another wall. The dirt floor in between boasted only rush matting and a few scattered pots and plates. "Not much is it?" Nebhotep said with a laugh, "But I call it home for now." He crossed to the table and lifted a cloth that lay over a clay dish, revealing bread, cheese and a handful of dates. "You are welcome to what I have, though I daresay Hay will bring you better soon." He gestured to the chairs. "Sit."

Khu sat and picked up a date, chewing on it carefully, but Scarab stood where she was, staring at the physician. "What has happened to Paramessu? Why can't I see him?"

Nebhotep stifled a yawn. "Forgive me, lady, I have been up all night." He poured water into the solitary cup on the table and offered it to Scarab. "No?" He drank deeply, his throat working convulsively. Wiping his mouth with one hand he put the cup down and faced the young woman again. "You can see him when he wakes. I gave him strong poppy not an hour ago. He will sleep the rest of the day."

"Thank you, Nebhotep. What is wrong with him?"

"Nothing that some elementary cleanliness would not have prevented. He took an arrow in the leg during the battle with the Amorites, pulled it out almost without knowing, and then carried on as if nothing had happened. He may be good to his men but they need a live general, not a dead hero."

"The wound went bad?" Khu asked, breaking open the loaf of bread. He stuck a slab of cheese on it and bit down, grimacing at the gritty texture. "Why do wounds go bad, anyway?"

Nebhotep snorted. "The army physicians say the gods dole out sickness and health, but I have never seen a rotten wound that wasn't dirty."

"So his wound became rotten?" Scarab asked. Her hands clenched and unclenched by her sides and her eyes stared at the physician, bright and glittering. "Tell me."

Nebhotep's eyes widened. "Easy girl, you'll do him no good by upsetting yourself. Sit down and take some food and I'll tell you everything."

Scarab opened her mouth to protest but the door opened and the scribe Hay entered with several servants. One laid fresh clothes on the bed, together with a small basket of pots which by the odors escaping into the room were filled with unguents and perfumes. Another spread a linen cloth on the table, while a third deposited several plates of food and a fourth a pitcher of wine and a jug of beer, along with some beautiful blue faience cups.

"From the General's rooms," Hay explained with a smile. He ushered the servants out and close the door behind him.

Scarab sat heavily on one of the chairs and poured herself a cup of wine. She drank it down in several long swallows and poured another one, raising an admonishing hand as Khu frowned. "Go on, Nebhotep. Tell me everything."

"Very well, my lady." The physician yawned again, putting a hand to his mouth. "The wound became badly inflamed, so much so that by the time the army doctors thought to bring him back to Zarw, he was close to death. A great fever took hold of him and his leg swelled so much the skin started to split."

"Did the army doctors not treat him?"

"Indeed. They dosed him with foul-tasting potions and covered him with the usual herbal poultices, reciting prayers over him until they became hoarse, but it had no effect. Then they tried fox urine and when that didn't work, the urine and saliva of a lion, though the gods only know where they found that."

"It didn't work?" Khu asked.

"Of course not. Then they tried honey, which I would have tried first, but by then it was too late. The poison had bitten deep into his leg."

"Poison? I thought you said it was a wound."

"It was an arrow wound but his body showed signs of a strong poison at work, either from something on the arrow or a poison introduced afterward. The other commanders had the servants put to the question but none would reveal who had introduced the poison. Luckily, they decided to bring him back here and the gods saw fit to bring me here within an hour of his arrival." Nebhotep grinned tiredly. "The gods smiled on our Paramessu, for I believe I have saved his life."

Scarab looked up from her wine cup. "Truly? You are not just saying that to ease my pain?"

"Nobody can cheat the gods, my lady," Nebhotep said in a gentle voice. "But he has recovered remarkably in the last two days. I believe he will live."

"And his...his leg?"

"He will keep it."

"I shall offer up a sacrifice to the Nine of Iunu," Scarab breathed. "Take me to him, Nebhotep. I must see with my own eyes that he still lives."

"He is asleep, my lady. Let me take you to him later." Nebhotep yawned again and glanced longingly at the bed.

"Now. I will see him now."

The physician sighed. "Learn from this Khu. Nobles are ever importunate, as are women. Put the two together and they are unstoppable. Come then lady; let us visit the sleeping man."

Scarab blushed. "I am sorry, Nebhotep. I know you are tired but I must see him."

"Tired?" Nebhotep shook his head as he opened the door. "Yesterday I was tired, last night I was exhausted. Today?" He shrugged. "Today I think I am dead already but do not know it." The physician led the way back along the corridor then up a flight of stairs to the upper floor where a servant sat cross-legged on the floor outside, the interior of the room visible from where he sat. The man scrambled to his feet as they approached.

"How is he, Nef?"

"Well enough, physician Nebhotep," replied the man, bowing deferentially. "I sponge him down and moisten his lips as instructed."

In a small room on the shaded north side of the building, a wasted man lay on a narrow cot. Covered only in a sheen of sweat, Paramessu lay in a troubled sleep, his ribs visible through his ashen skin. His eyelids trembled and his mouth muttered and mumbled, his limbs jerking uncontrollably at intervals.

"Oh, gods save him." Scarab ran to the cot and dropped to her knees beside the man, her hand reaching out to stroke his hot forehead. "I thought you said he was better, Nebhotep."

"He is. You should have seen him yesterday before I started cleaning out his wound."

Khu stared down at the Paramessu's left leg, at the gaping red wound in the upper thigh, and... "What...what is that? His leg is...is flyblown."

Scarab looked round, then down at the leg. Her eyes widened and rolled in her head and she clutched at the bed for support. Nebhotep looked puzzled for a moment then leapt to support her, dashing some water in her face. She spluttered and wiped her face off, before sitting back on her heels and staring in fascination and disgust at the wound. "Are those maggots?" she whispered. "I thought you said you cleaned the wound."

"That is exactly what they are doing, my lady." Nebhotep's voice, despite the exhaustion evident in it, also displayed a measure of pride. "Fly maggots will only eat dead flesh and the filth that is in wounds. I put them there myself and as you can see they have consumed almost all the rotten meat, leaving only healthy muscle behind. In a few hours I shall wash the maggots from the wound, apply a poultice of my specially prepared mould mixed with honey and bandage him up. Paramessu is strong. He will, with the gods' help, live many years yet. Who knows, he may even recover full use of his leg."

"This has worked before?"

"On occasion, I am told, though this is the first time I have tried it." Nebhotep leaned over and poked the flesh gently. "What the maggots are doing is cleaning the wound thoroughly, which should have been done immediately. Water would have sufficed then, and the scar would have been almost unnoticeable. Now, he will have a massive scar, and one that will be obvious to everyone." He allowed himself a small smile. "As he is a soldier, no-one will remark on it." Nebhotep straightened and yawned, loudly and at length. "Now I must insist, my lady. Leave Paramessu to his healing sleep. Nef will call me if there is any need." He ushered everybody from the room, nodding to his assistant who sat cross-legged again outside the room.

They helped the now staggering physician back to his room and onto his bed, where he sat, paying no attention as they quickly slipped into their new clothes. They sat at the table and folded some of the food into a cloth.

"Nebhotep," Khu asked casually. "How is it you are here? We left you in Waset three months or more ago."

The physician looked up blearily. "In the name of all the gods," he slurred. "Let me go to sleep." He shook his head wearily. "Ay tried to kill us all. Aanen and I escaped and I came looking for you."

"How did you know where to find us?"

"Who is there who could help you? I thought my lady might seek...seek assistance from her brother Akhenaten. Then where...? Not back south again...Men-nefer maybe? I found a young lad... 'menhot'...with a boat...he remembered...you... brought me to Zarw...up...canal..." Nebhotep collapsed backward onto the bed, unconscious within seconds.

Scarab straightened the physician's body on the cot bed with a smile. "May the gods bless you, Nebhotep, and the lad Amenhotep," she murmured. "I shall find a temple of the Nine and pray for both of you, and my Paramessu." She and Khu left the room with their cloth of food, closing the door quietly behind them.

Chapter 22

T he palace gardens of the western palace at Waset were relatively
new, despite dating to the time of the present king's father,
Nebmaetre Amenhotep. The palms stood proud and tall but in
the nearly two decades since the palace had been abandoned, the
shrubbery and formal gardens had grown into an untended riot of
vegetation. This tangle had been removed some six months past on the
accession of the new king and the gardens still struggled to grow.
Teams of slaves brought in water, soil from the fertile fields and loads
of animal dung. Skilled gardeners tended the young plants and trees
transplanted with care from other gardens, or scoured the countryside
looking for flowering and scented shrubs to please the king's eyes and
nostrils. But despite the efforts of hundreds of slaves, the grounds of
the western palace still looked raw and new--except in one place.

A corner of the orchard where the fruit trees still grew attracted the
attention of Huy, Overseer of the King's Gardeners. A small artificial
hill was constructed and planted with quick growing herbs and scented
bushes. Stone slabs were cunningly placed so that when water was
poured into a basin at the top, a series of small cascades was formed.
The splashing water humidified the air, cooling it and providing a
soothing background to the birdsong and thrum of insects. Often, in the
heat of the afternoon, the young king and his queen would sit on a
stone bench by the fish pool at the bottom of the cascade, spending
moments together in relative solitude, away from the cares of the
kingdom.

They did not concern themselves that behind the screen of trees, a hidden chain of slaves scooped water from the fish pond and passed it hand over hand to the rear of the hill and up to its summit. For an hour each afternoon, the waterfalls leaped and splashed for the king's pleasure.

Though a mere boy when he came to his coronation day, Nebkheperure Tutankhaten had become a god on that day, and had been admitted into the company of the many gods of the Two Kingdoms. The event changed his impressionable mind and he lost his boyhood together with his purely mortal status. The boy became, if not yet a man, at least a youth. And a youth married to a young, beautiful girl who had been raised in the belief that she ruled by right of birth. More and more, the boy king sought out her presence, and his mind turned from a regard for her as a companion and playmate to that of a queen and a wife.

Other things occupied Tutankhaten's mind though. Ever mindful of the gods, even before he became one, he was determined to honour them in the way he knew best, by ordering the enormous resources of the Two Kingdoms into the planning and erection of temples and statues. The great temple dedicated to the Aten at Gempaaten, near the third cataract in Nubia, was refurbished and enlarged, being rededicated to the gods Amun and Atum. Numerous statues in honour of Amun were started around Waset, and if they bore an uncanny resemblance to the young king, that was only because Tutankhaten, despite his name, was the earthly representative of Amun. Though the priest of Amun, at the coronation, had named him Tutankhamen, the young king still retained his birth name on the advice of his Tjaty.

"Do not be dictated to by a priest," Ay said. "It is your name and you will change it when the time is right."

"When will the time be right?"

"I will tell you."

Ay, ever mindful of the king's age and lack of experience, sought to relieve him of as many of the petty annoyances of everyday life as possible, assuming full political and judicial control. It was Ay who sat in judgment every day in the Hall of Justice, Ay who met with ambassadors and envoys, and Ay who held, with Horemheb, the army in the palm of his hand. This was an arrangement that gave the young king time to design his temples and statues, time to lead the prayers in

289

the temples, his high treble rising clear into the still air every dawn. If any thought that Ay assumed too much power, none dared say it, and so Ay grew in stature daily. Yet Ay's life was not completely one of work and responsibility. He took time off in the hot afternoons to sit in the king's gardens and enjoy the quiet, away from the court and his duties. On this one afternoon not long after the floods had receded, he sat on a bench with Horemheb, casually observing the king and queen by the fish pool, the cascade behind them successfully drowning out their young voices.

"They seem happy enough," Horemheb mused, stretching out his legs and kicking off his sandals. "I don't know why you are so worried. The boy is doing well."

"He is a remarkable young man," Ay agreed. "He has taken to kingship better than I thought he would."

"What basis do you have for saying that? Aside from his priestly duties you do not give him much opportunity to play the king."

"Nor will I until he is older. He is, as you say, just a boy and he has no real concept of the complexities of rulership."

"Then he should be thankful you are here to assume the burden."

Ay looked up sharply. "You mock me, Horemheb?"

"Perhaps. You cannot complain because you run the Kingdoms and are king in all but name, when you have been amassing power and wealth since Amenhotep's day."

"What I did, I did for Kemet, not myself."

"Of course." Horemheb fell silent and watched the young king and queen over by the fish pool. The sound of the falling water drowned out their voices except for an occasional burst of laughter, but he could read them through a study of the way they sat, how they leaned toward one another, a touch, and a look. "They are in love," he said, with a trace of surprise.

Ay nodded. "Such is my reading of the situation. He has always been a quiet boy, studious even, though he excels in archery. Still, he is a boy yet and only starting to discover the delights of a woman."

"At ten? He is precocious."

"He is the blood of Amenhotep, what can you expect?" Ay nodded toward the young queen. "What gives me greater concern is my grand-daughter Ankhesenpaaten. Though it pains me to say it, she is a true child of my own daughter Nefertiti. Hot-blooded, passionate and driven by a desire for power. She was the only choice for queen, I know, but unless that boy grows up fast and satisfies her lusts, there will be trouble."

Horemheb frowned. "She would be unfaithful to the king? What would she gain?"

"Her father took her young and awoke an appetite within her. She needs a man and she has a boy." Ay shrugged expansively. "Oh, the novelty and delights of being queen will hold her content for a while but sooner or later she will seek to quench the fire between her legs. A child that cannot be the king's would be disastrous."

"I find that hard to believe. They look happy, by the gods--even the queen. Look at them. That is a boy and a girl who love each other."

"I took my grand-daughter aside and explained certain matters to her. She knows that her surest path to what she wants lies through the king's bed. Once they are sleeping together, her appetites will diminish." Ay chuckled. "And who knows, maybe there will be an heir."

"I would have thought that was the last thing you wanted, old man. An heir cuts you out of the path to the throne."

"You put your finger on the nub despite your gibes, Horemheb. I am an old man. What chance do I have of surviving Tutankhaten? I want the future of Kemet in safe hands--my own for now, later that young man's, after him a son of his body on my grand-daughter. My line will rule Kemet even if I do not."

"If I thought differently, I would oppose you as I did once before. As it is, you rule Kemet even if your name is not carved on the monuments and the statues of Amun do not have your face."

Now Ay sat silently in the perfumed shade of the citrus trees, remembering. At length he sighed deeply. "I loved my daughter Nefertiti, for all she was headstrong and single-minded."

"Not unlike you."

"Maybe." Ay hesitated. "Is...is she..."

"She is alive, if that is what you are asking," Horemheb replied, keeping his voice flat. "And before you ask, I will not tell you where she is. Suffice it to say I get monthly reports from my spies and agents throughout the lands bordering on Kemet. She is alive."

"Thank you, Horemheb. Will you bring her home--for me? She is no longer a threat."

"No."

"Please, Horemheb. She is all I have. Will you do it for an old man who probably will not live much longer? I would be reconciled with her. Please."

"No, I will not. She was exiled for life and I will not break my word to Akhenaten--or his memory if he should accidentally die, so drive that thought from your mind too. Concentrate your affections on your other daughter, Mutnodjme."

"She has no great affection for me and stays in her estates in Ineb Hedj. I have no-one, Horemheb. No-one who loves me." Ay sighed deeply again.

"Your pain drives me to tears," Horemheb said, his voice oozing sarcasm. "Go find some woman of the streets. If you pay her enough, she will love you."

Ay got up and walked away from Horemheb, toward the far end of the fish pond and the end of the screen of trees on the far side. He watched for several minutes as sweating slaves dipped broad-mouthed clay pots into the pond and passed them along the line, circulating the water at great effort for the fleeting pleasure of a boy and girl. He nodded in satisfaction. It was right that the multitudes of Kemet toil for the comfort of the few. The old man stretched, his joints cracking, before turning back to look at Kemet's General on the bench under the citrus shade. The General was watching the king, ignoring Ay, who was the true danger. Smiling to himself, he thought over his recent conversation. *Hide your true thoughts. Misdirect those about you.* He did not care about Nefertiti--she had proved weak. Nor about her sister Mutnodjme. He had not seen her in years and truth be told, did not care if she lived or died. His lovely and lustful grand-daughter Ankhesenpaaten would serve her purpose for now and could be easily controlled. *If she produces an heir, so much the better.* If Tutankhaten showed signs of rebellion he could be removed and a younger boy put in his place. *I will live forever. I will rule Kemet forever.* Ay's shoulders slumped and he put on the mantle of an old man again, shuffling back to Horemheb.

"We might have a problem in Nubia," Ay said as he sat down again. "I am getting troubling reports of banditry in Kush."

"There are always bandits in Nubia. What makes this so important you would trouble yourself with it?"

"Most bandits are gangs of roaming thugs. The governor sends out a patrol and stamps them flat, hangs a few, and the region is at peace again until the next time." Ay turned to look at the other man from beneath hooded eyes. "This one is different. He is Kemetu rather than Nubian, and calls himself Son of Sobek, Son of the Crocodile god."

"So instruct the governor to send out his garrison. Do I have to tell you how to do your job?"

"He has sent out three patrols. All have disappeared."

"Really? Disappeared or killed?"

"I don't know. Does it matter?"

"Possibly not, but if they have just disappeared without trace they may have deserted or joined forces with this Son of Sobek. Do you know who he is?"

Ay shrugged. "Just a bandit, if a somewhat troubling one."

Horemheb turned to search the Tjaty's face. "Could it be Smenkhkare? He is supposed to have died by a crocodile, but no body was recovered. Now a Son of the Crocodile god emerges, a Kemetu, leading Nubian rebels. Is it just coincidence?"

"It is not Smenkhkare," Ay scoffed, though his eyes did not meet the general's. "Eyewitnesses saw him pulled under. He is definitely dead."

"Then we may have someone passing himself off as Smenkhkare. In some ways that could be even more dangerous."

Ay said nothing, just raised his eyebrows questioningly.

"The real Smenkhkare was a king who, if nothing else, loved Kemet. If he survived he would seek an open, just path back to power. He would not be inciting the provinces to rebel against the throne. If this Son of Sobek is just pretending to be the king, then he will try to appeal to past loyalties as well as attracting brigands in search of plunder."

Ay nodded. "You have put your finger on it again, Horemheb. Are you sure you do not want my job?"

"I am a soldier," Horemheb growled. "I like my enemies in front of me where I can keep an eye on them, not skulking around seeking power in dirty places."

"Then, my able General, I require you to confront the enemies of Kemet once again. Go to Nubia, track down and capture or kill this Son of Sobek, whoever he is, and restore peace to the province."

"And if he is Smenkhkare?"

"He is not. He cannot be. Smenkhkare is dead."

"And if he is?" Horemheb persisted. "What then?"

"Officially Smenkhkare is dead. We buried him for the entire world to see in the Great Place. Any bandit leader you capture will be an imposter, nothing more." Ay held Horemheb's gaze firmly. "An imposter would unbalance the nation, disturb Ma'at. He should be summarily executed." He paused, looking for any wavering of resolve in the general's face. "Is that understood?"

"Yes."

Ay continued to stare into the general's face. "But?"

"But nothing. I agree with you. I happen to like young Smenkhkare...or should I say I liked him, but his presence would be most unsettling at the present time. Three kings of Kemet at the same time would be unprecedented and would result in civil war." Horemheb shook his head. "No, the bandit leader in Nubia is an impostor, nothing more. I will find him and remove him."

"When will you leave?"

"Immediately. I will take the Amun legion as it would take too long to move troops down from the borders. Psenamy will command the few troops left in Waset. He is your creature, Ay, so talk to him. I expect him to guard the king well in my absence."

Ay nodded his acquiescence as Horemheb continued counting off points on his fingers. "I will want every scrap of information you have on this man's movements. I need to know what troops are in place in Nubia already, and any recent political appointments you have made. I am presuming I have full authority to act in this matter?"

"Yes, just don't exhaust the treasury," Ay said sourly.

"If you want him caught you must expect to pay the price."

"Have you any idea how much that boy..." Ay jerked his thumb in the direction of the king "...is costing me with his constant demands for new temples and statues?"

Horemheb laughed. "He is the king, after all."

"Well, I need more gold for the treasury. While you are down in Nubia, see if you can increase the production at the mines there."

"That is hardly my job. Who is viceroy?"

"Huy."

Horemheb shook his head. "I don't think I know him."

"He was Scribe of the Correspondence under Merimose in Amenhotep's time. He knows the country intimately, so make use of his knowledge. I might add that although he is about your age, he is a personal friend of the king."

"There was a Huy in the army in Asia just before I took over there. Him?"

"Very probably. He earned the title of 'His Majesty's Brave Warrior of Cavalry' before he came to court. He became 'Divine Father' and 'Fan-bearer on the King's Right', like me, so do not dismiss him as just another political appointee. Huy has real ability."

"Where is he based?"

"Sehotep-Neteru that the natives call Faras. There is a major garrison there, under Lieutenant Penno. You'd be advised to make use of him also. He knows how the Nubians fight."

Horemheb contemplated the old Tjaty cautiously. "If Huy and this Penno are so formidable, why do you need me?"

"Penno was one of the officers who came to Waset and swore his oath of fealty to Smenkhkare. Can you imagine what would happen if he came across this Son of Sobek and renewed his oath to him?"

Horemheb smiled. "Why would he if he is not Smenkhkare?"

"Just be sure you are the one to catch and kill him." Ay saw the king and queen get up from where they now sat on the grass by the fish pond and move toward them, hand in hand. He tapped Horemheb on the knee to catch his attention and stood up, bowing as the royal couple drew near. "Your majesties."

"Divine Father," Tutankhaten replied, graciously nodding his head, before spoiling the effect by grinning. "Horemheb, you have not been to see me in all the time you have been back in Waset. I want to hear some exciting stories of the rich lands you are conquering for me in Asia."

"Alas, your majesty, I have to leave for Nubia immediately."

"But I want you here," the king pouted. "Ay, tell him to stay. I want him to tell me stories."

"Tuti," Ankhesenpaaten said gently, laying her fingers gently on her small husband's arm. "There will be time for stories later. You should tell them of our good news."

"Good news, your majesty?"

"But...oh, all right. My beautiful Khesi and I have decided we are going to have a baby of our own."

Ay blinked. "Er, that is wonderful news, majesty." His eyes flicked to his grand-daughter who just smiled coolly. "When is this joyous event?"

"Well, Khesi has to show me what to do, but how hard can it be? I am the king after all. I can do anything."

"Indeed you can your majesty. I look forward to the day when Kemet's succession is assured." Ay bowed deeply again, hiding a smile.

Chapter 23

rumpets flared in the light, airy, sunlit halls of the king's palace at Akhet-Aten as King Waenre Akhenaten moved solemnly through the wide pillared corridors and halls toward the Chamber of Justice. Behind him marched the commander of the palace guards, Khaemnum, lately second in command of the Amun legion under General Psenamy, and now with an independent command guarding the king. He took his duties seriously, though he still suffered bouts of confusion as to whether he guarded the king from the people, or the other way round. Either way, he kept his men close and his eyes and ears open.

Servants threw open the double cedar doors of the Chamber of Justice. The space inside seemed larger for the scattering of people within it, a handful of the nobles of Akhet-Aten, merchants and shop-keepers, and a few common people, holding papers and documents in the hopes of finding the King's Justice.

The king looked round at his audience as he entered the chamber, a small smile twinkling his eyes. He turned to Khaemnum. "I think I have more guards here than petitioners," he said softly. "Could you not serve your purpose adequately by having half wait outside?"

Khaemnum grunted and spun slowly on his heel, surveying the small crowd carefully. With a nod, he gestured to his men, entering with only a small guard which ranged itself around the throne on the raised dais. He waited until all was still and Akhenaten seated comfortably before moving to the front of the dais and holding up his right hand.

"Behold and attend, citizens of Akhet-Aten. Your king, Waenre Akhenaten, comes before you to hear your pleas for justice. Approach now and present your evidence." Khaemnum lowered his hand and stepped back, gesturing to the Chamberlain, who immediately pushed the first man forward, onto his knees in front of the throne.

"Your majesty, this is Manku, a potter of the street 'Glory of Aten'. He brings suit against the grain merchant Nefneber who sold him a sack of moldy grain."

"Is the grain merchant here to answer this charge?"

"I am, your majesty." A small, rotund man, sweating profusely, threw himself to the floor and groveled before the king. "The grain was not moldy when I sold it, your majesty."

"Is the grain moldy now?"

"Yes, your majesty," replied the Chamberlain. "I examined the sack myself."

"Do either of you have witnesses to the state of the grain before today?" asked the king.

The Chamberlain consulted his papers. "The wife of Manku attests to the moldiness when she opened the sack three days ago and the slave of Nefneber to the fine state of the grain when sold."

"No help there, then," Akhenaten said. "A wife should support her husband and a slave is bound to his master." He thought for a few moments, one hand stroking his long chin. "When did the transaction take place?"

"There is some difference of opinion, your majesty," the Chamberlain said. "Manku says ten days ago whereas Nefneber says two months."

Akhenaten raised his eyebrows. "If it was only ten days ago and moldy already then Manku has a true grievance. On the other hand, if the grain was sold two months ago, then the dampness after the floods may well have affected it after it was sold. Do you have records of the transaction?"

"I...I do, majesty." Manku took a small fragment of pottery from his waist pouch and held it up. Khaemnum took it from the man's hand and passed it to Akhenaten.

The king turned it over, scrutinizing the marks on it. "It says twelve fine glazed pots were paid for one sack of good barley. Is this your sign, Nebnefer?" He held the pottery fragment up.

The grain merchant squinted at the shard then nodded. "It is, your majesty."

"And you say this transaction took place only ten days ago, Manku?"

The potter nodded. "Yes, majesty."

"There is no date on this shard. Is it not common practice to date transactions, Chamberlain?"

"Indeed sire, in the king's house and most...ah, elevated households."

"But seemingly not in this potter's house, nor in the grain merchant's." Akhenaten sat back and thought for a few moments, the forefinger on his right hand tracing a small circle on the armrest of the throne. "Do you keep your own records of your sales, Nebnefer?"

"Yes, majesty." He snapped his fingers and urged a naked slave out from the small crowd of petitioners. The man dropped to his knees and scrambled forward clutching a papyrus roll. "This is my record of the last two months, my lord." The papyrus was passed up to the king who unrolled it and examined the close lines of writing.

"Who wrote this? The penmanship is good."

"I employ a scribe to record my dealings, majesty."

"Is he here today?"

A man in the clean white kilt of a scribe stepped forward and bowed. "Scribe Ahmose, your majesty."

"Come up here and read this document for me."

Ahmose bowed again and walked up onto the dais until he stood beside the seated king. His head was above that of Akhenaten, so he quickly stooped, and then dropped to his knees beside the throne. Peering at the roll, he pointed to an entry near the beginning. "Here is the sale to the potter Manku, majesty. The twentieth day of the first month of Proyet, the Emergence. See, I have written his name here, receipt of twelve pots, and here the single sack of barley. These other entries are other transactions that took place all the way down..." The scribe gently unfurled the scroll in the king's hands. "...To a sale yesterday near dusk of three sacks of grain to the household of Lord Mahmose."

Akhenaten nodded, scanning the intervening entries. "There is another entry for Manku right here, is there not?" He pointed. "And only ten days ago."

The scribe looked closely, then nodded. "Indeed your majesty, you have sharp eyes."

The king sighed and passed a hand over his face. "All too rarely these days, I fear," he murmured. "But does this not open the question once more that Manku is right? The sale did take place ten days ago, as he said."

"With respect, your majesty," Ahmose said deferentially. "It shows a sale took place, not necessarily the sale in question."

"Explain."

"Here, sir. The original sale two months ago put the cost of grain at the end of Ahket, the Inundation, as twelve fine pots to a sack, yet here, ten days ago when the first early harvest was in, only three pots bought a sack."

Akhenaten nodded. "And the shard said twelve. It was the earlier sack that went moldy."

On the floor in front of the throne, Manku paled. He prostrated himself full length. "Have mercy, great king," he quavered. "I am a poor man, I only..."

"Silence!" Khaemnum snapped.

Akhenaten nodded. "The potter Manku stands convicted by his own mouth. Take him away, Khaemnum. I will decide on his fate later."

The soldiers dragged the weeping potter away and the defendant, his slave and his scribe bowed with varying degrees of humility and backed out of the king's presence. The Chamberlain presented the next case and the antagonists started their arguments.

Despite the few people in the Chamber of Justice, the cases dragged on and it was close to noon before the last case was heard and the judgment delivered. Akhenaten rose from his throne slowly, fighting back the urge to stretch and yawn. Instead, he bowed to the remaining lords and court officials, receiving their obeisance in return. The guards threw the doors open and the king walked out, enveloped by his retinue of soldiers.

"It is midday, Khaemnum," Akhenaten said. "I am hungry."

"Yes your majesty." The officer led his troops through the king's palace to a large colonnaded verandah that opened out onto gardens. Several large tables had been covered with fresh linen cloths and a variety of dishes and pots. The king walked over and poked a long finger into a few of them, grunting and nodding. He licked his finger and sighed, then reached up and removed the double crown of Kemet, setting it on the table near to a dish of goose meat swimming in its own grease.

"I do not like to eat alone. I will wait for my beautiful wife Nefertiti."

"Your majesty," one of the servants said. "The er...the queen...I mean, er...your daughter Meryetaten will be here shortly."

"Nonsense, my daughter Meryetaten is in Waset. She is married to my brother Smenkhkare. I will be eating with Nefertiti." He looked around the room suspiciously. "Where is my wife? Where have you hidden her?"

The servant cast a scared glance at Khaemnum and as the king was looking the other way, risked a gesture involving his forefinger and head.

Khaemnum coughed discreetly. "Your majesty, your queen has er, gone on a State visit and er, will be gone some time. Do you not remember? Your daughter Meryetaten has come down to Akhet-Aten to be with you during her absence."

"Gone?" Akhenaten picked up a slice of the roast goose and examined it as if it held the answer to Nefertiti's absence. "When did she leave? I don't remember...and my Meryetaten is here?" He bit into the meat and chewed noisily, grease dripping down his long chin. "Has she brought little Tashery with her?"

Khaemnum grimaced. "She left some time ago, majesty and no, your daughter Meryetaten came alone."

"A pity, I like little Tashery. I have a toy here for her somewhere." The king began lifting the dishes and looking under them. He emptied a flagon of beer onto the floor, splashing himself and the attendant servants in the process, before peering into the depths of the jar for the lost toy. "It is here somewhere, I know..." Akhenaten's voice trailed off and he dropped the last piece of goose onto the table, standing and staring at the beer flagon, his face slowly screwing up into a picture of misery.

"She died, didn't she? My darling little Tashery." Tears welled and spilled. "All my darling daughters...my Meketaten, my beautiful Neferneferouaten, lovely Neferneferoure and little Setepenre... all gone. Just like my wife Nefertiti, they have all left me and gone to be with the Living Aten, blessed be he. Even my little queens Merye and Khese. I am quite alone." The king held onto the table with one hand as his voice broke down into paroxysms of sobbing.

"Not alone, father. I am with you."

Khaemnum turned toward the door with a loud sigh of relief. "May the gods be praised, Queen Meryetaten."

The eldest of Akhenaten's daughters stood in the doorway. No longer having a beauty to rival that of her mother, the fabled Nefertiti, the woman had put on weight, together with the cares and sorrows of being an unloved queen. Following on the birth and subsequent death of her baby daughter by her marriage to her own father, Akhenaten had put her away in his quest to father a son. He married his only other surviving daughter, Ankhesenpaaten, sending his former queen upriver to Waset to marry his younger brother and co-regent, Smenkhkare. Trapped in a loveless marriage, one of form only and no substance, the bitter young woman withdrew into solitude. She turned away from the religious reforms being slowly introduced by the co-regent and took once more to the beliefs of her childhood, seeking the support of her father's god, Aten. Then Smenkhkare died and Tutankhaten became king, with her younger sister Ankhesenpaaten as queen. Meryetaten saw her opportunity to rejoin her father and left for Akhet-Aten as soon as she was able.

Meryetaten entered the room and took in the situation with a glance. She signaled the servants to leave, but restrained Khaemnum as he bowed and tried to leave with them. "Stay," she murmured. "I have need of you." Walking across to her weeping father, she put an arm around him and held him close. "It is all right, father," she said. "I am here to look after you." She waited patiently as her father continued weeping, his muffled cries ripped out of him by his suddenly released agony. After many long minutes, she led him across to a padded and cushioned couch and persuaded him to lie down.

"My eyes," Akhenaten whimpered. "They hurt."

Meryetaten wet a cloth from a pitcher of cool river water and rested it over her father's eyes, stroking his hand and whispering to him as he fell silent then, a while later, fell asleep.

"Has he been doing this a long time?" Meryetaten asked quietly. She stood, leaving her father sleeping on the couch, and crossed the room to where Khaemnum stood.

"What?"

"Imagining himself back in happier times."

"As long as I can remember," Khaemnum said. "But I've only been here since...less than a year. He is usually...well, normal, I suppose, but every now and then something inside him snaps and he doesn't seem to know where he is."

"I shall pray to the Aten for him."

Khaemnum frowned. "You think it will do any good? The Aten seems one of those gods that is rather...shall we say, remote."

Meryetaten lifted her chin and for an instant looked the image of a queen again. "The Aten is the only real god and my father enjoys a special relationship with him. He will not abandon him."

Khaemnum thought about this, trying to work out who was not going to abandon whom. He opened his mouth to ask but then decided it did not matter. "Can the doctors do nothing?"

Meryetaten shook her head. "No more than they can cure his blindness."

"His...Akhenaten is not blind."

"It is progressive, like his delusions. It started years ago when he tried to see his god in the sun's disc. He was blind then for days. He recovered under the ministrations of the physician Nebhotep, but the malady returns, worse each time. I'm surprised you have not seen it."

Khaemnum crossed the room and looked down on the cloth-covered face of his sleeping king. "Perhaps I have. There are times when he refuses to come out of his rooms, even to visit the temple. He never gives a reason, just turning away to face the wall."

"Naturally you will report this to Ay."

Khaemnum shrugged. "I do not see the point."

"Ay looks for a way to rid himself of the king. A blind, mad man is no king."

"He is still the anointed one. The gods..." Khaemnum smiled ironically and bowed to Meryetaten. "...Or god, perhaps, put him in his place. Who am I to contradict, ah, divinity?"

"You surprise me, Khaemnum. I thought you Ay's creature, full of hatred for us."

"I am a soldier, lady." Khaemnum smiled again. "I follow orders but I do not always agree with them." He walked to the table and gestured at the dishes. "Do you mind?" When Meryetaten shook her head, he poured himself some wine and broke off a piece of crusted bread, dipping it in the goose grease. He raised the cup to his lips before remembering his manners. "For you, my lady?"

"Some wine." Meryetaten took the cup and sipped. She sat on the end of the couch, near her father's sandaled feet and studied Khaemnum carefully. "So when the order comes to kill my father, you will obey, even though you may disagree?"

"Kill him? What in the gods' holy names are you talking about? I look after the king, protect him."

"And I thank you for it, Khaemnum. But what happens when my beloved grandfather Ay decides his hold over the boy king is secure enough? Do you not think he will have the true king removed? Will you be the one he uses?"

"He would not do that, lady. Killing a king is god-cursed. When he is judged in the Halls of Death, his spirit would be rent and cast into the flames of Ases. That would be my fate too if I obeyed such a command."

"And what if no man strikes the king down, but he dies nonetheless?"

Khaemnum looked blank, his forehead wrinkled as he stared at the princess-queen. "You are talking in riddles, lady. If the gods strike him down, who is to blame?"

"I can tell you what will happen one day, Khaemnum. You will get an order that simply says something like, 'Show the king to his god'. Who can say what that means? Ay will say, if any dare question him; that it was something innocent, meaning only that the king should be allowed more time to worship in the Aten's temple." Meryetaten placed her wine cup carefully on the floor and stood up. She crossed to where the soldier stood and looked up at him. "But you, faithful Khaemnum, will have received the true meaning beforehand, and will take my father out into the desert and leave him there, with a small flask of water and a loaf of bread, to die. You can say, should any ask you, that he was fit and well when last you saw him; that you left him with food and water and you are not to blame; that it was his father the Aten who took him."

"That...that is just supposition, lady. I cannot believe it of the Tjaty."

304

"You do not know him as I do. The real question is what you will do when the command comes. Will you obey a usurper or the true king of Kemet?"

Khaemnum stared down at the king's daughter. "Why do you tell me this, lady?" he asked in a shaky voice. "You have no great reason to love the king, despite being his daughter. You were also his wife and bore him a child, before he put you away. Many women would hate a father like that."

Meryetaten paled and spun on her heel, walking quickly to the edge of the verandah, where she stood and stared out at the gardens for several minutes.

"I did hate him," she said at last, her voice soft. "For so long I desired his death. But the gods did not grant my wish and I came to see that it must be--it can only be--that there is one true god, his god, the Living Aten. I then prayed to Aten and he answered me, Khaemnum." Meryetaten turned and looked at the soldier through tear-filled eyes. "He showed me that my father needed me, needed my love. I have come back to Akhet-Aten to be with him. I will not leave him again. I will share his fate, whatever it is. You will have to take both of us out to die in the desert."

"I...I could not do that."

"Then you will help us?"

Khaemnum was silent for a long time, his eyes unfocused and turned inward upon his own soul. At last he sighed raggedly. "I will think on it."

Akhenaten shifted on his couch and the drying cloth fell away from his reddened and inflamed eyes. He stirred in his sleep and smiled.

Chapter 24

Paramessu was a long time healing, despite Nebhotep's attentions and Scarab's devoted care. Throughout the time of the general's recuperation she hovered by his bed side, ever ready with water or a cooling cloth, holding the pot unashamedly as he relieved himself, feeding him and, under the physician's care, exercising his damaged leg. This last duty she had a hard time believing but Nebhotep assured her that a leg unexercised over months would waste away. So she stretched Paramessu's leg, pushing and pulling, ignoring his winces, until the day came when he could leave his bed with its stinking sheets and venture out into the sun. Progress was rapid and within ten days of his first steps he was exercising in the barrack yards, working his way slowly back to fighting fitness.

News came in regularly from the army up in Kenaan where Djedhor was in command of the army. The Amorites were quiet, as were the Hittites, though spies indicated something was being planned. A messenger from Horemheb in Waset a month past, when Paramessu still tossed feverishly on his sweat-soaked pallet, had confirmed Paramessu in his rank of Commander General of the Northern Army, and Djedhor as his second. Horemheb himself was staying in the south for the time being. The letter did not explain why, but the messenger thought it something to do with a Nubian uprising. Paramessu fretted for a while, eager to be back in command of his army, but Djedhor's reports, outlining the situation and the lack of news of the Amorite forces, calmed him. He started to devote himself to regaining his strength. On the first day of the second month of Shomu, he limped over to the stables and took out a fine roan stallion, determined to ride out into the countryside for fresh air, exercise and a welcome change of scenery.

The second day, Paramessu was once more at the stables, but waiting for him was Scarab, dressed a trifle inappropriately for a royal lady in a short military kilt and a thin shoulder wrap that fastened at the neck but hung loose and open to her midriff. She smiled at Paramessu as he stopped short of the stable doors, staring.

"I thought I might join you today, General Paramessu."

"Er, yes, of course, my lady." Paramessu recovered his wits and collected his stallion again, selecting a quiet gelding for Scarab. Leading the horses out into the courtyard, he hesitated as he handed the reins of the gelding to the young woman. "Can you ride, or do you wish to join me on my horse? Or we could take a chariot."

Scarab raised an eyebrow and grinned. "Have you forgotten you taught me to ride?" She took the reins of the gelding, grasped the mane and swung herself up in a lithe movement that had Paramessu blushing and looking away. He mounted his stallion with less grace, his weakened left leg letting him down, and pulled the horse's head round to face the compound gate, urging it forward with his heels. Scarab followed, her gelding trotting along behind.

They rode out of the city of Zarw, westward with the sun at their backs along the great canal. The great road that ran toward the delta of the Great River and the heart of the Lower Kingdom passed through small villages clustered around the city and its arterial waterway. Many people used the road and for maybe an hour they walked or trotted their horses, moving through the carts and herds, around people carrying produce. The land around was pasture, with herds of cattle and goats, lush and green for the most part though bare earth and close-cropped scrub showed through in areas where the grazing was heaviest.

Scarab urged her gelding alongside a silent Paramessu as they sat waiting for a herd of goats to pass a procession of laden carts, the oxen pulling them with heads held low, resigned to their thankless task. "Why do we follow the road?" she asked. "I thought a dashing soldier like you would be galloping across the countryside."

Paramessu turned and looked across at the young girl. "My lady, were I by myself I would, but a gentleman must know when to curb his desires."

Scarab clicked her tongue disapprovingly. "Then you must learn to be less of a gentleman." She jerked her reins, pulling her horse's head around and drummed her heels into its flanks. The gelding leaped forward, dashing between two carts, the oxen in the following one shying back with a bellow of surprise. The horse gathered itself and jumped across a narrow irrigation ditch, landing in the soft springy turf of the neighboring field. Scarab clung to her horse's back, her body leaning low over its neck, yelling encouragement as it laid its ears back and surged forward. Behind her, she briefly heard shouts and whistles and the crack of the ox-drivers' whips, before her attention was fully taken up with the task of staying on the galloping beast.

The end of the field drew rapidly closer and Scarab could feel her mount's muscles bunch as it faltered for a moment then launched itself at the drainage canal lying between two fields. For a wonderful moment the pounding, jarring movement beneath her ceased and all she felt was the wind in her hair, the sun on her back and the flapping of her kilt skirts around her waist. The ground rushed up to meet them, there was a dreadful impact and for an awful moment she thought she would lose her seat as she slid forward over the animal's neck. Recovering with difficulty she risked a quick glance over her shoulder and saw Paramessu's roan stallion soaring behind her, a grim-faced man on its back.

The gelding raced on, though its sides heaved and sweat slicked its flanks, saliva spattering back over Scarab's arms. She wondered how she was going to stop the horse or whether she would just have to let it run itself into exhaustion. Through the pounding of her horse's hoofs she heard another drumming, getting louder. Another glance saw Paramessu closing fast as he urged his stallion onward, his mouth open and apparently shouting, though she could hear nothing. She felt herself slipping and jerked, over-corrected and slid off the horse's back in the opposite direction. She threw her arms around its neck, gripping hard as her legs slipped, and she found herself hanging above the rushing ground, the gelding's forelegs slashing perilously close. The horse shied and dug its hoofs into the turf, pulling sideways and Scarab lost her grip, tumbling and rolling over the grass to end up on her back, half-stunned.

Paramessu, only a dozen or so strides behind, pulled back hard on the stallion's reins. Its hindquarters dropped and he was off its back and running toward the prone figure of Scarab before the horse had come to a halt. His weakened leg collapsed and he rolled, cursing, before forcing himself up again and limping to the girl's side. He knelt beside her, indecisive for a moment, then cradled her head in his arms and brushed the dirt from her face.

"My lady, are you hurt?" he muttered. "Oh gods, let no harm come to her, I beg you. I will do anything if only..."

Scarab groaned softly and fluttered her eyelids open. "Paramessu? What happened?"

"You little fool," he snapped, anger overflowing relief. "I taught you to ride sedately, not try and kill yourself."

Scarab smiled tremulously. "Don't be angry with me, Paramessu. I could not bear it. I just...I just wanted you to enjoy your ride with me, not feel constrained."

Paramessu let out a ragged breath. "I am not angry, my lady, but you must promise me never to do anything like that again."

"I will." Scarab struggled to sit up, wincing at the pain.

"Sit quietly, lady, you may have hurt yourself in the fall. Let me check your bones quickly. One learns these things in the army." He ran his hands gently over Scarab's arms and legs, then probed her neck and stomach with his fingers. "Does this hurt? Or this?"

Scarab shook her head. "I might fall again if this is how you treat me," she murmured.

"What?"

"Nothing." Scarab grinned as his hands fell back to his sides. "Am I all right?"

Paramessu nodded. "Nothing is broken, that I can see anyway, my lady. I'll get Nebhotep to examine you when we return though." He looked around and spotted the two horses grazing a little way off. "I'll get the horses and we can head back," he said, getting to his feet.

"Wait. I think I'll rest a little bit first." Scarab touched her thighs gingerly. "That horse's back is harder than I thought."

Paramessu trotted off to catch the horses and returned shortly with them walking sedately behind him. He tied them up to a small scrubby tree on the edge of the drainage ditch and let them graze again, before walking back over to Scarab and sitting back down on the springy turf. They sat in silence for a few minutes, each studiously avoiding the other's gaze.

"Could I persuade you to call me 'Scarab' instead of 'my lady'?"

Paramessu pondered for a moment. "It would not be proper. You are sister to...to the king. I am just a soldier."

"You did once before."

"You were but a girl then, a runaway, and I only half believed you when you said you were sister to the king."

"That is not true, Paramessu. Later, when you found out who I really am, you still were kind and gentle and called me Scarab."

"Things have changed, my lady. You have grown into a woman."

"Yes, things have changed, and not just in the way you think. My brother Akhenaten reigns still though he is all but deposed; my brother Smenkhkare has been murdered; and my brother Tutankhaten is now king in name only. My uncle Ay controls him and seeks my death." Scarab wrestled a small stone free of the black earth at the base of a clod of grass and threw it into the drainage ditch. A small white heron flew up with a cry of alarm, beating its wings frantically as it fled across the field. "Make no mistake, brave General Paramessu, I am no longer a princess. I am...I am a woman without skills, without means of support and probably without a future. I would think that a soldier could call such a woman 'Scarab' without impropriety."

Paramessu sat and stared at the ground in front of him, his hands plucking grass blades and ripping them into shreds, a frown on his face. At length he nodded. "A soldier might call such a woman 'Scarab', but you are not without resources. Many men in Kemet love you and would come to your aid." He turned to the young woman and smiled wryly. "In truth I would like to call you 'Scarab'. I often think back on those times and remember those days and nights we spent together."

"I remember them too," Scarab said softly.

"Then...Scarab, I shall be honoured to be your friend."

"Friend only, dear Paramessu? I am a woman and..." she blushed, looking away.

Paramessu's lips quirked upward in a smile but he quickly controlled his expression. "There too I would be honoured, my...Scarab. But you are young..."

"I am seventeen."

"...and I am considerably older than you--twenty years older. Why I have even been married."

"You are not now?"

"No Scarab. I married young, at my father's bidding, but she died after a year. I joined the army and have never sought the company of women."

"But you enjoy my company, do you not?"

"Indeed I do, young Scarab. You have a...a lively mind."

"That is not all I have," Scarab murmured. She rose to her feet and brushed the dirt and grass off her kilt. "We had best be getting back, Paramessu." She groaned as she started to move, clutching her buttocks. "I am sore and I'm not sure I can ride back."

"It is too far to walk, Scarab." Paramessu got up and walked over to her. "Come, I shall help you onto your horse." He held his hands cupped for her to step up, looking away politely as she swung her leg over the horse's back.

Scarab grinned down at him from the gelding's back. "Ever the gentleman, my Paramessu. I am tempted to test your resolve." Instead, she twitched the reins and started her horse back toward the road at a sedate walk. Paramessu scrambled onto his stallion and joined her.

The ride back to Zarw was amiable but quiet, both riders silent for the most part, each absorbed in their own thoughts. Several times, each rider found an excuse to drop back slightly and at those times, devoured the other with their eyes.

Rides into the countryside around Zarw became a daily event. Khu disapproved but could find no diplomatic way of voicing his jealousy, so withdrew sulkily.

Nebhotep on the other hand, heartily approved as he could see his patient's strength returning. *Besides,* he thought, *he enjoys her company and any fool can see she is infatuated with him.*

The heat of summer enveloped the land and the fields dried, the crops ripened and the harvesting finished. The green and springy fields of grass turned brown and sere and the air itself baked. The time came when the rides to the north and south and west of Zarw, into the rich farmlands of the Delta, no longer held an attraction. One morning, just before dawn, when a gentle coolness still enveloped the land, Scarab came down to the stables to find Paramessu waiting with an extra horse, laden with packs.

"I have something different planned today, Scarab."

Paramessu led them east toward the desert of the peninsula of Sin, the rising sun blinding them as they rode. Within an hour they left the last of the dry farmlands and entered a scrubby wilderness that stretched out ahead of them. The sun rose higher, a ball of fire that burnt the remaining vegetation away and rippled the dusty air. Breaths of wind, hot as if from a baker's oven, gusted over them, lifting the dust and sand into a stinging cloud and making them cough.

"Set's breath, we call it," Paramessu said. "Don't worry. It will not gain strength. It lasts only until the sun is about so high." He pointed to a spot in the heavens about halfway from the rippled horizon to the pale washed out blue of the zenith.

"Why are we out here?" Scarab gasped. "We'd be better off in the Zarw barracks."

"I want to show you something." Paramessu would not be drawn further but rode silently on until Set ceased his panting and the shadows shortened, walking beside them in the heat. He pointed off to the right, toward a small hill and turned the horses' heads, guiding them across sand and rock toward the rising land.

Close to the top they found a series of huge rocks that had split away from the stone core of the hill, and for the first time that day, a modicum of shade. They dismounted and Paramessu led the horses into the shelter of a large boulder where a dusty cavity in the shade told of desert animals that used the place for shelter. The horses shied at the rank animal stench but faced with the choice of baking sun or cool shadow, overcame their fears. Paramessu unpacked feed and gave each horse a drink of water from a collapsible leather bucket before carrying the rest of the packs around to the northeast flank of the hill. Working quickly, he erected a lean-to with the aid of two long staves and linen rope, thin linen cloth shading a tiny area of the hillside from the sun.

Scarab joined him in picking the rocks out from underneath the shelter and sweeping sand in to replace the larger ones, filling in the depressions. At the last, Paramessu spread a large army blanket over the sand and gestured, grinning.

"Lady, your palace awaits."

"Thank you, noble lord." Scarab sketched a bow and bending over, walked into the low shelter. She sank down onto her knees and looked at Paramessu as he entered and sat beside her, clutching the smaller pack. "So, what's this all about?" she asked. "It seems a lot of trouble to go to just to get me alone. I would have come to your room if you asked."

Paramessu chuckled. "Don't think I haven't thought about it. But I brought you out here for quite another purpose."

"Is it going to take all day?"

"Not long, Scarab, but it is important."

"Good." Scarab grinned and settled herself comfortably. "When you have finished showing me things, I will show you something too."

Paramessu raised an eyebrow but refused to comment further. He opened the pack and took out water, dried meat, bread and fruit. "First, we eat."

"No wine?" Scarab grumbled. "Don't I rate wine then?"

"Never drink wine or beer in the desert if you have water. Wine will make you thirsty and beer will make you want to...er, pass water. You must guard against thirst and water loss at all times."

Scarab reached out and helped herself to a small melon, digging her thumbs through the tough rind and into the orange juicy centre. "Is this going to be a lecture? You are starting to sound like one of the scribes in the palace." She broke off a piece and passed it to Paramessu, biting into another. The sweet juice flooded her mouth and trickled down her chin, dripping onto her breasts.

Paramessu sighed and pointed out into the desert, sweeping his hand to encompass the north and the east. "What do you see?"

Scarab shrugged, biting into the melon again. "Sand, sky, nothing. Why?"

"Kemet is blessed by the gods, Scarab. We have good soil, a never-failing supply of sweet water and an equitable climate. We are further blessed by gold and precious stones. Is it any wonder that the nations of the world, the lands of our nine enemies, covet Kemet? What is it that protects the Two Kingdoms?"

"The army?"

"In part. But if we had good gentle lands adjoining ours, the armies of our enemies would sweep in and conquer us whenever they chose. The land itself defends us--the desert, the sand, the sun."

Scarab frowned and tossed her melon rind down. She wiped her sticky hands on her kilt and took a small loaf of bread. Nibbling on the crust she folded her long legs under her. "You could have told me all this at Zarw, Paramessu. Why did you bring me all the way out here?"

"I wanted to show you the reality of it. My army is out there somewhere, maybe twelve thousand men, but the desert doubles my strength if I use it properly. A commander must always be aware of the land and look for ways in which he can ally himself with it." Paramessu fell silent for a while, brooding over the bare landscape. "There are gods out here, Scarab. The sun rules all, Re is king. But there are others--Geb is the land beneath us, Shu the wind that cools, blessed Tefnut that grants moisture if we learn where to look for her bounty, the star-spangled body of Nut during the night--even Set has his place."

"Set I can believe, out here in the desert," Scarab agreed with a shudder. "Why would anyone want a god like Set?"

Paramessu picked up a handful of dates and started eating them, talking around the sweet fruit. "You think of Set as evil, as the opposer of Asar and Heru. But the soldiers worship him, not just because he is violent but because he personifies the desert. Many soldiers are named for Set--even my own father is named Seti."

Scarab nodded. "I think I understand. When you talked of the gods of the desert I remembered the Nine of Iunu. I sidetracked to the temples of Iunu on my way to Zarw." She stopped with the half-eaten loaf at her mouth and put it down suddenly, breathing out raggedly. "I...I had a vision in the temple of Atum, the god spoke to me."

Paramessu turned to stare into her face, searching her eyes and expression for any hint of a jest. He found none. "Go on," he said gently. "What did the god say?"

"I'm not sure. I thought I understood it when I came out of the temple but my thoughts just disappeared like water on the sand." Scarab sat silently for several moments. "I think he said something about my brothers and I know he said I should honour the Nine."

"It is often the way when the gods speak." Paramessu nodded. "Yes, they speak clearly but to men's ears it is as a dimly remembered riddle. It will come back to you when it is fulfilled."

"What's the use of that? I want to know what's going to happen."

"Only the gods know the future. Men are better off not knowing."

Scarab made a face. "Men maybe, but I'm a woman."

Paramessu smiled. "Yes, I had noticed that."

Scarab looked at Paramessu with a neutral expression for a moment then looked down at the food and drink and the remnants of their meal. "What a mess we have made." She tidied away everything back into the leather bag and tucked it to one side of the lean-to. "I suppose we had better be thinking about going back."

"Not yet, it is too hot. Wait until the sun is sinking or we'll roast on the way home."

"If we left now it would be all right. It is not yet noon." Scarab leaned past Paramessu to look outside at the position of the sun and her arm brushed his bare chest.

For an instant he did nothing, then with a groan he reached for her, gripping her upper arms in his huge hands and pulling her close. His lips descended on hers roughly. Scarab stiffened and pulled back, starting to struggle then abruptly she flung herself forward, taking Paramessu by surprise and they both fell sideways, with Scarab on top. She raised her head and looked deep into the General's deep brown eyes.

"What took you so long?" she whispered.

"Scarab," Paramessu said shakily. "We shouldn't." But even as he said it, his hands fumbled with the catch around her neck and he drew the linen shoulder-shawl aside, exposing her firm young breasts, still streaked with sticky melon juice.

"I choose to, Paramessu. It is my right." Scarab eased off her man and sat beside him on the army blanket. She removed her kilt and lay back naked. "I choose you, Paramessu, my love."

Paramessu rolled over onto one elbow and looked down at the naked girl, his face flushed and his breathing coming hard. He flipped his kilt aside revealing his erection. Scarab's eyes widened and for a moment she drew back again, a flicker of fear in her eyes. Then, with a soft cry like the swallow chick that launches itself from its nest in the eaves of the temple of Amun for the first time; she opened herself and drew Paramessu down onto and into her.

She cried again then, piercingly, but with the gentle motion and the soft touch of hands and lips she calmed, letting her tears roll unhindered, crying out only once again as the motion of their bodies quickened toward the end.

A lifetime later she lay quietly, her hands stroking the great muscled chest and arms beside her as Paramessu dozed, exhausted by his exertions as battle never could. Scarab looked at him fondly and smiled, wondering what it would be like to live with such a man. Her life as a princess was over; maybe it was time to consider life as an army wife.

Chapter 25

T he river was much narrower above the first cataract; in places a strong man might throw a stone from one bank to the other. Certainly a man with a bow could have sent an arrow into anyone standing on the deck of a barge forging its slow way upriver. Horemheb stood in the prow of the lead barge, scanning the vegetation on either side, his demeanor as close to nervousness as anyone had ever seen him. Behind him, on the swiftly flowing river, was the Amun legion from Waset, aboard a dozen great barges, and another four or five loaded with arms and supplies.

The journey upriver from Waset had been long and drawn out, following a protracted period of preparation. Horemheb had barely contained his fury at the delays, eager to be heading south toward the bandit leader named Son of Sobek. Ten days of preparation followed by another twenty to reach the city of Abu, on the doorstep of the first cataract. Technically, they were already in Lower Nubia, the province of Wawat, yet most people regarded the cataract the real boundary. Just south of Abu the mountains ran together, pinching the wide river into a narrow gorge where the placid water they had been traveling on was transformed into something malevolent. Huge boulders sent spray crashing into the air and the roar of the waters thundered like a continuing hailstorm.

The barges could not be rowed or sailed up the cataract, even had a strong wind blown from the north. The only way upriver was for the barges to be towed through the gorge. Disgorging their cargo of soldiers, arms and food on the eastern bank of the river, opposite the great docks of the city Abu on its island, the lightened barges, now almost bobbing in the water, were drawn by their crews to the base of the swift water. Strong hawsers were attached and the men strung out along the narrow path beside the torrent. They hauled, bracing themselves against the rocks, the muscles in their arms and legs standing out like giant serpents, the sweat dripping off their bodies, as they pulled the barges upward, hand by hand.

With the sailors engaged in bringing the transport over the cataract, Horemheb organized his own men into a baggage train that crossed the hills an hour or two inland, bringing all their arms and supplies overland. The journey took the best part of two days but by the time they reached the once more placid river above the long cataract, the barges were there waiting for them, the sailors lounging around on the shaded banks, resting after their exertions.

Horemheb's legion re-embarked and the river journey began again, though through very different terrain. Northward, in Kemet, the land on either bank of the great river was farmed, and especially toward Abu, every hand breadth was planted, even under the date palms and fruit trees. In Wawat, having crossed the low mountains of the first cataracts, the land was dryer, the banks steeper, and the green areas around the dotted villages smaller. The soldiers stared out at a landscape that was barren even by Kemetu standards, rock and scree and sand interspersed by clumps of withered grasses and stunted thorn trees. Little moved in these barren lands except the ever-present vultures and hawks, circling far above and reminding them, comfortingly, that the gods of Kemet were present even here in the wilderness.

The river bent slowly west of south, not just a vagary of the river valley but a trend that hinted at other changes. The river, too, no longer ran smooth, long stretches of swiftly flowing but calm water broken by swirling whitecaps that had the sailors straining at their oars, soaked with sweat in the burning sun as the laden barges crept upriver. Nothing that could truly be termed a cataract, yet it was by no means the gentle life-giving water that they all knew from lower down. At intervals, the fleet passed temples, their serried ranks of pillars standing like groves of petrified trees on knolls and bluffs above the river. Forts too, of stone and mud brick, dusty signs that this land was under military control. A handful of soldiers turned out at each outpost, standing staring down at the passing barges. The Amun legion called and waved greetings to their lonely brethren, but rarely was their greeting answered. The sight of such massed force was too strange, too disturbing, to evoke feelings of comradeship. The river kinked almost north, briefly, with temples on both sides of the river and the great fort of Aniba standing guard over the wasteland, just where the river resumed its southwesterly course.

The voyage to the capital city of Wawat proved laborious. As nightfall approached each day, Horemheb pulled his fleet in to the calmer shore and set out an armed camp with two circles of guards and thorn bush hedges. He did not have his army forage off the land, partly because there was little to be gleaned from the parched terrain, but mostly because he wanted to reach the city of Sehotep-Neteru as fast as possible. The sooner he met with Huy, the Viceroy of Wawat, and Penno, the garrison commander, the better.

The journey took a month, far longer than Horemheb planned but he had not counted on the swiftness of the river in Wawat, nor the frequent stretches of rapids. According to his charts, only one cataract lay between Abu and Sehotep-Neteru and he had expected a smooth and easy passage. Instead, he thought, it might have been faster to march. Several times he caught himself contemplating the idea, and each time he put it firmly aside. He would need the barges later if the rebels crossed the river.

At last the fleet of barges drew alongside the city of Sehotep-Neteru, that the natives call Faras, and turned their prows in toward the western bank. The city itself was a strange mixture of Kemetu city and sprawling native village. The populace turned out to see the fleet put in to the docks, a great crowd of chattering Nubians in brightly coloured clothing interspersed with migrants from the north, scarcely paler in complexion and just as gaudily dressed. A military contingent was there too, soldiers smartly kitted out, standing impassively in a great double line between the docks and the army garrison.

Horemheb's barge docked and, restraining his impulse to leap out onto dry land after the month of enforced captivity aboard, Horemheb waited with a vague semblance of patience for the gangplank to be set out and the gold-threaded ceremonial matting laid down. At last all was in place and Horemheb strode onto the great dock and marched alone up to the waiting dignitaries. Snapping to attention, Horemheb,

General of All Kemet's Armies, saluted crisply before dropping to his knees and lowering his forehead to the ground.

Viceroy Huy, representative of his august majesty Nebkheprure Tutankhaten, waited the requisite interval of time in the shade of the ostrich feather fans before leaning forward and lightly touching the kneeling general on the back with his symbol of office, the royal flail.

"Arise, Horemheb, trusted servant of the king," he intoned formally for the benefit of his entourage. In a softer voice he continued. "Get up, Horemheb, the day is hot and I have cool wine from the Delta in my palace."

The general arose slowly then embraced Huy three times before stepping back a pace. The viceroy snapped his fingers and a scribe bustled forward bowing to Huy deeply and Horemheb less deeply. One by one, the scribe introduced the other prominent personages in the viceroy's retinue--Amenemipet, one of the deputy viceroys; Soleb, the high priest of the temple of Nebmaetre Amenhotep; Mermose, second prophet of Amun in Wawat; another Huy, this one merely the mayor of Sehotep-Neteru; and Penno, the lieutenant of the fortified garrison.

Horemheb bowed to them all, varying only the depth of his gesture with the rank of the recipient. The problem of Amenemipet was a ticklish one. Strictly, as foremost General of Kemet, Horemheb outranked him, yet on occasion, the deputy viceroy could stand in for the king himself. In the end, Horemheb bowed gracefully and low, but maintained firm eye contact. Amenemipet smiled slightly as he returned the compliment, making sure the depth of his bow accorded Horemheb equal rank. Penno, as befitting a junior officer, both bowed and saluted his General.

The viceroy climbed into a sedan chair and four burly Nubian servants quickly carried him up the hill to the vice-regal palace. Amenemipet ordered Penno to stay behind with a detachment of guards and organize the movement of the Amun legion into temporary accommodation near the garrison quarters. He then gestured in the direction the viceroy had taken, suggesting that Horemheb accompany him. The others followed, the two lines of soldiers falling in around them, maintaining a barricade between the dignitaries and the jostling crowds.

"You have troubles here?" Horemheb asked as he strode along beside the deputy.

Amenemipet waved a hand to disperse a small cloud of flies. "What makes you ask that?" he said lightly.

"Your guards. This crowd does not look dangerous."

"It is not. My men are here merely as an honour guard."

Horemheb raised an eyebrow, recognising the watchfulness of the soldiers and the unmistakable battle-readiness of the men. "I know men," he said flatly. "Tell me."

Amenemipet shrugged. "I do not expect trouble but it does no harm to be prepared. The rebels have struck in cities before, on market days and festivals."

The procession wound up the hill toward the threefold structure on the hill overlooking the river--the vice-regal palace, the temple of Amenhotep and the garrison commander's headquarters. The priests bowed as they reached the temple area and slipped through the cordon of soldiers, paying no heed to the remnants of the crowd that still clung to the route from the river. Amenemipet led Horemheb into the palace and took him to the western wing, his own quarters. On a spacious verandah on the shaded north side, where a cooling breeze fought back the heat of the day, servants brought river chilled wine and a selection of dried and fresh fruits for Horemheb's pleasure. The doors shut and the two men found themselves alone.

"I'd rather wait until Penno gets here," Horemheb said, forestalling the deputy's questions. "Will he be long?"

"I had not thought to invite him. He is only the garrison commander."

"Nevertheless, he is experienced. I would appreciate his presence."

Amenemipet scowled and called out to one of the guards outside the doors to fetch the garrison commander. Twenty minutes later, he arrived, out of breath, his eyes looking questioningly at the deputy viceroy and the General.

"All right, he is here. Now, we could argue about rank and precedence," Amenemipet said, "But it would not be productive. I propose that we forget we are viceroy and General and just attend to the matter at hand. Why are you here, Horemheb?"

"You know why I'm here. To catch this bandit king of yours."

"We can catch him ourselves," Penno said.

"That is true," added Amenemipet. "We do not need the great Horemheb up here implying we are incompetent."

Horemheb shook his head. "But did you not request help from Tjaty Ay? That was my understanding when he commanded me upon this venture."

"We asked only for men. We have generals enough."

Horemheb stared at the other men in silence for a long time. "I am General of all the Armies," he said quietly. "I am commanded by the king and his Tjaty to come to Wawat and put down this rebellion. Are you refusing to help me? Am I to consider you both rebels as well?"

"By all the gods," Amenemipet exploded. "You accuse me of treason? I am deputy viceroy of Wawat and the king's trusted servant. I could have you flogged for such insubordination."

"You could try," Horemheb agreed. "But the Amun legion is loyal to me and," he smiled thinly, "You really do not want to test them. Now, you said that we forget about rank and precedence and concentrate on the matter at hand. Why do we not do just that?" The general chose a comfortable looking padded chair and sat down, putting his feet up on another.

Amenemipet glowered but said nothing. Penno kept quiet also, very conscious of his relatively junior position. He busied himself pouring chilled wine into golden cups inlaid with precious and semi-precious stones.

Abruptly, the deputy viceroy nodded. "Very well, this matter needs to be resolved. For the good of the king's peace I shall let you assume command of the forces here in Sehotep-Neteru. Penno, you will place yourself at this man's disposal." Amenemipet whirled and stalked to the door, ignoring the cup Penno held out for him.

"You are not staying, my lord?" Horemheb asked gently.

"I have other duties. Penno knows as much as I."

"Actually, a good deal more," Penno murmured as the deputy viceroy swept out of the room, the guards quickly closing the doors behind him. He offered Horemheb the cup and took the other one in his hand to another chair nearby. "We'll leave the other cup for 'Ipet, if he deigns to return," he grinned.

Horemheb raised his cup. "It is customary to drink to the king's health, life and prosperity, but under the circumstances I think we will just toast the success of this expedition." He drank, thirstily emptying the cup. Stifling a belch, he put the cup down and turned to the young garrison Lieutenant. "So, tell me all."

"All? I, er, I hardly know where to start."

"Then tell me first who he is."

Penno shrugged eloquently, drinking from his cup. "He calls himself the Son of Sobek..."

"Why?"

"Er...because he is fierce? I don't know, sir. Is it important?"

"Never mind. Go on."

"Well, he came from the north less than a year ago, not long after we had news of the death of Djeserkheperu Smenkhkare. He only had a few men then but his band grew quickly."

"How? What incentive did he offer his men? Rape and plunder, I suppose, like any other bandit?"

"Strangely no. I have not received word of a single village attacked by this Son of Sobek. A few reports of massacre came in but all proved to be the work of other gangs."

"So how does he hold his men?"

"With gold, sir--King's gold." Penno frowned and got up to get more wine. He refilled Horemheb's cup and brought over a plate of sugared dates, placing them on a stool near the general's chair. "He attacks the king's gold mines and any small concentration of troops."

Horemheb popped a date into his mouth and chewed, spitting the stone out into his hand. "How is it that a gang of thieves can defeat even a smaller group of trained soldiers?"

"They are not just a gang, sir. Their leader commands them as would a general. A survivor from the Kumma attack last month told me..."

"A survivor? Did the man cut and run?"

Penno shook his head. "The fort was overwhelmed in the pre-dawn darkness. Only about ten were killed and the rest captured."

Horemheb put up his hand and rubbed his eyes, his head bending as he sighed. "Kemetu soldiers captured by bandits? I can understand being killed; death comes to us all, but allowing yourself to be captured?" He looked up at Penno. "What happened then? He killed them? How did your man escape?"

"Apparently he offered them a choice, sir. Serve him or return to Sehotep-Neteru unharmed." Horemheb gaped. "I'm sorry to have to say that several joined the Son of Sobek."

323

"This has happened before?" Horemheb croaked. "Soldiers turning traitor? How many?"

"All told?" Penno stared down at the floor miserably. "About a hundred. Add that to his native army and slaves he released from the mines and he commands a force of close to a thousand men."

"Gods!" Horemheb sat back and stared out the window. "Why have you allowed it to go on so long? Why did you not report this to the court in Waset immediately?"

"We did, sir. As soon as we knew the extent of the damage. It has only been in the last three months that things have become serious."

Horemheb arose and walked over to the edge of the verandah, looking out over the thatched rooftops of the city. A stench drifted up from the close-packed houses and streets--the usual mix of animal and human excrement overlain with sweat and rotting food, but here the sharp and tangy aromas of spices mingled with the foul air. The sounds of a city came to his ears too. He strained his senses to separate out the voices, to make sense of them, but after a while he gave up. The many tongues of Wawat defeated him. Shifting his gaze to the narrow strip of garden underneath the verandah, he calmed himself again as he watched the Nubian gardeners tending the manicured beds of flowers and the fruit trees. Close to the verandah, a few cubits from his own feet, Horemheb saw a pale-complexioned man, a Kemetu, his back turned, apparently monitoring the activities of the gardeners. *Who would want a job like that*, he thought. *Far from home, among provincials and overseeing the gardens of the viceroy.* Shaking his head he turned back to Penno.

"I have heard nothing but defeat in your narrative and in what Amenemipet said. Have you had no victories over this Son of Sobek? You are soldiers of the king, by all the gods."

"We have had victories," Penno said stiffly. "When we meet him on equal terms we prevail. He has attacked five towns and in four we beat him back."

"And in the fifth?"

Penno looked away. "He burned the fort to the ground."

"This was the attack you told me of earlier? In Kumma?"

"No sir, this was over the river, in Semna."

"So let me see if I have this right...this Son of Sobek appears out of nowhere less than a year ago. His rag-tag army of tribesmen, slaves and deserters do what they will, go where they please, attack what they like, and when you beat them off from a town, you call it a victory?"

"Sir, that is harsh..."

"You have given me no evidence that the army is doing anything. Instead you stay holed up in the towns and forts and react to whatever this man does. You think me harsh? I will show you harsh, Penno. I am going to take my Amun legion and every man you have and I will take the offensive. I will carry the attack to these rebels and I swear by my own god Heru that before a month is out I will have this Son of Sobek fed to his god's crocodiles or fleeing for his life." He rammed his right hand forward with each claim as if pushing his words at the junior officer. The wine in his cup splashed out with every gesture, staining his hands and clothing unheeded.

Penno flushed but refrained from saying anything.

Horemheb glared at the lieutenant, as if daring him to contradict his statements. When nothing was forthcoming, he nodded stiffly and put his wine cup down, grimacing at the purple splashes of wine on his kilt. "You have a map? I need to know the lay of the land."

"Yes sir." Penno got up and hurried out, returning a few minutes later with a large scroll of papyrus. Horemheb had, in the meantime, cleared a space on the table, and Penno unrolled the map, anchoring the corners with plates, Amenemipet's untouched wine cup and a pitcher of water.

Horemheb bent over the map, his eyes roaming, following the lapis line of the river and other unfamiliar symbols. "Where are we?" he asked.

"Here, sir." The great river curved up from the bottom of the map, bearing to the west and south in a great loop, almost running backward again, north and east before suddenly resuming its southerly course toward the top of the map. Penno tapped the papyrus not far past the start of the loop. "Here is Sehotep-Neteru, here and here are the forts he captured and..." His finger traced across the map, stopping briefly both north and south of the capital. "...here are the towns he attacked and was beaten off."

"Does he have a base?"

"Not that we know of, sir."

"Then where does he hide with an army of a thousand men? This may be a large province, but he still needs to feed and water them. My guess is he won't be far from the river."

Penno hesitated. "Er, there are wells, sir." He took a deep breath and pointed to the map once more. "Downriver, where the forts of Ikku and Kubban guard the road to the mines, there is a dry watercourse, a broad valley that only flows when the rains are hardest--there are wells dug that supply the mine slaves and guards." Reaching out to a dish of nuts he took a handful and started placing them on the map. "These are wells, sir, sources of water far from the river."

"Wells deep enough to supply a thousand men?"

"Few," Penno conceded. "Perhaps this one here on the road to the mines--they call it the Well of the King--another here, almost due east of us, and..." Penno searched the map carefully, looking for landmarks. "And here, sir. Perhaps two days march east of the temple of Amun at Amara in the province of Kush."

Horemheb retrieved the dish of sugared dates and replaced the nuts at the three points Penno had marked, with a piece of fruit. He stood back and considered the map, noting positions and the placement of the river and the wells. "Where would you hide, Penno?" he asked. "Put yourself in this character Sobek's sandals."

Penno gave the matter considerable thought, his fingers tracing patterns on the papyrus and his lips forming the sounds of the places on the map. Once or twice he absentmindedly picked up a well nut and ate it, crunching the seed as he worked. "A thousand places to hide if I were alone, but with an army? If I wanted just to hide, I'd pull back beyond the third cataract. Plenty of places there you could hide an army a hundred times the size."

Horemheb looked at the map, considering the distances involved. The room was quiet and he could just distinguish the faint sounds of the Nubian gardeners outside as they worked. "He won't go there. He needs to be close enough to strike at towns and forts."

"Then here at the well east of Amara."

"Not up nearer to the gold mines? The one east of us would be handy to everything he needs."

"Too close, sir. I agree he could be there but I think he'd run too much risk of discovery. Besides, he has another advantage with the

Southern Well. It is in Kush and so far he has not attacked Kushite towns."

"But Kush is a Kemetu province, as is Wawat. Are you telling me he is safe in Kush just because he does not prey there? Are the viceroys at war with each other?"

"No sir. There is no viceroy in Kush at present. He died of fever a year ago and has not yet been replaced. Until he is, our own viceroy Huy cannot formally ask for assistance." Penno shrugged. "Give me the simple life of a soldier any day."

"That makes the Kushite well a lot more attractive for this rebel."

"Oh, yes. I believe he is near the Amaran Road."

Horemheb nodded. "You've thought about this. All right, the Southern Well it is. How do we get there? What is the terrain like? What route would you take?"

Penno considered, idly eating the nuts that represented the wells as he thought. "There are two possible routes. The first is the easiest. The Amaran Road runs down this wide valley called Tanjur in the Nubian tongue. It has the advantage of being in very dry country without villages."

"Why a road if there are no villages?"

"It is a trade route that passes the well. For our purposes, the lack of villages means there will be no-one to warn the rebels."

"If they are there."

"Yes," Penno nodded. "If they are there." He traced a finger just north of Sehotep-Neteru, again on the eastern bank. "There is another road here, more of a track really, that starts near the temple at Abu Hoda and runs south into the mountains. Very steep and treacherous, but it comes out at the Southern Well. Overall, the land is bad in this loop of the Great River. Dry and sunbaked with nothing to recommend it except gold."

"You know the country, Penno. Which route would you take?"

"Both."

"You'd split our forces?"

"Normally, no, but in this case it scarcely matters. The Son of Sobek will not confront you head on. He will pick at you like you would a scab, until you bleed. Splitting our force may make him split his."

"I will force him to battle," Horemheb said firmly. "He will face me or lose any honour he pretends to."

Penno wisely refrained from commenting, busying himself with pouring more wine into their cups. "What do you plan to do then, General?"

"How many men can you raise, Penno? Strip the garrison; pull in any auxiliaries you can trust."

"Three hundred if I am to leave the city and the viceroy properly guarded." He caught his general's eye and stammered in agitation. "F...four maybe, if...then five, but the viceroy will object, sir."

"I will talk to him." Horemheb drained his wine and stifled a belch. "So, Penno, you will lead your five hundred men up the steep track through the mountains. You know the country. I will take the Amun legion south to Tanjur and strike inland. Together we will crush Sobek's balls." Horemheb brought his empty wine cup down on a stray nut that still adorned the papyrus map, scattering fragments over the mountains.

"You will need an excuse to take your men south so soon after you got here." Penno dug into his sash band and pulled out a scrap of papyrus, grinning. "By chance I have a report here that says the Son of Sobek has been seen near the temple at Soleb. You will need to follow that report up."

Horemheb snatched the scrap from Penno's hand and scrutinized the scribblings. "What do melons and cucumbers have to do with anything?"

Penno tried valiantly to look surprised. "It says that? That must be my shopping list for the quartermaster." He dug into the band of his kilt again. "Dear me, I appear to have lost it. I can only swear to you that the report came in."

Horemheb passed the piece of papyrus back, his face impassive. "So you did. I saw it before it was accidentally destroyed."

The two military men, General and Lieutenant, exited the wide enclosed verandah in the viceroy's palace in Sehotep-Neteru, also called Faras in the Nubian tongue, and marshaled their troops. Within a day, Horemheb's Amun legion had re-embarked to continue their journey south in pursuit of bandits, and Penno, with his much smaller army, headed north to Abu Hoda and the mountain tracks. The two men were pleased with the rapid departure and for added security, allowed the soldiers no contact with the native city. Nobody in the capital city knew their destination or route, not even the viceroy.

As the fleet moved south again a solitary man, Kemetu by complexion despite his lowly occupation as a gardener in the grounds of the viceroy's palace, watched them go. Fondling the crocodile tooth on a leather cord around his neck, he set off for the dock area to find a boatman willing to ferry him across the river.

Chapter 26

Т

he messenger from the northeastern border galloped down the Royal Road from the north, the dust of his passing a great column in the faded blue sky of high summer. The heat beat up at him from the baked earth of the withered fields that hung onto life grimly, waiting for the next inundation. He reached Zarw in the early afternoon, leaping from his foundering horse in the army barracks, his eyes red and raw in a dust-caked visage.

"Where is the General?" the messenger croaked. "I have an urgent message for General Paramessu."

Servants brought water for washing, sour beer and bread, while others raced to find the most senior officer in the city. Pemheb, the Lieutenant of the Zarw garrison came running, knuckling the sleep from his eyes and yelling at his subordinates to fetch wine, a scribe, and fresh clothing. Before interrogating the messenger he dispatched riders out into the countryside in all directions to seek out the general and the beautiful Khabiru girl in whose company he spent so much time.

"What in the name of Set is going on?" Pemheb snapped as he strode into the guard room, the scribe and two guards on his heels. Flicking a hand to dismiss the servants, he stared haughtily at the strange sight of the messenger seated at the rickety table cramming as much beer and bread into himself as possible. Water had been applied liberally to his head and upper body revealing its normal copper colour, but his lower limbs remained coated in a thick layer of pale dust, runnels of drying mud streaking him in an exotic pattern.

The man struggled to his feet and saluted, choking down his mouthful of food. "Paser, my lord, Leader of Five, Heru legion, General Djedhor commanding." He dropped to his knees, prostrating himself in front of the high officer. "I have an urgent message for General Paramessu," he mumbled.

"Get up," Pemheb said impatiently, nudging the man with one sandaled foot. He waited until the messenger stood before him again. "You have a written message?"

"Yes sir." His hand moved toward the pouch at his waist then hesitated. "I, er, I'm only supposed to give them to General Paramessu, sir."

"He is not here at the moment. In his absence I am the ranking officer. You may give them to me."

"My lord, I cannot." The man licked his lips nervously. "General Djedhor said..."

"Paser," Pemheb said with a hint of impatience. "If you wish to see your Five again and maybe rise in rank, you will give me the message right now." He held out his hand.

Paser hesitated a moment longer, then opened his pouch in a puff of dust and handed over a folded and crumpled piece of papyrus.

Pemheb held the paper delicately in forefinger and thumb for a moment before passing it to the scribe. "Here, Mener, read this to me."

The scribe bowed and unfolded the message, scanning the contents. "It is in a fair hand, sir, with well-formed characters boldly drawn..."

"The message, Mener, I am not a scribe to appreciate the finer points of the general's writing."

"I believe his scribe would have written this...er, yes, my lord. It says, 'To my lord General Commanding of the Northern Army, Paramessu son of...'"

"Skip the honourifics," Pemheb growled. "Get to the meat of it."

"Yes my lord. It says 'The Amorites have put an army into the field again, heading south from Taanach, perhaps fifteen thousand strong. I expect them to be at Lachish by the new moon. Request you bring all available men and arms.' It is signed Djedhor, Commander of the Heru legion."

Pemheb swore softly. "Today is two days shy of the full moon." A servant arrived with a small pitcher of wine and a cup, but the Lieutenant waved him away. Telling Paser to return to his meal,

Pemheb left, the scribe Mener hurrying after him, hurriedly jotting down notes as the officer fired off a series of commands.

"Have Hay and Wennere start rounding up every man in Zarw who has ever held arms...get the quartermaster to prepare a list of provisions available...the master-at-arms is to inventory the weapons. Immediately, Mener. Then get my senior officers to the upstairs room...not Hay and Wennere of course, and notify me immediately if Paramessu returns." Mener hurried off, leaving the Lieutenant to stand at the doorway to the guard post looking out at the flurry of activity as the news spread.

Paramessu and Scarab returned before the sun had moved another hand span across the dusty sky, escorted by one of the riders, and the General was ensconced with his officers within minutes. Scarab left the army to its business and went to the wash room to freshen up and find clean clothing.

Khu found her as she opened the door to her room in the block of rooms assigned to minor officials associated with the garrison. Several scribes shared apartments here, as did the physician Nebhotep. Scarab and Khu had been granted temporary accommodation at Nebhotep's behest to start with, but Paramessu, as soon as he recovered sufficiently, had made more permanent arrangements. Khu now assisted Nebhotep, and Scarab's official position was as an assistant to the garrison secretary. The last month, however, had seen her position become vaguer, less tenable, as she seldom returned to her room at night, spending most of her days and nights with the man who had become her lover.

Scarab turned in her doorway and smiled at Khu. "What is happening? All I know is some messenger has arrived and everyone is running around like ducks with their heads cut off."

Khu did not return her smile. "War, or so the rumor goes. An Amorite army is knocking on the gates of Kemet." His mouth turned down in a grimace as he looked at her closely. "You do not look well. You should consult Nebhotep."

"I'm fine. Just a bit hot from the desert still. I'll lie down in the dark for a little while."

Khu shrugged. "As you wish, but I still think you should see Nebhotep." He turned to leave.

"Khu?" Scarab asked, a trace of a frown on her forehead. "Is anything wrong? You seem...well, distant."

"Wrong? What could be wrong? I am in hiding in the farthest reaches of the kingdoms, pretending to be a doctor's assistant, while the princess I have sworn to protect puts herself in danger on a daily basis."

Scarab gaped, then shut her mouth and blinked. "What danger? I am with my...with Paramessu. What harm can come to me when he is with me?"

"You have to ask me that? Well, perhaps you do. You have led a sheltered life as a princess. Army men, particularly the professional ones, the officers, are tough and violent and are used to taking what they want. Paramessu wants you, Scarab; I can see it in his eyes. You are in danger."

The air chilled in the corridor as Scarab held onto her anger. "You forget yourself, Khu. I am a royal princess, daughter and sister of kings. I will not be spoken to like this--as if I were a spoiled child or a fool. I know my own mind--and that of Paramessu." She turned and went into her room, shutting the door behind her. Through the thin wood she heard Khu's last rejoinder "If you think you are a princess still, then announce it and see how long you live," before he stamped off down the hallway.

Khu went upstairs to the chamber Nebhotep used as his workplace. He found the physician standing by a rough bench erected along one wall, grinding dried herbs in a granite mortar. He looked up as Khu entered the room.

"You look as though you have eaten bitter herbs, Khu. Perhaps while you are in that frame of mind you would be so good as to take the plants in that basket by the door and remove the fruits?"

Khu nodded without speaking, picking up the basket and carrying it over to a table by the window. Pulling out a wilted branch he started removing the tiny fruits that hung singly or in small clusters. Some were green and some a deep bluish-purple that stained his fingers as he picked them. Without thinking, he raised his hand to his mouth.

"Stop that," Nebhotep snapped. "Do not taste those fruits, Khu. Wash your hands when you finish but do not allow the juice to come near your mouth or your eyes."

Khu stared at his stained fingers. "What are you doing with poisonous plants?"

"Anything is poisonous if you take too much of it. However, this plant has its uses provided only very small amounts are taken."

Khu grunted and resumed his work, trying hard not to get more of the juice on his hands than he had to. When he had stripped all the berries from the branches, he separated, under Nebhotep's guidance, the ripe berries from the green ones, and put them into a small jar, pouring a small amount of greenish olive oil over them. He threw out the green berries and the leaves before washing his hands thoroughly, scrubbing his hands hard with sand from a dish beside the water tub.

"Why the scowl, lad?" Nebhotep asked. "Something is troubling you."

Khu just shook his head, staring into the bowl as he scrubbed his hands.

"If you don't want to talk about it, that's all right, but my guess is, it's about Scarab."

Khu sighed and stopped scrubbing, resting his hands on the sides of the tub. "She won't see she is in danger."

Nebhotep stopped grinding dried herbs and dusted his hands off on a piece of cloth before turning to face the young man. "What danger?" he asked softly.

Khu shrugged. "Paramessu."

"How is he a danger?"

"He's a strong, violent soldier who could do anything to her...kill her even, and she refuses to see the danger, even when I point it out to her."

Nebhotep scratched his chin thoughtfully. "Paramessu is a general and a man of great intelligence and ability. Moreover, he knows who Scarab really is. I think he is less of a danger than you imagine." He looked closely at Khu. "Or do you have reason to believe he represents a danger other than violence?"

"They ride off together every day and as often as not she does not sleep in her room at night. I know--I sleep in the next room."

"So we come to it, lad. This girl whom you have known for the past four years has found herself a lover and you are jealous."

"I am not." Khu's face flushed and he looked away. "I...I do not think of her like that. I..."

334

"Lad, you would have to be made of stone not to think of her like that. You would not be the first to fall in love with someone far above your station. She is a beautiful and personable young woman with whom you have spent a lot of time. It is natural to feel something-- whether it is love or lust."

"That...that is not true. My feelings for her are noble and pure. I do not..." Khu shook his head and resumed washing his hands. "It is Paramessu who feels the lust."

"And apparently, so does Scarab. Well, what of it? Neither of them is married or betrothed. As long as consent is there, no law is broken, no morals disturbed."

"But she is a princess, and he only a common soldier."

"And you are only a farmer's son," Nebhotep muttered under his breath. Aloud, he said, "It would not be the first time a soldier has climbed to high office or favour over the open legs of a princess." The physician went and put his hand on Khu's shoulder. "Scarab is old enough to be master of her own fate. Leave it with the gods."

Khu looked round at Nebhotep, his face screwed up in anguish. "I could not bear to see her hurt."

"Life is hurt, young Khu, as you are finding out. Has she ever said anything to you to raise your own hopes?" Khu said nothing, just looked down. "I thought not. Then be a friend to her, Khu. A good friend is worth more than gold."

Khu nodded slowly, reluctantly. "Will you talk to her?"

"About what? I will not seek to counsel her on matters of love."

"Not that. She is not well. She is tired and flushed and I have heard her vomiting more than once lately."

Nebhotep's lips twitched but he kept his thoughts private. "Have her come and see me. Tell her I command it."

The meeting of the officers ended with a flurry of activity. Men from all over the city and surrounding countryside poured in as a result of the call to arms. The garrison masters-at-arms exhausted themselves finding gear for the new soldiers and the governor of the city opened the granaries, releasing a flood of grain to the developing army.

Scarab found herself neglected by Paramessu as he spent each day from before sunup to well after sunset busy with his duties, collapsing exhausted into a narrow camp bed set up in his headquarters. Whenever possible, she stayed close, sitting quietly in a corner and watching him at work, or dogging his footsteps like a puppy, thirsting for any look, or a stolen word or caress. When he could, he did, but for the next three days, Scarab felt as if she was already left behind.

"I will come with you," she said once. "I can stay in your tent and look after you."

Paramessu shook his head. "You cannot." He turned back to the scribe and continued dictating complicated instructions to his officers.

That night, Paramessu came to her room a little before midnight and scratched on her door. In a fit of pique, she cried out "You cannot," and turned her back. Minutes later she relented, but he was back in his headquarters, driving his scribes and secretaries relentlessly.

The army left at dawn on the fourth day after the messenger arrived. Though he wanted to lead his troops out of the city, Paramessu delayed, taking the time to farewell a tearful Scarab.

"How long will you be gone?"

A shrug. "Who can say? I cannot desert my post in the face of the Amorite enemy. A month, three, maybe longer."

"I cannot bear it. My heart longs for you already, my body too."

"You must bear it, Scarab. Remember who we are. If the gods will it, we shall be together again."

Scarab climbed to the top of the city wall and watched until the last soldier disappeared into the billowing dust cloud raised by the departing army. From there she went to the temple of Atum and prayed, spending time in each of the temples of the Iunu Nine after that. The temple of Set frightened her, the statue of the god was manlike, but the head that stared down at her was of no animal known to her. The long, strange snout and the prominent ears, surrounded by the gloom of the temple precinct, raised the hair on her neck, but she persevered, knowing that Set was the god of soldiers and the desert.

"Bring him home safe to me, divine ones."

She went and sat morosely in her room for the rest of the day until driven out by thirst. On her way to the now almost deserted dining hall she met Khu, looking disconsolate. Scarab tensed, not wanting another confrontation. Khu smiled however, and fell in beside her, finding bread and a scrap of beef, some figs and a small pitcher of sour beer. They ate in almost complete silence, what conversation there was, inconsequential.

Towards the end of the meal, Khu cleared his throat nervously. "Nebhotep wants to see you."

Scarab looked at Khu suspiciously. "Why? Have you been saying things about me?"

"Only that you did not look well." Scarab started to get up and Khu hurried on. "I have heard you vomiting, Scarab. If you are sick, you should see a physician. If not Nebhotep, then another."

Scarab paused, looking down at Khu's earnest and worried face. "I am not sick, but I will see Nebhotep. Are you satisfied?"

She found the physician in his workroom, seated at the window table, examining the dissected corpse of a dog. He looked up as she came into the room and beckoned her over. "Look at this," he said pointing into the mass of glistening entrails. "These large tubes that lead to and from the heart were filled with blood when I opened them. Why should that be, I wonder? The heart is supposed to be the seat of the intellect, but why would it need blood? The heart is hollow too, continuations of these tubes."

Scarab glanced at the splayed out animal and gasped at the stench before drawing back a few paces. She paled and fanned the air, leaning against the far bench. Nebhotep leapt to his feet and threw a linen sheet over the dissection. "My apologies, Scarab, I did not think how the sight and smell might affect you."

She shook her head weakly. "I did not think it would. I have seen...I'm sorry, Nebhotep. I think I'm going to be sick."

"Here." Nebhotep wiped his hands on a cloth and picked a small jar off a shelf, prising the lid off as he carried it across the room. A sweet, sharp scent filled the air, banishing the stench of the decomposing dog.

"Ah, thank you," Scarab gasped. She took a few deep breaths and sat down on a chair. "What is that? A perfume?"

"I suppose it could be used as such but it is very costly. It comes from far in the East. The merchant told me it was over a year in its travel, but I think he is lying. He said it comes from a place where the forests are so thick you cannot easily walk between the trees. When I heard that I knew he was just trying to push the price up. Everyone knows there are only deserts to the East. South into deep Kush is the only place for those forests." Nebhotep shrugged. "Wherever it is from, you can extract oil from it that eases toothache immediately. It also has a smell that is pleasant and overpowers others."

Scarab nodded. "Khu said you wanted to see me."

"Yes, he tells me you are not feeling well."

"It comes and goes. I have had a stomach flux of late but that could just be the bad water this late in the summer."

"Oh?" Nebhotep raised an eyebrow. "I did not realize you were a physician." He held up a hand to forestall a comment and took Scarab's face gently in his hands, turning her toward the light of his window. "Hmm." Releasing her head he directed her to stand before the window and raise her arms above her head. "Turn sideways...yes, like that. All right, you can put your arms down. Aside from vomiting, how do you feel?"

"Tired, but I'm out riding every day."

"When was your last moon?"

"My last...?" Scarab thought back, feeling uneasy suddenly. "It was seven days before the full moon, it always is."

"This full moon just past?"

"Yes, of course." Scarab's face fell. "No, it was before the last full moon. Oh, Nebhotep, I have missed my moon days. Am I...am I..."

"You are tired and vomiting, yet by your complexion and clear eyes I would say you are in excellent health. You have missed your moon days and your breasts, outlined against the light, are fuller than I remember them. Are your nipples sore?"

Scarab nodded. "A little. Am I with child, Nebhotep?"

"Very likely, my lady, but I would like to make sure." He took a wide-mouthed earthenware pot from a shelf and held it out. "I need you to pass water. You may use the far corner."

Scarab complied, squatting while the physician turned his back. She handed the pot back and held herself up straight, taking a deep breath before she spoke. "How long before you can be certain?"

"Ten days, maybe less. I have the emmer wheat and barley ready."

Seven days later, Scarab sat in Nebhotep's workshop once more looking at flat pottery dishes of soil, on which seeds were scattered. Some of the dishes stank of stale urine, others did not. White worm-like roots snaked out of some seeds but not others. Scarab looked from one dish to another, a perplexed frown on her face.

"What does it mean, Nebhotep? Am I with child?"

"Emmer and barley grown in your water and river water. None grow in the river water, but they do in yours. However, only the emmer seeds grow in your water, not the barley."

"So what does it mean?"

"You are with child, Scarab, and it will be a boy."

Chapter 27

Taanach, royal city of the Amorite king Aziru, lies close to the strategic pass known as Megiddo but further inland. The coast road running north through Kenaan turns inland at the great spine of a mountain running north-west to south-east from the sea. There are three ways across this mountain spine--the northern route through Jokneam, a middle route through the Pass of Megiddo, and the southern route where Taanach stands guard. In the days of the Kemetu king Menkheppere Tuthmosis, Taanach was a base for their campaign against the Kenaanite forces under the king of Kadesh. Those days were long past and Kemet was no longer the power it had once been. Now the armies of minor tribes in the days of Tuthmosis had become strong and challenged the weak kings of Kemet. All that stood in the way of Aziru's conquest of Lower Kemet was the Northern Army still technically under the command of Horemheb, one of Kemet's greatest generals. In point of fact, Horemheb was at the other end of the Two Kingdoms and the Northern Army remained under the aegis of Paramessu and Djedhor. This was a fact that suited Jebu, the Amorite general, extremely well.

There are two roads that lead out of Taanach. One leads north and west, skirting the plains of Megiddo before joining the coast road, a broad thoroughfare used by traders and armies both, and along which the Kemetu army had, in the past, many forts and garrisons. This main coast road passed through Jokneam, bypassing Megiddo and Taanach, as did all travelers without specific business in Aziru's city. Less traveled, and seemingly less useful to anyone heading south, was the road that led south-eastward, inland toward the hills and mountains that were the rugged backbone of Kenaan. Not far out of Taanach it turned south and west, joining up with the coast road again, but at that bend, another road branched off, running straight and true toward the rising sun. This was the one that Jebu took. He explained the situation to his Lieutenant Ephras the night before the army set out.

"You remember the battle in that little unnamed valley? What are our chances of doing that again?"

"Excellent, general," Ephras said confidently. "The men's morale is high and we have even more men than we had then."

"So you agree the Kemetu generals are all fools?"

"Eh? Er, no...I wouldn't..." Ephras' voice trailed off in confusion.

"Paramessu was a raw, untried general and I almost had him." Jebu smacked a fist into his other hand. "Somebody rallied their troops and saved their army. There may be inexperience in front of us, but no stupidity. So I'll ask you once more, Ephras; what chance do we have of repeating our almost-victory?"

A desire to agree with his general vied with a fear of appearing disloyal. "Er, not much...I suppose."

"Very good, Ephras, not much. In fact, I'd say almost no chance at all. So, next question--do we bring the Kemetu to battle?"

Ephras' forehead broke out in a light sweat. Either answer could land him in trouble, so Ephras opted for a hesitant question of his own. "Is this not what our king wants?"

"Yes, but he also says I am in charge." Jebu knew precisely how much reliance to place on a king's promises--none. If he defeated Kemet, Aziru would claim the credit for appointing the successful general; if he failed, it meant his own death. He looked at his Lieutenant for a few minutes, enjoying the man's discomfort, and knowing exactly the dilemma a junior officer found himself in when trying to guess what a general wanted to hear. He smiled to himself and relented.

"What are the advantages and disadvantages of facing the enemy in open battle? Advantages first, please."

Ephras' relief was almost tangible. "We outnumber them," he said promptly. "We are more familiar with the country round here, we have chariots, we know we can beat them."

"And the disadvantages?"

"They...they are better disciplined." Ephras stopped and thought hard. "They are fighting for their land whereas we...we..."

"Are fighting for plunder. Don't be afraid to admit it. What else?"

Ephras shook his head. "That is all I can think of, general."

"They are also fighting for pride. We almost beat them last time and we certainly bloodied their noses. They will be looking to avenge their comrades, and that General Paramessu will be looking to wipe out his shame."

"So do we meet them in battle, sir?"

"Yes, but at a time and place of my choosing."

"You have a place in mind, general?"

"Now, Ephras," Jebu continued as if he had not heard the question, "We must decide how we are going to fight without coming to battle until I am ready." He walked to the flap of his tent, pushing the heavy wool to one side and looking out. The guards standing outside snapped to attention and looked enquiringly at their general. Jebu waved them away and they saluted before turning back to their duties. He looked out on the sea of tents that represented the massed might of Amori and Hatti.

"Do you remember the old days, Ephras?"

"Sir?"

"When I was just a troop leader and we roamed the countryside as we pleased?"

"Yes, sir. They were hard days."

"True, but productive also. I lost count of the villages we burned, animals and farmers slaughtered and we accounted for a number of Kemetu soldiers too. Why were we never caught, Ephras?

The young officer shrugged. "We never stayed around to be caught. As soon as we hit a fort or a farm or a village, we moved on."

"So our twenty men killed about a hundred or so...and lost a handful. That's pretty good results for any troop of soldiers."

"Yes, sir."

"Would you like to do it again?"

"Er, do what, sir?"

Jebu sighed. "If I sent you out with say, a hundred men. That's enough to do some real damage but not so many you can't move fast. You take no food or baggage, just live off the land. Could you do it?"

Ephras nodded slowly. "Of course, but to what end? You'd have me attack villages again?"

Jebu turned and looked his Lieutenant directly in the eyes. "The Kemetu army."

Ephras looked at his general carefully, trying to decide if this was a jest he had missed. He reflected on the conversation and decided it must be. Smiling politely, he waited for Jebu to continue.

"I mean it Ephras. You and twenty other groups disappear into the countryside and harass the enemy. Never attack superior or even equal numbers; never attack where you cannot escape; never continue the attack long enough for reinforcements to come up."

"And the rest of the army does what exactly?"

"We divide the main army in two, Hittites and Amorites and we act as the bait, trying to goad the Kemetu army into pursuing one or both of us across Kenaan. An army in pursuit of a fleeing enemy is strung out and has eyes only for the prize ahead."

"You would run from them?" Ephras asked incredulously.

"Well, perhaps not run, but at least withdraw fast enough to make them lose their caution. Then, when their attention is fixed on us or the Hittites, the small groups fall on their flanks and their stragglers."

Ephras frowned, still not sure whether this was an obscure jest or evidence that his general had gone mad. "What would be the point? Our efforts would be a flea bite."

"If each man in these troops killed two Kemetu and we lost half our men, we would gain a great numerical advantage."

"Enough to be worthwhile, sir? The enemy will not just stand there and take it."

"That is what I am counting on." Jebu grinned, his teeth white in his black beard. "You've seen a bull maddened by biting flies in the summer? They are doing it no real hurt but the bull, if tormented long enough, strikes out blindly and without thought at whatever it perceives as its enemy." Jebu came closer and looked calmly into the eyes of his Lieutenant. "The Kemetu generals will be cautious after the last battle, but also eager to avenge their honour. We must drive them to unthinking action. We flee, they pursue, driven mad by our flea bites. When they lash out in anger, we turn and fall on them as a disciplined army. Can you and your men act like fleas, Ephras?"

Ephras thought it over carefully, then nodded and grinned. "When do we start?"

The legions of the Kemetu army moved northward along the coast road. Paramessu had joined up with Djedhor and the legions a little south of Lachish two days before the new moon. The men he brought with him from Zarw, hastily conscripted and almost untrained, presented a motley appearance in front of the disciplined legions. The officers unlimbered their whips and strode among them, picking out the best of them and marching them off into the Hundreds and Fifties of the legions.

The whole army waited on the hills and ridges above Lachish for the Amorite army, but nothing appeared. Scouts sent north returned empty handed and three days after the new moon, Paramessu, in consultation with Djedhor and the other commanders, decided their intelligence had been false. There was a very real danger that the Amorite army had slipped past them as they lay encamped by Lachish, and was even now marching south toward an unguarded Kemet. They sent out patrols in all directions, searching for any sign of a passing army. Those that returned reported movement toward the coast road. Several patrols disappeared, though not much attention was paid to the fact at the time. Any number of things could have delayed their return.

Paramessu ordered the army north and west to intersect the coast road. Thousands of men are difficult to move as a cohesive whole. Not only do the different units of an army--light infantry, archers, spearmen, chariots--move at different speeds, but they also have different needs. A foot soldier can venture where a chariot cannot, whereas horses can, for the most part, forage in places where men would starve. Thus the Kemetu army split up into dozens of smaller units, taking road and track and path, maintaining contact with each other, or at least those closest, but only loosely. Stragglers and small units that became separated had a habit of disappearing, though this was often not noticed until the army camped for the night. The men knew the enemy was around, but the disappearances could not be due to enemy action as no attack took place, no hint was seen of either

Amorite or Hittite. Officers, in touch with the deteriorating mood of the men, put the losses down to desertion and brutalized any soldiers genuinely caught slipping away. The full moon came and went.

Then a large Hittite army group was seen by scouts moving south toward them on the plains along the coast. Paramessu hurriedly drew his splintered army together and advanced to meet them, arriving on the flat plains near the town of Ashdod close to dusk. The legions spread out and took up a defensive position, but when no attack eventuated, set up camp for the night. Opposite them, a thousand fires flickered on the dark plain as the enemy too settled down for the night, in preparation for the battle that must certainly ensue the following day.

Paramessu met with the commanding officers of his legions-- Hednakht of Re, Khui of Set, Djedhor of Heru and Amentep of Ptah. The commander of chariots was newly appointed. Merybastet commanded only fifty chariots, those that had been in pieces, being repaired at the time that Khaenmaat had led his squadron to its death.

"Your thoughts, gentlemen." Paramessu looked round at the serious faces of his commanders. "What are your impressions of what lies before us?"

"We can take them, General," Amentep said firmly. "There are only four or five thousand of them."

"How can you tell?" Merybastet asked. "It was getting dark and we never saw them clearly."

"Count the watchfires. Hittites customarily sleep five or six to a fire and my men counted close on eight hundred fires tonight."

"We are sure they are Hittites?"

"They were your patrols that brought the news, Hednakht," Djedhor said.

"So where are the Amorites? I thought they were marching south with the men of Hatti."

"That is a matter of some concern," Paramessu interposed. "I do not want a surprise tomorrow when we attack."

"How much of a surprise could it be?" Amentep asked, smiling. "We outnumber them nearly three to one...No, let me finish." He held up a hand as Khui opened his mouth to speak. "We know the Amorite army is much larger, maybe eight or ten thousand, but how could an army that size be moved around without everyone knowing about it? It cannot be anywhere near. Certainly not within a day's march. I say we attack and destroy the Hittites immediately."

"But why would they separate?" Merybastet asked. "That is foolishness when you know the enemy is near."

"Exactly my thoughts," Khui growled. "As I was trying to say."

Amentep grinned. "Who can explain the mind of a woman, a goat or an Amorite? Isn't that the old proverb? Never mind why they separated, let's just take advantage of it."

"I like your balls, Amentep, though I could wish you thought before you leaped," Djedhor said slowly. "Incomplete intelligence has lost many a battle."

"You are getting too old for this," smirked Amentep. "Maybe you should let the younger blood take over command."

Djedhor's eyes narrowed and he clenched his fists by his side. "The day you manage your Ptah legion half as well as my Heru legion--that's the day I step aside."

"That'll be tomorrow then," Amentep jeered. "You just stay back with your men and guard the camp. My Ptah's could take those Hittites by themselves."

"Enough!" Paramessu snapped. "I will not have my commanders squabbling among themselves like children. I called you here to get reasoned argument, not vainglorious posturing. If you cannot control yourselves I will remove you from command and give your legions to someone else."

Djedhor bristled. "With respect, General, it was Horemheb who gave us our commands. It is he who will tell me to go, no-one else."

"And General Horemheb passed the command of this army over to me." Paramessu spoke softly, looking at the faces of his commanders one by one. "Each of you inherited a legion that existed under another commander, yet you have all made changes. Why? Because as commander you have the right, the duty even, to make changes for the good of your legion. Well, I have that same right, gentlemen, and I don't give a mouse's turd what you think of it. Defy me and I will break you, so hard and so fast you will pray that the ranks are as far as you fall. Do you understand? Amentep? Hednackht?" He continued around the circle of commanders, extracting words of acquiescence or at least a curt nod from each man in turn. "Djedhor?"

The commander of the Heru legion met Paramessu's eyes, his own smoldering with anger. Jaw clenched he gave a curt nod and turned away, staring out of the raised tent flap at the swarm of watchfires across the valley.

"So this is what we will do," Paramessu said. "We will attack the Hittites at first light, falling upon them with our superior numbers. Ptah on the left, Set in the centre and Heru on the right. Re and the chariot squadron will stay in reserve. If the Hittites have a surprise for us, I can deploy you as needed. If the Amorites somehow come up on us from the rear, then we will have warning. Now, see to your men and rouse them at moonrise. Be ready to move at first light."

The commanders bowed and left the General's tent, some with a smile, Djedhor still angered and stiff with resentment. The murmur of men on edge rose from the camp, the veterans trying to grab a few hours of sleep, the new recruits too keyed up to rest, sat or stood and watched the Hittite fires, their weapons in hand. A glimmer of light appeared in the east, too faint for the great barque of Re. The waning moon, now only a sliver, rose above the hills, casting a wan light. The great army gathered itself, moving as silently as possible into position on the darkened plain. Ahead, the Hittite camp lay in silence, the watchfires burning low in the chill pre-dawn air.

"Are they asleep?" Paramessu muttered to Hednakht as he waited by the Re standard at the rear of the army. "Well, it will be their last sleep so we will not disturb them just yet."

The moon slowly ascended the paling sky and a pink flush tinged the eastern sky. The valley plain became visible, and by degrees the deserted campsite of the Hittite army.

"They've gone," Hednakht said incredulously. "They've crept away in the night."

"They will not have gone far," Paramessu said grimly. "We will catch them and show them they cannot play games with us."

"Which way do you think they have gone, sir? If they know where the Amorites are they may try to join them."

Paramessu turned and called messengers to his side. "Tell Heru and Set to move toward the Hittite camp. Find out which way they have gone and signal us. Ptah is to move five thousand paces to the east and march parallel to the main column. Re will do the same to the west. Go." He watched impassively as the messengers raced off and a little later as the legions set off in the slowly strengthening light of the new day.

They found the trail of the retreating Hittites and set off in pursuit. As the day drew on the Kemetu army units slowly lost cohesion, spread out in a looser formation than the commanders liked, but the dust of the Hittites hung on the horizon and they fed their anger on the sight. Increasingly, reports of light fighting, skirmishing, came in from the rear and the extreme edges, but never in sufficient strength to warrant a response. The army picked up the pace, determined to close with the fleeing enemy.

Chapter 28

"I feel like a cow, a great gravid cow. How can any woman actually want to have children?"

Khu wisely refrained from comment. In the months since Paramessu had left Zarw, Scarab had, by degrees, swung from outright hostility toward the man responsible for her condition and, in his absence, any other man at hand; to weeping over her missing soldier and finding great delight in babies and young animals. Thankfully, her mood swings had calmed, as had her temper, though Khu knew enough to agree with most of her remarks but ignore others. Instead, he sought to divert her.

There was in fact very little to do in the almost deserted army garrison now that the able-bodied men had been swept from the city. Crippled men guarded the gates and old men, racked with infirmities and stiffening joints, polished weapons and mended equipment. The tasks which Scarab had attended to previously had almost disappeared and what little remained could be handled by the handful of low grade scribes left behind. Khu still assisted Nebhotep the physician, but here too there was little to do. The medical man had avoided conscription into Paramessu's band of reinforcements, quietly but firmly refusing the General's commands. He had a greater duty, he said, to the daughter of Nebmaetre. Paramessu had nodded and dropped the matter. Since the departure, Khu had filled the tiny workroom on the upper floor with a plethora of unguents, powders and pastes, all prepared under Nebhotep's careful scrutiny. Now with fewer patients,

Khu too had little to do. So he turned to Scarab and together they found diversions in the city.

After the streets of Waset, the alleys of Zarw were cramped and poor. Yet even here there were new sights and sounds and smells--different foods to be tasted, strange tongues to listen to, a whole new culture to absorb. This was a city on the borders of Kemet, open to the flow of traders still braving the war-torn barrier lands of Kenaan and Lebanon, bringing with them not only exotic trading goods, but also strange and wonderful people, far removed from the comfortable and comforting familiarity of Kemetu life.

Sex between consenting adults is a normal part of that life, providing neither party is married. However, precautions are taken to reduce the chance of an unwanted child. Scarab had not taken even the most elementary of these precautions--a linen plug soaked in honey and ground acacia seeds--and now paid the price. Pregnant women are seldom seen in public unless they are poor and must work. Scarab now ranked as poor but she had no work to allow her in public, so she dressed to conceal her condition. The thin linens of Kemetu women provided scant covering so she adopted the dress of her Khabiru kinfolk--voluminous woolen robes that hid all hint of figure, allowing only the head and extremities to be seen. Her flowing hair with its strong reddish tinge, courtesy of her mother, Queen Tiye, completed the disguise and none gave her a second glance.

Scarab and Khu stood in one of the market places of the sprawling city watching the ebb and flow of foreigners. They munched on honey cakes and sipped from a common pot of thin beer, bought with a piece of copper from the meager army wage allowed them for their services.

"They shouldn't be allowed in," Khu said firmly. "They are probably all spies for the Hittites and Amorites anyway."

Scarab laughed, crumbs of honey cake falling from her mouth. "Those aren't foreigners; they're mostly Khabiru, my own people. I can see a party of Cretans though...over there." She pointed. "...And that merchant probably hails from Syria or Lebanon. Some Nubians too, but I cannot see any spies."

"You wouldn't, that's the whole point. And Khabiru are foreign...well, as good as, though I suppose they've lived in Kemet so long they are almost the same as Kemetu."

The noise of the market place rose all around them, people crying their wares, men and women haggling and arguing, others in loud conversation. Children screamed and laughed, darting between the legs of the adults, with thin and hungry dogs keeping their eyes open for the opportunity to steal food from careless stall holders.

"You think Khabiru and Kemetu are the same, Khu?" Scarab shook her head. "They have kept their own language, their own customs, and their own gods. I don't know of another tribe that has kept so separate while living among us."

Khu grunted and stared sourly at a group of young Khabiru men passing by. They returned his stare and one called out an incomprehensible phrase. Khu rounded on Scarab as the youths swaggered away. "What did they say?"

Scarab shook her head again. "Nothing. It was just an impolite phrase concerning my choice in men. They don't like their women being seen with Kemetu, and they thought I was one, dressed like this." She plucked at her woolen robes.

"Well, if they don't like us, why don't they just go home? I certainly wouldn't miss them."

"Where would they go? Most of them were born here, as were their parents and grandparents. This is their home."

"I thought they came from Kenaan or the land of Sin-ai or something."

"Probably originally. My mother told me her father Yuya came to Kemet as a young man when famine struck Syria. Khabiru have been settling in Kemet for generations. Later, after he rose in power, his kinfolk came too. They talk of going home sometimes, somewhere north in a land of bread and wine, but I doubt they ever will. Life is too good here."

They continued walking through the market and though they had little copper in their purses, they stopped to examine the wares laid out on trestle tables beneath brightly dyed awnings. Carved figurines of the gods of Kemet jostled with piles of dates and olives; papyrus mats with tubs of live eels; loaves of bread still warm from the ovens, with cheap copper and faience jewelry.

Khu picked through the trinkets with one finger, occasionally holding a piece up to the light. "There's not much here," he grumbled. "Nothing like the quality you find in Waset or even Akhet-Aten."

"Well, there wouldn't be, would there?" Scarab replied. "In those cities you have a royal court to make jewelry for. Who could afford it here?"

"You would be surprised, young lady," cut in a deep voice in the Khabiru tongue. A tall man got up from a heavy-set chair in the shadows and approached the table. Dressed in the usual heavy wool robes despite the heat, and a full beard in the Khabiru fashion, his eyes burned beneath hooded brows and a long scar on his forehead stood out pale on his dark skin. The man continued in Kemetu, "There are a scattering of nobles around Zarw and besides, by the time the traveling merchants have sold their wares, there is gold to spend on elegant fripperies for wives and mistresses back home." The jeweler eyed Scarab and Khu doubtfully. "Perhaps you would care to see my finer work?"

"Yes, please," Scarab said eagerly.

The jeweler removed the seat cushion from the heavy wooden chair behind him and swung a hinged lid up. Lifting a tray from the depths, he carried it over to the trestle table.

"Aren't you worried about thieves?" Khu asked. "I mean, you've just shown us and whoever else is watching, just where your valuables are."

"That's why I pay the mayor extra for this site. See?" The jeweler jerked his head to either side. Looking round, Scarab and Khu saw two fully armed soldiers standing attentively a few paces away. They scanned the faces of everyone in the vicinity, but paid far more attention to the jewelry table. "I pay extra for the site, but I get two guards with it." He grinned. "Nobody steals from Jeheshua the jeweler."

"You are Khabiru." Scarab stated.

Jeheshua inclined his head gravely. "Indeed." He regarded the young couple before him. "The lad is Kemetu," he continued, speaking to Scarab in Khabiru again, "But you are Khabiru, are you not?"

A man pushed in from the side, reaching across Scarab to finger the bracelets and earrings scattered on the table. Picking up a copper bangle with green and blue glass paste inlaid in a swirling pattern, the man grunted and held it out. "How much?"

Jeheshua and the customer haggled for a few minutes, before the man nodded and dug into his purse, coming up with a small piece of silver. He held it out for inspection and it was Jeheshua's turn to nod. When the man had left he slipped the silver into the folds of his robe and turned back to Scarab.

"You are Khabiru, are you not?"

"On my mother's side."

Jeheshua nodded. "Of what tribe?"

Scarab hesitated. "I don't know. My mother said of the same tribe as Yuya."

Jeheshua lifted his eyebrows. "If that is true, then you are related to the king."

"Only distantly, I'm sure." Scarab smiled. "What have you got to show us?"

The jeweler lifted a cloth from the wooden tray and revealed a sparkling array of gold, silver and semi-precious stones. Khu murmured in appreciation and Scarab gasped at the beauty of the pieces. Necklaces of chalcedony and rich dark amber glowed up from the deeply dyed blue wool of the tray base, the stones, together with lozenges of glass paste in beautiful reds and blues held together by threads of gold. Delicate filigree work surrounded the centre stones, drawing the eye onward from one wonder to the next.

"These are...are beautiful, Jeheshua. No, they are more--you have a gift from the gods." Scarab found her fingers trembling with the desire to pick the pieces up and hold them against her throat, to feel them against her naked skin. With an effort she controlled herself, forcing an expression of calm onto her face. "The gods have given you a great gift that you can create such beauty."

Jeheshua shook his head, his dark locks glistening in the sunlight, his eyes dark and suddenly chilly above his hawked nose. "Do not speak to me of gods, young lady, there is but one."

"Are you an Atenist?" Khu queried.

Jeheshua swung to face him. "I am a servant of the Lord."

"What?" Khu stared in astonishment, the man's words taking him by surprise. In the Khabiru tongue, which Jeheshua had used, his words sounded very like the name A-khen-aten. "What did you say?"

Scarab recognized the similarity of the sounds and quickly laid a hand on Khu's arm. "Say nothing," she muttered. Turning back to the jeweler, she bowed her head. "I am sorry if I have given offence, Jeheshua. The beauty of your work overcame me and I spoke from my upbringing. My father's house was Kemetu and I know not my mother's ways."

Jeheshua bowed stiffly in response. "Then, young lady, I too retract my hasty judgment, for I would not turn a child of the people from the true way." He forced a smile and threw a cloth back over the tray of jewels. His eyes caught the look of disappointment on Scarab's face and he pondered a moment, before nodding suddenly in decision. "If you appreciate beauty, I have another piece." Taking the tray back to his chair he pulled out another tray before returning the one with the necklaces to the hidden depths of the seat. He brought the new tray back to the table and, after glancing around to make sure he was not overlooked, withdrew the cloth.

The piece of jewelry drew a gasp of amazement from both Scarab and Khu. A pectoral, heavy with gold, filled the tray. Scarab stretched out her hand and roughly measured it--over three times the length from her wrist to finger tips; it would stretch from a man's throat to his waist. A magnificent scarab of yellow chalcedony formed the centerpiece, its curved wings stretching out and up. The hind legs of the scarab were not beetle legs but the fierce talons of a hawk, clutching a lily and a lotus. Below hung heavy tassels in the form of lotus blossoms and buds, glass paste in red and blue, together with slivers of lapis. Rearing cobras, the sacred uraeus, framed the scarab on either side but instead of the usual ball of the sun pushed ahead of the translucent yellow representation of the sun god, was a boat containing the wadjet-eye and a crescent moon in brilliant gold, the body of the dark moon above it.

Scarab frowned, her finger tracing the plain unadorned surface of the dark of the moon. "Where is the name?" she asked. "Who is it for? Their name should be on this."

Jeheshua nodded. "Indeed there should, but who will buy it?"

"Who did you make it for?" Khu asked. "You don't just make something like this in the hope of finding a buyer."

"It can only have been a member of royalty, or one who would curry favour with the king," Scarab added softly. "You have put in the royal uraeus. It is treason for someone who is not of the king's line to wear this."

"If you are of the tribe of Yuya, you could wear it, young lady," Jeheshua said, his dark eyes searching Scarab's face.

"You are mistaken."

"I think not. You wore a wig then as any proper lady of the court should, but you are known in Waset and Akhet-Aten." Scarab backed away slightly, flicking a glance at the soldiers standing a few paces away, though thankfully out of earshot of normal conversation. Jeheshua noticed her agitation and hurried on. "There is nothing to fear from me, lady. I too, am of the tribe of Yuya. We stand by our own."

Scarab licked her lips. "What is it you want of me?"

Jeheshua spread his hands and smiled. "Nothing--and everything. I will not tell others of your presence, Handmaiden of the Lord, though several know of your presence here in Zarw. If news should come to me of others seeking you--an uncle say--I will contrive to send you warning."

Scarab stared into the tall man's eyes, searching out the feather of his soul, finally bowing her head slightly in acknowledgement. A movement to her right caught her eye and she picked up a ring at random from the table. "How much?" she asked loudly, half turning toward the man approaching the trestle. "I think he seeks to rob me."

The man looked startled, then grinned and moved on after a cursory glance at Jeheshua's wares.

Scarab turned back to the jeweler. "No man gives protection without wanting something in return. I have no money with which to pay you."

Jeheshua laughed. "You think I need money when I have this?" He gestured toward the pectoral, now covered in its tray.

"Then what?" Khu growled, moving beside Scarab and glaring at the man.

"Be at peace, lad, I mean your lady no harm." Jeheshua turned his attention back to the girl again. "The Khabiru have been a favoured people in Lower Kemet for many years, but this is coming to an end. The king in Akhet-Aten identified his god with ours too strongly. Now the Tjaty and others are bringing Kemet back to their old pagan gods. The one god, and those who worship him, will suffer for it. I seek help for my people wherever I may."

"I am Kemetu too," Scarab said quietly. "I worship the Nine of Iunu."

"You are young. The Lord will call you when He is ready for you. When the Tjaty's desires rule Kemet, you will help your mother's people."

Scarab inclined her head. "If I can do so without offending the Nine...or the One, I will do so." She turned to go but was drawn back to the pectoral again. "You never told us who you made it for."

"Your brother Smenkhkare, but he died. I will probably have to break it up and reuse the gold, though it took me three years to make."

"Then take it to the court of Tutankhaten at Waset."

"The boy?" Jeheshua grinned. "It would stretch from throat to knee and he could not bear the weight of it."

"But he will grow to be a man, if Ay lets him, and he loves beautiful things. Show it to Tutankhaten--put his name on the moon above the wadjet-eye. He will pay you well."

Jeheshua considered, his fingers stroking his short beard. "I have always wanted to see Waset. I will think on this."

Scarab and Khu took their leave of the jeweler and started back toward the barracks. Khu looked about distractedly as they walked, jumping nervously if any man walked too close.

"We will have to leave Zarw," he said. "It is too dangerous now that we are known."

"No. I am staying here until the birth of my son at least and maybe more. You heard him, Khu. Jeheshua said he would get me warning of danger."

"And you trust him? He is as much a fanatic for his god as your brother Akhenaten is for the Aten. You should not have said you worshiped the Iunu Nine."

"Possibly," Scarab agreed. "But I will not compromise my beliefs for any man. Besides, I trust him. We have things in common."

Khu looked incredulous. "What? Apart from the fact you are partly descended from that stiff-necked people."

Scarab smiled, but said nothing further, being distracted by the movement of the child in her belly.

Chapter 29

The expedition against the Son of Sobek had failed. Despite the security and rapid deployment of Horemheb's Amun legion south past the second cataract, word had somehow been passed to the rebels. Disembarking at the entrance to the Tanjur Valley, the legion struck up the Amaran Road, moving swiftly, weapons at the ready, but they saw no-one, not even the inhabitants of three tiny villages they ran through. They arrived at the Well of Amara barely hours ahead of Penno's force which had taken the longer, more arduous route over the Abu Hoda track. The rebels had been at the Well of Amara, that much was clear. Fires still smoked, and scattered baggage told a story of sudden departure, but of the rebels themselves, there were only tracks.

Horemheb and Penno rested the men, allowing them the opportunity to eat and catch up on a bit of sleep before the next task. They withdrew to the shade of a date palm near the Well to discuss just what that next task was going to be.

"There was an informer, there had to have been," Horemheb fumed.

"Of course," Penno agreed. "I tell you, this Son of Sobek has infiltrated every town and city, every fort and garrison. It was a gamble at best."

"Then what was the point of us hurrying like that?"

"I hoped we might provoke him into facing us."

"Well, we didn't, so where has he gone now? North to the other wells and the gold mines?"

"Possibly, but I'd wager he has gone south instead, deeper into Kush."

"Why? Your argument before was that he would not want to be too far from the cities."

Penno nodded. "But now he has a trained army to deal with. I believe he will lure us deeper into Kush until a time of his choosing, and cut us to pieces."

Horemheb scowled and, picking up a small rock, pitched it at a nearby goat. It missed but fell close enough to startle the animal into headlong flight. "Where will he head for?"

"Kergus and the boundary stelae of Tuthmosis between the fourth and fifth cataracts."

"That is being extraordinarily precise. Do you know something you aren't telling me?" He glared suspiciously at the Lieutenant.

Penno laughed. "Not really, general. He has fewer options than you might think. We came up two of the exits. I know he did not pass me. There is south or east across the dry lands--I would not want to try that by myself, let alone with an army. No, southeast down the Kurgus Valley is the way he went...I'd bet my life on it," he added, catching sight of Horemheb's skeptical look.

"I may hold you to that," Horemheb muttered.

An hour later the combined force of the Amun legion and the Sehotep-Neteru garrison were on the march again. Horemheb had them discard every unnecessary piece of equipment, retaining only their weapons, a bedroll, dried rations and as many pots of water as they could carry. They headed southeast into the dry and windswept mountains, following the traces left behind by the rebel force.

The passage to the crest of the ridge proved difficult, access being limited to a few narrow tracks more in use by wild animals than by human travelers. The legion struggled to the top and looked to the southeast, down the long rugged sweep of the Kurgus valley. The same tracks led down from the ridge on the other side, but in the distance, at about the point that the wind and the drought relented sufficiently in the depths of the valley for stunted trees to grow, they converged and expanded into a road. There was little cover on the higher slopes and the Kemetu force made good time, slipping and sliding down the loose hillsides, a mass of men moving downward in no good order, without the need to guard against surprise attack. Their feet kicked up a choking cloud of acrid dust that caked in their throats, causing them to cough and spit, wasting precious water.

Just short of the tree line, Horemheb called a halt and had his officers shepherd the troops into battle formation before moving down to the road. Once there, he threw out scouting groups and parties of skirmishers that flanked the main body, ranging widely through the scrub thickets, looking for any sign of the enemy. None was found, just the signs in the dust of the passage of many men on foot.

They made camp that night by a small depression in the valley floor that still displayed the recent presence of water. Penno had the men dig out a shallow pit which soon filled with muddy water. Strained through kilts, it was sufficient to restore the water used that day and provide a small ration for each man in which to soften their grain. Penno wanted to ban the use of cooking and watch fires at night, but Horemheb over-ruled him.

"They already know we are here. The men may as well be comfortable." He was careful to set a double ring of guards though. The night passed without incident or note, save for the distant roaring of lions.

The next day, and the ones following, was much like the first, hot and dusty and filled with the exhaustion of being continually on guard in unfamiliar territory where death might spring from behind any boulder, thicket or tree. Sometimes they found a seep or a tiny well to provide water at nightfall, sometimes not; but slowly the rations were used up and Horemheb was forced to send heavily armed hunting parties out into the hills surrounding the Kurgus to look for food. Despite the barren nature of the surroundings, they usually returned with enough game to enable the legion to travel further. They continued their progress southward, following the distinct track of hundreds of bare and sandaled feet.

Half a month later, the Amun legion arrived at a point where the Kurgus was joined by two other valleys, the ridged sides opening out into a lightly forested plain. Here, the prints of the rebel army, so distinct in the dust and earth, faded and disappeared. Horemheb and Penno joined the scouting group at the forefront of the column, squatting to examine the pristine road ahead of them.

"Did they leave the road somewhere and we missed them?"

Penno shook his head, pointing his finger in a broad sweep over the dusty surface. "Others use this road, even animals, yet there are no prints beyond this point. It has been swept clean, and recently."

Horemheb stood and scanned the scrub land, one hand shading his eyes. There were many places for men to hide and he felt his skin crawl at the thought of an arrow suddenly appearing out of the wilderness and striking him down. "We must find them. The legion stays here in a defensive position with outlying guards. I want five, no six, patrols, each of twenty men and a trumpeter, each under the command of a good officer. I will take one of these patrols and I want to see the other officers here before the sun has moved a finger span."

The patrols fanned out to cover the Kurgus valley in their line of advance, as well as behind, in case the rebels tried doubling back, and the two side valleys. They were under orders not to engage the enemy unless they had to, slipping back to the legion if they found anything significant. If they were discovered, an alarm was to be sounded by the trumpeter. Horemheb led his patrol out into the side valley that ran in a westward direction. Another patrol paralleled his but over a thousand paces distant.

The general organized his men simply. Their mission was to find the tracks of the rebel army so he spread his men out in line abreast, in pairs ten paces apart. One man scanned the ground continually while another scanned the surroundings, bow in hand and arrow at the ready. Horemheb followed with the trumpeter in the middle of the line. The vegetation was sufficiently thin that he could see the entire line most of the time, and felt confident that nothing would slip by them easily.

The day was hot, calm and silent except for the shuffle and slide of loose rock underfoot, the occasional curse as a thorn or rock penetrated careless skin, and the muted buzz of insects. When they first set out there had been a flurry of animal calls as the fauna of the area, though unseen, responded to the disturbance of their territory by men. That had died away, though a solitary creature, a bird, Horemheb guessed, still called from a point upslope from their flank. Horemheb counted off the paces to himself and after each hundred, halted his men and listened carefully for any hint of action from the other patrols.

The afternoon wore on and the sun sank behind the ridges to the west, throwing a cooler shadow over the valley. The ground became steeper and Horemheb called a halt, turning his men and calling them across to line up a hundred paces to the side.

"All right, back the way we came...stay alert, man," he rapped out as he saw a man fall over. The man lay sprawled and Horemheb cursed, turning toward him. Something whispered in the air, and again, the trumpeter stumbling against his general from behind, almost throwing him off balance. Somebody yelled and the bushes moved, suddenly filled with running men. Horemheb snatched for his sword, yelling at the trumpeter to sound the alarm. Cries filled the air but not the brazen cry of the trumpet and he turned, cursing once more as he saw the signaler dead on the ground behind him, an arrow in his back. Then he was fighting for his life, his sword swinging up to catch the downward curve of gleaming bronze. The man stumbled past, a Nubian farmer by the looks of him; his inexperience shouting out as Horemheb casually swept his blade across the man's belly. Without stopping to see the man fall he pushed forward at another man, ducking under a head-high sweep and stabbing for the throat. The man fell back and Horemheb followed, his pulse loud in his ears, knowing he was dead but determined to go down fighting.

Abruptly silence fell, broken only by the scuff of sandals on the ground and his own panting. Horemheb stopped, his sword held low and he swung slowly round, taking in the ring of armed men with the sour taste of defeat in his mouth.

"Throw down your sword, General Horemheb."

"Nobody orders me," Horemheb growled, taking a firmer grip on his sword. He crouched lower, ignoring the stinging sweat pouring into his eyes. "Come and take it if you can, for I obey none but my king."

"It is your king who commands you."

Something in the voice caught at his mind and he straightened, his sword point wavering. "Show yourself."

"I am here, Horemheb."

The circle of men drew back and faded into the scrub, leaving two men to face the general. He stared at them, looking for any sign of familiarity. They were both young men and not native to the country, but they were like few Kemetu Horemheb had ever seen. Their hair, obviously their own, hung long and lank, blending in to thick beards. Their bodies were hairless for the most part but horribly disfigured. Something had ripped away flesh from the torso of the taller one,

leaving twisted and puckered skin, shining pink and raw against the
bronzed limbs. The other man, smaller but stockier, favoured one leg,
the left being criss-crossed with savage scars. He held a bow, the arrow
pointing steadily at the general's chest.

Horemheb found himself staring at the terrible scars, trying to
imagine how such destruction had come about--and how the men had
survived. The wound on the taller man's torso narrowed toward his
right side and pale circular scars formed two roughly converging lines,
not unlike the snout of...

"So that is why they call you Son of Sobek."

"Only the crocodile god could have made them release me," the
man said softly. "Am I not therefore his son?"

"Smenkhkare." The statement was flat and without a hint of
question.

"You hold a weapon in the presence of the king," growled the
limping man, raising the bow to bring the arrow in line with
Horemheb's eye.

Horemheb looked down at his blood-stained curved sword and
grunted, throwing it to the ground. "Why have you killed my men?"

"Your men? Are not all soldiers the king's men?"

"A king does not kill except through necessity. You slaughtered
these men."

"Have a care," yelled the stocky man. He advanced a limping pace
forward, the point of the arrow barely moving as he did so. "I will kill
you if you insult the king."

"'Enough, Menkure," Smenkhkare said, laying a hand gently on the
archer's bowhand. "Horemheb is a friend...is he not, Horemheb?"

The general stared back at the pair, his mind in turmoil. "I am a
friend to the king," he said slowly.

Smenkhkare laughed; an edge of bitterness in his voice. "You'll
have to do better than that."

Horemheb suddenly tired of the word games, the politics. "Then
speak plainly."

"Very well. I am your anointed king, Ankhkheperure
Djeserkheperu Smenkhkare. It is agreed that my brother Waenre
Akhenaten rules in his City of the Aten and I rule the rest of Kemet.
Why then, does my Tjaty Ay crown that fool of a boy, my younger
brother Tutankhaten as king in my place?"

"Because you are dead, Smenkhkare. Dead and buried but you do not yet realize it."

"I want my kingdoms back, Horemheb."

The general shrugged. "Then take them. If the gods recognise your cause they will oust the usurper in Waset. Why have you not tried before now?"

"I was six months just recovering from my injuries. By then there was a new king on the throne of the Two Kingdoms and Ay was controlling matters behind the throne. I had only Menkure here," Smenkhkare reached out and touched the arm of the other man gently. "But no army. How could I claim what was rightfully mine?"

Horemheb nodded slowly. "With difficulty," he agreed.

"And you? Where do your loyalties lie?"

"With Kemet."

Smenkhkare smiled and moved into the shade of a large thorn tree. "Now I must ask you to speak plainly."

Horemheb moved into the shade also, keeping a few paces from the king and his glowering attendant. He sat down on a rock and stretched his legs out in front of him. "Kemet was strong in the days of your father Nebmaetre. Under Akhenaten and his heresy..."

"Which you supported," Menkure interrupted.

"Only that I might keep the army strong," Horemheb shot back. "As I was saying, Akhenaten weakened Kemet and you did little better."

Menkure growled, but said nothing. "I did not have much time," Smenkhkare observed mildly. "Even so, I reintroduced the old worship of the gods and curbed the worst excesses of the Amun priests. I also helped the common man."

"Who gives a fig for the common man? You neglected your power base, Smenkhkare, the army and the nobles. You alienated Ay and look where it got you."

"Ay was ruining the country with his greed. I would not allow his schemes so he tried to control me. I reminded him who was king and dismissed him. He was to retire at the end of the month."

"Ah, so that was the reason."

"The reason for what?"

"Your death."

"Explain yourself."

"Your death...or your apparent death...shook the country. There were riots and uprisings, quelled quickly and firmly by the army, I might add. Still, confidence was shaken and if Ay had not crowned Tutankhaten king after the seventy days, chaos would have resulted."

Smenkhkare grunted. "And if I return?"

"Many will flock to your banner. As many will support Ay, saying that you are an imposter. The balance, the Ma'at of Kemet, will be disturbed."

"Forget the many--what do you say, Horemheb? Am I Smenkhkare or an imposter?"

"Here and now, between the three of us, I say you are Smenkhkare."

"What will you say when you report to Ay?"

Horemheb raised an eyebrow. "I am to live then? I shall tell him the truth. That you are the king, that you survived his assassination attempt and that you intend to return."

Smenkhkare looked up sharply. "You knew of the attempt? You know for a fact of Ay's guilt?" His eyebrows came together in a suspicious frown. "Did you know of the plot before or after?"

"If I had known beforehand, I would have stopped it, even if it meant killing Ay."

Smenkhkare nodded, his face relaxing and a small smile struggling through his thick beard. "Of course. Upright Horemheb. I did not think you a traitor."

"Do not mock me, Smenkhkare. I do what is right for Kemet."

"What is right for Kemet then, in your eyes?"

"You are not the only one affected by all this. Many people live and die through an action of yours, a careless word, and an ill-considered judgment. Kings live so far above their subjects they think the laws do not apply to them." Horemheb leaned closer and stared earnestly into the bearded man's eyes. "Many died when you did."

Smenkhkare paled beneath his hirsute features and his hand trembled slightly. "Who has died? It was six months before I started to get news. Akhenaten is dead then? What...what of my sister?"

"Akhenaten still rules in his City of the Sun. Ay tried to kill the whole of the King's Council, but he did not succeed. Sutau is dead, so is Kensthoth, Meres, Kenamun..."

"I am not interested in those men. Tell me of my sister, of Beketaten. Is she dead?"

"No-one knows. She and the farm lad Khu disappeared on the night the Council was imprisoned. Aanen and Nebhotep escaped later. Mahuhy...well I would imagine he has gone back to his old haunts and is keeping out of sight."

"Nobody has seen my sister since?"

"Rumors only. You know what rumors are like. She is nowhere and everywhere."

"Then I will hope she is alive still," Smenkhkare said simply. "Now, what am I to do with you, General Horemheb? Will you and your legion support your rightful king?"

"What are your intentions?"

"To reclaim my throne of course. With your help I can march on Waset at once, without it I will have to delay another year or so until I build my army. What do you say?"

"I say no, Smenkhkare," Horemheb said gently. "I will not help plunge this land into civil war."

"You will not fight for me, but you will fight for the traitor Ay."

Horemheb shook his head. "I will fight for Kemet and its anointed king Tutankhaten. In the eyes of virtually everyone, you are dead. Be content with what the gods have given you. Go south and carve yourself out a kingdom if you must, but give up your thirst for Kemet."

"That is your final word?"

"It is."

"I should kill you," Smenkhkare said softly. "You are Kemet's best commander. I do not want you fighting for my enemies."

Horemheb shrugged and stood up. "Perhaps you should. I do not hate you but I will not allow you to destroy the Two Lands."

"Let me, your majesty." Menkure limped forward, the arrow back in his bow and the string of the short, strongly curved weapon hummed in anticipation. The honed bronze tip glinted in the afternoon sunlight as it came to bear on Horemheb's chest.

"No."

"Your majesty, he is dangerous and an enemy. Let me kill him."

"I command you, Menkure." An edge of bronze crept into the king's voice. The other man lowered his bow slowly and spat on the ground at the general's feet.

"I have a proposition for you, Horemheb. You came out here to catch or kill me. I am going to give you that chance. Five days march to the south, down the valley, lies an open plain, just before you get to the river. It is a perfect battleground, flat and firm. Meet me there with your legion in ten days and let us settle this issue."

"You would stand and fight me? Why?"

"You are a gifted General, but I have sharpened my skills these last four years. I also have a good army--small but a match for yours. Meet me in open battle and we can decide the future of Kemet. If you win I will take my men south, should I survive, and trouble you no more. If I win, you join me and help me take back the throne."

"You would do this?" An edge of excitement crept into Horemheb's voice and he damped it down quickly. Smenkhkare nodded. "Very well. I agree. Ten days time it is."

Horemheb left, walking through the men of Smenkhkare's army as they drifted back to join their king. Once out of sight, he set off at a run and soon made it back to the camped legion.

"Signal the recall, at once," he snapped. "Penno, come with me." Horemheb led the Lieutenant to one side and explained the situation to him.

Penno looked skeptical. "It is Smenkhkare then? He will fight us, in open battle? And you believe he will do so?"

"He wants me to fight for him. When I refused he offered this." Horemheb laughed. "The hot sun has addled his mind if he thinks his band of misfits and renegades can beat a trained legion. I intend to show him his mistake."

The Amun legion camped there for the night, though Horemheb still insisted on a fully guarded perimeter. The night passed without incident and at first light the general led the troops in a hymn of praise to Re before striking camp.

From a hillside overlooking the Kurgun Valley, two bearded men, both scarred terribly, stood and watched as the legion set off to the south, soon disappearing into the scrub.

"He fell for it," Menkure said.

"I thought he would."

"Why did you not just have me kill him and be rid of him that way?"

"He was a prisoner. It would not have been honourable. Besides, he is Kemet's foremost general, I cannot waste such talents. When I am king again and Kemet is at peace, he will give me his allegiance once more." Smenkhkare clapped his friend on the shoulder and grinned. "Assemble the men. We march at once."

"Yes, your majesty. In which direction?"

"North. We march for Waset. It is time to take my throne back."

Chapter 30

S carab knew the day and the hour of her child's conception. More important than the day of birth was the circumstance of begetting. The tiny tent in the desert where a man and a woman had engendered a new life was in itself a womb in the hostile wilderness of the northern plains. Whirlwinds danced in the baking air beneath their little hill of rock and sand, and the breath of Set moved in time with the rhythmic pulse of lust. Love was there too; else Scarab could not have brought herself to do it. A girlish fantasy, a longing for the strong and handsome soldier had slowly grown to become love and, when the man realized that he too felt something more than tenderness for the princess in his charge, love had found a way. Scarab knew the child was a boy. Nebhotep had done the tests with wheat and barley, and the Khabiru midwives confirmed it. In the weeks following her meeting with Jeheshua, she had grown to respect the old man and had acceded to his request that she get to know her Khabiru relatives.

"You will need proper midwives," he had said, "Not an army butcher."

The day fast approached when the boy was due, then it passed and Scarab grew anxious. The father, Paramessu, was in the north with the army, and she longed for his presence, his touch, his kiss, to dispel her fears and worries.

"First children are often late," said the midwives. "He will come in his own time."

There was another reason for Scarab's anxiety. Without the father, who would name the boy? She remembered her own childhood when her father Nebmaetre had been struck down just before her birth. Unable to utter her birth name she had remained nameless for four years, four years in which had she died, she would have wandered in darkness for eternity. To be nameless was hard for a girl but it was disastrous for a boy. Scarab was determined this would not happen to her son and had arranged for Nebhotep the physician to stand in for the father and utter the name at sunrise the next day. It was not according to custom but in the eyes of the gods it might suffice until Paramessu could repeat the ceremony when he returned.

She even knew the name, though they had never discussed it. In fact, Paramessu had left to rejoin his army never knowing his woman was with child. Scarab smiled to herself at the thought. She was 'his woman' and he had fathered a child on her, one who would be blessed by the gods for he would bear the name of a god, one of the Nine of Iunu. Set would be his name--to some a name of ill omen--but to a soldier a very fitting name. Set was god of the red deserts and he had been present when her son was conceived. It felt right, though she told no-one, least of all the Khabiru midwives. They identified the Kemetu god of chaos and destruction with their own Ba'al, a thunder deity of the north and adversary to their own nameless god. Scarab would not risk their certain displeasure before the birth. After, when they saw his beauty they would not care what his name was.

Nebhotep acted in a most peculiar manner during Scarab's pregnancy. Physicians were expected to have no part in the birth of a child and his keen interest in her, even to the extent of measuring her growth and examining her intimately at intervals was seen more as a perversion than good medicine. Scarab allowed it because she could see no harm in it and was in any case lonely and thrived on the attention. Khu was suspicious and steadfastly refused to leave her side during the examinations. Nebhotep's response was to nod and smile and put the lad to work grinding herbs and mixing unguents. Eventually, however, as her term neared its culmination, the Khabiru women got wind of the scandal and whisked Scarab off to their tents, refusing to let Nebhotep, or even Khu, anywhere near her. Birthing was women's work, always had been. The man's contribution was nine months in the past, and now the real work fell to the women, as usual.

Scarab was in pain. Labor itself was still hours or days away, there had been no hint yet of the trials ahead, but still she hurt. Under the care of Nebhotep and Khu she could still enjoy a shadow of the pampered life of a princess with two men at her beck and call. Here in the tents of the Khabiru she was expected to do her share of the chores. The only concession the tribeswomen made to her condition was to assign her a young girl, Meryam, to be her companion.

"It's not fair," Scarab whined. "I should be sitting down in the shade, not carrying bundles of washing to the canal." She stopped and threw her belly forward, one hand pressed to the small of her back. Despite the tented nature of the voluminous Khabiru robes, no-one could mistake her bulge for anything else. With a grimace she waddled on after her young companion. "Wait, Meryam. I can't walk as fast as you, and my feet hurt. I can't even see my feet," she added.

"Do all Kemetu complain so much, or is it just princesses?" Meryam grinned and turned back, hitching the bundle of linen and wool clothing under one arm. She took Scarab's elbow and gave her some support as they resumed their journey to the canal.

"You're not to call me that; we don't know who might be listening." She scanned the people nervously, but all seemed to be ignoring her, going about their own business. "My name is Scarab, Meryam, please use it."

"Yes princess Scarab," Meryam said meekly. She tried to dip in the strange half bow half squat her people called a curtsy, and almost dropped the washing.

With a laugh, Scarab steadied the young girl and together they went looking for a suitable place on the banks of the canal. The Khabiru had brought in stones and carved away a section of the bank to make a gentle slope to the water's edge, lining the basin with rock and building several small stone jetties in the shallow water. On these jetties, and along the bank of the canal, Khabiru women knelt, sat or squatted, or even stood knee-deep in the clear water, their robes tucked up into waistbands showing their brown legs unashamedly.

Meryam found a place several paces away from the other women and unrolled her bundle of washing. She dipped a robe into the water, pushing it under until the air trapped inside the fibres bubbled out and it sank. Fishing it out she dumped it on the rocks beside Scarab for her to rub the soap into the fabric. Scarab picked up the large bar of yellowish soap with a small moue of distaste and tentatively dabbed at the robe with the bar.

"Scrub it in hard," Meryam instructed. "Otherwise it'll never lift the dirt."

"It smells and it has bits in it. Don't you put in perfume? The soap in the palace always smelled of flowers."

Meryam shook her head. "We are a desert people. Where would we get flowers? And for that matter, why would we want to? Soap cleans perfectly well the way it is."

Scarab put a bit more effort into her scrubbing and when Meryam pronounced herself satisfied, passed the robe back to the young girl. She dunked it under the water again, rinsing it thoroughly before beating it against the rocks, sending a spray of soapy water over them both. While Meryam worked on getting the soap out, Scarab started on the next item of clothing. An hour or two later, the work was done, both girls were soaked and the clothes lay around them on the rocks, drying in the sun's heat. They lay back amongst the garments and dozed, letting the heat dry them.

Scarab scratched at her woolen robe where it mounded over her belly. She shifted awkwardly, trying to get comfortable. "I don't know how you can live in these heavy robes, Meryam. I've only been in them a few months and I still want to scratch and pull them off. I think our way is much better."

Meryam opened one eye. "What? Going around in your flimsy linens?"

"It's much cooler."

"But you're...you'd be almost naked." Meryam opened her other eye and propped herself up on one elbow. "People could...men could see your..." The young girl blushed deeply. "...Your breasts," she finished in a whisper.

Scarab looked at the embarrassed young girl with curiosity. "What of it? I used to walk around like that without a thought. Nobody looks...well, nobody who matters. When I was in Akhet-Aten I often saw the king and queen and their children wandering around naked or just with a thin dress that hid nothing." She smiled at Meryam's horrified expression. "Nobody thinks anything of it. And it is much cooler and freer," she added. "Besides, you've lived in Zarw all your life; you must have seen many naked or nearly naked Kemetu."

"Some," Meryam admitted. "But the young girls are not encouraged to leave our own city and not many Kemetu pass through our tents. She blushed again and hid her face. "I remember when you came to Zarw with that caravan a year ago and walked through the camp wearing only your thin kilt and dress that...that showed everything. Do you remember how the women reacted?"

Scarab nodded. "They called me a whore."

"I'm sorry, Scarab. They didn't know you. Among my people a woman who exposes her breasts and paints her face is announcing to everyone what she is selling. Some people call all Kemetu, whores. Not me, Scarab," Meryam added quickly, putting out a hand reassuringly.

"I suppose they think I'm one anyway, with this." Scarab indicated her rounded belly. "Having a child, but no husband."

"Children are a blessing from the Lord. That is what we believe."

"So do we. Children are loved and cherished by all."

"Of course, it is better if a woman has a husband. If not, she has to work to put bread on her table as well as do all her womanly duties." Meryam stroked Scarab's arm and leaned closer. "Your strong soldier, the father, will he marry you?"

"I don't know. I...I wanted him to but..." Scarab stopped in confusion. She thought for a few minutes. "One part of me wants to; the other part wants to stay free. I want to be with Paramessu and my Se...my son, being a wife and a mother, having other sons and daughters and living a good and peaceful life, but I also...I don't know what I want."

"Do you miss being a princess?"

Scarab looked around quickly before answering. "I miss my brother Smenkhkare. If he hadn't died, he would have married me and my life would be very different." The look of horror was back on the young girl's face. "What's wrong?"

"Your brother? You would have married your brother?"

"Only my half-brother," Scarab said hurriedly. "The king fathered us both but my mother was Queen Tiye, whereas his was the king's daughter Sitamen. We were always close, even as childr...what?"

Meryam looked as if she had eaten something rotten. "The king bedded his own daughter? I never knew such things happened...and to think I called Kemetu civilized."

"I'm not saying it is a good thing, Meryam, but the ruling family has to guard itself."

"By incest? How can you possibly justify such a sin?"

Scarab struggled to sit up, panting with the effort. She fixed the young girl with a hard look. "Your own ancestor committed incest, if the stories I hear are right."

"What? Never. How can you say such a thing?"

"Did not your ancestor Ibrahim marry his own sister Sarai? And Ibrahim's brother Loht father children with his own daughters?"

"That is different; our god told them to do it."

"Maybe one of our gods told us to do it. That would make it all right then, wouldn't it?"

"Did they? Did one of your gods tell your family to do it?"

"I don't know. If they did it was a long time ago. But there is a reason for it, Meryam. Imagine if I was still a princess and Paramessu wanted to marry me. Marrying into the royal family might give him a claim to the throne. If he was strong, with the army behind him and the king was weak, he might try and take over. The king might rather marry me himself, even if he is my brother, rather than risk bloodshed and chaos."

Meryam was silent for a while. At last she sighed deeply and smiled tentatively at Scarab. "I don't really understand it, but as long as I don't have to do it, I think I can live with it." Her smile became a grin as another thought occurred to her. "And it'll never happen to you now either. You'll marry your soldier and then you can't marry your brother...what's wrong?" Her smile slipped as she saw the expression on Scarab's face. "Oh, Scarab, I'm sorry, I forgot he was dead."

"No. No, that's not it. I...I think..." Scarab pressed a hand against her belly, grimacing as a spasm of pain twisted her face. "I think he's coming."

Meryam leapt to her feet and started tugging at Scarab's arm. "We've got to get you back quickly." Scarab was more concerned with the sudden cramping pains in her belly than in getting to her feet, so Meryam looked across to the nearest group of women washing clothes, recognizing one of them. "Tabita," she called. "Help me please, my guest is having a baby and I think her time has come. I have to get her to the birthing tent."

An older woman, portly and with a limp, hobbled across and, with a grunt, lent her weight to the endeavor. They pulled Scarab up between them and Meryam slipped her shoulder under Scarab's arm, partly supporting her weight.

"I've got her now, Tabita, thank you." She started moving back to the tents before remembering her washing. "Tabita, could you bring our clothes? I cannot carry them and support my guest."

Tabita waved them on, saying she would bring them later and not to worry. Meryam and Scarab hurried on as fast as they were able, though Scarab insisted on stopping every few paces and holding herself tightly, whimpering as another pain racked her.

"Can't I just sit down for a few moments, I...unh...oh Meryam, this is unbearable."

"Keep going. We need to get you to the birthing tent where the midwives can look at you and decide if the baby really is coming."

"What do you mean 'if'? Aaah...it is killing me."

"Don't be a baby yourself, Scarab. I've helped with many births and I know what is happening now is nothing to what's coming."

Scarab said nothing but shot her helper a look of pure hatred, to which Meryam replied with a sweet smile. They staggered on, Scarab eager to get to the tent where perhaps they would do something to stop the pain. Within sight of their destination, Scarab suddenly stopped again, embarrassment colouring her face.

"I've wet myself," she whispered, holding her robes close about her in an effort to conceal the growing puddle at her feet. The dry, dusty ground soaked up the moisture avidly but it was obvious she was in distress.

"Your waters have broken," Meryam said matter-of-factly. "The baby really is coming."

"I told you." Scarab lurched forward in a tottering run for the presumed haven of the birthing tent.

The midwives arrived within minutes, having been alerted by children sent scurrying by Meryam. They took charge quickly, opening up the sides of the tent in such a way as to allow cooling breezes to blow through, without allowing any outsiders to intrude. Stripping off Scarab's heavy woolen robe, now soaked and clinging, they rubbed her down quickly and slipped a short linen gown over her. For a people obsessed with modesty, the gown hid little, but it was designed more to comfort a woman becoming distressed by what was happening to her than to hide her private parts. Besides, a longer garment would just get in the way.

Lying down on a couch, Scarab was examined by an old woman called Debrah; though Scarab was not sure whether this was a name or a title. The other women were very respectful of the Debrah, and hurried to anticipate her wishes. The woman spread Scarab's legs and carefully examined her vulva, nodding to herself and muttering.

"No hair...shameless...well, it makes it easier to see." Debrah lowered her patient's legs and turned her attention to Scarab's belly and hips. "Tight muscles," she murmured. "But the baby is in place." She looked up at Scarab's pale face, lined with sweat-soaked hair. "Be strong girl, and push only when I tell you, not before."

Scarab gasped as another contraction rippled through her abdomen. It went on and on, before fading, leaving her with a general background ache. "Is the baby coming now?" she demanded, her facial expression a mix of hope and fear.

"Not yet," Debrah said. "You are young and this is your first. It could be many hours yet." The old woman withdrew, leaving the others to wipe Scarab down with cool, damp cloths and massage her hands and feet, slaking her thirst with tiny sips of water. Meryam sat by the head of the couch and whispered encouragement, telling her of births she had witnessed and the beautiful babies that had come from them.

The day dragged slowly past and Scarab dozed between the bouts of pain. Whenever her body went into spasm, she cried out or screamed, cursing the day Paramessu had forced himself on her, cursing what he had put in her.

"If he thinks he's coming near me again with that big...aah!"

As the contractions came closer together she found herself unable to relax, and she swore at Meryam and the women assisting in the birthing tent. Scarab fought against the muscles that pushed savagely at her womb, the sweat pouring off her body. Her hands gripped the bedding tightly and she tossed her damp hair from side to side as the pain gripped her.

"I've changed my mind," she panted. "I don't want it." Another scream was ripped from her, but weaker now as her strength faded.

Debrah came again, tutting over the state of her patient and examined her again. "Not yet," she muttered.

The light outside faded as the sun set and Meryam brought in and lit oil lamps, which cast a warm and gentle light over the scene. Two women erected a delivery seat in the middle of the tent, its polished wood glowing in the lamp light.

"What about the prayers?" Scarab muttered weakly. "There should be prayers to Bes and Taueret, Khnum and Het-Her."

"What place have those false gods here?" snapped one of the women setting up the delivery seat.

"Peace, Asherah," Meryam chided. "She has been raised a Kemetu. She does not know any better." She got up soon after and hurried out of the tent, returning a few minutes later. Resuming her seat, she leaned across and whispered in Scarab's ear. "I saw Khu outside. He will have the prayers said. Your gods will be with you."

Scarab looked at her with grateful eyes, squeezing her hand hard as another contraction gripped her.

When it was fully dark outside, Debrah returned. She examined Scarab once more and this time she nodded, her lined face cracking into a toothless grin. "He comes, child. Your baby is coming."

"I don't want him," Scarab muttered. "Send him back, he's too...ow!"

Debrah laughed and directed the other women to lift Scarab up and place her on the delivery seat. A rim of wood barely supported the back of her buttocks and the angle of the support held her upright. Knees bent, her feet fitted into slots that opened her up in a squatting position, very similar to one used in the privies. Long past the stage of being embarrassed, she allowed her short linen gown to be removed, sitting there naked in full sight of the midwives, and the weight of the baby pressing downward. She felt as if she was a thin skin stretched over something large and irresistible.

Another contraction rolled down and Scarab suddenly felt as if she were about to have a bowel movement, a large and painful one. She screamed weakly, now exhausted, and Debrah dropped to her knees in front of the seat, her attention fixed.

"He is coming. I can see his head. Wait until the contractions and push, child."

Scarab screamed for the last time and pushed as her muscles spasmed, another following moments later, then another. A huge boulder moved through her, ripping and tearing its way down her body, until she knew she could take no more. She was about to die...and suddenly she felt fluids rush from her and the agony vanished. *No*, she thought vaguely, *not gone but bearable*. She felt sore and battered and not quite sure where she was. Another spasm built and she cried out despairingly. *I thought it was over...*

Meryam squeezed Scarab's hand tightly, putting her mouth close to Scarab's ear. "It's the afterbirth. Nearly over."

Another slippery rush and a feeling of emptiness. Around her, the women bustled. She felt herself being washed and a cloth tied between her legs, a fresh linen gown slipped over her head--it felt gloriously clean on her skin--then they were helping her out of the delivery seat and back to the couch. Something was put in her arms and held there until she could collect her thoughts enough to grasp it.

Scarab looked down and saw a wizened, red face screaming back up at her. *He even looks like the god Set*, she thought. Under the gentle guidance of Meryam, she brought the baby's face to one of her breasts and as the tiny mouth grasped her nipple, as she felt the deep tug inside as her son suckled, her dammed up emotions broke and she burst into tears.

Chapter 31

"I think I've been duped," Horemheb snarled, staring across the open space of the clearing near the river. The journey south down the Kurgus Valley from the site of the ambush had taken five days. For another seven they waited for Smenkhkare and his army to arrive, during which time the general threw out guard posts in all directions with signal fires ready to be lit at the first sign of the enemy. A rocky escarpment at their backs protected them from a surprise assault and the men had been kept busy fortifying their position still further. Horemheb had doubted the defensive works would be necessary--he intended to attack Smenkhkare's army when it arrived-- but it was infinitely preferable that the men keep busy rather than lying around getting stale. Slowly, awareness of his mistake had grown into certainty. "He's not coming. I've been fooled, but why? What does he gain?"

Penno scratched himself absently as he watched a lone hawk wheeling in the faded blue sky far above them. "He means to attack Sehotep-Neteru while we are gone. The garrison we left there cannot defend the city against his army. The viceroy is in danger."

"Possibly, but you did not see him, Penno. You did not talk to him. He is obsessed with retaking his kingdom. I think that is exactly what he is trying to do."

"Is he mad? He cannot take on the armed might of Kemet with a thousand men."

"No, but who knows he is about to strike? Only us. He could be at the gates of Waset in two months if he pushes his men hard. The local garrison numbers no more than a couple of hundred now that I have the Amun legion down here." Horemheb shook his head. "I could get back there to find Ay and Tutankhaten dead and Kemet in turmoil."

"If that is what he is doing."

"He could have a smaller ambition, but we'll know it by the time we return to Sehotep-Neteru. If there is no word of him we will know he has gone north."

"Can we catch him, sir?"

"He is twelve days north of where we saw him, we are five days south. He has a smaller army more used to the country. We cannot hope to match his pace until we reach the barges at Tanjur. That is perhaps twenty days overland. By then he will be in Abu below the first cataract. There are barges in Abu if he can capture them." Horemheb broke off and smacked his fist into his palm. "May the gods curse him, Penno. He may have been a king but he lies and he has betrayed a trust. Now he brings civil war to Kemet."

"There might be another way," Penno said slowly. "The river."

"What about it? We don't have barges or even boats. That is why we have to get to Tanjur."

"Rafts, sir. The trees aren't large here but big enough to lash together. There are two cataracts between here and Tanjur and many smaller rapids but the river flows fast."

Horemheb swung round and stared at his Lieutenant. "Forget the rafts. How far is it by the river route? Could we march along the banks?"

Penno shook his head. "We are twenty days from Tanjur overland, three times that if we marched along the river, which we can't anyway. There are gorges. By water, maybe only ten days."

"Hapi save us." Horemheb smiled for the first time since he had returned from Smenkhkare. "Wait, how safe is this rafting? I do not want to lose my army by drowning before we ever meet the enemy."

"Safe enough, sir, if the rafts are properly built."

The Amun legion set to work within the hour, uprooting the camp and traveling the half day further south to the banks of the river, where they started to cut the largest trees, gangs trimming the branches and lashing the gnarled trunks together with ropes and, when they ran out, fixing them in place with wooden pegs cut from the trees and copper bands forged from melted down weapons. The first losses occurred during this time. Three men died when trees fell on them, seven to poisonous snakes that infested the area and one to the stings of savage hornets when the tree that housed their nest was felled.

The hundred rafts embarked on the third day and for several hours enjoyed a fast-paced but uneventful journey downriver. Then the banks rose about them and the pace of the water quickened, leaping into white-capped hummocks and beneath the rush of the water they could hear the grind of rocks in the riverbed.

"The cataract," someone screamed, and from his raft in the middle of the tossing flotilla, Penno yelled back, "Not yet. It's just rapids. Hold on."

The rafts weathered the first stretch of fast water, and the second, but the constant movement stretched the ropes, working the wooden pins loose and toward sunset on the second day, as they plunged into another swirling and tossing stretch, the first rafts came apart, throwing men and equipment into the water. Many could swim but most had little chance in the raging waters. A few made it to other rafts and clung on grimly until they could be pulled aboard, and others made it to shore, to watch in horror as their friends swept by and out of sight. There could be no going back for survivors, but watchfires were lit that night to guide any that lived to their camp just above the fourth cataract at a place called Napata.

There was a large temple to Amun at Napata and the fuddled priests scrambled to mobilize their stores of grain and wine when Horemheb marched into the temple precincts. The Meheila Road crossed a ridge of mountains to another temple at Kawa, but Horemheb knew he dare not take this route, despite the temptations. They could not carry the rafts over the steep and sometimes precipitous road and if there were no boats at Kawa, his army would be stranded. At least the Napata temple and the small city founded by Tuthmosis a hundred years before had rope and he set the army to repairing and strengthening the rafts before ferrying them overland past the cataract.

The voyage to the third cataract took another three days, without major loss of life. The banks of the river opened out into flat plains of brown and yellow grass, scattered with flat-topped thorn trees. Herds of game moved in the open spaces, stampeding away from the water as the strange flotilla of rafts came into view. Horemheb considered stopping for a day to hunt, as despite the priests' stores, his army was still short of food. Only the thought of Smenkhkare's horde descending on Sehotep-Neteru or Waset prevented him and grim-faced, he kept the rafts out in mid-river. The water ran as fast as ever, but there were fewer rapids and they were easily negotiated. The only incident came on the evening of the final day before reaching the cataract. They set up camp on the western shore and as the men foraged for food among the fields and huts of a seemingly deserted village, a hail of arrows preceded an attack by howling tribesmen bent on revenge for the pillaging of their livelihood. The attack was beaten off and the dead of both sides buried a little way into the desert. Priests of Amun recited prayers for the dead before the rest of the legion retreated behind hastily erected fortifications for the night.

Negotiating the third cataract where the river plunged over a shelf of rock, falling some three man-heights into the foaming pool beneath took most of the next day and the loss of three rafts with their men as ropes snapped, sweeping them into the maelstrom before anyone could even think of help. The river below the fall ran rapidly with vicious stretches of turbulence that required the use of ropes to winch the rafts down past the worst parts. The days passed rapidly and Horemheb chafed at the delay.

"Ten days you said, Penno. It has been twelve since we left the clearing at Kurgus."

"Ten days on the river," Penno reminded his general. "It will be ten days tomorrow and we have passed the temple of Amara. We have made good time."

"And lost over a hundred men," Horemheb snarled. "We would not have lost them going overland."

For Horemheb's peace of mind and Penno's health, it was as well that they swept past the inscription rocks at Tanjur the following morning, spotting the anchored barges in the small inlet that marked the base of the Tanjur valley less than an hour later. The men on the rafts, soaked and hungry, let out a bellow of exultation that brought the sailors on the barges running from their camp on the shore.

Horemheb allowed his troops just long enough ashore for a hot meal prepared from the stores on board the barges before heading down-river once more. "They can rest as we travel. I will not lose more time than I have to."

Not content with allowing the current to do its work, the sailors were pressed into rowing, sending the wallowing craft careening through the water. When darkness fell that night Horemheb had oil lanterns lit at the front and rear of each barge and a new constellation of stars moved through the dark Nubian night. Two boats went aground in the night, not being able to see the gravelbanks and sharp rocks beneath the surface and another found itself swept sideways after negotiating a difficult section of rapids. Hitting a sunken rock amidships, the barge tilted then capsized and sank, throwing fifty men into the dark waters. Horemheb cursed, but pushed his fleet on, refusing to delay by any rescue attempt.

Penno persuaded his general to beach his craft before they reached the second cataract however. They waited until the dawn light grew strong enough to illuminate the rushing roaring current that boiled through the narrow gorge. To the horror of the seasoned sailors, Horemheb announced that he would not waste a day letting the barges through slowly, each vessel anchored by straining men on the ends of thick ropes. The soldiers would not march around as they had on the voyage up-river--instead, everyone would ride the rapids together.

Nineteen barges entered the cataract but only sixteen came out into the wide pool at the base. The other three split apart as the force of the water drove them against the sides of the gorge, shattering on the monstrous rocks of the channel. Wreckage and bodies were left to the river and by afternoon the remnants of the Amun legion and Penno's garrison arrived at the docks of Sehotep-Neteru.

The town crowded the docks and nearby streets, jostling and yelling, demanding news of the expedition and soon the wails of bereaved women drowned out the crowds. The Viceroy Huy arrived in a sedan chair, his staff bustling around him, and he greeted Horemheb and Penno on the docks.

"He is defeated?" Huy asked anxiously. "For days we have seen bodies in the river and knew there had been a great battle."

Horemheb ignored the Viceroy and turned to Penno. "You see, I was right. He is heading for Waset."

"General, you will speak to me, not my officers."

Horemheb glanced at Huy to see the Viceroy's face darkening in anger and he realized he had become so caught up in his plans he was in danger of alienating the one man who could help him save Kemet.

He dropped to his knees and prostrated himself, arms extended forward.

"Forgive me, O great one of the divine Nebkheperure, I meant no disrespect. I have been pursuing the rebels down river for ten days, gripped by a fear that they would attack Sehotep-Neteru and put your life in danger."

Viceroy Huy contemplated the back of Horemheb's head for several long moments, a contented smile on his lips. "You may arise," he said graciously. "Now, what were you saying about Waset?"

Horemheb arose and dusted off his knees. "The rebel army evaded us and moved north. I have reason to believe they mean to attack Waset."

"Is your mind addled, General?" deputy viceroy Amenemipet sneered. "Too much hot sun perhaps? What would a bandit want with a city? Robbing farms and waylaying caravans is more his style."

Horemheb's eyes flicked over the deputy before returning to Huy. "Let your guard clear the dock, Viceroy. I have news that would rock the city if it became common knowledge."

"You intrigue me." Huy gave the orders and very quickly the dock area was cleared of townsfolk. The party of officials moved to one side of the dock, allowing the disembarking soldiers and sailors to move past and up the road to the garrison fortress. "Very well, what is this so important news?"

"The Son of Sobek is king Smenkhkare."

The Viceroy and the priests gaped. Huy the Lesser, the mayor of Sehotep-Neteru guffawed and Amenemipet the deputy viceroy smiled coldly. "You have gone mad."

"Not madness. I saw him and spoke to him."

"You spoke to him but did not at least capture him that we all might see this...this king of yours," Amenemipet asked.

"He overwhelmed the patrol I was leading and captured me, killing my men."

"You gave up so easily? I do not see a mark on you."

Horemheb ground his teeth then winced as a small chunk snapped off a lower tooth, a sharp stab of pain lancing into his jaw. "He captured me, I talked with him. He is Smenkhkare. Whatever you might believe, the king survived the crocodile--that is why he is called

Son of Sobek--and on the basis of that talk I believe he is determined to win back his throne."

"How?" Huy asked. "I cannot believe he would attack the garrison at Waset with his bandits and renegades."

"My lord, the garrison of Waset is here with me. The city is essentially defenceless."

"Then what will you do?" Mermose, second prophet of Amun in Wawat, pushed to the front and confronted Horemheb. "The king is in Waset. You cannot leave him to the mercy of...of..."

"Of his brother," Horemheb finished. "I don't know what will happen to our king Nebkheperure if Smenkhkare wins but I fear bloodshed and chaos will spread throughout our Kemet."

"Then you must make sure he does not win, General Horemheb."

"Then I will need your help, Viceroy."

"You have it." Huy nodded. "King Nebkheperure can count on my loyalty. Tell my deputy what you need," he went on, waving his hand nonchalantly at Amenemipet. "Whatever you need, he will find for you." The viceroy turned and got back into his sedan chair, signaling the slaves to take him back to the palace. A squad of guards ran ahead and beside of the sedan, clearing the inquisitive crowd away, and the mayor and priests trotted along behind, preferring the refined company of the Viceroy to that of the coarse soldiers.

Amenemipet regarded Horemheb coldly. "What is it you need?" he rasped.

Horemheb thought for a moment. "I need my barges provisioned. I intend to leave this afternoon, but I need food and beer for two thousand men for a month, arms too, we lost a lot..."

"That is impossible," Amenemipet interrupted. "The stores do not contain food for even five hundred for a month."

"Then I suggest you find it elsewhere...or perhaps your loyalty is not as certain as your viceroy? Must I inform him of your unwillingness to help your king?"

"Curse you," the deputy spat. "You shall have it." He spun on his heel and started away.

"I have not finished, Amenemipet," Horemheb snapped. "Swords, pikes, bows with extra bowstrings, all the arrows you can find, rope, acacia gum, sharpening stones...use your imagination. Put yourself in the king's place; what would you want the relieving army to have?" He paused for the space of two breaths. "What are you waiting for? Praise? You haven't done anything yet."

Amenemipet flushed and a snarl of anger broke through his lips. "I will not forget this, Horemheb." Wheeling away, he strode down the dock, yelling at his officers as they ran to his side.

Horemheb grinned at Penno. "That felt good."

Penno smiled in return. "It was good to see, sir, but you have made a bad enemy. He did not rise to be deputy viceroy without having powerful friends."

"And no doubt he has made many enemies too. Forget him; we have more important things to do."

The two men went up to the palace, availing themselves of the same room. After they had refreshed themselves with a good soak in the baths and put on fresh clothes, Penno sent for several of his officers and arranged for food and drink to be brought for all of them. Horemheb poured himself a long drink of sour beer and rose to his feet.

"You will forgive me if I do not ask your names or exchange pleasantries with you. All I need to know is that you are loyal officers of the king. Penno has assured me of your worth so I will accept it as fact. First, who knows the rivermen best? The sailors of the city?"

An officer raised his hand tentatively. "My brother is a fisherman, sir."

"Does he know the river between here and Waset, or just locally?"

The officer's face fell. "Just locally, sir."

"Never mind, he will know others with greater knowledge. Contact your brother and find me a dozen men who know the river north of here like the tits on their wives. Have them here within the hour." The officer saluted and left the room. Horemheb took a long drink of beer and wiped his mouth with the back of his free hand. He belched loud and long before turning back to the others.

"I intend to strip the city of its fighting men. I have nine hundred of the Amun legion and two hundred of the garrison. I want another thousand men."

"I'm sorry sir, we just don't have them," Penno said. "I could find you another two or three hundred perhaps, but you'd leave the city defenceless."

"I'll take your three hundred, Penno. Let the Medjay protect the city. Where else are there soldiers? Fighting men? Men?"

"How about the city?" asked a young officer, "The townsfolk..."

"...Would not know one end of a spear from the other," laughed another.

"They can learn." Horemheb pointed at the young officer. "Yours is the idea, yours the duty. Find me a hundred fit men. Promise them half a deben of gold when we get to Waset. Off you go, I want them at the docks in two hours time." Filling his mug with beer again he looked at the others. "Six hundred to go. Ideas?"

"The mines?" hazarded one.

"Too far," Penno said. "We leave this afternoon and even the nearest mines are three days away."

"What about the forts? Buhen and Migassa, even Serra and Askut on the far bank," another countered.

"Buhen maybe and Serra across the river," Penno said slowly. "They are close enough. Twenty men apiece."

"There are forts downriver. If we sent a courier ahead, they could have men ready to be picked up as the fleet got to them."

"How many forts are we talking about?" Horemheb asked.

"Aniba, Ikkur and Kubban. The last two are larger, being on the gold caravan trail." Penno quickly calculated. "A hundred and fifty?"

"We are still four hundred short, gentlemen. Where do we get them?"

There was a long silence before Penno stirred. "There is only one place, general, but we could never get them here in time. The forts of the second cataract. I could find you at least two hundred more there, but it will take five days to get them."

Horemheb nodded. "Get them. Penno, I am leaving you in charge in Sehotep-Neteru. You will go to the forts and get me my men. I will leave you two barges. Fill them, pack them in and send them down after me. You," he pointed at one of the officers. "You are responsible for sending couriers to the lower forts, and you," an older man, "to the nearby forts." Draining his mug, he grabbed a cold duck and ripped a leg off, filling his mouth with the fatty dark meat. He swallowed and waved the chewed leg at the men in the room. "You have your orders, gentlemen."

Penno approached his general after the officers left, picking at a loaf of bread. "I'd rather come with you, sir. I can detail an officer to cover the upper forts."

"No, I want you. You'll do it properly. You won't accept excuses. Besides, I need someone dependable up here in Wawat if things go wrong."

Penno nodded. "What do you want rivermen for?"

"Somewhere ahead of us is the rebel army. Going overland probably, but Abu has barges. If they take the barges they can be in Waset long before us. I will send messengers down to warn the governors of Abu, Djeba and Nekhen. If they can mobilize their garrisons we may delay or even halt the rebels. Another messenger will take the news to Ay in Waset, and another will go north, all the way to Zarw. If the worst befalls Kemet and Waset is taken, maybe even the king falls in death; I want the northern army ready to come to my aid. They cannot get to Waset until months have passed, but if I cannot stop Smenkhkare now, I will defeat him later."

Chapter 32

To a casual observer, the Hall of Justice in the Western palace of Waset reflected the care and attention any king of the Two Kingdoms should give to the welfare of his subjects. By ancient custom, the king presided over the law courts, listening to petitions brought by high-born and low-born, hearing arguments brought by plaintiffs and defendants, and dispensing justice equitably and without favour. For generations, the ancestors of Nebkheperure Tutankhaten had ably administered the daily affairs of the land. Even the king's brother up in Akhet-Aten gave of himself that his people might lead happier lives. And to this casual observer, the young king sitting on the great golden throne in the Hall of Justice was continuing this noble tradition.

The king, however, was bored. He did not enjoy these sessions that took place every morning and would gladly have dispensed with them, preferring more exciting pastimes like hunting, or playing with his carved wooden soldiers, or even the new-found pleasures of his young queen Ankhesenpaaten. The reason he did not run off and play was his uncle Ay. He feared his uncle, and while he did not think actual harm would follow from disobedience, he knew from bitter experience that Ay had many ways of imposing his will. The first time he had tried to assert his independence had been a scant two months after his coronation. He decided one morning to go duck hunting with his Nubian friends Hiknefer and Khai and blithely informed Ay of his decision as they left the palace. The Tjaty bowed and let them go. The next morning they played in the gardens and Ay again said nothing.

The following morning it was fishing. And so it went on for ten days until the afternoon when the young king summoned his entourage to view the progress at the new additions to the temple of Amun on the east bank.

"I regret to say, your majesty, that there has been no work on the temple." Ay bowed low then stood back, watching his king with a small smile creasing his eyes.

"Why not?" Tutankhaten demanded.

"There is a dispute that has brought work to a halt. It seems that the priests of Djehuti claim ownership of the land adjoining the Amun temple where your majesty's new building was to be erected."

The king frowned, trying to work out exactly what this meant. "So who does own the land?"

"That is the issue, your majesty."

"Cannot the courts do something? They can listen to both sides and make a ruling."

"Your majesty has a good grasp of the workings of the law." Ay bowed again. "However, may I suggest that your majesty is overlooking one point?"

"What?" Tutankhaten asked sulkily.

"The courts cannot function without the presence of the king." Ay stood as if in thought for a few seconds. "I believe the dispute was to have been heard on the morning you went duck hunting, your majesty."

The young king flushed and looked down at the tiles. After a few minutes he started scuffing his sandal against the floor. "It's boring. I don't like sitting there all morning."

"I remember your father, the great Nebmaetre, also did not enjoy sitting in the Hall of Justice day after day, listening to petitions. Yet he did it. Do you know why Nebkheperure?"

Tutankhaten grimaced and shook his head reluctantly, not looking up.

"He did it because he loved his people and he knew that just as the gods had granted him great glory, so too must he honour the people in his charge. It was his duty to represent the people before the gods, to bring them justice. He did this every day of his life unless he was too sick to stand." Ay dismissed the palace servants and put his hand on

Tutankhaten's shoulder. "Nebmaetre was a great king, one of the best these Two Lands have seen. Do you want to be a great king too?"

"Yes," Tutankhaten whispered. "I want to be the best."

"Then do your duty. We shall sit in court this afternoon and hear petitions instead of inspecting temples." Ay's voice grew harsher. "Then tomorrow morning, and every morning, you will preside over the courts. Do you agree?"

"Yes, Divine Father."

Somehow, Tutankhaten never got to hear the supposed dispute between the priests of Djehuti and those of Amun. When he visited the temple expansion a month later, the work was on schedule and there was no sign of discord. When asked, Ay merely said they had come to an agreement, and smiled. Since then, Tutankhaten had sat in court every morning, doing his duty as a king.

The droning voices of the court officials faded out and Tutankhaten looked up with a start. His feet, swinging beneath the seat of the throne, stilled, and he saw the ring of faces around him regard him questioningly. He racked his memory for the last thing said but came up blank. Looking round, he saw the familiar lined visage of Ay and sagged with relief, calling him over with a curved finger.

"What do I say, uncle?"

Ay sighed and leaned close to the boy's ear, whispering into it. "Did I not tell you to listen? Lord Mahmose has brought a suit against Lord Khefrure. Mahmose bought a hundred head of pure white heifers from Khefrure as the basis of a sacrificial herd for the temples. He has been awarded the supply contract for the Waset temples. But now the heifers are throwing calves that are less than pure in colour. Mahmose demands the matter be put right."

"How?" Tutankhaten screwed up his face as if he would cry. "I don't know what to do."

"It is as well that I am here then." Ay straightened and faced the ring of expectant faces. "May I convey the decision of the king in this matter, your majesty?" Ay asked in a ringing voice.

"Yes," Tutankhaten squeaked in relief. Recovering fast, he nodded solemnly. "Do so, Tjaty Ay."

Ay delivered a careful summing up of the case and delivered his verdict. If the decision favoured his friend Mahmose and seemed unduly harsh toward the Lord Khefrure, none commented on the fact, the parties bowing deeply to show their acquiescence. The lords retired and two more stepped to the front, and the next case started.

Tutankhaten, despite his recent embarrassment, found his attention wandering again. The day was hot and his crown was heavy. *Would anyone really mind if I took it off and swung my legs?* He put a finger between his shaved scalp and the edge of the stiffened linen of the crown, easing the burden slightly. Scraping his finger along the rim, he felt the headgear shift, the square red Deshret and tall white conical Hedjet crowns move as they started to overbalance. Someone coughed sharply behind him and Tutankhaten looked round, startled, his hands darting upward to rescue the symbols of royalty.

"Behave yourself, Tuti," Ankhesenpaaten hissed. His young queen sat primly on her own throne a pace behind the king's and a little lower. The greater height of the queen and the tall feathered crown with central sun disc destroyed the intended image of the lesser monarch. Whenever the two were together, the queen dominated her boy king. The nobles and commons attending the petition sessions were in little doubt as to who ruled when Ay was absent.

Tutankhaten stuck out his tongue at his wife, but he turned back to face the assemblage with a straight back, and for several minutes refrained from fidgeting. For a while he listened to the arguments as first one man, then another spoke about the intricacies of border markers in fields somewhere he had never been. He yawned widely and looked across to where he could see a splash of azure sky through an opening high on one wall. A ray of sunlight lit the Hall through this opening and the young king thought dreamily of the dark houses of the gods in contrast to the open halls of the Aten temples.

The arguments came to a close and once more Ay made a pretence of consulting the king before announcing the royal decision. The Tjaty smiled inwardly as the lords filed from the Chamber. Early in the reign he had debated whether to let the boy do as he please and dispense justice himself, in effect ruling the Two Lands. With a pang of regret he decided against it, weighing the satisfaction of being king in all but name against the certain enmity of the nobles and above all, Horemheb. Instead, he brought the boy king to heel and made him assume his duties, then set about making his days so boring he willingly let his Tjaty make all the decisions. Little by little, Ay gathered the actuality of power to himself, while the appearance of power still lay with the young king.

"Well, thank the gods that is over," Tutankhaten said. "I thought I was going to fall asleep there at the end."

Ay bowed low to his monarch. "May I commend your majesty on your forbearance? You displayed a regal posture which did not go unnoticed. And your decisions were a wonderful balance of justice and mercy. The goddess Ma'at could not have done better."

Tutankhaten simpered. "Really? Yes, I suppose I was. That comes from being a king and a god, uncle Ay. You are not royal so you can only guess at the uplifting presence of the godhead."

"Indeed your majesty." Ay bowed again. "May I ask what your pleasure is this afternoon?"

"I think some lunch. I'm hungry. Then I will visit the god Amun in his temple. I want to tell him about some ideas I had for the additions. I suppose I should tell the architects too." Tutankhaten shrugged. "Then I might go hunting wild fowl in the marshes." He turned and took off his great double crown, handing it to a servant. As the symbol of kingship passed from his hands, he became a little boy again, not giving another thought to his Kingdoms. "Lunch. I hope they have the honeyed quail I like." He jumped down off the dais and ran across the hall toward the open doors.

Ay flicked a hand in signal and two guards raced after the king, their eyes alert for any danger.

"Why do you fill his head with that nonsense, grandfather?" Queen Ankhesenpaaten arose from her throne gracefully and came across to stand next to Ay. She handed her tall feathered headdress with its golden sun disc to a servant and shook the braided locks of her wig. "He is quite an intelligent boy when he puts his mind to it, yet you give him nothing to do. He knew nothing about what happened here today, yet you made him believe he showed wisdom. Why?"

"Because he is just a boy, your majesty." Ay sketched a bow toward his granddaughter. "Time enough for him to learn these things when he is a bit more mature."

"He is the king, Divine Father," Ankhesenpaaten said sharply. "And you treat him like a servant to do your bidding."

Ay turned and gestured for the servants and guards to leave the chamber, waiting until the double doors closed, leaving them alone. He turned back to his granddaughter. "Your husband has been crowned king, but he is not king yet. Not really. He is a boy playing at being a king. You think I seek to deprive him of his power, belittling him." Ay shook his head, his thick white hair gleaming in a ray of sunlight from the tall windows. "On the contrary, I protect him from those who would lead him astray, who would weaken him, maybe even kill..."

"Like today?" the queen sneered. "You made the proceedings so boring he lost himself in daydreams. If I had not stopped him he would have tossed his crown aside and left the Chamber."

"Yes, I saw that and I thank you for it, your majesty. I try to balance the power he has as king with a sense of duty. Today I went a little too far. I am glad you were there to stop what might have been an unfortunate loss of face and authority."

"He would have looked foolish, but what authority are you talking about? He has none. Even I hold more power in the palace."

"You hold the power within the palace, I hold it outside." Ay paused and regarded the young woman standing before him, seeing hints of the beauty of her mother Nefertiti, judged by many to have been the most beautiful woman in the world. For a moment his heart cried out to his lost daughter, somewhere in exile, only Horemheb knew where. Then the old man took hold of his emotions with a grip of bronze and put his daughter from his mind.

"You are mistaken though if you think I hold this power for myself. When Tutankhaten came to the throne on the death of his brother Smenkhkare, I would not have given a ripe fig for his chances. What happens whenever a young boy succeeds to the throne? He dies; or if he is very lucky, someone rules for him until he is old enough to rule for himself. I did that for your husband. If I had not he would have died. He still may, he has enemies." Ay paused again, feeling for a convincing argument. "You do not believe he has enemies? Why? Because the people cheer him on the streets? They do that because I release wheat and barley from the city granaries in his name. Yes, the people cheer, but it is higher up that you should look for threats."

"The nobles are always seeking favours, looking for ways to gain an advantage," Ankhesenpaaten said. "I know these men; none of them is a serious threat--except perhaps you."

"You do me much honour," replied Ay with a laugh. "But I look higher."

"Higher? There are none higher. You mean the priests?"

"I mean the other king, your father, locked away in his little City of the Sun."

"My father is not a threat to Tuti," Ankhesenpaaten said scornfully. "Akhenaten approved of him, I know, I was there."

"Of course not, child. Your father is gentle...and weak. He could be used to gain power. In fact, it has already started. Prince Merneptah is reported to be gathering power for himself in the court at Akhet-Aten."

"Who is Prince Merneptah? I have never heard of him."

"I am not surprised. Your grandfather Nebmaetre spawned offspring on his junior wives and concubines like...like a frog in spring. This prince is the son of Mutia, one of the lesser concubines."

Ankhesenpaaten found herself smiling at the image conjured up by Ay. "He does not sound like much of a threat--a tadpole prince."

"Probably not, and my commander Khaemnum has him under observation, but there will be others. There will always be others as long as Akhenaten is there to act as a focus for power and disaffection."

"What are you saying?"

"Just that your father is dangerous. Not of himself, but of what others make him."

"So guard him from his enemies. You are still loyal to your king, are you not?"

Ay said nothing for a few moments, appearing to consider his answer. "He is the king, and I shall watch those around him diligently." His eyes met those of his granddaughter, and in the instant he exulted inwardly, knowing she was her mother's daughter. "I will watch him too for one of these days he will tire of others using him and he will act for himself."

Queen Ankhesenpaaten turned away to look across the deserted chamber, not wanting her grandfather to see her thoughts. "Would that be such a bad thing, Tjaty? Akhenaten is the king after all. Does he not have a right to rule our Kemet?"

"And what of Nebkheperure Tutankhaten? Do you think that your father, once he made the decision to pick up his crown again, would allow a sniveling brat a share of the kingdoms." Ay laughed scornfully. "No great loss to Kemet, your majesty, except..."

"Except what?"

"You would no longer be queen. Tutankhaten would be a disinherited prince, not even the co-ruler he is at present, and you would be just a wife, holding no power except over servants, no riches save those dispensed by a merciful king." Ay moved up slowly behind his granddaughter and leaned close, whispering in her ear. "What if your father takes another wife, Queen Ankhesenpaaten? It could happen, he is still not old. Imagine another woman living in your palace, commanding your servants, wearing your jewels. How would you feel?"

"My father married me once. He could do so again and I would still be queen."

Ay smiled at the tremor in the girl's voice. "You could only give him a girl child and a sickly one at that. No, he will take a strong woman for a wife, one who may yet give him sons."

Ankhesenpaaten suddenly laughed though the humor sounded strained. "There is no woman he can take to wife that would not immediately raise another family to royalty. He will not risk that."

"There is one--your aunt Beketaten."

The queen swiveled on her heel and stared at Ay. "She is dead, you told me so yourself."

Ay shrugged. "I thought so at the time, but there are rumors."

Ankhesenpaaten frowned. "She lives? Where is she?"

"Rumors only, as I said. She has been seen up and down the river from Kush to the Delta." Ay laughed. "One rumor even put her in Iunu talking to the priests of the Nine Gods."

"Is she a danger? I mean, apart from my father marrying her?"

"No. She is only as dangerous as any woman. I'd be on my guard in bed with her and I would not turn my back on her, but otherwise she is only a woman."

Ankhesenpaaten dropped her eyes, hiding the fury in them. "You think of me as harmless too? I am the queen. I could have you killed."

"Yes, you could, but your ability to do so stems from your boy-husband, the king. You do not have it in you, granddaughter," Ay took three rapid steps forward and gripped the queen by the throat, forcing her head up and back. He leaned forward breathing in her face. "Do not threaten me again, granddaughter. I made you queen, I can unmake you with a word. If you want to stay queen you will do as I say." He stared into Ankhesenpaaten's wide-open eyes, reading the fear in them. "Do you understand, little one?" he said gently.

Ankhesenpaaten nodded as much as the old man's hand allowed. "Yes," she whispered.

Ay smiled and let his hand drop. He turned his back on the young woman unconcernedly, feeling the hate boring into his back. "Hate me if you want, granddaughter, but do not forget to fear me too." Without waiting for a reply, Ay started across the chamber to the great cedar doors. Reaching them, he opened them wide, the guards outside crashing to attention. Turning back into the room, he addressed the young queen once more, his calm voice carrying without difficulty to the woman standing by the thrones.

"I shall keep you and your husband safe, Queen Ankhesenpaaten. I will act against all your enemies and protect our beloved Kemet." Ay bowed and slipped through the doors, leaving the young queen alone.

Ay walked quickly through the western palace, avoiding the area of the king's residence until he came to the set of rooms he claimed as his own. Servants scurried to obey his commands which he issued as soon as he stepped inside the suite. Food and drink were brought to his inner chambers and messengers hurried out to summon important officials to the Tjaty's audience.

By the time Ay had bathed and changed into a clean kilt, had his white locks greased with costly unguents and the barest hint of makeup applied to eyelids and lips, the first of his visitors had arrived. The others turned up by the time the servant had poured the wine and, bowing to the noble officials of the kingdom, left the room.

Ay waved the men toward the table of wine and food. "We have a decision to make and I have need of your counsel. You may speak freely; I can vouch for everyone here."

"What decision is there that could not be made at our usual meeting?" asked Maya, Intendant of the Treasury. "Are you about to declare war on somebody and need gold? If that is the case, where is General Psenamy?"

"It is not war," Ay said. "And Psenamy is sick with the bloody flux. The physicians do not expect him to live."

"Not much of a loss, if you ask me," Maya grunted. "I'm sorry if he was your friend, Ay. I know you picked him but really, the man was almost incompetent."

"I did not pick him, he was senior officer in Waset four years ago and he was eager to serve me. Nakhtmin here is my choice of General." Ay indicated the young man who stood modestly behind the Tjaty.

"Nakhtmin?" said the priest of Amun by the table, where he paused in the act of stuffing his mouth with a morsel of fatty goose. Bakt, First Prophet of Amun under Ay and Tutankhaten, had fattened considerably since his sudden rise in the hierarchy. The former First Prophet, Amenemhet, had died suddenly in Ineb Hedj at the time of Smenkhkare's demise. The Second Prophet Aanen, brother to Ay, was missing, and Bakt, with the blessing of Ay and, seemingly of Amun, had assumed the supreme position. He had used it to make himself an extremely wealthy man.

"Nakhtmin?" he repeated, "The son of Djetmaktef the landowner?"

Ay nodded. "He is a skilled warrior despite his youth. I have raised him to the rank of General of the Southern Armies."

"Which do not exist," Maya observed. "Horemheb has the Amun legion down in Kush seeking out bandits and there is only a meager force here. You have an easy job of it, Nakhtmin."

Nakhtmin said nothing, just bowed and smiled.

"A young man who knows when to keep quiet." Bakt heaved himself across the room and clapped the general on the shoulder with a greasy hand. "I like the man already."

"If I might have your attentions, I will tell you why I summoned you." Ay stared at the fat priest with distaste. "It has been four years since the heretic was toppled, though he remains under guard in his city. Tell me the mood of the people. You first, Bakt."

"Amun has grown in wealth again, which is pleasing to the gods."

"And to you it seems," Maya muttered softly.

"However," the priest went on. "The Aten is still worshiped openly and gold still flows into the temple coffers. Gold that is rightfully Amun's."

"I am surprised," Ay commented. "I did not think I was that out of touch with the common man. What is the attraction of the Aten? He was always a god of the heretic. I thought once freedom of worship was reintroduced, Atenism would fade away."

"It is because the king and queen still bear the name of the Aten," Bakt said. He looked longingly at the food on the table then with an effort turned his attention back to the Tjaty. "They were crowned Tutankhamen and Ankhesenamen. Why is it they still retain their birth names?"

"They wished it," Ay said. "It makes that much difference?"

Bakt nodded, and Maya joined him. "It is as Bakt says. In the course of my duties I see many traders and land holders. They all perceive the king as supporting Akhenaten, if not openly, at least tacitly by his adherence to the Aten name. The name means 'Living Image of the Aten', Ay. What do you expect people to think?"

"Then I will persuade them to change their names."

"You will need to do more," Bakt said. "The heretic is an abomination that must be stamped out. It should have been done four years ago, then we would not have these troubles." Bakt belched, stifling it with a pudgy fist. A taste of goose came into his mouth again and he glanced across to where the fat was congealing on the roasted bird.

"You are counseling I should kill Akhenaten?" Ay asked.

"When a cobra enters the chicken coop you do not catch it and turn it loose," Nakhtmin observed quietly. "You kill it, despite it being a symbol of royalty."

"Spoken like a farm lad," Maya said drily. "But he speaks truth, Ay. We could afford to let him live four years ago, but not now. We need a king who is totally on the side of Amun."

"I will do it," Nakhtmin said. "I will rid you of the heretic."

"No." Ay shook his head. "I have a man in place that is prepared for that deed. Besides, Nakhtmin, I see great things in the future for a man of your talents. I would not have even a hint of such a god-cursed action laid at your door." The Tjaty extended his hand to the door. "Thank you, gentlemen. Your counsel has been invaluable. I will attend to matters now."

"So the heretic will die?" Bakt asked. He edged closer to the table, eyeing the roasted goose.

"I will attend to matters. Now leave me."

The three men trooped from the room, one of them scowling at a missed opportunity to finish his meal. As they left, Ay's steward Mentopher entered. Ay called him in.

"Bring writing materials. I must prepare a letter. Then ready yourself for a journey."

"You want I should find a scribe too, master."

"No. I will write this myself."

When Mentopher arrived with pen, ink and papyrus, Ay sat down and composed a short letter to Khaemnum in Akhet-Aten. While it spelled nothing out--Ay was always careful--to the eyes of a man prepared it left no doubt as to the expected course of action. Sealing the letter with wax, he pressed his ring into it, leaving the mark of authenticity. Mentopher left immediately, and by sunset was well down the river, his passage aided by a stiff southerly breeze.

Chapter 33

Smenkhkare's army poured through the pass over the mountain range south of the city of Abu, and formed up on the cultivated plains opposite the great island city. The eastern bank of the river ran close to the island, the narrow strip of blue water being the only thing that protected the city as the southern army had no boats. The granite boulders of the island rose in grey billowings that resembled an elephant's back, formations that gave the city and island their names. Smenkhkare halted his army opposite the docks and looked longingly at the boats and barges tied up at them.

"How do we get them?" Menkure asked. The scarred young warrior with the limp approached his king and gestured across the narrow channel.

"I cannot see a way," Smenkhkare replied. He ran his hand over his freshly shaved face and head. He and Menkure had shaved when they neared the borders of Kemet. The lack of hair accentuated the livid scars that were the legacy of the crocodiles.

"Could we send swimmers across under cover of night?"

"Perhaps, though I think Governor Ka-Nakht will be waiting for us." Smenkhkare glanced involuntarily upriver to where the fog of the cataract misted the granite defile through the mountains. "Whatever we do, it will have to be soon. Horemheb will know we tricked him and be after us. He has barges. Unless we can get our own, he will be in Waset before us."

"Do you think the Governor knows of our presence?"

"If I was Horemheb, I would have sent messengers north. What I do not know is whether he has reached his barges yet. If he has, then you can be sure he will be spreading the news. There are enough boats on the river to take a hundred messages."

"Can we provoke the Governor to attack us?"

"How?"

Menkure looked around at the villages and fields full of ripening crops. "What if we torched the villages and fields? He would not want to see his property destroyed."

Smenkhkare considered the idea, weighing the injury that would be done to his subjects. He felt a tiny itch of guilt rise up in his mind but quickly pushed it away. "It may work. See to it, Menkure."

Curls of smoke soon lifted into the blue skies of Kemet as first the villages, then the crops in the fields were put to the torch. Screaming women and children were driven inland, many of the men willingly joining the rebels despite the destruction of their meager belongings. The gray and white clouds of smoke coalesced into a great pall that swept over the river and the northern part of the island, obscuring the sun and turning the light underneath the shroud into a dull orange glow. Lookouts posted on the cliffs reported activity within the city and shortly after, there came reports of soldiers massing near the docks.

"It's working, my lord."

"So it seems."

The first boats put out into the current shortly after, drifting downriver as they waited for others to join them. Soon, a mass of small boats and several oared barges crept slowly across the smoke-hazed water toward the eastern shore.

Menkure limped down from the heights to where Smenkhkare stood talking to his commanders. "My lord, there are twenty-three boats with an estimated five hundred soldiers."

"So few? Governor Ka-Nakht seemingly does not think much of us." Smenkhkare grinned. "We will not disappoint him. Kashta, Psuro, take your commands and hide in the palm groves. Wait for my signal. Kasaya, Shabaqo, take the irregulars and fall back across the burnt fields as the troops land. Draw them away from the river. Aspalta, take a hundred men and secure those boats when you hear the sounds of battle." The commanders raced away and in rapid order, half the rebel army faded away into the surrounding palm groves. The remainder, a motley looking rabble of men, milled around in the open space near the river, shouting and shaking their weapons in the air.

The first boats docked, running aground on the muddy banks, and the soldiers leapt out, quickly forming into ranks under the shouted commands of their officers. They spread out in a defensive cordon, allowing the other troops to safely disembark and form up into columns.

"They are well-disciplined, Menkure. It will be a pleasure to accept such men into my army."

"We have to defeat them first, my lord."

The troops from the Abu garrison advanced inland in battle order, the officers keeping the men under a form control as the rabble of men in front of them hurled rocks and taunts before falling back a few paces. The troops came on, spreading out as they entered the burnt fields, their sandaled feet and legs becoming blackened as they stirred up clouds of choking ash. The rebels fell back again, then scrambled into a loose formation, seemingly urged on by officers with whips.

The Abu troops halted fifty paces from the surging line of rebels. On a signal they crashed their curved bronze swords against hippopotamus-hide shields, let loose a full-throated challenge and charged the rebels. For a moment the rebel line hesitated then suddenly disintegrated, turning tail and running. A cry of triumph echoed across the smoke-filled field and the pursuing troops broke ranks, losing their cohesiveness as they raced after their foes.

A trumpet wailed somewhere in the murk and the pounding of feet. Determined men ran out of the smoke and crashed into the flanks of the Abu troops, rolling both ends of the line back into their fellow soldiers. At the same time the routed enemy turned and stood firm, pressing back, and weapons slashing. Outnumbered and demoralized by the sudden flank attack, the Abu garrison threw down their weapons and knelt on the ground, holding out their arms toward the rebels in a sign of surrender. Several were slaughtered by enthusiastic soldiers but their officers quickly got them under control. The prisoners were herded together to await the king's pleasure and the discarded weapons gathered up.

Aspalta sent a runner back from the river to report that all the boats had been captured. Smenkhkare nodded and, gathering his commanders, strode over to where the Abu garrison sat on the blackened ground, hands clasping their heads as their captors pointed weapons at them. The cordon of guards drew back as their king approached. Many of them knew what was about to happen, having seen it before, though never on such a large scale.

"Men of the Abu garrison," Smenkhkare called, pitching his voice to reach over the hundreds of men seated before him. "You need feel no shame at having been defeated by my men, for the gods of Kemet are behind me. Ask of your own god Khnum and his consort Satet. The gods of Kemet recognise the truth and justice of my cause, for I am Per-Aa, your anointed one, your king Ankhkheperure Djeserkheperu Smenkhkare. Perhaps some of you were in Akhet-Aten when I was made co-ruler or in Waset at my formal coronation in the temple of Amun. Speak up. Do any here recognise me?" He walked into the midst of the sitting prisoners and archers among the guards trained their arrows on the troops nearest him. "Disregard my wounds, look upon my face. Do you recognise me?"

"I do, my lord king," sobbed an older man.

"And I," said another. "I was there in Waset. It is the king, lads, no mistake."

A clamor of voices arose and many hands reached out toward Smenkhkare as he slowly walked through the prisoners. He left the circle and stood outside, staring back at them.

"I march for Waset to take my throne back from Tjaty Ay. He has laid hands on his anointed king and for that his life is forfeit. Who will join me?"

A deep silence greeted Smenkhkare's words. Menkure gestured angrily and shouted out. "What of the oaths you gave to your king? Are you traitors that you forget them so easily?"

One of the prisoners rose slowly and saluted. "I am Djutep, Leader of Fifty, my lord king." He hesitated, looking from Menkure's angry face to Smenkhkare's calm one. His eyes lingered on the horrific scars criss-crossing both men's bodies and he could not disguise a shudder. "What of our oath to Nebkheperure Tutankhaten, my lord? If we obey one oath we break another. You ask us to risk the anger of the gods as oath breakers no matter what we do."

"I have no quarrel with my brother," Smenkhkare replied. "It is Tjaty Ay who has sinned, not the young king in Waset. I will put Ay to death but Tutankhaten will be co-ruler with me. By joining my army you will not break any oath of loyalty. Rather, you will be reaffirming those you made to me."

"You swear this, my lord?"

"How dare you question the word of your king?" Menkure yelled. "Cut that traitor down where he stands." At once, two archers raised their bows.

"Hold." Smenkhkare's voice was conversational, but carried the expectation of instant obedience. One archer immediately dipped his bow, relaxing the taut bowspring. The other, a fraction faster in his reactions, threw his arm up despairingly as he loosed the arrow, sufficient for the projectile to whip over Djutep's head. The archer immediately dropped to his knees and prostrated himself on the ashen soil.

"Djutep, Leader of Fifty," Smenkhkare continued. "You are either a brave man or a foolish one. I do not need to give my word, for a king's statement is truth. However, I will do this. I swear by the gods that I mean no injury to my brother Tutankhaten. None who join me will break their oath to him."

"My lord." Djutep dropped to his knees and bowed his head. "I will follow you willingly."

"Who will join this officer?" Menkure asked loudly. Many prisoners scrambled up and knelt in the blackened fields, though others did not, sitting where they were or arguing with their fellow soldiers who knelt. "All who would follow their rightful king stand forth and make ready to re-take your oath of allegiance." Menkure gestured for the priests to come forward with the sacred objects.

Smenkhkare turned to go but whispered to Menkure as he did so. "Swear them in and kill the rest. Have the new recruits do it. It will be a test of their commitment. Kill any who refuse."

Sometime later, Menkure marched the men down to the riverside, where the rest of Smenkhkare's army stood. The city across the river resembled an ant's nest stirred with a stick. The remnant of the Abu garrison was whipping and beating the populace into a defence of the city.

"How many men did we lose?" Smenkhkare asked.

"Thirty," Menkure replied. "And twice that from wounds, no doubt."

"How many recruits?"

"Three hundred and some."

The king nodded and turned his attention back to the city across the river. "We do not have enough boats. We will have to capture more."

"A bloody business, my lord. Ka-Nakht will not be fooled again. We will have to fight for every span of ground. Could we not just march on Waset by river and land?"

"And leave them in our rear? Horemheb will no doubt be grateful for the reinforcements."

Menkure studied the island city. "We could land troops almost anywhere and march on the city itself. There are no walls. Under cover of night, maybe?"

Smenkhkare nodded. He glanced up to where the sun was dropping to the horizon through the thinning smoke. "Put the best troops on the boats and sail them north just before dusk. Have the rest of the army march along the bank in columns. We shall make them believe we are bypassing the city. We will return in the night and land on the western side. With the help of the gods we will succeed."

The small fleet set sail just before sunset when the shadows of the island of Abu fell across the narrow channel. The garrison ran to keep pace with them, shadowing their progress down the river until they reached the end of the island where they stood and watched them out of sight. The rebel army on the eastern shore marched away into the dusk too, then circled round out of sight of the river and returned to the blackened fields opposite Abu. Later, in the blackness of the night, lit only by the brilliance of the stars in the body of Nut, the boats returned, oared upriver slowly, turning into the western channel. Their cargo of soldiers were landed without incident on the rocky shore of the island and a handful of men guided the boats around Abu and through the narrow strait between the main island and the Isle of Amun to the south. They made landfall again in the darkness before dawn, just as the marching army returned to their starting point.

As dawn broke, lighting up the granite buildings of the city, as many as would fit into the boats clambered aboard, making a suitable amount of noise, and set a course for the main docks of Abu. The lookouts in the city spotted them almost immediately, and before they were half way across, the garrison was massed on the eastern shores of the island, preparing to throw back the invaders.

The boats stayed just offshore, weathering a desultory hail of arrows and men from the garrison who had changed sides the day before, starting yelling across the water to their fellow soldiers.

"It is the king returned," they shouted. "Smenkhkare himself. We have seen him, it is true. Surrender and he will be merciful."

The startling news caused some discussion in the ranks of the garrison soldiers and when the boats drew closer, fierce arguments raging allowed only a half-hearted response. As the soldiers stood about undecided, Smenkhkare and Menkure led a two-pronged attack on their rear, charging through the streets of the city and scattering the populace. The garrison turned to meet the threat and the boats disgorged their occupants onto the docks. Small pockets of resistance melted away as the garrison threw down their arms, bemused expressions on many faces as they recognized friends and fellow soldiers among their captors.

Smenkhkare addressed the captives and the men of the city, quickly convincing them all of his identity and most of them to renew their oaths of allegiance to him. Governor Ka-Nakht refused however, and forbade any of his immediate staff to join the rebel cause.

"A man is king until he dies, sir," he said stiffly. "Smenkhkare died and was buried after the seventy days. He cannot come back to life."

"Are you a fool, Ka-Nakht? Look at me. Do not tell me you do not recognise me. I put your staff of office into your hands myself."

"Smenkhkare confirmed me in my office as Governor, which your illustrious father Nebmaetre awarded me twenty..."

"So you acknowledge Nebmaetre as my father?"

"I know a son of Nebmaetre when I see one." Ka-Nakht sighed. "Young man, I do not doubt that you were once King Smenkhkare but you died to that position. No man returns from the House of the Dead unless he is granted rebirth."

"What makes you think I am not reborn?"

"Smenkhkare died four years ago, whereas you are more than twenty floods. You cannot be the king reborn. If you are not the king reborn I cannot offer you my allegiance." Governor Ka-Nakht drew himself up straight and looked Smenkhkare in the eye. "Will you now kill me, as I'm told you killed my men who did not join you?"

"If I leave you alive, what will you do when Horemheb arrives?"

406

"Assist him as best I can. My oath of loyalty to Nebkheperure Tutankhaten binds me."

"And if I succeed and become king again?"

"Then the gods will have spoken and I will swear my oath of loyalty to the new king."

Smenkhkare turned away and looked out through the window at the granite city of Abu spread below him. After several minutes he spoke quietly. "You have your life, old man."

"And what of my men?"

"If they choose to stay I will spare their lives also."

Governor Ka-Nakht nodded and smiled. "Yes, you were a king once. You are merciful to those you have conquered."

"I will take as many men as I can. I will take every boat, every bit of food I can, and the contents of your treasury as payment for those lives. I will not leave anything for you to help my enemies."

"We will starve. Without boats we cannot fish, nor can we fetch food from the fields, if you have left any unburned."

"Make do, Ka-Nakht. Perhaps Horemheb will help you. Or if you can hold out a month or two, I will help you. Once I am king again I will empty the Waset granaries to feed you."

The entire army squeezed aboard the fleet of boats and barges, loaded with men and food and gold until the water lapped close to the tops of the painted sides. Less than a hundred unarmed men stood with Governor Ka-Nakht and watched as the horde of small craft were carried out of sight by the current. When they were gone, Ka-Nakht busied himself with an inventory of the city, finding out missed food stores and reassuring himself that not all his treasury had been stripped. The granite quarries of Abu held more than just fine building stone-- they held a secure cache of arms and gold. When Horemheb arrived, he would find Abu ready and willing to help him.

Chapter 34

"Scarab! Scarab!" Khu raced through the Khabiru tent city, his black hair flying behind him and his kilt flapping. His eyes searched the tents, seeking a familiar pattern of colours and designs among the varied styles and patterns. He sought too a familiar face, but to Khu, the Khabiru face lacked the distinguishing features the Kemetu had. Several times he thought he saw Jeheshua, the jeweler, and as many times was disappointed. He looked for the women he knew were companions of Scarab, but they too seemed to be in hiding. At last he saw a woman who looked familiar and stopped, breathing hard, in front of her. His windblown hair and staring eyes alarmed her and she called out for assistance.

Khu understood very little of the Khabiru tongue and the words he had picked up were often not exactly what he wanted to say. He had been slapped once or twice by pretty girls so this time he restricted himself to names.

"Scarab," he said. "Meryam?"

The woman backed away, shaking her head. "Anah." She pointed at herself. "Anah."

"Not you, you silly girl," Khu groaned. "Where Meryam was at?"

Another woman joined young Anah and spoke to her, asking what she was doing with the Kemetu lad.

"I think he's looking for someone called Meryam," Anah explained. "But which Meryam? I know five and I'm sure there are more."

"Well, tell him. Ask him which one."

"I don't think he speaks Khabiru. His accent is terrible."

"Ask him anyway. See if saying a name will get him to recognise one."

Anah nodded and cleared her throat. "Meryam. Do you mean Meryam daughter of Uphiel...or Meryam daughter of Azarel...?"

"Yes, yes," Khu nodded vigorously as he heard the familiar name. "Meryam, Scarab. Where?"

"Which one?" Anah asked. "Ednah, can you talk to him?"

"What is that other word he used, the Kemetu word...scar-ab, was it?"

"It is the name of one of their gods, I think. The scar-ab beetle is their sun god," Anah explained.

"What a strange people, worshiping insects." Ednah's mouth fell open as a thought occurred to her. "Could he mean Meryam the whore? She lives over near the pagan temples."

"That must be it," Anah exclaimed. "Kemetu men think of little else...or so I've been told," she added wistfully. Now that the lad had calmed down a bit she noticed his deep brown eyes below his wavy black hair, his lips that looked as sweet as...

"Anah!" Ednah said sharply, jabbing a finger into the young girl's side. "Your Meryam is over there, young man." She pointed back toward the walled city of Zarw, close to where the many-pillared temples gleamed in the sunlight.

Khu understood the gesture if not the words and he frowned. "I've just come from there," he said. "I know Meryam's tent is over here somewhere, closer to the canal."

Ednah and Anah pointed again and Khu shook his head. "Meryam," he repeated. "Scarab."

"I think he means the young Kemetu girl who birthed last month. Meryam my sister attended her." A short, somewhat stout Khabiru man in the full beard favoured by every male old enough to grow one, strolled up to Khu and said in passable Kemetu, "I know the Meryam of whom you speak for I am her brother Eli, son of Abiezar. Come, I will take you to our tent."

"Thank you Eli." Khu bowed politely to the two women, then at the man. "I must find Scarab. Do you know where she is?"

"With my sister no doubt, playing with her baby." Eli sighed and led the way through the maze of tents. "This Scarab of yours is an intelligent woman with many stories of the court. Then just as she was getting interesting she has a baby and can now talk of nothing else. Why is this, Khu?"

"I don't know." Khu shrugged. "I have never understood women."

"You would not be alone. Our sacred writings say there are four things no man can know, an eagle in the air, a snake on a rock, a ship in the open sea and the heart of a woman." Eli grinned. "You are her husband?"

"No." Khu tried rather unsuccessfully to hide a scowl. "She is unmarried. She loves a soldier, a General in the northern army. I am a friend...just a friend."

"A friend is never 'just' a friend. Be steadfast, Khu, for friendship often outlasts love...ah, here we are." Eli pointed to a broad woolen and hide tent, richly embroidered in red and brown. He drew back the tent flap and bowed toward Khu. "Be welcome in our tent. Your presence honours us."

Khu entered the tent and blinked in the dimness, his eyes gradually becoming accustomed to the darkness. On the far side of the spacious tent, on carpets slightly threadbare with age, two young women sat on their heels looking down at something in front of them. Both were dressed alike, in the long woolen robes of the Khabiru and Khu felt a pang of annoyance that Scarab was not here after all.

Then one of the women turned and smiled. "Khu, what a lovely surprise. Come and see little Set."

Eli winced at the name but kept quiet. Why would any sane woman name her child for the destroyer?

Khu crossed the tent and knelt by Scarab. Her baby slept in a wickerwork basket, lined with a red woolen blanket. One thumb was tucked safely inside his mouth and every now and again he sucked on it in his sleep.

"Er, very nice. He, er, looks like...his father?"

"Doesn't he?" Scarab smiled and gently stroked the baby's bald head. "He will grow up to be a famous general, just like his father."

"Scarab," Khu whispered, plucking at her sleeve. "I have news. You must come at once."

"What is it?"

"A messenger from the south." Khu saw her look of alarm and shook his head. "Not from Waset, from Kush. There...there is news of your brother."

"Tutankhaten? Is he on an expedition to Kush? But he is just a boy. What is Ay thinking of?"

"Not Tutankhaten, Smenkhkare. He has been seen."

"If that is true, it means trouble," Eli muttered.

Meryam motioned her brother to silence, and put a hand comfortingly on Scarab's arm.

Scarab sat silent, staring down at the sleeping baby. "Don't," she whispered after a few moments. "Don't ruin my happiness with false rumors."

"I would not do that to you, Scarab," Khu said. "Not for all the gold in the Great Place. This is official. It is a messenger from Horemheb himself, bidding Paramessu bring troops down to Waset."

"H...how do you know, Khu? Why would you be told?"

Khu grinned. "Sometimes you learn more being a nobody. You know that pretty serving lass in the barracks kitchens? Tua? Well, I was in there passing some time with her and enjoying a pot of beer when this messenger comes in, all dusty and tired, and sits down with the officer of the guard. It seems he has just reported to Judge Seti, Paramessu's father, and given him official dispatches from Horemheb."

"Don't be silly, Khu. Dispatches are sealed and the Judge is not going to open them in front of a common messenger and read them out. The man's just guessing, spreading rumors."

Khu shook his head, his grin broadening. "No, that's where you are wrong. The messenger received the orders from the hand of Horemheb himself in...oh, I can't remember the name...some city in Kush--and the General told them why it was so urgent they get the news through. He said--this is Horemheb saying this, not the dispatches--that Smenkhkare was alive and marching on Waset with an army."

"But why would he...ah, he knows Ay...but how? What of the crocodile? Was that a lie too?" Scarab shook her head, a frown creasing her brow. "I must find out. I must get to Waset." She leapt to her feet then stood looking down at the sleeping infant. "What about little Set?"

"I can look after him," Meryam said. "I would be delighted to. I can find a wet-nurse easily."

"He would be safe here," Eli said reassuringly. "If that is what you want to do."

"Yes...no." Scarab looked from one to the other, then at the flap of the tent and back down to little Set. "I don't know. Of course I cannot leave him, I am his mother, but I must find out..."

"Why not leave him here while he is sleeping?" suggested Eli. "Go to Judge Seti and find out the truth. Then you can come back here and decide what you want to do."

"Sounds sensible," Khu added.

"Will Judge Seti see me though? He does not know me."

"I will find an elder to accompany you," Eli said. "We are on good terms with the Judge. He will see an elder if we request it."

Scarab looked puzzled. "Why would an elder do that for me?"

"Because of who you are," Eli replied.

"And because of who we know you to be," Meryam added.

Eli hurried out and returned about an hour later, an hour during which Scarab slowly became more and more anxious. She paced the tent, woke up her baby and played with him, put him down again and fretted when the infant would not fall asleep. Meryam picked Set up and rocked him and his fitful cries hiccupped to a halt. Scarab scowled and took her baby back firmly, rocking him and murmuring.

The tent flap was thrown aside and Eli entered with another man--a tall man with a scar across his forehead.

"Jeheshua," Khu exclaimed. "What are you doing here?"

"He is an elder of the tribe of Yuya," Eli explained. "Who better to represent Scarab, who is of Yuya herself, than an elder of her tribe?"

Scarab nodded and handed her baby to Meryam. "Can we go now? Anything could be happening. For all we know Judge Seti could have left the city by now and be marching down to Waset."

"Impatient, isn't she?" Eli grinned. "Is that the blood of Yuya showing?"

"I believe that statement is bordering on disrespect for your elder, young Eli," Jeheshua reproved mildly. "Are you calling me impatient too?"

"My apologies, revered elder," Eli said, bowing. He spoilt the effect by grinning. "Judge Seti is not going anywhere, Scarab. That's why we took so long. We petitioned Seti for an audience and he has granted one. We can leave whenever you are ready."

Seti greeted the small deputation in his house in Zarw. Recently retired after a long life of service within the army, he looked forward to a pleasant few years with his wife before making the last journey into the West. It was a vain hope. Such was the Judge's experience and wisdom that hardly a day went by without someone seeking him out for help with some knotty problem of law, both civil and military. He found he welcomed the disruptions as time hung heavy in a household too empty for too long. Only two of his children by his beloved wife Pentere had survived childhood, a son and a daughter. Paramessu had risen rapidly through the ranks of the army and was now a General, enough to make any man proud. But a man who is active in the army has little time for a family and at forty, Paramessu had still not re-married after his first wife and young son had died in the plague. Seti's daughter Nefertari was barren. Perhaps the worst fate that could befall a child-loving Kemetu, her husband had divorced her and she lived now with her parents. Seti and Pentere had all but despaired of having grandchildren.

The gate-keeper let the three men and a woman into the walled courtyard of the judge's residence and the steward of the small estate took them through to an inner courtyard where Seti awaited them. A fishpond filled one corner and an old tamarind tree overhung the still waters. Dragonflies danced above the reeds and waterlilies and bees hummed in the foliage of the perfumed flowering trees. An old man sat on a stone bench near the pond, reading a scrolled papyrus. He looked up as his steward crossed the courtyard, the sand scrunching beneath his feet.

"Ah, Jeheshua, come in, my friend, come in." The judge rose to his feet and embraced the old jeweler warmly. Looking beyond him, Seti examined the three younger people. "This must be the young woman I am hearing things about, but who are these men?"

Eli stepped forward and bowed respectfully. "I am Eli, son of Abiezar, sir. May I present Khu, son of Pa-it of Akhet-Re, and the lady Beketaten." Khu bowed deeply as he was introduced, but Scarab merely inclined her head gracefully.

Seti raised an eyebrow at her gesture. "I am Troop Commander and Judge of the king's forces in Zarw, young lady. You would do well to remember that."

"And I am a high-born lady of the royal court in Waset, Judge. You would do well to remember that too."

"She is high-spirited, Jeheshua," Seti commented. "Is she really the one?"

"You may address me directly, Judge," Scarab said with a trace of asperity creeping into her voice. "There is no need for a middleman."

"This middleman, as you call him, got you this meeting. A touch more respect for your elders and betters would not go amiss, young lady. Do they not teach manners in court any longer?"

Scarab opened her mouth to utter a cutting retort but Khu jabbed his elbow into her side hard. "Remember why you are here," he hissed.

Scarab controlled herself with an effort and bowed rigidly. "Your pardon Judge Seti, I am forgetting myself. Thank you for allowing me this meeting. I want to ask..."

"First, some refreshment. Steward, bring wine and I think some of those delightful honey cakes cook makes."

The steward bowed. "At once, my lord." He hurried off on his errand.

"Well," Seti said with a smile. "We shall await refreshments. Pray take a seat, Jeheshua." The old judge sat down on the stone seat next to the jeweler and looked up at the three young people standing in front of him. He gestured across the courtyard. "There are some chairs over there. Khu, Eli, be so good as to fetch them."

When everyone was seated, Seti looked Scarab directly in the eye. "You are the young woman my son Paramessu has bedded. You have had a child I believe. Is it his?"

Scarab's eyes flashed and her lips tightened momentarily. "Paramessu and I are lovers. We intend to marry. He will recognise the boy as his."

"As I said, Jeheshua, high-spirited. Not a bad thing in a horse or a woman." Seti's features softened slightly. "Have you told Paramessu he has a son?"

"I have written to him, but he has not replied."

"I would not read too much into that. It is notoriously hard to get a letter through to the army unless it goes by special messenger."

"On another matter, my lord Judge," Scarab said, allowing a little more respect into her voice. "You have had word from the south, I believe. May I know the content of the letter?"

"Ah, the wine. Besneb, please serve my guests." Seti watched as silver goblets were filled with chilled wine, moisture beading briefly

414

on the cold exteriors. "I have it shipped in from the Island of the Sea, Kretos, I believe it is called. Drink, tell me what you think." He waited for expressions of praise before accepting one himself. "The honey cakes are from an old recipe that my cook refuses to divulge." Seti shrugged and smiled. "I have no choice but to keep her on."

For a few minutes they ate and drank, with Scarab slowly becoming more agitated. At last she could not stand it any longer. "Judge, please, what was the message from the south?"

"First tell me why you are so interested? The contents of the letter are confidential at present but I anticipate it will be public knowledge before the month is out, sooner if the messenger is already spreading rumors. Cannot you be patient, young lady?"

"Is it to do with King Djeserkheperu Smenkhkare?"

Seti sighed. "Why are you interested in a fallen king?"

"Because he is my brother, sir."

Seti's eyebrows shot up. "Brother? You are a daughter of Nebmaetre? By a concubine perhaps?"

"By his queen Tiye."

Seti sat back and exhaled loudly. "Then you are full sister to Akhenaten and half-sister to Tutankhaten as well. What did you say your name was?"

"Beketaten."

"There was a princess of that name. I thought she died of the plague years ago."

"Obviously not, as you see."

"You swear this is true, not just an elaborate tale? Forgive me lady, but..." Seti looked at the three men. "This is true?"

"I was on the King's Council myself, sir," Khu said. "This truly is the lady Beketaten, sister of three kings."

"By all the gods," Seti muttered. He stretched out a hand to Jeheshua. "Forgive me, old friend, I mean your solitary god no disrespect."

"None is taken, sir," Jeheshua murmured. "The news is startling."

"The letter?" Scarab asked impatiently. "What did it say?"

"Er, yes." Seti seemed momentarily at a loss for words. He withdrew the papyrus scroll from his robe and unrolled it. Clearing his throat, he read. "Greetings from General Horemheb, Commander-in-Chief of the northern armies, fan-bearer on the king's...er, I'll leave out

415

the honourifics and greetings, shall I? Let's see, yes...The man calling himself Son of Sobek is in reality the former king known as Djeserkheperu Smenkhkare. I have it from his own mouth that he intends to wage war against the lawful authority of the Two Lands and will be approaching Waset with an army estimated at fifteen hundred by the full moon of Proyet. You are commanded to muster a force of at least two thousand men, fully armed and equipped, and transport them to Waset before this date. Er, he ends with the usual..."

"So he lives." Scarab suddenly burst into tears. The men looked at the ground, unsure of their supposed course of action. Khu lifted the linen cloth from the honey cakes and passed it to Scarab. She dried her tears, dabbing at her face with the cloth. "I'm sorry. I am happy really, I just...I just believed he was dead for so long."

"More wine?" Seti asked, lifting the wine pitcher.

Scarab shook her head. "I must go to him. When do you send the soldiers down to Waset to aid my brother? I will go with them."

"My lady Beketaten, I do not think that is their purpose," Jeheshua commented quietly. "General Horemheb's words have a different meaning."

"What other meaning could he have? He said he talked to my brother. He would not just talk if he had some other motive."

"No, he is right, Sca...lady Beketaten." Judge Seti shifted uncomfortably on his seat. He opened the papyrus scroll again and scanned it. "Horemheb plainly states Smenkhkare as saying he intends to wage war against the lawful authority. This means he regards himself as being in opposition to the...your brother and the men he requests from me are to fight him."

Scarab stared wide-eyed at the old judge, then around at the two Khabiru men and Khu. "You would send men to kill my brother? To kill your grandson's uncle--the true king? What of me? Will you kill me too?"

"Not while I am here," Khu growled, moving over to stand behind Scarab.

"Nor I," Eli agreed.

Judge Seti shook his head. "Please, please, there is no cause for alarm. Horemheb's request cannot be fulfilled anyway. I have no troops to spare in Zarw as they are all far north of here with my son's army.

The full moon of Proyet is just over a month away. I could not send troops in time even if I wanted to."

"And what of myself, sir? Will you hold me to ransom to force my brother's surrender?"

Seti smiled. "Do you imagine he would surrender his kingship for a woman? Even his sister?"

Scarab sat silently for a few minutes before shaking her head. "Nor would I want him to. But I am still going to him. You will not stop me."

"You will take your son--my grandson?"

"Of course."

"You would take a newborn babe on a dangerous journey knowing that a battle lies at the end of it? You would really risk his life?"

"I have no choice," Scarab said, her chin rising defiantly. "I must go to my brother and...and my little Set will have to come too."

"What is his name? Did you say Set?"

"Yes." Scarab smiled faintly, seeing a look of pride steal over the old judge's face. "I named him for the desert god of soldiers because his father told me how important the name was to him."

"Thank you," Seti whispered. He lowered his head and raised his hands to his face. After a few moments he looked up at the other men, his eyes glistening. "Gentlemen, would you leave me to talk with...with my daughter alone? She will be quite safe," he added, seeing Khu's face stiffen. "On my honour."

"It will be all right," Scarab said calmly. "Wait for me outside, Khu."

Seti waited until the men had left the courtyard before turning back to Scarab. He looked carefully at the girl in Khabiru clothing, her long reddish tinged hair so reminiscent of the old queen Tiye.

"You are determined to go south to aid your brother? No, do not bother to answer; I can see it in your eyes. Well, you will do what you must, but I ask you not to put the child at risk."

"Would you separate a child from his mother? What sort of a mother deserts her baby?"

"What sort of mother knowingly takes her baby into danger?" Seti snapped.

Scarab's eyes flashed again but she remained seated. She thought for the first time of the rigors of the journey and of the uncertainty that lay at the end of it. Smenkhkare and Horemheb would fight but only the gods knew the outcome. *Am I being foolish taking Set with me?*

"Forgive me," Seti said. "It was not my place to dispute with you, but with my son absent, the boy's father, I felt duty-bound to speak."

"I...I would leave him with his father if he was here," Scarab sobbed. "But I cannot just abandon him to the care of strangers."

"The Khabiru are your friends, your mother's people."

"They are truly kind, but my son is Kemetu not Khabiru." She tried a small, tremulous smile. "Besides he bears the name of a god that is an abomination to them. I don't think they'd feel comfortable with it."

"Khu then? He seems a likeable fellow."

"Khu would not leave me. You see, there is no-one. I must take him with me."

"There are his grandparents, lady Beketaten. Family who would love him as a treasured only grandson."

"You, judge?"

"And my wife Pentere. Our daughter is barren and though my son Paramessu was married, his wife and son died many years ago. Now you have arrived and given us another grandson. You must know we would protect him with our lives."

Scarab looked hard at Judge Seti's lined face, searching his eyes. She saw only sincerity and strength and felt herself drawn to the idea. She was not abandoning little Set, but leaving him for a short time with his grandparents. She did not know Seti or Pentere but they were Paramessu's parents and she knew he loved them. "I wish I could talk to Paramessu, tell him what I intend, ask his thoughts."

"Write him a letter; I will see he gets it. I have army messengers at my disposal and I am duty bound to tell him Horemheb's news anyway, so I will include your letter."

"What shall I say? That I go to help my brother reclaim his throne and not to come after me with the army?"

Seti chuckled drily. "Tell him you love him, child. Tell him of his son and that he will be in Zarw awaiting the arrival of his proud father. Tell him that you will be gone a short time only after which all three of you will be reunited." Seti got to his feet and drew Scarab up, walking across the sandy courtyard with her. "My scribe will write the letter if you wish. Just tell him what you want to say."

"I can write it myself. It would be better."

"Of course." He beckoned to a servant. "Take this lady to my study and provide her with writing materials. Bring her to me when she has finished."

Seti immediately turned and went to find his wife Pentere. He found her in the small herb garden outside the kitchens, supervising the kitchen staff as they dug through the sandy soil, pulling weeds and watering the burgeoning rows of vegetables. Pulling her to one side, he led her through into the shade of a small orchard where he informed her of the afternoon's events.

"Our son has a child by some loose Khabiru woman, a whore probably, and you want to adopt the brat?" Pentere tried to decide whether disgust or incredulity better mirrored her emotions.

"She is no whore, nor a Khabiru, though she is related to the late queen Tiye. She is..." Seti grinned widely, enjoying his wife's look of puzzlement. "...sister to both kings." He decided to say nothing about Smenkhkare. That would probably come to nothing anyway. It was not important; certainly not as important as whom she was. "She is of the Great House, and our son has brought her to child. Do you know what that means?"

Pentere shrugged, but a gleam of avarice lit her eyes. "Wealth?" she asked hopefully. "Comfort in our old age and a fine tomb?"

"Oh, much more, dear Pentere. The child, she even named him Seti, has title to the throne of Kemet. Neither of the kings has a son. If they die, we could yet see our grandson crowned King of the Two Lands." Seti rubbed his hands together as Pentere's eyes opened wide. "I've always rather fancied the title of Divine Father."

Chapter 35

K haemnum sat in the little room that served as his headquarters in Akhet-Aten. A table and chair filled most of the room, with a ramshackle set of shelves against the crumbling plaster of one wall. Scrolls filled the shelves and littered the floor and table as he scratched away with a splintery reed on coarse papyrus. The splayed tip of the reed caught on a knot in the uneven surface of the papyrus, releasing a flood of ink over the scroll. Khaemnum cursed and blotted at the scroll with a linen pad, seeking to lessen the disfigurement of the careful rows of pictographs.

Despite being the ranking officer in Akhenaten's capital city of the sun, Khaemnum preferred to do his own accounting and report writing. He had a scribe ready to do all his work for him, but he sent him away, enjoying a duty that occupied his mind, dragging it away from the mundane. For four years he had held the post of commander in Akhet-Aten, four years in which other more junior officers had been rotated out to other duties, had secured advancement and glory, while he played nursemaid to a forgotten king with a tiny detachment of guards. Akhenaten was truly forgotten outside of this little city, as no event of the king's life was recorded any longer. Once, the records might have stated 'On the eighth day of the third month of the sixteenth year of our glorious king Waenre Akhenaten...' but that had stopped in his seventeenth year. Events since then had been recorded as happening in the 'year of King Nebkheperure Tutankhaten'. Even the minor events, such as the arrival of a new batch of wine bore the ownership seals of the boy king rather than his elder half-brother. Here, Khaemnum sometimes felt the injustice of it and took a perverse pleasure in altering some of the seals. Only last month he had altered a new pressing of the sweet dark wine from Syria to read 'In the twenty-first year of Waenre Akhenaten', but no-one noticed. In truth, no-one cared. Akhenaten had already been relegated to the recesses of history.

Khaemnum sat back on his stool and stretched his arms up and back, feeling his muscles and tendons creak with the effort. Sweat trickled between his shoulderblades, running down to stain his kilt. He ran a tongue over his dry lips and glanced out of the small window toward the dark green slick of the river. The room usually caught the breezes off the river but today the air hung heavy and still, holding the stench of the city close instead of dispersing and cleansing it. A new city, raised pristine from the desert sands a mere twenty years before, Akhet-Aten possessed none of the overcrowded squalor of Great Waset, yet despite a falling population, the smells and filth had grown--another thing about which few people cared.

"Boy! Where are you, Hepu?" A tousle-headed boy stuck his head around the corner of the door. "Get me some beer, and make it cold." Khaemnum flipped a small piece of copper across the room. Hepu snatched it out of the air and ran. "A pitcher, mind. Not just a mug."

Khaemnum got to his feet and started tidying away the scrolls, sticking them in the shelves in no particular order. His scribe had tried to show him how to organize them but the commander soon gave up, content to have the scribe come in afterward and rearrange things. He poked his head out of the door and squinted up into the faded blue sky, judging the position of the sun. He felt a faint clenching in his belly and remembered he had eaten nothing since his breakfast of bread and dates at dawn before the king's daily audience. For a few minutes he debated whether to find some food, but his throat told him only to find drink.

Hepu arrived back, hauling a large stoppered pitcher of beer and a mug. The foaming liquid hissed and sputtered around the imperfect seal of the container's neck, and moisture beaded on the glazed pottery surface. Khaemnum's throat constricted at the sight and he poured himself a mug of the thin sour brew. He gulped but it felt as if his dry mouth soaked up the liquid before it got to his throat. He poured himself another but stopped with it half way to his lips as a shadow fell across the doorway.

"Commander Khaemnum?"

"Who asks?" Khaemnum reluctantly put the mug on the table beside the pitcher and stared at the man filling the open doorway. Thickset and muscular, he gave the impression of height, though the top of his bald head missed the door lintel by at least a hand breadth. Khaemnum's eyes traveled over the bulging muscles and pillar-like legs before coming reluctantly to the man's face. He drew a sharp breath but managed to control himself, covering his slip with a cough. Flint hard eyes stared back at him over a hawked nose and large loose lips that even in this savage heat were moist and glistening.

"You are Commander Khaemnum?" the man repeated. "I have a letter for you from Tjaty Ay."

"And you are?"

"I am Mentopher, his steward." The man reached into a pouch at his waist and pulled out a folded papyrus. He held it out for Khaemnum and as he did so, a white scar in the form of the hawk of Heru gleamed against the dark side of the man's chest. "Yes, Khaemnum," Mentopher said, noting the direction of the Commander's glance. "I am one of Ay's chosen ones."

Khaemnum accepted the folded letter and turned it over. There was no name on it, nor was the seal imprinted with any symbol. He cracked the wax and picked it away with his fingernails until the loose edge came away. Unfolding it, he scanned the few lines of script.

"You can read it, can you?" Mentopher asked. "Ay said you could read and wouldn't need a scribe."

"I can read it." Khaemnum sat on the edge of the table and read the message slowly. It was in Ay's rather stilted script and was short and to the point. Nothing in it could be construed as treasonous; indeed, if he had not had prior warning of the message it would be meaningless. He re-read it, in the hopes he might have missed something. It said, 'The time has come. Take him to the desert and let him commune with his god. The bearer will go with you as witness.' Looking up at Ay's hulking steward, Khaemnum asked, "You know what the letter says?"

"I cannot read, but Ay told me its contents. I am to come with you to see it done." Mentopher grinned, revealing stained and rotting teeth.

"Very well. I will give the matter some thought and determine a suitable time."

"What's wrong with now? The sooner we kill the bastard the better."

Khaemnum sighed. "We are not going to kill anyone. The killing of..." he dropped his voice, "...a king is god-cursed and anyway, Ay says nothing of killing, only of leaving him in the desert."

Mentopher shrugged. "So grab him and take him out and leave him now. You've got soldiers haven't you? Set's hairy buttocks, I could carry him myself."

"You would have a riot on your hands and that is something Ay would not want. There are still a lot of Aten worshipers here."

"So fix it, Commander." Mentopher picked up the pitcher and sniffed the contents, grinning delightedly at the sharp smell of the sour beer. He poured a mug full, splashing some carelessly on the table, and drained the contents. Belching loudly, he poured another mug. "Just don't take too long. I'm sure the Tjaty would not be happy to hear you are delaying unnecessarily."

"You can find a bed in the barracks. See the quartermaster. I will send for you when everything is ready."

"I will stay in the North Palace. Ay has told me to use his rooms there. The accommodation is better." Mentopher finished the mug of beer and dropped it onto the table before leaving.

Khaemnum carefully wiped the mug before pouring himself the last of the beer in the pitcher. Sitting on his stool, he tipped it back, leaning against the wall with his feet on the table. He sipped and thought about the king and his daughter Meryetaten. She had foreseen this situation over a year ago and had appealed for Khaemnum's help. Now the day had arrived but he still did not know what he was going to do. *It's a dreadful thing to kill a king, even just by exposing him in the desert heat, but disobeying the Tjaty is unthinkable. Isn't it? That is why Mentopher is here - to ensure my cooperation.*

Swinging his legs down, Khaemnum went to the door and looked out on the sun-baked city. The heat from the sun beat down on the anvil of the earth, the air itself shuddering and shimmering with each stroke. Pools of water appeared to lie in the streets, and the figures of distant people were distorted and strange. A man could die right here in the city if exposed to the Aten for a few hours. He recalled the ancient penalty for blasphemy against the sun god, Re. The criminal was staked out in the pitiless glare of the god. Madness took the blasphemer within hours, as he ranted and railed against his fate, followed swiftly by death. Could I do this if I thought of Akhenaten as a blasphemer? He did try to abolish the gods.

Khaemnum took a faded linen headdress from the shelves and draped it over his head, tying it in place with a flax cord before venturing out into the streets. He walked away from the marginally cooler area near the river toward the dazzling brightness of the painted palace in the heart of Akhet-Aten. In the rippling heat the sweat on his body dried instantly, leaving just a fine incrustation of salt behind. Inquiries determined that Lady Meryetaten was taking her ease in the shaded gardens of the women's quarters and was not to be disturbed. Khaemnum thought for a moment before handing the maidservant the folded and dusty letter from Ay.

"Take this to your mistress," he instructed. "She is expecting it."

The girl was back within minutes, and took the commander by a roundabout route to the gardens where Meryetaten stood waiting under the heavy shade of a citrus tree, the letter in her hand.

Dismissing the maidservant, the king's daughter handed the letter back to Khaemnum. "So, it has come at last. What do you intend to do?"

"Ay has sent his steward to see it done. If I do not do it, he will."

"He is your king," Meryetaten said softly. "You took an oath of loyalty to him."

"I know. And when I stand before the judges in the afterlife, I do not want to face them with such a sin weighing down my heart." Khaemnum sighed. "I will help you if I can."

"How exactly? I do not need ifs or maybes. I need a definite plan."

"Then let me think for a moment."

"Do it out loud," Meryetaten said. "It may be that something you dismiss is right."

"Very well." The commander started pacing, three steps, a turn, and three more, turn again. "I am to take Akhenaten out into the desert and let his god kill him. Mentopher is to go with me to see it done. I cannot kill him directly, even Ay does not command that, so I have to be able to say I left him with food and water." Khaemnum stopped and looked at the king's daughter. "Anything?" he asked hopefully.

"What if the Aten does not kill my father? He is his servant after all."

Khaemnum grimaced. "My lady, we are not talking about the godhead of the sun's disc, something spiritual; we are talking about a desert sun hotter than a coppersmith's furnace. Make no mistake, if he is left out there, he will die, king or not."

Meryetaten nodded. "So he will die under the desert sun. Look at it another way. What would save him?"

"Once he was out there?" Khaemnum considered the question. "Shade, water, rescue?"

"Let me ask something else, commander. You and Mentopher take my father out there. Do you leave him or watch him die? Do you go alone or take soldiers?"

"I...I suppose I would take soldiers, if it was my intent to leave him."

"What if Mentopher wanted to stay and see him die? Could you dissuade him?"

"If I had to, my lady. I would kill him."

"No, that you must not do. He is the witness that the deed was carried out. If there is even a hint that my father still lives, Ay will hunt him down and kill him for certain. If Mentopher wants to stay, you must find a way to dissuade him."

Khaemnum resumed his pacing, thinking through the lady Meryetaten's words. "So the king is alone with a small flask of water and a loaf of bread. How does he survive?"

"Leave that to me, Khaemnum. Do you know the desert between Akhet-Aten and the Eastern Sea?"

"Moderately well, my lady. I have been on patrols to about five days out."

"It is enough. Do you know the trade route that runs from just north of here to Gharib on the sea?"

"Yes, but Mentopher would never accept that. Too many people travel that route."

Meryetaten's lips tightened and she directed a glare at Khaemnum. "Did I suggest such a thing, Commander?" She waited, staring the man down until he lowered his eyes, murmuring an apology. "As I was saying, about half way along the road there is a well...it is called the Well of Khons, I believe. Turn south and travel half a day south to a pillar of rock that sticks out of the desert like...like a young man's member. You know it, Commander?"

"I know it." Khaemnum could not control a grin. "The soldier's call it 'King's Phallus'."

Meryetaten stared stony-faced. "Indeed? Then it must have been some other king they named it for." After a moment she relented, her face softening into a faint smile. "Well, that is where you will leave my father."

"Then what?"

"Then you leave him there and forget about him. What follows is none of your concern, and for the safety of all of us, it is better you do not know."

Khaemnum nodded. "I plan to leave after the dawn hymn tomorrow. I had better go and tell the king to prepare for the journey."

"You will tell him nothing. Spin him a tale if you must but do not even hint that he will survive this. Mentopher will read it in his face and it will all be for nothing."

"How is it that a well-born lady like you knows these things? The ways of the desert, the pillar of rock, a man you have never met?"

Meryetaten smiled. "Do not imagine that only Ay has spies. Never underestimate me, Khaemnum."

Khaemnum, with Mentopher and a squad of twenty soldiers, intercepted Akhenaten as he left the great Temple of Aten the next morning, just after the dawn hymn to the Sun. The soldiers slipped between the king and the few court officials that still bothered to accompany Akhenaten, and gently ushered him to one side, dissuading anyone else who tried to stay close.

"What is the meaning of this, Khaemnum?" Akhenaten asked querulously, peering about him with reddened eyes. "I don't have time for any other business today. My eyes hurt so much I can hardly see. I want to go and lie down."

"No, you are coming with us," Mentopher growled.

Akhenaten moved closer to the large man and looked up at him, moving his head from side to side in an effort to see him clearly. "Who are you? Why do you speak so disrespectfully? Don't you know I'm the king?"

Khaemnum pushed Mentopher aside. "My apologies, your majesty. He is Mentopher, a servant of your Tjaty, Ay. He meant no disrespect, just that we are here as you ordered, ready to escort you to the dedication of the new Aten temple in the desert."

426

"A new temple? I ordered...I do not..." Akhenaten's voice trailed off, not remembering, but also not wanting to reveal his forgetfulness. "Er, yes, that is right, but we will leave later. I am hungry."

"Your majesty, you gave strict orders. Food and drink have been prepared and we must leave immediately if we are to get there before nightfall."

Akhenaten allowed himself to be persuaded, though frowning at his own apparent forgetfulness. The squad of soldiers formed up around their king and, with Khaemnum and Mentopher at their head, marched through the city to the northern stela marking the official boundary. Waiting in the sparse shade of the rock wall were another small group of soldiers with a train of heavily burdened donkeys. The king was shown to one of them.

"I am not going to ride a donkey," Akhenaten stated. "Where is my sedan chair or my golden throne with my Nubian slaves? Even a chariot will do."

"The path is too steep and rocky for a sedan chair or a chariot, your majesty. You must ride the donkey."

The king acquiesced reluctantly and, with help from one of the soldiers, mounted the sturdy beast. Plunging into the shadowed gully that split the cliffs of the north and eastern walls of the city plain, the troop of men started working their way up the dry stream bed. If the way seemed neither as steep nor rocky as he had been led to expect, Akhenaten gave no sign, clinging on hard to the leather girth strap, his eyes fixed on the path just ahead of his animal.

At the top of the cliffs, the path opened out onto the dun-coloured desert that stretched away in great rolling sweeps of sand and rock to the north and east. The path itself curved westward toward the unseen river then north, following the top of the cliffs that closely bordered the valley at this point. From time to time a path would diverge from the main one, usually angling down the rocky slopes to a smudge of blue-green water and vegetation in the distance, less often heading east into the dry and inhospitable interior. The road was almost deserted, the only other travelers being merchants who, on sighting the strange figure of the king with his elongate face and limbs, his rounded belly and his ornate gold pectoral, fell to the ground and prostrated themselves. Akhenaten said nothing, perhaps because his vision obscured the details, but once or twice he moved his hand in the form of a blessing.

The troop traveled as fast as the donkeys would allow, the soldiers trotting alongside the animals and keeping them moving with judicious prods with spear handles, or if a beast became particularly recalcitrant, pricking it into renewed vigor with a spear point. They halted briefly at noon for a hurried meal, the blazing sun beating down on them from above, its fierce rays prickling their skin as if thousands of little hands reached down from the Aten in his glory to caress his subjects below. Akhenaten lifted up his voice in praise, the soldiers standing around patiently while the king sang.

"Why do we allow this folly?" Mentopher growled. "Bind him and be done with it. We could travel much faster."

"And if we were seen by some passing trader or farmer?" Khaemnum queried. "How would it look if we had the king captive? We have to be able to say we traveled at the king's command and when we left him, it was because he ordered us to do so."

Toward dusk they moved off the road and camped in the lea of a rocky outcrop. The king had fallen silent as the day progressed and now ate his frugal evening meal without comment or fuss. He curled up by the fire in a thick woolen blanket to keep out the chill night air, lying on his back and staring up at the blaze of Nut's body with the pale star track of Atum's semen splashed across the velvety blackness.

"I can scarcely make out even the brightest stars," he murmured. "What sort of a king does a blind man make?"

Khaemnum, lying closest to the king, heard him but could not think of anything to say until long past the moment. When he did, he thought the words, not daring to say them out loud. *Then give up being a king and worship your god in peace.*

The next day at dawn, Akhenaten was in good humor once more and led the group in praise of the rising sun. Afterward he smiled as he sat on the back of his donkey as they headed away from the road and into the face of the morning sun. Hours passed and the small party of soldiers moved deeper into the yellow-brown desert, over areas of rock, slipping over loose pebbles and trudging through hot calf-deep sand. As the sun passed the zenith and slipped toward the western horizon, Khaemnum left the troop to rest in the relative cool of a shaded gully and climbed a low hill to stare to the northeast. He returned quickly and ordered the men to set up camp, drawing Mentopher to one side.

"We are almost there. I could see King's Phallus from the top of the hill."

"Then why do we not push on and reach it tonight? Then we can leave him to his fate."

"Because I have a plan." He would say no more but returned to the tiny camp fire of dried donkey dung, joining the king on the upwind side.

"When do we get there?" Akhenaten asked.

"Tomorrow. Not long after dawn."

The king sat and stared at the smoky fire until night fell. He accepted food and water without comment, nibbling on it and sipping the water, at length laying the remnants down on the sand beside him.

"You have been kind to me, Commander Khaemnum. I fear though that the opportunity to repay your kindness is past." Khaemnum said nothing, just watched the dim profile of the king against the starlit heavens. "I am almost blind now," the king went on. "I can only see shapes, light and dark. As a blessing I can still see the Aten. But a blind king cannot rule. It would be better if I walked out into the desert and let my father the Aten take me, would it not?"

"My lord..." Khaemnum could not think what to say, so closed his mouth.

"That is what you mean for me to do tomorrow." Khaemnum found his cheeks wet and hurriedly brushed them away with the back of one hand, grateful the dark hid his shame. Akhenaten sat a few minutes longer, before lying down and pulling the wool blanket over him.

The king was up the next morning in the pre-dawn darkness. He led the soldiers in the hymn to the sun once more then turned to Khaemnum and Mentopher. "Let us do this thing," he said, turning and walking out into the full sun.

Mentopher ran after him and roughly grabbed his arm, pulling him round and shoving him up the slope of the hill. Khaemnum joined them after ordering the soldiers to stay behind, and all three men crested the hill and sighted the pillar of rock together.

"Set's buttocks," Mentopher growled. "Why did we not get closer last night? It will take us all day to get there." He sat down on a rock and wiped his face with his hands.

"Mid-morning," Khaemnum corrected. "Provided we leave now." He smiled at Akhenaten and started toward the distant pillar. The king joined him and so, a curse or two later, did Mentopher.

Three hot hours later, the three men staggered into the tiny patch of shade cast by the rocky pillar. Nothing moved in the heat except the rippling air, yet none of them sweated, the moisture being sucked off them before they even noticed it. Mentopher unplugged the water skin at his side and took a long drink, his throat working convulsively. Khaemnum followed, desperately wanting to drink his fill but knowing he must exercise restraint for the trip back. Akhenaten eyed the water skin, his tongue touching his lips, but he did not beg.

Mentopher saw the look and grinned. "Thirsty, heretic? Here." He tossed a small skin to the king, watching with eager eyes as the king unstoppered the flask with shaking fingers.

The king upended the skin and swallowed, grimacing and lowering it so precipitously that a few ruby drops spilt onto the sand, vanishing without trace in seconds. "Wine? You could not spare water?" he asked calmly.

"You be careful with that, heretic. In this heat wine will make you even thirstier." Mentopher put back his head and roared with laughter. "Never mind, I brought you something to eat too." He threw a small bundle at the king's feet. "Salted mutton."

"You are cruel, Mentopher," Khaemnum said. "There is no need to act like a barbarian." He handed the king the water skin. "One swallow, mind."

Akhenaten took a long pull at the skin and handed it back to the military commander. "I believe I will sit over here in the shade and contemplate the beauty of this land. You had better return, Commander, you will want to be out of the sun before the day gets hot."

Khaemnum nodded and looked to where Mentopher was already retracing his steps. "Wait here, my lord," he said quietly. "Do not despair. Your god will not forget you."

Akhenaten watched the two men walk away, the vagueness of their forms quickly swallowed up by the shifting air. He moved with the shadow as it slowly circled the pillar above him, doing no more than wetting his lips with the wine, resisting the temptation to drink. He ignored the salted meat entirely despite his growing hunger. As he sat, he thought about Kemet and the Aten, how his god both gave life and took it. He smiled at the thought that he would soon be with his god, beyond pain, beyond thirst. Staring into the setting sun the shadows closed around him, narrowing his vision until all he could see was a tunnel lit by his god at the end of it. Akhenaten stood and stretched his arms out, lifting his voice up in praise of the Living Aten one last time. All that issued from his throat was a hoarse croak and the failure made him reel.

As he fell into unconsciousness, he thought he heard a woman cry out, "Father!"

Chapter 36

For generations the walls of Waset had been an unnecessary luxury. They last served their purpose when the Hyksos invaders from the north penetrated into the inner part of the Two Kingdoms. Since then, the massive brickworks of the defensive wall had been allowed to fall into a sad state of disrepair. When the messenger had arrived from the south, his tiny craft flying before current and wind like a great bird, bringing news of another invader, Ay had marshaled the men of Amun's city and set them to work.

The city on the western bank lay defenceless. Built over years in a time of peace, palaces and temples and residential areas lay sprawled amid farmland and orchards. Leaving only a small crew of servants behind to maintain the palace against their return, Ay removed the court to the old palace, bringing with him the guards and masons from the Great Place. It irked him to leave the tombs unguarded but with the favour of the gods the usurper Smenkhkare would be defeated inside a month.

Ay stood on the walls of the old city and stared south along the river, General Nakhtmin beside him. General Psenamy had proved himself to be less than useful and Ay had promoted Nakhtmin, the son of Djetmaktef, over him. Around the two men, teams of men worked feverishly to shore up the defences, bringing freshly quarried stone from across the river and mud bricks newly sun-baked by the river where women and children had been conscripted to do the menial work.

432

"How long have we got?" Ay asked, shading his face with his hands.

Nakhtmin shrugged and leaned back against the rough parapet. "Not long. My spies tell me the rebel is moving north, capturing the cities as he advances. Abu and Edfu fell after fighting, Nekhen capitulated without a struggle, and he nears Esna. If they hold him there, he may be as long as ten days, if not, then a few days."

"Can we defeat him?"

"That is in the hands of the gods. I know if I had been Smenkhkare..."

"Don't use that name," Ay hissed. "He is a rebel, nothing more." He looked around to see if any of the workmen had overheard him. One of the men carrying bricks looked vaguely familiar and Ay frowned, trying to remember.

"Tjaty?" Nakhtmin touched Ay's arm.

Ay tore his attention away from the half-remembered face. "What?"

"I was saying if I was the rebel I would not have stopped to invest the other cities, knowing Horemheb was behind me. Abu maybe, he needed boats, but not the others. It is in our interests that he delays."

"Even if he strengthens his army?"

"Even then. What can he add? A few hundred men of doubtful loyalty. Time is what he does not have."

"So we can defeat him when he arrives?"

"We do not need to. We can sit inside our walls and wait for Horemheb's army to catch up."

"In other words, we cannot."

Nakhtmin smiled. "Tjaty, you must learn to think in a less direct fashion. Not every battle is won by dashing out and confronting the enemy head-on. We have a city we can defend against a larger army than Smen...the rebel has. Wait for Horemheb. That is my counsel."

Ay and General Nakhtmin moved away to stroll along the top of the wall, examining the reconstruction efforts and to view the mass of humans and animals pouring into the city from the surrounding countryside. No matter who fought, the common man ended up being killed, his property destroyed and his wife raped. Though Kemet had been at peace internally for generations, memories lingered and men moved with alacrity to avoid internecine conflict.

As the officials departed, the man carrying the bricks straightened and eased his back, watching the Tjaty with hate filled eyes. "I will be back," he muttered to the man beside him.

"Bring us back a beer, Mahuhy," the other man called.

Mahuhy clambered down the rickety ladder to street level and walked rapidly through the milling crowd of workers until he found himself in the darker, more deserted streets of the dock area. For the next hour or two he slowly worked his way through the taverns and brothels, staying a few minutes, usually just long enough for a few sips of water or beer, a muttered conversation or joke with one of the working girls, before moving on. Behind him, he left a flurry of activity as men, and a few women, hurried off intent on errands of their own.

Sunset saw him moving cautiously through the deeply shadowed streets where the river lapped the pilings of the jetties and piers. This was one area the city walls did not encompass, and to a water-borne army, would be a logical entry point. Earlier, Mahuhy had passed through squads of masons and architects intent on tearing down whole areas of slums and constructing a low wall to protect the exposed underbelly of the city. Naturally, many people objected to the destruction of their homes and the Medjay were kept busy maintaining the peace, or at least Ay's version of it.

Mahuhy, once a Councilor of the king, but now no more than a businessman of Waset, had not been able to openly return to his trade of brothel keeper since fleeing the clutches of Ay's soldiers. Disdaining to leave Waset, he had gone underground, fostering friendships with criminals and beggars, drawing on old favours and garnering new ones. Within a year of the coup that saw Tutankhaten come to the throne, Mahuhy was in a powerful position. He still ran his string of brothels though now through front-women, canny ex-prostitutes who had a head for figures and a sharp nose for profits. Add to that half the taverns in the poorer quarters and judicious contracts placed through venial priests to supply meat and grain from the temple farms to the households of the nobility, and Mahuhy could be reckoned among the richest and most powerful men in Waset. And this despite the fact that only a handful of men knew who he really was. Anonymity was a blessing though, if Ay found him he would die unpleasantly.

The great warehouse sat deserted and dark, down a street that no-one frequented after sunset. Mahuhy stepped up and rapped confidently on a small door in the side of the building, paused and knocked again. The door opened and he stepped through to find a bronze blade at his throat. A flare of light illuminated a group of men as the cover was removed from an oil lamp and Mahuhy grinned, pushing the hand that held the blade to one side.

"Who did you think I was?" Mahuhy asked. "Ay's guards do not politely knock."

The young man holding the dagger sheathed it and scowled. "How was I to know? It is better to be sure than dangling from a noose."

"Good man, Heb. You are learning." Mahuhy scanned the circle of faces in the dim light of the lamp. "Are we all here?"

"Kaha's not here, he got arrested."

"What? Why, for Hapi's sake?"

"Do not concern yourself, Mahuhy; it is nothing to do with our purpose. He got drunk and urinated in the porch of a priest. He will be out tomorrow."

Mahuhy nodded. "Kaha is a drunken idiot. If it wasn't for the fact that he controls the guild of corn merchants, I'd have nothing to do with him."

"Surely not," drawled a lean older man with a puckered scar down his left cheek. "He must spend a fortune in your brothels. I know my cut is substantial."

"Indeed, Rait, if it were not for you and Hay here," Mahuhy gestured at a young man with a cast in one eye. "I would be considerably richer than I am."

"We must all share the wealth that flows from the nobles," Hay murmured. "Though it seems to me that Rait and his 'Sons of Re' protect a better class of brothels than do my 'Sons of Set'. Why should more wealth flow to him, Mahuhy?"

"I would hesitate to call you mistaken," Mahuhy said cheerfully. "But you really must get your scribes to go over your accounts again. I try to be fair to all my friends and business partners. I am deeply indebted to the two largest and bravest gangs of warriors in Waset as I'm sure we all are." He gestured at the other men in the darkened warehouse, their leaping shadows stretching out from the single lamp in their midst. "Paser, your dock workers benefit from the Sons of Re and Set, do they not? And Roma, surely even the armorers are better off for peace in the streets?"

"Oh, indeed," burly Roma said, flexing the massive biceps on his arms, the result of a lifetime's expertise with hammer and anvil. "Their rapaciousness is only exceeded by Ay's Medjay."

"You would rather we withdrew our protection?" Rait asked in a voice as soft as spider silk.

"Or ours?" Hay growled. "It can be arranged."

"No, of course not," Roma grated. "Ay unfettered would be far worse."

"Would you say..." Mahuhy asked, "...That Ay is bad for business?"

The other men stared at the brothel keeper. "What stupidity is this?" A large man limped out of the shadows and confronted Mahuhy. The man's right leg was twisted and shorter than the other and he supported himself with a long staff. "Ay treads on everyone trying to earn a living in Waset. Even my beggars are hounded off the streets despite the valuable service we perform."

Paser snorted. "I don't begrudge your right to beg, friend Menmut, but how can you describe begging as a valuable service?"

Menmut grinned, revealing another deformity hidden by the shadows. One side of his face did not move, remaining leaden and still as the other side flexed and creased. "Why, friend Paser, our presence reminds those more fortunate that the gods smile on them, no matter how hard their lives."

"If I might ask again," Mahuhy said. "Is Ay bad for business?"

"Of course. We all know this."

"Then you will be interested to hear of who threatens Ay's peace of mind. Someone is coming to attack Waset."

"Old news," yawned Menmut. "My spies heard about the bandit horde five days ago."

"It is true," Hay agreed. "We have all known of this for days. What else has Ay been doing than prepare the defences?"

"What have you heard?" Rait asked sharply. "You would not waste our time with something as obvious as a gang of bandits."

"Indeed, no," Mahuhy said. "Who leads this gang?"

"One bandit is much the same as another," Roma growled, glancing at the leaders of the Sons of Set and Re.

"He calls himself the Son of Sobek, so I hear," Rait said. "If it's the same gang from Nubia."

"It is." Mahuhy found it hard not to grin. "And it's not some son of the crocodile god, it's Smenkhkare."

"Horse dung. He died. They buried him."

"They buried tokens only," Menmut said slowly. "One of my people saw the sarcophagus before it was sealed. His body was never found."

"That's because it was eaten. Our beloved king Smenkhkare lies as crocodile shit at the bottom of the river."

"Ay does not believe that and I'll tell you why," Mahuhy said. "I was on the King's Council and in the days immediately following the disappearance, when we were all in fear of our lives, I met a man whose brother works for Ay. He says this other man reported to Ay behind locked doors of what happened on the king's hunting expedition, and afterward, Ay had the man killed."

Menmut grimaced, though the expression could have been a smile. "Hearsay, Mahuhy. Have you nothing better to go on."

"I overheard Ay and General Nakhtmin talking on the walls this afternoon. They spoke of Smenkhkare and how they depend on Horemheb getting here in time."

"Would Smenkhkare be better for us than Ay?" Roma asked.

"Smenkhkare is more likely to support the army than the boy. A bigger army means more weapons for your guild to make."

"What of the dock workers?" asked Paser.

"A vigorous young man as king means a strong Kemet trading with the world. More trade, more ships, more work. And as for you others, well, I know Kaha as the guild of corn merchants will benefit from stability, and if Smenkhkare returns maybe his sister Beketaten will too..."

"If she's still alive," Heb interjected.

"Pray to Het-Heru she is. She was always kind to the poor and unfortunates of the city. Menmut, your beggars will benefit too."

"This is all very well," Rait said slowly. "You all benefit by Smenkhkare's return and I can see where this conversation is leading, but what's in it for us, Mahuhy? The last thing Hay and I need is a strong, stable government. That means a strong army and Medjay and the next thing you know, I'm hanging from the walls with the crows picking my eyes out." The gang leader shook his head. "No thanks, I'm better off if Ay rules."

Hay nodded his support and the two men started toward the door.

"There is one thing you might consider, gentlemen," Mahuhy said, making no attempt to block their exit. "Think back five years. Where did you find your wealth?"

Hay turned and cocked his head to one side. "What are you getting at?"

"You robbed the nobles, you intercepted rich caravans, and you took a cut of all the riches that poured into Waset. Where do you get it now?"

"From merchants and small businesses as protection," Rait stated. "A lot more work for less profit. Do you think things would return to the old days?"

"I cannot promise it, Rait," Mahuhy said. "Smenkhkare may tighten the laws but surely he will look favourably on any who assist him now?"

"What would you have us do?"

"What I would have you all do if Smenkhkare attacks the city. Use your followers to disrupt the defence, open the gates if you can, riot so that the Medjay are busy with you rather than fighting our king."

Menmut thought about it for a few minutes, the other men looking to him for his decision. At last the leader of the beggar's guild nodded. "If I can do it I will, but I will not risk my people in pitched battle with soldiers or Medjay. If Smenkhkare returns, I will help him." The others nodded their acceptance, the two gang leaders last of all.

"Thank you," Mahuhy said simply. "General Nakhtmin thinks we have five to ten days before the king arrives, so I suggest you use the time making plans."

General Nakhtmin was wrong. Two days later at dawn, the lookouts on the city wall sounded the alarm and the officer of the watch, General Psenamy ordered the gates closed. Within minutes, Ay and his main advisers joined Psenamy on the wall, looking south to where the river was now covered with a scattering of white sails, the waters chopped by oars stroking in time as the fleet sped toward the city.

"Your advice?" Ay asked.

"Sit tight." General Nakhtmin shrugged. "It is a very pretty sight but what can he do? Smenkhkare will sit outside these walls until Horemheb arrives."

"That is not honourable," Psenamy said vehemently. "When Smenkhkare arrives we should allow him time to rest his men then assemble the army. We must, of course, meet him in battle."

"Fool," Nakhtmin muttered. "Do you want to hand the city to him? Smenkhkare has twice as many men as us."

"I fear the general is right, Tjaty," Usermontju said. "My Medjay are zealous but they are no match for trained soldiers. I say we wait for Horemheb to arrive."

Ay looked at his other advisers. "What about you? Do you have an opinion?"

Bakt shook his head. "I will pray to Lord Amun. This is his city, he will not forsake us."

"I am only a scribe," said Treasurer Maya. "I can manage the financial affairs of the Kingdoms, but I am not competent to comment on military matters."

"At last, somebody who realizes it," Nakhtmin snarled. "There is nothing to see here, Ay. I suggest we head down for breakfast."

"You can eat at a time like this?" Maya's eyebrows rose.

"A soldier learns to eat when he can."

Smenkhkare's fleet landed a little south of the city and his army disembarked. He had the boats drawn up and secured, then set up a defensive perimeter and sent scouts out to survey the city defenses. By mid-day he was sitting in his tent, sipping fresh river water and contemplating the high walls of the city and planning his next actions.

Chapter 37

T he journey from Zarw to Waset occupied the worst month of
Scarab's life. The first day was the horror of saying goodbye to
her infant son, ameliorated only by the knowledge she was
leaving him in the hands of doting grandparents. Her letter to
Paramessu had gone with an army messenger, also taking the news of
her brother Smenkhkare's resurrection. She explained how she must go
to his side and help him if she could, but that she could only do this if
she knew her infant son Set was in good hands. "I will be back inside
three months--six at the most," she wrote. "I will be there to see his
first steps, to hear his first words. I am torn by my decision but I have
to do this." Pleading with Paramessu to return to Zarw at the first
opportunity, to see his son, she filled the rest of the short scroll with
protestations of her love. That first day, on a small fishing boat
scudding down the canal toward the great river, she nearly asked them
to turn around, to go back, as the pain in her heart grew too great.
Alone with three men--Khu, Nebhotep and a taciturn young boatman
the very antithesis of the garrulous Amenhotep of their voyage to Iunu-
-Scarab missed the company of Meryam and being able to talk of
womanly things.

"He'll be missing me. What if Set won't feed?" Scarab asked
anxiously of Nebhotep. "I have milk, he should be drinking mine."

"You were there, Scarab. We found him an excellent wet-nurse and
Paramessu's parents will provide him with the best of care. You could

not do better your..." Nebhotep bit his lip, but Scarab completed the sentence and burst into tears, running off to the stern of the small boat to look out into their wake longingly. For days, Scarab turned any conversation inevitably to the subject of her abandonment of her beloved baby and would not be consoled by any clumsy male attempts to soften the impact of her loss. For a reason that neither Khu nor Nebhotep could understand, the contradictory ideas that Set was better off without her or worse off, produced equally disastrous effects. In the end they decided her illogicality was something uniquely female and left her alone. This did not work either, as she then accused them of not caring.

By the end of the first week, at about the time they passed Ineb Hedj, aided by a fresh northerly wind, Scarab's milk was drying up. Mixed emotions flared again--relief at the cessation of soreness and the embarrassment of damp gowns, but sorrow that now she could not even pretend she was a mother. As long as she was producing milk she could cling to the notion that if by some miracle Set was restored to her, nothing would have changed. Now that her milk had ceased to flow, she could not even feed her own baby. She cried herself to sleep most nights.

"I should have brought Set. I could have sat up here in the bows and looked after him without getting in the way."

"Scarab, you know that's not true," Khu chided, forgetting his decision not to get involved in any 'baby' conversations. "We are going into a war. That is no place for a baby."

Scarab stamped her foot and turned her back on the men, refusing to speak again until the evening meal. As usual, the small craft did not risk sailing at night but was beached at dusk and, if no villages were nearby, they made a small fire and roasted fish caught during the day. If they were near habitation, their meal could be eked out with bread and vegetables. Judge Seti had provided them with a small box of copper and silver to provide for necessities. It was enough to last them until they arrived in Waset.

"I'm sorry, Khu," Scarab murmured that night as she accepted a roast fish from the lad. "I should not have been so rude. You are right; we are going into a war."

Khu blushed and muttered something indistinctly, turning his attention to his meal. He glanced at Nebhotep and winked.

"I have been thinking," Scarab went on. "Of what use are we going to be to my brother when we find him?"

"Use? I don't think the king will be looking for a use for his sister," Khu replied with a laugh. "Just having you there will be enough. Our physician too will be an asset. There will be a need for doctors after a battle. And as for me..." Khu flexed his arms. "A good strong man like me will probably be asked to lead the battle."

Scarab shied a pebble at Khu, hitting him on the leg. "Be serious. I'm not just going to sit around like the other women looking beautiful while men fight for my brother."

"What makes you think you're beautiful?" Khu laughed again and dodged another pebble. "Anyway, what can women do? Organize the servants maybe, or help Nebhotep?"

"I could fight. Meny taught me...don't look at me like that. When those thugs attacked us in Waset, I killed two of them while you just got yourself stabbed."

"That was just luck. You surprised them."

"I could take you, Khu."

Khu laughed and slapped his leg, looking at Nebhotep and the boatman for support. "If I was asleep, maybe."

"Try me." Scarab stood up and dusted the dirt off her hands. "Show me you're a better fighter."

"Come on, Scarab, I'm not going to fight you. What would it prove? I'm bigger and stronger and anyway, I wouldn't want to risk you getting hurt."

"You won't hurt me. You won't even touch me. We'll use twigs as daggers, Nebhotep can adjudicate and the fight ends after the first hit to the body."

Khu sighed noisily. "I don't want to fight you, Scarab. Nebhotep, help me out here. She shouldn't be doing anything strenuous so soon...er, you know..." All three men looked at Scarab warily, waiting for a fresh outburst of tears.

"So soon after I've had a baby, you mean," Scarab said with barely a tremor. "Tell him, Nebhotep. Physical exercise would benefit me."

The physician nodded. "That is true. The muscles need toning again. You will need to exercise care, but I cannot see any harm coming from it." He smiled. "Except perhaps injured pride."

Full night had fallen by now but they threw more wood on the fire and cleared a small area of stones and sticks. Nebhotep selected two twigs of equal size and handed them to Scarab and Khu.

"Now I don't want any injuries," Nebhotep admonished. "Arms and bodies only. Nothing near the head or below the waist. If either of you get hurt I will tell the king you recklessly endangered yourselves." He stepped back. "Fight."

Scarab stepped back two paces and unfastened her gown, letting it fall to the ground with a sibilant whisper. Below it she wore only a brief kilt, her breasts, though shrinking back to their former size, swung in a most provocative manner as she moved.

Khu's eyes left their watch of Scarab's, his attention wandering downward and Scarab leaped forward, her left arm suddenly raised at eye level, her right hand held low. Khu jumped and flinched away from her left hand, bringing his twig up even as he fell back, then cried out as her twig snapped on his ribs.

Scarab retreated and tossed the broken twig on the ground, grinning. "See? I told you I could take you."

"That's not fair," Khu said, rubbing his ribcage. "I was distracted."

"Yes, you were rather," Nebhotep laughed. "Still, in war you fight anyway you can just to survive. Scarab wins."

"Wait. As I said, I was taken by surprise. She could not do that again, now that I'm ready for her tricks."

"Up to you, Scarab." Nebhotep cocked his head enquiringly. "You won but you can fight him again if you want."

"Why not? I don't have to distract a man to win."

They faced each other again across a few paces of sand and circled slowly, each looking for an opening. Scarab feinted and as Khu made to block the blow, slashed, forgetting the twig had only stabbing capabilities. She leapt back out of the way and started circling again, her feet feeling the irregularities of the ground. Khu suddenly tossed the twig to his other hand and stabbed. Scarab backed away quickly, her defence confused by the switch and the twig grazed her stomach. She weaved her 'blade' to and fro, watching Khu's eyes follow it. Hiding a smile she moved it across at chest height then jumped, making her breasts bounce. At the same moment she swept forward with her hand, stabbing for his chest again. His hand came across, knocking her arm aside and his twig snapped against her side.

"Fornication," she shouted, throwing down her weapon. "That was too low. It was on my waist."

"My lady." Khu bowed and straightened, grinning. "Though I don't think such expressions are commonly uttered by of a lady of the court."

"A fair blow," Nebhotep confirmed. "Scarab, you cannot rely on men being distracted by your er, attributes."

"Again," Scarab grated. "I will not be beaten."

Khu shook his head. "Enough, Scarab. We have won one apiece. Let us call it a draw and be done with it."

Scarab bent and snatched up her twig from the ground and lunged at Khu, weaving and feinting. Unarmed, Khu fell back, his eyes watchful, circling the fire. "Stand still," Scarab muttered. She lunged again and Khu ducked to one side, grabbing hold of her right arm, pulling her off balance. Exerting his strength, he bent her arm forward, pressing it inexorably toward her chest, despite her flailing left fist. With a cry of anger she dropped the twig just before it touched her and Khu let go, pushing her backward and scooped it up as it fell. Leaping forward, he gave her no time to recover her balance and rammed the twig home against her ribs. Scarab sat down hard and swore colourfully.

Khu tossed the fragments of twig into the fire and extended his hand to the fallen girl. "Never fight angry," he said. "My father taught me that."

Scarab slapped his hand aside and scrambled to her feet, her eyes blazing. She snatched her gown up and stormed off into the darkness.

"Scarab, wait," Khu cried out and started after her.

"Leave her to cool down, Khu." Nebhotep put a hand out to restrain him. "Nobody likes losing, royalty least of all. Her pride is wounded, best let her heal by herself."

"But she's alone out there. Anything could happen. Bandits...or a lion."

"She's not gone far. She may be angry but she's no fool." Nebhotep stood with his back to the fire and looked out into the darkness. "There," he said, nodding in the direction of the river, "She's sitting by that tree."

Khu watched anxiously for a while, then sighed and joined the others on the blankets by the fire. The boatman, true to his nature, had watched the entire drama without saying a word or indicating by action that anything untoward was happening. Nebhotep was curled up snoring, and Khu settled down, determined to remain awake until Scarab returned to the fire.

Khu woke at dawn to find Scarab's blanket still unslept on. He leapt up in alarm before he saw her sitting against the tree, head bowed and resting on her arms, asleep. She woke as he crunched across the gravel toward her.

Scarab smiled tentatively as Khu approached. "I'm sorry. I behaved stupidly last night."

"That's all right," Khu replied. "You actually fought very well for a girl."

Scarab's lips tightened. "I'll try you again one day, Khu, but not just yet." She looked over at the embers of the fire where the boatman was attempting to coax a flame out of the ashes with some dried bark. "Is there any food? I'm starving."

The northerly breeze backed to the west after Ineb Hedj, then a few days later to the southwest, forcing them to run against the current and the winds. They passed Akhet-Aten under cover of night, not wanting to risk being seen by the guards.

"Akhenaten could help us," Nebhotep suggested.

Scarab shook her head. "More likely the guards Ay put on him would arrest us...or kill us."

The southwesterly wind freshened, deflecting off the river cliffs and swirling in random gusts over their boat, making the small sail flap and shake. Their progress slowed considerably and more ominously, as they crept southward they started to find scattered wreckage and one or two bloated bodies lodged in the reeds.

Nebhotep would not allow Scarab to see the bodies close up, but he examined them with a surgeon's eye and reported his findings. "They drowned, I'd say, and weeks ago."

"So they were fishermen?" Khu asked.

"No, they wore soldiers' kilts, but there were no wounds on them save for the fish and crocodiles." He patted Scarab's knee reassuringly. "There has been no great battle yet."

"But something is happening. And the battle may be on land anyway." Scarab turned to the impassive boatman. "How long to Waset?"

The man shrugged. "Four days...five maybe."

The river turned northeast just after that, as it flowed in the great loop named for the principal city on that part of the river, Iunet. Sacred to the goddess Het-Heru, the community was small and they felt no need to hide as they passed. The wind, which for the last day had been behind them as the river turned, now swung round to oppose them as they sailed past Iunet, and they found themselves drifting shorewards.

An oared warship put out from the Iunet docks, rapidly overhauling them. A grappling hook hauled them closer and soldiers poured over the sides into the small boat, hauling them up onto the deck of the warship and in front of the officer.

"Who are you and what is your business?" the officer snapped. "Quickly now, I am a busy man."

"Not good," Nebhotep muttered. "What side is he on?"

Scarab shook herself free of the soldier holding her and drew herself up, staring the officer down. "How dare you treat me in this way? I am returning to Waset from my estates and I do not appreciate your men man-handling me. What is your name and rank? I am going to report your behavior to your superior."

The officer flushed but stood his ground. "I am sorry for any hurt, lady. Perhaps if you would tell me who you are..."

"You are impertinent. I shall report you to the king."

"Ah!" The officer smiled. "Which king then?"

"What do you mean? The king in Waset, of course."

"Have you not heard, lady? There are two. King Smenkhkare has returned to claim his Kingdoms."

Scarab almost collapsed with relief and she heard Khu and Nebhotep exhale noisily. The boatman just looked on impassively. "You call Smenkhkare king still?" she asked. "Was he not killed by a crocodile?"

"No, lady, he was not. Now, what is your name?"

"I am Beketaten, sister to the king. You will take me to him immediately."

The officer heard the tone of command in the young woman's voice and his confidence wavered and fell apart. "Er, yes, lady Beketaten."

Scarab quickly scanned the open deck of the warship. "You will also rig a sail as a sunshade over there," she said, pointing aft. "I will require something to sit on, some decent food and wine. Please see to it, Captain..." She put a suitable amount of interrogation into her last comment, and the officer stumbled to reply, his voice losing its overlay of superiority.

"A...Amentes, my lady, and I...I is not a captain. I is a Leader of a Hundred."

"Then, Amentes, Leader of a Hundred, you have your orders." Scarab strolled toward the rear of the vessel, acting as if she owned it. Sailors and soldiers stared after her, grinning at their Leader's discomfiture. "Oh, one other thing, Amentes. Pay off our boatman, would you? Five pieces of silver should be sufficient. One of your men has my silver. Bring the rest to me when you have done so." Without waiting for an acknowledgment, Scarab carried on to the aft of the warship and sat on the deck, staring out over the water.

Khu and Nebhotep knelt beside her. "Most accomplished, my lady," Nebhotep murmured. "Your breeding shows in times like these."

"Thank you, Nebhotep," Scarab replied, her voice shaking. "It's been a long time and I wasn't sure I could carry it off."

The voyage to Waset took the rest of the day and a further day and night, the familiar landscape appearing out of the darkness with the dawn. The armed warship with its many oarsmen meant they did not have to pull into the shore at night, but could keep forging upriver. Amentes was most attentive, making sure that every small comfort that the fighting ship could provide was available for his guest. Scarab learned that Smenkhkare's army had arrived outside Waset only five days before, several ships sailing on past to secure any forces of the Tjaty that could later threaten them. They had found few men, Amentes said, and fewer supplies and had been about to return when they spotted her ladyship's boat.

"How is the king? Is he in good health?"

Amentes puzzled over that one. "Well, I don'ts gets to see him too much, if you knows what I mean, your ladyship. I mean, he's the king and all and I'm just a low officer. He was hurt bad by the crocodile though, that's I know, him and his friend Menkure."

"They are scarred?" Nebhotep asked.

Amentes nodded. "Right across the body." He drew his hands across his torso, demonstrating the extent of the wounds. "Some on his face too, and Menkure has a awful limp."

Scarab shuddered and tried to prepare herself for the sight of her brother as the ship drew up to the eastern bank of the river just south of the city. Amentes immediately hailed another officer and sent him to warn the king while he and a squad of his men escorted Scarab through the sprawling camp.

The king's tent sat on a low knoll about a thousand paces from the river, overlooking the southern gate and the great pylons of the temple of Amun. The tent sides were folded back and the figure of a man sat on a high-backed chair staring out toward the city. Beside him stood another man leaning on a long staff and Scarab knew as they approached that this was her long-lost brother and his close friend Menkure. Her initial idea of running forward to throw her arms about him died as she saw his unmoving regard of the small procession winding its way through the camp.

"He has changed," Khu muttered.

"Wouldn't you?" Nebhotep asked. "He has literally been in the mouth of a god and returned to tell of it. That would change any man."

"He is my brother," Scarab murmured. "But he is also the king."

The procession came to a halt at the bottom of the low knoll and Amentes saluted before dropping to his knees in the sandy soil, followed by the men in his squad. "Great king, I bring the one who calls herself Lady Beketaten."

The man on the throne stared down at the woman standing among the kneeling men of the guard. He nodded and said something to the man standing behind him, who limped forward.

"Let the lady and her companions approach and make obeisance to Djeserkheperu Smenkhkare, King of Upper and Lower Kemet, Lord of the Two Lands, Ankhkheperure, Son of Re, Lord of Crowns, Holy of Manifestations, Given life forever continually."

Scarab, with Khu and Nebhotep trailing behind, approached the throne. She fell to her knees and bowed her head to the ground three times before sitting back on her heels with her head bowed. Behind her, her companions followed her lead.

"My lord Smenkhkare," Scarab said quietly. "My heart rejoices to see you. I thank the gods of our Kemet that you have been restored to us."

"Lady Beketaten, sister, you are welcome."

"May I present my companions, and your loyal Councillors, Lord Khu and Lord Nebhotep?"

The king nodded, the scarred tissue of his face twisting as he spoke. "They too are welcome."

"What is your pleasure, my lord king? We exist to serve you."

Smenkhkare sat silent for a long time, staring down at the three kneeling figures in front of his throne. "My wish," he said at last, "Is that you rise and greet your brother as you used to."

Scarab looked up and saw Smenkhkare stand. She gasped as the gown draped over his shoulders fell away, revealing the scarred and puckered body that was the legacy of the crocodile god Sobek. She wept as she rose to her feet and embraced her brother, feeling the ridges of scar tissue criss-crossing his back.

"Do you still call yourself Scarab, or has that gone the way of childhood's things? You have grown to be a woman, a beautiful one that rivals my brother's wife Nefertiti."

"I am still known by that name, my lord."

Smenkhkare released his sister and bade the men stand. "Nebhotep, there will be work for a physician soon."

"My skills are at your disposal, great king."

"And Khu, the faithful one. I shall have to give you lands as befits a noble lord. Come to me when I retake my throne and we will choose your estate together." The king grinned, a hungry grin without humor. "One of Ay's estates, I think. He will not need them."

"Thank you, great king."

"Stay close to my Scarab for now, Lord Khu. She is precious to me." He nodded, dismissing them and turned to his sister once more. "You have come just in time, Scarab. Ay rejects my demands." He pointed out over the plain to a single stake with a small rounded object atop it. Crows wheeled above it, landing briefly and taking off again. "See his messenger," he laughed. "Now he can see my response."

"Brother," Scarab gasped. "Why did you kill him? He was surely just a messenger?"

"He brought unwelcome news." Smenkhkare shook his head. "No matter, he was just a man. Many more will die before I am on my throne again."

"What will you do?"

"I have waited outside the gates of my Waset long enough. It is time to take the city. Menkure, have the trumpets sound. Muster my army."

As Menkure turned to go, a distant ram's horn sounded urgently from upriver, then another, closer. Smenkhkare wheeled and stared toward the river, where a great roar of voices arose into the rippling morning air. A man, a Nubian officer bearing the badges of his rank on his linen headdress, ran up and prostrated himself briefly before rising and saluting his king.

"My lord king, ships on the river, many of them. Horemheb has come."

Chapter 38

"Horemheb has the gift of timing," Smenkhkare said with a wry grimace. "However, I am glad the waiting is at an end." He strode down the hillock toward the river with the camp in an uproar as the officers strove to get their men into ranks. "Menkure, send Kashta and Shabaqo with their archers to the river. They are to harass the landing. Psuro is to take his shielded spearmen and oppose the landing physically. He is to throw them back if he is able, the archers to support him in that if they establish a landing."

Menkure saluted and limped off, bellowing orders to his officers. For all that the camp resembled a kicked ant's nest; the trained discipline of the soldiers quickly became apparent. Smenkhkare turned to Scarab.

"What am I to do with you, sister? And your friends?"

"Give me a sword and I can fight. So can Khu, he is almost as good as me."

"I think not." He beckoned to Amentes, who had not gone far after delivering his charges to the king. "Amentes, you will guard my sister with your life, as will you Khu. Physician, there will be many men seeking your help shortly, both to stay in this life and to leave it. Make yourself useful where you can." He gathered the rest of his guards around him and set off for the river at a fast jog.

Smenkhkare caught up with Menkure and Psuro's spearmen as they started to set their formations, phalanxes of men with hippopotamus-hide shields and helmets and armed with bronze-tipped spears twice the height of a man. The ships on the river slowed and turned toward the eastern shore, coming under a cloud of arrows as they drew within range.

"There are not as many as I thought there would be," the king said.

"He must have lost more coming through the cataracts."

The Nubian infantry under Kasaya and Aspalta signaled their readiness and Smenkhkare gave the order to advance down through the rough ground near the river's edge. Kashta's archer company hurried round to cover the attempted landing while Shabaqo's continued to torment the ships. As they got closer, a hail of arrows returned and men started falling. The boats shuddered as they grounded, sliding up onto the muddy banks, men leaping from them and dying. Others jumped over the bodies pushed forward, their curved bronze swords at the ready. Officers yelled orders, their calls mixing with the screams of the wounded.

"Forward!" Psuro called and the spearmen responded, moving down through the hillocked scrub. The rough ground interfered with their steady movement and gaps appeared in the line, which Horemheb's soldiers exploited. The spears were too long for the soldiers to get to grips with their enemies though and gradually the hundreds of men landed from the boats were pushed back toward the water.

"We have them," Menkure exulted. "Come on, men, another push and the dogs will run." The ram's horn blew again and the lighter infantry started around the edges of the spearmen, cutting into Horemheb's men as they tried to squeeze out from between the spears and the water.

"Where's Horemheb?" Smenkhkare asked, scanning the line of battle. "It is not like him to miss a fight." The king suddenly frowned. "How could he miss the fight unless..." He turned and looked inland and upriver where a cloud, alone in the blazing hot blue of the sky, drifted slowly down toward him. He called a runner to him and sent him off, out of the battle to investigate the cloud. He was back within minutes.

"Soldiers, lord king, an army. They will be here within minutes."

Smenkhkare swore. "It is Horemheb," he yelled at Menkure over the cacophony of the battle. "The cunning bastard landed his main force south of here. This is just a decoy to keep us busy."

"We must withdraw then, my lord. This ground is too rough to stand against a proper army."

The horns sounded again, urgently, and the combatants separated, Smenkhkare's troops streaming back, away from the river to the plains near their camp. As they ran they could see another army racing toward them from the south and fear gave them strength. They reached their positions mere hundreds of paces ahead of Horemheb's troops and they turned on the shouted orders of the officers, readying themselves for the onslaught.

Horemheb's men came on as a roaring tide of men, all semblance of order lost in the wild race across the plain. Then trumpets blared stridently, cutting through the din, and the mass of men slowed and stopped. Panting, exhausted men staggered back and formed into their units while keeping a wary eye on the army ranged in front of them.

"I was hoping they'd just keep coming," Menkure said. "They'd lost all cohesion and we could have smashed them."

"I keep telling you, Horemheb's no fool. He's one of Kemet's best generals and he knows the art of warfare." Smenkhkare grinned. "What he doesn't know is that I'm better."

The two armies stood and faced each other across two hundred paces of sand and rocky earth. Smenkhkare's men stood in five companies--spearmen in the middle, their long bronzed spears glittering in the bright sunlight; on either side a company of light infantry; and on the flanks, the mobile archers. Horemheb chose a more conventional array, concentrating the bulk of his men in the centre and two long curving arms of men out to either side like the horns of a bull.

"He thinks to charge us like the strong bull of Heru and envelop us with his horns," Smenkhkare grinned. "Well, I have the answer to his tactic."

Fifty paces behind the king, with Amentes guarding her, stood Scarab. She scanned the field of what would soon become a raging battle, noting but not fully understanding the arrangements that General and King were making. The thought of another king touched her mind and she turned and stared up at the walls of the city. She thought she could recognise two of the many lining the top--an old man and a boy-king.

On the south wall of Waset, high above the great carved wooden South Gate, and shaded by the massive pylons of the temple of Amun, Ay looked out on the plains with Tutankhaten and Queen Ankhesenpaaten at his side. Their spirits had risen, fallen and risen again over the last hour as the initial stages of the battle played out beneath them. Cheering had broken out from the multitudes of courtiers lining the walls as the fleet hove into view, a hush descending as the rebel army threw the rescuers back. Then came the unexpected appearance of Horemheb's main army, flying the banner of the Amun legion, and joy won out again. Now they stared down at two evenly matched armies.

"What will you do, Tjaty?" Usermontju asked. "My Medjay are ready for any task."

"Do? The Tjaty will do nothing. I am king; I will lead my troops into battle."

Everyone turned, startled, to where the young king Tutankhaten stood with the queen, his cousin Ankhesenpaaten. Looking out over the dusty plain to where the armies stood facing each other, the king no longer looked like a little boy, but rather a young man showing a rare spark of courage, a determination to have his own way.

"I am your king," he repeated. "It is my right and my duty to lead my people." Without conscious thought, the nobility gathered around broke into applause. Tutankhaten beamed and stuck his chest out. "I will lead my loyal troops into battle and win a glorious victory over the enemies of our Kemet."

"My lord king, that is not a good idea." Ay stood with his fists clenched and a black scowl on his face. The applause died away to a few desultory claps and faces turned, cautious but expectant, waiting for the clash of the king with his Tjaty and uncle. "You have never led troops into battle and those enemies you say you will defeat are fellow Kemetu for the most part. This is not a time for glory but for survival."

Tutankhaten paled and his queen gasped in outrage. "How dare you speak to me like that?" the king said, his voice rising into a shrill treble. "Guards, guards, a...arrest the Tjaty."

Ay did not even trouble to look at the sudden flustered indecision of the guards but reached out and grabbed the boy king by his upper arm and strode across to the edge of the wall, dragging Tutankhaten with him. He ignored the cries of 'Sacrilege' and 'Treason', instead pointing out toward the armies. Ay lowered his voice and spoke quietly but very firmly into the king's ear.

"Men are dying out there--for you. Willingly for the most part, but it is not a game, it is not an exercise with toy soldiers; it is not an opportunity for glory. They are doing it so we can stop the greatest danger we have faced in many years. That is your brother Smenkhkare who faces us. He wants to rip Kemet apart in a civil war and kill you so he can rule alone. Make no mistake, young Nebkheperure, your brother is a skilled soldier and if you went out there he would cut you down without having to think about it." Ay relaxed his grip on the king's arm and put his arm around his shoulders. "You will not go out there. Do you understand?"

Tutankhaten sniffed loudly and rubbed his bruised upper arm with his other hand. "I told them I would. I cannot go back on my word." His words shook as he fought down the fear that consumed him whenever he heard anger in his uncle's voice.

"You can and you will," Ay snapped. "General Nakhtmin will lead our troops out to help Horemheb, when I judge the time to be ripe. Now, you have something to tell your court, do you not?"

Tutankhaten shivered and brushed away years. "What...what do I say, uncle?"

Ay smiled and stroked the boy's head gently. "You say that you have reconsidered the situation, taking into account the advice of your experienced counselors and have decided to place General Nakhtmin in command. In such an important battle, nothing must be left to chance." He pushed his king gently back toward his scowling queen and unhappy courtiers.

Tutankhaten stumbled through his speech before seeking solace in the arms of Ankhesenpaaten. The young woman adopted a scornful visage but refrained from saying what was obviously on her mind. The courtiers decided it was really none of their business and tried to look disinterested in the whole affair.

Ay addressed Nakhtmin and formally ordered him to assemble the garrison troops and Medjay together by the South Gate, in preparation to leading them out against Smenkhkare's rebels. Nakhtmin saluted and strode off, barking orders to his officers.

Standing to one side, his face muffled by bandages and a thin cloak, Mahuhy heard the orders and, murmuring to the men standing beside him, issued his own instructions. The group of ordinary citizens left their duties on the wall and hurried after the general. As they started down the wooden scaffolding that was the means of access for the common people, Mahuhy heard a woman scream with excitement, "Look, the battle is starting!"

From the plains to the south of the city, arose a roar of men's voices. Horemheb's soldiers drummed their short, curved bronze swords on their small, circular leather shields, the rhythmic noise stirring the senses as men's heartbeats matched the pounding beat. With a yell of derision they leapt forward, charging down on the spearmen.

Smenkhkare's men stood firm, their long spears leveled and poking out a full man length ahead of them, a great bronze-tipped forest of death. Soldiers threw themselves forward and died, impaled. Others took their places, screaming insults to keep their courage up, hacking futilely at the spearmen still out of reach. Then a young man fell, the enemy's spear ripping through his chest and out through his back. The spearman could not free his weapon and it was plucked from his grasp as his victim collapsed. A friend of the young man danced into the gap and plunged his sword into the defenceless spearman. Others in the formation could not turn their spears swiftly enough, nor, being engaged in fighting for their lives, could they put their spears down and attack the enemy in their midst with swords. The hole grew larger, then another appeared and between one thrust of the spears and the next, the whole company disintegrated, the front lines of both armies breaking up into pairs of soldiers desperately trying to kill each other.

The weight of Horemheb's centre started to push the disorganized spearmen back. At the same time, the long horns of the army started forward and out, running lithely across the sand as they drew the enemy out of his formation in an effort to remain in contact. Smenkhkare's infantry companies stretched and lost their cohesiveness, becoming another column of running men, matching the movements of their enemies.

"Curse the man. They are breaking our formations," Menkure yelled, forgetting himself so much in the excitement of the moment that he thumped his king on his arm.

"I see it," Smenkhkare agreed. "Send the archers out." The ram's horn sounded again and Shabaqo and Kashta led their squads of archers out wide, racing a hundred paces past the infantry columns before spreading out. They knelt and proceeded to unleash a devastating hail of arrows into the flanks and backs of Horemheb's army. A flint-barbed missile struck the priest holding the banner of Amun aloft and the emblem of the Amun legion disappeared into the clouds of dust churned up by thousands of feet. Smenkhkare's men roared in triumph, but a few moments later it rose again as another priest raised it aloft.

Horemheb gave a command and squads of men ran out to engage the archers and halt their depredations. The Nubian commanders were under no illusions as to their men's ability to withstand armed and armored soldiers and they all took to their heels. Being unencumbered by anything heavier than bows and bundles of arrows, they quickly outdistanced them, before suddenly turning and delivering a concentrated hail of arrows on their pursuers. The survivors from Horemheb's squads limped back to the relative security of the massed army and the archers moved in again.

Three times Horemheb tried to smash the archers and three times he failed. The trumpets sounded at last and the horns of the bull withdrew into the head. Here the heavily armed men were still moving forward, pushing the centre of Smenkhkare's army back. The spearmen now lost all cohesiveness and as their ranks disintegrated, they threw down their long spears and hefted the swords and clubs they carried in their belts. The battle became a milling mass of men fighting a thousand duels, stabbing, thrusting and hacking.

The weight of numbers started to tell and though there were no specific commands given or tactics displayed, Horemheb's men started to push Smenkhkare's men back toward Waset, slipping and stumbling over the blood-slicked ground and the bodies lying like a wheat field after a summer storm. Many of the fallen still lived and hauled themselves with limbs crushed or amputated, entrails spilling out, toward the others still, daggers in hand. Those who had lost their weapons found more strewn about the battlefield, or else forsook arms altogether, using fingernails and teeth to extract the life of the enemy. Above everything hung the stench of blood and burst guts, and a cry ascended through the choking dust to the azure heavens from a thousand tortured bodies.

"We cannot go on," Menkure screamed, his eyes wide in his dusty and sweat-soaked face. He slashed at a soldier who stumbled within reach and took a step backward. "The only men we are not using are the archers and they cannot shoot for fear of hitting us."

Smenkhkare laid about him with his own sword, his right arm covered with bright blood. His once-white kilt now was streaked and stained with sweat and gore and he panted as he fought, grudgingly retreating before the press of the enemy. "If we lose here...we are dead...they'll never...leave us...alive."

Psuro fought his way to the king's side. A savage cut across his chest had released a flood of blood, now caked and drying on his dark skin. "You must retreat, my lord king. My spearmen, such as they are, will hold the enemy long enough to give you a chance."

Smenkhkare scowled, but dropped back, leaning on his wounded commander. "Hold them to a count of a hundred, Psuro. No more. Then you turn and run. If we can get a gap between the armies again, the archers could yet win for us."

Psuro nodded and turned away, seeking out his surviving officers and forcing some order into the struggling remnants of his command. Smenkhkare sent runners to Shabaqo and Kashta if they still survived and gathered the signalers with their ram's horns. He saw Scarab and her friends under the care of Amentes and grimaced, limping across to them.

"There is no safe place, sister," the king said simply. "I need Amentes, so you must stay close to me."

"You are wounded. Let Nebhotep treat your leg."

"It is nothing. He can do so later, if we live."

"Then let me fight, brother. You need swords."

"I need the gods more, can you deliver them?" Smenkhkare laughed humorlessly. "Yes, arm yourselves and do what you can. I am about to throw the dice one last time."

Smenkhkare limped off again with Amentes and his squad. The horns sounded, a wail of despair, and Smenkhkare's army turned and ran, suddenly opening a ragged gap between the two armies. Horemheb's men rushed after but the remains of Psuro's spearmen threw themselves forward, many onto the swords of the enemy, clutching their opponents as they died. The gap opened a little more. The horn sounded again and through the dust clouds a storm of arrows fell again, slaughtering the spearmen and the front ranks of Horemheb's army. Psuro threw himself forward and disappeared under a crush of struggling men.

"He has done it!" Menkure exulted. "Stop running, you fools," he yelled as his own men streamed past him. "Turn and fight again."

The insistent sound of the horn and the officers with the whips of their rank rallied the men and forced them into a rough semblance of company formations again. Another swathe of the enemy fell under a volley of arrows and the front ranks of Horemheb's army wavered. In the instant before the general's army fell back, the Great South Gate of Waset creaked open and five hundred garrison guards and Medjay poured out, the powerful figure of General Nakhtmin at their head.

Smenkhkare raised his sword to signal the attack on Horemheb's wavering army but the noise made him turn and stare at the tight formation of armed men charging into his rear. His shoulders slumped and he frantically yelled to the rear ranks to turn. Too slowly they answered the call and the Waset troops, inexperienced but fresh, crashed into the rear of Smenkhkare's line, rolling them up. Moments later, as Horemheb saw what was happening; he threw his own men forward in one last effort and caught the king's army in a vice of hardened bronze.

Within the city, Mahuhy's summons had brought the beggars and the dock workers, the idle and the criminals out in force. Many of them remembered the former king and his sister fondly and entertained visions of the gratitude he would show when he was restored to his throne. The gang leaders were less enthusiastic and opted for the less dangerous and infinitely more rewarding task of relieving the citizenry of the city of their remaining wealth while their attention lay elsewhere. If their arson and violence helped Mahuhy, well, they would be sure to remind him of it later. Instead of the thousand men Mahuhy hoped to lead against Ay's men, he found himself leading a rabble of cripples and totally inexperienced fighters out of the South Gate minutes after the troops ran through. Mouthing curses, he set off at a run for the battle, screaming at the others to follow.

A stiffening of street fighters from the Sons of Re and the Sons of Set might have made Mahuhy's tiny army a force to be reckoned with. Instead, they broke on the rock of older legionnaires and Medjay and smashed apart. They died fast, but they provided a distraction and even brought about a few deaths in the rampaging madness of the battle. Smenkhkare's men extricated themselves and inched back toward the river, laboriously defending themselves.

A knot of soldiers saw the king under his banner, only a few ranks from the ragged front line. Yelling fiercely they launched themselves at him, hacking down the intervening fighters, friend and foe alike. Amentes saw them coming and screamed a warning, interposing himself and dying bloodily under their blades. The king, with Menkure by his side, stabbed and slashed, taking their toll. Menkure fell with a spear through his thigh, leaving his king's back exposed. Khu rushed in, killed a man and fell back before the onslaught of another two. Scarab, dirty and bloodied and gasping for breath, stumbled forward to protect her brother's back and fell beneath a backswing of a sword as it reached the end of its curve. A wound opened on her forehead and blood drenched her face, blinding her. Nebhotep grabbed her and hauled her back out of the way, whipping off his kilt and wrapping it around her head.

Smenkhkare dispatched another man and lowered his sword, holding his side and looking around in a lull in the fighting. He saw Menkure on the ground and stumbled toward him, concern on his face.

"Are you hurt, old friend?"

"I'll live, my lord king." Menkure tried to grin and winced. His eyes widened suddenly. "Behind you, Djeser."

An officer bearing the insignia of one of Horemheb's Leader of One Hundred leaped forward, his bronze blade high and sweeping down toward the king's unprotected back. Smenkhkare turned, his blade rising slowly, knowing he could not stop death. A man jumped forward, unarmed and threw himself into the path of the curved sword. It bit deep and blood fountained out of the man's lungs, bright and frothy as he screamed briefly. He was knocked back into the king and Smenkhkare stumbled, feeling the body tugged aside as the soldier tried to free his blade. The king's blade flashed and the officer fell.

"Who was he?" Smenkhkare panted, pointing at the corpse of the unarmed man. "He deserves to be remembered for his valor."

Menkure, now back up on one knee, shook his head. "Never seen him before. We had a lot join up since Edfu."

Nobody else knew either and very soon, the king had other things on his mind. The battle had swung against him and despite his fury and determination to carry on the fight; he knew this battle was lost. He directed the remnants of his army back to the river where his boats lay, and they fought for every pace, leaving the plains of Waset littered with Kemetu and Nubian dead. Horemheb led the charge, determined that Smenkhkare would not escape; while General Nakhtmin swept over the battlefield with his elderly troops and Medjay, routing the last pockets of resistance.

Two boats pulled away from the bloodied banks of the river and turned upriver, crabbing slowly across the current as exhausted men fought now against the river's flow as they had fought all day against the troops loyal to Ay and King Tutankhaten. The ships lay heavy in the water, though none then thought to ask why. It was only days later when all pursuit ceased, that the holds were examined and the contents of the crates revealed. The two boats contained the royal treasury of Smenkhkare--not a great sum as compared to that of his father Nebmaetre, whom men called 'golden', but far more than that of his brothers Akhenaten and Tutankhaten. They put in to the western shore and carried it to a safe spot for burial until such time as the king would have need of it.

Smenkhkare stood in the stern of the second boat as it crept round a bend in the river, watching the tall pylons of Waset disappear into the distance and the dusk. Tears filled his eyes as he recalled so many good men killed and maimed. So few had survived and even his sister had been wounded fighting for him. He lifted his arms and cried out loudly, "May all the gods of Kemet bear witness to my oath. I will return and wrest my crown back from the traitor Ay."

Epilogue

"I am not sorry to be leaving Waset behind. I loved the city of my birth and my childhood, the people in the streets, the cool dark temples and the loud and gaudy festivals, but my uncle Ay has changed all that. Waset to me now is a place of suspicion and death, somewhere I'd rather not be. I know we will return one day, for my brother means to be king again, but in the secret places of my heart I hope it is not soon.

"My brother Smenkhkare has changed in the year or more we have been apart. That is not surprising, looking at what he has been through. He fell from the highest position in the Kingdoms into death, only to be resurrected again. The story is not unlike that of Asar, whom Set killed and who resurrected into great Heru. All that is missing is the presence of Asar's faithful wife Auset. In some ways I have been cast as Auset, one of the Nine of Iunu, yet I will not marry my brother, even for the sake of the gods. Another has claimed my heart and body and I will marry him as soon as the gods bring us together again, and we will spend the rest of our lives raising our son Set to be a soldier like his father.

"I miss him so. The further south we travel the more my heart is ripped apart. I know my son is in good and loving hands, his grandparents will dote on him, and my all-but-husband Paramessu will raise him until I can be there. I pray to the gods it is soon.

"My brother has an almost impossible task ahead of him. The armies of Kemet commanded by the best generals will surely contest his claim to the throne. Smenkhkare will need to find an army from somewhere. He believes Kush to be the answer, but that may be only because he once found help there. It was not enough then and I fear it will not be again, but what else is he to do? He is king--Ankhkheperure Djeserkheperu Smenkhkare, anointed one of the Two Kingdoms, King of Upper and Lower Kemet, Son of Re, Lord of Crowns--may he live forever. And I? I was once Princess Beketaten, daughter and sister of kings, but of what use is a princess now? I will be Scarab again, truly Scarab, Khepri, aspect of the Sun, and I will find a way to help my brother regain his throne, find a way to be reunited with my Paramessu, and find a way to love and care for my son.

"We sailed past Asna, Nekhen and Edfu, but news had already reached those cities of our status. The remnants of the population lined the river and sent volleys of arrows against us. They fell well short of course, as we had the whole river to use, but the fact that the common people turned against us hurt deeply. Not being able to put in at the cities, we were forced to scavenge for food and supplies in the farmlands near villages. Many of our wounded died in the days following the battle at Waset, despite the good efforts of Nebhotep and a handful of other physicians. Where we could, we buried them in the hot, dry sands of the desert edge where they stood a chance of immortality, their bodies drying before decay could set in, preserving the shell of the person for later spirit resurrection.

"And so we came to Abu again, where we found the Governor Ka-Nakht prepared to defend the island and the city..."

The chamber plunged into darkness, the lights briefly glowing dull orange before fading to a stygian gloom, not even a hint of light leaking in from the research tent where the generator still purred throatily. Doris screamed and Angela said, "Can it, Doris," very matter-of-factly.

"What the hell is going on?" Marc roared, swinging round in what he thought was the direction of the entrance. "Al, are you playing silly buggers again?"

"I'm over here," said an aggrieved voice. "Minding my own bloody business."

"There's a light over there, boys and girls," Daffyd observed in his Welsh lilt. "I believe it's coming from the next chamber."

Flickering yellow beams swung and tracked like drunken searchlights and they could hear footsteps scrunching on the sandy floor of the first chamber.

"Who's out there?" Marc growled. "Speak up, or do I have to come and find out?" He bent to clamber through the low hole in the wall and was blinded as two flashlight beams speared the blackness, blinding him.

"You will please all move away from the entrance and make no sudden movements." The voice that echoed from the first chamber spoke slowly and clearly in English, though with a strong Syrian accent. "Doctor Hanser? Do you hear me? You will please to do this, I wish no-one any harm."

"I hear you," Dani called. "Who are you?" She called to the others in the almost complete darkness, "Get back everyone, away from the entrance."

Boots scraped on the sandstone floor and the unmistakable sound of quality leather-soled shoes scrunching over the fine debris from the removal of the stone blocks came to their ears. The flashlight beams moved closer then flashed up, blinding the circle of archeology students before carrying on with a quick sweep of the new chamber. Behind the lights, Dani could make out dim shapes of men.

"Who are you?" she repeated. "This dig is carried out under the auspices of the Syrian Ministry of National History. You have no right to interfere."

"I am well aware of who you are, Doctor Hanser," the cultured voice continued. "I signed your permit myself."

"Under-Minister Bashir?" Dani's voice sounded incredulous. "What are you doing here? We received no word of your intended visit."

"That is perhaps just as well." Bashir said. His shoes scraped as he altered his position slightly. "Lights, Yusuf, if you please."

The lights flickered and came on strongly, flooding the chamber with incandescent brilliance again. Everybody blinked and shaded their eyes against the floodlights, gradually becoming aware of the rifles pointing at them from several soldiers standing behind the Under-Minister.

"Bloody hell," Al muttered.

Bashir was dressed in a crisp, clean, charcoal-gray Italian suit and shining black leather shoes. Tall and lean, his swarthy features sported a pencil-thin moustache and deep-set intelligent eyes under an immaculately trimmed head of black hair. He smiled, bestowing his largesse on everyone in turn, lingering a trifle longer on Angela's physical attributes. Switching his attention back to Dani, he repeated his last words to her.

"As I was saying, Doctor Hanser, it is perhaps as well that I sent no word. If I had, I think I would presently be examining some rather dull ditches in the earth rather than an unexpected Kemetu tomb."

Dani hesitated before saying quietly, "There is an explanation for that."

"I am sure you have one," Bashir said drily. "I am most interested in hearing it, but not here. My assistants," he waved a hand negligently at the soldiers behind him, "Will escort you all to your tents, where you will remain under guard. Except you, Doctor Hanser, and..." Bashir looked around the others before nodding his head at Daffyd. "And you, Doctor Rhys-Williams. I will talk to you both together right here." The Under-Minister stood aside to let the students out, waiting until all the soldiers but one had left.

The soldier did not carry a rifle but held a handgun. He slipped it into a leather holster and clipped the cover over it before coming to attention. "You wish me to bring in the furniture, Minister Bashir?" he asked.

"Thank you, Nazim, if you would be so kind." While he waited, Bashir strolled around the perimeter of the chamber, examining the columns of tiny hieroglyphs. He came to the end panel and stood looking up at the huge mural in silence for several minutes, the only sound in the chamber being the muted purr of the generator. "Magnificent," he said at last. "I have not seen its equal even in Kemet." He swiveled on his heel and stared back up the length of the room at Dani and Daffyd. "And you thought to hide this treasure?"

Dani was about to speak when Nazim reentered, holding three small folding chairs under one arm and a tiny folded card table under the other. He carefully set them up, two chairs on one side of the table, one opposite.

"Will there be anything else, Minister Bashir?"

"No Nazim. If you would be so good as to wait outside, I need to talk to these people alone." As the soldier hesitated, Bashir smiled. "I shall be perfectly safe, Nazim." He ostentatiously drew his jacket to one side to reveal a small gun in a holster under his left armpit. The soldier saluted and withdrew.

Bashir waved Dani and Daffyd to the pair of chairs, taking the single one himself and sitting down, tugging gently on the knees of his immaculately pressed trousers as he did so. He crossed his legs carefully, flicking at a bit of dust on one cuff, before turning his attention back to the scientists.

"Now, Doctor Hanser, you were about to tell me why you were keeping this national treasure a secret."

"We're not exactly keeping it a secret, Under-Minister. It is just that we are not sure what we have found. We do intend to inform the Ministry."

Bashir said nothing, just staring at Dani. After a while he looked across at Daffyd. "What do you have to say, Doctor Rhys-Williams?"

"Basically the same as Doctor Hanser," Daffyd replied quietly. "We found this cavern by accident and have been exploring it to see what it was." He shrugged. "After all, it could have been a hoax and how would we have looked wasting the Ministry's time?"

"Very thoughtful. And is it a hoax?"

"No." Dani shook her head. "I'm not an Kemetologist but I'd stake my reputation..."

"Should it survive this incident," Bashir murmured.

"...That this is genuine eighteenth dynasty narrative."

"So you have decided it is a genuine find. You intended to inform the authorities?" Bashir noted the two slow nods and smiled to himself. "It is understandable you would not want to commit yourselves until you were sure so you can be forgiven a month's delay in reporting it. That is how long it has been, is it not? The workers here report a lot of work up here in the front of the cave this last month."

Daffyd risked a hard stare at Dani and tried to nudge her leg with a foot but she ignored it or did not see his warning.

"Yes, about that," she confirmed.

Bashir frowned. "So what am I to make of a letter that arrived last week from one Peter Burrows?" He looked from one to the other, noting the blank looks. "Not familiar? He is the brother of one Robert

Burrows, archaeologist. Ah, I see some recognition at last. This Peter sent a letter addressed to his brother Robert at the 'Kemetu Dig', care of the Ministry. Naturally, the letter was opened and you can imagine the Minister's astonishment to hear that an Kemetu tomb had been discovered under his nose." Bashir uncrossed his legs and recrossed them, carefully pointing the sole of his shoe away from Dani. "The only troubling note about this letter was the intimation that this tomb was discovered last year. Last year, Doctor Hanser?"

Dani nodded, not trusting herself to speak.

"So I must now ask myself whether you ever meant to reveal its existence. Perhaps this delay is so you can first remove all the grave goods." He leaned forward suddenly and stared into Dani's eyes. "What was here, Doctor Hanser? A gold sarcophagus? Jewelry, artefacts? What?"

"There was nothing, boyo," Daffyd drawled. "What you see is what you got. A lot of writing and a couple of magnificent paintings."

"No gold?" Bashir rapped out, still staring at Dani.

"N...no," she stuttered, suddenly very much aware of the golden scarab in the pocket of her jeans. "You can search the camp if you like, you won't find anything."

"We already have. There is nothing." Bashir sat back again and recrossed his legs. Staring at Dani he saw something curious, the woman was suddenly nervous. "Turn out your pockets, both of you, on the table there."

"I really think I must refuse, boyo," Daffyd said. He took out his tobacco tin and papers and slowly rolled himself a cigarette. Striking a match, he lit it, blew a cloud of blue smoke into the air and replaced the items in his jacket pocket. "That's all I have, anyway."

"You will empty your pockets now or I will fetch Nazim in here to do it for you. I assure you he will not be gentle, even with the good lady doctor."

Daffyd sighed and stood up. He started emptying his pockets onto the torn green baize of the card table--his cigarette makings, a battered leather wallet, a grubby handkerchief. After a moment, Dani joined him, though her pockets were emptier save for her notebook from the previous season and the heavy gold scarab. Hand trembling slightly, she laid the gleaming piece on top of her notebook and sat down again, muttering under her breath.

Bashir poked through the jumble of things for a moment then he smiled. "Ah, what have we here?" He reached out and picked up the golden scarab, glanced at it and put it to one side, lifting up the notebook under it. "Your notebook from last year. This will tell me everything." He started leafing through it, becoming engrossed in the detailed notes written in her small but neat handwriting.

Daffyd raised a bushy eyebrow at Dani and mouthed a query. "What happened? Why is he ignoring the scarab?"

Dani shrugged slightly, and moved a hand up to cover her mouth should the Minister look up. "I don't know." She formed the words clearly with her lips in silence. "I don't think he saw it."

Daffyd frowned. "One of your pagan gods?" he mouthed.

Bashir looked up and tossed the notebook down on the table. "This is only one notebook. You have others? I want to see them."

Dani nodded. "They are back in my tent." She hesitated a few moments before continuing, addressing the Under-Minister in respectful tones. "You can see from my notebook that we were meticulous in recording everything we found. Aside from some minor damage, nothing has been harmed and the contents are intact, just waiting for Kemetologists to study them."

"Except for the gold." Bashir picked up the scarab again and hefted it as if judging the weight before replacing it on the worn green baize. "Every tomb has something in it, even the ones that have been robbed. Your notes indicate no evidence of robbery, so where is the gold?"

Dani shook her head and Daffyd shrugged. "Who knows, boyo? Maybe in some deeper chamber."

Bashir looked down the length of the chamber to the mural covering the back wall. "Behind there, you mean? I can have my men break through there in no time."

"You can't do that," Dani gasped. "You wouldn't. That is art beyond anything that has come out of Kemet."

"It would be regrettable," Bashir admitted. "But what am I to do? The Minister believes you have stolen the treasures of this tomb, our treasures that belong to the people of the United Arab Republic. Both Syria and our brother-state Kemet are being robbed by western imperialists again." The Under-Minister grimaced and rubbed the thumb of his right hand gently against the first two fingers. "If I had something to show Minister Al-Siluzi, we could let you continue to investigate the site."

"A bribe, you mean," Daffyd said distastefully.

Bashir frowned. "Of course not. I am disappointed that you would consider me so venal. I am talking about baksheesh."

"Same thing, isn't it?"

"By no means. The term refers merely to a gift one would give to an official who is deserving of respect. In return you would be granted certain privileges."

"So if we give your minister gold, he will let us continue to work here?" Dani asked. "The problem is, we don't have any gold."

"None? You are sure?"

"What you see is what there is."

"Then I am afraid you must consider the dig closed," Bashir said with a tone of finality. "You will all be placed under arrest and taken back to Damascus where you will be tried and deported." He picked up the golden scarab again and tossed it from hand to hand. "Not even a small amount?" he asked. "As a token of good faith, you understand." He held up the scarab between forefinger and thumb. "Even this amount would do," he said with a smile.

Dani's shoulders slumped. The Under-Minister had been playing with them all along, pretending not to notice the golden scarab. "You...you can have it," she whispered, feeling her heart tear within her.

A flash of anger crossed Bashir's face. "This? What would I want with this stone?" He flung the scarab down on the table and Dani grabbed it, sticking it back in her jeans' pocket.

"There is a treasure," Daffyd said slowly.

Bashir swiveled to stare at the Welshman as he rolled himself another cigarette and lit it. "What treasure?" he asked softly. "Where is it?"

"I'll show you." Daffyd got up and strolled across the chamber to the place where Dani had been translating when the lights went out. "There is your treasure." He pointed at the columns of hieroglyphs.

Bashir scowled. "I cannot read that. What does it say?"

"It says, 'The two boats contained the royal treasury of Smenkhkare--not a great sum as compared to that of our father Nebmaetre, whom men called 'golden', but far more than that of his brothers Akhenaten and Tutankhaten. They put in to the western shore and carried it to a safe spot for burial until such time as the king would have need of it.'" Daffyd turned to Bashir with a grin.

Bashir was still scowling. "What does this have to do with a treasure?"

"The account says King Smenkhkare buried an enormous wealth of gold and went away," Daffyd explained. "It is known that Smenkhkare was buried with little ceremony, so where is the gold? I think it is right where they buried it three thousand years ago."

The Under-Minister licked his lips. "How much?"

"In today's dollars or pounds? Millions? Maybe billions."

"Where?"

"Ah, now that we do not know. Not yet, anyway," Daffyd hurried on as Bashir opened his mouth. "But somewhere in all this," he waved his hand around the chamber, "Somewhere in all this is a description. With luck it will lead us to the royal treasury."

Bashir considered this idea for a long time, scanning the walls avidly as if by sheer determination he might decipher the writings. At last he nodded. "Very well, you may continue your investigations, but I will be present at all times. Nothing is to be translated unless I am here. Is that understood?"

"Of course, Under-Minister Bashir," Dani said quietly, her hand resting unobtrusively over the scarab in her pocket. "We understand completely. We are partners."

"Then if we are partners, Doctor Dani, you may call me Ahmed." He bowed and smiled. "Come, let me escort you to my tent and we can toast the future of our enterprise with a rather superior Turkish coffee I have."

The three people left the chamber and a few minutes later the generator coughed and died, the floodlights dying to a sullen orange glow before plunging the chamber into the darkness that had enveloped it for over three thousand years.

The Main Characters in Scarab-Smenkhkare

The pronunciations given below are hardly definitive. As vowels are unknown in ancient Kemetu, we can only guess at the proper pronunciation. I have tried to select spellings and pronunciations that are common among English speakers, though where the accent lies is anyone's guess. If you prefer another form, please feel free to use it.

Aanen (Ah-nen) - second prophet of Amun, brother of Ay

Ahhotep (Ah-hoh-tepp) - glass maker of Waset

Akhenaten (Ah-ken-ah-ten) - the heretic king, husband of Nefertiti

Amenemhet (Ah-men-em-het) - first prophet of Amun, high priest

Amenemipet (Ah-men-emm-ee-pet) - deputy viceroy of Nubia

Amenhotep III (Ah-men-hoh-tepp) - king, father of Amenhotep IV (Akhenaten), Smenkhkare, Tutankhaten and Beketaten

Amenhotep IV - king, son of Amenhotep III, later changed his name to Akhenaten

Amentep (Ah-men-tepp) - commander of Paramessu's Ptah legion

Ankheperure (Ann-kep-er-oo-ray) - Living Manifestations of Re; throne name of Smenkhkare

Ankhesenpaaten (Ann-kess-en-pah-ah-ten) - third daughter of Akhenaten and Nefertiti

Ankhesenamen (Ann-kess-en-ah-men) - name taken by Ankhesenpaaten when

Tutankhaten changed his name

Ashraz (Ash-razz) - Aziru's spymaster

Aspalta (Ass-pal-tah) - commander of Smenkhkare's Nubian army

Ay (Eye) - father of Nefertiti and brother to queen Tiye, holds title of Divine Father, Tjaty to Akhenaten, priest of Amun and later of Aten

Aziru (Azz-ee-roo) - king of the Amorites

Bakt (Bar-k-tt) - third prophet of Amun, elevated by Ay

Beketaten (Beck-ett-ah-ten) - youngest daughter of Amenhotep III and Tiye

Djedhor (Jedd-hore) - commander of Paramessu's Heru legion

Djeserkheperu (Jess-er-kep-er-roo) - Holy of Manifestations; part of the family name of Smenkhkare

Ephenamen (Eff-en-ah-men) - priest of Amun

Ephras (Eff-rass) - aide of Jebu

Hednackht (Head-nah-k-tt) - commander of Paramessu's Re legion

Hiknefer (Hick-neff-er) - Nubian prince, companion of Tutankhaten

Horemheb (Hore-emm-heb) - general of the eastern borders, later of all armies during reign of Akhenaten

Huy (Hoo-ee) - 1. Viceroy of Nubia, 2. Mayor of Sehotep-Neteru, 3. Overseer of the King's Gardeners

Iteru (Ee-tare-oo) - The Great River, the Nile

Jebu (Jeb-oo) - Amorite general

Jeheshua (Jee-hesh-you-ah) - Khabiru jeweler of Zarw

Kasaya (Cass-eye-ah) - commander of Smenkhkare's Nubian army

Kashta (Cash-tah) - commander of Smenkhkare's Nubian army

Kenhirkhoshef (Ken-her-co-shef) - Overseer of the Great Place (Valley of Tombs)

Kensthoth (Kens-thoth) - high-ranking scribe of Waset, a King's Councilor

Khai (Kay) - Nubian prince, companion of Tutankhaten

Khaemnum (Kay-em-noom) - Psenamy's second in command, guardian of Akhenaten at Akhet-Aten

Khaenmaat (Kay-enn-mart) - commander of Paramessu's Chariots

Khu (Coo) - farm lad of Akhet-Re, a King's Councilor

Khui (Coo-ee) - commander of Paramessu's Set legion

Mahuhy (Ma-who-he) - King's Councilor and businessman of Waset

Meketaten (Meck-ett-ah-ten) - second daughter of Akhenaten and Nefertiti

Mena (Men-ah) - an alias of Khu

Menkure (Men-coo-ray) - friend and aide of Smenkhkare

Mentopher (Men-toe-fur) - steward of Tjaty Ay

Meny (May-knee) - Leader of Fifty under Paramessu

Meryetaten (Merry-ett-ah-ten) - oldest daughter of Akhenaten and Nefertiti

Mutaril (Moo-tar-rill) - Hittite ambassador to King Aziru

Nakht (Nar-k-tt) - assistant and adopted son of Ahhotep

Nakhtmin (Nar-k-tt-minn) - son of a Waset landowner, general of Ay's army

Nebhotep (Neb-hoh-tepp) - court physician in Akhet-Aten

Nebkheperure (Neb-kep-er-roo-ray) - Lord of the Manifestations of Re; throne name
of Tutankhamen

Nebmaetre (Neb-my-tray) - The Lord of Truth is Re; throne name of Amenhotep III

Neferkheperre-Waenre **(Neff-er-kep-er-ray-wah-en-ray)** - Beautiful are the Manifestations of Re--the Only of Re; throne name of Akhenaten

Neferkhepre (Neff-er-kepp-ray) - an alias of Scarab

Neferneferouaten-tasherit (Neff-eh-neff-eh-oo-ah-ten-tash-eh-rit) - fourth daughter of Akhenaten and Nefertiti

Neferneferoure **(Neff-eh-neff-eh-oo-ray**) - fifth daughter of Akhenaten and Nefertiti

Nefertiti (Neff-eh-tee-tee) - daughter of Aye, wife and queen of Akhenaten

Paatenemheb (Pah-ah-ten-emm-heb) - name that Horemheb took to please Akhenaten

Pa-it (Pah-eet) - farmer of village of Akhet-Re

Paramessu (Pah-ram-ess-ee) - son of Seti, a friend of Horemheb, who becomes a general of the Northern Army

Pa-Siamen (Pah-see-ah-men) - priest of Amun

Penno (Pen-oh) - Lieutenant of garrison at Sehotep-Neteru

Pentere (Pen-teh-ray) - mother of Paramessu

Psenamy (Sen-a-me) - General at Waset, Confidant of Ay

Psuro (Sue-row) - commander of Smenkhkare's Nubian army

Scarab - nickname of Beketaten

Set (Seth) - son of Beketaten and Paramessu

Setepenre (Seth-eh-pen-ray) - sixth daughter of Akhenaten and Nefertiti

Seti (Seth-ee) - judge and troop commander of Zarw, father of Paramessu

Shabaqo (Shab-are-ko) - commander of Smenkhkare's Nubian army

Shubbiluliuma (Shoo-bill-ool-ee-oo-ma) - king of the Hittites

Smenkhkare (Ss-men-kah-ray) - son of Amenhotep III by his own daughter Sitamen

Sutau (Soot-ow) - treasurer under Smenkhkare

Tiye (Tee) - wife and queen of Amenhotep III, sister of Ay

Tutankhamen (Too-tank-ah-men) - name taken by Tutankhaten when he revives the worship of Amun

Tutankhaten (Too-tank-ah-ten) - son of Amenhotep III by his own daughter Iset

Usermontju (Oo-sir-mont-jew) - Chief of the Medjay (Police) in Waset

Yuya (Yoo-yah) - Khabiru Tjaty of Tuthmosis IV, father of Ay, Tiye and Aanen

Gods of the Scarab Books

Amun (Ah-moon) - the hidden one; a sun god, lord of the sky and king of gods; became increasingly powerful during the eighteenth dynasty; worship was centered on Waset.

Asar (Ah-sar) (Osiris) - god of the dead; one of the Nine of Iunu

Aten (Ah-ten) - the sun as a disc, distinct from Re; elevated from a minor god in the eighteenth dynasty; became the supreme god during Akhenaten's reign.

Atum (Ah-toom) - Creator god; the unified light; one of the Nine of Iunu

Auset (Ow-seth) (Isis) - goddess of family love and loyalty; one of the Nine of Iunu

Djehuti (Jeh-hoot-ee) (Thoth) - god of the moon and of wisdom; patron deity of scribes and knowledge

Geb (Gebb) - god of the earth and growing things; one of the Nine of Iunu

Hapi (Hah-pee) - god of the Nile River

475

Heru (Heh-rue)(Heru) - a sky god; the Ascending Light

Het-Her (Hathor) - goddess of love, beauty and fertility

Khepri (Kepp-ree) - an aspect of the sun god epitomized by the actions of the sacred scarab beetle which rolls balls of dung (representing the ball of the sun) containing its eggs; the Dawn Light.

Khnum (Kk-noom) - god of the source of the Nile; the Divine Potter; creator of human children

Min (Minn) - fertility god.

Nebt-Het (Nebb-tt-het) (Nephthys) - goddess of secrets and mysteries; one of the Nine of Iunu

Nekhbet (Neck-beth) - vulture goddess of Upper Egypt

Nut (Noot) - goddess of the sky and direction; one of the Nine of Iunu

Ptah (Tar) - god of craftsmen.

Re (Ray) - one of the sun god; the Midday Light

Satet (Sah-teth) - goddess of the inundation of the Nile

Set (Seth) - god of the desert and destruction; associated with the colour red; one of the Nine of Iunu
Sobek (Sob-eck) - the Crocodile god

Shu (Shoo) - god of air and dryness; one of the Nine of Iunu

Tefnut (Teff-noot) - goddess of moisture; one of the Nine of Iunu

Wadjet (Wadge-eth) - cobra goddess of Lower Egypt

Wepwawet (Wepp-wah-wet) - Opener of Ways; the god of war and funerals

About the Author

Max Overton has travelled extensively and lived in many places around the world--including Malaysia, India, Germany, England, Jamaica, New Zealand, USA and Australia. Trained in the biological sciences in New Zealand and Australia, he has worked within the scientific field for many years, but now concentrates on writing. While predominantly a writer of historical fiction (Scarab: Books 1 - 6 of the Amarnan Kings; the Scythian Trilogy; the Demon Series; Ascension), he also writes in other genres (A Cry of Shadows, the Glass Trilogy, Haunted Trail, Sequestered) and draws on true life (Adventures of a Small Game Hunter in Jamaica, We Came From Königsberg). Max also maintains an interest in butterflies, photography, the paranormal and other aspects of Fortean Studies.

Most of his other published books are available at Writers Exchange Ebooks, http://www.writers-exchange.com/Max-Overton/ and all his books may be viewed on his website:
 http://www.maxovertonauthor.com/

Max's book covers are all designed and created by Julie Napier, and other examples of her art and photography may be viewed at www.julienapier.com

If you want to read more about other books by this author, they are listed on the following pages...

A Cry of Shadows
{Paranormal Murder Mystery}

Australian Professor Ian Delaney is single-minded in his determination to prove his theory that one can discover the moment that the life force leaves the body. After succumbing to the temptation to kill a girl under scientifically controlled conditions, he takes an offer of work in St Louis, hoping to leave the undiscovered crime behind him.

In America, Wayne Richardson seeks revenge by killing his ex-girlfriend, believing it will give him the upper hand, a means to seize control following their breakup. Wayne quickly discovers that he enjoys killing and begins to seek out young women who resemble his dead ex-girlfriend.

Ian and Wayne meet and, when Ian recognizes the symptoms of violent delusion, he employs Wayne to help him further his research. Despite the police closing in, the two killers manage to evade identification time and time again as the death toll rises in their wake.

The detective in charge of the case, John Barnes, is frantic, willing to try anything to catch his killer. With time running out, he searches desperately for answers before another body is found...or the culprit slips into the woodwork for good.

Publisher: http://www.writers-exchange.com/A-Cry-of-Shadows/
Amazon: http://mybook.to/ACryOfShadows

Adventures of a Small Game Hunter in Jamaica
{Biography}

An eleven-year-old boy is plucked from boarding school in England and transported to the tropical paradise of Jamaica where he's free to study his one great love--butterflies. He discovers that Jamaica has a wealth of these wonderful insects and sets about making a collection of as many as he can find. Along the way, he has adventures with other creatures, from hummingbirds to vultures, from iguanas to black widow spiders. Through it all runs the promise of the legendary Homerus swallowtail, Jamaica's national butterfly.

Other activities intrude, like school, boxing and swimming lessons, but he manages to inveigle his parents into taking him to strange and sometimes dangerous places, all in the name of butterfly collecting. He meets scientists and Rastafarians, teachers, small boys and the ordinary people living on the tropical isle, and even discovers butterflies that shouldn't exist in Jamaica.

Author Max Overton was that young boy. He counted himself fortunate to have lived in Jamaica in an age very different from the present one. Max still has some of the butterflies he collected half a century or more ago, and each one releases a flood of memories whenever he opens the box and gazes at their tattered and fading wings. These memories have become stories--stories of the Adventures of a Small Game Hunter in Jamaica.

Publisher: http://www.writers-exchange.com/Adventures-of-a-Small-Game-Hunter/
Amazon: http://myBook.to/AdventuresGameHunter

Haunted Trail A Tale of Wickedness & Moral Turpitude
{Western: Paranormal}

Ned Abernathy is a hot-tempered young cowboy in the small town of Hammond's Bluff in 1876. In a drunken argument with his best friend Billy over a girl, he guns him down. Ned flees and wanders the plains, forests and hills of the Dakota Territories, certain that every man's hand is against him.

Horse rustlers, marauding Indians, killers, gold prospectors and French trappers cross his path and lead to complications, as do persistent apparitions of what Ned believes is the ghost of his friend Billy, come to accuse him of murder. He finds love and loses it. Determined not to do the same when he discovers gold in the Black Hills, he ruthlessly defends his newfound wealth against greedy men. In the process, he comes to terms with who he is and what he's done. But there are other ghosts in his past that he needs to confront. Returning to Hammond's Bluff, Ned stumbles into a shocking surprise awaiting him at the end of his haunted trail.

Publisher: http://www.writers-exchange.com/Haunted-Trail/

Amazon: http://mybook.to/HauntedTrail
Ascension Series, A Novel of Nazi Germany
{Historical: Holocaust}

Before he fully realized the diabolical cruelties of the National Socialist German Worker's Party, Konrad Wengler had committed atrocities against his own people, the Jews, out of fear of both his faith and his heritage. But after he witnesses firsthand the concentration camps, the corruption, the inhuman malevolence of the Nazi war machine and the propaganda aimed at annihilating an entire race, he knows he must find a way to turn the tide and become the savior his people desperately need.

Series Page (all books):
Publisher: http://www.writers-exchange.com/ascension-series/

Book 1: Ascension
Fear prompts Konrad Wengler to forget his Jewish heritage. After fighting in the Great War, he turns to law enforcement and joins the Nazi Party as a Lieutenant of Police. War breaks out and Konrad witnesses firsthand the atrocities being committed upon his fellow Jews. When his origin is discovered, he's sent to a concentration camp where he's forced to face what it means to be a Jew and fight for survival.
Publisher: http://www.writers-exchange.com/Ascension/
Amazon: http://mybook.to/Ascension1

Rest of the books at Amazon:
Book 2: http://mybook.to/Ascension2

Kadesh, A Novel of Ancient Egypt

Holding the key to strategic military advantage, Kadesh is a jewel city that distant lands covet. Ramesses II of Egypt and Muwatalli II of Hatti believe they're chosen by the gods to claim ascendancy to Kadesh. When the two meet in the largest chariot battle ever fought, not just the fate of empires will be decided but also the lives of citizens helplessly caught up in the greedy ambition of kings.
Publisher: http://www.writers-exchange.com/Kadesh/
Amazon: http://mybook.to/Kadesh

Fall of the House of Ramesses Series,
A Novel of Ancient Egypt
{Historical: Ancient Egypt}

Egypt was at the height of its powers in the days of Ramesses the Great, a young king who confidently predicted his House would last for a Thousand Years. Sixty years later, he was still on the throne. One by one, his heirs had died and the survivors had become old men. When Ramesses at last died, he left a stagnant kingdom and his throne to an old man--Merenptah. What followed laid the groundwork for a nation ripped apart by civil war.

Series Page for all books:
Publisher: http://www.writers-exchange.com/fall-of-the-house-of-ramesses-series/
Amazon: http://bit.ly/FOTHRSeries

Book 1: Merenptah:
Egypt was at the height of its powers in the days of Ramesses the Great and the young king confidently predicted that his House would last for a Thousand Years. Sixty years later he was still on the throne and one by one his heirs had died and the survivors had become old men. When he at last died, he left a stagnant kingdom and his throne to an old man - Merenptah. What followed laid the groundwork for a nation ripped apart by civil war.

The northern tribes rebelled and joined forces with the Sea Peoples, invading from the north; while in the south the king's eldest son, angered at being passed over in favour of the younger son, plotted to rid himself of his father and brother. An ageing king takes to the field to fight for the House of Ramesses.
Publisher: http://www.writers-exchange.com/Merenptah/
Amazon: http://mybook.to/FOTHR1

Rest of the books at Amazon:
Book 2: http://mybook.to/FOTHR2
Book 3: http://mybook.to/FOTHR3

Glass Trilogy
{Paranormal Thriller}

Delve deep into the mysteries of Aboriginal mythology, present day UFO activity and pure science that surround the continent of Australia, from its barren deserts to the depths of its rainforest and even deeper into its mysterious mountains. Along the way, love, greed, murder, and mystery abound while the secrets of mankind and the ultimate answer to 'what happens now?' just might be answered.

Series Page (all books):
Publisher: http://www.writers-exchange.com/glass-trilogy/

GLASS HOUSE, Book 1:
   The mysteries of Australia may just hold the answers mankind has been searching for millennium to find. When Doctor James Hay, a university scientist who studies the paranormal mysteries in Australia, finds an obelisk of carved volcanic rock on sacred Aboriginal land in northern Queensland, he knows it may hold the answers he has been seeking. And when a respected elder of the Aboriginal people instructs him to take up the gauntlet and follow his heart, James, Spencer, an old friend and an award-winning writer, Samantha Louis, along with her cameraman and two of James' Aboriginal students, start their quest for the truth.

   Glass House will take you deep into the mysteries that surround the continent of Australia, from its barren deserts to the depths of its rainforest and even deeper into its mysterious mountains. Along the way, the secrets of mankind and the ultimate answer to 'what happens now?' just might be answered. Love, greed, murder, and mystery abound in this action-packed paranormal/thriller.
Publisher: http://www.writers-exchange.com/Glass-House/
Amazon: http://mybook.to/Glass1

Rest of the books at Amazon:
Book 2: http://mybook.to/Glass2
Book 3: http://mybook.to/Glass3

Hyksos Series, A Novel of Ancient Egypt

The power of the kings of the Middle Kingdom have been failing for some time, having lost control of the Nile Delta to a series of Canaanite kings who ruled from the northern city of Avaris. Into this mix came the Kings of Amurri, Lebanon and Syria bent on subduing the whole of Egypt. These kings were known as the Hyksos, and they dealt a devastating blow to the peoples of the Nile Delta and Valley.

Series Page(all books):
Publisher: http://www.writers-exchange.com/hyksos-series/
Amazon: http://bit.ly/HyksosSeries

Book 1, Avaris:
When Arimawat and his son Harrubaal fled from Urubek, the king of Hattush, to the court of the King of Avaris, King Sheshi welcomed the refugees. One of Arimawat's first tasks for King Shesi is to sail south to the Land of Kush and fetch Princess Tati, who will become Sheshi's queen. Arimawat and Harrubaal perform creditably, but their actions have far-reaching consequences.

On the return journey, Harrubaal falls in love with Kemi, the daughter of the Southern Egyptian king. As a reward for Harrubaal's work, Sheshi secures the hand of the princess for the young Canaanite prince. Unfortunately for the peace of the realm, Sheshi lusts after Princess Kemi too, and his actions threaten the stability of his kingdom...
Publisher: http://www.writers-exchange.com/Avaris/
Amazon: http://mybook.to/avaris

Rest of the books at Amazon:
Book 2: http://mybook.to/conquest
Book 3: http://mybook.to/TwoCities
Book 4: http://mybook.to/Possessor-of-All

More coming soon!

Scythian Trilogy
{Historical}

Captured by the warlike, tribal Scythians who bicker amongst themselves and bitterly resent outside interference, a fiercely loyal captain in Alexander the Great's Companion Cavalry Nikometros and his men are to be sacrificed to the Mother Goddess. Lucky chance--and the timely intervention of Tomyra, priestess and daughter of the Massegetae chieftain--allows him to defeat the Champion. With their immediate survival secured, acceptance into the tribe...and escape...is complicated by the captain's growing feelings for Tomyra--death to any who touch her--and the chief's son Areipithes who not only detests Nikometros and wants to have him killed or banished but intends to murder his own father and take over the tribe.

Series Page (all books):
Publisher: http://www.writers-exchange.com/scythian-trilogy/

Book 1: Ascension
   A small boy discovers that being a Jew in Germany can be a dangerous thing. Fear prompts Konrad Wengler to put his faith aside and he tries desperately to forget his heritage.
   He fights in the Great War and is wounded, becomes a policeman in his tiny Bavarian town, where he falls under the spell of the fledgling Nazi Party. He joins the Party in patriotic fervour and becomes a Lieutenant of Police and Schutzstaffel (SS).
   In the course of his duties as policeman, he offends a powerful Nazi official, who starts an SS investigation of this troublesome police Lieutenant. When war breaks out, he joins the Police Battalions and is sent to Poland where he has to witness the atrocities being committed upon his fellow Jews.
   The SS investigators have discovered Konrad's origins and follow him into Poland. He is arrested and sent to Mauthausen Concentration Camp. Suddenly, Konrad must face what it means to be a Jew and fight for survival. He has friends on the outside, a wife and a lawyer, but will they be enough to counter the might of the Nazi machine?
Publisher: http://www.writers-exchange.com/Ascension/
Amazon: http://mybook.to/Scythian1

Rest of the books at Amazon:
Book 2: http://mybook.to/Scythian2
Book 3: http://mybook.to/Scythian3

Sequestered
By Max Overton and Jim Darley
{Action/Thriller}

Storing carbon dioxide underground as a means of removing a greenhouse gas responsible for global warming has made James Matternicht a fabulously wealthy man. For 15 years, the Carbon Capture and Sequestration Facility at Rushing River in Oregon's hinterland has been operating without a problem...or has it?

When mysterious documents arrive on her desk that purport to show the Facility is leaking, reporter Annaliese Winton investigates. Together with a government geologist, Matt Morrison, she uncovers a morass of corruption and deceit that now threatens the safety of her community and the entire northwest coast of America.

Liquid carbon dioxide, stored at the critical point under great pressure, is a tremendously dangerous substance, and millions of tonnes of it are sequestered in the rock strata below Rushing River. All it would take is a crack in the overlying rock and the whole pressurized mass could erupt with disastrous consequences. And that crack has always existed there...

Recipient of the Life Award (Literature for the Environment):
"There are only two kinds of people: conservationists and suicides. To qualify for this Award, your book needs to value the wonderful world of nature, to recognize that we are merely one species out of millions, and that we have a responsibility to cherish and maintain our small planet."
Awarded from http://bobswriting.com/life/
Publisher: http://www.writers-exchange.com/Sequestered/
Amazon: http://mybook.to/Sequestered

We Came From Konigsberg
{Historical: Holocaust}

Based on a true story gleaned from the memories of family members sixty years after the events, from photographs and documents, and from published works of nonfiction describing the times and events described in the narrative, *We Came From Konigsberg* is set in January 1945.

The Soviet Army is poised for the final push through East Prussia and Poland to Berlin. Elisabet Daeker and her five young sons are in Königsberg, East Prussia and have heard the shocking stories of Russian atrocities. They're desperate to escape to the perceived safety of Germany. To survive, Elisabet faces hardships endured at the hands of Nazi hardliners, of Soviet troops bent on rape, pillage and murder, and of Allied cruelty in the Occupied Zones of post-war Germany.

Winner of the 2014 EPIC Ebook Awards.
Publisher: http://www.writers-exchange.com/We-Came-From-Konigsberg/
Amazon: http://mybook.to/Konigsberg

487

Strong is the Ma'at of Re, A Novel of Ancient Egypt
{Historical: Ancient Egypt}

In Ancient Egypt, C1200 BCE, bitter contention and resentment, secret coups and assassination attempts may decide the fate of those who would become legends...by any means necessary.

Series Page for all books:
Publisher: http://www.writers-exchange.com/strong-is-the-maat-of-re-series/
Amazon: http://bit.ly/MaatOfReSeries

Book 1, The King: Ramesses III fights foreign foes, builds temples throughout the Two Lands, and looks forward to a long, illustrious life on the throne of Egypt--all as Ramesses the Great, his hero grandfather, had. Alas, his reign is not meant to be. Ramesses III faces troubles at home, troubles that threaten the stability of Egypt and his own throne...
Publisher: http://www.writers-exchange.com/The-King/
Amazon: http://mybook.to/StrongIsTheMaatOfRe1

Rest of the books at Amazon:
Book 2: http://mybook.to/SITMOR2
Book 3: http://mybook.to/SITMOR3

TULPA
{Paranormal Thriller}

From the rainforests of tropical Australia to the cane fields and communities of the North Queensland coastal strip, a horror is unleashed by those foolishly playing with unknown forces...

A fairy story to amuse small children leads four bored teenagers and a young university student in a North Queensland town to becoming interested in an ancient Tibetan technique for creating a life form. When their seemingly harmless experiment sets free terror and death, the teenagers are soon fighting to contain a menace that reproduces exponentially.

The police are helpless to end the horror. Aided by two old game hunters, a student of the paranormal and a few small children, the teenagers must find a way of destroying what they unintentionally released. But how can they stop beings that can escape into an alternate reality when threatened?
Publisher: http://www.writers-exchange.com/TULPA/
Amazon: http://mybook.to/TULPA

The Amarnan Kings Series, A Novel of Ancient Egypt
{Historical: Ancient Egypt}

Set in Egypt of the 14th century B.C.E. and piecing together a mosaic of the reigns of the five Amarnan kings, threaded through by the memories of princess Beketaten-Scarab, a tapestry unfolds of the royal figures lost in the mists of antiquity.

Series Page for all books:
Publisher: http://www.writers-exchange.com/the-armarnan-kings/
Amazon: http://bit.ly/ScarabSeries

Book 1: Scarab -Akhenaten: A chance discovery in Syria reveals answers to the mystery of the ancient Egyptian sun-king, the heretic Akhenaten and his beautiful wife Nefertiti. Inscriptions in the tomb of his sister Beketaten, otherwise known as Scarab, tell a story of life and death, intrigue and warfare, in and around the golden court of the kings of the glorious 18th dynasty.

The narrative of a young girl growing up at the centre of momentous events--the abolition of the gods, foreign invasion and the fall of a once-great family--reveals who Tutankhamen's parents really were, what happened to Nefertiti, and other events lost to history in the great destruction that followed the fall of the Aten heresy.

Meticulously researched; the book unfolds a tapestry of these royal figures lost in the mists of antiquity.
Publisher: http://www.writers-exchange.com/Scarab/
Amazon: http://mybook.to/ScarabBook1

Rest of the books at Amazon:
Book 2: http://mybook.to/ScarabBook2
Book 3: http://mybook.to/ScarabBook3
Book 4: http://mybook.to/ScarabBook4
Book 5: http://mybook.to/ScarabBook5
Book 6: http://mybook.to/ScarabBook6

You can find ALL our books up at Amazon at:
https://www.amazon.com/shop/writers_exchange

or on our website at:
http://www.writers-exchange.com

All of Max's Books:
http://www.writers-exchange.com/Max-Overton/

All our Historical Novels
http://www.writers-exchange.com/category/genres/historical/

Printed in Great Britain
by Amazon

69401112R00280